STAR WARS®

The Jedi Academy Trilogy

STAR WARS®

The Jedi Academy Trilogy

JEDI SEARCH
DARK APPRENTICE
CHAMPIONS
OF THE FORCE

Kevin J. Anderson

GuildAmerica Books

Published by arrangement with:
Bantam Books
1540 Broadway
New York, NY 10036

ISBN 1-56865-120-1

CONTENTS

CONTENTS

JEDI

SEARCH

1

The black hole cluster near Kessel reached out for the *Millennium Falcon* with jaws of gravity, drawing it close. Even in the mottled blur of hyperspace, Han Solo could see the huge distortion as a bruised whirlpool, trying to suck them down to infinity.

"Hey, Chewie! Don't you think that's too close?" He stared at the *Falcon*'s navicomputer, wishing they had chosen a course that would take them a safer distance from the Maw. "What do you think this is, an old smuggling mission? We got nothing to hide this time."

Beside him, Chewbacca looked disappointed and grunted an excuse, waving his hairy paws in the stifling air of the cockpit.

"Yeah, well we're on an official mission this time. No more skulking about. Try to act dignified, okay?"

Chewbacca groaned a skeptical reply, then turned to his navigational screens.

Han felt a pang at returning to his old haunts, reminded of when he had been just on the other side of the law, running spice, being chased by Imperial scout ships. When his life had been free and easy.

On one of those frantic missions, he and Chewbacca had practically shaved the bottom plating off the *Falcon*, taking a shortcut and skimming closer to the Maw cluster of black holes than had ever before been recorded. Sensible pilots avoided the area, using longer paths that kept them clear of the black holes, but the *Falcon*'s speed had carried them to safety on the other side, making the Kessel run in under twelve parsecs. But that "guaranteed sure thing" mission had ended in disaster anyway; Han had dumped his load of spice just before being boarded by Imperials.

This time, though, Han was returning to Kessel under different circumstances. His wife Leia had appointed him an official representative of the New Republic, an ambassador of sorts, though the title seemed somewhat honorary.

But even an honorary title had its advantages. Han and Chewbacca no longer had to dodge scout ships, or duck under planetary sensor nets, or use the secret compartments under the deck plates. Han Solo found himself in the unlikely, and uncomfortable, position of being *respectable*. There was no other word for it.

But Han's new responsibilities weren't just quaint annoyances. He was married to Leia—who could have imagined *that*?—and he had three children.

Han leaned back in his flight chair and locked his hands behind his head. He allowed a wistful smile to cross his face. He had visited the kids as often as he could, in their protective isolation on a secret planet, and the twins were due to come home to Coruscant in a week. Anakin, the third little baby, had filled him with wonder as he tickled the tiny ribs, watching an expression of amusement cross the infant's face.

Han Solo, a father figure? Leia had said a long time ago that she liked "nice men"—and that was exactly what Han was turning into!

He caught Chewbacca looking at him out of the corner of his eye. Embarrassed, Han sat up straight and frowned down at the controls. "Where are we? Shouldn't it be about time to end this jump?"

Chewie growled an affirmative, then reached out with a furry paw to grasp the hyperspace controls. The Wookiee watched the numbers tick away on his control panel; at the appropriate moment he hauled backward on the lever that dropped them back into normal space. The mottled coloring of hyperspace fanned into starlines with a roar that Han felt more than heard; then they were surrounded by the expected tapestry of stars.

Behind them the spectacle of the Maw looked like a garish finger painting as ionized gas plunged into multiple black holes. Directly in front of the *Falcon*, Han saw the blue-white glare of Kessel's sun. As the ship rotated to align them with the ecliptic, Kessel itself came into view, potato-shaped and maned with the tendrils of escaping atmosphere, orbited by a large moon that had once housed a garrison of Imperial troopers.

"Right on target, Chewie," Han said. "Now let me have the controls."

Kessel looked like a wraith coasting along its orbit, too small to hold on to its own atmosphere. Huge generating factories constantly processed the raw rocks to release oxygen and carbon dioxide, making it possible for people to survive outside with simple breath masks instead of total environment suits. A good portion of the newly manufactured atmosphere escaped into space, wisping behind the small planet like the tail of a giant comet.

Chewbacca barked a short, nasal comment. Han nodded. "Yeah, it looks great from up here. Too bad it's so different when you get a closer look. I never liked the place."

Kessel was a major planet for spice production and seat of heavy smuggling activities, as well as the site for one of the toughest prisons in the galaxy. The Empire had controlled spice production except for what smugglers managed to steal from under Imperial noses. But with the fall of the Emperor, the smugglers and the prisoners in the Imperial Correction Facility took over the planet. Kessel had laid low during the depredations of Grand Admiral Thrawn and the recent resurrection of the Emperor, keeping quiet and trying hard not to be noticed, answering no one's request for help.

A low growl rumbled in Chewie's throat. Han sighed and shook his head, "Look, I'm not happy about going back there either, buddy. But things are different now, and we're the best people to do it."

With the civil war ended and the New Republic once again firmly seated on Coruscant, leaving scattered groups of Imperial warships to fight each other, it was time to reopen negotiations. *Better to get them on our side than to let them sell out wherever they can,* Han thought, *which is what they'll probably do anyway.* As representative of the new unified smugglers, Luke's old nemesis Mara Jade had tried to contact Kessel and been flatly rebuffed.

The *Millennium Falcon* approached Kessel, firing aft thrusters to help them catch up with the planet's motion, preparing for insertion into orbit. On the helm's scanner screens, Han checked their approach. "Vectoring in," he said.

Chewie made a quick comment and pointed at the screens. Han looked down to see blips already in orbit around the planet, emerging from the blanketing clouds of the atmosphere. "I see 'em. Looks like about a half dozen ships. Too far away to determine the types."

Han brushed aside Chewie's uneasy growl. "Well, then we'll just tell them who we are. Don't worry. Why do you think Leia made such a fuss about getting us proper diplomatic ID signals and everything?"

He switched on the New Republic beacon that automatically pinged out their identification in Basic and several other languages. To his surprise, the orbiting ships changed their vector in unison and increased speed to intercept the *Falcon.*

"Hey!" Han shouted, then realized he had not switched on the audio pickup. Chewie roared. Han toggled the switch on. "This is Han Solo of the

New Republic ship *Millennium Falcon*. We are on a diplomatic mission." His mind raced, wondering what words a real diplomat would use. "Uh, please state your intentions."

The two closest ships raced in, first growing into distinct points of light, then taking on shapes. "Chewie, I think you'd better get our forward deflector shields up. I've got a bad feeling about this."

He reached for the communications switch as Chewbacca brought up the shields, but then he looked through the front viewport. The two incoming ships roared toward him at unbelievable speed, spreading out on either side. The sight of their squared-off solar panels and central pilot compartments turned Han's blood to ice water.

TIE fighters.

"Chewie, get over here. I'm taking the laser cannon."

Before the Wookiee could reply, Han hauled himself up the access tube into the gun well. He grabbed on to the gunner's chair, trying to reorient himself in the new gravity field.

The TIE fighters came in for a two-pronged attack, spreading above and below the *Falcon* and firing their lasers. As the ship lurched from the impact, Han managed to throw himself into the gunner's chair, grabbing for the harness buckle and strapping himself in. One of the attacking ships swooped overhead, and the *Falcon*'s sensor panels howled with the sound of Twin Ion Engines, from which the TIE fighter took its name. The enemy vessel fired again, but the beams streaked harmlessly through space.

"Chewie, take evasive action! Don't just fly straight!"

The Wookiee shouted something from below, and Han yelled back. "I don't know—you're piloting, *you* figure it out!" Obviously Kessel had not rolled out the welcome mat for them. Had some vestige of the Empire taken over the planet? If so, Han needed to get that information back to Coruscant.

Other ships were approaching now, and somehow Han didn't think they were coming to help. Up ahead, the two TIE fighters swooped up in a tight arc, executing a complete one-eighty and roaring back for a second attack on the *Falcon*.

But this time Han had managed to strap himself in and power up the laser batteries. On his scope the TIE fighter made a digitized target, growing larger. The enemy ship came closer and closer. Han tightened his grip around the firing levers, knowing the TIE pilot would be doing the same. He waited, feeling sweat build up on his neck. He realized he was holding his breath. One more second. One more second. The targeting cross showed dead center on the starboard wing of the fighter.

The instant Han pressed the firing button, Chewbacca threw the *Falcon* into an evasive roll. The laser blasts went wide, spraying toward the distant stars. The TIE fighter's shot also missed, streaking in the opposite direction and coming perilously close to striking the second TIE fighter.

The second fighter managed to readjust his aim quickly enough that his two shots scored the *Falcon*'s shields. Han heard sparks spraying from the control panels. Chewie bellowed a preliminary damage report. Aft shields gone. Forward shields still holding well. That meant they had to take the TIE fighters head-on.

As the first fighter swung around for a third pass, Han swiveled his gun turret as far as it would go and stared at the targeting screen again. This time he would forget about finesse and perfect accuracy. He just wanted to blast the sucker. His lasers were fully charged, and he could afford to waste a few shots, as long as this wasn't going to be a prolonged battle.

As soon as the targeting cross touched the image of the fighter, Han squeezed his firing buttons at full power, strafing his deadly laser across the path of the incoming ship. The Imperial fighter swooped in but could not change its course quickly enough, plowing through the shower of laser bolts.

The ship erupted into a flame-flower of exploding fuel tanks and expanding atmosphere. Han and Chewbacca shouted their triumph in unison. Even euphoric, Han didn't sit around patting himself on the back.

"Let's go after the other one, Chewie." The second TIE fighter swerved outward in a long trajectory, then headed back toward Kessel. "Hurry, before those reinforcements can get here."

He wondered if perhaps he and Chewbacca shouldn't turn and flee immediately. But part of him refused to let anybody take pot-shots at the *Millennium Falcon* and just walk away from it.

Chewbacca increased speed, closing the gap between the *Falcon* and the TIE fighter. "Just get me one good shot, Chewie. One good shot."

He was in an unmarked modified light freighter—why would the TIE fighters come out shooting at them in the first place? Was it the New Republic ID beacon? What was going on at Kessel? Leia sat around thinking about details like that, analyzing the possibilities, and coming up with scenarios. With her tremendous load of diplomatic duties, she was becoming more and more of a thinker each day, trying to solve things by committee and negotiation. But a political solution wouldn't work if an Imperial TIE fighter came in shooting at you.

Another ship soared up from behind as they chased the TIE fighter toward Kessel. Han shot off a few bursts from his laser, but they all missed; then he turned his attention to the ship tailing them. The *Falcon* had no operational shields back there.

Chewbacca called out again from below; then Han got his second surprise for the day. "I see it, I see it!"

An X-wing fighter approached from the rear, slowly gaining on the *Falcon* as they neared Kessel. Han took another potshot at the TIE fighter. Even from this distance the X-wing fighter seemed old and battered, as if it had been repaired many times.

"Chewie, contact the X-wing and tell him we'd appreciate whatever help he can give us." Han pressed his back against the firing chair and focused his attention on his target.

The fleeing TIE fighter soared into the wispy tail of atmosphere behind the planet. Han could see a bright pathway as the speed of the ship ionized the gas.

Then the X-wing fired on the *Falcon* from behind. The lasers scored a direct hit, incinerating the protruding sensor dish mounted on the top of the ship.

Han and Chewie shouted at each other, scrambling to figure what to do. Chewbacca took the *Falcon* into a tight dive closer to the atmosphere of Kessel.

"Turn us around! Turn us around!" They had to get their unprotected aft section out of the X-wing's line of fire.

The X-wing shot again, burning metal on the hull of the *Falcon*. All the lights went out inside the ship. From the lurch of the cabin Han knew the hit had been a bad one. He could already smell something burning below decks. Emergency lights clicked on.

"We've got to get out of here!"

Chewbacca barked the Wookiee equivalent of "no kidding."

They ducked into the atmospheric tail, buffeted by the suddenly dense gas particles pelting the ship. Around them streamers of heated gas glowed orange and blue. The X-wing came in from behind, still firing.

Han's mind raced. They could skim around Kessel in a tight orbit, then slingshot back out of the system. With the black hole cluster so close at hand, no one would risk jumping into hyperspace without intensive prior calculations, and neither he nor Chewie could spare the time to do them.

With the *Falcon*'s sensor dish slagged, Han couldn't even send out a distress call or try to sweet-talk the traitorous commander of the X-wing. He couldn't even surrender! Talk about being stuck. "Chewie, if you have any suggestions—"

He stopped talking as his mouth dropped open. As they swept around Kessel, Han detected wave after wave of fighter ships launching from the garrison moon, raising a defensive curtain the *Millennium Falcon* would never be able to cross.

He saw hundreds of ships of every size and make imaginable, salvaged warships and stolen pleasure cruisers. Reaching the safety of numbers, the second TIE fighter did another tight loop to join the rest of the group. And they all came in shooting with a blur of turbolaser bolts that looked like a fireworks display. Despite the motley appearance of the Kessel fleet, Han's sensors showed that their weapons worked just fine. The attacking X-wing scored a direct hit. The cabin shook.

The *Falcon* took a turn upward as Chewbacca tried to flee the oncoming wave of ships. Han sent a barrage of laser fire into the cluster and was gratified to see the engine pod of a small Z-95 Headhunter fighter burst into flames. The snub fighter dropped out of the attacking fleet and wobbled toward Kessel's atmosphere. Han hoped it would crash.

Seeing that it would serve no purpose to keep firing against overwhelming odds, Han dropped back down the access shaft of the gun turret to the cockpit to see what he could do to assist Chewbacca.

Then the fleet of ships began pummeling them. The X-wing fired again, scoring a second direct hit. A firestorm of laser blasts struck their forward deflector shields. Chewie slewed the *Falcon* from side to side in a futile evasive maneuver.

Han settled himself into the other pilot's chair just in time to see the indicator lights for the forward shields wink out. They were now unprotected from the front and from behind.

Another hit rocked them, and Han's chest smacked against the control panel. "There goes the main drive unit. We're space-meat in the next barrage. Take us down, Chewie. Get us into the atmosphere. It's the only thing we can do."

Chewbacca started to express his disbelief, but Han grabbed the controls and sent them lurching down toward Kessel. "It's gonna be a bumpy ride. Hold on to your fur."

The swarm of attacking ships whirled in space as the *Falcon* plowed into the white atmosphere of Kessel. Han grabbed his seat as the ship struck the clouds. He suddenly felt the buffeting winds caused by gouts of air escaping into space. From his control panels and the stench leaking from the back compartments, Han knew that his maneuvering capabilities would be minimal. By the groaning sounds from his copilot, he knew the Wookiee had realized the same thing.

"Think of it this way, Chewie. If we land this thing in one piece, our skill as pilots will be legendary from one end of the galaxy to the other!" Han said with a humor he did not feel. *I knew I shouldn't have come back to Kessel.*

The *Falcon* was going down. Both Han and Chewbacca fought to keep a steady downward course that would not burn them up in the insubstantial atmosphere.

Kessel's main defensive fleet swept into orbit and prepared for an orderly descent. One sleek, insectile ship, which Han recognized as a black-market-built Hornet Interceptor, peeled off, streaking downward in the *Falcon*'s backdraft.

Chewbacca saw it first. The ship, aerodynamically perfect, slid through the atmosphere like a vibroblade, ignoring the heat generated on its hull. The ship fired surgical strikes of turbolasers at the *Falcon*'s maneuvering jets, disabling them further.

"We're already crashing!" Han bellowed. "What more do they want?" But he knew: they wanted the *Falcon* to be destroyed on impact, all occupants erased. Han suspected he didn't need any help from the Hornet Interceptor.

As they plunged downward, the *Falcon* approached one of the giant atmosphere factories, a huge smokestack mounted on the surface of Kessel, where immense engines catalyzed the rock and cooked out gases into a cyclone of breathable air.

The Hornet Interceptor fired again. The *Falcon* lurched from a near miss. Chewbacca's face was grim. His fangs showed as he concentrated on keeping them alive.

"Chewie, pull as close to the plume as you can. I've got an idea." Chewbacca yowled, but Han cut him off. "Just do it, buddy!"

When the Hornet tried to outflank them, Han swept the ship aside as the towering plume of atmosphere boiled into the sky. The Hornet Interceptor tried to second-guess his move, but Han lurched sideways again, driving the Hornet into the roaring upward flow of wind.

An aileron strut in the delicate insectile wing snapped off, and the Hornet spun into the cyclone. Other parts of its hull broke apart as the ship tried to escape but lurched deeper into the danger zone. Han gave a cry of triumph as the ship exploded into flames that were pulled to tatters by the atmosphere factory's vortex.

Then the surface of Kessel rushed up at them like a gigantic hammer.

Han fought with the controls. "At least we'll have a soft landing with the new repulsorlifts we installed," he said.

He grabbed at the panel, priming the controls. Chewbacca barked at him to hurry. Han activated the repulsorlifts as he simultaneously heaved a sigh of relief.

Nothing.

"What?" He slammed his fingers on the switch again and again, but the repulsorlifts refused to operate. "I just had those fixed!"

Han yelled above the noise of screaming wind as he fought to bring the *Falcon* under some semblance of control. "Okay, Chewie, I am definitely open for suggestions!"

But Chewbacca had no time to answer before the ship crashed into the rugged surface of Kessel.

2

The towers of Imperial City rose to the sky, high above the shadowed surface of the planet Coruscant. The cornerstones of the towers had been in place for more than a thousand generations, dating back to the formative days of the Old Republic. Over the millennia higher and higher structures had been built on top of the ruined foundations.

Luke Skywalker stepped onto a shuttle-landing platform that jutted out from the scarred, monolithic face of the former Imperial Palace. Gusts of wind whipped around him, and he pulled back the hood of his Jedi robe.

He looked into the sky, pondering the thin layer of atmosphere that protected Coruscant from space beyond. Wrecked ships still rode in haphazard orbits, debris from the vicious battles when the Alliance had recently recaptured the planet from Imperial control during civil war in the remnants of the Empire.

Higher than the tops of the towers, kitelike hawk-bats rode thermal currents rising from the canyons of the city. As he watched, one hawk-bat swooped down, down, into the dark crevasses between ancient buildings, finally emerging a moment later with something cylindrical and dripping— a granite slug, perhaps—in its claws.

Luke bided his time, using a Jedi meditation technique to quell the anxiety inside him. As a younger man he had been fidgety and impatient, filled with uncertainty. But Yoda had taught him patience, along with so many other things. A true Jedi Knight could wait as long as necessary. The New Republic Senate had been in session for only an hour, and they would still be working on mundane issues. Luke wanted to startle them after they had been talking for a while.

The immense metropolis of Imperial City bustled around him, little changed now that it was the seat of the New Republic instead of the Empire; prior to that it had been capital of the Old Republic. The capitol building, formerly Emperor Palpatine's palace, was made of polished gray-green rock and mirrored crystals, sparkling in the hazy sunlight of Coruscant as it towered over all other structures, even the adjoining Senate building.

Much of Imperial City had been laid waste during the months of civil war following the downfall of Grand Admiral Thrawn. The various factions of the old Empire had fought over the Emperor's home world, turning vast districts into graveyards of crashed ships and exploded buildings.

But the tide of battle had turned, and the New Republic had driven back the vestiges of the Empire. Many Alliance soldiers now turned their efforts to repairing the damage, his friend Wedge Antilles among them. Top priority had been given to rebuilding the former Imperial Palace and the Senate chambers. The Emperor's own construction droids ranged through the battle-scarred wastelands, automatically scraping up raw materials from the wreckage for conversion into new buildings.

In the distance Luke could see one of the enormous droids, forty stories tall, wrecking a half-collapsed building shell and plowing a path where its programming had deemed a new elevated transport path should be routed. Its girder arms toppled the stone face of the building, pulling free metal support structures and feeding the debris into a processing mouth where the materials would be separated and new components extruded.

During the previous year of violent strife, Luke had been whisked away to the resurrected Emperor's stronghold in the galactic core, and there he had allowed himself to learn the dark side. He had become the Emperor's chief lieutenant, just like his father, Darth Vader. The struggle had been great within him, and only with the help, and the friendship, and the *love* of Leia and Han had he been able to break free. . . .

Luke saw a diplomatic shuttle dropping down from orbit with its locator lights rippling in a complex sequence. Its jets turned off with a whining sound as it coasted toward a landing pad on the far side of the palace.

Luke Skywalker had been through the fire now. Inside, his heart seemed a diamond-hard lump. He wasn't merely another Jedi Knight—he was the only remaining Jedi *Master*. He had survived tests and rigors more potent than routine Jedi training prepared him for. Luke understood more about the Force now than he had ever dreamed possible. Sometimes it terrified him.

He thought of the days when he had been idealistic and adventuresome, riding the *Millennium Falcon* and dueling blindly with a practice remote as Ben Kenobi watched. Luke remembered also the skepticism he had felt as he swooped down upon the first Death Star during the Battle of Yavin, trying to locate a tiny thermal-exhaust port; Ben's voice had spoken to him then, telling him to trust in the Force. Luke understood much more now, especially why the old man's eyes had held such a haunted look.

Another hawk-bat swooped down into the dark maze of the lower levels of buildings, flapping its wings as it climbed back up, holding a squirming prize in its claws. As Luke watched, a second hawk-bat dove in on an intercept course, grabbing the prey out of the first's grasp. Far away, he could hear their cawing sounds as they slashed and tore at each other. The squirming prey, no longer heeded, fell through the air, buffeted by rising currents, until it struck ground somewhere in the alley dimness. The two hawk-bats, locked in mortal combat, also fell as they struggled with each other, until they too smashed into an outcropping of the abandoned lower levels.

A troubled expression crossed Luke's face. An omen? He was about to address the New Republic Senate. The time had come. He turned and walked back inside the cool corridors, pulling his robe tightly around himself.

Luke stood at the entrance to the Senate assembly chamber. The room swept down to a giant amphitheater in which sat the inner circle of appointed senators and outer rows of representatives from different planets, different alien races. Realtime holos of the proceedings would be broadcast around Imperial City and recorded for transmission to other planets.

Sunlight filtered through the fragmented crystal segments in the ceiling high overhead, fanning out the spectrum in a rainbow effect over the most important people at the center of the room, scintillating around them as they moved—designed, Luke knew, by the Emperor himself to strike awe into those observing him.

As she spoke now on the central dais, Mon Mothma, the New Republic's Chief of State, seemed uncomfortable in the grandeur of the assembly chamber. Luke allowed a smile to cross his face as he remembered the first time he had seen Mon Mothma describing the plans of the second Death Star as the Rebels approached Endor.

With her short reddish hair and soft voice, Mon Mothma did not look like a tough-as-nails military commander. As a former member of the Imperial Senate, Mon Mothma seemed to be more in her element now, trying to forge the pieces of the New Republic into a strong, unified government.

Beside Mon Mothma sat Luke's sister Leia Organa Solo, straight-backed and listening to every moment of the proceedings. Leia had been performing more and more important diplomatic activities with each passing month.

Around the dais sat the members of the Alliance High Command, important figures in the Rebellion given roles in the new government: General Jan Dodonna, who had led the Battle of Yavin against the first Death Star; General Carlist Rieekan, former commander of Echo Base on the ice planet Hoth; General Crix Madine, an Imperial defector who had been invaluable in planning the destruction of the second Death Star; Admiral Ackbar, who had led the rebel fleet in the Battle of Endor; Senator Garm Bel Iblis, who had brought his Dreadnaught ships against Grand Admiral Thrawn.

Battlefield credentials did not necessarily imply that these brave leaders would be gifted politicians as well, but since the hold of the New Republic was still shaky, as the recent devastating civil war had shown, it made good sense to keep military commanders in positions of power.

Finishing her speech, Mon Mothma raised her hands. For a moment it looked as if she were about to give a benediction. "I call for any new business. Does anyone wish to speak?"

Luke's timing had been perfect. He stepped into the light at the entrance archway and drew back his hood. He spoke softly, but used his Jedi powers to project with sufficient strength that everyone in the entire amphitheater heard him.

"I would address the assembly, Mon Mothma. If I may?"

He walked down the steps with a gliding stride, quickly enough that the others would not lose patience, but with enough grace to imply his own strength of character. Appearances could deceive, Yoda had said, but sometimes appearances could be very important.

As he descended the long ramp, Luke felt all eyes turn toward him. A hush fell over the assembly. Luke Skywalker, the lone remaining Jedi Master, almost never took part in governmental proceedings.

"I have an important matter to address," he said. For a moment he was reminded of when he had walked alone into the dank corridors of Jabba the Hutt's palace—but this time there were no piglike Gamorrean guards that he could manipulate with a twist of his fingers and a touch of the Force.

Mon Mothma gave him a soft, mysterious smile and gestured for him to take a central position. "The words of a Jedi Knight are always welcome to the New Republic," she said.

Luke tried not to look pleased. She had provided the perfect opening for him. "In the Old Republic," he said, "Jedi Knights were the protectors and guardians of all. For a thousand generations the Jedi used the powers of the Force to guide, defend, and provide support for the rightful government of worlds—before the dark days of the Empire came, and the Jedi Knights were killed."

He let his words hang, then took another breath. "Now we have a New Republic. The Empire appears to be defeated. We have founded a new government based upon the old, but let us hope we learn from our mistakes. Before, an entire order of Jedi watched over the Republic, offering strength. Now I am the only Jedi Master who remains.

"Without that order of protectors to provide a backbone of strength for the New Republic, can we survive? Will we be able to weather the storms and the difficulties of forging a new union? Until now we have suffered severe struggles—but in the future they will be seen as nothing more than birth pangs."

Before the other senators could disagree with that, Luke continued. "Our people had a common foe in the Empire, and we must not let our defenses lapse just because we have internal problems. More to the point, what will happen when we begin squabbling among ourselves over petty matters? The old Jedi helped to mediate many types of disputes. What if there are no Jedi Knights to protect us in the difficult times ahead?"

Luke moved under the diffracting rainbow colors from the crystal light overhead. He took his time to fix his gaze on all the senators present; he turned his attention to Leia last. Her eyes were wide but supportive. He had not discussed his idea with her beforehand.

"My sister is undergoing Jedi training. She has a great deal of skill in the Force. Her three children are also likely candidates to be trained as young Jedi. In recent years I have come to know a woman named Mara Jade, who is now unifying the smugglers—the former smugglers," he amended, "into an organization that can support the needs of the New Republic. She also has a talent for the Force. I have encountered others in my travels."

Another pause. The audience was listening so far. "But are these the only ones? We already know that the ability to use the Force is passed from generation to generation. Most of the Jedi were killed in the Emperor's purge—but could he possibly have eradicated all of the descendants of those Knights? I myself was unaware of the potential power within me until Obi-Wan Kenobi taught me how to use it. My sister Leia was similarly unaware.

"How many people are abroad in this galaxy who have a comparable strength in the Force, who are potential members of a new order of Jedi Knights, but are unaware of who they are?"

Luke looked at them again. "In my brief search I have already discovered that there are indeed some descendants of former Jedi. I have come here to ask"—he turned to gesture toward Mon Mothma, swept his hand across the people gathered there in the chamber—"for two things.

"First, that the New Republic officially sanction my search for those with a hidden talent for the Force, to seek them out and try to bring them to our service. For this I will need some help."

Admiral Ackbar interrupted, blinking his huge fish eyes and turning his head. "But if you yourself did not know your power when you were young, how will these other people know? How will you find them, Jedi Skywalker?"

Luke folded his hands in front of him. "Several ways. First, with the help of two dedicated droids who will spend their days searching through the Imperial City databases, we may find likely candidates, people who have experienced miraculous strokes of luck, whose lives seem filled with incredible coincidences. We could look for people who seem unusually charismatic or those whom legend credits with working miracles. These could all be unconscious manifestations of a skill with the Force."

Luke held up another finger. "As well, the droids could search the database for forgotten descendants of known Jedi Knights from the Old Republic days. We should turn up a few leads."

"And what will you yourself be doing?" Mon Mothma asked, shifting in her robes.

"I've already found several candidates I wish to investigate. All I ask right now is that you agree this is something we should pursue, that the search for Jedi be conducted by others and not just myself."

Mon Mothma sat up straighter in her central seat. "I think we can agree to that without further discussion." She looked around to the other senators, seeing them nod agreement. "Tell us your second request."

Luke stood taller. This was most important to him. He saw Leia stiffen.

"If sufficient candidates are found who have potential for using the Force, I wish to be allowed—with the New Republic's blessing—to establish in some appropriate place an intensive training center, a Jedi academy, if you will. Under my direction we can help these students discover their abilities, to focus and strengthen their power. Ultimately, this academy would provide a core group that could allow us to restore the Jedi Knights as protectors of the New Republic."

He drew in a deep breath and waited.

Senator Bel Iblis raised himself slowly to his feet. "A comment, if I may? I'm sorry, Luke, but I have to raise the question—we've already seen the terrible damage a Jedi can cause if he allows himself to be swayed by the dark side. We just recently fought against Joruus C'baoth, and of course Darth Vader nearly caused the death of us all. If a teacher as great as Obi-Wan Kenobi could fail and let his student fall to evil, how can we take the risk of training an entire new order of Jedi Knights? How many will turn to the dark side? How many new enemies will we make for ourselves?"

Luke nodded somberly. The question had been working at the back of his own mind, and he had pondered it deeply. "I can only say that we have seen these terrible examples, and we must learn from them. I myself have touched the dark side and come through stronger and more wary of its powers than ever before. I agree there is a risk, but I cannot believe the New Republic will be safer *without* a new force of Jedi."

A murmur rippled through the chamber. Bel Iblis stood a moment longer, as if he meant to say something else, but instead he sat down, looking satisfied.

Admiral Ackbar got to his feet and applauded with his flipperlike hands. "I agree that the Jedi's request is in the best interests of the New Republic," he said.

Jan Dodonna also stood. After narrowly surviving the Battle of Yavin, Dodonna had treated Luke with complete trust. "I agree as well!"

Soon all the senators were standing. Luke saw a broad grin on Leia's face as she too stood. He felt the rainbows around him from the crystal ceiling, seemingly full of power, and he felt warm inside.

Mon Mothma sat, nodding gravely. She was the last to stand up, and she raised her hand for silence. "I give you my hopes for the rebirth of the Jedi Knights. We will offer whatever help we can. May the Force be with you."

Before Luke could turn, applause from the audience rolled like a storm through the chamber.

3

Leia's quarters were among the most spacious and accommodating in the Emperor's abandoned palace—and the room echoed with emptiness. Leia Organa Solo, formerly a princess, currently the New Republic's Minister of State—felt tired and worn as she returned to her rooms at the end of a long day.

The high point had been Luke's triumphant address before the assembly, but that was merely one detail in a day filled with problems. Confusing contradictions in multilingual treaties that even Threepio couldn't fathom, alien cultural restrictions that made diplomacy nearly impossible—it made her head spin!

As Leia looked around her quarters, a frown etched her face. "Illumination up two points," she said, and the room grew brighter, driving some of the quiet shadows farther away.

Han and Chewbacca were gone, ostensibly to reestablish contact with the planet Kessel, although she believed it was more of a vacation for him, a way to relive the "good old days" of gallivanting across the galaxy.

Sometimes she wondered if Han ever regretted marrying someone so different from himself, settling down with diplomatic entanglements on Coruscant. He tolerated endless receptions during which he had to dress nicely in clothes that obviously made him uncomfortable. In conversations he had to speak with a measured tact that was completely foreign to him.

But Han was off having fun at the moment, leaving her stuck in Imperial City.

The New Republic's Chief of State, Mon Mothma, gave Leia more and more assignments, letting the fate of planets hang on how well she accomplished her tasks. So far Leia *had* performed well, but the seven years since the Battle of Endor had been filled with many setbacks: the war against the alien Ssi-ruuk Imperium, the resurgence of Grand Admiral Thrawn and his bid to reassemble the Empire, not to mention the resurrected Emperor and his gigantic World Devastator machines. Though they seemed to be enjoying a time of relative peace at last, the constant warfare had left the New Republic on shaky ground.

In a way it had been easier when they had the Empire to fight against, to unify all the factions of the Alliance. But now the enemy was not so clearly defined. Now Leia and the others had to reforge links between all the planets that had once been crushed under the Imperial boot. Some of those worlds, though, had suffered so much that now they wanted to be left alone, given time to lick their wounds and heal. Many wanted no part of a galaxywide federation of planets. They wanted their independence.

But independent worlds could be picked off one by one if other powerful forces ever allied themselves against them.

Leia walked into her bedchamber and stripped off the diplomatic clothing she had worn all day. This morning it had been crisp and bright, but the fabric lost its vigor after too much time under the rainbow lights of the grand audience chamber.

Within the next week or so, Leia would have to arrange meetings with ambassadors from six different worlds in an effort to convince them to join the New Republic. Four seemed amenable, but two insisted on complete neutrality until their planets' specific issues were addressed.

Her most difficult task would be two weeks hence, when the Caridan ambassador would arrive. Carida was deep in territory still held by vestiges of the Empire, home of one of the primary Imperial military training bases. Even though Emperor Palpatine was dead and Grand Admiral Thrawn overthrown, Carida refused to face reality. It had been a major victory that the ambassador agreed to come to Coruscant at all—and Leia would have to entertain him, no doubt smiling pleasantly the entire time.

Leia turned on the controls of the sonic bath and set it for a gentle massage. She eased herself into the chamber, letting out a long sigh, wanting just to blank out the troubles from her head.

Around her, fresh-cut flowers from the Skydome Botanical Gardens brightened the room with their faint perfume. Mounted on the wall were nostalgic scenes from the planet Alderaan, pictures of the planet where she had grown up, the planet Grand Moff Tarkin had destroyed to demonstrate the power of his Death Star: the peaceful, sweeping grasslands that whispered in the wind, the soaring kite creatures that ferried people from one smooth tower city to another, the industry and deep settlements built into the walls of wide cracks plunging into Alderaan's crust . . . her home city rising from the center of a lake.

Han had procured those pictures for her just last year; he wouldn't say where he had found them. For months the images wrenched her heart every time she looked at them. She thought of her foster father, Senator Bail Organa, and her childhood as a princess, never suspecting her true heritage.

Now Leia looked on those pictures with bittersweet fondness, as an indication of Han's love for her. He had, after all, once won a whole planet in a card game and had given it to her for the other survivors of Alderaan. He did love her.

Even though he wasn't here now.

After only a few minutes the sonic bath unknotted her muscles, revitalizing and refreshing her. Leia dressed again, this time in something more comfortable.

In the mirror she looked at herself. Leia no longer spent the meticulous time with her hair that she had when she was a princess on Alderaan. Since then she had borne three children, the twins, who were now two years old, and recently a third baby. She was able to see them only a few times a year, and she missed them terribly.

Because of the potential power carried by the grandchildren of Anakin Skywalker, the twins and the baby boy had been taken to a carefully guarded planet, Anoth. All other knowledge of the planet had been blocked from her mind, to prevent anyone from prying it out of her thoughts.

During their first two years, Luke said, Jedi children were most vulnerable. Any contact with the dark side could warp their minds and abilities for life.

She activated the small holodais that projected recent images of her children. The two-year-old twins, Jacen and Jaina, played inside a colorful sculptured playground artifact. In another image Leia's personal servant Winter held the new baby, Anakin, smiling at something out of view. Leia smiled back, though the static images couldn't see her.

Part of that long loneliness would soon be over. Jacen and Jaina could now use some of the Jedi powers to protect themselves, and Leia could shield the twins as well. Within little more than a week—no, it was exactly eight days—her little boy and girl would be returning home.

Knowing that the twins were coming to stay lightened her mood. Leia eased back into the self-conforming chair as she turned on the entertainment synthesizers, playing a pastorale melody written by a famous composer from Alderaan.

The door chime sounded, startling her from her reverie. She glanced down to make certain she had remembered to dress herself, then went to the entryway.

Her brother Luke stood in the shadows, cowled in his brown hood and cloak. "Hello, Luke!" she said, then gasped. "Oh, I forgot completely!"

"Developing your Jedi powers is nothing to take lightly, Leia." He frowned, as if scolding her.

She gestured him to come inside. "I'm sure you'll have me make it up with extra practice sessions."

When seen from a distance, the huge construction droid moved at a plodding pace, lifting its immense support pods only once every half hour to shuffle a step forward. But standing right beneath it, General Wedge Antilles and his demolition teams saw the construction droid as a blur of motion, its thousands of articulated arms working on structures to be disassembled. The walking factory plowed deeper into the morass of collapsing and half-destroyed buildings in an old sector of Imperial City.

Some of the droid's limbs ended with implosion wrecking balls or plasma cutters that sent explosive jolts into the walls. Collector arms sorted through the rubble, yanking out girders, shoveling boulders and steelcrete into dispensing receptacles. Other raw wreckage was scooped directly into the churning mandibles and conveyor belts that brought the resources down to elemental separators, which in turn pulled out the useful substances and processed them into new building components. The heat rising from its internal factories rippled in miragelike waves, making the immense machine glow in Coruscant's star-filled night.

The construction droid continued to work its way through the buildings damaged from the devastating firefights during the recent civil warfare. With so much to repair or destroy, sometimes the droid's collector arms and debris nets were not sufficient.

Wedge Antilles looked up just in time to see a packed receptacle split from its moorings. "Hey, keep back, everybody! Under cover!" The demolition team scrambled under the protection of an outcropping of wall as the debris fell twenty stories.

A rain of boulders, transparisteel, and twisted rebars crashed with explosive force into the street below. Someone yelped into the comlink, then promptly silenced himself.

"Looks like this main building is going to go any minute," Wedge said. "Team Orange, I want you to keep at least half a block away from that thing. There's no telling what that droid's going to do, and I don't want to shut it down. It takes three days to reinitialize and get it working again." Wedge had not been thrilled with using the outdated and unpredictable technology of the construction droids, but they did seem to be the fastest way to clear the wreckage.

"I copy, Wedge," the Orange Team Leader said, "but if we see any more of those feral refugees, we're going to have to try and rescue them—even if they are faster and hide better." Then the comlink channel broke into chatter as he ordered other team members to move.

Wedge smiled. Even though he, like Lando Calrissian and Han Solo, had been promoted to the rank of general, Wedge still felt like "one of the guys." He was a fighter pilot at heart, and he liked it that way. He had spent the last four months in space with the salvage crews there, hauling wrecked fighters into higher orbits where they would pose no risk to the incoming ships. He had salvaged the vessels not too badly damaged and self-destructed those that posed too great a hazard in the orbital traffic lanes.

Last month Wedge had requested a ground assignment for a change, though he loved to fly in space. Now he was in charge of almost two hundred people, supervising the four construction droids that churned through this section of the city, restoring it and erasing battle scars from the war against the Empire.

The construction droids each had a master plan deep in their computer cores. As they repaired Imperial City in swaths, the droids checked the buildings in front of them, fixing those that needed minor repairs, demolishing those that didn't fit into the new plan.

Most of the sentient life forms had been evacuated from the deep under-world of the ancient metropolis, although some creatures living in the darkest alleys could no longer be classified as fully human. Shabby and naked, with pallid skin and sunken eyes, they were the descendants of those who had long ago fled to Coruscant's darkest alleys to escape political retribution; some looked as though they had not seen the sun their entire lives. When the New Republic returned to Coruscant, an effort spearheaded by the old veteran of Yavin 4, General Jan Dodonna, had been to help these poor souls, but they were wild and smart, and eluded capture every time.

The streets—or what had been streets centuries ago—were covered with dank moss and a lush growth of fungus. The smells of decaying garbage and stagnant water swirled around them anytime Wedge's team moved. Microclimates of rising air and condensing moisture created tiny rainstorms in the alleys, but the dripping water smelled no fresher than the standing pools or gutters. Wedge's teams deployed floating repulsor-lights, but clouds of settling dust from the demolition work filled the air with thick murk.

The construction droid paused in its work for a moment, and the relative silence sounded like a thud in Wedge's ears. He looked up to see the droid extending two of its big wrecking-ball arms. It swung the balls with mammoth force, toppling the wall in front of it. Then the droid levered its support-pod legs forward to take a step into the collapsing building.

But the side of the wall did not slough inward quite as Wedge expected; something inside had been reinforced more than the rest of the building. The construction droid tried to step down, but the wall would not yield. The titanic droid began making loud, hydraulic sounds as it attempted to regain its balance. The forty-story-tall mechanical factory tilted sideways and hung poised on the verge of toppling. Wedge jerked out his comlink. If the construction droid fell, it would take out half a block of buildings with it, including the area where he had just sent Team Orange to take refuge.

But then a dozen of its arms locked together and extended to the adjacent wall of buildings, splaying out, breaking through in places, but steadying the droid's weight just long enough for it to regain its balance. A rustling noise came over the comlink as Wedge's teams let out a collective sigh of relief.

Wedge tried to see by the light of the shimmering aurora overhead and the floating lights they had strung. Hidden behind an edifice indistinguishable from the rest of the buildings stood solid metal walls, heavily reinforced but buckled and ruptured by the enormous foot of the construction droid.

Wedge frowned. The demolition teams had encountered a lot of ancient artifacts in the ruined buildings, but nothing that had been so powerfully shielded and hidden. Something told him this was important.

He looked up with a start to see that the construction droid had reoriented itself and returned to the reinforced building that stood in its way. Bending down its scanner-dome head, the droid inspected the tough walls of the shielded room, as if analyzing how best to rip it to shreds. Two of the explosive electrical claws extended downward.

The construction droid knew nothing about what secrets these buildings might contain. The droid merely followed the blueprint in its computer mind and carried out its programmed modifications.

Wedge felt an agonized moment of indecision. If he shut the droid down to inspect the mysterious building, it would take three days to reset all the systems and power it up again. But if the droid had indeed uncovered something important, something the Cabinet should know about, what would a few days matter?

Blue-white lightning flickered on the ends of the construction droid's explosive claws as it reached toward the shielded walls.

Wedge picked up his comlink and made ready to shut down the droid— and then his mind blanked. What was the code?

Beside him Lieutenant Deegan saw his moment of panicked confusion and snapped the answer. "SGW zero-zero-two-seven!" Wedge instantly keyed it into the comlink.

The droid froze just as it was about to discharge its electrical claws. Wedge heard the hissing rumble as the factories inside went into standby mode, powering down and cooling off. Wedge hoped he had made the right decision.

"Okay, Purple and Silver Teams come on in with me. We're going to do a little exploring here."

Summoning a cluster of floating lights to follow them, the teams converged at the foot of the construction droid and then moved into the wreckage. Loose dust flickered down.

They scrambled over the rubble, careful not to cut themselves on shattered transparisteel and protruding metal. Wedge heard the skittering sounds of small life-forms hiding in the new cracks. The patter of falling stones continued to fall as the collapsing walls shifted and reshifted. "Watch your backs—this place is still falling apart," Wedge said.

Ahead a wide cavelike gash had opened in the heavily shielded room, showing only a lightless interior.

"Let's go in. Nice and easy." Wedge narrowed his eyes at the shadows around them. "Be ready to retreat at a moment's notice. We don't know what's in there."

A deafening screech sounded far above, reverberating in the night. The demolition teams jumped, then forced themselves to relax when they found it was only the cooling construction droid venting waste heat.

Wedge stepped to the edge of the darkened hole. The buckled crack in the wall was completely dark, showing nothing.

The moment he poked his head into the darkness, the monster lunged forward, all fangs and spewing saliva.

Wedge cried out and stumbled back, bouncing against the jagged edge of the opening as the locomotive of claws and fur and armored body plating charged at him.

Before he could straighten his thoughts—before he could even imagine shouting an order to his troops—a spiderweb of crisscrossed blaster fire erupted into the night. Most of the beams struck home with a smoking hiss into the creature's body. A second round of blaster fire lanced out.

The monster roared in explosive surprise and pain before collapsing with enough force to start a small avalanche in the debris. Its death sigh sounded like steam escaping from a furnace.

Wedge slumped to the ground and suddenly felt his heart begin beating again. "Thanks, guys!"

The rest of them stood, frozen in surprise and terror, gawking at their own reflexively drawn blasters and at the heaving, dying hulk of the monster that had dwelled within the shielded building.

The thing looked like a huge armored rat with spines along its back and tusks coming out of its mouth. It had the tail of a krayt dragon, flicking in its final convulsions as black-purple blood oozed around burned craters of blaster wounds in its hide.

"Guess it got hungry waiting in there," Wedge said. "Your fearless leader needs to be a little more careful from now on."

He sent the bobbing lights through the opening to illuminate the chamber ahead. Nothing else seemed to be moving inside. Behind them the giant armored rat shuddered with a last groaning sigh, then sagged.

In pairs they pushed through the opening into the isolated chamber. The metal-plated floor was strewn with cracked bones and skulls from the subhumans that lived in the city's lower levels. "I guess it found something to eat after all," Wedge said.

On the far side of the dark room, they found another tunnel from deeper underground where a grate had been peeled aside. The grate was rusted, but bright score marks from large claws showed where the rat-thing had torn its way through.

"Not it—a *she*," Lieutenant Deegan said. "And now you can see why she was so upset." He pointed to the corner where the worst damage had occurred.

Broken blocks of building material lay piled on the rat-thing's nest. Bright smears of blood showed where three of the creature's young—each one the size of an Endorian pony—had been crushed by the boulders.

Wedge stared for a moment before he looked around the rest of the gloomy room. Adjusting the light-enhancers on his visor, he could see dark gadgets, consoles, bed-platforms with manacles and chains. Parked and dormant on two stands were glossy black Imperial interrogation droids; secret computer ports stared gray and dead like amphibious eyes.

"Some sort of torture center?" Lieutenant Deegan asked.

"Looks like it," Wedge answered. "Interrogation. This could yield a lot of information the Emperor didn't want us to have."

"Good thing you shut down the construction droid, Wedge," Deegan said. "It's worth the delay."

Wedge pursed his lips. "Yeah, good thing." He looked at the cruel interrogation droids and the torture equipment. A part of him wished he had never found this place.

The sculpture on Leia's crystal table jittered forward, stopped, then rose into the air.

The figure was a fat man with spread palms and a grin wide enough to swallow an X-wing fighter. The dealer had assured Leia that it was a genuine

Corellian sculpture, that it would make Han think fond memories of his own world just as Han's images of Alderaan did for her. Upon receiving the anniversary gift, Han had thanked her profusely, but could barely control his laughter. He finally explained that the statue was a trademarked figurine stolen from a chain of cheap Corellian eating establishments. . . .

"Keep concentrating, Leia," Luke whispered into the silence, leaning closer. He watched her intently. Her eyes were focused in the far distance, not seeing the sculpture at all.

The statue continued to levitate, rising higher off the table; then suddenly it bumped forward to topple onto the floor.

Leia heaved a sigh and slumped back in the self-conforming chair. Luke tried to cover his disappointment as he remembered his own training. Yoda had made him stand on his head while balancing rocks and other heavy objects. Luke had received other training from the twisted Joruus C'baoth, and he had learned the depths of the dark side from the resurrected Emperor himself.

His sister's training had been much less rigorous, and more haphazard as she continually rescheduled lessons to accommodate her increasing diplomatic duties. But Leia concerned him: he had been working with her for more than seven years now, and she seemed to be blocked, having reached the limit of the powers she could master. Given her heritage as the daughter of Anakin Skywalker, Leia should have been easy to train. Luke wondered how he would manage to instruct a large group of students at his proposed Jedi academy if he could not succeed with his own sister.

Leia stood and picked up the fallen statue from the floor, setting it back on the table. Luke watched her, keeping his face free of any downcast expression. "Leia, what is it?" he asked.

She looked at him with her dark eyes and hesitated before answering. "Just feeling sorry for myself, I guess. Han should have arrived on Kessel two days ago, but he hasn't bothered to send a message. That's no big surprise, considering him!" But Luke saw more wistfulness than sarcasm in her eyes.

"Sometimes it wears on me not to have my own children here. I've been with the twins for only a fraction of their lives. I can count on one hand the number of times I've visited the baby. I haven't had time to feel like a mother. The diplomatic chores won't give me a rest." Then she looked directly at him. "And you're about to go off on your great Jedi hunt. I feel like I'm missing out on life."

Luke reached out to touch her arm. "You could become a very powerful Jedi if you would only devote some concentration to your work. To follow the Force, you must let your training be the focus of your life and not become distracted by other things."

Leia reacted more strongly than he had anticipated, drawing away. "Maybe I'm afraid of that, Luke. When I look at you, I see a haunted expression in your eyes, as if a vital part of you has been burned away by the personal hells you've walked through. Trying to kill your own father, dueling with a clone of yourself, serving the Dark Side for the Emperor. If that's what it takes to be a powerful Jedi, maybe I don't *want* the job!"

She held up her hand to stop him from saying anything until she had finished. "I am doing important work for the Council. I'm helping to rebuild a whole republic of a thousand star systems. Maybe that is my life's work, not being a Jedi. And maybe, just maybe, I might want to fit being a mother in there, too."

Luke looked at her, unmoved. No one could read his expressions anymore; he was no longer innocent. "If that is your destiny, Leia, it's a good thing I'll start training other Jedi soon." They stared at each other in an uncomfortable silence for a few moments. Luke looked away first, retreating from that line of conversation.

"But you still need to protect yourself from the Dark Side. Let's work a little more with shielding and your inner defenses, and then we'll call it a night." Leia nodded, but he could sense that her spirits had sunk further.

He reached out with his fingers to touch her dark hair, drifting over the contours of her head. "I'm going to try to probe your mind. I'll use different techniques, different touches. Try to resist me, or at least pinpoint where I am."

Luke let his eyes fall half-closed, then sent faint tendrils of thoughts into her mind, deftly touching the topography of her memory. At first she didn't react, but then he could feel her concentrating, building an invisible wall around his probe. Though slow, she succeeded in blocking him off.

"Good, now I'm going to try different places." He moved his touch to a different center. "Resist me if you can."

As he kept probing deeper, Leia became better at fending him off. She parried his attempts with greater speed and stronger force as he guided her to put up barriers. He grew more pleased as he worked with her, touching random spots in her mind, trying to take her by surprise. He could feel her own delight with her improving abilities.

Luke reached to the back of her mind, an area of deep primal memories but little conscious thought. He doubted he could get any defensive reaction there, but no attacker would be likely to strike at such places. Her thoughts were like a map laid out in front of him, and Luke touched inward to an isolated nub in her mind. He pushed—

And suddenly felt as if a giant invisible palm had planted itself on his chest and shoved backward. Luke stumbled to keep his balance, taking two steps away from her. Leia's eyes went wide, and her mouth dropped open in surprise.

Luke said, "What did you do?" in the same moment Leia said, "What did I do?"; then both answered, "I don't know!" simultaneously.

Luke tried to reconstruct what he had done. "Let me try that again. Just relax."

She seemed anything but relaxed as he probed her again, reaching to the back of her mind, finding the isolated nub among her instinctive centers. Touching it, he found himself knocked away again with physical force.

"But I didn't do anything!" Leia insisted.

Luke allowed himself to smile. "Your reflexes did, Leia. When a medical droid taps your knee, your leg jerks whether you want it to or not. We may have just stumbled upon something a potential Jedi has that others don't. I want you to try it on me. Here, close your eyes and I'll give you an image of what I did to you."

"Do you think I'll be able to?" Leia asked.

"If it truly is instinctive, all you need to do is find the right spot."

"I'll try." Her face wore a skeptical expression.

"Do, or do not. There is no try. That's what Yoda always said."

"Oh, stop quoting him. You don't need to impress me!"

Leia touched her brother's temples, and he took a deep breath, using Jedi relaxation techniques to drop his guard. He had erected so much mental armor in the past seven years that he hoped he could still let her inside. He felt the touch of her thoughts, delicate mental fingers tracing the contours of his brain. He directed her search toward the back, where primitive thoughts slept. "Can you—"

Before he could finish his question, Leia stumbled backward into the self-conforming seat. "Wow! I found the nub, but when I touched it, you knocked me off my feet."

Luke felt wonder tingle through him. "And it was completely unconscious on my part. I wasn't aware of doing anything."

Luke touched his lips as new thoughts raced through his mind. "I need to try this on other people. If it's completely a reflex reaction, this could be a very useful test for finding people who have latent Jedi powers."

Next morning, the metropolitan shuttle skimmed over the rooftops of Imperial City, like a bus on the thermals rising from chasms between the tall buildings. The strip of buildings newly erected by the construction droids looked like a gleaming stripe through the ancient city.

Admiral Ackbar piloted the shuttle himself, holding the controls in his articulated fin-hands as he watched the skies with his widely set fish eyes.

Behind him, strapped into their seats, rode Luke Skywalker and Leia Organa Solo. The bright dawn spread long shadows in the lower levels of the city.

Ackbar leaned forward to the comlink. "General Antilles, we are on approach. I can see the construction droid up ahead. Is everything cleared for our landing?"

"Yes, sir," Wedge's voice sounded clearly from the speaker. "There's a good spot just to the right of the droid that should be perfect for landing."

Ackbar cocked his head to peer through the curved viewplate, then brought the metropolitan shuttle in, aligning it with gaps in the buildings, descending to the unexplored street levels.

Wedge came out to meet them after Ackbar had settled the shuttle beside the powered-down construction droid. Ackbar emerged first into the rubble-strewn clearing, tilting his domed head up to look at the strip of sunlight coming from high above. Luke and Leia stepped out side by side as the vehicle hummed into its standby/cooldown mode.

"Hi, Wedge!" Luke called. "Or should I say, General Antilles?"

Wedge grinned. "Wait until you see what the demolition crew found. I just might get promoted again."

"I'm not sure you'd want to," Leia said. "Then you'd be stuck with diplomatic duties."

Wedge motioned for them to follow. The construction droid blocked out the sun. Luke could hear teams scrambling up access ladders and automated lifts on the outer shell of the droid. Maintenance crews were taking advantage of the shutdown time to check the internal factories and resource processors, to modify some of the programming inside the droid's computer blueprint.

The stripped carcass of a large beast lay in the rubble just outside the opening of the shielded room. Wedge gestured to it. "That thing attacked us last night, and my team killed it. Sometime when we were up in the construction droid's pilot lounge, napping and cleaning up, other scavengers came out and stripped the meat off its bones. Too bad. The xenobiologists might have wanted to classify it, but now there's not much left."

Wedge ducked inside the breached metal walls of the shielded room. Luke could hear people shuffling and banging inside. He saw Leia wrinkle her nose at the strange smells wafting out.

Luke's eyes took a moment to adjust to the glowing yellow illumination of the floating lights posted around the chamber. Something powerful had gone berserk in here. At first he saw broken equipment scattered on the floor, wires torn out, smashed computer terminals. Long claw marks gashed the walls. A black spherical Imperial interrogation droid lay split open in one corner. He saw Leia's eyes fix on it, and he sensed a wave of revulsion pass through her.

Several people from Wedge's team had wrestled a heavy metal grate back into place against one wall and were now laser-welding it into its channel. The grate had been horribly bent.

"More excitement last night," Wedge said. The welders looked up from their work, waved to Wedge, then bent back to their beams. "The mate of that rat-creature came back up through the tunnels, found its companion killed, and smashed everything it could." He frowned. "Ruined most of the old equipment here, but we still might be able to salvage something. The Emperor kept the place under tight security. Seems to be some kind of deep interrogation facility."

"Yes, indeed," Ackbar said, striding through the wreckage. Broken circuit boards crunched under his wide feet. "We wouldn't want any of this to fall into the wrong hands."

Luke's attention drifted over to a tangle of wires and flat sheet-crystal readers on the floor. His forehead furrowed with concentration as he went to look more closely. "Is that what I think it is?" he mumbled.

"What did you say, Luke?" Leia asked, following him.

He didn't answer her as he bent over the equipment, pulling wires and cables and trying to sort through the mess. "It looks like there were three separate units here. They're probably all destroyed." But he felt a growing excitement within him. Maybe they would be able to piece the components together.

"What is it?" Leia asked again.

Luke uncoiled one of the cables and found an intact sheet-crystal reader at the end. It looked like a glassy silver paddle longer than his hand. "I've read about this in my research on the old Jedi Knights. The Emperor's hunter teams used it to seek out Jedi who were hiding during his great purge."

He found a second intact sheet-crystal paddle, then picked the control pack that looked the least damaged. With his cyborg hand, Luke brushed aside some of the dust, then jacked the cables into either side of the pack, holding the paddles, one in each hand. He flipped the power switch on the control pack and was gratified to see a warm flurry of lights as the unit went through its initialization diagnostics.

"The Emperor's teams used equipment like this as sort of a Force detector, for his henchmen to read the auras of people they suspected of having Jedi talent. According to the records, the remnants of the Jedi Knights held this thing in great fear—but maybe we can use it to restore the Jedi."

He grinned, and for a moment he felt like the fresh, excited farm boy he had been back on Tatooine. "Hold still, Leia. Let me test this on you."

She stood back, alarmed. "But what does it do?" Both Wedge and Ackbar had stepped over to watch.

"Trust me," Luke said. He held the sheet-crystal paddles at arm's length, bracketing Leia. When he tripped the scan switch, a thin slice of coppery light traced down Leia's body from head to toe. Suspended in air above the control pack, a smaller echo of the copper scan-line reappeared in reverse motion, assimilating the data and constructing a tiny hologram of Leia.

It looked different from the small holo of Leia that Artoo Detoo had projected for Ben Kenobi. Instead, it was a wire-frame silhouette of her body, with color-coded lines tagged to readings that projected a column of numbers in the air. Surrounding the outline was a corona of flickering blue, faint but definite.

"Can you understand anything from that, Luke?" Admiral Ackbar said, peering closer.

"Let's get another one for comparison." This time Luke pointed the paddles at Wedge, who flinched as the coppery scan line ran up and down his uniform. When his wire-frame holo appeared beside Leia's, most of the color-coded details were similar—but his image showed no blue corona.

"Now let's try you, Admiral." He extended the paddles toward the Mon Calamarian, adjusting the control pack to take Ackbar's alien physiology into account. When his scanned image appeared, it too lacked the blue aura.

"Leia, would you do it to me, just so we can be more sure?"

Leia handled the equipment reluctantly, as if uneasy to touch a device that had been used by those who had designed the interrogation droid. But she operated the scanner easily, holding the sheet-crystal paddles on either side of Luke.

His image bore the bright corona.

"This is very valuable," Luke said. "You don't need any particular skill with the Force to use this equipment. We can find people with Jedi potential just by scanning them. It will be a great help in finding candidates for my academy. Maybe some good will come of this device after all these years."

"Very good, Luke," Ackbar said.

Luke pursed his lips. "Wedge, I want to try something. Would you relax for a minute and let me do a mind touch on you?"

"Uh," Wedge said, then saw his team members looking at him. He straightened. "Whatever you say, Luke."

Luke wasted no time, reaching out to touch Wedge's temples, running a mental probe over the surface of his mind, back to the primitive area, the surprising nub in the contour of thoughts—

But when Luke touched it, nothing happened. Wedge probably didn't even know he was being probed. Luke pushed harder, but he triggered no reflexive counteraction, no uncontrolled push as Leia had given him. "What was that all about?" Wedge asked. "Did you do anything?" Luke smiled. "I just strengthened a theory of mine. We have gotten a lot closer to bringing back the Jedi Knights."

4

At least the ship didn't explode on impact.

That was the first thing Han Solo thought as painful consciousness returned. He blinked his eyes, listened to the hissing of atmosphere streaming through breaches in the *Millennium Falcon*'s hull. Somehow they had survived a crash landing. He wondered what planet he was on.

Kessel!

His eyes widened as he saw red splashes across the control panels. His own blood. His leg felt as if it were on fire, and he tasted liquid tin in his mouth. As he coughed, more blood splashed out. Han had not managed to strap himself in before the crash. It was a good thing he had not stayed up in the gun well. From his skewed vantage he could see that the ship had spun on impact, with the top gun well crushed beneath them.

He hoped Chewbacca had fared better. Turning his head, Han felt as if shards of ground glass were rubbing his spine. In the copilot's chair, the Wookiee lay motionless, his pelt matted with discolored blood oozing from wounds hidden by his shaggy fur.

"Chewie!" he managed to croak. "Say something, okay?"

Han heard the thud of a small explosive charge on the primary hatch; then someone from outside managed to hot-wire the ramp. The rest of the *Falcon*'s air spurted into Kessel's thin atmosphere. "Great," he mumbled. With the shattering pain in his ribs, it had already been hard enough to breathe.

Heavy footsteps marched up the ramp. Han wanted to pull out his blaster or at least knock a few enemies down in a fistfight. But he could barely raise his eyes, expecting to see an orderly column of white-armored stormtroopers. That would be an appropriate end to a day like this.

Instead, the intruders wore a hodgepodge of armor, some parts modified from prison-guard uniforms, other plates adapted from stormtrooper equipment. None of it made any sense to Han, but his mind had already maxed out with things that should never have happened. A TIE fighter and an X-wing fighting side by side? Against him?

The boarding party wore oxygen masks fitted over their faces to let them breathe the thin atmosphere of Kessel. Their voices were muffled as they shouted orders to each other.

One man, looking scarecrowish with impossibly long arms and neck, strode into the *Falcon*'s cockpit. Han felt recognition stir inside him, but he couldn't pinpoint a name. The scarecrow wore armbands from an Imperial prison, but at his side he carried a modified double-blaster that was patently illegal on most planets. The scarecrow turned wide-set, flinty eyes on Han.

"Han Solo," he said. Though the breath mask covered his lower face, Han could tell the man was grinning widely. "You're going to wish you never survived landing on Kessel."

With a flash of memory, the scarecrow's name came to Han. *Skynxnex.* That was it! But Skynxnex had been locked up in the Imperial Correction Facility, barely avoiding a death sentence. Questions had just begun forming in his mouth when Skynxnex brought an armored fist down on Han's head, sending him back into unconsciousness. . . .

Kessel. Spice. His thoughts mixed into nightmares as he fought to come back to himself.

Han had always been proud to boast that the *Falcon* had made the Kessel run in record time, but he rarely recounted the whole tale, that he had actually been fleeing Kessel with a full load of spice in his secret belowdecks compartments, when Imperial tariff ships had tagged him.

Han got the shipment, as always, from Moruth Doole, the froglike man in charge of skimming black-market spice from Imperial production quotas. Doole was some sort of official in the gigantic Imperial prison complex, from which came most of the spice-mine laborers. The Empire maintained strict control over the spice output, but Doole managed to keep quite a little side market of his own. Han Solo and Chewbacca had run spice for him, whisking it past Imperial patrols and putting it into distribution channels run by gangsters such as Jabba the Hutt.

But Moruth Doole had a habit of stringing along his helpers until he decided he could gain bigger favor by turning them over to the authorities. Han had never been able to prove it, but he suspected that Doole himself had tipped off the tariff ships on the *Falcon*'s flight away from Kessel, providing the exact coordinates where Han planned to enter hyperspace.

Han had been forced to jettison his entire cargo of glitterstim spice, worth a fortune, just before being boarded. When Han tried to circle back later and retrieve the floating cargo, the Imperials had given pursuit. During the chase he had desperately skimmed closer to the gravity influence of the immense black hole cluster than the navcharts claimed was possible. One of the tariff ships had been lost in the swirling maelstrom of hot gases plunging into a bottomless singularity. But the *Falcon* had survived, breaking into hyperspace and fleeing to safety.

Temporary safety. The lost cargo of spice alone had been worth 12,400 credits and Jabba the Hutt had already paid for it in full. Jabba had not been pleased. . . .

The thought of all those months frozen in carbonite, motionless, hanging on Jabba's wall, made him shiver. The cold was black around him, and he couldn't see. His teeth chattered together—

"Cease your thermal convulsions!" a raspy metallic voice snapped. It sounded like a plasma saw cutting through rock. "The temperature in the medical center has been lowered to minimize surgical shock to your metabolism."

Opening his eyes, Han stared up into the bulletlike face of a medical droid. Most of the metal was a primary green, but a black hooded attachment extended over its optical sensors. Segmented mechanical arms reached toward him, displaying a wide variety of out-of-date medical implements, all of them sharp.

"I am the prison medical droid. I have not been programmed for anesthetics or the niceties of making you comfortable. If you fail to cooperate, your treatment will only be more unpleasant."

Han rolled his eyes back. This was a far cry from traditional medical droids who were programmed specifically with the patient's comfort in mind.

Han tried to move. Around him the prison medical center was white and cold, with gleaming medical appliances and empty bacta tanks mounted on the wall. Han vaguely sensed several guards standing near the doors. When he turned his head, the medical droid reached out with cold metal hands to clamp against his temples. "You must remain motionless. This will hurt. A great deal. Now relax—immediately!"

Out of sight on the other side of the room, Chewbacca let out a great roar of pain. Han was relieved to know the Wookiee was still alive. *Before* treatment, at least.

Han winced as the medical droid began to work on him.

• • •

Chewbacca shook him awake with a hairy, enthusiastic, and grateful hug. Han groaned and blinked his eyes, but the room was so dim he had to stare for a few minutes before anything came into focus. His entire body felt as if it had been beaten instead of healed.

Chewbacca groaned and hugged him again. "Take it easy, Chewie! You'll send me back to that medical droid!" Han said. Instantly, the Wookiee released his grip.

Han mentally assessed how he felt. He sat up, flexed his arms, then got to his feet. Two, no *three* of his ribs, as well as his left leg, tingled with the maddening bee stings that indicated where bone knitters had repaired the fractures. Han remained weak, but replacement/nutrient solutions had probably brought him back up to nominal levels.

Chewbacca also looked scruffy and haggard. Patches of fur had been shaved from his body, and Han could discern lumpy scars where medical droids had made quick patchwork with no finesse. After treatment the two of them had been tossed into this dank place.

Finally, Han took a deep whiff of the air inside the chamber. "What died in here?" He suddenly realized that wasn't just a joking comment.

Chewbacca answered by pointing to the hulking form that occupied a third of the space in the cell. Han blinked again to be sure his vision was adjusting properly.

The thing was huge and hideous—part crustacean, part arachnid, and judging from the rows of dagger teeth, entirely carnivorous. Its claw hands were as big as a human was tall, and its jointed body armor was covered with scablike bumps. The only good thing about it was that it was dead. The carcass reeked.

The first time Han had been near a rancor, he had been blind from hibernation sickness after being thawed in Jabba's palace. Jabba fed the monster below his throne room with his enemies—or anyone else at random. Han had seen many more rancors on the planet Dathomir during his courtship of Princess Leia. One of the beasts had somehow died here in the Imperial Correction Facility. The rancor had decayed as far as it was going to, and then mummified the rest of the way.

The prison itself, from what Han knew of it, was a cross between a zoo and a correctional facility, because the different life-forms had different degrees of sentience. The only factor in common was that they were all violent.

Their cell was gigantic, as far as cells went—large enough to hold the rancor and give it room to maneuver. Brittle, moldy bones lay scattered around the floor, many of which had been gnawed and pulverized, as if in a desperate attempt by the starving rancor to find more food. Green and blue smears of slime oozed down the walls. Tiny dripping sounds were the only noises Han could hear.

"How long have we been here, Chewie? Do you know?"

Chewbacca didn't know.

Han ran it over again in his mind. They had come to Kessel, they had identified themselves both by name and with a New Republic call sign. A fleet of ships had come out to attack them—TIE fighters and X-wings and a motley bunch of other ships. Obviously, the people in charge of Kessel were up to something, and they didn't want the New Republic to know about it.

Then he remembered scarecrow-like Skynxnex, who had boarded the crashed *Falcon*. Skynxnex had been a thief and an assassin, the primary point of contact between Moruth Doole and the spice smugglers. Skynxnex had wrangled a nominal post as a prison guard in the correction facility, but now he seemed to have changed jobs . . .

Han heard the click and hum of the deactivation field around the cell doors, and then a grating whirr as hydraulic lifts hauled the huge door upward. As the door raised, garish white light flooded into the room. Han clapped a hand over his eyes. He hadn't realized the cell was so dim.

"Get ready, Chewie!" Han whispered. If there weren't too many guards, they could rush them, slug their way out, and escape. But then he felt a twinge of pain from his recently broken ribs, and dizziness washed over him. Chewbacca leaned weakly against one of the damp walls of the rancor's cell and groaned.

Well, maybe if there's only one guard, who has poor eyesight and is recovering from weeks' worth of dysentery . . .

"Never mind, Chewie. Let's see what they have to say."

The skeletal figure standing in the door was obviously Skynxnex. As Han's eyes adjusted to the light, he could see four other guards behind Skynxnex, wearing not-quite prison uniforms, patches of body armor to protect sensitive areas but showing no rank or insignia.

"So, Han Solo, I trust you appreciate our . . . hospitality?" Skynxnex asked.

Han smirked and looked behind him at the dank cell, the dead rancor. "Yeah, you guys are really turning Kessel into a resort world. Just like the planet Ithor."

Skynxnex followed his gaze to the mummified monster. "Ah yes, during the turmoil when we took over the prison, someone forgot to feed the rancor. It was a pity. Months passed before we remembered him. A double pity, too, because by the time we thought of him, we had plenty of Imperial prisoners we needed to dispose of. That would have been fun to watch. Instead, we had to send them all into the spice mines."

Skynxnex smiled for just an instant; then his face took on its flat, mechanical composure again. "I hope the medical droids helped you recover from your crash injuries. It's important that you both are healthy enough to withstand interrogation. We want to learn exactly why you came to spy on Kessel."

It occurred to Han that for once he could actually tell the truth and be completely open about his mission. "Ready when you are, Skynxnex." Somehow he was afraid the truth wouldn't be good enough in this case.

The gangly man allowed another flash of a smile. "So you do remember me, Solo? Good. Moruth Doole will want to talk to you immediately."

Han raised his eyebrows. That meant Doole was still alive, still running things—but Han had no idea how the pieces fit together. "I'd love to talk to old Moruth. It's been a long time. He was a good buddy of mine!"

Skynxnex snickered at that, then stopped. The other guards behind him also chuckled. "Yes," Skynxnex said, "I do believe I've heard him mention your name. Several times."

The lift took them out of the main cell-block areas, along a tube to the outer corners of the correctional facility. They rocketed skyward along the angled metal tracks.

Looking through the scratched transparent walls of the elevator, Han could see that the prison itself was a massive tan-and-gray edifice made of plasteel and synthetic rock. The flat front face sloped backward at about a forty-five-degree angle; elevator turrets glided along each of the corners. A glassed and mirrored substructure protruded from the slanted face, housing the administrative offices and prison personnel.

In the racing elevator car Skynxnex watched both of them with flickers of amusement, keeping his modified double-blaster trained on them. The two guards, armed with more conventional weapons, also stood tense and ready.

Seeing this, Han felt ironically impressed. He didn't know what he had done to instill such fear in these people.

Both Han and Chewbacca had been strapped into stun-cuffs, a restraining fixture across the wrists that sent paralyzing jolts of electricity directly into the nervous system, proportional in strength to the amount of struggle a prisoner exerted. Han controlled himself well enough and received only an unpleasant tingle along his forearms. As usual, Chewbacca could not keep his temper in check and managed to stun himself into a stupor.

When the elevator doors opened, Skynxnex prodded the two prisoners forward. Han complied and walked easily ahead, trying to put a self-confident spring in his step. He'd had his troubles with Moruth Doole, and he did not trust the man a bit—but as far as he knew, there was no powerful grudge between them.

Skynxnex escorted them through administrative offices, many of which had been ransacked or burned. They went past a broad anteroom to a huge office faced by giant windows that looked out upon the barrens of Kessel. In the distance Han could see the crumbled salt flats. Great jets from the atmosphere factories sent gouts of oxygen, nitrogen, and carbon dioxide into the pinkish sky, keeping the planet barely habitable. Powerful radiation shields in orbit filtered out a large percentage of the deadly X rays and gamma rays pouring from the nearby Maw. If not for the precious spice, no one would bother trying to live on Kessel.

The original sign on the desk-unit announced this to be the warden's headquarters, but someone had crossed out the previous ID tag and mounted a hand-lettered sign in Basic: DOOLE'S PLACE. On the wall to the right of the desk-unit hung a man captured in final throes of agony, frozen in carbonite. Doole had taken a lesson from Jabba, displaying some old nemesis for all to see. Han shivered just to look at the trophy.

Next to the window a barrel-shaped form stood silhouetted by the garish light. Han recognized Moruth Doole immediately.

Doole was a Rybet, squat and soft-skinned. His bright-green coloring and tan highlights looked like worm stripes up and down his cheeks, arms, and shoulders. His skin was dry, but so smooth it looked slimy. As always Doole dressed in the skins of less-fortunate reptiles. His waistcoat looked like something from an ancient history vid. Doole sported a bright-yellow cravat, which meant he was in mating readiness, though Han couldn't imagine where on the planet Doole would ever find a willing female of his own species.

Doole turned around, displaying a much-changed face, jittered with nervous tics and paranoia. His Rybet eyes were overlarge, lanternlike, with vertical slits—but one of his eyes was now milky white, like a half-cooked egg. He wore a mechanical focusing device over his other eye, strapped onto his smooth head with brown leather straps.

Doole fiddled with his mechanical eye, and the lenses clicked and whirred into place, like a camera unit. His Rybet fingers were long and wide at the end, showing signs of vestigial suction cups as he adjusted the focus and pressed his face close to Han's. The blind eye stared milkily off in another direction. After a long inspection he finally hissed in recognition. "It *is* you, Han Solo!"

Han frowned. "Been hitting the spice too heavily, I see, Moruth. Always gets the eyesight first."

"It wasn't spice that did this," Doole snapped, tapping the contraption on his eye. He drew in another long sputtering breath that sounded like a

carbonated drink spilled on hot coals. "Why are you here, Solo? I want you
to tell me, but maybe I want you to resist just a little bit so I can make
this *hurt*."

Chewbacca roared in anger. Han tried to spread out his hands, but the
stun-cuffs zapped him. "Wait a minute, Moruth! You'd better explain a few
things to me. I don't quite know—"

Doole didn't hear him, rubbing his splayed hands together and smiling
with his squishy lips. "The hardest part is going to be restraining myself from
having you dismembered right here where I can watch."

Han felt his heart pound. "Can we be reasonable for just a minute? We
were business partners, Moruth, and I never crossed you." Han didn't mention
his suspicions that Doole had crossed *him* in that last spice run. "I apologize
if I did something to upset you. Can we work it out?"

He remembered his conversation with the hit man Greedo in the Mos
Eisley cantina. Once offended, Jabba the Hutt had never been interested in
working anything out. He hoped Doole would be more reasonable.

Moruth Doole stepped backward, fluttering his long-fingered hands.
"Work it out? What are you going to do, buy me a droid replacement for
my eye? I hate droids! Because of you, Jabba tried to have me killed. I had
to beg them to take only my eye. I had to *beg* them to take my *eye!*" He
jabbed at his boiled-egg blind side.

Skynxnex shambled closer to Doole, lowering his voice. "I think you're
confusing him, rather than frightening him, Moruth. Maybe he really doesn't
know what happened."

Doole sat down at his desk and straightened his lizard-skin waistcoat,
regaining his composure. "When you dumped your load of spice, Jabba
blamed it on me! He put out a contract on my life. All because of your
cowardice."

Chewbacca roared in outrage. Han barely kept his anger in check. "Jabba
put out a contract on me too, Doole. Greedo tried to assassinate me on
Tatooine. Boba Fett captured me on Bespin and I was trapped in carbonite,
just like your friend there"—he gestured to the gruesome trophy on the wall—
"and I got sent to Jabba anyway."

Doole waved a hand in dismissal. "Jabba's men had already infiltrated
the spice-mining operations, and he wanted to expose me, so his own people
could procure the glitterstim directly. One of his hit men fried my eye and half
blinded the other. He was about to do more, but Skynxnex killed him."

At the doorway the scarecrow smiled with pride.

"Jabba forced my hand, and I had to act. We staged the prison revolt.
The warden himself was Jabba's man, but half of the guards were on my
side. I paid them well, you see. Luckily, the Empire was thrown into chaos
right about the same time. We took Kessel for ourselves. There were a few

other upstart slave lords on the other side of the planet, but they didn't last long. I've been stockpiling spice supplies and building up a massive defense fleet with everything I can scrape together. Nobody—and I mean *nobody!*— is going to come here and take things away from me."

Doole grabbed his head with his long fingers in a gesture of weariness. "Everything was going just fine before you had to get Jabba angry at me! Everything was safe. I knew just how to play the game. Now I'm jumping at shadows, afraid every moment."

Doole stared at Han with his mechanical eye. "But ruining my life once isn't good enough for you, is it? You come back here broadcasting a message from the New Republic. Somehow I thought remnants of the Empire would try to grab the spice mines back first, but big governments are all the same. You are a spy, a particularly inept one. Did you think you could just fly into our space, look around, and go back to your Republic with all the information they need to come take us over?" He slapped his palm on the desktop with a damp splat. "We'll strike the first blow by killing their spy, and we will be ready to blast them out of the sky the moment your attack ships come out of hyperspace!"

"You haven't got a chance!" Skynxnex sneered.

Han allowed himself to smile, then actually chuckled. "You boys have it all wrong. Absolutely wrong." Chewbacca grunted his agreement.

Skynxnex scowled. Doole stared at Han in silence for a moment. "We'll see about that."

Doole reached into the pocket of his waistcoat and withdrew a small ancient-looking key, which he inserted into one of the drawers of the former warden's desk. He fumbled with the lock, then opened the drawer. Reaching in, he pulled out an armored strongbox. He hefted the strongbox to the table, then dug in another pocket of his waistcoat to extract a second key.

Han watched, his curiosity piqued, as Doole opened the strongbox and withdrew a smaller sealed container. Doole meticulously slipped both his keys back into his pockets before looking at Han.

"I'd like to spend time interrogating you thoroughly, but I want to know exactly when the New Republic plans to come in and take over, how many ships they are sending, what type of forces they will use. I'll get the information now, but I may have time to enjoy interrogating you later, just on general principle."

Doole placed his webbed Rybet palm on the top of the sealed container. With a slight hum a beam of light curled around his fingers in an ID scan; the small container burped as the airtight seal was broken. The lid slid away to reveal a padded interior compartment.

The box was filled with slender, black-wrapped cylinders about half as long as a finger. Han recognized them immediately. "Glitterstim," he said.

Doole looked at him. "The most potent form of spice. With it I'll be able to read the truth of what you say. Your errant thoughts will betray you."

Han felt a sudden sense of relief. "But what if I don't have any hidden thoughts to betray?"

Skynxnex struck Han's head with the back of his hand, sending him reeling. Chewbacca tried to stagger forward, but the stun-cuffs silenced his bellows and made him sway dizzily, barely able to keep his balance.

Doole selected one of the slim black cylinders and held it in his fingers. With a deft motion he peeled off the opaque outer wrapper and withdrew a thin bundle of transparent glassy fibers. As Doole held the inert glitterstim up to the light pouring through the broad viewing window, the light-sensitive spice began to scintillate and glow from within, ripening.

Han watched until it was ready for Doole to consume. He swallowed a dry lump in his throat.

Doole opened his mouth when the segment of glitterstim glowed a pearlescent blue. He extended his sharp purplish tongue to wrap around the crystalline fibers, which he drew back into his mouth. The glitterstim crackled and fizzed; as Doole flexed his lips, tiny sparks seeped out the corners.

Han stared as Doole closed his blind eye and breathed deep, watery breaths. The spice would act on Doole's mind, pump up his latent powers. The automatic focusing gears of Doole's mechanical eye clicked and whirred, spinning around as it tried to make sense of the visions pouring through the Rybet's mind. Then Doole turned to face Han and Chewbacca.

Han winced as he felt tiny fingers clawing around in his brain, picking through the lobes of memory, images he had stored in his thoughts . . . searching, searching. He tried to shrink away but knew he could keep no secrets from anyone pumped on glitterstim.

Skynxnex chuckled, then immediately fell silent, as if afraid of directing Doole's attention to himself, where his own brain could be picked.

Han felt anger growing, outrage that Moruth Doole could dissect the private moments he had with Leia, could observe the births of Han's three children. But the spice effects lasted only a few moments, and Doole would be concerned mainly with learning why Han and Chewbacca had come to Kessel.

"I really was telling you the truth, Doole," Han said quietly. "We are on a peaceful mission to reestablish diplomatic contact with Kessel. The New Republic is trying to open up trade and welcome you. We came in peace, but you just declared war on yourself by shooting down their first ambassadors."

Chewbacca growled.

Skynxnex stiffened, then took a few awkward steps forward. "What is he talking about?"

Han raised his voice. "Read the truth in my mind, Moruth."

The Rybet's mouth hung slack, and Han could see glitterstim sparks sputtering around his cheeks. He felt the tiny probing fingers crawl deeper and deeper into his mind, scrabbling around. Doole was frantically trying to find some proof of his suspicions as the spice enhancement faded away.

But Doole could find nothing; there was nothing to find. The only thing he did learn was the power of the Alliance forces that would be arrayed against him. A fleet that had succeeded in overthrowing the entire Empire would certainly be sufficient to destroy a ragtag outlaw operation on Kessel.

"No!" Doole wailed. He whirled to glare at Skynxnex. "What are we going to do? He's telling the truth!"

"He can't be!" Skynxnex said. "He's a—he's—"

"The spice doesn't lie. He's here for exactly the reasons he said. And we shot him down. We took him prisoner. The New Republic is going to come after us, and they'll wipe us out."

"Kill the two of them now," Skynxnex said. "If we work fast, we can cover everything up."

Han felt sudden fear return. "Now, wait a minute! I'm sure we can fix this with a few careful messages. I *am* the ambassador, after all! Diplomatic credentials and everything. I wouldn't want a simple misunderstanding—"

"No!" Skynxnex said, keeping his attention fixed on Doole. "We can't risk that. You know what Solo has done before. He knows you tipped off the Imperial tariff ships to go after him."

Actually, Han hadn't been certain until that very moment. "Now, there's no need to panic," he said again. "I can talk to the New Republic Senate. I know Mon Mothma personally, and my wife Leia is a cabinet member, and—" His mind whirled, trying to think of how Leia would handle this. Many times he had watched her smooth diplomatic problems. She had a finesse with words, a way of approaching other people's concerns and stroking them, delicately maneuvering opposing sides into a compromise. But right now Leia wasn't with him.

"Yes, I think I agree," Doole said, tapping a finger against his swollen lips. Han let out a sigh of relief. "I agree with *Skynxnex.* I'll review the battle tapes, but I don't believe you transmitted any messages after coming out of hyperspace. One of our fighters shot off your subspace antenna dish. The New Republic has no way of knowing you arrived safely. With no evidence they will conclude you got swallowed up by the Maw."

Doole began to pace in front of the large viewing window. "We'll delete any mention of you from our records. Instruct all my mercenaries to forget about the attack. Yes, that'll be the safest alternative!"

"You're making a big mistake!" Han said. He could barely restrain his urge to yank at the stun-cuffs.

"No," Doole replied, tapping his squishy-tipped fingers together. "I don't think so."

Chewbacca bellowed a loud string of guttural words.

"My best bet would be to kill you right away," Doole answered; then he rubbed his fingers against his blind eye. "But you still owe me for this, Solo. Even if you worked every day for a hundred years, it would never repay me for the loss of my eye. You both are going down into the spice mines, the deepest and most distant tunnels. They've been needing quite a few replacements lately."

Doole grinned with his wide froglike mouth. A final flicker of blue sparks rippled at the corner of his lips.

"No one will ever find you down there."

5

The former Imperial Information Center lay buried deep beneath the old palace, covered by layers of shielding walls and guarded by tight security at every entrance. To keep the temperatures within tolerable limits for the great data archive machines, vast heat-exchanger systems and powerful cooling units filled the room with a background roar.

Hunched over fourteen consoles were lumpy dull-gray slicer droids, hardwired into the terminals as they meticulously hacked at the security encryption codes and backup viruses set up in the Emperor's mainframes. The slicer droids had been working for a full year, ferreting out vital tidbits from the labyrinthine databases. Already they had exposed twenty-three Imperial spies in deep cover trying to sabotage the burgeoning New Republic.

The hum of the cooling units and the motionlessness of the slicer droids blanketed the Center with an echoing emptiness. Lonely and fidgety, the protocol droid See-Threepio paced back and forth, his servomotors whirring, as he viewed the room with his optical sensors for the hundredth time.

"Haven't you found anything yet, Artoo?" he said.

Jacked into one of the information ports, Artoo-Detoo bleeped an impatient negative and continued whirring as he tunneled through the overwhelming amounts of information.

"Don't forget to double-check everything," Threepio said, and began pacing again. "And don't be afraid to follow unlikely leads. Master Luke would call them hunches. This is very important, Artoo."

Artoo hooted indignantly.

"And remember to check every planet from the Old Republic. The Empire didn't necessarily have time to update its information on all of them."

This time Artoo did not bother to reply but continued to work.

A moment later Threepio heard the outer doors open, and a shadowy figure moved toward them with silent grace. As always, Luke Skywalker wore his Jedi cloak, but this time the hood was draped casually over his shoulders. Luke walked with an eagerness in his step.

Threepio was glad to see a resurgence of the excited boyishness that had so characterized young Luke when the droids first met him after they had been purchased from the Jawas on Tatooine. Of late Luke's eyes had not been able to hide the haunted look and the barely contained power of a Jedi Master.

"Master Luke! How good of you to check on us!"

"How's it going, Threepio? Found anything yet?"

Artoo beeped an answer, which Threepio translated. "Artoo says he's going as fast as he can, but he wishes me to remind you of the enormous amount of data he must inspect."

"Well, I'll be leaving in a few hours to follow up on some earlier leads I uncovered by myself. I just wanted to make sure you two have everything you need before I take off."

Threepio straightened in a gesture of surprise. "Might I ask where you are going, Master Luke?"

Artoo chittered and Luke turned to him. "Not this time, Artoo. It's more important that you stay here and continue the search. I can fly by myself."

Luke turned to answer Threepio's question. "I'm going to Bespin to check on somebody there, but first I want to go to an old outpost called Eol Sha. I've got reason to believe that at least one lost Jedi descendant might be there." With a swish of his cloak, Luke turned to depart from the Information Center. "I'll check back with you when I come home." The door slid shut behind him.

Threepio spoke immediately to Artoo. "Punch up the data on Eol Sha— let's see where Master Luke is going."

Artoo obliged, as if the idea had been in his own circuits. When the planetary statistics came up on the screen accompanied by ancient two-dimensional images, Threepio raised his golden mechanical arms in horror. "Earthquakes! Geysers! Volcanoes and lava! Oh my!"

• • •

When Luke emerged from hyperspace, the starlines in the viewport funneled into points. Suddenly brilliant pastel colors splashed across the universe—magentas, oranges, and icicle-blues of ionized gas in a vast galactic ocean known as the Cauldron Nebula. The automatic dimmers in the pilot's compartment muted the glare. Luke looked at the spectacle and smiled.

Leaving the hyperspace node, he punched in the co-ordinates for Eol Sha. His modified passenger shuttle arced through the wispy gas, leaving the nebula above him as the engines kicked in. The double wedge-shaped craft descended toward Eol Sha.

He had wanted to take his trusty old X-wing, but that ship was a single-person craft, with room for only an astromech droid in the back. If Luke's hunches about Jedi descendants proved correct, he would be bringing two candidates back to Coruscant with him. . . .

According to outdated records, the settlement on Eol Sha was established a century before by entrepreneurs who intended to use ramjet mining ships to plow through the Cauldron Nebula and scoop up valuable gases. The mineship pilots would distill the gaseous harvest into pure, rare elements for sale to other outposts.

Eol Sha was the only habitable world close enough to support the commercial venture, but its days were numbered. A tandem moon orbited very close to the planet, spiraling in on a death plunge as gravity dragged it down. Within another hundred years the moon would crash into the planet, smashing both into rubble.

The nebula mining scheme had never paid off. The incompetent entrepreneurs had not counted on the true costs of ramjet ships and the unremarkable composition of the Cauldron's gases. The outpost on Eol Sha had been left to fend for itself. At about that time the Emperor's New Order had begun, and the Old Republic had crumbled to pieces. The few survivors on Eol Sha had been forgotten in the chaos.

The outpost had been rediscovered two years ago by a New Republic sociologist who had visited them briefly, recorded his insights, and filed a report recommending immediate evacuation of the doomed colony—all of which was promptly forgotten in the already blossoming bureaucracy of the New Republic and the depredations of Grand Admiral Thrawn.

The item that had attracted Luke's attention, though, was that a woman named Ta'ania—an illegitimate descendant of a Jedi—had been one of the original colonists on Eol Sha. Luke would have suspected the Jedi's bloodline had ended there, except for one small detail.

According to the sociologist's report, the leader of the ragtag colonists, a man named Gantoris, was said to be able to sense impending earthquakes, and he had miraculously survived as a child when his playmates were killed in an avalanche. Somehow Gantoris escaped injury while the others, a mere arm's length away on either side of him, had been crushed.

Luke attributed many of these stories to exaggeration in retelling, for even someone with a great deal of Jedi potential could not control such things without training—as he himself knew. But still the clues and the circumstantial evidence led him to Eol Sha. He had to follow every lead if he was to find enough candidates for his Jedi training center.

Luke took the modified shuttle on a figure-eight trajectory around the looming moon and vectored in on the remnants of the outpost on Eol Sha. After crossing the terminator where the planet's night fell into day, Luke looked out the viewport at the scabbed and uninviting surface of the planet.

His hands worked the controls automatically. As he swooped low, he could see the decrepit and shored-up habitation modules that had been battered by natural disasters for decades. In the near distance hardened mounds of lava sprawled around a volcanic cone from old eruptions. Curling smoke rose from the heart of the volcano, and glowing orange smudges showed where fresh lava seeped through cracks in its side.

Luke took the shuttle past the battered settlement and beyond a stretch of cratered, jumbled terrain. The shuttle settled onto the rocky hardpan, and Luke exited through flip-up doors behind the passenger seats.

The air of Eol Sha smoldered in his nostrils, filled with acrid sulfurous smoke and chemical vapors. The gigantic moon hulked on the horizon like a platter of beaten brass, casting its own shadows even in daylight. Murky clouds and volcanic ash hovered in the air like a hazy blanket.

When Luke stepped away from the passenger shuttle, he could feel the ground hum beneath his boots. With senses heightened from the Force, he could touch the incredible strain the close moon placed on Eol Sha, squeezing and tearing it with tidal forces that grew worse each passing year as the moon spiraled closer. A hissing white noise permeated the air, as if the innumerable steam vents and fumaroles breathed out gasps of pain from the world.

Pulling the dark cloak about him and securing the lightsaber at his belt, Luke strode across the rough terrain toward the settlement. Around him small craters and deep pits dotted the ground, encircled by white and tan mineral deposits. Sounds of gurgling steam came from deep beneath them.

Halfway to the settlement Luke fell to his knees when a jolt went through the ground. The rocks bounced and the earth rumbled. Luke spread his arms to keep his balance. The tremors rose, then fell, then increased again before stopping abruptly.

Suddenly, the random craters around him crackled, then belched towers of steam and scalding droplets of water. Geysers, all of them—he had walked into a field of geysers, triggered by the earthquake to erupt simultaneously. Steam rolled over the ground like a dense fog.

Luke pulled the hood over his head for protection and took shallow breaths as he trudged forward. The settlement was not far away. On all sides of him the geyser field continued to gasp and howl, gradually lessening as the spumes declined in intensity.

When Luke finally emerged from the steam, he saw two men staring at him from the doorway of a rusted and ancient prefab shelter. The outpost on Eol Sha had been built from modified cargo containers and modular self-erecting shelters. By the looks of the hovels, though, the maintenance subsystems had failed decades before, leaving the forgotten people to eke out a crude existence. The rest of the settlement seemed deserted and quiet.

The two men stopped their work shoring up a collapsed entranceway, but they didn't seem to know how to react to the presence of a stranger. Luke was probably the first new person they had seen since the sociologist had visited them two years earlier.

"I have come to speak with Gantoris," Luke said. They looked at him with bleak expressions. Their clothes appeared worn and patched, sewn together from pieces of other garments. Luke's gaze held one of the two men. The other shied back into the shadows. "Are you Gantoris?" Luke asked softly.

"No. My name is Warton." He fumbled for words; then they came out in a rush. "Everyone is gone. There's been a rock slide in one of the crevasses. It buried two of our youngest, who went out to spear bugdillos. Gantoris and the others are there, trying to dig them out."

Luke felt a stab of urgency and grasped Warton's arm. "Take me there. Maybe I can help."

Warton allowed himself to be nudged into motion, and he took Luke along a winding path through jagged rocks. The second man remained behind among the collapsing shelters. Luke and Warton descended through switchbacks down the steep wall of a crack in the ground, a split wrenched apart by tidal forces. Down here the air seemed thicker, smellier, more claustrophobic.

Warton knew exactly where to find the other survivors in the maze of side channels and partial landslides. Luke saw them shoulder to shoulder in an elbow of the crevasse, scrambling over newly fallen rock, working to haul boulders aside. Every one of the thirty people there wore the same implacable expression, as if their optimism had burned away but they could not allow themselves to give up their duties. Two of the women bent over the rubble, calling into the cracks.

One man worked with twice the effort of the others. His long black hair hung in a braid on the left side of his face. His eyebrows and eyelashes had been plucked away, leaving his broad face smooth and angular and flushed with his exertion. He shoved rocks aside, which the other people hauled away. They had already managed to clear some of the debris, but they had not yet uncovered the two victims. The dark-haired man paused to glance at Luke, failed to recognize him or understand his presence, then returned to his efforts. By the way Warton and the others looked to him, Luke guessed the man must be Gantoris himself.

Before Warton had taken him to the base of the rockfall, Luke stopped and, with a quick glance, took in the positioning of the boulders. He let his arms fall to his sides, rolled his eyes back in concentration, and reached out through the Force, using the strength he found there to feel the boulders, to move them, and to keep other rocks from doing further damage. When Yoda had trained him to lift large stones, it had been merely a game, a training exercise; now two lives depended on it.

He paid no attention to the astonished sounds as the colonists stepped back, ducking out of the way as Luke mentally hurled boulder after boulder from the top of the rock pile, tossing them into other parts of the crevasse. He could feel life down in the shadowy depths, somewhere.

When the rocks began to show splashes of blood, and he exposed a pale arm, part of a shoulder hunched in the secret shadows of the avalanche, several people rushed forward. Luke made an extra effort to keep the unstable pile of rocks steady enough for the rescue operations. He continued to remove fallen boulders.

"She's alive!" someone shouted, and several helpers rushed into the debris, brushing away stones and hauling free a young girl. Her face and legs were battered and bloody, one arm was obviously broken; she began weeping with pain and relief as the rescuers pulled her out. Luke knew she would be all right.

Near the girl, however, the young boy had not been so lucky. The avalanche had crushed him instantly. The boy had been dead long before Luke arrived.

Luke continued to work grimly, until they had excavated the body. Amid sobs of grief, he released himself from his semitrance and opened his eyes.

Gantoris stood directly in front of him. Barely suppressed anger seethed beneath his controlled expression.

"Why are you here?" Gantoris asked. "Who are you?"

Warton stepped up beside Luke. "I saw him walk out of the geyser field. All the geysers went off at once, and he just strode out of the steam." Warton blinked in awe as he looked at Luke. "He says he has come for you, Gantoris."

"Yes—I know," Gantoris muttered to himself.

Luke met the other man's eyes. "I am Luke Skywalker, a Jedi Knight. The Empire has fallen, and a New Republic has taken its place." He drew a deep breath. "If you are Gantoris and if you have the ability, I have come to teach you how to use the Force."

Several of the others walked up, bearing the broken, rag-doll body of the dead boy. The man carrying the boy let his stony expression flicker for just an instant.

The look on Gantoris's face seemed a frightening mixture of horror and eagerness. "I have dreamed of you. A dark man who offers me incredible secrets, then destroys me. I am lost if I go with you." Gantoris straightened. "You are a demon."

Surprised, especially after his efforts to save the two children, Luke tried to placate him. "No, that isn't it."

Other colonists gathered around the confrontation, finding a focus for their anger and suspicion. They looked at Luke, at this stranger who had arrived in time to usher in the death of one of their dwindling number.

Luke glanced at the people around him and decided to gamble. He stared directly into Gantoris's eyes. "What can I do to prove my intentions to you? I am your guest, or your prisoner. What I want is your cooperation. Please listen to what I have to say."

Gantoris reached out to take the body of the boy in his own arms. The man who had been carrying him looked forlorn and lost as he stared at the bloodstains on his sleeves. Gantoris nodded back to Luke. "Take the dark man."

Several people reached forward to grasp Luke's arms. He did not struggle.

Bearing the dead boy, Gantoris led a slow procession out of the chasm. He turned once briefly to glare at Luke. "We will learn why you are here."

6

Leia stood in the private communications chamber, heaving a sigh as she glanced again at the chronometer. The Caridan ambassador was late. He was probably doing it just to spite her.

Out of deference to the ambassador, she had reset her clock to Caridan local time. Though Ambassador Furgan had suggested the transmission time himself, it seemed he couldn't be bothered to abide by it.

Two-way mirrors displayed empty corridors outside the communications chamber. At this late hour most sensible people were deeply asleep in their own quarters—but no one had ever promised Leia Organa Solo that diplomatic duties kept regular hours.

When such obligations crept into her schedule, Han usually grumbled at being awakened in the depths of the night, complaining that even pirates and smugglers kept their activities to more civilized time slots. But this evening Leia's alarm had awakened her to empty and silent rooms. Han still had not called.

A cleaning droid puttered along the corridor, polishing the walls and scouring the two-way mirrors; Leia watched its lampreylike scrubbers do their work.

With a burst of static from poorly tuned holonet transmitters, the image of Ambassador Furgan of Carida formed in the center of the receiving dais. Maybe the poor transmission quality was deliberate—yet another rude reaction. The chronometer told Leia that the ambassador had made his transmission a full six minutes past the time he himself had insisted on. Furgan made no attempt to apologize for his tardiness, and Leia studiously avoided calling attention to it.

Furgan was a barrel-chested humanoid with spindly arms and legs. The eyebrows on his squarish face flared upward like birds' wings. Despite the Emperor's known prejudice against nonhuman species, apparently the Caridans had been acceptable enough to secure the Emperor's business, since Palpatine had built his most important Imperial military training center on Carida.

"Princess Leia," Furgan said, "you needed to discuss certain planning details with me? Please be brief." He crossed his arms over his broad chest in clearly hostile body language.

Leia tried not to let her exasperation show. "As a matter of protocol I would prefer if you could address me as minister rather than princess. The planet on which I was a princess no longer exists." Leia worked hard to keep the scowl off her face.

Furgan waved her comment aside as if it were of no consequence. "Very well then, Minister, what did you wish to discuss?"

Leia took a deep breath, quelling the hot temper rising behind her cool expression. "I wanted to inform you that Mon Mothma and the other Cabinet members of the New Republic will be hosting a formal reception in your honor when you reach Coruscant."

Furgan bristled. "A frivolous reception? Am I supposed to give a warm and glowing speech? Make no mistake, I am coming to Coruscant on a pilgrimage to visit the home of the late Emperor Palpatine—not to be pampered by an upstart, illegitimate band of terrorists. Our loyalty remains with the Empire."

"Ambassador Furgan, there *is* no centralized Empire." It took all her effort not to rise to the bait. Her dark eyes burned with obsidian fires, but she smiled instead at the ambassador. "Nevertheless, we will extend to you every courtesy in the confidence that your planet will find a way to adapt to political reality in the galaxy."

The Caridan's holographic image shimmered. "Political realities change," he said. "It remains to be seen just how long your rebellion will last."

Furgan's image fizzled into static as he cut the transmission. Leia sighed and rubbed her temples, trying to massage away the headache lurking behind her eyes. She left the communications chamber discouraged.

What a way to end the day.

Deep underground in the Imperial Information Center, all hours looked the same, but See-Threepio's internal chronometer told him it was the middle of Coruscant's night. A pair of repair droids worked at dismantling one of the great air-exchange systems that had burned out. The repair droids dropped tools and discarded pieces of metal shielding with reckless abandon, making the echoing chamber sound like a war zone. Threepio much preferred the humming loneliness of the previous day.

Buried in their own universe of data networks, the hunched slicer droids worked undisturbed. Artoo-Detoo slavishly continued his days-long search without pause.

With a loud clatter the repair droids dropped an entire three-bladed fan assembly. "I'm going to give those droids a piece of my mind!" Threepio said.

Before Threepio could march off, Artoo jacked out of the data port and began chittering and whistling. In his excitement the little astromech droid rocked back and forth, bleeping.

"Oh!" Threepio said. "You'd better let *me* check that, Artoo. It's probably another one of your false alarms."

When data scrolled up on the screen, Threepio could see nothing that would have captured Artoo's interest—until the other droid recompiled the information to emphasize his point. A name popped up beside every entry— TYMMO.

"Oh, my! It does appear suspicious when you look at it that way. This Tymmo person seems a likely candidate indeed." Threepio straightened, suddenly at a loss. "But Master Luke isn't here, and he gave us no further instructions. Whom can we tell?"

Artoo bleeped, then whistled a question. Threepio turned to him with offended dignity. "I will not wake Mistress Leia in the middle of the night! I am a protocol droid, and there is a proper way to go about these things." He nodded in affirmation of his decision. "We will inform her first thing in the morning."

The levitating breakfast tray brought itself to Leia's table on the park balcony high in the Imperial towers. The sun gleamed on the city that stretched across the entire landmass of Coruscant. High in the air flying creatures rode the morning thermals.

Leia scowled down at the food the breakfast tray presented to her. None of it looked appetizing, but she knew she had to eat. She selected a small plate of assorted pastries and sent the breakfast tray on its way. Before it departed, the tray told her to have a pleasant day.

She sighed and picked at her breakfast. She felt exhausted mentally as well as physically. She hated to feel so dependent, even on her own husband, but she never slept well while he was away. Han should have arrived on

Kessel three days ago, and he was due back in two days. She didn't want to cling, but it disappointed her that he had not yet transmitted so much as a greeting. With diplomatic duties that kept her busy at all hours, they saw too little of each other even when they were both on the same planet.

Well, the twins would be coming home in another six days. Han and Chewbacca would be back by then, and their entire lifestyle would change. A pair of two-year-olds running around the palace would force Han and Leia to look differently at many of the things they took for granted.

But why hadn't Han gotten in touch? It shouldn't have been so difficult to send a holonet communiqué from the *Falcon*'s cockpit. She wasn't quite ready yet to admit she was worried about him.

With a greeting signal from the archway of the park balcony, an older-model protocol droid marched into view. "Excuse me, Minister Organa Solo. Someone wishes to see you. Are you accepting visitors?"

Leia set down her breakfast pastry. "Why not?" It was probably some lobbyist wanting to complain to her in private, or a panicked minor functionary who needed her to make a decision on some uninteresting detail, or one of the other senators trying to hand off some of his own duties.

Instead, with a flourish of his vermillion cape, Lando Calrissian walked through the arch.

"Good morning, Madame Minister. I hope I'm not disturbing your breakfast?" He flashed a broad, disarming smile.

Seeing him, Leia felt her mood immediately lighten. She stood up and met him near the archway. He gallantly kissed her hand, but she was not satisfied until she had given him a friendly hug. "Lando, you're the last person I expected this morning!"

He followed her back to the table overlooking the skyline of Imperial City and pulled up a chair, sweeping his cape over its back. Without asking, Lando took one of her untouched pastries and began to munch on it.

"So what brings you to Coruscant?" she asked. She realized how eager she was just to have a normal conversation without diplomatic entanglements and hidden agendas.

Lando brushed crumbs from his mustache. "I just came to see how you all are doing in the big city. Where's Han?"

She grumbled. "That seems to be a sore subject this morning. He and Chewie went off to Kessel, but I think they just used it as an excuse to go joyriding and remembering their glory years."

"Kessel can be a pretty rough place."

Leia avoided his eyes. "Han hasn't bothered to call in six days."

"That's not like him," Lando said.

"Oh, yes, it is—and you know it! I suppose we'll have words when he comes back day after tomorrow." Then she forced an artificial air of brightness. "But let's not talk about that right now. How can you find time to trot around visiting people? A respectable man like yourself has so many responsibilities."

Lando averted her gaze this time and began fidgeting. He stared at the expanses of gleaming new buildings visible through the metropolis. For the first time Leia noticed a slight scruffiness to his appearance. His clothes seemed a bit ragged around the edges, the colors faded as if from too much wear.

He spread his hands, then took another breakfast pastry. "To tell you the truth, I'm . . . um, in between engagements right now." He gave her a lopsided grin, but she frowned back at him.

"What happened to your big mining operation on Nkllon? Didn't the New Republic replace most of your destroyed machinery?"

"Well, it was still a lot of work, and not paying off—bad publicity after the Sluis Van attack, you know. And Nkllon is a hellish place—you were there. I just needed a change."

Leia crossed her arms and looked at him skeptically. "All right, Lando. The appropriate excuses are logged and recorded. Now, what really happened to Nkllon?"

He squirmed. "Well, I lost it in a sabacc game."

She couldn't keep herself from laughing. "So you're out of work?" His expression of wounded pride was obviously faked. Leia considered for a moment. "We could always reactivate your commission as a general in the New Republic. You and Wedge were a great team on Calamari."

His eyes widened. "Are you offering me a job? I can't imagine what you would want me to do."

"Formal receptions, state dinners . . . plenty of wealthy backers wandering around," Leia said. "The possibilities are endless."

Just then the old protocol droid shuffled through the arch again, but before he could announce his business, See-Threepio and Artoo-Detoo bustled around him, making a direct path to Leia. "Princess Leia!" Threepio could not contain his excitement. "We've found one. Artoo, tell the princess. Oh, General Calrissian! What are you doing here?"

Artoo launched into a series of electronic sounds, which Threepio dutifully translated. "Artoo was checking the records of various winners in different gambling establishments throughout the galaxy. We seem to have encountered a man who has extraordinary luck at the Umgullian blob races."

Threepio handed a hardcopy printout of the winning statistics to Leia, but she passed it on to Lando. "You're better trained to understand this than I am." Lando took the page of figures and stared at them. He didn't appear to know what he was looking for.

Threepio added his own commentary. "If it is displayed only as wins and losses, Mr. Tymmo's record shows nothing out of the ordinary. But when I had Artoo plot the magnitude of wins, you will note that while Mr. Tymmo loses quite often in minor races, in every instance when he bets more than a hundred credits on a particular blob, that blob wins the race!"

Lando tapped the sheet of numbers. "He's right. This is pretty unusual. I've never seen the Umgullian blob races myself, and I'm no expert in the nuances, but I'm inclined to say that these odds are next to impossible."

"This is exactly the sort of thing Master Luke asked us to look for." Threepio moved his arms up and down, whirring the servomotors until they whined in protest. "Do you think Mr. Tymmo could be a potential Jedi for Master Luke's academy?"

Lando looked at Leia with questions in his eyes. He had obviously not heard of Luke's recent speech. But Leia's eyes sparkled. "Someone needs to check this out. If it's just a scam, we need a person who knows his way around gambling establishments. Lando, isn't that a job you could do?"

She knew his answer before she even asked the question.

7

The cracked and gasping wastelands of Kessel always made Moruth
Doole hungry. Staring out the landscape window, Doole's mechanical eye
focused to the far distance.

Kessel's surface was whitish and powdery, with a few hardy transplanted
weeds trying to survive in the crevices. Great plumes from the atmosphere
factories gushed into the pinkish sky in a losing battle against the weak
gravity. Unseen radiation from the Maw crackled against the atmospheric
shields. The garrison moon housing Kessel's defense fleet was just setting
on the horizon.

Doole turned from the window and went to an alcove in the former
warden's office. Time for a snack.

He withdrew a cage of fat and juicy flying insects, pressing his face close
to the mesh so he could see better with his dim eyesight. The insects had
ten legs, iridescent body cases, and succulent abdomens. They panicked the
moment he moved the cage.

Doole rapped spongy fingers on the mesh, stirring them up. The insects
flew around the confined space in a frenzy. Somehow terror released a hor-
mone that made their meat sweeter. He licked his swollen Rybet lips.

Opening the mesh door, Doole thrust his entire head into the cage. The
insects fluttered around his eyes, his ears, his cheeks. Doole's sharp tongue
shot out again and again, spearing the insects and slurping them into his

mouth. He snapped up three more, then paused to swallow. Their squirming legs tickled the inside of his mouth. Giving a sigh of pleasure, Doole lapped up another pair. One insect flew directly into his open mouth, and Doole swallowed it whole.

Someone knocked on his door and marched in before he could respond. Wearing the insect cage over his head, Doole turned around to see Skynxnex, his gangly arms and legs jittering. "I have a report, Moruth."

Doole extricated his head from the insect cage, then sealed the opening. Three bugs managed to escape and flew to the wide picture window, flinging themselves against the transparisteel. Doole decided to catch them later. "Yes? What is it?"

"We have finished overhauling the *Millennium Falcon*. All identifying marks are removed, replaced with fake serial numbers. We made a few other modifications in addition to the regular repairs it needed. With your permission I'll have it flown up to the garrison moon where it can be incorporated into our space navy. Light freighters aren't the best warships, but with a good pilot they can still cause plenty of damage—and the *Falcon* is closer to a fighter than a freighter."

Doole nodded. "Good, good. What about our work on the energy shield generators? I want them functional as soon as possible, just in case the New Republic comes after us."

"Our engineers on the moonbase think they can reroute the circuits so we won't need all the parts we're missing. Kessel will be impregnable before long."

Doole's single eye lit up with eagerness. "Have Han Solo and his Wookiee gone into the mines yet?"

Skynxnex tapped his fingertips together. "I've reserved an armored personnel transport and will make the delivery personally within the hour." He fingered his double-blaster. "If they try anything, *I* want to be the one to deal with it."

Doole smiled. "I look forward to them rotting in the dark." He waved his splayed hands. "Well, what are you waiting for?" Moving with his jerky walk, Skynxnex left the warden's chambers.

Doole smiled at the thought of his revenge on Solo, but uneasiness tugged at him. The New Republic seemed far away and insignificant, but from his scan of Han's mind, he knew the magnitude of firepower that could be directed against him. Not since Doole had taken over the prison facilities from Kessel's upstart slave lords had he felt such impending doom.

Under the old system it had been so much simpler. By blackmailing or paying off prison guards, Doole had managed to set himself up as a kingpin of spice smuggling right under the Empire's nose. He sold maps and access codes for Kessel's energy shield, fostering small-time spice operations on other parts of the planet. Hapless entrepreneurs would work their new mines, then sell the product in secret to Doole. Once the spice veins began to play out, Doole (acting as a loyal prison official) would "discover" the illicit operation and report it to his Imperial contact. When Imperial troops raided those illegal mines, Doole's handpicked guards made certain that anyone who could point a finger at Doole never survived capture. The other helpless lackeys would be put to work in the primary mines. It was a win-win situation for Doole.

During the prison revolt Doole targeted his primary rivals and made the toughest guards go after the worst smugglers until they slaughtered each other. This left Moruth Doole in charge, with Skynxnex as his right-hand man.

Doole had captured the warden, sending him to work in the spice mines until he was broken. Then, for the entertainment value, Doole had planted spice grubs in his body. As the grubs chewed up his insides, the warden had gone through marvelously theatrical convulsions, in the middle of which Doole encased him in carbonite, using freezing equipment that had once been used to prepare violent and dangerous prisoners for transport.

Reminiscing always aroused him. Reaching into a drawer of his desk, Doole withdrew the bright-yellow cravat that signified his readiness to mate. He secured it in place, then drew in a long hissing breath as he refocused his mechanical eye and glanced at his reflection. Irresistible!

Doole rubbed his palms along his ribs to straighten the lizard-skin waistcoat, then strutted out of his office, down the corridor. He entered the secure wing, keying in the access code that only he knew; then he sucked in a deep breath. Flicking his tongue in and out, he could pick up the pheromones from the air.

Inside their cubicle-cells, the captive Rybet females huddled in the corners, trying to hide in the shadows. Doole's yellow cravat seemed very bright in the dimness.

Alone on Kessel, Moruth Doole had been frustrated for many years. But now that he ran the planet, he could afford to have dozens of female slaves shipped from his homeworld. Sometimes the females did not cooperate, but after years of working in the correctional facility, Doole had plenty of experience in dealing with unruly prisoners.

Lately, his only difficulty had been in *choosing* among the females. As he sauntered down the narrow corridor, setting his mechanical eye to high focus and peering into the cells, Moruth Doole's writhing lips formed a huge, lustful smile.

Kessel's landscape rushed beneath the armored prisoner transport. Han Solo could see only a narrow strip through the window slits in the prisoners' compartment. He and Chewie had been strapped into their seats and linked to resistance-feedback electrodes that would knock them unconscious if they struggled too much. Chewbacca had even more trouble with the full-body restraint than he had with the stun-cuffs.

Skynxnex hunched over the pilot controls, circling the transport away from the battlements of the Imperial Correction Facility. An armored guard sat in the copilot's seat, directing his blaster rifle toward Han and Chewie.

"Hey, how about pointing out some of the landmarks, Skynxnex?" Han said. "What kind of tour is this, anyway?"

"Shut up, Solo!" Skynxnex said.

"Why should I? I bought a full-price ticket."

Skynxnex sent a painful jolt through the restraining electrodes. Chewbacca roared. Han muttered, "There goes your tip, Skynxnex."

The scarecrow guided the transport around a huge open pit that plunged deep into the ground. Rusted girders and support structures stood like skeletal fingers propped up in the whitish barrens. It took Han a moment to realize this was a shaft bored into the crust by the giant atmosphere factories, chewing through the rocks and dissolving out oxygen and carbon dioxide to replenish the constantly fading air. After the huge factory had sucked out the viable breathing gases, it had left access to an entire network of underground tunnels for spice mining.

Skynxnex set the prisoner transport down on the rocky ground and fitted a breath mask over his nose and mouth; he gave another mask to the guard.

"What about us?" Han said.

"You won't be out very long," Skynxnex said. "A little light-headedness will do you good."

Punching a button on the control panel, Skynxnex released their restraints. Han stretched his sore arms. Instantly, the guard snapped up his rifle, and Skynxnex whipped out his modified double-blaster, both pointing the deadly barrels directly at Han.

Han froze. "Just . . . stretching. It's okay. Calm down!"

When Skynxnex opened the side door to the transport vehicle, Han felt his ears pop. Moist air flashed into white vapor, wafting in the rarefied atmosphere next to the open pit.

Han felt oxygen being stolen from his lungs. Instinctively, he drew in a deep breath, but that helped little. He and Chewbacca stumbled out of the craft as Skynxnex and the guard prodded them.

At the rim of the crater they found an elevator cage on tracks that plunged deep into the pit. Skynxnex seemed to be moving with deliberate slowness. Unable to breathe, Han tried to hurry, stumbling into the elevator cage and gesturing Chewbacca after him. He gasped and wheezed. Black spots began to appear in front of his eyes. When he did manage to breathe an entire lungful of the thin air, the cold of Kessel bit into his chest.

"A few years ago we had the atmosphere factories running full tilt," Skynxnex said, his words muffled behind the facemask. "Doole figured it was a frivolous waste of energy."

The guard shut the wire mesh door, and Skynxnex operated the elevator controls. The cage descended at a rapid clip until the window of sky shrank to a small spot of blue light high above.

They saw openings into the rock wall sealed off with steel doors. At each level a ring of light encircled the pit, but many of the illuminators had either burned out or been broken.

Chewbacca hung on to the bars of the elevator with his long hairy arms, panting for air. His pink tongue protruded, turning purplish from lack of oxygen. Han, shivering and dizzy and starved for breath, slumped to the bottom of the elevator.

When the elevator abruptly stopped, the jolt slammed Han's head into the mesh. As he looked down through the open cage floor, he saw the pit continuing immeasurably far below them.

"Get up!" Skynxnex said, kicking him. "No time to sleep. Come on, you'll get a breath of fresh air inside."

With some help from Skynxnex, Han managed to haul himself to his feet. The smaller guard had much more difficulty manhandling Chewbacca forward.

Opening the gate of the elevator, they had access to one of the sealed metal doors. Skynxnex cranked the hatch, and all four of them staggered into a small tiled chamber.

Han could barely see anymore. His ears buzzed. His eyesight was a mixture of black specks, roaring blood, and dim shadows of the objects around him. But as soon as Skynxnex sealed the door, glorious oxygen flooded the chamber.

Before the captives could recover, the guard shoved the barrel of his blaster rifle under Chewbacca's chin, and Skynxnex held his own weapon against Han's head. "Almost there," Skynxnex said. "No funny stuff now."

Han, happy just to be breathing again, couldn't dream of doing anything. At least not yet.

On the other side of the airlock was a large muster room filled with lethargic-looking workers ready to begin their shift in the spice mines. The muster room had been blasted out of solid rock, and a tall bank of bunks ran along one side of the room. An empty eating section with long tables took up the central area.

Cameras stared down at the activity from perches on the walls. Guards in hodgepodge stormtrooper uniforms waited behind screens in the control rooms. Other guards kept an eye on the people moving about in the muster area. All the workers looked pale and haggard, as if they had been underground and underfed for years.

A burly man strode up to meet them, keeping his eyes fixed on Skynxnex. The man had a lumpy face, a lumpy chin covered with bristly black stubble, and lumpy arms as if his massive muscles had all been attached at the wrong places.

"You brought me two more?" the man said. "Only two? That's not enough." He reached out to grab Chewbacca's hairy arm. Chewbacca roared and flinched away, but the lumpy man didn't notice. "Well, the Wookiee's worth three men, but I don't know about the other one. This doesn't take care of half the people I've lost."

Skynxnex glowered at him. "So stop losing people," he said with a voice of ice, then nudged Han. "This is Boss Roke. He's in charge of breaking you. He gets extra points with Moruth Doole to make your life miserable."

"He doesn't seem to be doing a very good job of keeping track of his workers," Han said.

Roke flashed him a withering glare. "Something's taking my men down in the deep tunnels. I've had two more missing since yesterday. They vanish without a trace—no locators, nothing."

Han shrugged. "It's hard to get good help these days."

Skynxnex pulled out his double-blaster and shoved it in Han's face again, but he spoke to Boss Roke. "Get thermal suits for these two. We'll watch them while they get into uniform."

Roke snapped his fingers, and two guards went rummaging through some cubicles. "The human won't be difficult, but the Wookiee—we don't carry much in that size."

In the end the guard found a large misshapen suit that had once been worn by some alien creature that had three arms, but it fit Chewbacca well enough after they sealed off the third arm; the empty sleeve and glove dangled down his chest.

A heater-pack between the shoulder blades powered the whole thing to keep them warm down in the frigid mine tunnels. Han was relieved to see a small breath mask attached to the suit.

Skynxnex backed toward the elevator. The guard had already entered the airlock chamber. One last time, as if he felt he hadn't used enough tiresome threats for one afternoon, Skynxnex pointed the double-blaster at Han. "Next time maybe Moruth will let me use this."

"If you clean up your room without being told, and if you eat all your vegetables," Han taunted, "then he might let you have a special treat."

"Shift alpha, ready for work detail!" Boss Roke bellowed into the muster room, and dozens of weary people shuffled to squares painted on the floor.

Roke pointed to two empty squares. "You two, positions eighteen and nineteen. Now!"

"What, no new-employee orientation?" Han asked.

With a sadistic grin on his face, Boss Roke shoved him toward the squares. "It's on-the-job training."

At some unspoken signal the workers mounted breath masks on their faces. Seeing this, Han and Chewbacca followed suit. A big metal door on the far side of the wall slid open to reveal an illuminated chamber a hundred meters long, in which floated a centipedelike mine transport of little cars linked together by magnetic attractors.

A high-pitched tone *pinged* through hidden speakers, and the workers took their seats on one of the floating mine cars. As people climbed aboard, the separate sections of the cars swayed back and forth.

Chewbacca grunted a question. Han looked around, blinking. "I don't know any more about this than you do, buddy." Now that Skynxnex had departed, he no longer needed to continue his blustering. Fear started to trickle into his limbs.

Boss Roke took a seat in the pilot car; other guards were stationed evenly throughout the open tram. All the guards wore infrared goggles. Every one of the prisoners sat motionless. Behind them the metal door slammed shut. Everyone seemed to be waiting for something.

"Now what?" Han mumbled to himself.

All the lights went out. Han and Chewbacca plunged into an absolute suffocating blackness like a blanket of tar.

"What the—" Han drew a sudden deep breath. The blackness was palpable. He couldn't see a thing. Beside him Chewbacca groaned in alarm. He heard the other workers moving, shuffling. Han's ears strained as his imagination tried to understand what was going on. He heard a clunking, sliding sound. "Hold on, Chewie," he said.

A metal door at the opposite side of the chamber opened up. The sound of its movement along rough metal tracks echoed in the enclosed space. Wind rushed around their ears as the air spilled outward into the mine tunnels of Kessel.

In a sudden panic Han pushed his breath mask tighter against his face just as he felt the atmosphere grow thin. The fleeing air took with it whatever heat had remained, making his exposed skin tingle with cold.

The mine cars lurched on their repulsorlifts, picking up speed. Acceleration slammed Han into his hard, uncomfortable seat. He could hear the air roaring past his head, feel the tunnel walls around him. The transport whipped around a curve, and Han grabbed the cold metal railing to keep himself from flying out of his seat. The mine cars whisked along, tilting downward, then lurching sideways. He had no idea how Boss Roke could possibly see where he was going unless the whole system was computer controlled.

Behind them, just after they had passed under an echoing archway, a heavy metal door slammed shut with a sound like an avalanche of scrap metal.

Han couldn't understand why the spice miners didn't string up at least some cheap illuminators as guideposts along the tunnels. But then it came to him like a slap in the face: the realization that since glitterstim spice was *photoactive*—made potent in the presence of light—it obviously had to be mined in total darkness or else it would be ruined.

Total darkness.

Han and Chewbacca would spend their days at hard labor in the mines without ever being able to see each other, or where they were, or what they were doing. Han had to blink his eyes just to make sure they were open instead of closed—not that it made any difference.

A shiver went down his back. Boss Roke had said that some unknown thing deep in the mines was preying on helpless workers, snatching them unawares. How could anybody run from a carnivorous attacker while surrounded by complete darkness?

The quality of the sound changed off and on. As Han's mind grew accustomed to processing information through his ears, it became obvious whenever the rushing mine car passed side tunnels, because of the sudden hole in the wind. Breathing through the mask, he could smell nothing other than flat recycled air.

The mine car wobbled from side to side, rocking as somebody moved about in the seats, climbing over the individual cars. The person slowly clambered over one seat back, then another, approaching their position. Han thought he heard someone breathing, straining, growing nearer.

"You there! Number fourteen! Sit down!" a guard shouted.

Number fourteen? Han thought. How could the guard possibly see which one had been moving about? Then he remembered the infrared goggles. The guards could probably see everyone, bright silhouettes against the backdrop of blackness.

The car stopped jostling for a few moments, but then the rocking started again. The mysterious person kept moving toward them. Somebody heaved himself over the seat to the empty spot right behind Han and Chewbacca.

"Hey, I told you to sit down!" the guard shouted.

"This is my new seat," a voice said.

"That's your new seat!" the guard said, strangely repeating the words before he fell silent.

Han forced himself not to speak. Since he couldn't see anything himself, the intruder must be just shifting about, unable to tell where he was going.

Or could he have his own set of infrared goggles? Had Skynxnex or Moruth Doole hired some assassin to get rid of Han and Chewbacca while no one was watching? A quick slash from a vibrator knife? A shove that knocked him off the floating transport, abandoning him down in the empty labyrinth of tunnels? In the darkness Han would never be able to find his way back. He wondered if he would starve, freeze, or suffocate first. He didn't want to find out.

He heard the faint, echoed breathing of someone speaking behind a breath mask, leaning closer. Beside him Chewbacca bristled in anticipation.

"Are you really from the outside?" the voice said. "I haven't been above ground for years." It seemed hopeful, soft, and tenor, but muffled behind the breath mask and the rushing wind. Han couldn't tell if it was the voice of an aged man, a deep-voiced woman, or a quiet and meek clerk from the former Imperial prison.

Han's mind pictured a skeletal old man with long scraggly hair, tattered beard, and ragged clothes. "Yeah, we're from out there. A lot of things have changed."

"I'm Kyp. Kyp Durron."

After a moment's hesitation Han introduced himself and Chewbacca. Suspecting some kind of trap, he decided not to give too much information. Kyp Durron seemed to sense this and talked about himself without asking too many prying questions.

"You'll get to know everybody here. That's just the way of it. I've lived most of my life on Kessel. My parents were political prisoners, exiled on this planet when the Emperor started cracking down on civil unrest. My brother Zeth was taken off to the Imperial military training center on Carida, and we never heard another word from him. I got stuck here in the spice mines. I always thought they'd come back and haul me to Carida too, but I guess they forgot."

Han tried to imagine Kyp's life going from bad to worse. "How come you're still down in the mines?"

"During the prison revolt they didn't much care who ended up here. Now most of the workers are the old Imperial prison guards. Nobody thought to let me out when they changed everything up top. I've never been important enough."

Kyp made a sound that must have been a bitter laugh. "People say I have good luck in all sorts of things, but my luck has never been good enough to let me have a normal life." He paused, as if gathering hope. In that moment Han wished he could see the stranger's face. "Is it really true the Empire has fallen?"

"Seven years ago, Kyp," Han said. "The Emperor was blown up with his Death Star. We've been fighting battles ever since, but the New Republic is trying to keep everything together. Chewie and I came here as ambassadors to reestablish contact with Kessel." He paused. "Obviously the people of Kessel weren't interested."

Han snapped his attention to the front as he heard something happen to the cars ahead. The front car split off; he could hear it echo with a diminishing *swoosh* down one of the side tunnels. A few moments later another two cars separated themselves and went down another side tunnel as their sounds diminished in the hollow distance. The rest of the floating mine car continued down the main tunnel.

"They're separating the mining teams," Kyp said. "I wanted to be with you. Tell me everything."

"Kyp," Han said with a sigh, "it looks like we'll have plenty of time to give you the details."

The audio hum of the mine cars' repulsorlifts deepened. Han felt the breeze on his face dwindle as they slowed. His hands and face were numb; his ears tingled with the cold, but the rest of his body seemed comfortably warm in the heated thermal suit.

The guard who had shouted at Kyp spoke when the floating cars stopped. "Everybody out. Link up. March to the work area."

The remaining cars swayed as the prisoners climbed off and stood in silence on the crumbled ground. Their equipment grated against each other in the darkness, and their boots scuffed the dirt. A pandemonium of little sounds echoed in the claustrophobic tunnel, making the blackness press in even more heavily.

"Where are we going?" Han said.

Kyp grabbed a loop on Han's belt. "Just hold the person in front of you. Believe me, you don't want to get lost down here."

"I believe you," Han said. Chewbacca made his own noise of agreement.

When the work detail had lined up, the front guard began to march them along. Han took small shuffling steps to keep from stumbling over rubble on the floor, but he still tripped into Chewbacca several times.

They turned to pass through another tunnel entrance. Han heard a faint thump and a yowl of pain from the Wookiee. "Watch your head there, buddy," he said. He heard the rustle of fur inside a thermal suit as Chewbacca bent down to pass through the arch.

"Here's the rail," the guard said. "Stop here, take your time, and go down."

"What's a rail?" Han asked.

"Once you touch it, you'll figure it out," Kyp answered.

The noises he heard made no sense to Han. He couldn't determine what was actually happening. He discerned sliding sounds of fabric, bitten-back outcries of surprise or fear. When Chewbacca shuffled up, he voiced a guttural complaint, shaking his entire body in refusal.

The guard lashed out with something hard that struck Chewbacca. The Wookiee roared in pain and swung his arm trying to hit the guard, but apparently smacked only the rock wall instead. Chewbacca grew more upset, flailing right and left. Han had to duck to keep from being battered.

"Chewie! Calm down! Stop it!" The Wookiee slowly regained control of himself at the sound of Han's voice.

"Do what I tell you!" the guard shouted.

"It's okay," Kyp added his own encouragement. "We do this every day."

"I'll go first, Chewie," Han said, "whatever it is."

"Down there," the guard snapped.

Han bent over, fumbled with his hands, and felt a big hole in the floor like a trapdoor to lower tunnels, with piled rubble all around it. His fingers found a cold metal railing about the size of a typical steel girder, polished smooth and plunging downward, like a slide or a metal banister.

"You want me to ride that?" Han asked. "Where does it go?"

"Don't worry," Kyp said again. "It's the best way down."

"You've got to be kidding!"

Then he heard Chewbacca laughing, a nasal, chuffing sound. That made up Han's mind for him. He sat down on the metal rail and wrapped his legs around it, placing his hands behind his hips and gripping the rail as best he could. The slippery fabric of the thermal suit immediately started him sliding. The darkness grabbed at him as he picked up speed. Han imagined sharp stalactites just centimeters above his head, waiting to take off the top of his skull if he sat up at the wrong moment. He continued to accelerate. "I don't like this!" he said.

Suddenly the rail disappeared beneath him, and he tumbled onto a mound of powdery sand. Another two workers scrambled forward to yank him clear of the end of the rail. He brushed dust off his thermal suit, though he couldn't see the dirt anyway.

A few moments later Chewbacca came down with a long, echoing howl, and shortly after that came Kyp Durron and the guard. "Line up again!" the guard said.

Chewbacca grunted and huffed a few words. Han snorted. "Don't tell *me* it was fun!"

The guard marched them ahead. When the ground dropped out from under them, they splashed into a shallow lake. The pressure of the water pushed against the legs of Han's suit. The captive miners sloshed ahead, holding on to each other in their blindness.

The water had a sour, brackish smell, and Han's stomach clenched, anticipating a drop-off that would plunge him in over his head. Chewbacca whined but kept his comments to himself.

Under the water something soft and fingerlike poked against Han's legs. Other contacts nudged at his feet, prodding and coiling around his calves. "Hey!" He thrashed about with his feet. The ghostly, touching things swarmed about him. Han pictured soft blind grubs, hungry in the darkness; their mouths would be filled with fangs, waiting for something to eat, something helpless in the dark—as he was. He splashed again to drive them away.

"Don't call attention to yourself," Kyp Durron said in a low voice. "That will only bring more of them."

Han forced himself not to overreact, to walk with gliding, even strides. None of the other prisoners cried out; apparently, no one had been eaten alive yet, though the small probing fingers or suckers or mouths continued to play around his legs. His throat felt very dry.

He wanted to drop to his knees when they finally reached the tunnel on the other side of the subterranean lake. Behind them dripping water and tiny splashing sounds echoed in the grotto.

An unknown time later they arrived at the actual spice-mining area. The guard withdrew an apparatus from his pack, making shuffling and clinking noises as he did so. Unseen, he set it up along the walls of the tunnel.

"We have to go deep to get the good spice deposits," Kyp said. "Down here the glitterstim is fresh and fibrous, instead of old and powdery like in the higher mines. The spice veins are laid in crisscross patterns along the walls of the tunnel, never going much below the surface of the rock."

Before Han could say anything else, a high-pitched, teeth-jarring hum pounded against the tunnel. Chewbacca roared in pain. Then a skin of rock along the inner tunnel sloughed off. The guard had used an acoustic disruptor that penetrated only a few inches into the rock, crumbling it down. "Get to it!" he said.

Kneeling on the rubble-strewn floor, Kyp showed Han and Chewbacca how to sort through the crushed rock, feeling with cold-numbed fingers through the broken pebbles and debris to pluck out strands of glitterstim, like tufts of hair or asbestos fiber.

Han's hands felt raw from the work and the biting cold, but none of the other prisoners complained. They all seemed beaten. He could hear them breathing and gasping as they continued to exert themselves. Han stuffed fragments of glitterstim into the gathering pouch at his hip. He felt a sinking feeling, like a knife twisting inside him. He could be at this job for a long, long time.

After the team finished sifting through the rubble, the guard moved them farther down the tunnel, then activated his acoustic disruptor to bring down another section of the wall.

As they huddled in the tunnel, picking at broken rock, Han could think only of his aching knees, his burning fingers. Of how nice it would be to be back with Leia again. No one had told him how long a shift was—not that he had any way of telling time in the darkness. He grew hungry. He grew thirsty. He kept working.

During a lull Han felt a tingle go up his spine. He looked, knowing he could see nothing in the dark. But his ears, now attuned as his primary sense, picked up a distant rustling, a thousand whispering voices growing louder, picking up speed like a hydrolocomotive bulleting down a tube. A pearly glow seemed to seep out of the air.

"What—?"

"Shhh!" Kyp answered. The prisoners had stopped working. A faint glittering dazzle like a dense cloud of faint fireflies shot through the tunnel, humming and chittering.

Han ducked. Around him he heard the others also falling flat on the debris-covered floor.

The glowing thing shot down the hollow tube, rolling and roiling. Once it passed them and went beyond the point where they had mined spice from the walls, the glowing thing suddenly curved right and plunged straight into the solid rock, vanishing like a fish falling back into a dark pool.

Behind them, along the curving lengths of the tunnel, tiny blue sparks flickered from the exposed spice that had been activated by the light source whizzing past. The blue sparks sputtered and flickered, and quickly faded.

Han's eyes ached from the sudden barrage of light—a light that was probably too dim for him to have seen under normal circumstances, but his eyes had been yearning in blackness for hours now. "What was that?" he shouted.

He heard Kyp panting beside him. "Nobody knows. It's about the fifteenth one I've seen over the years. We call them bogeys. They've never hurt anybody, or so we think, but nobody knows what's grabbing those people down in the deep mines."

The guard himself seemed shaken, and Han could hear a quaver in his voice. "That's enough. End of shift. Let's make our way back to the cars."

That sounded like a good idea to Han.

When the string of mine cars returned to the long holding grotto and the metal door closed behind them, Han heard the sound of weapons being drawn. All workers were ordered to strip out of their thermal suits. Han could understand the precautions—with a brief mental boost from stolen glitterstim, a prisoner might be able to stage an escape . . . although Han had been to the barren surface of Kessel and wondered where an escapee might go.

When the standard lights finally came back on, the blinding glare was enough to make Han crouch over, as if someone had punched him in the gut. He shielded his eyes.

He felt a hand take him and lead him into the muster room. "It's okay, Han. Just follow me. Let your eyes get used to it. There's no hurry."

But Han was in a hurry to see what Kyp Durron looked like. He kept blinking away tears and forcing his pupils to contract enough that he could make sense out of the brilliant images showering around him. But when he finally discerned Kyp's form, he blinked again—this time in surprise.

"You're just a kid!" Han saw a dark, tousle-headed teen who looked as if he cropped his own hair with a blunt object. He had wide eyes surrounded by dark rims, and his skin was pale from years of living in the darkness of the spice mines. Kyp was wiry and tough looking. He stared at Han with hope and a little intimidation.

"Don't worry," Kyp said. "I do the best I can."

Kyp reminded him of the brash and wide-eyed young Luke Skywalker Han had first met in the Mos Eisley cantina. But Kyp seemed tougher than Luke had been, not quite so naive. With the rough life Kyp had had, growing up on Kessel and locked in the spice mines without anyone to watch over him, it was no wonder the kid had a hard streak in him.

At the moment Han couldn't decide which he hated more—the Empire, for inflicting such hardships on Kyp and his family, or Moruth Doole for perpetuating them . . . or himself, for getting Chewie and him into this mess in the first place.

8

Night on Eol Sha offered little rest. Falling darkness fought against the simmering orange glow from the nearby volcano, the pastel blaze of the Cauldron Nebula, and the looming spotlight of the too-close moon. Hissing blasts from the geyser field broke the quiet at irregular intervals.

Luke sat alone in the cramped storage module Gantoris had given him for sleeping accommodations. Never intended as a living area, the module had few comforts: a basin of filmy water and a cloth-covered mound of dirt for a bed. Gantoris took a perverse pleasure in telling Luke that it had been one of the dead boy's favorite places to play. Either the refugees blamed Luke for not being able to save both children, or perhaps Gantoris just wanted to keep him off balance.

Luke had his lightsaber and all the powers he had learned from Jedi training, should he decide to escape. But that was not the reason he had come to Eol Sha. Cupping his chin in his hands, he stared out at the hostile night. He needed to convince Gantoris to listen to him, to see the need for rebuilding the Jedi Knights—but why would someone from an isolated colony, with no conception of galactic politics, bother to care?

If Gantoris was indeed a descendant of the long-ago Ta'ania, Luke had to make him care.

When the other people drifted to their quarters for the evening, Warton brought him a steamed bugdillo to eat. Luke poked at the glossy black shell of the crustacean, splitting open the cracks in its multiply segmented body to get at the pinkish meat. That afternoon a boy had been killed trying to spear these small creatures. . . .

At any time Luke could leave the battered module, walk to the passenger shuttle on the far side of the geyser field, and retrieve his own rations; but he didn't want to leave, not until Gantoris agreed to come with him. Luke ate the sour-tasting meat, chewing in silence.

"Come with me." Gantoris stood silhouetted in the square doorway of Luke's quarters.

Luke blinked and came out of his trance, refreshed and surprised to see the gray morning light shining through cracks in the module. Without a word, he stood up and stepped outside.

Gantoris wore the faded uniform of a trader captain. It fit him poorly, but he carried himself with pride. The uniform must have been passed down from generation to generation as the hopeful colonists waited for the ramjet gas miners to return and make their settlement a booming town.

"Where are we going?" Luke asked.

Gantoris handed him a woven pouch, then slung a similar one over his own shoulder. "To get food." Tossing his thick black braid behind him, he marched toward the geyser field.

Luke followed across the rugged terrain, sidestepping the lime-encrusted network of geysers and steam vents. The planet of Eol Sha hummed with the tidal strain, like fading vibrations from a struck gong.

Gantoris moved with outward confidence, but Luke sensed trepidation, an uncertainty in him. Luke decided this might be a good time to talk about the Force and its powers.

"You must have learned something about the order of Jedi Knights," he began. "For a thousand generations they served the Old Republic as guardians and keepers of order. I believe one of your own ancestors—Ta'ania—was the daughter of a Jedi. That is why I've come to you. She was among the people who established this colony on Eol Sha.

"The Emperor hunted down and killed all the Jedi Knights his assassins could find, but I don't believe he could have traced every descendant, every bloodline. Now the Empire has fallen and the New Republic needs to reestablish the Jedi Knights." He paused. "I want you to be one of them."

He gripped Gantoris's shoulder. The other man flinched, and pushed Luke's hand away. Luke's voice took on a more pleading tone. "I want to show you the powers of the Force, the infinite doors it can open. With this new strength you'll be able to help hold the entire galaxy together. I promise we'll take your people and move them to a safe planet, one that will seem like a paradise after Eol Sha."

Luke realized he was proselytizing. Gantoris looked at him with dark, unfathomable eyes. "Empires and republics mean nothing to me. What have they cared for us before? My universe is here, on this world."

He stopped in front of the wide opening to a geyser and peered into its depths. The creeping stink of rotten eggs wafted into the morning air. From his hip pouch Gantoris withdrew a battered old datapad and consulted a column of numbers that looked to be some sort of timetable. "Here. We will go inside the geyser and harvest."

Luke blinked. "Harvest what?"

Without answering Gantoris lowered himself over the lip of the geyser hole. Luke shrugged off his Jedi cloak and left it beside the geyser rim, then followed the other man underground. Was Gantoris just trying to see if Luke would follow him down into the belly of the geyser?

The shaft was a narrow, winding chimney through porous rock, a pipeline to gush superheated water. Colorful mineral deposits sparkled white and tan and blue, powdery in his hand. Luke found plenty of footholds as he followed Gantoris into the honeycombed passages. The rock felt warm and slimy. Acrid vapors rising from below stung his eyes.

Gantoris worked his way into a side crevice. Luke asked, "What do you want me to do?"

In answer Gantoris wedged himself deeper into a crack and shrugged the woven pouch off his shoulder. "Look in the dark pockets, the ones protected from the scalding water." Gantoris dug his fingers into a crevice, felt around, and pulled out a handful of rubbery tendrils. "With the heat and the mineral deposits, the lichens have a rich growing ground. It takes a great deal of processing, but we can make something edible out of this. On our world we don't have many choices. My people must take what we can find."

Luke likewise removed his pouch and began to search in the cracks, probing with his prosthetic hand. What if something poisonous lurked in the crevices to sting him? He could read ominous intentions from Gantoris but couldn't pinpoint them. Was Gantoris looking for a simple way to kill the "dark man" from his dreams? On his third try Luke found a mass of spongy growth and yanked it out.

Gantoris looked over his shoulder at Luke. "It would be better if we split up. If you stay by me, you will find only my leavings. I can never feed our people that way." Gantoris's voice changed to a mocking tone, and his forehead crinkled, raising his shaven eyebrows. "Unless your Force can miraculously create a banquet?"

Keeping his handholds, Luke edged over to another crack as Gantoris worked deeper into his own fissure, turning a jagged corner. A flurry of uneasiness shot through him, but Luke began to search among the crevices.

The lichen wasn't difficult to find, and Luke quickly filled his pouch, crawling through narrow openings. Perhaps Gantoris had expected him to get lost among the fissures. But even disoriented underground, Luke could always retrace his path. He had heard nothing from the other man, and, deciding that he had fulfilled his obligation, Luke began to work his way back to where they had split up.

When he reached the joined passage, Luke saw that Gantoris was no longer there. He crawled deeper into the fissure, looking for the other man, all the while expecting a trap but confident he could deal with it. He would have to impress Gantoris with his Jedi abilities.

The passage ended in a blocked wall of eroded stone. The smells of sulfurous smoke grew stronger, engendering a deep sense of claustrophobia in him. Luke recalled the two children buried under the avalanche, bright blood splashed on the bottoms of the fallen rocks. The ground around him hummed with barely contained murderous energy—what if another earthquake happened while he was wedged in the narrow cracks underground?

Gantoris was nowhere in sight. "Gantoris!" he called, but heard no answer. Looking up the shaft of daylight poking through from the surface, Luke finally saw the man's silhouette nearly at the top. Gantoris scrambled up the jagged walls, climbing as fast as he could manage, leaving Luke behind.

He was fleeing something.

Luke sensed rather than heard the buildup of pressure deep within the planet, the water table heated against magma crouching near the surface, coming to a boil, rising up, finding the most direct way to escape.

Gantoris had carried his own timetable. The geysers must erupt at regular intervals. He intended to trap Luke underground, where he would be cooked to the bone by curtains of superheated steam.

Luke grabbed for a handhold and hauled himself up, scrabbling with his boot for a place to rest his foot. He clambered up the bumps and corners of the chimney leading up. The heat increased around him, making it difficult to breathe. He gasped and blinked burning tears out of his eyes. Steam curled upward, as if seeping out of the very rocks.

His foot slipped and he nearly plunged downward, but his prosthetic hand flashed out, grabbing on to an outcropping and refusing to let go. When he finally regained his balance, the outcropping crumbled to pieces.

Luke had lost precious seconds. The light above shone brighter, urging him on. He held on to another corner, crawled up another few feet, reached out again.

Briefly he saw a shadowed head peer down into the geyser chimney, watching him. Gantoris. But he offered no help.

Luke clawed his way up, ignoring his torn flightsuit, climbing as fast as his limbs could carry him. Then he ran out of time.

He heard the explosion deep beneath him, the rumbling roar of a plume of boiling water rushing to the surface. Luke braced himself and knew he had one chance.

He had done this in Cloud City on Bespin, and during his training with Yoda, and other times. As the jet of steam and deadly water blasted toward him, Luke gathered his strength, his concentration, and sprang straight *up*, hurling his body out of the geyser shaft. He used the Force as a springboard to throw himself high and free, just as if he were lifting an inanimate object.

Luke shot out of the geyser chimney, flailing his arms as he dropped to the rugged ground. He tucked his shoulder and rolled, striking with enough force to knock the breath from him.

A second after he hit the ground, a wall of steam and superheated water belched from the geyser. Luke shielded his exposed flesh from the scalding droplets and waited for the blast to dwindle.

The geyser eruption lasted several minutes. When Luke finally crawled to his knees, he saw Gantoris and the other people of Eol Sha walking toward him, their faces grim, as usual. They had set him up, trapped him, tried to kill him.

But the anger faded quickly. Hadn't Luke challenged Gantoris to test him, to let him prove his intentions? Luke gathered his drenched Jedi cloak from the geyser rim and waited for them.

Gantoris crossed his arms over his chest and nodded. His face looked wide and bleak without eyebrows or eyelashes. "You passed my first test, dark man." Luke sensed both eagerness and terror from the man. "Now come and face your last trial."

As the people stepped forward to take him again, Luke did not resist. He had decided to take whatever risks proved necessary to rebuild the Jedi Knights.

He hoped the risks would be worth it.

It was like a religious procession. With Gantoris in the lead, the people of Eol Sha began a long march up the slope to the cracks of lava. Luke walked straight and proud, determined not to show fear, though the people had already proved their murderous intentions. Despite his Jedi training, he was in very real danger. The oppressive moon hung overhead like a gigantic fist.

Spires of lava rock jutted out of the hillside like rotten teeth. Gantoris did not slow his pace when the slope took a steep turn, but he stopped when they reached a sheltered opening in the volcano wall. Overhead a pall of smoke and ash hung in the air.

"Follow me inside," Gantoris told Luke. The others filed past, continuing along the rugged path. Luke stepped after him. He needed to earn Gantoris's respect, if not trust. In this circumstance Gantoris was making all the rules.

Gantoris strode confidently down the narrow passage into the dense shadows, a lava tube blasted through the side of the cone to ease pressure from an ancient eruption. Up ahead a fiery orange glow lit their way. Luke felt growing anticipation mixed with dread with each step they took.

The lava tube spread out, revealing a boiling lake of fire. Though the fissure opened to the sky, and other openings let in gusting cross-drafts, the chamber felt like the blast of an oven. Luke ducked his head, trying to shield his face with the damp Jedi hood, but Gantoris seemed unaffected.

Squinting through noxious gases belching from the lava, Luke watched the other people arrive on the far side of the chamber, lining up and waiting. All faces turned toward him.

Gantoris had to raise his voice over the growling sounds of the churning magma. "Walk across the fire, dark man. If you reach the other side safely, I will allow you to teach me whatever you wish." Without waiting for a reply Gantoris disappeared back into the darkness of the lava tube.

Luke stared after him for a moment, wondering if Gantoris could be serious—but then he noticed dark objects in the blaze of bright lava. Hard stepping stones of denser rock that did not melt but made a precarious path across the lake of fire.

Was Gantoris testing his courage? What did the man want, and what did his dreams of a demonic "dark man" portend?

Luke swallowed, but his throat was dry as parchment. He stepped to the edge of the simmering lava. The stones beckoned, but common sense warned him to go back, to return to his shuttle and fly away. He could find other candidates for his Jedi academy. Threepio and Artoo must have uncovered some leads by now, and he himself had another possibility on Bespin. Luke hadn't even tested Gantoris yet; why should he risk his life for someone who might or might not actually have Jedi potential?

Because he had to. Forming a new order of Jedi Knights would be difficult, and if he flinched from the first test of his own powers, how could he consider himself worthy of attempting such a task?

Impossible heat swirled around him. Stepping to the edge of the fire, Luke looked at the broken sky above him. Then he set his foot down on the first stepping stone.

It supported his weight. Luke looked ahead, fixing his gaze on the opposite side. The gathered people kept watching.

Lava bubbled around him, belching noxious gases into the air. He tried to breathe in shallow gasps. He took another step. The other side seemed very far away.

Blinking irritated tears from his eyes, he counted the stones ahead of him. Fourteen more. Luke stepped to the next one.

Gantoris appeared on the far side, joining the other refugees of Eol Sha. Luke didn't expect them to cheer him on, but they remained too eerily silent.

Another step. Around him the lava gurgled like the belly of a giant beast, a hungry beast.

Luke moved to another step, then another. A tendril of euphoria began to rise within him. This wasn't as difficult as he had feared. He would be able to pass this test. With reckless courage and speed, he strode to the halfway point.

Then the lava began to bubble and hiss more forcefully, gushing as something stirred below. The volcanic chamber throbbed with a sound that drummed from just below his range of hearing, but enough to vibrate his teeth. He felt his stomach plunge with apprehension. He tensed, waiting to see what horror awaited him.

Something lived within the lake of lava. Something moved.

Suddenly a serpentlike creature burst above the surface, hissing like rocket fuel caught on fire.

The fireworm had a triangular head and pointed ear tufts. Crystalline scales armored every inch of its body. Its wide eyes were jewels glowing with a fire of their own. Insulated air intakes sucked in the hot atmosphere, filling bladders deep within the creature's core and making it rise to the surface of the lava pool, huge and fierce. The silicon armor plates glittered like mirrors in the firelight.

Luke kept his precarious balance on the stepping stone, avoiding sudden death in the molten rock, then leaped to the next rock. As the fireworm rose and coiled above him, he knew he could never outrun the monster. He stopped and found secure footing. Instinctively, he drew his lightsaber, igniting it with a snap-hiss. The green glow of his blade fought against the fiery orange of the lava chamber.

On the far side of the lava lake, the gathered people of Eol Sha watched in silence, unmoving.

The fireworm glared down at Luke with its viper's head. It opened a vast metallic mouth and spewed congealing lava at the wall. Armored intakes continued to suck air, raising coils of the behemoth's body to the surface. Luke held up his lightsaber, but it seemed pitifully small to fight a lava dragon.

With an ultrasonic bellow the fireworm dove beneath the magma again, splashing molten rock into the air. Luke danced from stepping stone to stepping stone, trying to avoid the deadly firefall. Globs of lava set his Jedi cloak on fire, but Luke managed to yank it over his shoulders and toss it into the bubbling pool, where it burst into bright flames.

He held his lightsaber in front of him. His eyes widened. He reached out with his Jedi senses, trying to second-guess the creature. His every nerve was tuned, ready to respond, but he saw only the restless surface of the lava.

"Where are you?" he whispered.

The fireworm's head exploded out of the lava on the other side, rearing up to strike. It plunged down, opening its huge mouth to reveal fangs like stalactites. Luke whirled, bringing up his lightsaber and dancing back to the previous stepping stone.

As the fireworm struck, Luke slashed with his humming green blade. But when the lightsaber smashed against the mirrored armor plates, the glowing green edge refracted into a thousand components, splitting and ricocheting around the chamber. Sparks showered all around him. The energy blade that could supposedly slice through anything broke only one small silicon armor plate.

On the other side of the chamber, the people of Eol Sha ducked to escape the flying shards of green power. Splintered rock fell into the magma lake. Luke knew he could not use the lightsaber against the monster again.

The fireworm yowled in surprise more than pain, then dove for refuge under the lava. Luke crouched, desperately trying to figure out what he should do next. He turned, ready to run to the other side where the people waited for him.

The fireworm would return any minute. He didn't know how much time he would have.

Suddenly, the creature launched itself out of the lava, roaring and hissing and making sounds too horrible for Luke to describe. He turned, lightsaber in hand and ready to die in battle—but now the monster had no interest in him at all.

Gouts of acrid smoke poured from the chink in the silicon armor, where lava ate its way into the fireworm's body core. The creature writhed and tossed, spewing lava into the air. Molten rock devoured the fireworm's internal organs like acid, killing it from the inside out. Burning within, the fireworm thrashed in agony, spraying lava as flames and foul smoke boiled out of the tiny breach in its armor. When the fiery rock burned through to the fireworm's inflated air bladders, the creature exploded.

Splatters of hardening lava rained down. Luke managed to deflect most of the burning chunks with the Force, but some scorched his back and shoulder. The fireworm's death throes churned waves in the molten rock, then gradually subsided.

Luke raised his eyes, blinking in disbelief. The people of Eol Sha still waited for him.

Most of the stepping stones had been washed away in the turmoil. Nothing but impassable lava remained between him and Gantoris. He could not finish his journey. Giddy with terror and a backwash of possibilities from the Force, Luke stared at the impassable river of flames between him and his goal.

He thought of the potential for his proposed academy, for the return of the Jedi Knights. The New Republic needed him. He had to complete his promise. He would gather candidates to teach the ways of the Force. He *would*. Without a doubt in his mind, still throbbing with the Force after his battle against the fireworm, he closed his eyes.

Luke walked across the lake of fire.

He did not think about it. The lava refused to touch his feet. Only the Force burned bright around him. One step after another, he strode across the flaming rock, letting himself see nothing but his goal until he stood again on solid ground on the far side of the lake of fire, with Gantoris and his people.

When he reached safety, he nearly collapsed with relief, but he could not allow himself to show a change of expression. He tried not to think about what he had just done.

Gantoris stood before him, an expression of awe on his broad face. The others backed away, but Gantoris remained motionless. He swallowed as he met Luke's gaze. "I will abide by my promise." He drew a deep breath. "Teach me how to use this mysterious power within me."

Without a thought Luke reached forward with trembling hands and touched Gantoris's head. He sent mental fingers inward, probing to the back of the other man's mind, searching until he found the mysterious nub in Gantoris's subconscious, and pushed—

The strength of his reflexive reaction knocked Luke backward so that he had to catch his balance before tumbling into the lava. Gantoris did indeed have the Jedi potential, enough to make him a formidable candidate for the Jedi academy.

Luke allowed himself a sigh of relief. The terror and the testing had been worth it. He took Gantoris's hand, then looked at the gathered survivors of the abandoned colony.

"We will find a new home for your people. But first you will come with me to Coruscant."

9

Lando Calrissian's ship, the *Lady Luck*, received clearance from a bored-sounding traffic controller to land in the spaceport of Umgul. As the ship coasted through the misty atmosphere, Lando was amazed at the number of private ships, space yachts, and luxurious ground skimmers bustling around the landing center.

Lando cruised with the other traffic over flatlands surrounding a broad river on his way to Umgul City. Fleets of sail barges drifted over the sluggish river. Looking down, he could see flashing lights and gyrating bodies that spoke of wild parties on the barge decks.

A moist planet, but cool, Umgul was frequently blanketed by dense fog and low-hanging clouds; even now, in the middle of the day, wisps of mist drifted up from the river and spread across the lowlands. Though unremarkable in resources and strategic importance, Umgul had earned galactic fame as a sports center, home of the renowned Umgullian blob races.

The *Lady Luck* followed her designated vector to a spaceport carved into limestone bluffs rising above the river. Accompanied on either side by tiny two-person pleasure skimmers, Lando brought his ship through the cavern mouth. He barely managed to avoid hitting a blue zeppelin full of tourists. Inside, hairy attendants wearing bright-orange vests directed the *Lady Luck* into her parking stall by waving handheld laser beacons.

Lando turned to the two droids next to him in the pilot's compartment. "Are you boys about ready to have fun?"

Artoo beeped something Lando could not understand, but Threepio straightened in indignation. "We are not here to have fun, General Calrissian. We are here to assist Master Luke!"

"*I'm* here as a private citizen going to the blob races." Lando jabbed a finger at him. Being in close quarters with Threepio for only a day had already been enough for the prissy droid to get on his nerves. "*You* are my protocol droid, and you'd better play the part—or I'll have you run a complete diagnostic of all the sewage-control systems on Umgul City."

"I . . . understand clearly, sir."

As the *Lady Luck*'s ramp tongued out, Lando stepped into the chaos of the Umgullian reception center. Voices blurred by background noise made perpetual announcements over the intercom systems. Roars from departing vehicles echoed in the grotto. Acrid smells of exhaust fumes and engine-fueling ports stung Lando's nostrils.

Nonetheless, he held his head high and strode down the ramp, swirling his cape and beckoning the two droids to follow. "Threepio, can you understand any of those announcements? Figure out where we're supposed to go."

Threepio scanned the data walls that listed services offered by Umgul City. Text scrolled out in several languages.

Four stubby vendors rushed over to the new visitor, pushing trinkets and souvenirs at Lando. The scruffy-looking hucksters were Ugnaughts, the ugly little maintenance creatures that filled the lower levels of Cloud City. "Why not bring a baby blob home for the kids, sir?" The Ugnaught thrust out a greenish, oozing mass that looked like a fist-sized wad of phlegm.

"How about some blob candy, sir? Best in the city! My secondary mate makes it at home." The gelatinous blob candy looked identical to the baby blob the first Ugnaught had offered.

"Good-luck charm?" said a third Ugnaught. "Works for all religions!"

Lando waved them away. "Threepio, where are we going?"

"Adjusting for local time, sir, I believe there is an important blob race beginning in less than one standard hour. The Umgullian mass-transit systems will take us directly to the blob arena. I believe the mass-transit access is—"

The four Ugnaught souvenir vendors began falling over each other offering to guide the fine gentleman to the arena.

"—immediately to our left." Threepio gestured to a brightly painted tunnel entrance.

"Come on," Lando said and, without looking back, walked over to the mass-transit entrance. The disappointed Ugnaughts hurried off to hunt for other customers.

The mass-transit trip was like a roller-coaster ride without wheels. A slim tubelike car shot through the tunnel up to the top of the bluff, splashing through high-rising fog and rushing over woodlands where trees crammed into notches in the weathered limestone. The ground was a crazy quilt of bright signs describing tourist attractions, eating establishments, pawnshops, and high-interest, no-questions-asked gambling loans.

At the great entry kiosks to the blob arena, streams of people and other creatures pushed in, paying their credits and obtaining seat assignments. Lando paid for himself but argued with the ticket-taking computer over whether his two droids were companions (and thus needed to buy tickets) or subservient information-processing attendants; Lando won the argument, though Threepio seemed insulted at being classed as little more than an appliance.

The blob-racing stadium was a vast sinkhole that had collapsed into the top of the bluff, a circular pit in the rocky ground. The Umgullian stadium management had carved thousands of seats, stalls, pits, and sockets out of the sloping rocky walls to accommodate all manner of bodily configurations.

Giant whirring fans had been mounted around the rim of the sinkhole, generating a hefty breeze to shove back the encroaching fog that pushed in from all sides, driving it into the open air, where it dissipated.

After pushing his way along the crowded halls, Lando found his seat, pleased to see that it had a good view of the entire "blobstacle course" below. The odds panel in front of his seat listed information about the fourteen blob challengers for the day's first heat and also counted down the twenty minutes remaining before the next race would begin.

A grin spread across Lando's face as he took in the smells of treats and condiments, saw whirring robotic drink dispensers drifting through the stands. He was enjoying this already. It brought back plenty of old memories.

As baron-administrator of Bespin's Cloud City, Lando had spent much of his time in the high-class casinos, watching the tourists and high rollers. He had never seen blob racing before, but the excitement in the air made his heart beat faster.

Threepio fidgeted, looking at the crowd. A white ursine creature nearly knocked him over as it pushed its way to a seat farther down the mezzanine.

Lando couldn't forget the primary reason why he was here, though. Mounted to Artoo's body core was the power pack of the Imperial Jedi-detecting device, and Lando kept the sheet-crystal detector paddles secured to his own side.

"Okay, Artoo. Let's see if we can find our friend Tymmo. Jack into the stadium computer and see if he's bought a ticket or placed a bet. If so, let's find out where he's seated."

The announcer's voice echoed around the arena. "Sentient beings of all genders—welcome to the galaxy-renowned blob races of Umgul! Before we begin this afternoon's first heat, we'd like to call your attention to next week's special gala blob derby to be hosted in honor of a visiting dignitary, the Duchess Mistal from our sister planet Dargul. We hope you'll all attend."

The apathetic reaction from the crowd told Lando just how many visiting dignitaries Umgul must host throughout the year.

"For this afternoon's event we'll be running fourteen thoroughbred racing blobs through a twelve-point blobstacle course that has been thoroughly inspected and certified by the galactic racing commission. All data on the age, mass, and viscosity of our racing blobs is available at the terminal in front of your seat."

Lando smiled grimly at that. Umgul City claimed to run clean blob races, and cheating was a capital offense. "What does he mean by 'thoroughbred racing blobs'?" he asked.

Threepio heard him. "This species of blob has several variants that are used for different purposes throughout the system. Some upper-class people actually keep them as pets. Others have seen certain medicinal value in blob treatment, such as letting a blob ooze across one's back for massage therapy or soaking one's aching feet in the warm gelatinous mass."

"But these are racers?"

"Yes, sir, bred for speed and fluidity."

The announcer finished reading several standard disclaimers. "At this point we officially declare all betting substations to be closed. The odds computer will post final probability tables, which are now available at your terminals. We shall begin the race in just a moment. Please enjoy a refreshment compatible with your biochemistry while you wait!"

Hearing a ratcheting sound, Lando directed his attention to the rear of the playing field. Conveyor mechanisms raised the blob platforms to a high ramp, stopping in front of a gate that held the oozing blobs back from the launching slide. The fourteen separate chutes in the steep, lubricated ramp were designed to boost a blob's momentum at the starting signal.

"On your mark!" the announcer said.

Lando could sense a blanketing hush through the stadium as the spectators craned forward, staring at the chutes and waiting for the blobs to emerge.

A loud electronic tone reverberated through the air, like a bullet hitting a brass bell, and suddenly the gates flew open. The ramps tilted forward, spilling the multicolored blobs down the lubricated chutes.

Fourteen syrupy masses tumbled and oozed pell-mell down the slides, striking the low walls and slithering as fast as they could to the bottom of the ramp. The blobs showed a range of colors, primarily grayish green but laced with bright hues. Variegated strands of vermillion stood out on one, turquoise on another, lime-green on a third. Each blob had a holographic number imprinted in its protoplasm; the number somehow stayed upright no matter which way the blob oriented itself.

With the chutes equally lubricated, all fourteen blobs struck the bottom of the ramp at about the same time. When the low walls no longer separated the tracks, the frantic blobs began to make their way helter-skelter around each other, gushing forward into the blobstacle course.

One contender, Blob 11—a dark-green specimen laced with a striking amethyst pattern—burst onto the flat of the track with pseudopods already extended, as if trying to scramble away the moment it hit the bottom of the ramp. It squirted forward, clenching itself together and oozing its body core ahead.

The amethyst blob had pulled a small lead by the time it hit the first obstacle, a tall metal screen with a wide mesh. Blob 11 hurled itself onto the mesh grid with its full body and began to push its entire self through, dribbling in a hundred tiny segments out the other side, where it flowed its gelatinous mass back together again. It managed to push itself halfway through before the next blob struck a different part of the screen. Lando decided to cheer for the amethyst blob, though he had no money riding on the race. He still liked to root for winners.

The second blob took a different tactic, concentrating its body into a narrow streamer that spouted through one of the mesh holes, pouring its mass to the other side.

The amethyst blob finished reassembling itself on the bottom of the grid, took no time to rest, and pushed onward.

By this time all the other blobs were struggling to get through the first obstacle. The amethyst blob frantically mushed ahead, increasing its lead as if fleeing in terror.

"Go!" Lando shouted.

The second major obstacle proved more formidable. A tall ratline made of chain links led up to another steep, luuricated slide that dropped into a sharp, banked curve.

Blob 11 reached the bottom of the ratline and extended a pseudopod up to the first loop of chain, wrapping the jellylike tendril onto the flexible rung and extending another pseudopod again and again until it flowed like a tentacled amoeba, desperately hauling its amorphous form upward faster than gravity could slurp it back down.

The amethyst blob slipped, and a large segment of its body mass drooled downward, barely connected to the main core by a thin stream of mucus. According to the official rules posted in front of Lando's seat, the entire body mass of a blob had to get to the finishing circle; it could not leave portions of itself behind.

The second and third blobs reached the bottom of the ratline, also trying to scramble up.

The amethyst blob hovered on the ratline, sagging as it worked to siphon its precariously balanced appendage back into the main core. The chain links began to work through the soft organic material, but the blob moved faster, finally drawing itself up, and hooked over another loop of chain.

Behind it the next two blobs managed to ascend to the second level of chain loops.

Back at the first blobstacle, the last of the blobs squeezed through the mesh and began creeping at top speed toward the ratline.

Blob 11 reached the top of the ratlines and, coiling its mass, shot onto the steep, greased slide, rolling and spinning and tumbling. Its holographic number remained upright all the while. The blob reached the high banked curve at the bottom of the slide, rebounded, and gushed toward the next blobstacle.

The crowd was roaring and shouting now. Lando felt exhilaration burst through him. He decided he'd have to return to Umgul when he had more time to relax, to make a few real bets.

"Excuse me, sir, but are we expressing enthusiasm for Blob Eleven?"

"Yes, Threepio!"

"Thank you, sir. I just wanted to be certain." The droid paused, then amplified his voice. "Go, number eleven!"

The second and third blobs reached the top of the ratlines simultaneously, and both leaped onto the lubricated slide, squirting down at an alarming rate. Many of the spectators jumped out of their seats and screamed with excitement.

The two blobs tumbled next to each other, grappling with pseudopods and rolling. The steep, banked curve rose up in front of them like a wall.

"Oh, I can't watch!" Threepio said. "They're going to crash!"

The two blobs both struck the corner at the same instant and splattered into each other, forming one giant ball. The crowd roared with absolute delight.

"Total fusion!" the announcer cried.

The spectators continued to cheer. The two blobs had combined into one much larger mass, and they seemed to be working at cross purposes, trying to lumber over to the side of the track and out of the way of other oncoming blobs. Meanwhile, the amethyst blob increased its lead.

"Those two are out of the race," Lando muttered.

Artoo returned, bleeping with excitement. "Excuse me, sir," Threepio said, "but Artoo has located our man Tymmo. He has indeed come to the races and placed a very large bet. We have his seating assignment. We can go see him now if you wish."

Lando was startled to be interrupted during the race; then he jumped to his feet. "We found him already?"

"Yes, sir. And as I said, he has placed a very large bet, if you take my meaning, sir."

"Let me guess," Lando said. "On Blob Eleven, right?"

"Correct, sir."

"Looks like he's done it again," Lando said. "Let's go."

They pushed past other spectators who had not bothered to take seats, then emerged into the flagstoned halls. Lando allowed Artoo to lead, puttering down near-empty interior corridors. Lando was reluctant, wanting to see the outcome of the competition. "Hurry up, Artoo."

The little droid hummed downhill toward the lower levels of the sinkhole stadium. Through a graffiti-scrawled archway they passed into the section of least expensive seats filled with desperate-looking people, the ones who had staked everything on guessing the winner of just one race. Somehow Lando hadn't expected a winner as lucky as Tymmo to be in the low-rent section. Maybe he was trying to keep a low profile.

Though support pillars and debris screens crowded the view this far down in the crater, Lando could see that Blob 11 had increased its lead substantially, a full obstacle ahead of the remaining nine blobs. Farther back on the track two blobs lay motionless and rubbery in a bed of desiccant, too slow to cross the deadly obstacle before they suffered terminal dehydration.

The surviving blobs worked at stringing themselves through a sequence of metal rings dangling on ropes, each swaying and trying to extend a pseudopod to the next ring before the pendulum motion stretched it to the breaking point.

The amethyst blob had already crossed the desiccant trap and the rings and was now oozing precariously over a long bed of sharp spikes that continually poked through its outer membrane. Tireless, Blob 11 threw itself forward with wild abandon, not heeding the spears jabbing through its body.

Artoo whistled, and Threepio pointed to a man three benches down. "General Calrissian, Artoo says this is the man we want."

Lando squinted at Tymmo. Young and attractive, but with a fidgety, furtive look, he had a disreputable air. Though his blob was winning by a wide margin, he did not seem elated. The other people around him cheered or wailed, depending on where they had cast their bets, but Tymmo just sat and waited, as if he already knew the outcome.

Blob 11 dragged the last of itself off the bed of nails, tugging to remove a few clinging strands from the spike points. The nails had slowed it to a crawl just in front of the next obstacle—a slowly turning propeller blade with razor edges.

The amethyst blob poised itself but seemed too panicked to plan the best way through the spinning blades. It squirted forward, elongating to gain speed, then shoved its body into the gap between the whirring fan blades. About a quarter of the blob made it through before the sharp edges slashed through, bisecting it.

Mucus squirted but clung in one long, liquid thread on the propeller blade. One segment of the blob waited safely on the other side of the blobstacle. The remaining three quarters hunched, then lunged through the next gap in the blades. This time half of its mass passed successfully through, and the second segment oozed forward to rejoin the first small mass. The rest of Blob 11 made it through with only a nick in its posterior portion, but as the fan blades spun around again, droplets of slime on the edges congealed into a small lump and dropped off, rolling to safety, where all the portions conjoined once more.

The crowd cheered. Some of the losers in the lower levels began throwing drink containers against the guard mesh in front of them. Blue sparks flickered from the electrified wires. Tymmo hunched forward in his seat, keeping one hand in his pocket. Lando wondered if he carried some kind of weapon.

Tymmo looked around, blinking his eyes in alarm as if he suspected he was being watched. Lando winced, knowing that his fine clothes and rich cape made him appear painfully out of place in the lower levels. Tymmo noticed Lando and the two droids, tensed, then forced himself to watch the end of the race.

Blob 11 approached the final blobstacle, hauling pseudopods over the rungs of a ladder as it dripped down. It seemed burned to exhaustion, but still it pushed on as if demons were chasing it. Its bright amethyst tracings had faded to mere speckles.

Reaching the top of the ladder, the blob descended into an array of wide funnels that had exit holes of varying sizes, many of which were sealed shut. The amethyst blob thrust extensions of itself into various funnels, poking around until it found one with a large enough hole in the bottom.

Behind, the nearest other blob began negotiating the bed of nails in front of the whirling propeller.

Choosing an acceptable funnel, Blob 11 dumped itself into the cone and pushed. A pasty stream ribboned out the narrow end, rolling and piling on the ground as the blob re-collected itself. The thin strand of blob went on and on, coming out in spurts near the end until finally the tail plopped out of the funnel.

Blob 11's entire body shimmered as it trembled with exhaustion. It charged toward the finishing circle and looked as if it intended to keep going.

The crowd continued to cheer, but the race was clearly over. Lando watched Tymmo. The other man adjusted something in his pocket.

Blob 11 came to a sudden halt in the finishing circle. Blob wranglers in coveralls rushed onto the track with wide shovels and a levitating barrow to scoop up the exhausted thing and return it to the blob pens for rehydration and a long rest. The audience then began to root for which blobs would place and show.

Tymmo slid out of his seat and flicked a quick glance from side to side, but Lando had already stepped behind a support pillar. Tymmo jostled the spectators still watching the rest of the race, making his way toward one of the cashiering stations where other winners had already queued up. Most of the winners jumped up and down, chattering with shared excitement; even the more reserved ones wore broad grins. Tymmo, though, showed only a metallic, unreadable expression. He seemed very nervous.

Lando and the two droids eased themselves into the line, butting through the crowd. Tymmo kept glancing back, but he did not see them again. Over the loudspeakers the announcer listed the order of winners in the blob race.

Lando pulled the cable jacks to the sheet-crystal Jedi detectors out of his sleeves and plugged them into the power pack on Artoo's body. He slid the flat paddles into the palms of his hands, ready for a chance when he could scan Tymmo to confirm whether or not he had the bluish aura of a possible trainee for Luke's academy.

Threepio seemed very excited. "Why don't we just go up to him and tell him the good news, General Calrissian?"

"Because something's fishy here," he said, "and I want to make sure before we get ourselves in too deep."

"Fishy?" Threepio asked, then looked around as if to locate any aquatic spectators at the blob races.

"His turn is next at the terminal. When he keys in his betting chit, it'll take a minute to process and cash in his winnings. He's effectively trapped until the transaction is done, unless he wants to throw away a lot of credits."

Of course, Lando remembered, cheating was punishable by death on Umgul, and Tymmo might be happy enough just to get away with his life. What had he been hiding in his pocket?

As Tymmo stepped up to the terminal and inserted his chit, the announcer broke through the background noise to remind everyone once again of the next week's races in honor of the visiting duchess from Dargul. Tymmo flinched visibly, but keyed in his ID code and inserted his account card to collect his winnings.

"Come on," Lando said, stepping out of line and moving toward the cashiering station. He flicked the power switch on the scanning pack; its warm-up hum vanished in the background noise.

Tymmo looked intently at the display on the cashiering station, punching in his access code and transferring his winnings as quickly as he could. Lando stepped up beside him and swept either side of the man with the detector paddles before Tymmo realized what was happening.

Tymmo looked up, saw Lando holding something that might have been a weapon, saw the two droids that might have been armed mechanical body-guards, and panicked just as the terminal ejected his account card and called for the next customer. Tymmo snatched his card and fled, scattering a pack of Ugnaughts as he ran into the crowded stands.

"Hey, Tymmo, stop!" yelled Lando. The man was swallowed up in the surge of spectators exiting the stands after the race.

"Sir, aren't we going to follow him?" Threepio asked.

Other spectators had turned to stare. The next winner, grinning and oblivious, stepped up to the cashiering station.

"No." Lando shook his head. "We've got a reading for now. Let's check it out."

In a shadowed corner, not caring if anyone saw what they were doing since nobody would understand it anyway, Lando watched the power pack of the Imperial detector reconstruct a holographic aura mapping of Tymmo.

As Lando had unfortunately expected, Tymmo's reading showed a per-fectly normal outline: no bluish haze of Jedi potential, nothing at all out of the ordinary. "He's a fraud."

Threepio seemed disappointed. "Can you be certain, sir? I should point out that many people were standing around, and they could have disturbed the readings. You also scanned him very quickly, and none too closely. Remember, too, that the detector itself is extremely old and may not be completely reliable."

Lando gave the protocol droid a skeptical frown, but Threepio's argu-ments did have some merit. He should take the trouble to be sure. Besides, Lando was enjoying himself on Umgul so far. "All right, we'll check him out a little further."

Relieved that the New Republic would pick up the tab, Lando relaxed in his spacious hotel accommodations. From the dispenser he ordered a cold punchlike drink popular on Umgul and went to the balcony to watch thick evening mists curl along the streets. He sipped the drink, unable to remove his perplexed frown or smooth his creased forehead.

"Could I get you anything else, sir, or shall I power down for the time being?" Threepio asked.

"Please do!" he said, realizing how nice it would be to keep the protocol droid quiet for a while. "But leave the circuit open in case Artoo tries to get back in touch."

"Certainly, sir."

Posing as a maintenance droid, Artoo had gone poking around the blob stables to see if he could uncover anything out of the ordinary. The little astromech droid had tuned his communication frequency to Lando's comlink so he could send a message.

Now with Threepio quiet Lando could finally think. He went over to the room's courtesy terminal and punched in a request for information. The screen automatically displayed a complete schedule for the next three weeks of blob racing, but Lando selected another menu.

The Umgullian Racing Commission was fanatical about being forthcoming with all information relating to the races and the blobs themselves. A sample of protoplasm was taken from each blob before and after any race, then subjected to rigorous analysis, the results of which were available to the public.

With help from the information assistant built into the terminal, Lando was able to collate the before-and-after tests for all of Tymmo's high-stakes winners. He didn't know what he was looking for, but he suspected some drug used to urge the blobs to greater speed, some incentive that would affect only the winners.

"Run a correlation," Lando said. "Is there anything unusual about these particular winners? Something found in these blobs, but not in the others?"

Tymmo bet only once in a while, and if his manipulation was subtle enough, Lando could imagine that the Umgullian racing commission might have missed a tiny modification. But Lando knew that one variable tied these particular winners together apart from the other blobs. Since hundreds of people bet and won on each race, the commission would have no reason to look at only those particular races where Tymmo had cashed in.

"One minor anomaly found in all cases," the information assistant said.

"What is it?"

"Faint traces of carbon, silicon, and copper in the postrace chemical tests of each winner in this subset."

"This wasn't noticed before?" Lando asked.

"Dismissed as irrelevant. Probable explanation: minor environmental contaminants from the blobstacles themselves."

"Hmmm, and these same traces show up on every one of the winners?"

"Yes."

"Do they show up on any of the other blob tests, winners or losers, in any race?"

"Checking." After a pause the terminal answered, "No, sir."

Lando looked at the test results. The amounts of contaminant were absolutely trivial, nothing that should have had any effect. "Speculation on what might have caused this?"

"None," the terminal answered.

"Thanks a lot," Lando said.

"You're welcome."

Threepio sat bolt upright, startled out of his recharging state. "General Calrissian! Artoo has just contacted me." Threepio bumped the comlink with his golden finger, and bleeping noises burst through the speaker. "Mr. Tymmo has appeared at the blob corrals, disguised as a blob wrangler. Artoo has verified his identification. What could he be doing there?"

"Let's go," Lando said. "I didn't expect him to try again so soon, but now we've got him, whatever he's doing."

Lando grabbed his cape and slung it over his shoulders before he swept out of the room. Threepio raised his hands in alarm but shuffled off as fast as he could, his motivators whirring.

The two ran through the darkened, misty streets of Umgul City. Around them blockish limestone dwellings rose high, stacked upon each other like cracker boxes, lacquered to a high gloss with moisture sealants. Streetlights hung at the street intersections, shedding a pearly halo into the mist. Workers climbed on scaffolds, tearing down old banners that advertised the visit of one dignitary and putting up new ones welcoming the Duchess Mistal to Umgul City.

Lando sprinted up the cobblestoned streets with Threepio scurrying stiffly behind. Steep thoroughfares climbed the bluffs. Ahead and adjacent to the sinkhole arena, they could see a large lighted structure where the blobs were kept and monitored.

Lando ducked through a service entrance to the blob corrals, and Threepio followed. Strange smells, damp and musty, filled the air. Cleanup droids chugged through the halls, while others checked temperature controls for the blob pens. The lights had been dimmed for the evening, encouraging the blobs to rest.

"Threepio, do you know where we're going?"

"I believe I can locate Artoo, sir," Threepio said, and turned in slow circles before he pointed the way.

Down another level they reached a shadowy chamber cut into the limestone. The lights inside had been set to their lowest illumination, and moisture generators kept the room damp and clammy. "Artoo is in here, General Calrissian."

"Okay, be quiet. Let's see what's going on."

"Do you really think Mr. Tymmo could be cheating, sir? Even with the threat of capital punishment?"

Lando frowned at him. "No, I'm sure he has a perfectly legitimate reason to be wearing a blob wrangler's uniform, slipping into the blob corral late at night, and skulking around in the darkness."

"What a relief, sir. I'm glad to hear he may yet be a Jedi candidate."

"Shut up, Threepio!"

They crept through the entrance into a room lined with blob pens. Banks of about twenty small enclosures blocked his line of sight in the shadowy room. Within each pen a gelatinous blob burbled and vibrated as it rested.

From the far side of the room came a rattling noise: a blob pen being eased open. Lando crept silently down the rows of blob enclosures, letting his eyes adjust to the dimness.

In the shadows of the far row of pens, Lando spotted a human form. He recognized Tymmo's build, his furtive movements, his lanky dark hair. Tymmo hunched over a cage, reaching inside, doing something to the blob in front of him.

Lando leaned close to Threepio and breathed words in the faintest of whispers, knowing he would not be overheard in the general stirring of the blobs. "Enhance your optical sensors so you can make out what he's doing, and record everything for later playback. We may need proof if we're going to get this guy."

Before the droid could answer, Lando clamped his hand over Threepio's mouth to keep him silent. Threepio nodded and turned to stare at the man in the shadows.

With a whirring sound Artoo-Detoo puttered down the walkway between the pens. Tymmo looked up, startled, but Artoo carried a cleaning attachment and scrubbed the floor under the pens. He whirred right by Tymmo, ignoring the man just as a cleaning droid would do. Lando nodded in admiration for the little astromech.

Tymmo turned back to his work, shaken by Artoo's appearance and apparently wanting to be out of there as soon as possible.

"Sir!" Threepio cried. "He just implanted a small object in the protoplasm of that blob!"

Tymmo whirled and grabbed at one of the pockets of his jumpsuit. Lando didn't need greater illumination to recognize a blaster being drawn.

"Thanks a lot, Threepio!" he said as he tackled the droid. An instant later a blaster bolt sparked off the wall near where they had been standing a moment before. "Come on!"

He scrambled to his feet and ran over to where Tymmo had been hiding, ducking to take advantage of the cover the blob pens offered. Another blaster shot ricocheted through the dimness, missing them by a wide margin.

"Artoo!" Threepio wailed. "Sound the alarms! Call the guards! Alert the corral owner! Anybody!"

Tymmo shot at them again, and Threepio gasped as sparks erupted close to his head. "Oh, dear!"

Inside the corral the blobs awakened and stirred, rearing up against the bars of their pens.

He heard Tymmo crash into the corner of a cage. They reached the pen where Tymmo had been meddling. Lando kept his head low. "Threepio, see if you can tell what he planted in that blob."

"Do you really think that's wise right at the moment, sir?"

"Do it!" Lando had his own blaster drawn, scanning the shadows for Tymmo's form.

Ratcheting alarms rang out. "Good work, Artoo," Lando mumbled.

Seeing a hunched, moving form, Lando risked a shot on stun but missed. An indignant series of electronic noises told him he had almost deactivated Artoo. "Sorry about that."

By firing his blaster Lando had given away his position. Tymmo shot back, but his energy bolt spanged off the wall. Lando fired again, and as the stun beam expanded outward, he saw several blobs in its path curl up and condense sideways.

"A shoot-out at the blob corral," Lando said to himself. "Just the way I wanted to spend my vacation."

Threepio stood next to the pen trying to determine exactly what Tymmo had been doing. The blob itself, riled by the disturbance, reared up against the bars, leaning into the cage door. Dim light glinted off Threepio's polished body, offering a clear target; but this time when Tymmo fired, his blaster bolt incinerated the lock on the pen. With the pressing weight of the blob, the door flung open, and the entire gelatinous mass dumped onto Threepio's head, oozing down his body. The droid's muffled cries of panic came through the wet protoplasm.

Seeing Tymmo's form move through the shadows, Lando sprinted after him. The other man made for the archway exit as fast as he could move in the murkiness. "Tymmo! Hold it right there!"

Tymmo turned to glance in Lando's direction, then put on a burst of reckless speed. At that moment Artoo scuttled out of the shadows, placing himself directly in the running man's path. Tymmo crashed into the droid, somersaulted into the air, and landed on his back.

Lando pounced, grabbing Tymmo's blaster arm and yanking it behind his back until the weapon dropped free. "Good job, Artoo."

Tymmo thrashed and struggled as the alarms continued to sound. "Get away from me! I won't let you take me back to her!"

"Help me! Help!" Threepio cried. He waved his arms, frantically trying to wipe blob material from his outer shell.

Guard droids and human security officers scrambled into the grotto.

Lights flared on as somebody upped the illumination. Tymmo fought more frantically.

"Over here!" Lando called.

The guard droids took possession of Tymmo, clamping their restraining arms around him. Another reached out to grasp Lando, and he suddenly realized he had no good reason to be in the blob corral either.

"What in the bleeping miasma is going on here!" a deep voice roared. A hirsute man who looked as if he had dressed hurriedly strode into the corral area. "And shut off those blasted alarms! They're upsetting my blobs, and they're giving me a headache."

"Over here, Mr. Fondine," one of the human guards answered.

The man came over to see Tymmo struggling in the guard droid's straitjacket grasp. Lando caught his attention. "I've uncovered a possible sabotage of the races, sir. This man here has been tinkering with the blobs."

The man gave Tymmo an acid glance, then turned back to Lando. "I'm Slish Fondine, owner of these stables. You'd better tell me who you are and why you're here."

Lando realized, with some surprise, that he had nothing to hide. "I'm General Calrissian, a representative of the New Republic. I have been investigating this man, Tymmo, as part of an entirely different mission, but I believe you will be very interested to study his track record of wins."

Tymmo glared at Lando. "You'll never take me back to her! I couldn't stand that—you don't know how she *is*. I'll die first."

Slish Fondine shushed him with a wave of his hand. "That can be arranged, if what the general says is true. On Umgul cheaters are executed." The alarm sirens finally fell silent.

"Will somebody please help me!" Threepio cried.

Fondine saw the droid struggling with the dripping greenish mass and rushed over to assist him. Brushing the protoplasm back up into the main mass, Fondine shushed and cooed the blob. "Easy now." He spoke to Threepio as well. "Stop struggling! The blob is as afraid of you as you are of it. Just be calm." He lowered his voice. "They can sense fear, you know."

Threepio tried to remain still as Fondine gently coerced the blob to reincorporate back toward its pen. Threepio suddenly grew excited again. "Sir! I've just found a near-microscopic electronic object inside this blob's protoplasm. Magnifying . . . it appears to be a micro-motivator!"

Lando suddenly understood what Tymmo had been doing. A micro-motivator implanted in the blob could send out a powerful internal stimulus, provoke a frantic flight response in any creature. If tuned properly, the micro-motivator could give a blob the speed born of absolute terror. The gadget was so tiny that Tymmo could self-destruct it after the blob had successfully won a race, leaving only minuscule traces of a few component elements in the blob tissue. And no one would ever know.

Slish Fondine glared daggers at Tymmo. "That is vile blasphemy against the whole spirit of blob racing."

Tymmo squirmed. "I had to have the money! I had to get off planet before she gets here."

In exasperation Lando said, "Who are you talking about? Who is *she*?" He freed himself from the guard droid's grip.

Tymmo's eyes goggled at Lando's question. "Didn't she send you to get me? I saw you spying on me at the races. You tried to catch me, but I escaped. I'll never go back to her."

"Who?!" both Lando and Slish Fondine bellowed in unison.

"The Duchess Mistal, of course. She clings to me every second, she blows in my ear, she won't let me out of her sight—and I couldn't stand it anymore. I had to get away."

Lando and Fondine looked at each other without comprehension, but Artoo trundled up, chittering an explanation. Threepio, extricated from the blob mass, stepped forward to translate.

"Artoo has run a check. The Duchess Mistal of Dargul has posted a million-credit reward for the safe return of her lost consort—apparently, he ran away from her. The man's official name is Dack, but his description precisely matches that of Mr. Tymmo here."

Tymmo hung his head in misery. Fondine crossed his arms over his chest. "Well? What have you got to say for yourself?"

"Yes, I'm Dack." He heaved a huge sigh. "The Duchess Mistal reached her age of marriage two years ago and decided to find the perfect consort. She advertised across the galaxy for likely candidates, and she received millions of applicants. I was one of them. Who wouldn't want the job? She was rich and young and beautiful. All the consort would have to do is live in total opulence and be doted upon by the duchess."

Tears sprang to Tymmo's eyes. "My particular talent was electronic wizardry. I built those micro-motivators from scratch. When I applied for the consort position, I knew my odds were small. But I succeeded in hacking into the central computer in Palace Dargul, sabotaging the other applicants, planting an algorithm so that the computer would spit out my name as the perfect choice."

Slish Fondine looked nauseated at the mere concept of cheating in such a heinous manner.

"The duchess and I were married, and everything seemed exactly as I had expected—at first. But the duchess was convinced I was her perfect match, fated to be with her forever. Every waking moment of the day she refused to let me move more than arm's length away from her. She would wake me up at all hours of the night, find me during her meal breaks. She would trap me in the gardens, in the libraries."

Tymmo's eyes grew wild, shining with panic. "I thought she would get tired of me—or at least *used* to having me around—but it went on for more than a year! I couldn't sleep, I jumped at shadows. I was a wreck, and that made her feel sorry for me . . . so she clung even tighter!

"And I couldn't leave! On Dargul they mate for life. Life! She'll never give up searching, and she'll never take another mate as long as I live." Tymmo looked as if a scream hovered on his lips. "I'll never be free of her! I had to escape."

"Well, it looks like you've finally found a way out," Slish Fondine said in an angry voice. "As an admitted scam artist, you'll be promptly executed under the laws of Umgul."

To Lando's surprise Tymmo didn't even try to defend himself. He seemed resigned to his fate.

But Lando wasn't so sure about the idea. "Let's think about this a minute, Mr. Fondine. Did you say there's a *million-credit* reward for his safe return to the duchess, Artoo?"

Artoo chirped an affirmative.

"Now, Mr. Fondine, think of what a wonderful gift of state this would be for the upcoming visit of the duchess, returning her consort in time to ease her loneliness."

Tymmo groaned in misery.

"On the other hand, if you were to execute him, *knowing* he is her missing consort, things could get very unpleasant between Umgul and your sister planet. Might even be cause for war."

Fondine's face darkened with the possibilities, but his honor had been so offended that the choice was not clear to him.

He sighed. "We will leave it up to the prisoner himself. Tymmo, or Dack, or whatever your name is—do you wish to be executed or returned to the Duchess Mistal?"

Tymmo swallowed hard. "How long do I have to think about it?"

"It's not a trick question!" Lando said.

Tymmo sighed. "Can I at least be allowed to rest until she gets here? I'm going to need all my strength."

The *Lady Luck* cruised out of the huge grotto of Umgul's spaceport, rising above the mists into the sky. Slish Fondine had insisted, out of fairness, that he would transfer half of the duchess's reward into Lando's account when she arrived.

No longer penniless, Lando would have seed money to invest in some new operation, some other scheme that could excite him. He had tried the molten metal mines on Nkllon, and the Tibanna gas mines on Bespin. He wondered what he might find next.

Though he had tried his best to track down a worthy candidate for Luke's Jedi academy, he hated to return empty-handed to Coruscant. But he knew there would be others.

Threepio remained uncharacteristically silent as the *Lady Luck* burst into hyperspace, heading home.

10

Images of starships whirled through space like pinpoints of fire around Coruscant. The holographic map of the system showed the locations of all vessels in range and plotted approved approach orbits on a huge spherical grid. Data terminals spewed information on vessel sizes and landing requirements, keeping track of anyone reporting impaired control. A scattering of red danger zones marked debris clouds of wrecked ships that had not yet been removed from the battle over Coruscant.

Dozens of space-traffic controllers stood at their stations around the 3-D map of the planet, pointing at images with light pens and drawing safe-approach vectors or prioritizing landing patterns. One of the war-damaged spaceports on the western end of Imperial City had just been brought back on-line in the last week, and much of the shuttle traffic was being rerouted there to ease the burden on landing platforms around the Imperial Palace.

Leia Organa Solo stood beside one of the traffic controllers. Seeing how busy the woman was directing space traffic, Leia tried not to ask too many questions, but she found it difficult to wait.

"There's something." The traffic controller reached up with the light pen to indicate a squarish violet icon used for *Small Starship—Type Unknown*. "Could that be the one you're waiting for, Minister Organa Solo? Just popped out of hyperspace. Unable to determine previous vector."

Leia felt a surge of excitement. "Yes, that's the one. Have they requested clearance yet?"

The traffic controller touched a receiver implant at her temple. "Coming in now. The pilot sends only her name. Sounds like some kind of code. Winter?"

Leia smiled. "No, that's her real name. Give her clearance to land on the top northside platform of the Imperial Palace, my authorization." She drew in a deep breath, feeling her heart pound faster. "I'll go meet her personally." She turned and took two quick steps away before she remembered to thank the traffic controller for her help. "Come on, Threepio," Leia said as she bustled past him.

The protocol droid snapped to attention, then hurried after her with his stiff-legged gait. He had returned to Coruscant with Artoo and Lando three days earlier and spent four hours in a luxurious lubricant-and-scrubber bath. Now he gleamed like new, with all traces of blob mucus removed from his finish.

Leia heard Threepio's motivators humming as he followed. She ignored him, lost in her own conflicting thoughts. Han should have been back from Kessel two days ago, but still she had heard no word from him. He'd probably fallen in with some of his old smuggling buddies, had too much to drink, gambled far into the late hours, and completely forgotten about his other obligations. It was a good thing Chewbacca had sworn a blood oath to protect him, because Han was going to have to face *her* when he got back, and he was going to need a Wookiee's protection. How dare he forget something like this?

For now, Leia would welcome her twin children home. Alone.

Standing on the top deck of the palace, Leia craned her neck and searched the hazy skies. Coruscant's aurora shimmered through the twilight, eclipsed by the complex matrix of the great orbiting shipyards.

"Threepio, tell me the minute you see them coming." The breeze tossed loose strands of hair in front of her eyes.

"Yes, Mistress Leia. I'm searching." In an imitation of a human gesture, Threepio cupped two golden hands around his optical sensors as if it would help him focus better. "Don't you think it would be wiser for us to step back slightly from the edge?"

Leia held her breath. Her children were coming home. They had not set foot on Coruscant for nearly two years, but now they would be back to stay. She could be a real mother to them, at last.

Just after their birth the twins had been sequestered on a secret planet uncovered by Luke and Admiral Ackbar. It was a world unrecorded on any chart, but habitable and protected. Luke and Ackbar had established a heavily guarded base there, leaving Leia's trusted servant Winter behind to watch over the Jedi children.

She suspected Luke had given the children a bit more than just Winter for protection, though.

During their protective isolation Leia had managed to visit Jacen, Jaina, and Anakin every few months, usually with Han in tow. At a prearranged time Winter would pop out of hyperspace in a long-distance shuttle. Without ever knowing their destination, Leia and Han would climb aboard the shuttle, be sealed in the back passenger compartment, and Winter would take them to the protected planet. The New Republic Senate was appalled at Leia's mysterious movements, but Luke and Ackbar had silenced their objections.

Leia hoped she would be able to find the time to visit her baby boy, little Anakin, now that she had the twins to watch over. It would be a tragedy if she had to be even less of a mother to the baby than she had been to these two.

"There it is, Mistress Leia!" Threepio pointed up at a flickering point of light that grew brighter every second. "A shuttle is coming down."

She felt a spasm of anxiety mixed with a thrill of excitement.

The shuttle approached, winking red and green lights in the twilight sky. It circled the former Imperial Palace, then activated its repulsorlifts to come down with a gentle sigh on the landing platform. Angular and buglike, the shuttle bore no markings, no indication of its planet of origin.

With a hiss of equalizing pressure, the hatch of the shuttle's passenger compartment split open, gently extending a ramp. Leia bit her lip and took a step forward, squinting into the sharp shadows. The shuttle blocked most of the breeze, leaving the area still and silent.

The young twins stepped out side by side and waited at the top of the ramp. Leia stared at Jacen and Jaina, both self-composed and dark-haired, with wide avid eyes and small faces that looked like the ghosts of Han and Leia.

After a second's hesitation Leia ran up the ramp, gathering the children in her arms. Both Jacen and Jaina hugged their mother. "Welcome home!" she said, whispering.

She sensed fear and reservation in them; Leia realized with a pang that she was a virtual stranger to them. Winter had been their nanny for as long as they could remember. Leia had been just a visitor whenever she could find time in her duties. But she would make it up to them. She promised herself that much.

All the outstanding obligations rose up in her mind, haunting her with the specter of duty. She still had to deal with the Caridan ambassador and a thousand other delicate tasks to hold the New Republic together. Dozens of planetary systems were on the verge of joining the Republic if a skilled representative—Leia herself—showed good faith by making a visit of state. If Mon Mothma summoned Leia to help ratify a treaty, or to take her place at a state dinner, how could Leia refuse? The fate of the galaxy hung in the balance, clearly dependent on what she did.

How could mere children take precedence over that? And what kind of a mother did it make her even to think about it?

"Where's Daddy?" Jacen asked.

Anger went through Leia like a spear of ice. "He's not here right now."

Winter finally worked her way back from the pilot compartment. Leia looked up at her friend and confidante, and warm memories washed over her. Winter had had snow-white hair for as long as Leia could remember, a serene face that rarely allowed even a twinge of anger to show through. Noticing Han's absence, Winter raised her eyebrows, filling her face with questions, but she remained silent.

"Where's baby Anakin?" Jaina asked.

"He has to stay with me for a while longer," Winter said, nudging the two children down the ramp. "Come, now, we'll take you to your new home."

The two children dutifully marched ahead, with Leia following close beside them. Threepio didn't seem to know what he was expected to do during the reunion, so he just followed, waving his arms and making flustered exclamations.

"How long we stay here?" Jacen asked.

"Where's our room?" Jaina said.

Leia smiled at the questions and took a deep breath before answering them. From now on she had a feeling she would be hearing a lot of questions.

When Leia finally kissed the twins good night, Threepio couldn't decide whether mother or twins looked more exhausted. Leia pushed loose dark hair away from her eyes as she stood at the doorway to their room and blew another kiss.

After adjusting his servomotors to allow a little more flexibility in his joints, Threepio hunkered down between the twins' beds. He had already taken care of important details such as providing fresh cups of water for the children and installing small night-lights in the dark corners.

"You two be good for Threepio," Leia said. "He'll stay here until you go to sleep. You've had exciting things happen today, and we'll do a lot more tomorrow. I'm so glad to have you back." Leia flashed a heartfelt smile at them, showing joy even through the weariness on her face.

"I'm certain I can handle this, Mistress Leia," Threepio said. "I have reviewed most of the available child psychology databases, except for those recommended by the Emperor, of course."

Leia's answering look seemed to carry a bit of skepticism, which puzzled Threepio.

"Don't wanna go sleep," Jacen said, sitting up in bed.

Leia still smiled. "But you need your rest. Maybe Threepio will tell you a bedtime story if you're good." She waved once more, then faded back into the main living area.

The children had indeed had a busy day. After their journey with Winter they had been taken on a quick tour of the Imperial Palace, then shown their new quarters. Even with her duties as Minister of State, Leia had managed to redecorate the twins' bedchamber in warm, soothing colors. Threepio would have offered his own assistance in the project, but at the time he had been with Lando Calrissian at the blob races. Thinking back, Threepio would have preferred the decorating chores.

Several times during the tour Leia was interrupted by insistent calls, documents that needed to be authorized, brief conversations that could not be delayed. Each time Leia looked guilty, as if realizing this was an indication of things to come.

The twins, though filled with excitement and wonder of the new things around them, grew cranky as they became tired. They had been overwhelmed by too much strangeness in one day, given a new home, and told to sleep in an unfamiliar room. According to the information Threepio had recently uploaded, it was perfectly normal for the children to cause minor difficulties.

"Don't wanna bedtime story," Jacen said, crossing his small hands over his chest and looking defiantly at Threepio.

"No story," Jaina echoed.

"Of course you do," Threepio insisted. "I have scoured the collected works of children's literature on thousands of planetary systems. I have selected what I believe will be a truly enjoyable story. It is called *The Little Lost Bantha Cub*, a classic that has been popular for generations with children of your age."

He had been looking forward to telling this story, recalling how much he had enjoyed telling the Ewoks of his adventures with Master Luke and Captain Solo. He had even selected some very exciting sound effects for appropriate points in the *Bantha Cub* story. Threepio had never actually been close to a live bantha during his time on Tatooine, but bantha riders— the Tusken Raiders—had dismantled him during their first attack on Master Luke. He supposed that gave him some small claim to expertise.

"Don't wanna story!" Jacen repeated. Both children had unruly dark hair, and the deep brown eyes of their mother. Right now the young boy had a determined and stubborn look on his face that Threepio had often seen on Han Solo.

Threepio realized that the issue at hand had very little to do with the actual story. According to his new information on young children, the twins were right now feeling displaced and helpless. With so many things out of their control, they needed to exert their power, to insist on some tiny spot of stability. Jacen needed to see that he could have some effect on his surroundings. Right now the boy was very upset; Jaina, picking up on her brother's distress, seemed on the verge of tears.

"Very well, young Master Jacen. I will tell you the story some other time."

Threepio knew just the trick to keep the twins happy and let them drift off to sleep. He was, after all, fluent in over six million forms of communication. He could sing lullabyes in any number of languages, any number of styles.

He selected a few that were guaranteed to please the twins. Jacen and Jaina would be asleep in no time. He began to sing.

"*Now* what are they crying about?" Leia said, sitting up sharply and looking toward the bedroom. "Maybe I should go and see."

Winter reached out to touch her wrist, stopping her. "It'll be all right. They're tired, they're frightened, they're anxious. Bear with them. And since you're new to them, they'll be testing your limits every moment, finding out how they can manipulate you. Don't teach them that you'll come running every time they make a sound. Children learn those sorts of things very quickly."

Leia sighed and looked at her personal servant. For years Winter had advised her in many things, and she was usually right. "Looks like *I'm* the one who needs to learn things quickly."

"Every part of it is a learning process. You must balance your love for them with their need for stability. That's what parenting is all about."

Leia scowled as hidden concern began to drown out her happiness at having the children back with her. "I might be doing this all by myself."

Winter's gaze seemed incisive, and she asked the question that had been on her mind for hours. "Where is Han?"

"He's not here—that's where he is!"

Not wanting Winter to see her flustered outrage, Leia stood up and turned her back. Over and over, she had imagined possibilities of Han hurt, lost, attacked . . . but she found it safer to believe other possibilities. "He's flying around in the *Falcon* with Chewbacca. He should have been back two days ago. He knew when the twins were coming home, but he couldn't bother to be here! It's bad enough we've been practically nonexistent as parents for the first two years of their lives, but he can't even spare the time to greet Jacen and Jaina when they finally come home."

Han had felt the razor of Leia's words many times, and her tongue had grown more precise with years of diplomatic practice. A small part of her was glad he was not here to bear the brunt of her anger. But then again, if he had been here, she would not have had cause for such anger.

"Where did he go?"

Leia waved her hand, trying to sound casual. "Off to Kessel, to see if he could convince any of the old spice miners to join the New Republic. He hasn't bothered to call since he left."

Winter gazed at her, not blinking. Winter's intense periods of thought always unsettled Leia. "Let me tell you this, Leia. I think I'm right. If it were anyone else on a mission like this, two days overdue and no contact for a week or so, you would be concerned. Very concerned. With Han, you are making an assumption that he is just being irresponsible. What if something happened to him?"

"That's crazy." She turned away again, to keep Winter from seeing that the same worries had been plaguing her.

Winter's grave expression did not change. "According to the reports I have seen, Kessel is relatively hostile territory. Not only the spice mines, but the Imperial Correction Facility, with some powerful defenses in place to keep prisoners from escaping. The entire system has been out of contact with us for some time."

Winter paused, as if accessing other memories. "When Mara Jade and Talon Karrde unified some of the smugglers two years ago, Jade noted that Kessel might cause certain problems. Shouldn't you check with a diplomatic contact there to make certain nothing has happened to the *Millennium Falcon*?"

Leia blinked her eyes, annoyed at Winter's suggestion, though she had thought of it herself dozens of times. "Seems like overreacting, doesn't it?"

Winter regarded her calmly. "Or are you just unwilling to show your concern because it would embarrass you?"

The private communications chamber looked different in the bustle of a bright morning on Coruscant. The last time Leia had stood inside the room had been to contact the infuriating Caridan ambassador in the dead of night.

Now, as she looked out the mirrored walls, Leia watched minor functionaries hurrying to daily assignments, administrative and service personnel who had probably worked in Imperial City for years, caring little for what overall government ruled the galaxy.

Not long ago, Leia thought, the Alliance had been made up of the bravest and most dedicated fighters, those willing to die for their ideals. How could the New Republic degenerate into bureaucracy so quickly? She thought of heroes she had known, like Jek Porkins and Biggs Darklighter, who had died to destroy the first Death Star; she hoped their spirit still remained somewhere in the new government.

At the transmission console Winter made a small noise to attract Leia's attention. "This has been difficult, Leia, but I think I have a contact. The entire city of Kessendra seems to be abandoned, but I was able to obtain communications codes for the Imperial Correction Facility. With further inquiries I have tracked down a person who seems to be at least nominally in charge of what passes for a government there. His name is Moruth Doole, originally in the administration of the prison. Somehow he is now overseeing the spice-mining operations.

"There seems to be quite a bit of chaos there. My first contact was with the garrison station on Kessel's moon. Everyone seems quite alarmed at being contacted by the New Republic. I was bounced to several others before Moruth Doole finally agreed to speak with us. He is waiting for you now."

"Go ahead," Leia said. Winter checked her board, then initiated contact. Leia stepped into the transmission field.

A small hologram of a froglike creature appeared above the dais. Static caused by poor transmission equipment on the Kessel end smeared Doole's coloring into yellowish green. His archaic waistcoat and bright-yellow cravat made him look a comical figure.

"You must be Minister Organa Solo?" Doole said. He spread his hands toward her image in a placating gesture. She noticed that he wore some sort of mechanical contraption, a focusing mechanism perhaps, over one of his lanternlike eyes. "I am extremely pleased to hear from a representative of the New Republic, and I apologize for any difficulty in getting in touch with me. We've had some social turmoil over the past couple of years, and I'm afraid we have not yet managed to quell all disturbances."

His fleshy amphibian lips stretched upward in what must have been meant as a smile. A long, sharp tongue flicked out as he spoke, but Doole talked so quickly that Leia could not get a word in edgewise. In her years of diplomatic service Leia had learned not to count too much on reading body language from nonhumans, but could this be a sign of nervousness?

"Now then, Minister, how can I help you? Believe me, we have been considering sending a representative to establish relations with the New

Republic. I would like to extend an invitation for you to send an ambassador to our world, in the interests of maintaining harmony. On Kessel we like to think of the New Republic as our friends."

Doole stopped talking abruptly, as if he realized he had said too much. Leia frowned inwardly but controlled her expression. Moruth Doole was saying exactly what she wanted to hear, giving perfect political answers without her having to ask the questions. Odd. What was he thinking? "Actually, Mr. Doole—I'm afraid I don't know your proper title. How do you wish to be addressed?"

Doole stared with his one eye and fiddled with the mechanical lenses, as if he had never considered the question before. "Uh, Commissioner Doole will do nicely, I think."

"Commissioner Doole, I welcome your offer of openness and cooperation, and I hope we have not already acted prematurely. One of our representatives went to Kessel more than a week ago, but we have heard nothing from him. He was due to return three days ago. I am contacting you to see if you could verify that he did indeed arrive safely?"

Doole raised his long-fingered hands to his cheeks. "A representative, you say? Here? I am aware of no such arrival."

Leia kept her face placid, though her heart grew cold. "Could you check to see if his ship, the *Millennium Falcon* arrived? We had some difficulty tracking down a person in charge just moments ago. Perhaps he reported to someone other than yourself."

Doole sounded doubtful. "Well, of course I can check." He punched at a data terminal unseen beyond the fringe of the transmission field. Almost immediately—too fast, Leia thought—Doole straightened. "No, I am sorry, Minister. We have no record of a ship called the *Millennium Falcon* ever arriving in Kessel space. Who was piloting the ship?"

"His name is Han Solo. He is my husband."

Doole straightened in shock. "I'm terribly sorry to hear that. Is he a good pilot? As you may know, the black hole cluster near Kessel makes for extremely hazardous flying conditions, even in hyperspace. The Maw is one of the wonders of the galaxy, but if he was to take a wrong path through the cluster . . . I hope nothing happened to him!"

Leia leaned deeper into the transmission field. "Han is a very good pilot, Commissioner Doole."

"I'll muster a search team at once, Minister. Believe me, Kessel will offer whatever assistance we can in this matter. We'll scour the surface of the planet and the moon, and we'll search space for any disabled ship. I will inform you immediately of any progress we make."

Doole reached forward to the controls of his holotransmitter, then paused. "And of course we look forward to formally receiving any other ambassador you choose to send. I hope the next time we speak will be under happier circumstances, Minister Organa Solo."

As Moruth Doole's image fizzled into static, Leia let her stony expression fall into a scowl of confusion and suspicion.

Winter looked up from her controls. "I detected no outright contradictions of fact, but I am not convinced of the total truth of what he was saying."

Leia's gaze focused on something far away. Anxiety twisted her insides, and she felt very foolish for being angry with Han. "Something is definitely wrong here."

11

When Han Solo's temper finally snapped, he hauled off with a roundhouse punch that knocked the guard backward. Han leaped on the man, punching him again and again in the chest and stomach, cracking his knuckles on the scuffed stormtrooper armor.

The other guards in the muster room scrambled toward him, knocking Han to the floor. Behind the transparisteel observation cubicles, shift monitors sounded the alarm and summoned assistance. The door slid open from the communal areas, and four more guards charged in, drawing their weapons.

Chewbacca let out a thunderous Wookiee roar and waded through the other guards, yanking them off Han's back. His life debt to his partner took precedence over common sense.

Han continued to swing, yelling incoherently at his captors. Chewbacca smashed two of the guards' heads together and dropped their limp bodies. The reinforcements looked up at the Wookiee, and they goggled as they saw the wall of fur and muscle in front of them. They drew their weapons.

Young Kyp Durron bent low and dove into the knees of the closest armed guard, knocking him to the floor. Kyp scrambled out of the way, yanking at boots and legs, tripping two more men.

With nothing to lose, other prisoners joined in the brawl, indiscriminately punching anything nearby, guards or other prisoners. Many of the captive spice miners were themselves former prison guards who had been on the wrong side during Moruth Doole's rebellion—and the other prisoners hated them.

With a *whoop* of energy, blue arcs of a blaster set on stun lanced out and knocked Chewbacca flat on his back, where he coughed and groaned and tried to raise himself on his elbows.

The alarms kept ringing, a throbbing sound that increased the chaos in the muster room. More guards rushed out of the communal area. Blue stun bolts rippled through the air, mowing down the rioting prisoners and taking out other guards at the same time.

"Enough!" Boss Roke shouted into a microphone on his collar. The voice exploded through the muster-room speakers. "Stop it, or we'll stun you all and then *dissect* you to learn what's wrong with your brains!"

One more stun bolt was fired, dropping two struggling workers to the floor like sacks of gelatin.

Han yanked himself free of the guards and rubbed his split knuckles. Anger continued to seethe through his mind, and he had to work double time to calm himself so he wouldn't get shot.

"Everybody to the bunks! Now!" Boss Roke said. His lip curled; bluish-black stubble looked like a smear of dirty oil on his chin. His lumpy body seemed coiled and dangerous.

Kyp Durron lifted himself up, but as he caught Han's gaze, he flashed a smile. No matter what their punishment would be, Kyp had enjoyed lashing out.

Two very uneasy guards hauled Chewbacca to his feet, draping his hairy arms over their shoulders. Another guard wearing a battered old stormtrooper helmet trained his gun on the Wookiee. Chewbacca's arms and legs twitched as if still trying to struggle, but the stun bolt had thrown his nerve impulses into turmoil. The guards tossed him into one of the holding cells and activated the door before Chewbacca could engage his muscular control. He sagged to the ground in a flurry of mussed brown hair.

His eyes dark with anger, Han moved with taut readiness. He followed Kyp to the line of metal bunks. The guards brushed themselves off and glared at him. Han climbed into his uncomfortable sleeping pallet. Around him the metal rods holding the mattresses and bunks apart seemed like another cage.

Kyp climbed to the upper bunk and leaned down. "What was that all about?" he said. "What set you off?"

One of the guards rapped a stun stick against the side of the bunk. "Keep your head inside!"

Kyp's face popped back into his own area, but Han could still hear him moving. "Just touchy, I guess," Han mumbled. He felt a hollow sorrow inside. "I just realized that today is the day my kids are coming home. I wasn't there to be with them."

Before Kyp could acknowledge, Boss Roke flicked on the sleep-generating field that pulsed around the bunks and sent Han, still resisting, on an endless plunge into dull nightmares.

Standing outside the doorway of the spice-processing annex, Moruth Doole fitted an infrared attachment into place over his mechanical eye. He hissed in his own uneasiness, flicking his tongue in and out to taste the air, to keep himself safe.

The recent transmission from Solo's woman made him very nervous about what the New Republic might do to him. In the warm darkness of the spice-processing rooms, he could relax. Looking at the blind and helpless workers that did his bidding hour after hour made him feel stronger, more in control.

The heavy metal door thudded into place, sealing out the light. The secondary entrance slid open to a womblike vault that glowed in his IR attachment, warm and red from the body heat of the workers. Doole took a deep breath, sniffing the musty dankness of the gathered life-forms.

He looked at the blurry orange images crouched over the processing line. They stirred, silently afraid of his presence. That made Doole feel good. He strode in among them, inspecting their work.

Hundreds of blind larvae, pale and wormlike with large sightless eyes, fumbled with four slender arms to handle the delicate spice crystals. They wrapped the fibrous segments in opaque paper and loaded them into special protective cases, which would then be ferried up to the shipyard and transfer base on Kessel's moon. With the larvae working comfortably in the total darkness necessary for spice processing, Doole's operation ran much more smoothly than it had under Imperial control.

The brief telepathic boost offered by glitterstim spice had made the substance a valuable commodity tightly controlled by the Empire. Other planets had a weaker form of spice, sometimes known as the mineral ryll, but Kessel was the only place where glitterstim could be found. The Empire had kept an iron fist around Kessel's spice production, keeping the glitterstim for espionage and interrogation purposes, as well as checks on loyalty and the granting of security clearances.

But there had always been a vast demand on the invisible market: lovers wanting to share an ephemeral telepathic link, creative artists seeking inspiration, investors trying to obtain inside information, scam operators wanting to dupe rich clients. Many smugglers delivered the spice to Jabba the Hutt and other gangster distributors.

But the Empire no longer controlled spice production. Doole had expected to have no further problems—until Solo came back.

Doole had been waiting for the call from Coruscant for days. He had rehearsed his answers over and over, knowing exactly what he should say. Perhaps he had rehearsed too much, coming up with snap answers that might make Minister Organa Solo suspicious.

Skynxnex told Doole he was overreacting, that they just needed to play their part. Solo and the Wookiee had been safely exiled to the spice mines. No one would ever find them. But there was always a chance something could go wrong. Maybe it would be best if he just ordered Solo killed and got rid of all the risks.

Doole walked along the rows of larval workers. His vision in the blurry infrared was not much worse than the normal eyesight from his mechanical eye. The caterpillarlike larvae bowed in silence, working slavishly. Doole had taken them from the egg sac and raised them here, centering their existence on processing spice. He was a god to them.

As Doole passed, one of the largest males reared up in a defensive posture, waving his frail arms as if to ward off Doole from his territory. To his shock Doole noticed that the male larva had nearly reached maturity. Had time gone by so quickly? This one would soon shed his skin and emerge as a strong adult.

Doole would have to kill him well before that. The last thing he needed right now was competition—even if it did mean killing one of his own children.

Boss Roke stood in the muster room with hands on his hips, giving the workers a lumpy, appraising smile. "We lost another team yesterday. A guard and four workers, down in the deep new tunnels." He waited for that to sink in, but most of the prisoners had already noticed the missing workers.

"The samples brought up earlier show that this could be one of the richest strikes of spice we've found, and I'm not going to let incompetence and superstition cheat me out of a big payoff. I need some volunteers to go down with me to the lower tunnels and check it out—and if I don't get volunteers, I'll pick them anyway." Boss Roke waited. "Don't all volunteer at once."

He scanned the room. Watching him, Han knew that because of his part in the brawl the day before, he would be one of those picked. But he didn't mind—not if his suspicions were correct. Rather than give Roke the satisfaction of coercing him, Han stepped forward. "I'll volunteer. Beats another day of getting dirt under my fingernails."

Roke looked at him in surprise, then narrowed his eyes in suspicion.

"I'll go along, too." Kyp Durron stepped beside Han. Han felt a happy warmth swell up inside him, but he pushed it back. He didn't want to explain anything, not just yet.

Chewbacca yowled in surprise, then grunted a question about Han's sanity.

"What did he say?" Boss Roke asked.

"He's volunteering, too," Han said.

Chewie let out an uncomfortable snort of denial but made no further argument.

"One more volunteer," Roke said, then scanned the room. "You, Clorr." He pointed to a former prison worker who had done a lot of damage in Han's brawl. "I'm taking one guard and you four. Suit up. Let's go."

Roke didn't waste any time. By now Han had grown used to pulling on his thermal suit and adjusting the breath mask. He switched on the power pack to start warmth pulsating through his suit. Chewbacca looked ridiculous with his suit's empty third sleeve limp and taped flat against his torso.

Kyp and Chewbacca kept staring at Han, wondering what he had in mind. Han moved his hands slightly to quell their questions for the time being. Of course he had a plan.

One of the other guards, looking fidgety and uncomfortable, shifted a blaster rifle from shoulder to shoulder.

"Let's go!" Boss Roke said, and clapped his hands.

The four volunteers and the second guard lined up at the opening to the long metal chamber that housed the floating mine cars. They entered, and Boss Roke disengaged three cars from the long train. Roke and the guard sat up front, while the others crammed into the remaining two cars.

"Hey, how about some of those infrared goggles?" Han called. "If there really is something out there, we'll need to be able to see where to run."

Roke contemptuously put his own goggles over his eyes. "You're expendable." He activated the guidance system on the front car's controls. The lights went out, and the opposite door groaned open, flooding the compartment with cold, thin air.

"So much for that idea," Han said, then scrambled to put his breath mask in place.

The unenthusiastic prisoner, Clorr, groaned in dismay. Then the floating cars lurched into motion, gaining speed until they bulleted through the tunnels. The air whooshed as the car sped close to crumbling rock tubes from which generations of spice miners had peeled glitterstim deposits.

When the wind of their passage drowned out other noises, Kyp leaned closer to Han, speaking through his breath mask. "Okay, so tell me what we got ourselves into."

Han shrugged. "I have an idea, and if I'm right, we can all get out of this mess."

Chewbacca made a skeptical sound but ended in a question.

"Think about it, Chewie. People have been disappearing off and on from the same place—what if they found a way to escape? They've been working new tunnels, going into unexplored areas looking for spice, then suddenly a bunch of them don't come back. You and I know there are plenty of abandoned shafts from the illicit miners that slipped through Imperial security. This planet is honeycombed with entrances to the spice tunnels."

Han paused, hoping they had already figured it out. "Roke's teams usually have one guard and five blind prisoners. What if they came around the corner and suddenly found an opening to the surface, letting them see again. They could overpower the guard and make their way to freedom.

"Once Roke discovers the way out, though, he'll block it up and we won't have another chance. If we're ever going to get out, if I'm ever going to get back and see Leia and the kids, I've got to try. I thought maybe this desperate gamble would be worth it."

"Sounds like a good chance," Kyp said. "I've been down here so long, I'm willing to try anything."

Chewbacca agreed, but with somewhat less enthusiasm.

They plunged down and down, whipping around sharp corners. Several times Han thought the rocky walls brushed within a handbreadth of his head, and he tried to crouch down inside the car. He didn't want to imagine what would happen if Chewbacca's head struck an outcropping at the speed they were moving.

In the black spice mines Han rapidly lost all conception of time. He had no idea how long they traveled, how far they went, or how fast the floating cars moved through the tunnels. Boss Roke brought the vehicle to a stop and called for the prisoners to dismount. The guard noisily unshouldered his blaster rifle.

Han paid extra attention to the small noises he heard, building the best mental picture possible of where Boss Roke and the guard were standing at all times. That was something he would need to know if he had to make a quick escape. But they had gone down so deep now, he could not imagine finding a passage to the surface.

"Follow me," Boss Roke said. "I want one prisoner up front ahead of me and the guard taking the rear."

Han heard a shove and a gasp, then someone stumbled forward. Was it Kyp? No, from the unpleasant groan he determined that the point man would be Clorr, the former prison worker.

Boss Roke rustled in his pack, withdrawing some piece of equipment. Han heard an electronic clicking and pinging sound. It was some sort of detector. Han strained his ears, listening to the tones change as Roke moved the scanner from side to side.

"Spice all around us," Roke said. "Just as we thought, and the concentration seems even higher up ahead. Move forward."

Clorr stumbled into the blackness, followed by Boss Roke. Han walked blindly. He felt Kyp taking hold of his waist, and he heard Chewbacca's breath echoing behind his breath mask.

As they went farther, the tunnels grew colder and colder. Han's naked fingers crackled when he bent them. He turned up the heat in his suit, but the warmth comforted him little.

The electronic clicks from Roke's detector grew louder. "Concentration increasing," he said. "These are some of the densest, freshest veins of spice we've ever uncovered. There'll be a lot more work for you prisoners to do."

The detector clicked, and they shuffled ahead. Other than their own noises, the spice tunnel seemed a mouth of silence.

Han thought he heard a sudden scuttling noise farther down the passage, something massive that moved, stopped, moved again, then slowly began to come back, as if stalking. Up front Clorr muttered to himself, but Han heard Boss Roke shove him onward.

"The reading gets stronger right up around the corner." Boss Roke's gravelly voice carried a childlike hint of excitement. "I'm going to have to recalibrate this sensor."

Han heard the distant skittering sound again, but it seemed farther ahead. It wasn't a noise that anyone in their party had made. It sounded like sharp metal points ticking against glass.

The tenor of shuffling human footsteps changed as they turned the corner. "Spice reading is off the scale!" Boss Roke cried.

Suddenly Clorr screamed.

"Hey!" Roke said.

Clorr screamed again, but the sound came from much deeper in the tunnel, as if something had yanked him away and fled, carrying him to a secret lair.

"Where are—" Roke said, then he, too, gave a startled shout.

Han heard booted feet turning around, running back. Han nudged Kyp aside, back the way they had come. "Watch yourself!"

Boss Roke stumbled into Han, then fell backward. Han reeled against the rocky wall but kept his balance. Roke clawed at the floor, desperate to flee.

"Turn around!" Han shouted to Kyp, giving the young man a push toward the floating cars. "What is it?" he yelled to Boss Roke. He heard the pointy, ticking sound again, moving closer, skittering like many sharp legs that ended in stiletto claws.

Roke screamed, then gave an *oooof!* as the air was knocked out of him.

Han heard a thud as the man hit the ground, but Roke clambered to his feet again, or at least to his knees, crawling forward.

As Han started to run, Roke grabbed his leg and held on. Han tried to jerk free, shouting, "Stop it! We've got to get out of here!"

But before Roke could let go, something behind him—something very large and very, very close—grabbed Roke and yanked him backward, breaking his grip. Roke's fingernails were like claws as he tried to grasp the slick fabric of Han's thermal suit, but with a quick whisking sound he was dragged away down the tunnel, still gurgling and crying out.

In the darkness Han could see nothing at all.

"Run!" Han shouted.

Chewbacca roared, then plowed like a demolition vehicle into the guard behind him. Kyp followed the Wookiee and leaped over the fallen man, but Han stumbled on him, sprawling flat on the broken rocky floor. Nobody could see anything.

The guard scrambled to his knees and started thrashing and pummeling as if Han were the enemy. But Han, blinded and desperate, grabbed for something else. He snatched at the infrared goggles on the guard's face and pulled them free.

The walls were closing in around him. The screams and sounds of panicked fleeing and the *tick tick* noise of the approaching monstrous thing made claustrophobic thunder around him.

The fallen guard's wail of sudden blindness and dismay was muffled by his breath mask. He clutched at Han, but Han knocked the breath mask free. The escaping oxygen made a whistling sound. The guard had to release Han to replace his mask.

Han scrabbled forward. He had to see. They needed to find the floating cars so they could get away. "Run, Chewie! Straight ahead! Make sure Kyp goes with you!"

He slapped the goggles over his head. He heard the scuttling, thumping sounds of the sharp, scampering legs again. Had an army of the things come to attack, or was it just one very large specimen with many legs?

Looking through the goggles, he could see the bright blob of the fallen guard's infrared signature and the fleeing brilliant shapes of Kyp and Chewbacca. He heard the thunder of hard, pointed legs coming back up the tunnel, stampeding down on them.

The guard moved, clambered to his feet, and began stumbling behind Han, but the man could not see. He weaved back and forth and struck the wall, smacking his head on a hard outcropping.

Running, monstrous feet came closer, like a patter of meteorites pelting the side of a ship. The guard screamed.

Han turned around to watch him, but he saw nothing else in the blackness

of the tunnel, no shape, no signature, no body heat from any creature—
nothing that was alive.

The guard suddenly froze, as if a giant invisible hand had grabbed him
from behind. Then Han saw, to his horror, the *silhouette* of a long, spindly
leg reaching around in front of the guard's waist and another one clipped
over his shoulder, totally black, like a cutout from the infrared form of the
guard. The man struggled and wailed.

The guard yanked at something—his blaster rifle. Han gasped as a
brilliant lance erupted in the pitch darkness, striking against the multilegged
thing, illuminating it for the shaved splinter of a heartbeat. Han saw what
seemed to be a writhing mass of sharp twigs, a rat's nest of spindly legs and
claws and fangs intermixed with eyes—many, many eyes. Then the creature
absorbed all the light, plunging the tunnels back into opaque blindness.

The guard was lifted high in the air and turned around. Other shadows
of the icicle legs wrapped around him. The glowing rectangle of the thermal
suit's battery pack burned brilliantly in the infrared, but one of the sharp claws
thrust into it like a stinger. Sparks flew into the darkness, leaving glimmers
in front of Han's eyes.

As Han ran backward, stumbling and tripping, he saw the man's infrared
outline grow dim as he became as cold as his surroundings. The creature,
whatever it was, must be draining or feeding on energy, on body heat or
anything it could find in the cold empty tunnels.

"Keep running!" Han yelled, now that he could see the forms ahead.
He made out a dim glow of warmth still radiating from the floating mine
transport. "The car's right in front of you, Chewie! Get on it!"

The Wookiee bumped into the metal side of the vehicle and dragged
himself to a stop. Chewbacca reached over and grabbed Kyp, hauling him
into the seat of the car.

Then Han heard the clacking, scrambling footsteps behind him again,
charging down the tunnel. He was the next one in line. He dashed ahead,
gasping, tripping on debris and bumping into walls he could not see. His
blood had turned to ice water.

Chewbacca fumbled along the control panel of the floating mine car,
trying to distinguish the buttons in the dark. Han kept running. The sounds
of the sharp legs grew louder, rumbling.

Han risked a glance over his shoulder. Though he could hear the thing
charging at top speed after him, he could see nothing in the darkness, nothing at all.

He reached the floating car and leaped in. "Just punch RETURN, Chewie!
Hit anything!"

Chewbacca hit the start button, and the car pivoted on its axis to move
back in the direction they had come.

The galloping sounds of the ice-pick-legged creature skittered faster and faster. The floating mine car picked up speed, but the creature kept coming behind it. Han still couldn't see it with the infrared goggles.

With a loud *spang* something struck the back car, rocking it sideways and slamming it against the side wall of the tunnel. Sparks flew as it scraped along the rocks, but the vehicle continued to accelerate.

Han heard a hollow roar behind them, and then they left the noises farther and farther away. The creature ceased chasing them. The darkness rolled ahead like a great black vacuum.

Han knew they were automatically heading back to the muster room. Chewbacca groaned and roared at him. Kyp sat panting in terror. "What did you see?" Kyp asked.

"I don't know," Han said. "Nothing like I've ever seen before."

Chewbacca chuffed in anger and annoyance and immense relief, and Han sighed. "I agree. This wasn't one of my smarter ideas."

12

Luke Skywalker showed Gantoris the wonders of the universe. He took his passenger into orbit in the modified shuttle, letting the man look down on the doomed planet of Eol Sha. The too-close moon hung above the world like a raised fist against a curtain of stars.

Igniting the shuttle's sublight engines, Luke soared into the blazing wonder of the Cauldron Nebula as Gantoris stared out the viewports into the chaotic, glowing gases. Then they plunged down the endless, other-dimensional hole through hyperspace, shortcutting across the galaxy.

To Bespin.

During the uneventful trip Luke began telling Gantoris about the Force, about the training the candidates would undergo at the proposed Jedi academy. Now that he had agreed to come along, Gantoris seemed willing and even eager to understand the strange echoes and feelings that had touched his mind throughout his life.

The hum of the shuttle's powerful engines and the giddy, abstract swirls of hyperspace were conducive to beginning a few exercises for awakening Gantoris's potential. Luke was surprised at the man's powers of concentration, at how he could close his eyes and sink into his mind undistracted. Luke had been an impatient young man during his own Jedi training; Gantoris had had a much harsher upbringing, making him grim and enduring.

"Reach out and feel your mind, feel your body, feel the universe surrounding you. The Force stretches around and through everything. Everything is a part of everything else."

Luke paid close attention to what he asked Gantoris to do. Obi-Wan Kenobi had spent some time training Luke, and Yoda had spent much more. But Luke had also undergone the abortive training of Joruus C'baoth as well as learning the powers of the dark side during his time with the resurrected Emperor.

Luke could not forget that Obi-Wan's training had also transformed Anakin Skywalker into Darth Vader. Would it be worth bringing back the Jedi Knights if the price was the creation of another Vader? Gantoris's ominous dreams of a "dark man" who would show him power and then destroy him made Luke very uneasy.

By the time Luke brought the shuttle out of hyperspace on an approach to Bespin, he thought Gantoris might be overwhelmed with new sights. But the stern man gawked out the viewports like a child, awed by the roiling gas planet where Lando Calrissian had once run Cloud City. The sight of the swirling planet suddenly brought back some of the greatest horrors in Luke's life. He squeezed his eyes shut as he felt the sting of those memories.

Gantoris, in the passenger compartment behind him, bent forward. "Is something wrong? I just sensed a strong flow of emotions from you."

Luke blinked. "You could detect that?"

Gantoris shrugged. "Now that you've taught me how to feel and how to listen, it came through very clearly. What's disturbing you? Are we in danger?"

Luke opened his eyes and looked out at Bespin again. He thought of his friend Han Solo kidnapped and frozen in carbonite for delivery to Jabba the Hutt; he thought of the duel with Darth Vader on the catwalks of Cloud City that had cost Luke his hand. And, worst of all, he recalled Vader's deep voice pronouncing his terrible message. "Luke, *I* am your father!"

Luke shuddered, but he turned to look back into Gantoris's dark eyes. "I have powerful memories of this place."

Gantoris kept his silence, asking no further questions.

Airborne mining installations rode Bespin's wind currents—floating automated refineries, storage tanks bobbing above the clouds, and facilities to scoop valuable gases from the cloud banks. Not all of these floating installations had proved profitable, though. The drifting colossus of Tibannopolis hung empty, a creaking ghost town in the sky.

Luke tracked the derelict floating city on his navigation screens. The construction hovered over the dark clouds as a storm gathered. The city tilted due to malfunctioning repulsorlift generators.

"Is that where we're going?" Gantoris said.

The roof, decks, and sides of Tibannopolis had been picked over by scavengers hauling away scrap metal. It looked like a skeleton of its former self, with buckled plates and twisted support girders in a broad hemisphere; dented ballast tanks hung below. Numerous antennae and weather vanes protruded from the joints.

"We're going to wait for someone here," Luke answered.

He brought the shuttle down on a primary landing deck that looked sturdy enough to support his ship. The crisscrossed structural beams were covered with scaled plating, but in some spots the seams had bent upward, popping their welds.

Luke emerged from the shuttle, and Gantoris joined him. The other man's long dark hair whipped around him like a mane, no longer braided, but he stood proudly in his hand-me-down pilot's outfit. His black eyes glittered with wonder.

The high wind gusting through the carcass of Tibannopolis made a moaning sound. The swaying metal groaned as rusted joints rubbed against each other. The wind had a bitter chemical tang from trace gases wafting to higher altitudes.

Black birdlike creatures with triangular heads clustered in the open gaps of buildings, nesting on stripped girders. As Luke and Gantoris moved forward, the flying creatures stirred and rustled leathery wings. Their mouths snapped open and closed with croaking sounds.

Below and around Tibannopolis, the clouds had turned the smoky gray of impending thunderstorms. Flashes of lightning rippled through the cloud bank below.

"What now?" Gantoris asked.

Luke sighed and gathered some inflatable blankets and a sleep roll from the passenger shuttle's storage compartments. "We've spent two days cooped up in the ship. I have no way of knowing when Streen might come back, and I think we should try to get a good rest."

"Streen?" Gantoris asked.

"The man we're waiting for."

The storm came through that night and rinsed off the exposed surfaces of Tibannopolis, causing fresh blooms of rust and patina on the construction alloys. Luke and Gantoris had found shelter in the decaying buildings of Tibannopolis, resting on the slanted floor because of the derelict city's tilt.

Awash in a Jedi trance more restful than sleep, Luke paid little attention to his surroundings but kept a small window open in his mind, ready to flick him back to wakefulness.

Gantoris surprised him. "Luke, I think someone's coming. I can sense it." Luke became instantly awake and sat up from under the sheltered metal alcove, looking out at the washed-clean swirls of clouds. It took his mind only a moment to locate the approaching presence of a human—but he was impressed that Gantoris had been able to sense the distant stranger at all.

"I was practicing," Gantoris said, "reaching out and looking with my mind. There isn't much around here to distract me."

"Good work." Luke tried to keep the pleased expression from his face but failed. "This is the man we've been waiting for."

He used his sense to focus on a black shape approaching across the skyscape of rising gases. Luke saw an amazing cluster of lashed-together platforms and bulbous tanks held aloft by balloons and maneuvered with propellers that stuck out at all angles. The hodgepodge vehicle drifted toward them, riding the winds.

Luke smiled at the bizarre construction, while Gantoris stared in awe. They could make out the silhouette of a single man standing at the helm as buffeting breezes rippled trim sails at the sides of the main platform. Streen, the gas prospector, was returning home.

Luke and Gantoris made their way down to the landing platform to wait for him. As the collection of gas tanks, balloons, and flat walkways approached, Streen finally noticed them.

At the controls of his contraption he swerved and circled around the ruined city, as if frightened and reluctant to land. But somehow, seeing only the two of them waiting, he regained his nerve and rode the breezes in.

Streen did not land his vehicle, merely bringing it to the edge of the landing platform and lashing it to support posts mounted at the rail. Luke held on to the fiber-chains and helped Streen secure his vessel.

No one spoke. Streen kept surreptitiously slipping glances in their direction.

Luke sized him up. Streen was approaching old age, bearded, with brown hair so intermingled with strands of gray that it had turned to a creamy color. His skin bore a leathery look, as if the rough winds and harsh open air had sucked something essential out of his flesh. The prospector was clad in a well-worn jumpsuit studded with pockets, many of which bulged with hidden contents.

As Streen stepped onto the landing area, four of the black birdlike creatures fluttered up from roosts among the platforms, venting stacks, and gas tanks of Streen's vessel, returning to the jungle of construction frames in the floating city.

"Tibannopolis hasn't been inhabited for years," Streen said. "Why have you come here?"

Luke stood tall and faced the man. "We came to see *you*."

• • •

Gantoris stood patiently beside Luke Skywalker, feeling odd to be in a different position now. He had joined the Jedi to learn from him, swept up by his visions of a restored order of Jedi Knights and the powers they could tap through the Force.

This time Gantoris listened as Skywalker began to tell Streen of his plans for an academy, of his need for potential candidates who might have a talent for using the Force. He watched the skepticism on Streen's face, similar to what he himself must have shown at first. But unless Streen had suffered the same dark dreams or premonitions, this hermit on Bespin should be a more open-minded listener than Gantoris himself had been.

Streen hunkered on the corroded surface of the landing platform and squinted into the sky before looking back to Skywalker. "But why me? Why did you come here?"

Skywalker turned instead to Gantoris. "There are many valuable substances dissolved in Bespin's atmosphere at various layers. The floating cities are huge mining operations that remain in place as they draw gas from below the cloud layers. But Streen is a cloud prospector. At certain times some storm or a deep atmospheric upheaval will make a cloud of volatiles belch up, waiting to be siphoned off. Streen goes out on the winds with his tanks, looking for the treasure.

"Bespin has computerized satellites to detect these outbursts and to dispatch company men—but Streen always gets there first. He somehow knows an upheaval is going to happen before it does. He is there waiting with his empty tanks to siphon off whatever comes bubbling up and sell it back to the independent refineries."

Skywalker squatted next to the hermit. "Tell me, Streen—how do you know when a gas layer is going to rise? Where do you get your information?"

Streen blinked and fidgeted. Now he looked even more frightened than when he had first seen the strangers waiting on the landing platform. "I just . . . know. I can't explain it."

Skywalker smiled. "Everyone can use the Force to some extent, but a few have a stronger innate talent. When I form my Jedi academy, I want to work most closely with those who already have the talent but don't know how to use it. Gantoris is one of my candidates. I think you should be another one."

"Come with us," Gantoris added. "If Skywalker is right, think of all the things we could accomplish!"

"How can you be sure about me?" Streen asked. "I always thought it was just luck."

"Let me touch your forehead," Skywalker said. When Streen did not move away, Skywalker tentatively reached forward with his fingers, brushing the man's temples. Gantoris couldn't figure out what Skywalker was doing until he remembered the test Luke had performed on him down in the lava chamber.

Skywalker's face looked blank and lost in concentration for a moment, then suddenly he jerked backward as if his body had been burned. "Now I'm sure, Streen. You do have the talent. There is nothing to fear."

But Streen still looked nervous. "I came out to this place because I need to be alone. I'm not comfortable around people. I feel them pressing in around me. I like people. I'm lonely, but . . . it's very difficult for me. It's all I can do to be around them just while I deliver my cargo. Then I have to run away.

"Seven or eight years ago, when the Empire took over Cloud City, everything got much worse. The people were agitated. Their thoughts were full of chaos." He looked up at Skywalker in dismay. "I haven't spent much time with people for eight years."

Gantoris could sense the man's emotions winding toward panic—and just when Gantoris felt certain Streen would refuse, Skywalker held up a hand. "Wait," he said. "Why not just watch us train for a while? Maybe you'll see what I'm talking about."

As if pleased at having an option that did not require him to make an immediate decision, Streen nodded. He looked toward his floating platforms and gas tanks with a palpable stab of regret, as if wishing he had never come back to Tibannopolis. Gantoris could feel an echo of the other man's emotions, the yearning for freedom that Bespin's clouds offered, the solace of being alone.

"Show me your new Jedi exercises, Master. Teach me other things." Skywalker seemed to flinch at being called "Master," and Gantoris wondered what he had done wrong—was not Luke Skywalker a Jedi Master? How else should he be called?

Skywalker brushed aside the comment. He pointed to the thicket of girders and rusted metal bars in which flocks of the leathery black creatures made their homes, chittering and moving about in the afternoon. Far below, the clouds thickened into what could become another storm.

"Those flying creatures," Skywalker said. "We will use them."

Streen stiffened. His face grew dark and ruddy. "Hey, don't disturb my rawwks." Then he lowered his eyes, turning away as if embarrassed by his outburst. "They've been my only company all these years."

"We won't harm them," Skywalker said. "Just watch." He lowered his voice to speak as an instructor to Gantoris. "This city is a complex mechanism. Every girder, every metal plate, every life-form from those rawwks to the airborne algae sacks and everything around us, each has its own position in the Force. Size matters not. Tiny insects or entire floating cities, each is an integral part of the universe. You must feel it, sense it."

He nodded to the derelict structures around them. "I want you to look at this city, imagine how the pieces fit together, find the girders with your mind, tell me what you can sense and how one thing touches another. When you think you have found the intersection where a rawwk and girder touch, I want you to reach out and *push* with your mind. Make a little vibration."

Skywalker curled his forefinger around his thumb and stretched forward as he nodded toward a lone rawwk sitting on the end of a weather vane. He flicked out his finger, as if to shoo away a gnat, and Gantoris heard a distant *pinnngg*. Startled into the air, the rawwk flapped its wings and cried out in alarm.

Gantoris chuckled and, eager to try, flicked his own finger in imitation of what the Jedi had just done. He imagined seeing a whole flock of the rawwks take flight—but nothing happened.

"It is not that easy," Skywalker said. "You aren't concentrating. Think, feel yourself doing it, envision your success—then reach out with your mind."

More serious this time, Gantoris pursed his lips and squinted, looking for his target. He saw a delicate many-branched antenna on which five rawwks sat. He pictured the antenna, knowing his target, and stared. He took a deep breath and *pushed*. He still didn't quite know what he was doing, but he felt something happening in his mind, something working, some outside . . . *force* linking him and the antenna.

He watched as the antenna slowly swayed. The rawwks stirred but remained on their perches. Anyone else watching might have assumed the wind had shifted at that moment, but Gantoris knew he had done it.

"Good attempt. You have the right idea, but now close your eyes," Skywalker said. "You're letting your sight blind you. You *know* where the antenna is, you know where the rawwks are. You can sense their place in the Force. You don't need to see with your eyes. Tighten your focus. Feel it, know what you want to do."

Skeptical, Gantoris closed his eyes; but as he concentrated, he could indeed see vague outlines of what he had just looked at, tiny afterimages imprinted on the Force with tendrils reaching out and connecting them to everything else.

He reached out with his fingers to make the flicking gesture again but hesitated. He realized he did not need that either. Flicking the fingers was simply an example for Skywalker to make his point. Whatever actions he made, waving his hands or muttering spells were just so much mumbo jumbo. Understanding the Force was what allowed him to do what he needed.

Pleased with this sudden insight, Gantoris kept his eyes closed and folded his arms. He flicked out an imaginary finger, feeling the metal, picturing his fingernail striking the hard surface. In his head he heard the hollow *bong* as it struck, then opened his eyes to watch the five rawwks burst into flight, cawing at each other as if casting blame.

"Good!" Skywalker said. "I'm impressed. I thought this was going to be much more difficult." Still grinning, he looked at Streen, who had been watching them in silence. "Would you like to try it? You have the potential. I could show you how."

Streen balked. "No, I . . . I don't think I could do that."

"It isn't as difficult as it looks," Gantoris said. "You'll feel a different strength come into you."

"I don't want to," Streen said again, defensively. Then he lowered his eyes and patted his pockets, as if looking for something he didn't expect to find. Gantoris thought he was just making distracted movements.

The old man swallowed, then looked back at Skywalker. "If you teach me how to use this . . . sense I have—can you also teach me how to *switch it off*? I want to learn how *not* to feel the people around me, not to be bombarded by their moods and prying thoughts and sour ideas. I'm tired of having only rawwks for company. I'd very much like to be part of the human race again."

Skywalker clapped him on the shoulder. In his dark jumpsuit he looked like a benevolent god. "That much I can show you."

Luke watched as Streen cut loose the fiber-chains holding his floating hodgepodge ship to the Tibannopolis docking area. Standing on the docking platform, he gave his ship an unnecessary shove out into the breezes. The empty barge of platforms and balloons, propellers and gas storage tanks, drifted out to be caught up by swirling air currents.

Streen had emptied the pockets in his jumpsuit and now looked at Luke. "I know I'm not coming back. That old life is over."

The three of them climbed aboard Luke's passenger shuttle and made ready to depart Bespin. Luke felt a glowing satisfaction, not just to be leaving the gas planet that held so many dark memories, but to have both passenger seats filled, to have two new candidates for his Jedi academy.

He raised the shuttle off the landing platform, then began a steep climb toward orbit. Below them, in the opposite direction, Streen's abandoned platform continued drifting on its own, widening the gap between it and the derelict city.

Streen looked out the passenger window, staring with a bleak sadness that struck Luke's heart with pity. Below, the ghost town of Tibannopolis was truly empty again.

Then Luke watched something amazing happen. The city came alive with movement, swarming as tiny black figures took to the air. Thousands and thousands of rawwks that had made their home with Streen suddenly took flight, departing the abandoned metropolis in a huge flock that kept coming and coming and coming, spreading out among the clouds in a farewell salute to Streen.

Looking out the window and watching this, Streen smiled.

13

Skynxnex inserted a new charge pack into his double-blaster, smiled at the weapon, then thrust it into the holster. "Thank you, Moruth," he said. "You won't regret this."

Doole tapped his spongy fingers on the former warden's desk. One of the loose iridescent insects fluttered around the room, battering itself again and again on the wide landscape window.

"Just try not to make a mess of it," Doole said. "I want Solo gone and all traces removed. Nothing left. It's only a matter of time before the New Republic comes nosing around. We've got to be absolutely clean. Is the energy shield functional yet?"

"We're testing it this morning, and our engineers are confident it'll work. Solo and the Wookiee will be dead by then," Skynxnex said. "My personal guarantee."

Doole's lips curled like a rubbery gasket stretched out of shape. "Don't enjoy yourself too much."

Skynxnex smiled back at him and turned to leave. His black eyes glittered. "Only as much as necessary," he said.

The mine car roared through the tunnels in total blackness. Han had no choice but to trust the computer guidance system.

Chewbacca had found the accelerator button and punched it repeatedly, trying to get farther away from the multilegged horror deep in the mines.

Han gripped the sides of the car with hands gone white from cold and terror. Each time they shot past a gaping side tunnel, his imagination heard noises of skittering legs and scythelike claws reaching out to pluck them from the passing car.

"Our course is taking us back to the muster room," Kyp said. "This could be our chance to escape."

"Where else should we go?" Han asked. He felt his heart pounding. Chewbacca groaned a question, and Han translated it. "Do you know any other way out of these tunnels?"

"I don't," Kyp said, "but maybe I could find one."

Han fought to contain a sudden fit of shudders. "I don't know about you, but I'm in no mood to go wandering through dark tunnels feeling for a way out—not with that thing chasing after us." The thought of a freezing death in the energy-draining fangs of the monster made the option of imprisonment in the spice mines seem not so terrible after all.

Before they could form some sort of alternative plan, the floating mine cars coasted to a halt in the long holding chamber. The metal door at the far end slammed shut behind them. With his infrared goggles, Han could see the activation controls on the wall next to an inner door. His knees were weak; his hands trembled as he punched access for the muster room.

Light flooded around them, and the three survivors staggered inside, holding each other. Chewbacca used his hairy arms to keep both Han and Kyp on their feet.

Dazzled, Han cupped his hands over his eyes and let the infrared goggles dangle on his neck. "Boss Roke is dead," he croaked to no one in particular. "There's a monster in the tunnels. It attacked the guard. We barely got away."

"Han—" Kyp said.

Chewbacca sniffed, then roared in anger.

Han fought to focus his vision. He heard people rustling in the muster room. He saw only shadows in the glare. Finally, he could make out a tall, gangly form with dark hair and sunken eyes on a skull-like face.

"Glad you're back, Solo," Skynxnex said from the other side of the room. He drew the double-blaster at his hip.

Everything seemed to move slowly for Han. He had not yet come down from the boost of adrenaline caused by utter terror. Han saw the gun, saw Skynxnex, saw the man's cadaverous face. Doole had sent his henchman to kill them.

Han wasted no time, shoving Chewbacca backward. "Back in, Chewie! We've got to get out of here!" He yanked Kyp through the open doorway.

Chewbacca let out a yowl and lunged into the dark chamber where the floating mine cars waited.

"Hey!" Skynxnex began to run in long, leaping strides that carried him across the muster room. Han sealed the door in his face, scrambling the lock mechanism.

"It'll take him a second to figure the access code. Get in the car, now!" Han leaped onto the swaying pilot seat. "Looks like we're going to try one of those alternatives you wanted, Kyp."

He powered up the rocking vehicle. From the other side of the door came pounding and then the sounds of blasters striking the metal. Skynxnex was going to disintegrate his way through. They had to get to the relative safety of the tunnels right away.

Han punched up the computer guidance system and let the vehicle go. The great metal door on the far side of the long holding tunnel slid open with a grinding sound as the mine car accelerated back down the central tunnel from which they had just come.

"I hate to go back there," Han said. Chewbacca roared a comment, and Han nodded. "Yeah, I hate even worse to be blasted."

"Do you know Skynxnex?" Kyp asked, regaining his breath.

"We're old buddies," Han said. "That's why he wants to kill us."

The floating car rushed through the half-open metal gate just as the door from the muster room melted open, spilling a wedge of light into the tunnel.

"They're only going to be a minute behind us," Han said. With his infra-red goggles he could see the pilot controls now—but none of the coordinates meant anything to him. The only exit he knew of was back through the muster room. "Any ideas, Kyp?"

"It's an automated course," Kyp said. "If I had time to think and get my bearings, I might be able to figure out something."

"We don't have that luxury right now."

The great metal door did not close behind them after they passed through. Wind whipped past their ears as Han kept his finger on the accelerator button. From behind they heard shouts, other people climbing into waiting mine cars. Han leaned over the controls, but the repulsorlifts could go only so fast.

Unable to see, and without any knowledge of the labyrinth of underground tunnels, Han did not dare fly the car manually. He would have to hope he could get far enough ahead so that Skynxnex could not follow . . . but then what? They would be lost in the cold, dark maze. How many other multilegged monsters waited for them in the shadows?

The sound of another mine car came roaring up behind them. Han had three cars linked together, hauling three riders with only one engine. If

Skynxnex and the others took one car each, they would travel faster. They would be in blaster range within moments.

"Solo!" Skynxnex bellowed.

"Hold on!" Kyp said.

Han instinctively braced himself as the computer guidance system yanked them to the left-hand fork in an unseen tunnel, then plunged them steeply downward. Before Han could wonder if they had lost their pursuers, he heard the echoing whine of repulsorlift vehicles soaring down the tunnel after them.

"I'm open to suggestions," Han said. He looked behind them with his infrared goggles and saw the glowing target of Skynxnex and two other piloted vehicles. In the cold darkness his own body heat would be just as apparent to the pursuers.

Chewbacca held on to Kyp, pushing him down to safety in the second car. The Wookiee reached behind him, fumbling with the catch to the empty third car. Skynxnex and the two guards closed the gap. With a growl at the pursuers, Chewbacca decoupled the magnetic bearing from the third car.

Suddenly released, the empty car swung out behind them, dropping toward the ground. Skynxnex cried out as he swerved up to avoid a collision. The other two guards both curved to the left, battering into each other, but somehow all three pursuers kept their balance. They roared after Han.

"Nice try, Chewie," Han said.

Skynxnex pulled out his modified double-blaster, powered it on, and aimed. When he fired, the two barrels sent their beams out at slight intersecting angles to each other. A short distance beyond the muzzle, the two beams coalesced and *phased*, forming a staccato series of bursts, each one containing a brief impulse of power ten times that of a single blaster beam. Though the weapon looked impressive, it was almost impossible to aim, and most other users—even hardened criminals—had dropped them in favor of more reliable weapons.

The phased double beam poured out, striking the ceiling of the tunnel ahead of Han. The explosion of heat and light blinded him through the infrared goggles. Somehow Kyp reacted with molten speed and yanked the floating car sideways. Miraculously, they swerved around the debris that fell from above, struck only by the patter of small pebbles.

"Everybody okay?" Han said.

Chewbacca grunted. "So far," Kyp said.

Han turned to look as Skynxnex zoomed safely through the tiny avalanche he had caused. Falling rocks and debris pelted the next car, though, making it spin out of control. The car struck the rough tunnel wall in a shower of sparks, then exploded, spewing shards of metal everywhere.

"One down," Kyp said.

Echoing sounds came from the open tunnel mouth ahead. Through the infrared goggles Han could see other spots of warmth, a caravan. They shot past the side tunnel just as another train of floating mine cars emerged. "They've got reinforcements!" Han said in dismay. But then he saw the cars were all linked together—another mining party on its way back to the muster room at the end of a shift.

Skynxnex and the other guard plowed right into them. Their accelerating cars rode up and over, knocking three hapless workers out of their seats and leaving them blind and lost in the tunnel. The driver of the work train slewed out of the way, ramming into the rocky wall of the tunnel.

Skynxnex spun in the air but somehow kept his seat. The second guard fared even better, pulling up beside Skynxnex as they zoomed away from the site of the wreck and the shouting work crew.

Han had no idea where they were going, but they were getting farther and farther away from anyplace good. With Skynxnex and his double-blaster behind them, they had no choice but to keep fleeing deeper into the tunnels.

Ahead in the inky blackness a sudden clump of pearlescent glitters sprang out of a bare rock wall, wavering in the air. Then the luminescence started traveling down the tunnel away from them, as if trying to outrun the approaching cars.

"Another bogey!" Kyp cried.

Their floating car followed the bogey, closing the gap. But as they neared, the swirling glowing thing accelerated, as if taunting them by flying ahead, whipping around curves just in front of them. By the faint glow Han could actually see the winding curves of rock.

Skynxnex and the other pursuer zoomed along in their wake.

"Uh-oh," Kyp said. "I think I just figured out what course we're on. All this feels very familiar."

"What?" Han said. "How can you tell?"

"The most recent set of destination coordinates in this navigation computer was programmed by Boss Roke. We're going back down to where that monster was!"

The glowing bogey roiled ahead of them, dipping up and down but refusing to pop back into the spice-covered walls. As it rushed along, the bogey's bodily illumination activated threadlike veins of glitterstim, leaving a patchwork of blue sparks in their wake.

In a long, straight stretch of tunnel Skynxnex fired his double-blaster again.

As if he could sense the blast coming, Kyp rocked the car to one side as the intense pulsed bolt shot down the tube, passed through the bogey without harming it, and struck a distant wall. The impact blew open a huge aperture into another grotto.

Seeing an escape, the bogey ducked through the new opening.

"Put it on manual," Kyp said. "Let me fly it." By now their eyes had grown accustomed to the bogey's glow, and they could actually see where they were going.

"I don't want a free return trip to where that monster is waiting." Han relinquished the controls. Without a moment's pause Kyp launched the car into the wide-open section of wall that led to an unknown maze.

"This is the same series of tunnels," Kyp said.

As they plunged into the new grotto, something long and fibrous stung Han's face like a sharp wire whipping past him.

The bogey shot into the vast chamber, flying across the darkness to the far wall. Upon striking the rock face, though, it did not melt through and vanish as the first bogey had done days earlier. Instead, the glowing ball stuck on the rough rock surface. It glittered and spangled and pulsed, as if struggling.

Another whiplike strand struck Han's face as they flew through the air.

Around the bogey in the glow, wide veins of spice fizzled blue as the illumination activated them. The light crackled and spread outward in a network, geometrical crisscrossings along the wall. All of the spice in the chamber began to race around in long lines as the light increased in a chain reaction. The pattern looked familiar.

"Like a web!" Han said.

The bogey struggled frantically as the spice around it grew brighter and brighter. Han saw long fibers of free-hanging glitterstim draped through the open air of the grotto.

From behind them Skynxnex fired again in a long continuous blast that missed them in the wide space. The powerful pulsed beam struck the far ceiling of the chamber, making it erupt with hot broken stone that poured down from the roof of the tunnel. The images in Han's infrared goggles were blindingly bright.

The bogey stretched and struggled as parts of the spice web tore away in the avalanche, yanking portions of the glow with it.

Then Han saw the monstrous creature rise up from its lair on the grotto floor—a huge spider made of blown glass, all sharp edges, with a hundred legs and a thousand eyes. The bristling legs moved in a blur as it clambered up the debris toward the glowing bogey struggling in the spice web.

Han wrenched the floating car around, ready to plow his way out and away from the monster that had almost captured him in the tunnels—even if he had to fly right down Skynxnex's throat.

On the rocks below, tossed aside like wadded sheets of used paper, lay the crumbled forms of Boss Roke, Clorr, and the guard, frozen solid and drained of every drop of their bodily energy.

The creature must lay down deposits of spice as its web to capture bogeys, Han thought, *or any other warm creature it can find down in these tunnels.* That was why light activated the glitterstim spice—to trigger the bogeys' capture in the trap.

Skynxnex and the pursuing guard roared into the grotto. The scarecrow fired again, paying little attention to where he was going. His blast ricocheted off the wall, activating more spice.

The spider-thing glowed a dull blue with electric arcs crawling up and down its needlelike limbs, as if the creature itself were made out of activated spice. Attracted to the approaching heat source, it reared up.

Skynxnex did not see it until he had driven his floating mine car nearly into the grappling-hook claws. In the last instant Skynxnex pointed his hot double-blaster down and fired at the voracious creature—but the energy spider absorbed the blaster's power and snatched out with a dozen limbs.

Skynxnex tried to leap out of the doomed car, but the spider thing speared him with a sharp leg, raising his scarecrow body higher. With the last of his strength, Skynxnex flailed his arms as his body grew cold.

The multilegged creature began to feed.

The pursuing guard rebounded sideways as he struck a thick mass of spice fibers dangling from the ceiling. The glitterstim sparked and glowed in the growing illumination. As the guard saw Skynxnex captured, saw the huge energy spider and the collapsing ceiling of the grotto, he whirled his floating mine car around and fled back out the cavern entrance as fast as he could go.

Han, though, saw an open passage in the ceiling and noticed a dim trickle of light coming from it. He wanted only to be out of there before the thing came scrambling after them, clawing its way up glasslike strands of glitterstim. . . .

"Up there!" Han urged.

Kyp plunged the car upward into the ceiling opening and suddenly came upon another network of tunnels. But these catacombs looked man-made. At last, one of the illicit mining shafts dug by spice smugglers searching to find active veins.

Han let out a whoop of delight. "This is it! We're out of here now!" Chewbacca clapped him on the back, nearly belting Han out of the pilot's seat.

They raced upward. The distant daylight pierced through the jagged obstacles of the passage. Han did not want to slow down. Kyp accelerated toward the light.

The floating car burst into the thin open air of Kessel, where watery light blinded them like a supernova. Blinking and struggling to see, Han yanked off his goggles and took back the pilot controls. He evened out their trajectory above the flat, desolate surface of the small planet.

Off to their right he saw the towering stack of an atmosphere factory gushing white steam and air vapor into the sky. "That way," Kyp said. "We'll be able to find a ship."

"Good idea," Han said.

As they approached the enormous construction, flying low enough to avoid notice, he kept an eye out. Moruth Doole would not know of their escape until the lone surviving guard returned to the muster room and made his report. Han, Kyp, and Chewbacca would have a few moments to get a head start, but not very long.

Adjacent to the atmosphere factory, Han did indeed see a broad landing pad with four craft on it. Two of the ships were local landskimmers and useless to them—but the others were small supply shuttles, spaceworthy enough, though they wouldn't go fast.

Holding the breath mask against his face, Han pointed with his other hand. "Down there. Get one of those ships and we're away from Kessel." He grabbed Kyp's shoulder. "We can go home."

14

When Luke returned to Coruscant, he had a joyous reunion with Han and Leia's two-year-old children, whom he had not seen for some time, not since he and Ackbar had set up the secret, protected planet for them.

He waited in Leia's living quarters, playing with the twins, tossing them in the air and juggling them using his Jedi powers. Jacen and Jaina squealed in delight, giggling and intuitively trusting that their Uncle Luke would never let them fall.

Children were a wonder to him. Raised with his Uncle Owen and Aunt Beru on the parched world of Tatooine, Luke had had little time for playing with children because the life of a moisture farmer was wrapped up in such hard work.

When he left Tatooine with Ben Kenobi, Luke had joined the Rebel Alliance, spending time as a fighter pilot and in Jedi training with Yoda. He never had time or opportunity to see children—and now he felt as much pleasure playing with them, watching their wide-eyed innocence, as they seemed to enjoy having him around.

"Faster! Faster!" Jacen cried.

Instead, just to tease him, Luke stopped the boy cold in the air, letting him hang motionless as Luke orbited Jaina around him. The little girl squealed and stretched out her hand, trying to grab her brother's ear as she spun.

Tiring of that, Luke let Jaina drift into a cushioned seat while he reached out to catch Jacen as the boy descended, holding him in his arms. Jaina squirmed and reached her pudgy arms up, wanting to be held too.

Luke made faces at the little boy, puckering his lips and wiggling them back and forth. He spoke in a funny head-cold voice that sounded something like Yoda's. "The Force is strong in this little one, hmmmm? Yes!" But then Luke wrinkled his nose and noticed something he didn't need Jedi powers to understand. "Or maybe that's not the Force I sense. Leia, I think you need to perform a motherly duty." He held Jacen in front of him.

Threepio bustled into the room. "Allow me to take care of that, sir. I have been getting a great deal of practice in the past day or two."

Luke smiled at the thought of Threepio trying to manage squirming twins. He noticed the droid looked a bit scuffed and battered. "Was that part of your protocol programming?"

"My manual dexterity is sufficient to the task, Master Luke." Threepio flexed his golden motorized fingers, then took Jacen from Luke's grasp. "And believe me, I enjoy these duties much more than gallivanting through space, getting shot at by Imperial fighters, or getting lost in asteroid fields."

Leia came into the room. She forced a smile that Luke could tell was a mask. She looked very tired. It wasn't just the strain of combining her diplomatic duties with being a mother; something else deeply concerned her, but she hadn't said anything. Luke did not pry—he could have reached in and taken the secret from her mind, but he would not do that to his sister. And she might even have figured out how to block him by now. He would let her broach the subject in her own way.

"The prep unit will have the meal ready in just a few minutes," Leia said. "I'm very glad you're back, and the twins seem to be pleased too."

Luke realized that he hadn't seen Han since his return; but because of their busy schedules, seeing Han and Leia in the same place at the same time was a rare occurrence anyway. It was a wonder they had somehow managed to have three children! Could Han's absence have something to do with Leia's hidden concern?

Luke picked up Jaina with the Force again, raising her into the air. She giggled and began flailing her arms and legs as if swimming through the open spaces of the room.

"Leia, I need your help in a couple of bureaucratic matters," Luke said.

"Sure." She smiled wryly at him. "What can I do?"

"I still need to contact Mara Jade and a handful of other possible Jedi candidates. But now that I have two trainees here and waiting, I've got to find a place where we can begin our Jedi studies. And I have to find it soon.

"I've spoken with Streen and Gantoris, and it's clear to me that Coruscant is not appropriate. Streen doesn't like to be around people, and he's not going to be very comfortable anywhere in Imperial City. All of Coruscant is covered with metropolis, buildings on top of buildings.

"And—" He hesitated, but this was a private conversation with Leia; he could not hide any of his worries from her. "There is some danger about what we might do. Who am *I* to be teaching all these Jedi potentials? I have no way of knowing what might trigger a disaster like one of the Emperor's Force storms. It would be better if we found someplace isolated, a place of solitude where we can conduct our training without interference."

"And in safety." Leia's dark eyes met his, and he knew that both of them were thinking of Darth Vader. "Yes, I agree. I'll try to find you an appropriate place."

"And while you're looking," Luke continued, "we also need to relocate all of the people on Eol Sha. There's only about fifty of them left on that outpost, but the planet is doomed. When I took Gantoris, I promised we would find a new home for the survivors. See what you can do."

"For a group of people that small, it shouldn't be difficult," Leia answered. "Anyplace sounds better than the planet they're leaving."

Luke laughed. "Or you could always have Han win another planet for them in a card game!"

She looked at him as if stung. *Yes indeed*, he thought. It was something to do with Han. He bounced Jaina up in the air again, touching her to the ceiling, then letting her fall back down.

Suddenly Lando Calrissian burst into the room unannounced. "Leia! Winter just told me that Han hasn't come back yet. Why haven't you talked to me about it?"

Startled, Luke let Jaina fall and barely managed to catch her in the air a handbreadth above the hard floor. Jaina giggled deliriously, confident that the whole thing had been planned.

Lando looked upset and angry as he glared at Leia, planting his hands on his hips, pushing back the cape to hang behind him. Then he noticed Luke standing in the room. "Luke, are you going to do anything about this?"

"I don't know what you're talking about—but I think Leia was just about to tell me."

Both men looked at her. She sighed and sat down. "Yes, Han is missing. He went off to Kessel about two weeks ago, but now he's four days late coming back. He never contacted me, so yesterday I got in touch with Kessel. I spoke to someone who seems to be in charge, a Rybet named Moruth Doole.

"Doole says that Han and Chewie never arrived. Kessel has no record of the *Millennium Falcon*. Doole suggested they might have gotten lost in the black hole cluster."

"Not Han!" Lando said. "And not in the *Falcon*. He knows how to fly that thing almost as well as I do."

Leia nodded. "All through the conversation I sensed something wrong with the way Doole was acting. His answers were too pat, and he seemed nervous. I had the distinct feeling he was expecting my call and had already made up appropriate excuses."

"I don't like that," Lando said.

"Well, if Han is missing and you knew since yesterday, why didn't you send out a fleet of New Republic scouts?" Luke said. "A formal search party? What if he *is* lost in the Maw somewhere?"

Leia sighed. "Think about it, Luke. If I mobilized an official force, I could create a galactic incident just when we're trying to get Kessel into the New Republic. And besides," she admitted, "you know Han. There's a very real chance he's just goofing around. He forgot his kids were coming back. Maybe he found a good game of sabacc or started talking old times with some of his spice-smuggler buddies—that's why he wanted to go on the mission in the first place."

"We'll go look for him ourselves," Lando said.

Luke could tell by the way Leia's face brightened that this was what she intended to ask all along. "We'll go snoop around," he said. "There won't be any official dispatch or record of our mission."

Lando said, "We'd better take the *Lady Luck.* She's just a privately owned yacht with some pretty good punch in her engines."

Leia stepped forward and plucked Jaina out of Luke's lap and cradled her. "I'll watch over Gantoris and Streen while you're gone."

Luke nodded and spread his hands wide. "You see, *that's* why you're a diplomat—you think of details like that. Just don't let the two of them get into any trouble."

"We should take Artoo with us," Lando said. "That little droid sure helped me out at the blob races."

Luke had heard of Lando's exploits with the scam artist Tymmo. "You can tell me all about it on our way there. Leia's waited long enough."

"Let's go to Kessel," Lando said.

15

They managed to steal the second shuttle.

Han and Chewbacca wasted precious time in the first cargo ship on the atmosphere factory's landing pad, trying to cross-circuit the controls as Kyp Durron kept watch in the open hatch. The air was cold on their exposed skin, and they didn't know how much stray radiation from the Maw actually penetrated the atmospheric shield; the sounds of breathing hissed behind their breath masks. No one had seen them. Yet.

After only a few minutes, Han accidentally triggered the shuttle's automatic lockout systems. He slammed his hand on the panel. "Should have known I couldn't beat the high-level security interlocks!"

Chewbacca pulled off an access plate and tossed it into the back compartment with the sound of a crashing landspeeder. Roaring in his Wookiee language, he began yanking wires out of the controls and jamming them into override ports, but the few lights still functioning on the panels continued to burn red.

"Forget it, Chewie. We'll try the other ship," Han said. "I think I know what I did wrong last time."

Kyp kept watch on the tiny doors of the atmosphere factory's massive stack. "Still no movement from inside. We're clear."

They raced across the open spaces of the landing field to the second cargo shuttle, an old Imperial model with scarred armor and long planar wings that made it look like a mechanical flying fish. Han and Chewbacca had flown a similar *Lambda*-class shuttle on their guerrilla mission to Endor; but this model looked even older. Prison facilities must have low priority for new equipment acquisitions, he thought.

Chewbacca opened the hatch, and Han ducked inside, moving straight to the controls. The Wookiee clambered after him as four guards marched into view around the perimeter of the atmosphere stack. The squad wore cobbled-together uniforms of old stormtrooper armor and thermal suits from the mines.

Kyp plastered himself to the wall just inside the open hatch. Looking across the landing field, he saw that they had forgotten to close the doorway on the first shuttle, and now their tampering was painfully obvious. He swallowed. "Better hurry, Han. We've got company, but they haven't seen us yet."

"If this doesn't work, we're in deep bantha dung," Han muttered, punching up the command screens and removing the access plate to the security override.

The squad of guards marched on what was probably a routine patrol. Han glanced up to see them through the shuttle's windowport, but the reflectorized transparisteel would prevent them from observing the pilot's compartment. He wondered how many times a day the guards walked around the circular perimeter of the atmosphere stack. He hoped they were sleepwalking by now.

He tried to fire up the shuttle's engines. The control panel gave him an ERROR message. "Bantha dung it is, then," he said. But he had one more thing to try.

The lead guard suddenly stopped and gestured toward the open hatch in the first shuttle. He tilted his head to speak into his helmet comlink, then went cautiously forward. He took another guard with him, while the remaining two drew their weapons and spread out, looking from side to side.

"Oh boy," Kyp said.

Han rewired the security circuit, feeding the password-checking mechanisms back into themselves; then he snapped the plate back on. "Let's try it. Kyp, get ready to close the hatch. If this works, those guards are going to be upset. If it doesn't work, *I'm* going to be upset."

The two guards poked their heads out of the first shuttle, gesturing wildly. They had seen the sabotage. The other two jabbered into their helmet radios, then sprinted toward the second shuttle, drawing their weapons.

Kyp slapped the button that slammed the hatch shut. All the guards began running, pointing their blasters at the shuttle.

Han punched the start controls. With a merciful whine and hum, the engines ignited. Power surged through the shuttle. Han gave a whoop of triumph, but Chewbacca knocked him back into the pilot's seat as he furiously worked the controls with his big hairy hands to lift them off the pad.

The guards fired blasters at the shuttle. Han heard the sizzling thumps as the beams struck, but the ship's armor could withstand attack from minor hand weapons.

At the base of the atmosphere stack, doors opened and an entire squad of guards boiled out like Anoat lizard-ants in mating season. One bright laser bolt splashed across the transparisteel directly in front of Han's eyes, dazzling him. "Time to leave this party," he said.

Chewbacca raised them off the ground, maneuvering the shuttle away from the other vehicles on the landing pad.

Two guards wrestled a blaster cannon into place, erecting it on its tripod and cranking up the aim point. Chewbacca growled, and Han took over the controls. "I know. That thing could be real trouble if we don't get some altitude fast."

A flurry of hand-blaster bolts pinged against the lower hull. Han flew the ship higher, adjacent to the gigantic stack, spiraling upward and using the curving walls as a shield. The guards managed to fire only one shot from the blaster-cannon, but the beam scattered wide as Han corkscrewed up, keeping the stack between him and the troops. Below, the guards ran around the perimeter to keep within firing range, but Han flew the shuttle beyond the reach of small weapons fire.

"We're out of here!" Han said. "Punch it, Chewie!"

Then the massive laser turrets mounted on the atmosphere tower began firing at them.

"What!" Han cried. "What are they doing with weapons on an atmosphere stack? It's a factory, not a garrison!"

One brilliant green bolt struck the starboard planar wing of the shuttle, sending the vessel into a roll. Han and Chewbacca grappled with the controls as they spun, and Kyp clung to the supports of the pilot's chair.

They careened into the gushing white updraft from the stack, knocked from side to side by manufactured air dumping into Kessel's atmosphere. "Hang on!" Han yelled. He did not want to crash on the planet again.

At the shuttle's top acceleration, he took them along the stream of air, roaring upward like a boat riding the rapids. Green blasts from the turret lasers continued to streak up, but by riding the center stream, Han kept the shuttle in the blind spot of their targeting mechanisms.

They zoomed toward the fringes of the atmosphere. Han looked at both Kyp and Chewbacca. "Well, so much for sneaking out of here. Now Moruth Doole is going to know we escaped."

As if on cue the shuttle's comm crackled, and they could hear Doole's croaking voice in the background. "Is this it? Did you get the right override channel this time?"

"Yes, Commissioner."

"Solo! Han Solo, can you hear me?"

"Why, it sounds like my old friend Moruth Doole!" Han said. "How are you doing, buddy? I hope you feel better than your assistant Skynxnex."

"Solo, you have caused me more grief than any other life-form in the galaxy—including Jabba the Hutt! I should have squashed you when I had you in my office."

Han rolled his eyes. "Well, you missed your chance, and I don't plan on giving you another one."

Doole chuckled, a hissing heh-heh-heh laugh like a fat man choking on sand. "You won't get away. I'll mobilize everything against you. Better start thinking about the afterlife now."

Kyp squinted out the port, as if deep in concentration. The atmosphere thinned around the fleeing ship at the far limit of where Kessel's gravity could keep hold. He saw Kessel's moon and suddenly shivered uncontrollably. He blinked in confusion.

Chewbacca bellowed into the speaker mesh. "You tell him, Chewie," Han said, then switched off the radio.

Kyp scrambled forward and grabbed the controls, activating the maneuvering rockets and making the shuttle lurch forward with enough force to slam Han and Chewbacca against their seats. Kyp tumbled backward, unable to keep his balance in the acceleration.

"What did you do that for?" Han demanded, glaring at Kyp.

But Chewbacca made an alarmed noise and dragged Han back to the console. Just below them the atmosphere shimmered and crinkled as an impenetrable ionized screen appeared, blanketing the planet.

"They've got their energy shield operational!" Han said. The workers on Kessel's moonbase had repaired the protective screen that blocked off the prison planet. If Kyp hadn't punched their acceleration exactly when he did, they would have been sizzled in the bath of power or trapped beneath the shield, unable to escape.

"How did you know?" Han said, looking over his shoulder at Kyp. Kyp picked himself up off the floor, shaking his head to clear his thoughts. "Never mind. Are you okay?"

"Yeah. Just get us away from Kessel."

Han spun around to the shuttle's controls. "Chewie, contact the New Republic. No waiting this time. They've got to learn what's going on here, just in case we don't make it back."

The Wookiee bent over the comm controls as Han struggled with the navicomputer. Han gawked at the task in front of him. "Damn! This thing's an old five-hundred-X model! Haven't seen one of these outside a museum. I hope they gave us a scratchpad to do backup calculations. That might be faster *and* more accurate!"

Chewbacca moaned and pounded his hairy fist on the console with enough force to buckle the panels. Han flashed a sidelong look at him. "What do you mean we're being jammed? Who's jamming us?"

Kyp turned to the side viewport, said in a low voice, "Here they come."

The garrison on Kessel's moon spewed fighters, dozens of rejuvenated battle craft, armored freighters, slim and heavily armed X-wings, and TIE fighters. Many of the ships must have been damaged during the recent war and then salvaged. Now Doole had also gotten his planetary defense shield running again. Kessel would be a veritable stronghold against any attack.

Streams of X-wings and Y-wings coursed out, flanked on either side by a squadron of TIE fighters. They roared through the wispy tail of atmosphere in Kessel's orbital wake, leaving a glowing window of ionized gas from their sublight engines.

"Strap yourselves in," Han said. "This is going to be a hell of a ride." He reached for the controls, preparing to fight, then felt a boulder drop in his stomach. "What? This ship is *unarmed!*" He frantically scanned the console. "Nothing! Not a single laser! Not even a slingshot!"

Kyp held the back of Han's pilot chair, bracing himself. "We stole a supply ship, not a fighter. What did you expect?"

"Chewie, pump everything into our shields—and I mean *everything*, including life support. We've got enough air in here to last longer than this ship is likely to hold. Boost shields until they're off the scale. We're going to have to outrun them."

The first wave of TIE fighters soared in, their Twin Ion Engines howling over the cockpit's feedback speakers. Laser spears shot out, pummeling the shuttle, but the shields held. X-wings attacked from the rear.

"Can't this ship go any faster?" Kyp asked. The lights dimmed as Chewbacca reinforced the shields.

"Like you said, kid, we stole a cargo shuttle. This isn't a racing ship, and it sure isn't the *Falcon*. Get ready for a jump to hyperspace as soon as this fossilized navicomputer gives an answer." He stared at the readout, then pounded on the panel. "It'll be another ten minutes before it coughs up a safe trajectory. Damn! The black hole cluster is screwing up the calculations."

Chewbacca interjected a loud, bleating comment.

"What did he say?" Kyp asked.

"He said our shields are going to fail in about two minutes. I wish I had weapons—I'd even settle for a rock to throw out the window!" His eyes were wide and suddenly empty of hope. "There's no way we can last long enough, and Doole sure won't take prisoners a second time. Sorry I got you into this, kid."

Kyp bit his lip, then turned to point out the front windowport. "Go there."

The Maw.

Swirling clouds of gas looped into the bottomless pits of black holes, making space look like a tangled skein of incandescent yarn. Gravity waited to tear apart any ship that came too close. The inexorable Maw cluster was destined to swallow up the Kessel system itself in only another thousand years—but Han didn't want to feed its appetite any sooner than that.

Chewbacca roared something that needed no translation. "Are you crazy?" Han asked.

"You said we're dead anyway."

Four Y-wings fired simultaneously on the port side of the shuttle, rocking it. A shower of sparks blasted from the comm unit, and Chewbacca struggled to reroute the circuits.

"There are supposed to be safe paths through it," Kyp said. "There must be."

"Yeah, and about a million paths that are sudden death!"

"It'll be flying a razor's edge all the way through." Kyp's young eyes looked immeasurably old as he stared at Han. "Do we have a better chance staying here and fighting?"

The enormous gravity wells of the Maw made a maze of all the hyperspace and normal space paths through the cluster. Most of the routes were either dead ends or went right down the gullet of a black hole. "We'd never find the right course," Han said. "It'd be suicide."

Kyp gripped Han's shoulder. "I can show you the way."

"What? How?"

A TIE fighter looped overhead, rotating in flight and firing at the hijacked shuttle. Cruisers from the moonbase approached, closing the gap. Against the capital-ships' turbolasers, the escapees would be vaporized within moments. Chewbacca groaned as their rear shields weakened and failed.

Han scrambled with the controls; both he and Chewbacca tried to reinforce weak points by draining the stronger shields up front. Lights in the cabin dimmed as the shields gulped more power.

"I helped you navigate through the dark spice tunnels when we were running from Skynxnex, didn't I?" Kyp said. "I knew when Doole was going to switch on the energy shield! I can find the right path into the Maw."

"That still doesn't tell me *how*, kid!" Han shouted.

Kyp wore an embarrassed expression for a moment; then he spoke quickly. "This is going to sound like a hokey old religion—but it works! An old woman who spent part of her sentence in the spice tunnels told me I had some sort of tremendous potential. She showed me how to use something called 'the power' or 'the strength' or something."

"The Force!" Han cried in relief. He wanted to grab Kyp and hug him. "Why didn't you say so? Who was this woman?"

"Her name was Vima-Da-Boda. Down in the spice mines she taught me only a few things before the guards hauled her away. I never saw her again, but I've been practicing what she taught me. It's helped a few times, but I don't really understand how."

"Vima-Da-Boda!" Han said, remembering the withered fallen Jedi he and Leia had found on Nal Hutta. During her guilt-ridden hiding, Vima-Da-Boda had somehow spent time in the spice mines, long enough to train Kyp in a few essential skills. Han hoped that would be good enough.

"I don't like this," Han said. Another pair of fighters soared by, firing repeatedly. "But I like it better than our other options right now."

He altered course, swinging around and heading straight toward the seething cluster of black holes. He hoped the shuttle's weakened shields would last long enough to get them there.

The first of the capital ships reached them and fired, looping overhead, then returning, as if to ram them. The shape of the attacking freighter made Han's blood turn to water, and he stared in silent dismay for a full second before he managed to cry out. "That's the *Millennium Falcon!* That's my ship!"

The *Falcon* came straight at them, firing again and again as the shuttle's forward shields tried to compensate for the pummeling. At the last moment Han wrenched the stolen shuttle into a steep dive so the *Falcon* scraped by overhead. One of the shots passed through the wavering shields to scar the armor of the shuttle.

"That does it!" Han said. "Now I'm mad. Chewie, at my order drop shields and dump everything into thrust. Pump every last erg into our engines and take us straight into the Maw." He glanced down at his readouts. "Shields are failing in less than a minute anyway, and the navicomputer needs another six to finish its calculations. Blasted five-hundred-X models!"

Another wing of fighters strafed them, then roared by, leaving a gap to their rear as a huge Lancer frigate closed the distance. A wave of system-patrol craft and Carrack cruisers followed, ready to bring a full armada of turbolasers to bear. Moruth Doole was taking no chances this time.

"Go, Chewie!" Han said.

The Wookiee dropped shields and channeled all power to the sublight engines. The shuttle burst forward in an unexpected spurt of speed, startling the pursuing ships.

"Surprise is only going to help us for a few seconds," Han said. "Then we're on our own."

"By that time we should be in the grip of the Maw," Kyp whispered. "If you're not right about this, kid, we'll never know it."

Curtains of incandescent gas blazed in front of them, swirling residue heated by friction as it spiraled in complex orbits through the Roche lobe of one black hole and down the gullet of another. Deadly x-rays filled space, forcing the transparisteel to dim itself to protect the eyes of the passengers.

"Only a complete idiot would try something like this," Han said. Chewbacca agreed.

The Kessel ships poured on additional acceleration, desperately trying to catch the escapees before Han could reach the Maw cluster. Han hunched over the controls, white-knuckled, as if to increase their speed by sheer force of will.

The fighters unleashed a laser firestorm, but the Maw's huge gravitational distortions spread out their focus and sent them on long arcs away from the target.

"Let's just hope these guys aren't idiots too!" Kyp said. Han drove toward the blazing shreds of hot gas.

The Kessel ships pursued until the last instant, then peeled off at full thrust with their maneuvering engines, letting their prey go to certain death.

Han's ship plunged into the gravitational jaws of the black hole cluster.

16

Leia suppressed a dignified smile as she led Gantoris into the projection chamber. The dark-haired man stared in his puppetlike way as he tried to gawk at everything at the same time.

Gantoris was resplendent in a new uniform, tailored to match the generations-old pilot suit he had worn as leader on Eol Sha. Leia had loaded a tailor droid with patterns from the archives and presented the uniform to Gantoris as a gift. He had been delighted, puffed with admiration.

Even after getting to know him, Leia felt uncomfortable around Gantoris. Though Luke assured her of the strong Jedi potential in the man, Leia did not like the thought of the deadly "tests" Gantoris had given Luke before he would agree to leave Eol Sha. Gantoris had lived a hellish life, she admitted, but he seemed too intense, his dark eyes fiery pits of contained fury. He had the look of a man accustomed to power suddenly shown how small he is in the grand scheme of things.

But the other side of Gantoris intrigued Leia. She watched him flick his eyes back and forth, craning his head to stare at the tall building spires rising to the fringes of Coruscant's atmosphere. He gaped in astonishment at the sparkling audience chambers, at the minor personal amenities in the quarters Luke had obtained for him. He had never before seen or even imagined things that Leia considered commonplace.

Now, as they entered the projection room, Gantoris stared at the giant windows that filled the walls with broad vistas of Coruscant and the centuries-old buildings that girdled the world. The two of them were not really high enough for such a view, Leia knew; the projection room was actually a deep internal chamber, and the "windows" were high-resolution screens displaying images from cameras mounted at the top of the Imperial Palace.

"What is this place?" Gantoris asked.

Leia smiled, folding her arms over her robe. "Right now this is just a room. In a moment, though, I'll give you a new world."

She stepped to the control dais in the middle of the room and called up images she had compiled from the archives, records left over from Old Republic surveys and the dossiers compiled during the Alliance occupation.

The window screens flickered, and the images changed, startling Gantoris. He whirled as the landscape suddenly showed a completely different planet. His eyes grew wide and panicked, as if Leia had just transported him across the galaxy.

"I'm showing you a new home. This is Dantooine, the place we have chosen for the people of Eol Sha."

Around them the window screens displayed vast plains of grassland and spiky trees. Purplish hills rolled across the distant horizon. A herd of small, hairy beasts roamed across the savanna; in the air a cluster of bright balloonlike things, either plants or rudimentary animals, drifted about; a few had snagged on pointed branches of the spiky trees. Two moons, one lavender and one greenish, soared overhead.

"We established one of our first Rebel bases on Dantooine. It has a mild climate, abundant life-forms, plenty of water. A few nomadic tribes roam up and down the coasts of the ocean, but for the most part the planet is uninhabited."

Leia had used Dantooine as a decoy when Grand Moff Tarkin interrogated her aboard the Death Star. To save her beloved planet of Alderaan, Leia had divulged the location of the old Rebel base on Dantooine rather than naming the real base on Yavin 4; but Tarkin destroyed Alderaan anyway, because Dantooine was too remote for an effective demonstration of the Death Star's power. Now, though, Dantooine could be put to use again, as a home for the refugees of Eol Sha.

"Do you think your people would like to live on a place like this?" Leia raised her eyebrows.

Gantoris, who had so far seen only his own blasted world, the gas planet of Bespin, and the city-covered surface of Coruscant, seemed impressed. "This looks like a paradise. No volcanoes? No earthquakes? Plenty to eat, and no sprawling cities?"

She nodded. Before Gantoris could say anything else, the door to the projection room opened. Leia turned, surprised to see the Chief of State, Mon Mothma, coming to join them.

The auburn-haired woman walked with a sure step that made her glide across the floor. The leader of the New Republic extended a hand to Gantoris. "You must be one of Luke Skywalker's first Jedi trainees. Please let me welcome you to Coruscant and wish you the best of success in becoming part of a new order of Jedi Knights."

Gantoris took Mon Mothma's hand and nodded to her with a slight bow; but Leia caught a fleeting impression that he considered himself a leader meeting an equal.

"Mon Mothma," Leia said, "I was just showing Gantoris some images of Dantooine. We are considering moving the refugees from Eol Sha to our old base there."

Mon Mothma smiled. "Good. I'm aware of the plight of your people, and I would like to see them safely on Dantooine. I always thought it was one of our most pleasant bases, not quite as rigorous as Hoth or Pinnacle Base, without the dense jungles of Yavin 4." She turned to Gantoris. "If this world meets with your approval, I'll direct Minister Organa Solo to begin the relocation work immediately."

Gantoris nodded. "If these are representative pictures, this place Dantooine would be a perfect new home for my people."

Leia felt a surge of relief. "I was thinking of putting Wedge . . . I mean General Antilles in charge of the relocation duties. He's been supervising the reconstruction of the lower city levels for months, and frankly, I think that's a waste of his talents."

"I agree," Mon Mothma said. Though buried under more diplomatic entanglements and bureaucratic decisions than Leia could imagine, Mon Mothma somehow maintained a calm energy. "Also, my calendar just reminded me that the Caridan ambassador will be arriving in two days. Are all the preparations going smoothly? Can I offer my assistance in any way?"

"Just plan to be there. That's the most I can ask of you. I have decided to move the reception to the Skydome Botanical Gardens, rather than holding it here in the Imperial Palace. Since Ambassador Furgan seems hostile to our cause, I didn't want to exacerbate his reactions by receiving him in the former seat of the Emperor's government. In fact, the ambassador is trying to disguise his mission here as a mere pilgrimage to visit the site of various Imperial landmarks."

Mon Mothma nodded slightly but gave a smile. "At least he's coming. That's the best signal of all."

"I suppose." Leia remained skeptical.

"By the way, I never received your report on Han's mission to Kessel. That was a brilliant idea to send him instead of a formal ambassador. Han can speak to those people in their own language, and reopening the spice channels away from the black market might do wonders for the new economy. Did he have any success?"

Feeling awkward, Leia dropped her gaze to the floor. "He has been delayed, Mon Mothma, so I don't have any information at the moment. I'll give you a full report as soon as he gets back. Let's hope his mission is a success."

"Agreed." Mon Mothma's expression hinted that she suspected there was more to Leia's story, but she asked no further questions. "I have to go debate with the Ugnaught representatives about salvage rights for the wrecked ships in orbit around Coruscant. I'm afraid it's going to be a long afternoon, and I just wanted to greet you while I had the chance. Gantoris, it was a pleasure."

Mon Mothma turned to go but flashed a glance back at Leia. "By the way, you're doing a fine job, Leia. Too often in government we get inundated by so many dissatisfied interest groups, so many complaints, that we forget the things we're doing right. You are doing a *lot* of things right."

Leia couldn't cover an embarrassed smile. If only she hadn't lost her husband, she might have been a lot happier.

The twins began bawling in unison as soon as Winter stepped onto the ramp of her unmarked shuttle. Leia's personal servant stopped, keeping her back turned to Jacen and Jaina, and then slowly faced them.

Leia gripped the shoulders of the two children, but they still treated their mother as a stranger, even after several days. She held on tightly, which she realized might not have been the best thing to do, but she felt suddenly possessive of the twins.

Winter's face was cold and impassive beneath her white hair. "Children, stop crying this instant."

Jacen snuffled. "We want you to stay, Winter."

Winter thrust out one hand, pointing her finger like a spear at Leia. "*That* is your mother. I was only taking care of you. You are big children now, and it's time for you to be at your own home. I have to go back and take care of your baby brother."

Leia kept herself from trembling. She had known Winter a long time; the woman had total recall of anything she had ever seen or heard, and she rarely showed any sort of emotion. Now Leia thought she could detect a sadness in her, a sense of loss as she finally gave over care of her two wards.

Leia knelt beside the twins. "You'll be staying with me now, both of you. And your daddy should be home soon. We'll have lots of fun together."

The twins turned to look at her; Winter took that moment to slip inside the shuttle. Before Jacen and Jaina noticed she had gone, Winter activated the doors, sealing herself inside.

Leia stood beside the children on the windswept landing pad. The shuttle's repulsorlifts whined, powering up. Leia stepped backward, nudging the twins with her. "Out of the way now. Back where it's safe." Jacen and Jaina still sniffled, on the verge of crying again. In her untrained way Leia tried to send them calm, loving thoughts.

She spoke into a comlink on the lapel of her robe. "Grant departure clearance to unmarked shuttle on top northside platform of the Palace, authority of Minister Organa Solo."

The orbital traffic controllers acknowledged, and Winter's shuttle rose from the platform, pivoted, then angled into the sky. Leia raised her hand in a farewell salute. "Wave to Winter," she said.

The twins flailed their pudgy arms in the air. Winter flashed the lights in the shuttle at them; then the orbital-burn rockets kicked in, and the vessel shot into the aurora-streaked distance.

"Come on, you two," Leia said to them. "I've got a lot of lost time to make up for."

Streen sat atop the ruined and abandoned skyscraper where he had made his home. When Luke brought him to the yammering mass of Imperial City, where millions of people covered the planet with all their thoughts and all their feelings, Streen had begged for a place where he could have some solitude until they moved off-planet to their Jedi training center. Luke showed him the abandoned parts of the city, and Streen had selected the tallest building. Being high up reminded him of the clouds of Bespin.

Now Leia brought the twins with her, keeping a firm grip on each of their hands as she led them into the barely functional lift, which took them to the rooftop. They walked out onto the upper platform where Streen sat alone on the edge. The old man dangled his feet over the sides, unperturbed by the unbroken kilometer drop below him. He looked up and out at the unrelenting cityscape, the geometric spires of sprawling buildings. He watched the tiny shapes of hawk-bats riding thermals.

Leia walked across the rooftop. She had never been afraid of heights, although with the young children at hand she felt an altogether different kind of fear, a stomach-clenching paranoia of the millions of things that could bring danger to her children. Jacen and Jaina wanted to dash to the edge of the platform and look over, but she refused to release her grip.

Upon hearing them approach, Streen turned. Leia noted that he still wore his many-pocketed jumpsuit, not wanting to change into the warmer or more comfortable clothes she had offered him.

"We just came to check on you, Streen. With Luke gone I wanted to make sure there was nothing else you needed."

Streen paused a moment before answering. "What I'd like is solitude, but I fear there's no place I can have that on this entire planet. Even in the quietest places on Coruscant, I can still hear a constant hum of whispering thoughts and voices. It'll be very difficult for me here, until I learn how to block it out. The Jedi Master promised to teach me how to do that."

"Luke should be back shortly," Leia said.

They approached the edge, and Leia insisted on standing a safe distance away. But Jaina pulled forward to the full reach of Leia's arm, to where she could peer over the edge and gape all the way down. "That's far!" Jaina said.

"Too far to fall," Leia told her.

"I won't fall."

"Me neither," Jacen said. Then he insisted on straining forward to look over the edge as well.

Streen stared at them with a kind of wonder. "You're better than the others. The children's minds are simple and straightforward, and they don't bother me. It's only when thoughts are complex and filled with a thousand subtexts that it makes my head ache. And you, Minister Organa Solo, are quieter and more focused than most other people."

"Luke taught me how to control my own mind. I don't leak out the thoughts and feelings that bother you so much. I keep from broadcasting them to anyone else."

Streen gave a wan smile, then stared out at the vast sky. On various parabolic courses, blinking lights of incoming and departing diplomatic shuttles traveled across the sky.

"I hope all the Jedi trainees can learn to be as silent as you are, Minister. I'd very much like to be around other people, part of a community like yourself and the Jedi Master. How long will it be, do you think?"

He looked deeply into her eyes, and she pulled the children away from the edge. "Soon," Leia said. "As soon as possible."

She vowed that she would find a place for Luke's academy before he returned from Kessel. It had to be the right place, and she had to find it without delay.

Leia and Threepio insisted on giving the twins a warm ripple bath before bedtime. Leia ran the water as Threepio checked to make sure its temperature was perfect.

Leia shooed Jacen and Jaina toward the rippling water. Jacen balked. "Put bubbles in first!"

"I'll put the bubbles in while the water's still running. Now just get in."

"Winter puts bubbles in first," Jaina said.

"Well, this time we'll do it a little different," Leia explained a bit testily.

"I want bubbles now!" Jacen cried.

"Dear me! Perhaps we *had* better put the bubbles in, Mistress Leia," Threepio said.

But the twins' defiance had awakened Leia's own stubbornness. "No, I told you to get in the bath. I don't care how Winter did it. This is the place you live now. Sometimes we do things differently."

Jaina began to cry.

"It's all right!" Leia said. "It's still a nice bath. Look." She splashed her hand in the warm water. "It doesn't make any difference when you put the bubbles in."

"I put bubbles in?" Jaina asked.

"If you get in, you can add the bubbles."

Jaina promptly climbed into the water and held out her hands. Leia gave her an amber-colored sphere that would dissolve in the agitation of the ripples.

Jacen jumped into the ripple bath. "Now I put bubbles in!"

"Too late," Leia said. "Next time it'll be your turn."

"Perhaps we should let them add another sphere of bubbles?" Threepio said, bending over to situate the children in the water.

Jacen used both of his hands to fling water into the droid's face. "I want home!"

"This is home, Jacen. You live here now. I'm your mother."

"No. I want *home*!"

Leia began to wonder why her diplomatic skills were failing her now. The twins began splashing each other. It looked like light play at first, but suddenly—for no apparent reason—they both began to cry. Perhaps this would be good preparation for meeting the Caridan ambassador, Leia thought.

She squeezed her eyes shut as the two continued wailing. Threepio, growing more and more flustered, frantically tried to determine what the difficulty was.

Leia wished she knew where Han was.

17

The stolen shuttle plummeted into the Maw. Maelstroms of hot gas buffeted them from side to side as Kyp fought to guide Han along their tenuous course. The safe path was convoluted and treacherous where the gravitational singularities canceled each other out.

The Maw itself was one of the wonders of the galaxy. The very existence of a black hole cluster seemed astrophysically impossible and had led to much conjecture about its origin. Old Republic scientists cited probability arguments, that among the near-infinite stars in the universe, *something* like the Maw had to occur at least once. Other speculations, including those voiced by superstitious smugglers, suggested that the Maw had actually been *built*, assembled by a vastly powerful ancient race that had created the black holes in a barely stable configuration to open gateways into new dimensions.

At the moment, Han Solo cared only that the Maw was likely to be the cause of his death.

The shuttle's interior was dark and hot and stuffy. The wild colors and blazing light made psychedelic fireworks outside the ship and weird shadows inside. All lighting, life support, and temperature regulation had been shut down to increase power to the failing shields.

Han sweated in the pilot seat, watching the navigational controls he had relinquished to Kyp. Though he had been fighting for his life almost constantly during the past week, he missed Leia very much. She had no idea what had happened to him, and she must be terribly worried—but no doubt too proud to show it. Han hated even more to know that his children had finally returned from their sanctuary planet, and he hadn't been there to greet them.

But he would never see any of them again if the shuttle didn't survive passage through the Maw. Everything depended on Kyp Durron's mysterious abilities.

Kyp struggled with the controls, guiding the shuttle through some of the most delicate, most difficult maneuvers Han had ever seen—and Kyp kept his eyes closed! The young man seemed to be seeing through a different set of eyes, looking at some path not apparent with normal vision. Staring at the deadly black holes all around the shuttle, Han wanted to close his own eyes, too.

Kyp continued to negotiate the implacable obstacle course intuitively, threading through fragile points of stability. Chewbacca sat frozen with his own tension, afraid to disturb the young man's concentration.

Sparks flew on one of the far control panels as a shield gave out. Chewbacca growled as he jammed long fingers down on the controls, rerouting and spreading the remaining protection evenly around them. If a single gap appeared in the shields, the x-rays and fiery gases would tear them apart.

Kyp didn't flinch. "Coming up on the end of this ride," he said without opening his eyes. "There's a gravitationally safe island in the middle of the cluster, like the eye of a storm."

Han felt relief rush through him. "We'd better hide there for a while, recharge the power sources and make a few quick-and-dirty repairs." Chewbacca grunted his agreement.

"And take a good long rest," Kyp said. Han noticed a sheen of perspiration on his forehead. Despite his outward calm Kyp seemed to be concentrating enormously, straining his fledgling abilities. "We still have to find our way back out, you know."

The swirling ionized gases parted like a curtain thrown aside to reveal the gravitational oasis in the cluster's core, a safe haven for them to recuperate before returning to Coruscant.

"Made it!" Han said in a whisper.

But someone else had already found the hiding place.

Orbiting a small rocky island in the center of the Maw hung four gigantic Imperial Star Destroyers, bristling with weaponry.

Within a moment of their arrival swarms of TIE fighters poured out of the Star Destroyer hangar bays in a truly impressive show of force.

Han stared, unable to speak. They had just escaped execution at the hands of Skynxnex, the energy-spider attack in the spice mines, battle with the entire space fleet of Kessel, and destruction in the gravitational maze of the Maw. Now the shuttle's shields were failing, they had no weapons—and an Imperial armada had just been launched at them.

"The way things are going, we'll end up accidentally destroying the galaxy before suppertime," Han said. "Kick all the engines back on, Chewie! Let's turn this thing around. Kyp, find us another path out!"

"There aren't many paths to choose from," Kyp said.

The ship shuddered as if someone had kicked it from behind; then sparks sprayed out. Chewbacca groaned in dismay.

Han looked at the readouts. "All our shields just went out." He stared at the four Star Destroyers and the waves of TIE fighters and TIE Interceptors surging toward them. "I feel like we've got a big targeting cross painted right on our hull," Han said. "They can wipe us out with just a potshot." He glanced around, searching for something hard enough to kick; he found a bulkhead and lashed out at it.

The comm crackled, and for a moment Han expected another threatening message from Moruth Doole, but the ionized gases and distortions of the black holes would ruin any transmission passing through the outer shell of the Maw.

Gruff words spilled out of the speakers. "Imperial shuttle, welcome! It has been a long time since we received word from the outside. Please provide your security access code. Our TIE squadron is coming to escort you."

Han stiffened, remembering that they had stolen an old Imperial shuttle. They would have a few seconds before they were blown out of the sky. But a security access code? He had to think fast.

Han toggled the transmitter switch. "This is Imperial shuttle, uh . . . *Endor* coming in. We've, uh, had a rough ride through the Maw, and most of our computer systems are down. We request assistance." He paused, then swallowed. "Just how long has it been since you got news from the outside anyway?"

A loud click came from the other end. The TIE fighters continued toward them. Han squirmed, knowing his bluff couldn't work, that they were an unprotected target to be blown away by itchy Imperial trigger fingers.

The voice came back, gruffer and crisper this time. "Imperial shuttle *Endor*, we repeat—what is the security access code? Transmit immediately!"

Han turned to his copilot. "Chewie, how long until we get those shields?"

The Wookiee had removed the access panels on the side power compartments, yanking out masses of wires as he strung them through his fingers and tried to straighten the connections. Chewbacca sniffed to find burned circuits. It would be a long time before they had the systems even marginally functional again.

Han opened the transmitter circuit once more. "Uh, as I said, we've sustained substantial computer damage. We are unable to—"

"Unacceptable excuse! The code phrase is verbal."

"Just checking," Han said. "The code phrase is—" He looked to Kyp, desperately hoping that the young man would be able to pull the code out of the air, but even Luke Skywalker was unlikely to do something like that. Kyp could only shrug.

"Uh, the last code phrase we have is RJ-two stroke ZZ stroke eight thousand. Awaiting your confirmation." He clicked off, then looked at Chewbacca and Kyp, spreading his hands. "It was worth a try."

"Improper response," the gruff voice snapped.

"What a surprise," Han mumbled.

The transmission continued. "You have obviously not been sent by Grand Moff Tarkin. Shuttle *Endor*, you are to be taken prisoner immediately and brought aboard Imperial Star Destroyer *Gorgon* for deep interrogation. Any attempt at escape or resistance will result in your being destroyed."

Han wondered if he should bother to acknowledge, then decided against it. He was puzzled by the mention of Grand Moff Tarkin, the brutal governor who had built the first Death Star. Tarkin had been destroyed along with his doomsday weapon ten years before. Could these people have been out of touch for that long?

The shuttle lurched as if a giant invisible hand had grabbed it. Han could hear the metal plates groaning as pressure constricted the outer hull. "It's a tractor beam," he said.

The giant arrowhead shape of the flagship Star Destroyer loomed up at them. Chewbacca groaned something, and Han agreed. He had a bad feeling about this, too.

"Don't even bother, Chewie. We could never break that tractor beam, we could never run out of here fast enough, and we could never survive another passage through the Maw."

A squadron of TIE fighters surrounded the hijacked shuttle like a cocoon, making it impossible for them to deviate from the direct path of the tractor beam. The Star Destroyer *Gorgon* opened its huge receiving bay to swallow the prisoners. TIE fighters streaked up and into the cavernous metal mouth.

Han remembered being taken captive aboard the first Death Star in much the same way, flanked by Imperial starfighters, fighting against a powerful tractor beam. But that time he had been flying his own ship, and they had been able to hide in the *Falcon*'s secret storage compartments. Now they didn't even have uniforms to steal; they wore only the thermal prison suits used for working in the spice mines of Kessel.

"We're not going to make a very good impression," Kyp said.

The four Star Destroyers hovered over a cluster of interconnected rocky bodies at the very center of the Maw. Other constructions and skeletal debris orbited low to the asteroid archipelago.

Han wondered again what all this was. A staging area? A secret base? Why would the Empire have squandered so much firepower to protect the little clump of rocks below?

The tractor beam lifted the shuttle into the *Gorgon*'s bay and hauled it over to an isolated landing area. As the shuttle came to rest, Han heard faint groaning and ticking sounds, like a chorus of mechanical sighs of relief from the battered ship. Armed stormtroopers hustled into position, running in regimented columns that showed they were still well drilled, still highly trained. They carried old-model blasters held at the ready.

"We'd better see what they want," Han said. "Any bright ideas?"

"Only dim ones," Kyp answered with a shake of his dark head.

Han sighed in resignation. "Let's go out together. Hands up and move very slowly."

Chewbacca grumbled that he had no particular aversion to dying while fighting, if they were going to be executed anyway.

"We don't know that," Han said. "Let's go."

Chewbacca, the most intimidating, took the central position while Han and the smaller form of Kyp Durron flanked him. They walked out and surrendered. The stormtroopers instantly directed their weapons toward the three. Han wondered how he could have earned himself such an unrelenting streak of bad luck.

At a signal for attention the back ranks of stormtroopers snapped erect, shouldering their weapons, while the front ranks held unwavering aim at the prisoners. Han watched as doors at the rear of the landing bay slid open and a tall woman strode through, accompanied by a bodyguard on each side.

She had a slender build and precise movements. She wore an olive-gray jumpsuit and black gloves. She marched forward, paying little attention to those around her, as if the troops were mere fixtures. She fastened her gaze on the prisoners.

Her most striking feature was a full head of hair that billowed around her shoulders and disappeared to some unknown length down her back. Her hair was the color of hot copper and seemed to crackle with an electric life of its own. Her eyes were green and piercing, like turbolaser bolts.

She walked straight toward them. Han saw the insignia at her collar and was taken aback to recognize the rank of a full admiral. Han had attended the Imperial academy himself when he was young and knew that a woman reaching the rank of admiral was unheard of. Emperor Palpatine had had a well-known prejudice against nonhumans, but he sustained more subtle discrimination against women, rarely promoting even those who passed the rigorous tests. For this woman to have the rank of full admiral—especially of a small fleet of Imperial-class Star Destroyers—was remarkable. Han put himself immediately on guard; this was no person to be trifled with.

She stopped at the foot of the ramp and looked stiffly up at them. Her features were as finely carved and as cold and rigid as a statue's. Her lips barely moved as she spoke.

"I am Admiral Daala, in charge of the fleet guarding Maw Installation." She flashed her green glance to each of them in turn. "You three are in a lot of trouble."

18

Luke and Artoo had little to do as Lando Calrissian piloted the *Lady Luck* toward Kessel. A nebulous haze of escaping atmosphere surrounded the potato-shaped rock, while the jagged garrison moon rode in its close orbit.

"Welcome to the garden spot of the galaxy," Lando said.

Luke thought of his home planet of Tatooine, the Dune Sea, the Great Pit of Carkoon, the Jundland Wastes. "I've seen worse," he said. Artoo bleeped in agreement.

Lando leaned closer to the viewports. "Yeah, well don't make any hasty judgments. We haven't looked at this place up close yet." He opened a comm channel. If Kessel had a good tracking network, the station should have pinpointed the *Lady Luck* the moment they came out of hyperspace. "Hello, Kessel! Is anybody listening? I'm looking for someone named Moruth Doole. I've got a business proposition for him. Please respond."

"Who is this?" a startled-sounding voice broke in. "Identify yourself."

"Name's Tymmo, and if you want any other information, have Doole ask me himself." Lando grinned at Luke. They thought using the fake name of the scam artist from the blob races added another bit of irony to their mission. "In the meantime my associate and I have some money to dispose of—half a million credits, to be exact—so run along and fetch Doole."

The speaker remained silent, evidently while the communications officer conferred with someone; then the answer came back. "We're transmitting parameters for a holding orbit, Mr., uh, Tymmo. Follow these instructions precisely. Our energy shield is currently operational and will disintegrate you if you make an unauthorized attempt to land. Do you understand?"

Luke looked at Lando, and they both shrugged. Lando spoke into the comm channel, "We'll wait right here for Doole to roll out the welcome mat. But if he takes too long, I'll go spend my cash somewhere else." He laced his fingers behind his head and leaned back in the pilot's chair. Below, Kessel filled the viewports. It was Lando's job to fast-talk them into places, while Luke would keep his eyes and Jedi senses open for any trace of Han.

Before leaving Coruscant they had doctored up false personal backgrounds for themselves, removing any mention of the New Republic but keeping enough hints at shady dealings and fast transactions to provide corroborating evidence. Luke would remain nameless, if at all possible.

A raspy voice finally burst out of the speakers. "Mr. Tymmo? This is Moruth Doole. Do I know you?"

"Not at the moment . . . but I've got a large and liquid credit account that says you might want to."

They heard a bubbling intake of breath. "And what might that mean? My communications officer said something about half a million credits?"

"I recently hit it big at the Umgullian blob races. I'm looking for a place to invest the credits, and I've always thought there was money to be made in spice mining. You willing to talk?"

Doole barely paused. "Half a million credits is certainly worth talking about. I'll send a flyer escort for you. They'll take you through a safe corridor in the energy shield."

"I look forward to meeting you face-to-face," Lando said.

Doole only made a hissing, froglike sound.

Lando left the *Lady Luck* on the landing pad of the Imperial Correction Facility, surrounded by scout vehicles, ground transports, and other ships that had been cannibalized for functional parts. He stood dressed in finery, smiling and bright-eyed. Beside him Luke wore a nondescript jumpsuit from which all insignia had been removed.

A squad dressed in hodgepodge stormtrooper armor and prison uniforms led Luke, Lando, and Artoo-Detoo toward the enormous trapezoidal edifice of the correction facility. The brooding mass of the prison seemed to throb with years of pain and punishment, working at Luke's enhanced senses. He remained silent, on guard. At least the escorts kept their weapons holstered and behaved in as welcoming a fashion as they could manage.

They rode the tube elevators that climbed the sloping front wall of the prison. Through the transparisteel Luke watched the wastelands of Kessel spread hopelessly in front of them.

When the elevators opened into the mirrored administrative substructure, the guards motioned them to follow. Clerks, bureaucrats, and seedy-looking functionaries bustled through the halls, looking busier than they wanted to be. Luke wondered if Doole had staged this activity as an impressive show for Lando; but the frantic scrambling seemed more chaotic than efficient.

Moruth Doole himself met them in one of the corridors. The squat amphibian rubbed his splayed hands together and bobbed his head at them. A mechanical contraption covering one eye focused and refocused itself.

"Welcome, Mr. Tymmo!" Doole said. "Let me apologize for our turmoil here. You haven't picked a very good time to visit. Yesterday I lost my right-hand man and my primary shift boss in a tunnel mishap. Please excuse me if I seem a bit . . . flustered."

"Quite all right," Lando said, shaking Doole's extended hand. "I've been administrator of several large mining operations myself. Sometimes the planet itself doesn't want to cooperate."

"Very true!" Doole said, opening and closing his mouth like a young rawwk begging for food. "Interesting way of looking at it."

"I hope the disaster didn't hurt your spice production too much?" Lando said.

"Oh, we'll be back up to full output in no time."

Lando gestured to Luke. "My associate is here to help me check out the details of spice mining and to advise me on its potential as an investment." He took a deep breath. "I know I must have taken you by surprise. Tell me, is there any part of your operation that I might invest in?"

Doole motioned for them to follow toward his office. His lizard-skin waistcoat rippled in the uncertain light of the corridors. "Come in, and we'll talk some more."

Doole waddled ahead, turning his head from side to side as if he had trouble seeing where he was going. Inside the former warden's office Doole indicated for them to take a seat. Artoo idled beside Luke.

Glancing around the office, Luke noticed the carbon-frozen man hanging on one wall; the life-support indicator lights on the control panel were all dark. "Friend of yours?" he asked.

Doole sputtered a hissing laugh. "A former rival. He used to be warden of the prison here, before our little revolution brought genuine capitalism to the spice-mining industry." He sat down heavily behind the desk. "May I offer you any refreshment?"

Once seated, Lando folded his hands in his lap. "I'd rather talk business first. If our negotiations look promising, maybe we can celebrate with a drink."

"Good policy," Doole said, rubbing his hands again. "Now then, I've been thinking ever since your transmission, and I may well have something that could be the perfect investment. It so happens that just before his demise, our shift boss uncovered an exceptionally rich deposit of glitterstim spice. It'll take a good amount of money and effort to make repairs in the collapsed tunnel and to exploit this resource, but the payoff can be greater than your wildest dreams."

"I have some pretty wild dreams," Lando said, flashing his broadest smile.

Luke interrupted with a stern, skeptical voice. "Those are extravagant claims, Mr. Doole. Would you allow our Artoo unit to tap into your network and inspect the profit/loss picture of your operations for, say, the past two years? That will give me hard data on which to make a recommendation to Mr. Tymmo."

Doole squirmed on being asked to open his records, but Lando pulled his credit-transfer card from his pocket. "I can assure you the droid will do no damage to your data system, and I'd be happy to give you a small deposit, if it would make you feel more comfortable. Say, five thousand?"

Doole was trapped between his own uneasy wish for confidentiality and his need to appear aboveboard in front of a potential big investor—not to mention wanting the five thousand credits for its own sake.

"I suppose that would be all right. But I can give your droid access for only five minutes. It shouldn't need any more time than that to find the information."

Luke nodded. "That'll be fine, thank you." Artoo wouldn't waste effort checking out bogus profit/loss reports anyway. He would begin immediately trying to track down any record of Han Solo, Chewbacca, or the *Millennium Falcon*.

Humming forward, Artoo jacked into the terminal port beside Moruth Doole's desk. His data-link arm whirred as it accessed the information buried in the prison complex's computer.

While they waited, Lando continued his discussion with Doole. "I'd like to see all aspects of your spice mining and production. I'm sure you can arrange a tour immediately. Let us observe firsthand how the business works. *Including* these collapsed tunnels of yours—maybe I'd like to invest in repairs, if a good payoff seems likely."

"Uh," Doole said, looking behind him as if to find an excuse. "As I said, now is not a very good time. Perhaps we could arrange a more convenient time for you to come back—" Doole spread his squishy hands.

Lando shrugged eloquently and stood as if to leave. "I understand. If you're not interested, I can go someplace else. This money is burning a hole in my account. I want to do something with it, right *now*. There are other spice mines on other planets."

"Ah, but they are sources of ryll spice, not glitterstim—"

"They are still profitable."

Artoo withdrew and chittered to Luke. Though Luke only partially understood the droid's language, he heard enough to know that Artoo had not found Han, nor anything particularly incriminating as far as Doole was concerned. If the information banks had held any record of the *Falcon*, they had been wiped clean.

"Well, what's your droid's opinion?" Doole asked, hearing the bleeps.

"He finds nothing out of the ordinary," Luke said. He exchanged a dejected glance with Lando.

Doole stood up, beaming. "All right. I understand your concerns, Mr. Tymmo. Sometimes inconvenience must take precedence in business matters. I wouldn't want you to leave Kessel with any doubts. Come, I'll show you the spice-processing line, then we'll arrange a tour of the newly opened tunnels."

He burbled off, leading the way as they followed, still looking for any sign of Han.

A floater car took them across the surface to the entrance shaft of the collapsed tunnels. Luke and Lando ducked involuntarily as they sped into the narrow corkscrew passage.

"This was the site of an illegal mining operation back when the Imperial Correction Facility was in full control," Doole said, raising his voice above the sound of the speeding engines. "The perpetrators were caught, and this access shaft was sealed off until a recent avalanche opened everything up again."

Doole took them down into a wide grotto where part of the ceiling had fallen in. Wan light spilled down, illuminating the open areas. Workers had strung lights around the perimeter as they hammered and hauled broken rock. A crew of thirty or so milled around the chamber, shoring up walls and removing debris. The tunnels out of the grotto had been blocked by portable pneumatic doors that sealed the rest of the tunnels in blackness.

"This is a rare opportunity, Mr. Tymmo," Doole said. He had grown more and more loquacious after showing them the spice-processing rooms where the blind larvae packaged glitterstim. "Spice must be mined in total darkness, so we almost never get to see the tunnels in direct illumination. But the avalanche let in sunlight that spoiled all this glitterstim anyway. We sealed off the other shafts to preserve the rest."

"So what really happened here?" Lando asked, looking around.

"Tectonic disturbance," Doole said.

Luke could see the blackened marks where powerful blaster strikes had scored the stone walls, and he knew there was much more to this than simple seismic activity.

He felt a surge of startled fear from Lando. "What's that thing!" Lando pointed to the other side of the grotto.

Buried under a pile of jagged rubble, dozens of glassy spearlike legs protruded at all angles. Dim jewellike nodules dotted the spherical body core, eyes glazed in death. The rest of the body seemed to be made entirely of fangs. Falling chunks of rock had crushed it, and the creature's whiplike legs lay askew as if it had tried to flail the boulders aside.

Doole strutted over to the carcass. "That, my friends, seems to be the thing that creates the spice itself. It's the first such creature we've encountered, but there must be others deep in the tunnels. We're getting a xenobiologist to study it. The bulk of its body seems to be made of glitterstim itself, and the strands we pull from the tunnel walls are what it uses as a web." Doole stopped short of actually touching the fallen monster.

The guard in charge of dissection joined them. He nudged one of the sharp crystalline legs with his boot. "We want to see if we can extract raw glitterstim from the web sac and spinnerets in the dead body."

Doole bobbed his head up and down. "Wouldn't that be something? Absolutely pure glitterstim!"

Lando nodded noncommittally. Luke, playing his part, fished around for more information. "So how does this affect your safety record? Did this creature prey on any of the miners?"

"Yes, it killed several, including the shift boss and my assistant—the ones I told you about. How many bodies have you found so far?" Doole asked the guard.

"Three fresh ones and two old ones, and we think it killed a bunch more. There's a big Wookiee and some other prisoners still unaccounted for."

Doole scowled at the guard, but quickly regained his false smile.

Luke felt cold upon hearing the news. Of course, there was no way of knowing whether the Wookiee in question was Chewbacca—the Empire had taken a great many slaves from the Wookiee homeworld of Kashyyyk, and many survivors could well have been shipped off to Kessel. Luke met Lando's gaze, and the other man shook his head ever so slightly. "Very interesting," Lando said.

"Come on, there's more to see," Doole said as he strode back to the floating cars. "I hope all this is impressing you."

"Certainly is," Lando said. "You have an amazing operation here, Moruth."

Luke remained silent. All day long he had been straining his senses, searching for some echo of Han or Chewbacca, but he had found nothing.

Plenty of others wallowed in pain and misery here, but Luke found no hint of the ones he sought.

Han Solo might never have reached Kessel, and he was certainly no longer there. At least not alive.

19

The admiral's quarters on an Imperial-class Star Destroyer were spacious and functional, and they had been Daala's only home for more than a decade.

Year after year she operated in a vacuum, alone as always, following Tarkin's parting instructions with no further input from the Grand Moff. The great distortion of the Maw itself blacked out all external holonet transmissions. Her fleet had been isolated, and the crew on her four Star Destroyers had fallen into a routine, but Daala did not relax her grip. She was afraid to wonder about events outside in the galaxy, confident at least that she could count on the Empire with its unbending rules, sometimes cruel but always clear-cut.

But now, in her turmoil, she was glad her quarters were sealed and locked, quiet and empty, so no one could see her like this. It would ruin her image entirely. Everything had been cut-and-dried before the interrogation of the new prisoners. . . .

Daala punched up the recording and watched it again, though she had already replayed the sequence a dozen times. She could mouth the words as the prisoner spoke them, but this tiny image could not convey the impact she had felt when watching him firsthand.

The man, Han Solo, sat strapped in a nightmarish, convoluted chair with steel tubes and wires and piping tangled around him. The gadgetry looked sharp and ominous—most of it served no purpose other than to increase the prisoner's terror, and in that it proved effective.

On the recording, Daala stood by Commander Kratas, the captain of her flagship, the *Gorgon*. She could smell the prisoner's fear, but his demeanor was full of bluster and sarcasm. He would crack easily.

"Tell us where you come from," Daala said. "Is the Rebel Alliance crushed yet? What has happened in the Empire?"

"Go kiss a Hutt!" Solo snapped.

Daala stared woodenly at him for a moment, then shrugged, nodding to Kratas. The commander punched a control pad, and one of the metal bars across the restraining chair hummed.

The muscles in Solo's left thigh began to spasm, jittering. His leg bounced up and down. The spasms grew worse. He had a puzzled, confused look on his face, as if he couldn't understand why his own body was suddenly behaving so strangely. The involuntary seizure clenched the muscles under his skin.

Daala smiled.

Kratas adjusted one of the controls, and Solo flinched as the muscles along the left side of his rib cage also began spasming, tightening his body, but the chair would not let him move. Solo fought back an outcry.

The seizures were not so painful as they were maddening. Daala had found that a most effective interrogation technique was simply to induce an unrelenting facial tick that made the eyes blink over and over and over again for hours without end.

"Tell us about the Empire," she said again.

"The Empire is in the garbage masher!" Solo said. Daala could see the whites of his eyes as Solo tried to look down at his rebellious leg muscles. "The Emperor is dead. He died in the explosion of the second Death Star."

Daala and Kratas both snapped their heads up. "Second Death Star? Tell me about it."

"No," Solo said.

"Yes," Daala said.

Kratas adjusted another button. The bars in the labyrinthine chair hummed, and Solo's right hand began twitching, his fingers scrabbling against the smooth metal, jittering and shaking. Solo tried to look everywhere at once.

"The second Death Star?" Daala asked again.

"It was still under construction when we set off a chain reaction in its core. Darth Vader and the Emperor were on board." Solo resisted, but he seemed to delight in telling the news.

"And what happened to the first Death Star?" Daala said.

Solo grinned. "The Alliance blew it up, too."

Daala was skeptical enough that she didn't believe him entirely. A prisoner would say anything, especially a defiant one like this. But in her gut she feared it might be true—because it explained other things, such as the years of silence.

"And what about Grand Moff Tarkin?"

"He's in a billion atoms scattered across the Yavin system. He burned with his Death Star. He paid for the lives of all the people on Alderaan, a planet he destroyed."

"Alderaan is destroyed?" Daala raised her eyebrows.

Kratas increased the power vibrating through the chair. Tiny pearls of sweat appeared on his own forehead. Daala knew what the commander was thinking: during all these years of isolation they had been assuming the Emperor would maintain his iron grip, that the fleet of all-powerful Star Destroyers and the secret Death Star would cement Imperial rule across the galaxy. The Old Republic had lasted a thousand generations. And the Empire . . . could it have fallen in just a few decades?

"How long since the explosion of the second Death Star?"

"Seven years."

"What has happened since?" Daala finally sat down. "Tell me everything."

But Solo seemed to gain inner strength and clammed up. He glared with his dark, angry eyes. Daala sighed. It was like a rehearsed show they had to perform. Kratas adjusted the controls until Solo's entire body was a writhing, spasming mass of twitching muscles, as if a storm were happening inside his body.

Gradually, the prisoner spilled the entire story of the other battles, the civil war, Grand Admiral Thrawn, the resurrected Emperor, the truce at Bakura, the terrible conflicts in which the waning Empire had been defeated again and again—until finally she had Kratas release him. The loud humming of the chair suddenly stopped, and Han Solo slumped into exhausted bliss at being freed from the onslaught of his own muscles.

Daala motioned outside the door of the holding cell, summoning a glossy black interrogation droid that floated in with hypodermic needles glistening like spears in the dim reddish light. Solo tried to cringe back, and Daala could see the fear in his eyes.

"There," Daala said. "Now the interrogator droid will confirm everything you told us." She got up and left.

Later she had found out that Solo was indeed telling the truth in everything he said. Alone in her quarters, Admiral Daala switched off the recording. Her head pounded with a gnawing, throbbing ache like dull fingernails scraping the inside of her skull.

One of the Maw Installation scientists, learning that the new prisoner had actually been on board the completed Death Star, demanded to speak with him. Daala would send the scientist this interrogation report—after she edited it, of course. Sometimes it was impossible to keep these prima donna scientists happy. They had such a narrow view of things.

Right now Daala had greater worries. She had to decide what to do with this new information.

In her quarters Daala stood between two full-length curved mirrors that projected a reflection of her body, head to toe. Her olive-gray uniform showed no wrinkle, only crisp creases and near-invisible seams. Through a strict regimen of exercises and drills, she had not added a fraction to her weight during her long assignment; her appearance, though older and harder now, still pleased her.

Daala wore her bright admiral's insignia proudly over her left breast: a row of six scarlet rectangles set above a row of blue rectangles. To her knowledge she was the only woman ever to wear such a rank in the Imperial Navy. It had been a special promotion, given directly by Grand Moff Tarkin himself, and it was possible the Emperor did not even know of it. He certainly did not know about the Maw Installation.

Her coppery hair flowed over her shoulders, rippled down her back to below her hips. More than a decade ago Daala had arrived at Maw Installation with her hair cropped short and bristly, part of the humiliation the Imperial military academy inflicted upon female candidates.

After being sealed inside the Maw, though, Daala was placed in charge by direct order from Tarkin. Asinine regulations-for-the-sake-of-regulations meant nothing to her anymore. She refused to cut her hair, as a gesture of her own independence: rank had its privileges. She felt Tarkin would have approved. But Tarkin was dead now.

Turning, she dimmed the lights, then activated the door. Outside, two bodyguards snapped to attention and continued staring ahead. Despite Maw Installation's isolation, Daala insisted on peak performance, regular drills, war-gaming sessions. She had been trained in the Imperial military mold; though the system had done its best to squash her ambitions, Daala followed its tenets.

Beneath their armor the two guards were well built and attractive; but Daala had not taken a lover since Grand Moff Tarkin. After him fantasizing had been enough.

"Escort me to the shuttle bay," she said, stepping into the corridor. "I'm going down to the Installation." She strode off, hearing the bodyguards march behind her, weapons ready. "Inform the duty commander that I have a meeting with Tol Sivron." One of the bodyguards muttered into his helmet comlink.

She strode down the corridors, pondering the complexity of her ship, the troops, the support personnel. In the Imperial fleet a single Star Destroyer housed thirty-seven thousand crew and ninety-seven hundred troops, but because of the secrecy of the Maw Installation, Tarkin had assigned her only a skeleton crew—people without families, without connections to the outside, some recruited from worlds devastated by the early battles of the Empire.

Even under rigid discipline, though, her crew had been trapped here for eleven years with no furloughs, no R and R other than the meager amusement facilities available on board. Her troops had grown weary of the entertainment libraries—restless, bored, and angry at being placed on standby alert for so long without word from the outside. They were well armed and itching to go out and *do* something—as was Daala herself.

At her fingertips Daala had the might of sixty turbolaser batteries, sixty ion cannons, and ten tractor-beam projectors, one of which had just been used to capture the battered Imperial shuttle. Inside the hangar bays the *Gorgon* alone carried six TIE fighter squadrons, two gamma-class assault shuttles, twenty AT-AT walkers, and thirty AT-ST scout walkers.

Three more identical ships, the *Manticore*, the *Basilisk*, and the *Hydra*, orbited Maw Installation, also under Daala's command. Years ago Moff Tarkin had taken Daala herself to the Kuat Drive Yards to watch her four Star Destroyers under construction.

Tarkin and Daala had flown a small inspection shuttle around the enormous superstructures being assembled in orbit. The two remained silent for the most part, staring at the enormity of the project. Around them in space the tiny lights of workers, transport vessels, rubble smelters, and girder extruders made a hive of activity.

Tarkin had placed a hand on her shoulders, squeezing with a grip made of steel cords. "Daala," he said, "I am giving you enough power to turn any planet to slag."

Now, aboard the Star Destroyer *Gorgon*, Admiral Daala entered a personnel lift that took her and her bodyguards from the command quarters below the bridge tower to one of the hangar bays. She did not announce her arrival when the doors slid open. Daala was pleased to see her troops bustling about the TIE fighters, the shuttles, and service vehicles. After so many years of boredom, her personnel kept every system functioning perfectly.

Only months after the completion of Maw Installation, Daala had noticed a malaise creeping through the personnel. Part of it was because of her, she was sure; commanded by the only female flag officer, assigned to baby-sit a bunch of scientists in the most protected spot in the galaxy, the troops had grown lax. But a few graphic executions and continual threats kept Daala's crew constantly on edge, honing their skills and making it inconceivable for them to shirk their duties.

That tactic had been one of Tarkin's prime lessons. *Command through the fear of force rather than force itself.* Daala had 180,000 people at her disposal, not counting the weapons designers in Maw Installation itself. She did not want to waste them.

She glanced up and down the hangar, her molten-metal hair trailing behind her. Inside an electromagnetic cage that shielded the entire vessel, technicians scoured the battered Imperial shuttle *Endor* that had been brought in by the new captives. *Endor*—what kind of name was that? She had never heard the term before. The technicians would be checking for service markings, locator beacons, and course-log files.

For a moment Daala considered taking the battered shuttle itself down to Tol Sivron, the chief scientist of Maw Installation; the effect would probably shock him into paying attention to her for once. But that would be a childish gesture. She let the technicians continue their work and chose instead the Imperial shuttle *Edict.*

"I can pilot this myself," she said to her bodyguards. "Leave me." On the flight down she wanted time alone. She knew what Sivron would say on hearing the news, but this time she would not let him get away with it.

The bodyguards dropped back and to the side as Daala stepped up the ramp into the shuttle. She moved with quick, habitual movements, powering up the engines, running through the automated checklist. She mounted the headset nodes to her temple and to her ear, listening to her course vector as she raised the *Edict* from its pad and arrowed it out through the magnetic shields that closed off the hangar bay from the vacuum of space.

Surrounding her was the colorful, deadly shell of gases swirling into the endless gullets of black holes. Below hung Maw Installation itself, a cluster of planetoids crammed at the exact center of the gravitational island. The surfaces of the barren rocks touched in some places, grinding together. Immense bridges and bands held the asteroids in place. Access tubes and transit rails connected the cluster of drifting rocks.

Under Grand Moff Tarkin's direction Imperial constructors had ferried the rocks across space and through the obstacle course into the Maw. The insides of the asteroids were hollowed out into habitation chambers, laboratory areas, prototype assembly bays, and meeting halls.

If we present the citizens with a weapon so powerful, so immense as to defy all conceivable attack against it, a weapon invulnerable and invincible in battle, that shall become the symbol for the Empire. Daala had read a draft of the communiqué Tarkin had sent to the Emperor, urging the creation of superweapons. *We may need only a handful of these weapons to subjugate thousands of worlds, each containing millions upon millions of beings. Such a weapon must have force great enough to dispatch an entire system, and the fear it shall inspire will be great enough for you to rule the galaxy unchallenged.*

After getting permission for his scheme, Tarkin had used his new authority as Grand Moff to put together this supersecret think-tank installation, where he could isolate the most brilliant scientists and theoreticians, giving them orders to develop new weapons for the Emperor. Since Tarkin took credit for everything without citing his sources, the Emperor himself did not know of the installation's existence.

The workers and architects who built the place had boarded a return ship, thinking their job finished, but Daala had reprogrammed their navicomputers herself with an incorrect course out of the Maw. Instead of flying to their freedom, they had plunged straight into the mouth of a black hole. No loose ends.

The secret of Maw Installation had been protected. After Tol Sivron and his teams proved the initial concept of the Death Star, Grand Moff Tarkin had taken one of the Installation's top scientists, Bevel Lemelisk, to the Outer Rim to oversee actual construction of the first production-model Death Star.

Tarkin's last words to the Maw scientists had been a challenge: "Good. Now create an even more powerful weapon. Surpassing the Death Star may seem inconceivable, but we must maintain our superiority, we must maintain a sense of fear among the citizens of the Empire. The Death Star *is* terrible. Think of something worse. That is your reason for existence."

Tarkin gave them nine years to develop his next-generation ultimate weapon. And now, since Tarkin was dead and no one else knew Maw Installation even existed—Daala could make her own decisions, plan her own course of action.

Finally reaching the small gravity field of the central administrative asteroid, Daala secured the shuttle *Edict* in the docking bay. She stood beside her shuttle, breathing deeply of the dusty, exhaust-laden air and already wishing she could be back on the gleaming and sterile decks of the *Gorgon*. She would deal with Tol Sivron quickly, then return.

A contingent of stormtroopers assigned to ground duty bustled to assist her. "Follow me," she said. A show of force would smother any protests from the scientist administrator.

She did not announce her arrival but strode directly through the anterooms, startling the various clerks and administrative assistants. The stormtroopers stood at attention. The clerks stared at them, then slowly took their seats again and refrained from making any outbursts.

"Tol Sivron, I need to speak with you," Daala said, entering his office. "I have some important news."

The scientist administrator's office was cluttered, but with all the wrong things. More a bureaucrat than a scientist, Tol Sivron required the theoreticians and designers to build concept models and tiny prototypes of their ideas, which Sivron left on shelves, on furniture, in alcoves. Daala guessed that Sivron played with them as toys during dull moments.

Around the office lay piles of proposals, design studies, regular progress reports, charts of optimized parameters that the scientist administrator required in hardcopy. His clerks studied these reports, then wrote their own reports summarizing them and referencing still further documents. Daala didn't believe the administrator read any of them.

Tol Sivron swiveled his chair to look at her with a bored expression. "News? We haven't had any news in a decade."

Sivron was a Twi'lek, pasty-faced and hairless, with two whiplike head-tails that dangled from his skull. The tentacles fell over his shoulders like two skinless blood-eels sucking the back of his cranium. Sivron's close-set piglike eyes and mouthful of jagged teeth heightened Daala's disgust. Twi'leks were generally a disreputable lot, slinking around with smugglers and acting as henchmen for crime lords like Jabba the Hutt. Though Daala rarely questioned Grand Moff Tarkin's decisions, she didn't understand how Tol Sivron had obtained his position here.

"Well, we have news today. We captured three prisoners who blundered into the Maw in a stolen Imperial shuttle. We have put them all through deep questioning, and I see no reason to doubt the veracity of this information, as unpleasant as it may seem."

"So what is this unpleasant information?"

Daala kept her face absolutely rigid. "The Emperor is dead, the Rebels have won. A few warlords tried to put the Empire back together, but they merely caused years of civil war. A new Republic is now the primary government in the galaxy."

Sivron sat up in shock. In a nervous gesture his head-tails coiled behind his neck. "But how could that happen? With our Death Star design—"

"Grand Moff Tarkin built one Death Star, but the Rebels managed to steal the plans, and somehow they discovered a flaw, a thermal-exhaust port that allowed one small fighter access to the reactor core. The Rebels destroyed the Death Star and killed Tarkin."

"I'll assign a team to look over the plans so we can correct this flaw!" Sivron said, a matter of pride to him. "At once!"

"How is that going to help anything now?" Daala snapped. "Tarkin had Bevel Lemelisk with him on the outside. After the first Death Star was destroyed, the Emperor himself asked Lemelisk to design a larger model, this time eliminating the known flaw. The second Death Star was still under construction when the Rebels destroyed it."

Sivron scowled, as if trying to figure out how he could solve a problem already several years old. As the years stretched out with no word from outside, Sivron had sent self-destructing drones through the fiery walls of the Maw, carrying coded transmission bursts, updates for Tarkin. Daala had strict orders not to leave Maw Installation, and so they waited. And waited.

Daala's primary mistake had been overestimating the abilities of her mentor, Tarkin. She had graduated from the Imperial military academy on Carida, one of the toughest training grounds for military service in the Empire. She had excelled in every curriculum, defeated many warriors in single combat, used her strategic skills to wipe out entire armies in war games.

But because she was a woman, and because female officers were extremely rare in Imperial military service, the Caridan academy assigned Daala to difficult, thankless jobs, while they promoted the less talented men—men she herself had bested time and again—into positions of authority.

Out of frustration Daala had created a false persona in the computer networks, a pseudonym under which she could make suggestions that would be listened to. After a handful of these truly radical ideas paid off, Moff Tarkin had come to Carida to find this brilliant new tactician—but his detective work had uncovered Daala instead.

Luckily, Tarkin was more innovative and open-minded than the Emperor. He quietly reassigned Daala to his personal staff, took her to the Outer Rim territories on his fleet of Star Destroyers, and let her work with him.

They became lovers, two like minds, hard in spirit and unforgiving. Though he was older than she, Tarkin had a power and a charisma that Daala admired. Gaunt and tireless in his quiet viciousness, he had a self-confidence so great that he did not flinch even in the presence of Darth Vader.

To keep Daala hidden, Grand Moff Tarkin gave her four Star Destroyers and charged her with the task of guarding Maw Installation. But now that she had obtained new information from the captives, everything was changed. Everything.

Sivron stared at her with anger glowing in his eyes. "Where are these captives now?"

"In detention cells on board the *Gorgon*. They are recuperating from the . . . rigors of interrogation."

"What if someone comes looking for them?" He turned to glance out the transparisteel window on his office wall.

"They were escapees from the spice-mining operation on Kessel. They had no idea where they were going. They'll be presumed lost in the Maw— I myself can't understand how they survived the passage through the cluster in the first place."

"Why didn't you just dispose of them?" Sivron asked.

Daala maintained her patience with an effort. This was yet another example of Twi'lek shortsightedness. "Because they are the only link with the outside we've had in a decade. Qwi Xux has already requested an interview with the prisoners to ask them for details about the actual Death Star. We may need to pump them for further information—before we decide what to do next."

Sivron blinked his piggish eyes. "What to do? What do you mean? What *is* there to do?"

She crossed her arms over her chest. "We can take the new Sun Crusher and destroy the New Republic system by system." She stared at him with her green eyes, not blinking.

The Twi'lek squirmed. "But the Sun Crusher isn't finished yet. We still have tests to run, reports to file—"

"You have been procrastinating for two years. You are behind schedule thanks to your bureaucracy and ineptness. Grand Moff Tarkin is not coming back, and you no longer have an excuse to delay. I need the weapon now, and I'm going to take it."

Her mind kept replaying the words Tarkin had told her while inspecting the Kuat Drive Yards. *I am giving you enough power to turn any planet to slag.* And with the newly designed Sun Crusher weapon, she could bring the New Republic to its knees.

"If Solo is telling the truth," Daala said, "then my fleet could be the most powerful remnant of the Imperial Navy." She picked up one of Tol Sivron's small models. "We can't just wait here any longer. Now it's our turn to show them what we can do."

20

The Caridan ambassador arrived with his entourage on the recently repaired west landing platform, far from the Imperial Palace. His diplomatic shuttle looked like a glossy black beetle, bristling with weapons that had been remotely neutralized before the ship was allowed to approach Coruscant.

On the landing platform Leia waited to greet Ambassador Furgan with a full contingent of New Republic honor guard. The wind picked up, blowing around the tall buildings, as if trying to push the Caridan delegation back in the direction it had come. She wore her formal government robes as well as rank insignia for the Alliance forces.

Carida, with its powerful military training center, was one of the most important strongholds still loyal to the Empire. If she could crack open negotiations with them, her coup would not be soon forgotten. But the Caridan system was going to be a tough jewel-fruit to crack, especially with a rude and icy ambassador like Furgan.

The shuttle's hatch hissed open as the denser air of Carida rushed out. Two stormtroopers marched down the ramp, shouldering ceremonial blaster rifles equipped with bayonets. Their white armor gleamed from meticulous polishing. They moved like droids, walking off the ramp and stepping to either side, then freezing in position as a second pair of stormtroopers followed them down and waited at the end of the ramp.

Ambassador Furgan strode down, stubby-legged and self-important, as if to ceremonial music. His uniform was spattered with more badges, insignia, and ribbons than any person could possibly have earned in a lifetime.

After two more stormtrooper officers followed the ambassador down, Furgan drew a deep breath, looking into the distance and ignoring Leia. "Ah, the air of Imperial Center." He turned toward the waiting reception committee, beetling his thick brows. "Smells a bit sour now, though. The taint of rebellion."

Leia disregarded the comment. "Welcome to Coruscant, Ambassador Furgan. I am Minister of State Leia Organa Solo."

"Yes, yes," Furgan said impatiently. "After Mon Mothma's words about the extreme importance of Carida, I expected her to send more than a minor official to greet me. A slap in the face."

Leia had to fall back on some of Luke's temper-controlling exercises, a Jedi mind-blanking technique that allowed her to quell the surge of anger. "I see you have not taken the time to familiarize yourself with the structure of our government, Ambassador. Though Mon Mothma is the New Republic's Chief of State, the Cabinet is the actual governing body, of which the Minister of State and my subordinate diplomatic corps comprise perhaps the most important arm."

Leia stopped herself, angry with Furgan for goading her, and angry with herself for letting him manipulate her into petty games. Mon Mothma had instructed her to extend every diplomatic courtesy to the ambassador. She wished Han or Luke were there beside her.

"Mon Mothma has a great many other duties, but she has arranged for a brief face-to-face meeting with you later in the day," Leia said. "Until then, would you like me to show you to your quarters? Some refreshment, perhaps, after your journey?"

Furgan's eyes looked like small, overripe berries as he directed his gaze at her. "My bodyguards will go to my quarters first. They will sweep every inch of the rooms, every appliance, every wall and floor to remove hidden listening devices or assassination tools. The remaining guards will be with me at every moment. They will provide my food and drink from our own supplies to ensure against any possibility of poisoning."

Leia was appalled at his insinuation. She stopped herself from insisting that Furgan's actions were not necessary, since that would no doubt play directly into his hands. Instead, she showed him a small indulgent smile. "Of course, if such things make you feel more comfortable. . . ."

"In the meantime," Furgan said, "I would like an immediate tour of the Imperial Palace. Arrange one. I came on a pilgrimage to see my Emperor's home and to pay my respects."

Leia hesitated. "We hadn't planned on—"

Furgan held up a hand. Beside him the stormtroopers snapped even more stiffly to attention. The ambassador took one step closer to Leia, as if trying to look intimidating. "Nevertheless, you will arrange it."

That afternoon Mon Mothma stood in the dimmed audience chamber, waiting at the base of the holoprojector's controls. Though she had a thousand other duties to attend to, Carida seemed the likeliest flash point of resistance to New Republic stability. She had made it clear to Leia that she considered her sacrifice of time an investment to avert a possible war.

Without moving Mon Mothma seemed to fill the room with her quiet, commanding presence. Leia never ceased admiring her subtle but undeniable power, which Mon Mothma managed to exhibit even without Jedi training.

Leia followed Ambassador Furgan as he strode down the ramp to the base of the holoprojector. Grumpy, he looked behind him to where his stormtrooper bodyguards waited at the entrance to the chamber. Furgan had refused to leave them behind, and Mon Mothma had refused to let even disarmed Imperial stormtroopers near her. The power play had been brief and sharp, but in the end Mon Mothma allowed the stormtroopers to wait within sight of the ambassador, though outside the chamber.

But she had also won a seemingly minor concession. Mon Mothma required the stormtroopers to remove their helmets while they remained in her presence. The soldiers stood unmasked, holding the skull-like helmets under their arms, revealed to be humans, young cadets dressed in armor but with their anonymity taken away.

"Stand right there, Ambassador Furgan," she said without formally greeting him. "I would like to show you something."

The holoprojector shimmered, and the known galaxy filled the room, billions of star-specks flung in swirling arms throughout the enclosed chamber. The lights automatically dimmed as the sea-spray of stars came into focus. At the doorway the stormtroopers craned their necks to stare up at the huge image. On the chamber floor both Mon Mothma and Ambassador Furgan seemed insignificant.

"This is our galaxy," Mon Mothma said. "We have meticulously plotted every recorded system. These stars"—she waved her hand, and a wash of blue spangled across the arms of the galaxy—"have already sworn their allegiance to the New Republic. Others have remained neutral, though not unfriendly to our cause." A sprinkling of green appeared among the stars.

"The darkened area is what remains of the Ssi Ruuk Imperium." She indicated a splotch covering a portion of one spiral arm. "We have not yet fully explored their worlds, though it has been seven years since Imperial and Alliance forces joined hands at Bakura to drive out the invaders.

"Finally," Mon Mothma said, "we know of these systems that still remain loyal to the fallen Empire." A much smaller splash of red dusted the image, concentrated primarily toward the galactic core, from which the resurrected Emperor had launched his forces. "As you can see, your support is dwindling rapidly."

Furgan did not seem impressed. "Anyone can paint dots on a map."

Inwardly outraged, Leia marveled at the quiet way Mon Mothma handled the situation. Her voice did not grow louder; she merely looked at him with her calm, deep eyes. "You are welcome to speak to any of the ambassadors from these worlds to confirm their allegiances."

"Ambassadors can be bribed as easily as colors can be changed on a projection map."

This time Mon Mothma's voice grew just a bit brittle. "There are no bribes that can change the facts, Ambassador Furgan."

"If that is the case, then sometimes the facts themselves must be changed."

Leia could not keep herself from rolling her eyes. In a way this was amusing, but it seemed like a waste of time. Furgan was as unchangable as a man frozen in carbonite.

The entire planetary surface of Coruscant had been covered with layer upon layer of buildings, rebuilt, demolished, and rebuilt again. Galactic governments changed over the millennia, but Coruscant had always been the center of politics.

The complex construction patterns and towering metal and transparisteel pinnacles made weather difficult to predict. Occasionally, unexpected storms coalesced out of water evaporating from millions of exhaust vents, condensing and rising from the skyscraper forests, making small squalls that dumped rain down upon the hard surfaces of the buildings.

As the various diplomats gathered in the Skydome Botanical Gardens for Ambassador Furgan's reception, a sudden flurry of raindrops pattered down on the transparent panes, masking the bright curtains of Coruscant's aurora.

In the distance, near the horizon, the rebuilt Imperial Palace stood like a cobbled-together cathedral and pyramid, showing signs of many different eras. Leia had not wanted Furgan's reception to be held in any place that recalled the fallen Emperor's opulence and grandeur.

The Skydome Botanical Gardens rested on the level roof of an isolated skyscraper. Constructed by an Old Republic philanthropist who had grown rich by establishing the Galactic News Service, the giant terrarium was a carefully tended place with compartmentalized environments to house and display otherwise extinct or exotic flora from various systems in the galaxy.

Leia arrived with Threepio and her two children in tow just as the rain began to fall against the transparent ceiling. As Leia stepped through the door, she held herself defensively, her justifications on the tip of her tongue. She knew the presence of the twins might cause a stir at a stuffy diplomatic reception, but she did not care.

Throughout the day Furgan had pushed her around, complaining, demanding, acting generally rude. Leia had given up all of her time with the twins to be with the ambassador, and she decided that it was no longer worth the misery. She might be an important Cabinet member in the New Republic, but she was also a mother, still trying to adapt to the new demands on her time. In her quarters while changing clothes for the reception, Leia had felt her simmering resentment come to a boil. If she was going to be gone all the time anyway, she might as well have left Jacen and Jaina with Winter!

Besides, Threepio accompanied them, and he was a protocol droid. He could watch the twins and also help out with the fine points of the reception and translation if need be.

Since Han had disappeared, she was worried to the point of nausea much of the time. Luke and Lando had sent no word yet. She needed to have some stable point in her life. Leia almost hoped someone would challenge her about bringing the twins, so she could lash out.

When she passed through the door, Furgan's stormtrooper goons stopped her. The still-helmetless stormtroopers looked uncomfortable at meeting her eye to eye, but they stood firmly in her path. Behind them an equal number of New Republic guards stood at attention, watching the stormtroopers.

"What is the problem"—she glanced at the stormtrooper's insignia and deliberately misread it—"Lieutenant?"

"*Captain,*" he corrected. "We're checking everyone. A precaution against assassins."

"Assassins?" she said, deciding to be amused rather than upset. "I see."

One of the stormtroopers removed a handheld scanner and played it over Leia's body, testing for hidden weapons. Leia icily submitted to the scan. "This is for the ambassador's safety," he said. He looked disapprovingly at Jacen and Jaina. "We weren't informed there would be children attending."

"Are you afraid one of *them* is going to murder Ambassador Furgan?" Leia stared at the man's naked, pale face, scowling until he flinched. "That doesn't say much for your skills as a bodyguard, does it, Captain?" His flustered fidgeting was worth any amount of inconvenience he might cause her, Leia thought.

"Just routine precautions." The captain scanned Jacen and Jaina, showing visible discomfort at having to do so. When his task was complete, he still refused to move aside.

Leia crossed her arms over her chest. "Now what?"

"Your droid, Minister," the captain said. "We need to run a complete systems check. He could have assassin droid programming."

"Me, sir?" Threepio said. "Oh, my! You can't be serious."

Leia rolled her eyes at the mere thought of the prissy protocol droid being an assassin. "And how long will this complete systems check take?"

"Not long." The captain took a different scanner that trailed disconnected leads.

"Mistress Leia, I object!" Threepio's voice carried an edge of panic. "If you will recall, I have been maliciously reprogrammed in the past! I never want to trust a strange probe again."

Leia spoke to the droid but let her gaze bore into the stormtrooper captain's eyes. "Let him do it Threepio. And if your programming is altered in the slightest, this man will be responsible for a galactic incident that could well lead to war—a war in which his own home system of Carida would be the prime target for the combined forces of the New Republic."

"I will be very careful, Minister," the stormtrooper said.

"Indeed, sir, you will!" Threepio insisted.

When they finally managed to get through to the reception area, the rainfall dwindled to a trickle. People wandered along the tour-paths to observe the brilliant and bizarre shapes of alien plant life. As the guests stepped through forcefield environmental barriers, the humidity and temperature changed drastically to provide proper growing conditions for various types of plants. Tiny placards displayed scientific names written in a dozen different alphabets.

Holding their mother's hands, Jacen and Jaina stared with amazement at the people garbed in diplomatic finery, the exotic plants from distant worlds.

In a bright desert scenario at the center of the chamber, a monstrously large tentacle-cactus served hors d'oeuvres, waving its thick stalks back and forth and displaying tiny sandwiches, fruit slices, sausages, and pastries stuck on its long spines. Guests snatched snacks from the spines whenever the tentacle-cactus waved in their direction.

Stocky Ambassador Furgan seemed the center of attention, but everyone looked at him from the corners of their eyes rather than speaking to him directly. Feeling her political obligations, Leia sighed and walked toward him, the children trotting beside her.

Furgan fixed his gaze on the twins and drained the drink he was holding. She watched as he held the empty glass to a pump flask at his right hip. Furgan depressed the button and squirted himself a new drink of honey-greenish liquid. *Of course,* she thought, *anyone paranoid about poisons would bring his own supply.* He wore an identical flask on his left hip.

"So, Minister Organa Solo, these are the famous Jedi twins? Jacen and Jaina, I believe you named them? Don't you have a third child as well, named Anakin?"

Leia blinked, unnerved that Furgan knew so much about her family. "Yes, the baby is elsewhere—safe and protected." She knew he could not possibly have uncovered the location of the sheltered planet, but a mother's instinct magnified her fear.

Furgan patted Jaina on the head. "I hope you protect these two as well. It would be a shame for such sweet children to become political pawns."

"They are very safe," Leia said, suddenly feeling helpless. Keeping an eye on the ambassador, she turned the twins around. "You two take Threepio and go play now."

"It will be a very educational experience for them, Mistress Leia," Threepio said, bustling the children off to look at the plant exhibits.

Furgan continued his conversation with Leia. "If you want my opinion, it's too bad the Emperor didn't manage to wipe out all of the Jedi. Incomplete tasks always end up causing trouble."

"And why are you so afraid of the Jedi Knights?" Leia said. Though she disliked this line of conversation, she might glean some information from Furgan.

The ambassador took a long sip from his drink. "My feeling is that with our sophisticated technology, we should not cringe in fear of sorcery and bizarre mental powers that belong only to a few random individuals. It seems elitist. Jedi Knights? They were like strongmen for a weak old government."

Leia took up the debate. "The Emperor whom you revere so much was very powerful in the Force, as was Darth Vader. How are they so different?"

"The Emperor is *entitled* to special powers," Furgan said, as if stating the obvious. "After all, he's the Emperor. And Vader turned out to be a traitor in the end. As I understand it, he was the one who actually killed the Emperor. All the more reason to outlaw such powers."

Leia knew he must have seen Luke's widely broadcast speech to the Council. "Nevertheless, the Jedi *have* managed to survive, and the entire order of Jedi Knights will be restored. My brother will see to that. Within a few years the new Jedi Knights will fill the same role as the old, as protectors of the Republic."

"Too bad," Furgan said, turning away to seek other conversation, but no one seemed to want to talk to him.

Threepio lost track of the twins almost immediately, when they decided to play hide-and-seek among the flora exhibits, crawling under guardrails too low for Threepio to manage, then chasing each other around areas marked DO NOT ENTER. When the droid called for them to come back,

Jacen and Jaina developed a selective hearing difficulty and continued to dash away.

He chased them through a grove of mucus trees that dripped yellow pollinated ooze all over his polished body shell; but at least the slime left a trail of footprints for him to follow. Threepio wailed in dismay when he saw the small footprints leading directly into the "Carnivorous Plants" area.

"Oh, my!" he said, imagining bloodthirsty shrubs already digesting pieces of the small children. Before he could sound an all-out alarm, though, Threepio heard Jacen's high-pitched giggles, joined by his sister's laughter. Using directional locators, Threepio bustled back to the center of the exhibit.

Sitting in the middle of the giant tentacle-cactus, the twins played with the waving fronds, oblivious to the thorns. Somehow they had blithely eased their way past the daggerlike points and made a pillow out of the central mass of fine new bristles.

"Master Jacen and Mistress Jaina, come out of there this instant!" Threepio said in a stern voice. "I must insist!" Instead, Jaina giggled and waved to him.

In a tizzy Threepio wondered how he could rescue the children from the great plant without dislodging any of the hors d'oeuvres.

A lull fell in the conversation, the type of pause that often occurs in forced social situations. During the quiet Ambassador Furgan made his move. "I require your attention!" he called.

Leia watched him suddenly step away from her. Not knowing what he might do, she tensed, ready for anything.

The few conversations stuttered to a halt. All eyes turned to the Caridan ambassador. Mon Mothma had been chatting with General Jan Dodonna, the aged tactician who had planned the strike on the first Death Star. Mon Mothma raised her eyebrows, curious at Furgan's call for silence. Jan Dodonna stopped telling his tale and held his hands in midgesture as he stared.

Furgan took his empty glass and dropped it to his hip, filling it from the left hip flask this time. Leia wondered if he had already emptied the right flask.

Raising his glass high, he took one step toward Mon Mothma, grinning. Leia watched in disbelief. Was the rude ambassador going to propose a toast?

Furgan looked around the enclosed Skydome, making certain he had everyone's attention. Even the patchy rain had ceased. "To all gathered here, I wish to be heard. As ambassador of Carida, I have been empowered to speak for the Imperial military training center, my planet, and my entire system. Therefore, I must deliver a message to you all."

He raised his voice and raised his glass. "To Mon Mothma, who calls herself leader of the New Republic—" With a vicious sneer he hurled his drink into her face. The honey-green liquid splashed on her cheeks, her hair, her chest. She staggered back, appalled. Jan Dodonna caught her shoulders, steadying her; his mouth gaped open in astonishment.

The New Republic guards at the door immediately drew their weapons but somehow refrained from firing.

"—we denounce your foul rebellion of lawbreakers and murderers. You have tried to impress me with the number of other weak-minded systems that have joined your Alliance, but no amount of rabble can erase your crimes against the Empire."

He smashed his empty glass on the floor and ground the shards under his boot heel. "Carida will never surrender to your so-called New Republic."

With a flourish Furgan took his entourage and stormed off. At the doorway the gathered stormtroopers triumphantly placed the white helmets back on their heads, hiding their faces, and followed the ambassador out. The New Republic guards stared after them, weapons ready but not knowing what to do.

After a shocked silence the crowd erupted into a babble of outraged conversations. Leia ran to the Chief of State. Dodonna was already swabbing at Mon Mothma's damp robes.

The sticky drink drying on her face, Mon Mothma forced a smile for Leia. Into the rising hubbub of indignation she said, "Well, we didn't lose anything by trying, did we?"

In her disappointment Leia could not answer.

The tinny voice of Threepio burst over the background noise. "Excuse me, Mistress Leia?"

Leia frantically looked around for the twins, afraid Furgan had somehow kidnapped them during his diversion, but was relieved when she saw Jacen and Jaina standing with their faces pressed against the curved window looking out at the skyline of Imperial City.

Finally, from the corner of her eye, she noticed a golden arm flailing about in alarm. Somehow Threepio had gotten tangled in the tentacle-cactus exhibit; even from across the room Leia could see how badly scratched his plating had become. Hors d'oeuvres lay scattered about the floor.

"Could anyone assist me in getting free from this plant?" Threepio cried. "Please?"

21

Han Solo seemed to be drowning in a syrup of nightmares. He could not escape the drugged and painful interrogation, as the hardened and porcelain-beautiful face of Admiral Daala stared at him and pummeled him with questions.

"Just put him over here," a woman's trilling voice said. Not Daala.

His body was being dragged like luggage across a floor.

"We have been ordered to stand guard," said a fuzzed voice filtered through a stormtrooper helmet.

"Stand guard, then, but do it outside my lab. I want to talk to him in peace." The woman's voice again.

"For your own protection—" the stormtrooper began. Han felt himself dropped to the floor. His limbs didn't seem to remember how to bend.

"Protection? What is he going to do—he doesn't seem to have the energy to sneeze. If you left any unscrambled memories in his head, I want to pick at them without any interference."

Han felt himself hauled upright again, his arms wrapped behind him. Cold, smooth stone pressed against his back. "Yes, yes," the woman's voice said, "chain him to the column. I'm sure I'll be safe. I promise to stay out of reach of his fangs."

He heard the marching boots of stormtroopers leaving the room. His mind became active long before his body figured out how to respond. He remembered parts of the interrogation, but not all of it. What had he told Admiral Daala? His heart began pounding harder. Had he divulged any crucial secrets? Did he even *know* any crucial secrets?

He was fairly certain he had told her the basic events about the fall of the Empire and the rise of the New Republic—but that caused no harm, and it might even lead to benefits. If Daala knew she had no chance, perhaps she would surrender. And if banthas had wings . . .

His eyes finally opened grudgingly, letting light slam inside. He flinched away from returning vision, but eventually his eyes focused. He found himself in a spacious room, some kind of laboratory or analysis center, not his detention cell on the *Gorgon*. He heard singing and the sound of flutes.

Han turned his head to see a willowy alien woman standing in front of a device that seemed to be a combination musical keyboard and data-entry pad. He had heard her voice arguing with the stormtrooper. She hummed a complex string of notes as her fingers played on the musical keys; in front of her a rotating blueprint of a three-dimensional triangular shape took form, like a shard of glass capped with a tetrahedron and some sort of energy pod dangling from the lower point. With each tone the woman processed, additional lines appeared on the complicated diagram.

Han worked his tongue around in his mouth and tried to talk. He meant to say, "Who are you?" but his lips and vocal cords would not cooperate. The sounds came out more like "Whaaaaa yuuuurrrr?"

Startled, the female alien fluttered her slender hands around the 3-D geometrical image. Then she pranced over to where Han lay. She wore a badge on her smock, imprinted with her likeness and glittering holograms of the kind used for cipher-locks.

She was an attractive humanoid, tall and slender, with a bluish tint to her skin. Her gossamer hair seemed like strands of pearlescent feathers. When she spoke, her voice was high and reedy. Her eyes were wide and deep blue, carrying an expression of perpetual astonishment.

"I've been waiting for you to wake up!" she said. "I have so many questions to ask you. Is it true that you actually set foot on the first Death Star, and you got a look at the second one while it was under construction? Tell me what it was like. Anything you can remember. Every detail would be like a treasure trove to me."

The babbled questions came at him too quickly to assimilate. What did the Death Star have to do with anything? That was ten years ago!

Instead, Han focused his gaze past her. Pastel gases glowed on the other side of the broad window, swirling around the insatiable mouths of the black holes. He counted all four Star Destroyers in orbital formation high above. That meant he must be somewhere in the little cluster of planetoids in the center of the gravitational island.

And he was alone. Neither Kyp nor Chewbacca had ended up here with him. He hoped they had at least survived Daala's vicious interrogation. He worked his mouth, trying to form words again. "Who are you?"

The alien woman touched her badge with one of her long-fingered hands. "My name is Qwi Xux. And I know that you are Han Solo. I've read a hardcopy of the debriefing you gave Admiral Daala."

Debriefing? Did she mean the interrogation, the torture chair that made his entire body spasm?

Qwi Xux's entire demeanor seemed superficial and distracted, as if she were paying only a small amount of attention to details while she kept her mind preoccupied with something else. "Now then, please tell me about the Death Star. I'm very eager to hear what you remember. You're the first person I can talk to who was actually there."

Han wondered if the interrogation drugs were still muddling his brain, or if there really was a reason why someone should want him to talk about the defunct Death Star. And why should he tell this Imperial scientist anything anyway? Had he divulged anything important to Daala? What if she took her four Star Destroyers and attacked Coruscant?

"I've already been interrogated." He was pleased to hear his words come out clearly enough to be understood this time.

In one bluish hand Qwi held up a short printout. "I want your real impressions about it," she continued. "What did it sound like? What did it feel like when you walked down the corridors? Tell me everything you can remember." She wrung her hands in barely restrained excitement.

"No."

His response apparently shocked Qwi enough that she took a step backward and let out a startled musical squawk. "You have to! I'm one of the top scientists here." Her mouth hung partly open in confusion. She began to pace around the pillar where he had been bound, forcing Han to turn his head. The effort nearly made him pass out.

"What good does it do to withhold information?" Qwi asked. "Information is for everyone. We build on the knowledge we have, add to it, and leave a greater legacy for our successors."

Qwi struck him as being impossibly naive. Han wondered how long she had been sheltered in the middle of the black hole cluster. "Does that mean you share *your* information with anyone who asks?" he said.

Qwi bobbed her head. "That's the way Maw Installation works. It is the foundation of all our research."

Han barely managed a grin of triumph. "All right, then tell me where my friends are. I came in here with a young man and a Wookiee. Share that information with me, and I'll see what I can remember about the Death Star."

Qwi's uneasy reaction told him that she had never before considered anything but clear-cut cases. "I don't know if I can tell you that," she said. "You don't have a need to know."

Han managed a shrug. "Then I see how much your own code of ethics means to you."

Qwi glanced toward the door, as if contemplating whether to summon the stormtroopers after all. "It is in my charter here as a researcher that I have access to all the data I need. Why won't you answer my few simple questions?"

"Why won't you answer mine? I never signed your charter. I'm under no obligation to you."

Han waited, fixing his eyes on her as she fidgeted. Finally, Qwi pulled out her datapad and hummed as she keyed in a request.

She looked at him with wide deep-blue eyes that blinked rapidly. Her hair seemed like a glittering waterfall of fine down spilling to her shoulders. When she whistled again, the datapad gave a response.

"Your Wookiee companion has been assigned to a labor detail in the engine-maintenance sector. The physicist formerly in charge of concept development and implementation always swore by Wookiee laborers. He had about a hundred of them taken from Kashyyyk and brought to the Installation when it was formed. We don't have many left. It's hard and dangerous work there, you know."

Han shifted his position, still finding it difficult to move. He had heard rumors that Wookiee slaves had been put to work during the actual construction of the first Death Star. But Qwi spoke of these things with simple frankness.

"What about my other friend?" Han asked.

"Someone named Kyp Durron—is that him? He is still aboard the *Gorgon* in the detention area, high security. I don't see much of a report from his debriefing, so apparently he didn't have much to tell them."

Han frowned, trying to assess the information, but Qwi became animated again. "All right, I've shared the information you wanted. Now tell me about the Death Star!" She stepped closer to him but remained well out of reach.

Han rolled his eyes but saw no reason not to. The Death Star had been destroyed long ago, and the plans were safely locked inside the protected data core of the former Imperial Information Center.

Han told Qwi about the corridors, the noises. He knew the most about the hangar bay, the detention area, and the garbage masher, but she didn't seem much interested in those details.

"But did you see the core? The propulsion systems?"

"Sorry. I was just running interference while someone else knocked out the tractor-beam generators." Han pursed his lips. "Why are you so interested in all this anyway?"

She blinked her eyes. "Because I *designed* most of the Death Star!"

Before she could notice Han's shocked response, she trotted over to the near wall and worked a few controls that turned a section of the metal plating transparent. Suddenly a dizzying panorama replaced his narrow view of the bright gases. He could see the other clustered rocks that made up Maw Installation.

"In fact, we've still got the prototype Death Star right here at the Installation."

As Qwi spoke, a gigantic wire-frame sphere as large as any of the asteroids rose behind the shortened horizon of the nearest planetoid like a deadly sunrise. The prototype looked like a giant armillary sphere, circular rings connected at the poles and spread out for support. Nested in the framework and superstructure hung the enormous reactor core and the planet-destroying superlaser.

"This is just the functional part," Qwi said, staring out the window with admiration in her eyes. "The core, the superlaser, and the reactor, without a hyperdrive propulsion system. We didn't see any need to add the structural support and all the housing decks for troops and administrators."

Han found his voice again. "Does it work?"

Qwi smiled at him, her eyes sparkling. "Oh yes, it works beautifully!"

Kyp Durron felt like an animal trapped in a cage. He stared at the dull confining walls of the detention cell. Illumination came through slitted grills in the ceiling, too bright and too reddish to be comfortable on his eyes. He sat on his bunk, stared at the wall, and tried not to think.

Leftover pain still throbbed through his body. The interrogator droid had been vicious in finding the pain stimuli in his body, damping endorphins so the slightest scratch seemed like agony. The sharp hypodermic needles felt like spears as they plunged into his flesh; the will-breaking drugs flowed like lava through his veins.

He had begged his memories to divulge some detail the interrogators would find useful, if only to stop the questioning—but Kyp Durron was nobody, a hapless prisoner who had spent most of his life on Kessel. He didn't *know* anything to tell the Imperial monsters. In the end they had found him worthless.

Kyp stared at the self-making meal the door dispenser had given to him. By opening the lid of the pack, he spontaneously heated the textured protein main course and chilled the synthetic fruit dessert; after a short time the utensils themselves began to break down and could be eaten as snacks. But Kyp could find no spark of hunger inside him.

His thoughts drifted again to Han Solo's predicament. Unlike Kyp, Han knew a great deal about the New Republic and had many secrets to divulge. Han's interrogation would have been far more thorough than his own. And Admiral Daala's ministrations had been worse than anything Kyp had experienced during his years in the Imperial Correction Facility. At least down in the spice mines he knew how to avoid calling attention to himself.

Since the age of eight, Kyp had lived on Kessel, coping with the rules, the torturous work, the miserable conditions under the old Imperial rule or under the chain of usurpers and slave lords such as Moruth Doole. His parents were dead, his brother Zeth conscripted away to the stormtrooper academy, but Kyp had learned how to lie low, to survive, to endure.

Not until Han Solo's arrival, though, had he considered escape. Han showed that a small, determined group could break free of a prisoner's shackles. That they had stumbled into an even worse situation inside the Maw seemed irrelevant.

Piloting the stolen shuttle, Kyp had used his fledgling powers to steer them safely through the black hole cluster. In the years since the withered Vima-Da-Boda had taught him the fundamentals of her Jedi skills, Kyp had made little use of his own affinity for the Force.

He remembered Vima-Da-Boda's face as shrunken and leprous; and she had a habit of huddling in corners, of pulling shadows around herself as if to hide from immense prying eyes. The fallen Jedi had a guilty conscience that suffocated her like a blanket, but she had taken the time to teach Kyp a few things before the Imperials whisked her away. "You have great potential," she had told him in one of her last brief lessons.

Kyp had paid little attention to that, until now.

He stared fixedly at his untouched meal. Perhaps if he concentrated, focused his abilities on manipulating something, moving a tiny object, he could turn that skill into an escape.

Escape! The word rang through his heart, conjuring images of hope. He was not certain how he did what he did. Sensing the best route through darkened spice tunnels seemed perfectly natural to him. When flying the shuttle through the fiery gas clouds, he had listened to the mysterious whispering voice directing him. Kyp turned and altered course, spinning and whirling whenever it *seemed right*.

But now that he needed to make use of the Force, he didn't know where to begin.

He fixed his gaze on the flimsy foil covering of the instant meal, trying to bend it. He pushed with his mind, picturing the thin metal twisting and crumpling into a ball—but nothing happened. Kyp wondered how much of Vima-Da-Boda's ramblings had been simple superstition and craziness.

His parents had no special sort of powers. On the Deyer colony of the Anoat system, they had both been outspoken local politicians. Upon hearing of a growing rebellion against the Emperor's rigid policies, they decided to work from within, speaking out against Palpatine to make him more moderate rather than overthrow him entirely. They resoundingly protested the destruction of Alderaan—but their efforts had only gotten the two of them and their sons Zeth and Kyp arrested.

Kyp remembered that night of terror, when the stormtroopers had melted down the door of the family dwelling even though it was unlocked. The armed soldiers marched into the living quarters, kicked over the fragile fiber-grown furniture. The stormtrooper captain read an arrest order through the filtered speaker in his helmet, accusing Kyp's parents of treason; then the stormtroopers drew their blasters and stunned the two astonished adults. Kyp's older brother Zeth had tried to protect them, so the troopers stunned him as well.

Kyp, with tears streaming down his face, could only stare in disbelief at the three crumpled forms as the stormtroopers linked stun-cuffs around his wrists. He still couldn't imagine how they had considered him a threat, since he had been only eight years old at the time.

Kyp and his parents were taken to Kessel, while fourteen-year-old Zeth was hauled off as a brainwashed recruit to the Imperial military academy in Carida. They had never heard from Zeth again.

After little more than a year Kessel went into enormous internal upheavals, with prison revolts, the Imperials overthrown, slave lords taking over. Kyp's parents had died during the commotion, executed for being on the wrong side at the wrong moment. Kyp himself had survived by hiding, becoming silent and invisible. He had rotted in the darkness of the tunnels for eight years, and now he had escaped.

Only to be captured again.

Somehow, it seemed, the Imperials were always there to wreck his aspirations. On Deyer the stormtroopers had stolen him away from his home; on Kessel they had thrown him into the spice mines. Now that he and Han had finally escaped, the stormtroopers had clamped around him again.

Kyp's anger focused into a projectile, and he tried again to use his ability on the meal tray. He pushed, and a drop of sweat fell into his eyes, blurring his vision. Had the tray moved, jerked a little? He saw a small dent in the textured protein patty that formed the main course. Had he done that?

Perhaps anger was the key to focusing his latent energies.

He wished Vima-Da-Boda had spent more time instructing him down in the mines. He concentrated on the walls, on his narrow surroundings. He had to find some way of escaping—Han had already proved that it could be done.

Kyp vowed that if he did manage to get away, he would find someone to teach him how to use these mysterious powers. He never wanted to be left so helpless again.

Looking at the delicate, birdlike Qwi Xux, Han somehow could not imagine her as the developer of the Death Star. But she worked willingly in the Maw Installation, and she had admitted her role in a matter-of-fact way. "What's a nice girl like you doing in a place like this?" he finally said.

"This is what I do. This is what I'm best at." Qwi nodded her head absently, as if considering her answer. "Here I have a chance to grapple with the greatest mysteries of the cosmos, to solve problems that others have claimed are unsolvable. To see my wild ideas take shape. It's very thrilling."

Han still could not understand. "But how did this happen to you? Why are you here?"

"Oh, that!" Qwi said, as if suddenly understanding the question. "My home planet was Omwat, in the Outer Rim. Moff Tarkin took ten young Omwati children from various cities. He placed us in intense forced-education camps, trying to mold us into great designers and problem solvers. I was the best. I was the only one who made it through all the training. I was his prize, and he sent me here as a reward.

"At first I worked with Bevel Lemelisk to bring the Death Star to fruition. When we had the blueprints completed, Tarkin took Bevel away, leaving me to create newer and better concepts."

"Okay," Han said, "so I'll ask you again, *why* do you do this stuff?"

Qwi looked at him as if he had suddenly grown stupid. "It's the most interesting thing I can imagine. I have my pick of the challenges, and I'm usually successful. What more could I want?"

Han knew he wasn't getting through. "How can you enjoy working on things like this? It's horrible!"

Qwi took another step backward, looking baffled and hurt. "What do you mean by that? It's fascinating work, if you think about it. One of our concepts was to modify existing molecular furnace devices into autonomous 'World Devastators' that could strip raw materials from a planet's surface, feed it into huge automated onboard factories, and produce useful machines. We're quite proud of that idea. We transmitted the proposal off to Tarkin shortly after he took Bevel with him." Her voice trailed off. "I wonder what ever happened to that idea."

Han blinked in astonishment. The terrifying fleet of World Devastators had attacked Admiral Ackbar's home planet, laying waste part of the beautiful water world before the juggernauts were destroyed. "The World Devastators have already been built," Han mumbled, "and put to very efficient use."

Qwi's face lit up. "Oh, that's wonderful!"

"No, it isn't!" he shouted into her face. She sprang back. "Don't you know what your inventions are used for? Do you have any idea?"

Qwi backed off, straightening up again defensively. "Yes, of course. The Death Star was to be used to break up dead planets to allow direct mining of the heavy metals trapped in the core. The World Devastators would be autonomous factories combing asteroids or sterile worlds to produce a wide range of items without polluting inhabited planets."

Han snorted and rolled his eyes. "If you believe that, you'll believe anything. Listen to their names! *Death Star, World Devastator*—that doesn't sound like something for peacetime economic development, does it?"

Qwi scowled and turned her back on it. "Oh, what difference does it make?"

"The Death Star's first target was the planet Alderaan—my wife's home world! It murdered billions of innocent people. The World Devastators were turned loose on the *inhabited* world of Calamari. Hundreds of thousands of people died. Those efficient factories of yours manufactured TIE fighters and other weapons of destruction, nothing else."

"I don't believe you." Her voice did not sound confident.

"I was there! I flew through the rubble of Alderaan, I saw the devastation on Calamari. Didn't you read about it in my interrogation report? Admiral Daala pressed me over and over again for those details."

Qwi crossed her slender bluish arms over her chest. "No, that wasn't in your debriefing summary, which you so melodramatically call an 'interrogation.' "

"Then you didn't get the whole report," Han said.

"Nonsense. I'm entitled to all data." She stared at her feet. "Besides, I only develop the concepts. I make them work. If someone on the outside abuses my inventions, I can't be held responsible. That's beyond the scope of what I do."

Han made a noncommittal sound, simmering with anger. Her words sounded rehearsed, like something that had been drilled into her. She didn't even seem to think about what she was saying.

Qwi flitted back to her 3-D display panel, tapping on the musical keys and humming to sharpen the long, angular image she had been constructing when Han opened his eyes. "Would you like to see what I'm working on now?" Qwi asked, studiously avoiding any mention of the previous discussion.

"Sure," Han said, afraid that when she no longer needed to talk to him, Qwi would send him back to his detention cell.

She gestured to the image of the small craft. Four-sided and elongated, it looked like the long shard of a firefacet gem. From the diagram he could see a pilot's compartment with space enough for six people. Small lasers studded strategic areas; the bottom of the long point carried a strange toroidal transmitting dish.

"Right now we're working on enhancing the armor," Qwi said. "Though the craft is not much larger than a single-man fighter, we need it to be completely impervious to attack. By introducing quantum-crystalline armor, where only a few layers of atoms are stacked as densely as physics permits, laminated on top of another thin film just as tough but phase shifted, we can be confident that nothing will harm it. Not so much as a dent."

Han nodded to the laser emplacements; he couldn't see well from his vantage chained against a support pillar. "Then why add the weaponry if the ship is indestructible?" He had visions of a fleet of these things replacing the TIE fighters; a small force of indestructible assault craft could fly into any New Republic fleet and carve the ships up at their leisure.

"This craft is highly maneuverable, and small enough not to be noticed on a systemwide scan, but they still might encounter some resistance. Remember, the Death Star was the size of a small moon. This accomplishes through finesse what the Death Star brought about through brute force."

With a cold fear inside Han did not want to know the answer to his next question. How could she compare this small ship to the Death Star? But he couldn't stop himself from asking, "And what is it? What does it do?"

Qwi looked at the image with awe, pride, and fear. "Well, we haven't actually tested it yet, but the first full-scale model is basically completed. We call this concept the Sun Crusher, tiny but immensely powerful. One small, impervious craft launches a modulated resonance projectile into a star, which triggers a chain reaction in the core, igniting a supernova even in low-mass stars. Straightforward and simple."

In his horror, Han could think of nothing to say. The Death Star destroyed planets, but the Sun Crusher could destroy whole solar systems.

22

Luke and Lando stood with Moruth Doole high inside one of Kessel's atmosphere stacks. They held the rusted guard railing at the edge of a catwalk, staring down the dizzying drop. Leaning into the stack, they breathed the manufactured air boiling into the sky; it reminded Luke of the great air shaft in Cloud City.

Doole shouted into the roaring background noise. "According to one old Imperial study, there's only enough raw material in Kessel's crust to keep the atmosphere in equilibrium for a century or two at our present rate of consumption." He shrugged, hunching his bumpy shoulders in a sort of seizure. "A few years ago the output was higher so that the slaves could walk around and breathe the air—but what's the point in allowing that?"

Lando nodded sagely, as if still interested, while Luke said nothing. Doole had been their tour guide for an entire day, talking more than even the long-winded senators on Coruscant. Doole wanted Lando's half million credits and went about extolling Kessel's virtues like a representative from the planetary chamber of commerce.

Wherever Doole took them, Luke strained his Jedi senses, reaching out to find some sign of Han or Chewbacca. But Luke could feel no tickle in the Force, no ripple of his friends' presence. Perhaps they were truly dead after all.

Lando continued his conversation with Doole, shouting into the rushing wind that rose through the stack. "A lot can change around here by the time the air runs out. What matters is what you accomplish during your own lifetime."

Doole's hissing laugh was swallowed by background noise. He reached up to lay a hand on Lando's shoulder. "We think alike, Mr. Tymmo. Who cares what happens after we're space dust? I'd rather squeeze Kessel dry while I've got it in my fist."

"You seem to have such an enormous operation. Why are you still running it solo?" Lando asked.

Doole flinched at the term "solo," and Luke knew Lando had chosen his word carefully; both of them caught the Rybet's reaction. "What do you mean?" Doole asked.

"Well, when the Imperial confiscation of spice ended, I would have thought you'd open all your markets, get a thousand representatives to spread the product. Jabba the Hutt is dead. Why didn't you link up with the unified smugglers under Talon Karrde and Mara Jade? That must have hurt your profits."

Doole pointed one gummy-ended finger at Lando. "Our profits are growing enormously, now that we get *all* the glitterstim, rather than just what we can steal from under Imperial noses. And after being so long under the yoke of the Empire, I didn't want to get into the same position with the New Republic. Everybody knows that Jade and Karrde are just puppets."

Seeing Lando's skepticism, Doole waved his hands. "Oh, but we are considering it, of course. In fact, I've already spoken with a minister from the New Republic, opening up a line of communication that may eventually lead to an alliance."

"Sounds like good news," Lando said in a noncommittal voice.

Doole led them back along the catwalk to the access doorway, where Artoo waited. Shutting the heavy door behind them, Doole paused a moment for their ears to adjust to the sudden silence. "As you can see, a great deal is changing around here. You, my friend, have chosen a good time to join in."

"*If* I decide to invest," Lando said firmly.

"Yes, yes, if you decide to invest. The truth is, this could be even more important, Mr. Tymmo. Since the death of Skynxnex, I'll be needing a new, er, *assistant* for running the spice mines."

Lando fluffed the cape behind him in a self-important gesture. "If I'm investing half a million credits, Doole, I'd expect to be more of a *partner* than an assistant."

Doole practically kowtowed. "Of course. Trivial details can be worked out. I'll also need a new shift boss. Maybe your companion here would be interested in the work?" He looked at Luke, squinting with his egg-white eye.

Luke met the Rybet's mechanical eye and stared into the focus-changing lenses, trying to pry some secrets from Doole's brain. Luke said, "I'll have to think about it."

Doole ignored him, focusing his attention back on Lando. "Now then, you've seen practically everything. Is there anything else I can show you?"

Lando looked to Luke, who pondered a moment. Thoughts of the jagged moon and its security base kept troubling him. If Han was not on Kessel itself, perhaps he was imprisoned on the moonbase.

"Aren't you worried about attack from remnants of the Empire?" Luke asked. "Or consolidation forces from the New Republic?"

Doole brushed aside the comment. "We have our own defenses. Don't worry."

But Luke persisted, trying to sound like a cautious business associate. "If we're going to invest, we should see these alleged defenses. We know about the energy shield left by the Imperial Correction Facility. But do you have a fleet of any sort?"

Doole began to sputter, but Lando took charge. "Moruth, if there's something you don't want us to see . . ."

"No, no, it's no trouble at all. I'll just have to arrange a shuttle up to the moonbase. I don't want you to think we have anything to hide!"

Doole bustled off to arrange for the shuttle, leaving Luke and Lando to exchange skeptical glances.

Lando did not like the idea of leaving the *Lady Luck* behind on the landing pad of the Imperial Correction Facility, but Doole continued to play the gracious host. Luke silently tried to console him as they lifted off in the short-range shuttle, but Lando kept looking out the small window as if he would never see his ship again.

Kessel's moon approached, looking like a hollowed sphere with most of the rock scooped out to house a large internal hangar and the enormous generators and transmitters that created the protective energy shield surrounding the planet.

After they landed, Moruth Doole strutted out of the shuttle, gesturing them to follow with an impatience that made Luke curious. Doole stood waiting for them as Artoo worked his way down the ramp and into the giant grotto. Behind a transparent atmosphere-containment screen, Luke could see stars and the trailing wisps of gas looping around the black hole cluster.

Doole seemed prouder of his defensive fleet than he was of any other aspect of the Kessel operations. "Follow me."

He waddled across the rock floor of the hangar bay, leading them along rows and rows of fighter craft arranged in seemingly random order. They passed ships Luke found familiar and others so exotic he could not even identify them. He called on his knowledge as a fighter pilot to assess the fleet: X-wings, Y-wings, powerful Corellian Corvettes, a single B-wing, TIE fighters, TIE interceptors, four TIE bombers, several Skipray blastboats, gamma-class assault shuttles. In space, like prizes around the ragged opening of the moon, hovered larger attack ships—three Carrack cruisers, two big Lancer frigates, a single Loronar strike cruiser.

"After we drove out the Empire," Doole said, "I placed the highest priority on a defensive fleet. I bought every fighter I could find, no matter what its condition, and hired experienced mechanics from the Corellian sector of Nar Shaddaa."

He grinned with his amphibian lips. "We just got the energy shield operational again two days ago. I can heave a big sigh of relief now. With the shields finally up and our new fleet as a backup, Kessel is safe and independent. We can set glitterstim prices across the galaxy without interference from anybody."

"Sure is a lot of ships," Lando agreed. "I'm impressed."

Luke recalled how much trouble the New Republic had obtaining sufficient fighting ships during Admiral Thrawn's guerrilla campaigns. If Moruth Doole had been pulling all the strings he could to obtain every functional ship in the sector, no wonder supplies had been so limited.

"We should be able to defend against spice pirates, don't you think?" Doole said.

They kept walking along the rows of parked ships. Suddenly Lando froze, and Luke felt a surge of shocked emotion from him. Artoo began chittering wildly. Luke looked around until he saw one modified light freighter of Corellian manufacture—a ship that looked decidedly familiar.

"What is it?" Doole asked, looking down at the droid.

Lando took a moment to regain his composure. He rapped his knuckles on Artoo's top dome. "Stray cosmic ray, I suppose. Occasionally these old astromech units frazzle a circuit." He swallowed. "Could I speak with my assistant for a moment in private, Moruth?"

"Oh, uh, of course." Doole discreetly backed away. "I'll go make sure the mechanics are prepping the shuttle for our return to Kessel." He turned to Luke and forced humor into his tone. "Now, don't go talking your boss out of making an investment here!"

The moment Doole moved out of earshot, Lando nodded excitedly to the freighter. "That's the *Falcon*, Luke! I know her like a krabbex knows its shell!"

Luke looked at the ship, recognizing it himself but wanting more proof. "You positive?"

"It's the *Falcon*, Luke. I owned her, remember, before Han stole her from me in a sabacc game. If you look, you can see the streaking scar on top where I knocked off the subspace antenna dish trying to zip away from the Death Star."

Luke also noticed scorch marks from a recent space combat. "They could have changed the markings, wiped the memory core. Is there any other way we can prove it?"

"Just get me inside the cockpit. Han's made some modifications to the ship nobody else would know about."

When Doole returned, Lando said, "My assistant wants to be sure you've been doing thorough maintenance on these ships. If you're not taking care of them, they don't make much of a defensive fleet. Let's take a look inside one at random . . . say, that Corellian ship over there."

Doole seemed taken by surprise, glancing at the *Falcon*. "That one? Uh, we have plenty of top-notch fighters you can check out. That one is something of a . . . piece of junk."

Lando waggled his finger. "If *you* choose the ship for us, Moruth, that contradicts the whole point of a random inspection, doesn't it? Open this one up. Go on."

Reluctantly, Doole worked the external controls that dropped the *Falcon*'s ramp. Lando took the lead, followed by Luke, while Artoo puttered so closely behind Doole that he nearly ran over the Rybet's heels.

Inside, Lando strode to the cockpit, ostensibly to check out the systems. Running his fingers lovingly over the stained, worn surfaces, he flicked a few switches. "Ion-flux stabilizer checks out as optimal, so does the stasis-field generator. Should we go back and check out the power converter? Those things are notorious for breaking down in Corellian freighters."

Lando backed down the narrow corridor leading from the cockpit to the central living section of the ship. Turning left toward the entry ramp, he stepped carefully on the main deck plates. From the control panels he had unlatched the hidden locks, and when he stomped on the appropriate plates with his boot heel, they popped up, revealing the seven secret compartments Han had personally installed as spice-smuggling bins beneath the floor.

"Caught you, Doole, you bastard!" Lando grabbed him by the yellow cravat at his throat. "What have you done with Han and Chewbacca?"

Doole seemed completely astonished, flailing his splayed hands in the air. "What are you talking about?" he croaked. As Lando glared down into the Rybet's huge eyes, Doole slipped one of his hands into his waistcoat and yanked free a small "hold-out" blaster pistol. Luke saw it and reacted instantly, shoving with his mind and using the Force to hurl Moruth Doole away from Lando.

The blaster went off, sending a deadly beam ricocheting around the *Falcon*'s corridor. Doole fell backward, then scrambled to his feet. He fired at them again, but his mechanical eye had no time to focus, and the beam went wide. Doole dove down the ramp, bellowing for the guards. His mechanical eye fell off, clanging and rolling across the floor. He scrambled after it in a panic, feeling blindly with his hands.

Luke smacked the door controls, raising the ramp and sealing the hatch, "We should have kept him as a hostage," he said. "Now it's going to be a lot more difficult to get out of here."

Outside, Doole raised the alarm. Guards scrambled through the parked ships, drawing blasters, fastening their armor.

"Artoo, get to the computer!" Luke said.

Lando jumped into the chair behind the controls. "I doubt we can do anything for Han anymore. We need to get back and tell Leia. She can bring a full-scale occupation force to Kessel. We'll go over this place with a high-res scanner."

"If we get out of here alive," Luke said.

"Artoo," Lando called, "jack into the copilot's computer and tie into the hangar controls." The astromech droid chittered his willingness to help and rolled toward the navicomp console.

Outside in the hangar, security horns sounded. People ran around every which direction, not knowing where to go. Luke saw immediately that these mercenaries had far less experience working together than the sloppiest Imperial regiment. But the moment Lando lifted the ship off the landing-pad floor, everyone had an unmistakable target.

"Artoo, get that door field down!" Lando shouted.

Using maneuvering thrusters, he edged the ship forward, picking up speed as they rose over the other parked fighters. Pilots scrambled into their ships, ready for a space battle. In orbit around the moon, the capital ships did not yet seem aware of the situation.

Lando accelerated toward the wide hangar opening to space. They could not see the invisible shield. Artoo bleeped and whistled, but the sounds were not positive. "Get the shield down!" Lando insisted.

Artoo's interface jack whirred as he worked with the hangar bay's computer, trying to skirt the password controls.

"We need the shield down *now,* Artoo!" Luke said.

The *Falcon*'s rear thrusters kicked in and they lurched forward, gaining speed. "Come on," Lando said to the ship. "You can do it. Do it one last time for Han."

Artoo bleeped in triumph a moment before they shot through the opening. Luke flinched, but the shield dropped just in time.

Alert lights began to wink on in the big battleships riding in orbit. Weapons systems warmed up, targeting modules locked on to aimpoints.

The *Millennium Falcon* soared into open space as, behind them, the Kessel forces scrambled in pursuit.

23

Hunched in his dark robes, Tol Sivron came to visit Qwi Xux in her research room. He drew in a long, hissing breath, and his head-tails twitched with uneasiness as he stared at her setup. The Twi'lek administrator gave the impression of never having set foot inside an actual laboratory before—which seemed odd to Qwi, since he was in charge of the entire installation.

Qwi stopped her musical calculation with an atonal squawk. "Director Sivron! What can I do for you?"

Tol Sivron demanded regular written reports, feasibility studies, and progress summaries; he hosted a weekly meeting among the scientists to share their ideas and their work in a frank and stimulating exchange.

But Tol Sivron did not make a habit of *visiting*.

He shuffled around the room, poking at things, kneading his knuckles, and looking at the standard equipment as if deeply interested. He brushed his clawed fingertips over the calibration gauge of a weld-stress analyzer, muttering, "Mmm hmmm, good work!" as if Qwi herself had invented the common instrument.

"I just came to commend you for your consistently fine efforts, Dr. Xux." Sivron stroked one of the vermiform head-tails draped around his neck; then his voice grew stern. "But I hope you are about finished with your endless iterations on the Sun Crusher project. We're past Grand Moff Tarkin's target date, you know, and we must move soon. I insist you write your final report and get all the documentation in order. Submit it to my office as soon as possible."

Qwi blinked at him in annoyance. She had submitted five separate "final" reports already, but each time Sivron had asked her to rerun a particular simulation or to retest the structural welds in the Sun Crusher's quantum armor. He never gave any reasons, and Qwi got the impression that he never read the reports anyway. If it had been up to her, the Sun Crusher would have been ready for deployment two years ago. She was getting bored with it, wanting to move on to a new design she could start from scratch and get back to the enjoyable, imaginative work again.

"You'll have the report by this evening, Director Sivron!" She would just send a repeat of the last one.

"Good, good," Sivron said, stroking his head-tail again. "I just wanted to make sure everything is in order."

For what? Qwi thought. *We're not going anywhere*. She hated it when the administrators and the military types kept sticking their noses in her work. Without another word Tol Sivron left.

Qwi stared after him, then activated the rarely used privacy lock on her door. Returning to her imaging terminal, she continued trying to crack the wall of passwords in front of her. She did like challenges, after all.

Qwi could not stop thinking about what Han Solo had told her. At first it was a new puzzle to solve, but then she finally began paying attention. To her all the prototypes she developed were abstract concepts turned into reality through mathematical music and brilliant intuitions. She kept telling herself that she did not know, or care, what her inventions were used for. She could certainly guess, but she tried not to. She didn't want to know! She blocked those thoughts before they could surface. But Qwi Xux wasn't stupid.

The Death Star was supposed to be used to break apart depleted, dead planets to provide access to raw materials deep in the core. Right! Had she thought up that excuse afterward? The World Devastators were supposed to be immense wandering factories taking useless rubble and fabricating scores of valuable industrial components. Right! Tarkin had been with her during the immense pressure of her original training. She knew what the man was capable of.

And the new Sun Crusher was—"What?" Han had said, raising his voice so that it hurt her fragile ears. "What in all the galaxy could the Sun Crusher be used for *other than to completely wipe out all life in systems the Imperials don't like*? You don't even have a bogus excuse like rubble mining. The Sun Crusher has one purpose only: to bring death to countless innocent people. Nothing more."

But Qwi could not possibly have the responsibility for lives on her hands. That wasn't part of her job. She just drew up blueprints, toyed with designs, solved equations. It exhilarated her to discover something previously considered impossible.

On the other hand, she was perfectly aware of what she was doing . . . though feigned naïveté provided such a nice excuse, such a perfect shield against her own conscience.

In the Maw databanks Qwi had discovered the complete "debriefing" of Han Solo—protected by a password she had easily broken—full video instead of just a transcription. Sivron and Daala had indeed kept much of it from her—but why?

As Qwi watched the entire torture session, she could not believe her eyes. She had never suspected the information had been taken from him in that manner! The words on paper seemed so cool and cooperative.

But on a deeper, professional level she was outraged at Admiral Daala. Access to data was supposedly open to all Maw scientists. She had never been denied a single information request in twelve years inside the black hole cluster! But this was even worse. She hadn't just been denied access to the full report—she had been *deceived* into thinking Han's debriefing held no more data.

But information is meant to be shared! Qwi thought. *How can I do my work if I don't have the pertinent data?*

Qwi had little trouble breaking through the various passwords. Apparently, no one had expected her to bother looking. She read the full report with sickened astonishment: the destruction of Alderaan, the attack on Yavin 4, the ambush of the Rebel fleet over Endor, the huge hospital ship and personnel carriers blown into micrometeoroids by the second Death Star's superlaser.

"What did you think they were going to be used for?" Han had said. Qwi closed her eyes to the thought.

Focus on the problem. It had been a mantra of her childhood. Be distracted by nothing else. Solving the problem was the only important thing. Solving the problem meant survival itself. . . .

As a child she remembered spending two years in the sterile, silent environment of the orbital education sphere above her homeworld of Omwat. Qwi had been ten standard years old, the same age as her other nine companions, each selected from different Omwati honeycomb settlements. From orbit the orange and green continents looked surreal, blurred by clouds and dimpled with canyons, blemished by upthrust mountains—nothing like the clean maps she had seen before.

But beside Qwi's educational sphere orbited Moff Tarkin's personal Star Destroyer. It had been a mere Victory class ship, but powerful enough to rain death and ruin down on Omwat if the students should fail.

For two years life for Qwi had been an endless succession of training, testing, training, testing, with no other purpose than to cram the total knowledge of engineering disciplines into pliable young Omwati minds—or to burst their brains in the process. Tarkin's research had shown that Omwati children were capable of amazing mental feats, if pushed properly and sufficiently. Most of the young minds would collapse under the pressure, but some emerged like precious jewels, brilliant and creative. Moff Tarkin had wanted to test that possibility.

The gaunt, steel-hard man had stood in his dress uniform during important examinations, staring at the surviving Omwati children as they wrestled with problems that had stymied the Empire's best designers. Qwi remembered how alarmed they had been when one of her classmates, a young male named Pillik, suddenly fell to the floor in some kind of seizure, grasping his head and screaming. He managed to climb to his knees, weeping, before the guards grabbed him. He still grasped for his examination paper as they hauled him away, yelling that he wanted to finish his work.

In silence Qwi and her three surviving classmates went to the window of the educational sphere so they could watch as turbolasers from the Victory-class Star Destroyer obliterated Pillik's honeycomb settlement in punishment for his failure.

Qwi could not be distracted by consequences. If her concentration faltered, everyone would die. She had to lock away all caring. Problems were pure, and safe, to be solved for their own sake. She could not allow herself to think beyond the abstract challenge at hand.

In the end Qwi had been the only one of her group who made it through the training. She received no instruction in biological sciences, saving her memory space for more physics, mathematics, and engineering. Tarkin had whisked her off to the new Maw Installation and placed her under the tutelage of the great engineer Bevel Lemelisk. Qwi had been in the Maw ever since.

Problems had to be solved for their own sake. If she allowed herself to be distracted by feelings, terrible things would happen. She remembered images of burning Omwati cities winking like faraway campfires from orbit, the laser-ignited wildfires that swept across the savannas of her world—but she had too many calculations to finish, too many designs to modify.

Qwi had salved her conscience by laying the responsibility on others. But the truth was, she created devices that had directly caused the deaths of entire civilizations, the destruction of whole worlds. With the Sun Crusher she could wipe out solar systems with the push of a button.

Qwi Xux had a lot of thinking to do, but she didn't know how to go about this kind of pondering. This was an entirely new and different type of problem to solve.

• • •

Chewbacca stood like a statue, refusing to move and daring the keeper to use his power-lash again.

The keeper did.

Chewbacca roared at the pain lancing across his skin; his nerves writhed in the aftermath of the charge. He raised his hairy arms, seething with the desire to rip the fat, placid man's limbs from his spherical torso.

Fourteen stormtroopers leveled their blasters at him.

"Are you going back to work, Wookiee, or do I have to nudge the power setting up a couple more notches?" The keeper tapped the handle of the power-lash against his palm, gazing at Chewbacca with a bland expression. His complexion was dusty-looking and bloodless, as if no hint of life had ever passed beneath the skin.

"Any other time I might have enjoyed the challenge of breaking you, Wookiee. I've been here fourteen standard years with an entire crew of Wookiee slaves. We lost a few during the process, but I cracked them all, and now they follow orders and do their work. But Admiral Daala insists that everything be in top-notch condition for mobilization by tomorrow."

He flicked the sizzling green tip of the lash in the air in front of Chewbacca's face, singeing some of the fur. Chewbacca peeled back his black lips and growled.

"I don't have time to play games right now," the keeper said. "If I have to waste any more time disciplining you, I'm going to dump you out into space. Do you understand?"

Chewbacca considered roaring in his face, but the keeper looked serious. At the very least Chewbacca had to survive long enough to find out what had happened to Han. A long time ago Han had rescued Chewbacca from other enslavers, and he still owed the man a life debt. He gave a low grunt of acquiescence.

"Good, now get back to that assault shuttle!"

Chewbacca wore gray work coveralls with pockets to hold engine diagnostic tools and hydrospanners. None of the tools could be used as a weapon; Chewbacca had already checked that much out.

The gamma-class assault shuttle took up a good portion of the *Gorgon's* lower hangar bay. Chewbacca had a small databoard listing the configurations for the tractor-beam projector and the deflector-shield generators. He had worked on other ships before, and he knew the *Falcon* inside out thanks to the many on-the-spot repairs he and Han had been forced to make. With the specs on the databoard he could easily service decades-old Imperial technology.

On the rear of the assault shuttle Chewbacca checked the exhaust nozzles of the thrust reactors and grudgingly tested the blaster-cannon mountings.

In the front of the vessel a convenient boarding hatch allowed access for the command crew, but Chewbacca opted for the more rigorous method of popping open and climbing through one of the foldaway launch doors used to disgorge zero-G stormtroopers during a space assault.

Inside, he had access to the engineering level, where he tinkered with the power modulators and the life-support systems. He restrained his urge to rip out circuits and damage the equipment—the keeper would execute him immediately, and such a minor sabotage would accomplish nothing. Even subtle damage was likely to be discovered in the initial checkout procedure.

The assault shuttle's spartan passenger section held only benches for its complement of spacetroopers, as well as power-coupled storage compartments for their bulky zero-G armor. Up front Chewbacca powered up and checked out the command console, did a test run of the twin-tandem flight computers . . . and thought about uprooting the chairs on which the five members of the command crew would sit.

Outside in the *Gorgon*'s hangar bay the fat keeper shouted and lashed at the air. Chewbacca felt a surge of anger upon hearing cries of agony from the other cowed Wookiee slaves. He knew nothing about his fellow captives; he had been held in a separate cell, and they were not allowed to speak to each other. Chewbacca wondered how long it had been since these exhausted slaves had touched the branches of their home trees.

"Get working!" the keeper yelled. "We have a lot that needs to be done today! Three hundred ships on the *Gorgon* alone!" And Chewbacca knew the three other star destroyers had an equal number of TIE fighters, blastboats, and assault shuttles.

Chewbacca clenched his fist around an upraised storage lid, bending it noticeably. He wanted to know why Admiral Daala insisted on such desperate speed.

Qwi Xux did not like to be muscled around by stormtroopers. In her years at the Maw Installation, she had learned to ignore the rigid troopers marching around the corridors in white armor, in endless robotic training and formations that made no sense at all. Did they all have faulty memories, or what? Once she learned something, she didn't need to keep drilling, drilling, drilling. Qwi paid little attention to them anymore—until a squad marched into her laboratory and insisted that she follow them.

Only moments earlier Qwi had shut down her illicit database searches, and she had disengaged the privacy lock on her lab's entryway. She had no reason to think the stormtroopers suspected anything, but she still felt unreasoning terror.

The troopers folded around her in a protective bubble as they marched her along the tiled corridors. "Where are you taking me?" Qwi finally managed to ask.

"Admiral Daala wishes to see you," the captain said through the filtered speaker on his helmet.

"Oh. Why?"

"She'll have to tell you that herself."

Qwi swallowed a cold lump in her throat and put a haughty tone in her voice. "Why couldn't she come to me herself?"

"Because Admiral Daala is a busy person."

"I'm a busy person, too."

"She is our commanding officer. You aren't."

Qwi asked no further questions but followed in silence as they took her across an access tube to another asteroid in the main conglomeration, then aboard a small shuttle in the landing bay.

When they arrived aboard the Star Destroyer *Gorgon*, Qwi could not keep herself from staring in wide-eyed fascination. Though the enormous ships had hung in the sky above Maw Installation for as long as she could remember, Qwi rarely had an opportunity to board them. Her stormtrooper escorts took her directly to the *Gorgon*'s bridge.

The trapezoidal command tower rose high above the arrowhead-shaped main body, giving a panoramic view overlooking the vast landscape of the ship. Qwi stood and stared out the front viewport toward the cobbled-together collection of rocks that made up Maw Installation. For a moment she remembered watching from the orbiting educational sphere as Moff Tarkin obliterated Omwati cities far below. . . .

Command crew bustled about their stations, intent on their work as if in the middle of an important drill. In the corridors stormtroopers marched by at a brisk pace. Overlapping intercom messages peppered the air. Qwi wondered how the troops could be so busy after a decade of doing nothing.

Admiral Daala stood by her command console, staring at the deadly swirling gases that blocked her from the outside. Qwi saw her trim, perfect figure masked by an aurora of chestnut hair that flowed like a living blanket down her back. When Daala turned to face her, some of the hair remained where it hung, wrapping around her waist while other strands arced behind her.

"You wanted to see me?" Qwi asked. Her reedy voice quavered despite her efforts to control her nervousness.

Daala looked at her for a moment, and Qwi had the impression of being placed under a magnifying lens in preparation for dissection. Then Daala suddenly seemed to recognize her. "Ah! You are Qwi Xux, in charge of the Sun Crusher project?"

"Yes, Admiral." She paused a moment, then blurted, "Have I done something wrong?"

"I don't know. Have you?" Daala answered, then turned back to the broad window, staring out at her other ships. "I can't get any straight information out of Tol Sivron, so I'll tell you directly. If you have any further work to do on your Sun Crusher, finish it now. We are mobilizing the fleet."

Daala misinterpreted Qwi's shocked silence. "Don't worry—I'll authorize whatever assistance you need, but everything must be done within a day. You've had two years longer than Grand Moff Tarkin gave you. It is time to put the Sun Crusher to use."

Qwi took a deep breath, trying to keep her thoughts from spinning. "But why now? Why such a rush?"

Daala whirled back at her, wearing a sour expression. "We have received new information. The Empire lies wounded and vulnerable on the outside, and we can't just sit here and wait. We have four Star Destroyers, a full fleet the Rebellion knows nothing about. Since the Death Star prototype is not capable of hyperspace travel, it is useless to us in this operation—but we will have the Sun Crusher. Your beautiful Sun Crusher." The lights of the fiery gases outside glimmered in Daala's eyes. "With it we can destroy the New Republic, system by system."

All of Han's warnings echoed as loud as screams in Qwi's head. He had been right about everything.

Daala dismissed her, and Qwi stumbled as the stormtroopers escorted her back toward the waiting shuttle. Qwi would have to make her decision sooner than she had expected.

24

In her own quarters images of planets scrolled in front of Leia's eyes. Statistics, populations, resources—cold data that she had to absorb and assess to make her decision. She rejected most of the worlds out of hand; others she marked as possibilities. So far nothing had jumped out at her as the *perfect* place for Luke to establish his Jedi academy.

It hadn't seemed like such a difficult request, since the New Republic encompassed so many possible planets. She had found Dantooine as a new home for the survivors from Eol Sha—why was an academy site causing her so much trouble?

After meeting Luke's first two trainees and seeing how *unusual* they were, Leia suspected the Jedi studies would require complete isolation. She had spoken again to Gantoris and Streen in the past day and was discouraged to find both of them feeling miserable and abandoned. If only Luke would come back soon—with Han!

As she thought of other places, Leia pondered how Yoda had trained Luke on the swampy planet of Dagobah, a place completely devoid of other intelligent life. Her brother would want someplace similar for his own trainees.

Okay, what about Dagobah itself? she thought, putting a fingertip on her lower lip. The swamps had hidden Yoda for centuries, and it was certainly isolated from the mainstream of galactic traffic . . . but Dagobah had no appropriate facilities either. They would have to erect an academy from scratch. Mobilizing the New Republic construction forces, Leia could get the job done in short order—but she wasn't sure that was the right answer. Somehow she felt the right site would jump out at her. Because the restoration of the Jedi Knights meant so much, Luke would be very selective about the proper site. She just hadn't found it yet.

The message center buzzed. Again. Though it was barely midmorning, she had already lost count of the interruptions. With a sigh Leia answered it, seeing the image of another minor functionary take shape in the central focus.

"Minister Organa Solo," the functionary said, "I'm sorry to call you at home, but we need you to decide on a meal selection for the Bimmini banquet. The deadline is today. The choices are grazer fillets with tart sauce, nerf medallions with sweet fungi, broiled dewback—"

"I'll take the nerf medallions. Thank you!" She switched off the receiver, then calmed herself before returning to the images of the planets.

In the bedchambers Jacen burst into loud sobs, joined in a moment by his sister. Threepio cooed sounds of consolation, then began another one of his lullabies, which set them to crying louder. Part of Leia wanted to hurry into the children's room to see what was the matter, while another part of her just wanted to seal their door so she could have a little more quiet.

On the morning after the reception at the Skydome Botanical Gardens, both children had come down with a cold. Slight fever, congestion, and general crankiness—the type of frequent minor illness the twins would no doubt suffer for another few years—but Leia didn't want to just abandon them to the care of Threepio.

After some refresher programming, the protocol droid had proved himself capable of caring for the two-year-olds. But Leia felt a defensiveness in herself. She was their *mother;* while it was a new set of responsibilities for her, Leia did not want a droid to watch them all the time, no matter how competent his programming. The children had already spent so much of their lives with Winter that Leia wanted to make up for lost time—if her political duties would only give her the chance!

Before she could call up the file on another planet to consider, the message center buzzed again. "What is it?" she said, mustering every scrap of civility she still possessed. She did not recognize the alien administrator in the image.

"Ah, Minister Organa Solo, I am calling from the office of the deputy assistant minister of industry. I was told you might be able to offer a suggestion about a type of music that would be appropriate to play during the arrival of the Ishi Tib delegate?"

For a moment Leia reconsidered her time as a prisoner of Jabba the Hutt. At least the sluglike crime lord had not required her to do anything more than sit there and look beautiful. . . .

Before she finished signing off, a message came in from Admiral Ackbar. Though she liked the Calamarian admiral, she found it difficult to keep her temper from boiling. How was she supposed to get anything done with all these interruptions?

"Hello, Admiral—can I help you quickly? I'm in the middle of a rather large project right now."

Ackbar nodded graciously, swiveling his big fish eyes to the front in a gesture of courtesy. "Of course, Leia. I apologize for the interruption, but I'd like to solicit your comments on the speech I have just written. As you remember, I am giving it before the Cabinet tomorrow, and you agreed to provide me with data on the rezoning of embassy sectors in the devastated areas of Imperial City. I did write the speech without your input, but I need to have the information before tomorrow. I've marked clearly where you need to add your thoughts. Would it be possible—"

"Of course, Admiral. I'm sorry I haven't been more attentive. Please send it to my personal network address, and I'll get to it right away. I promise."

Ackbar nodded his salmon-colored head. "Thank you, and I apologize again for the interruption. I'll let you get back to work."

When he signed off, Leia could do no more than sit with her eyes closed, hoping for a few moments of silence. In quiet times, though, she began to worry too much about Han. . . .

The door chime sounded. Leia almost screamed.

Mon Mothma stood at the doorway in her flowing white robes. "Hello, Leia. Do you mind if I come in?"

Leia stuttered, trying to regain her composure. "Uh, please!" Mon Mothma had never come visiting, never shown the slightest inclination to make any sort of social call. Though calm and quietly charismatic, the Chief of State had always distanced herself from anyone else.

During the early days of the Rebellion, Mon Mothma had sparred with Leia's father Bail Organa on the floor of the Senate. Mon Mothma was a new senator then, a firebrand insisting on rapid and sweeping changes that dismayed the seasoned and cynical Bail Organa. Eventually, though, they joined forces to oppose Senator Palpatine in his quest to become President; when they failed and Palpatine proclaimed himself "Emperor," Mon Mothma began to speak of open rebellion. A horrified Bail Organa had not seen the need until after the Ghorman Massacre, when he finally realized that the Republic he had served for so long was truly dead.

The death of Bail Organa and the destruction of Alderaan had affected Mon Mothma deeply. But she had never hinted that she wished to become friends with the daughter of her old rival. "What can I do for you, Mon Mothma?" Leia asked.

Mon Mothma looked around the private quarters, fixing her gaze on the sweeping landscapes of Alderaan mounted on the walls, the grasslands, the organic-looking tower cities, the underground settlements. The faintest sheen of tears seemed to film her eyes.

"I learned that your children are sick, and I wanted to offer my consolations." She fixed a sharp gaze on Leia. "And I have also learned that Han and Chewbacca never returned from their Kessel mission. I wish you hadn't tried to hide that from me. Is there anything I can do?"

Leia looked down. "No. Lando Calrissian and my brother Luke have already gone to see what they can find. I hope they bring back news soon."

Mon Mothma nodded. "And I also wanted to commend you on the job you are doing. Or perhaps *console* you is the better word."

Leia could not hide her surprise. "The reception for Ambassador Furgan was a disaster!"

Mon Mothma shrugged. "And do you think anyone could have performed better than you did? You did a perfectly adequate job with the Caridans. Some battles simply cannot be won. Given the Caridans' potential for galactic mayhem, I think getting a drink thrown in my face is a relatively minor debacle."

With a faint smile Leia had to admit that the Chief of State was right. "Now, if only I could find a place to house Luke's Jedi academy, I'd feel like I'm making some progress through this whole morass."

Mon Mothma smiled. "I've been thinking about that too, ever since Luke made his speech. I believe I have a suggestion."

Leia's dark eyes widened in surprise. "Please!"

Mon Mothma indicated the data terminal in Leia's living chamber. "May I?"

Leia gestured for her to use the system. Though a lifelong politician, Mon Mothma set to work on the database; she was obviously no stranger to doing her own research.

When images of the new planet crystallized in the projection zone, Leia felt the tingle of excitement creep through her. The confident feeling that this was the *right* place grew in her heart. She wondered how she had overlooked something so obvious.

"Consider," Mon Mothma said, smiling. "It has everything he could possibly need—privacy, good climate, facilities already in place."

"It's perfect! I don't know why I didn't think of it myself."

The message center buzzed again.

"What?" Leia barked at the caller. She realized she should have been more restrained, but she had reached the end of her fuse. Mon Mothma remained at the data terminal, watching from outside the field of view.

The caller also dispensed with tact. "We need your report right now, Minister Organa Solo. The orbital debris committee is deliberating on the disposition of wreckage around Coruscant. You were supposed to attend our discussions this morning—"

Leia recognized the functionary as Andur, the vice-chairman of the committee. "My aide has already canceled my appointments for today. I'm sorry I was unable to attend."

"We received your cancellation, but we didn't receive your report. You agreed to write a summary and distribute it to us at this session. It's past due! Sick children do not make the New Republic stop functioning."

Seeing red, Leia remembered standing in Jabba's palace, holding the pulsing thermal detonator in her hand, waiting for it to explode and kill them all. Five, four, three, two . . .

Somehow she restrained herself. Perhaps spending a day with Ambassador Furgan had toughened her calluses. "I may be the Minister of State, Mr. Andur, but I am also a mother. I have to do both jobs—I can't sacrifice one for the sake of the other. My children need me now. The committee can wait."

Miffed, the vice-chairman raised his voice. "It would have been much easier to complete our deliberations if you had been here rather than home playing nurse—couldn't you hire a medical droid to take care of your kids' runny noses? This is an important issue we're dealing with, affecting the fate of all space traffic approaching and leaving Coruscant!"

Leia stiffened. "This is an important issue I'm dealing with here, too! How can you expect me to care about the whole galaxy if I don't even care for my own family? If you wanted mindless devotion to duty without caring about people, then you should have stayed with the old Empire!" She reached for the controls. "My report will be issued to you *in due time*, Mr. Andur." She switched him off before he could say another word.

At the end of her outburst, Leia slumped into her self-conforming chair, suddenly remembering her guest. Her face turned scarlet with embarrassment.

"That committee meets weekly, and there's no reason why they couldn't have waited until next time," she said in a simmering, defensive voice. "I'm really not going to let any important negotiations go down the drain. I know my duty."

Mon Mothma nodded, sharing one of her placid, heartfelt smiles. "Of course you won't, Leia. I understand. Don't worry about it." The Chief of State looked at Leia with what seemed to be a new and surprising respect.

Leia sighed and stared at the planetary image on the data terminal. "Maybe I should go off and spend a few months at the Jedi academy myself as soon as Luke gets it under way—though I know that'll never happen. Taking a vacation from Imperial City is about as easy as walking away from a black hole. Affairs of state swallow up my entire day."

She caught herself complaining and quickly added, "But of course restoring the order of the Jedi Knights is very important. I have the potential to use the Force and so do the twins. But thorough training will take a lot of time and concentration—two commodities I don't seem to have."

Mon Mothma looked at her gravely, then squeezed Leia's shoulder. "Don't worry too much. You have other important things in store for you."

25

Han rolled over with a groan in the detention cell. The hard ridges on the surface of his bunk—Han thought of them as "discomfort stripes"—made sleep itself a nightmare.

He awoke from a dream about Leia, perhaps the only enjoyment he had experienced in three weeks. The dim reddish light filtered down, hurting his eyes without providing useful illumination.

He blinked his eyes open, hearing people move outside his cell door, the clank of stormtrooper boots on the floor gratings, muffled voices. The cyberlock clicked as someone activated the password code.

He sat up, suddenly alert. His body ached, his mind still buzzed from the interrogation drugs, but he tensed as the door opened. He had no idea what this was, but he felt certain he wouldn't like it.

Corridor light flooded in, and Qwi Xux stood beside an armed stormtrooper. She looked battered and abused by her own thoughts, which gave Han a smug grin. He hoped she had lost a lot of sleep after learning of the devastating use to which her inventions had been put. She might be able to fool herself, but she couldn't fool him.

"What, have you come back to discuss a few more moral issues, Doc? Am I supposed to be your conscience?"

Qwi crossed her pale-bluish arms over her chest. "Admiral Daala has given me permission to interrogate you again," she said coldly, though her body language did not match her tone. She turned to the guard, her pearlescent hair sparkling in the dim corridor. "Would you accompany me inside for the interrogation, Lieutenant? I'm afraid the prisoner might not cooperate."

"Yes, Dr. Xux," the guard said, following her into the cell. He slid the door partially closed behind him.

While his back was turned, Qwi withdrew a blaster from the utility pocket on her smock, pointed it at the guard, and fired a stun blast. Rippling arcs of blue fire surrounded him, then faded as he crumpled to the floor.

Han leaped to his feet. "What are you doing!"

Qwi stepped over the fallen stormtrooper. The previous day she had seemed more fragile; the Imperial-issue heavy blaster pistol looked huge in her delicate hand. "Admiral Daala is mobilizing this entire fleet in less than a day. She plans to take the Sun Crusher and her four Star Destroyers to wipe out the New Republic. Your friend Kyp Durron is also scheduled for termination this afternoon." She raised her feathery eyebrows. "Does that add up to enough of an excuse to escape as soon as we can?"

Han's mind reeled. At the moment all he could think of was seeing Kyp and Chewbacca again, then getting back to Coruscant so he could be reunited with Leia and the twins. "I don't have any appointments I couldn't be persuaded to cancel."

"Good," Qwi said. "Any questions?"

Han smirked as he began to pull on his disguise of stormtrooper armor. "No, I'm used to doing this sort of thing."

Kyp could sense the difference in the air—his first indication that his efforts to focus the Force were actually accomplishing something. He studied every slight change in air currents, in the sluggish odors around the cell, the myriad tiny sounds that echoed through the metal walls.

Stretching his mind through invisible webs of the Force, Kyp could feel a *surge* from the guards when they walked past his cell. He could sense a *twinge* each time someone dispensed the food tray through the door. But their attitudes had changed. Over the whole ship he could catch faint ripples of activity, tension, growing anxiety.

Something was about to happen.

Closer at hand, he understood a deeper gut-wrenching truth. The emotions had been so clear in the guard stationed beside his door the previous sleep period. Kyp Durron was not to be part of whatever activity the Star Destroyers were preparing. A young man from the spice mines of Kessel could provide no useful information; they had no reason to keep him alive.

Admiral Daala had already scheduled Kyp's termination. He had not much longer to live. His lips curled back in an angry snarl. The Empire had been trying to destroy him all his life, and now they were about to succeed.

When he heard voices outside his door, he sensed the barrage of their uneasiness, the curdling plans of violence behind the forefront of their minds. He had no way to defend himself! Despairing, Kyp slid his head against the cool metal wall of the door, trying to pick out a few select words of the conversation.

"—scheduled for execution this afternoon."

" . . . know that. We are . . . take him. Admiral . . . authorization right here."

" . . . irregular. Why . . . want him?"

"Weapons test . . . target . . . new concept . . . vital to the fleet's new armaments . . . right away!"

" . . . need specific . . . only a general authorization."

"No . . . good enough!"

The voices rose, but Kyp couldn't make out more of the words. He tried to decipher three voices talking all at once.

Kyp made ready to lash out the moment the door slid open. He knew he would be cut down by blaster fire in no time—but at least it would be over, and he would be shot on his own terms, not the Empire's.

" . . . check with . . . first. Wait—"

Suddenly Kyp heard a thump and a muffled blast. A heavy object smashed against the doorway. Kyp flinched back as the door whisked open.

The dead stormtrooper guard sprawled backward into his cell with a clatter of white armor. A smoking hole oozed steam from the waist joint in the brittle uniform.

Another stormtrooper stepped inside holding the still-warm blaster pistol. Beside him stood a willowy alien woman, looking delicate but outraged at the same time.

"I hope *that* was sufficient authorization," the stormtrooper said, then pulled off his helmet.

"Han!" Kyp cried.

"I really hate red tape," Han said, nudging the dead guard with his foot. "Think you can fit into that uniform, kid?"

"No, I don't want one of the slow old ones!" Qwi snapped at the keeper of the Wookiee work detail. Through the narrowed field of view in his stormtrooper helmet, Han watched the delicate woman play the part of a tough, impatient researcher.

The rotund man glanced at his hairy charges, unintimidated as if he were accustomed to being shouted at by prima donna scientists. The keeper's face looked like pale, wet clay.

Han fidgeted, sweating in the cramped uniform. The helmet had nose filters, but the suit still smelled of body odor from its former owner. The stormtroopers at Maw Installation lived in their uniforms and likely disinfected the interiors much less often than they polished the exteriors.

The keeper shrugged, as if Qwi's impatience did not concern him. "These Wookiees have been worked hard for over a decade. What do you expect from them? They're all slow and worthless."

Han could see that most of the other Wookiees wandering around the hangar bay had patchy fur and stooped shoulders, bringing them almost to the height of a human. These slaves looked as if their will had been crushed over years of harsh servitude.

"I don't want to hear your excuses," Qwi said. She tossed her head, making the feathery pearls of her hair shimmer. "We've been ordered to get a lot of work done before the fleet departs, and I need a Wookiee with some energy. Give me that new prisoner you have. He'll do the work."

"Not a good idea," the keeper said, wrinkling his pasty forehead. "He's unruly, and you'd have to double-check his work. Can't trust him not to try sabotage."

"I don't care how unruly he can get!" Qwi snapped. "At least he won't fall asleep on the job."

On the far side of the bay a tall Wookiee stepped out of a gamma-class assault shuttle. He straightened from the cramped quarters and looked around the bay. Han had to force himself not to yank off his helmet and call out Chewbacca's name. The Wookiee seemed ready to strike, barely restraining himself from flying into a suicidal rage. With his bare hands Chewbacca could dismantle five or six TIE fighters before the stormtroopers took him down. The keeper glanced at Chewbacca, as if considering.

"I have authorization from Admiral Daala herself," Qwi said, holding out a curled hardcopy bearing Daala's seal. Han glanced at the other stormtroopers standing guard in the engine pool. He could not invoke the same violent "authorization" he had used to spring Kyp Durron from his cell.

Beside Qwi Xux, Kyp—wearing the smaller of the two stolen stormtrooper uniforms—stood stock-still. Han knew the kid must be terrified, but Kyp had snapped to attention and done everything Han suggested. Han felt a rush of warmth inside, and he hoped Kyp could get out of here to the normal life he deserved.

"All right, but you take him at your own risk," the keeper finally said. "I won't be responsible if he ruins whatever you have him working on." He whistled and motioned for a pair of stormtroopers to bring Chewbacca over.

The Wookiee growled in anger, glaring around with hard, dark eyes. He did not recognize Han, nor did he know Qwi Xux. Chewbacca glared at them, resenting another assignment.

"A little more cooperation!" the keeper yelled, then struck out with his energy lash, burning a smoking welt across Chewbacca's shoulder blades.

The Wookiee howled and snarled but somehow restrained himself as the other stormtroopers hauled out their blasters, ready to stun him if he went wild. Han tensed, clenching his fists as much as the armored gloves would allow. More than anything he wanted to shove the generating handle of the energy-lash down the keeper's throat and switch it on full power.

But instead Han stood at attention, doing nothing, saying nothing. Like a good stormtrooper.

The four of them marched out of the hangar bay. The keeper ignored them as he strode to the other captive Wookiees and began to strike left and right with his energy-lash, venting his anger. Han felt his stomach knotting.

Chewbacca kept looking from side to side, as if searching for his chance to escape. Han just hoped they could get someplace private before the big Wookiee decided to tear them all apart.

The doors closed, leaving them in a harshly lit white corridor. "Chewie!" Han said, pulling off his stormtrooper helmet. After breathing through the sour nose filters, even the musky scent of a Wookiee smelled sweet to him.

Chewbacca bleated in delighted surprise and grabbed Han in a huge hug, wrapping hairy arms around him and lifting him off the floor. Han gasped for breath, grateful for the protection of the armor. "Put me down!" he said, trying to stop himself from chuckling. "If somebody sees you, they'll think you're killing me! Wouldn't that be a stupid reason to get blasted?"

Chewbacca agreed and lowered him back to the floor.

"Now what?" Han asked Qwi.

"If you can pilot us out of here, we can escape," Qwi said.

Han grinned. "If that's our only problem, we're home free. I can pilot any ship—just give me the chance."

"Then let's get out of here," she said. "Time is running out."

When they boarded the shuttle back down to Maw Installation, Han could ask no further questions. Surrounded by other stormtroopers rigidly minding their own business, neither he nor Kyp could speak with Qwi. Casual conversation seemed forbidden.

Qwi fidgeted, looking at the shuttle walls, the narrow windows showing the deadly barrier of the Maw itself with its secret pathways—if they could escape.

Han desperately wanted to see Leia and the twins again. They filled his thoughts more and more, preoccupying him at times when he should have fixed every iota of attention on the peril around him. He ached to hold Leia again—but thinking of her while he wore a stormtrooper uniform seemed to taint the emotion.

Beside him sat Kyp, unreadable behind a stormtrooper mask. But the eyeholes of the helmet continued to turn toward Han, as if seeking reassurance. Han wished he had more to offer—but he did not know Qwi's plan.

Why were they returning to Maw Installation, rather than just stealing a ship and racing off into space? It would be a breakneck run, no matter when they started—and Admiral Daala's attack preparations grew more complete with each hour.

Han had to warn the New Republic of the disaster about to befall it. First, he had been concerned about the concentration of space power around Kessel—but the fleet of four Star Destroyers and the Maw Installation's secret weapons looked infinitely worse than whatever Moruth Doole had pieced together from the scrap heap.

Chewbacca wore mechanic's overalls, looking like a worker assigned to perform maintenance on some piece of equipment down in one of the laboratories. He made grunting sounds to himself, content to be reunited with his friends but anxious for action.

Qwi remained uncommunicative, keeping her thin bluish hands folded in her lap. Han wondered if he had gone too far in his accusations of her naïveté and the evil nature of her work. He wished he knew what she was thinking.

When the shuttle landed in one of the Installation's asteroids and the stormtroopers disembarked, Qwi led Han, Kyp, and Chewbacca away from the rocky hangar through a tunnel high enough to allow the movement of ships. "This way," she said.

Han did not recognize where she was taking them. "Aren't we going back to your lab, Doc?"

Qwi froze in midstep before turning to him. "No, never again." Then she moved on.

When they reached a tall metal doorway guarded by two stormtroopers standing at attention, Qwi took out her badge again, flashing the imprinted holograms in the light. The stormtroopers straightened to attention.

"Open up for me," Qwi said.

"Yes, Dr. Xux," the head guard said. "Your badge, please?"

She handed him her badge with a barely controlled smile. Han began to grow uneasy. These guards recognized Qwi by sight, and she seemed more comfortable now than she had been during other parts of their escape. Was this some kind of treachery? But to what purpose? He and Kyp turned toward each other, but the stormtrooper helmets kept their expressions unreadable.

"The Wookiee is here to do heavy maintenance on the engines—a complete coolant overhaul before tomorrow's deployment of the fleet," Qwi said. "These two guards are specially trained to prevent him from acting up. This Wookiee has caused some damage before, and we can't afford delays." Han tried not to cringe. Qwi was talking too quickly, letting her nervousness show through.

"Just give me the proper authorizations," the guard said. "You know the routine." He slid her badge through a scanner to log Qwi in, then handed it back to her. The stormtrooper seemed unconcerned, as if glad to be posted here rather than in the middle of frantic preparations for deployment.

Qwi went to the door's data terminal and punched up a request, then she handed him the hardcopy printout of Admiral Daala's permission again. Han wondered how many times she was going to use the same piece of paper!

"There, you'll see the approved work request for the Wookiee with a notation for special handlers. It's been authorized by Tol Sivron himself."

The guard shrugged. "As usual. Let me scan the service numbers of these two troopers. Then you're free to go in." He entered Han's and Kyp's numbers, then worked the door controls.

The great steelcrete doors ground to each side, revealing a hangar lit by levitating globes of light. Overhead, wide rectangular skylights let in the eerie glow of swirling gases around the Maw. Qwi stepped inside the chamber, and her whole demeanor changed, as if she had suddenly turned breathless. Han, Kyp, and Chewbacca followed.

The guard worked his controls, and the doors slid closed, sealing them inside. Qwi visibly relaxed.

Han stared up at a ship like none he had ever seen before. Smaller than the *Millennium Falcon*, this craft was oblong and faceted, like a long shard of crystal. Its own repulsorlifts kept it upright, with an actual ladder leading to the open hatch. Defensive lasers bristled from the corners of its facets.

The armor plating was multicolored and shimmering, like a constantly changing pool of oil and molten metal. At the lower vertex hung the oddly fuzzy torus of an immensely powerful resonance-torpedo transmitter. Though not much larger than a fighter craft, the Sun Crusher hummed with deadly potential.

"We're going to steal that?" Han cried.

"Of course," Qwi Xux said. "It's the greatest weapon ever devised, and I've spent eight years of my life designing it. You didn't expect me to leave it here for Admiral Daala, did you?"

26

The *Millennium Falcon's* subspace engines flared white hot as the ship blasted away from Kessel's garrison moon. A swarm of fighters streamed after it, peppering space with multicolored blaster fire. Large capital ships began to nose into the *Falcon's* flight-path like sleeping giants roused by stinging insects.

Lando Calrissian did his best to dodge the concentrated blaster fire. "The sublight engines are still optimal. Either Han's been maintaining her with a real mechanic for a change, or Doole reconditioned her for his fleet," he said. "Let's see how well the weapons systems work."

A pair of wasplike Z-95 Headhunters streaked after them, shooting fire-linked banks of triple blasters; close behind followed three battered Y-wing long-range fighters.

Luke spun around and whistled in surprise. "Headhunters! I didn't think anybody used those anymore!"

"Doole couldn't be choosy, I guess," Lando said.

The *Falcon* rocked with several direct blaster hits; the fresh and fully charged shields held, though, for the moment.

Lando dropped the blaster cannon through its ventral hatch, then fired back at the pursuers. After five prolonged shots, Lando managed to hit the exhaust nacelle of a Y-wing, forcing it to break formation and peel off for repairs.

"One down—only about a thousand more to go," Lando said.

The Z-95 Headhunters pummeled them with repeated blaster fire, as if to punish the *Falcon.*

"Go down close to the planet and skim the atmosphere," Luke said. "Let's burn them up in the energy shield."

Lando set course for the lumpy world of Kessel as he voiced his complaints. "We can't detect that energy shield either. How do you know we won't get disintegrated ourselves?"

"We've got better reactions than they do."

Lando didn't seem convinced. "I've already almost flown into an energy shield once during our attack on the Death Star. I'm not anxious to repeat the process."

"Trust me," Luke said.

Kessel swelled in front of them, pockmarked and wreathed in a cottony halo of escaping air. "We're getting close."

Luke held the back of the pilot chair, his eyes half-closed. He breathed regularly, reaching out, sensing the pulsing power generated as a protective blanket by the garrison moon.

"Don't fall asleep on me, Luke!"

"Keep flying."

The Headhunters swooped after, flanked by the remaining pair of Y-wings.

"The aft deflector shield is starting to feel the pounding," Lando said. "If these guys get any closer, they're going to fly up my exhaust ports!"

"Get ready," Luke said.

Kessel filled their entire viewport now, boiling with its turbulent thin-air storms, tiny plumes from the numerous atmosphere factories tracing lines above the landscape.

"I'm ready, I'm ready! Just say the word and I—"

"Pull up, now!"

Lando's tension helped him react like a spring-loaded catapult. He hauled up on the controls, ripping the *Falcon* straight up in a tight cartwheel. Taken by surprise, all four of the attacking ships splattered into clouds of ignited fuel and ionized metal as they slammed into the invisible energy shield.

"Missed it by a couple of meters at least," Luke said. "Relax, Lando."

Artoo bleeped, and Luke answered him after looking at the expression on Lando's face. "No, Artoo, I don't think he's interested in an exact measurement."

They soared just above the atmosphere on a tight orbit that took them around Kessel's poles. The curtain of stars rolled out from the edge of the planet as the landscape sped beneath them; then they looped back into space in a mad dash to escape.

They ran straight into the wave of fighters belching out of the garrison moon.

Yelling in surprise, Lando launched a pair of Arkayd concussion missiles from the front tubes. The density of approaching ships was so great that even the wild shots scored twice, taking out a TIE fighter and a blast boat, while the hot debris cloud destroyed a heavily armed B-wing.

"Let's not get cocky because we took care of a couple of ships. I've got only six more missiles."

"We will not surrender now," Luke said.

"No, I just mean we're running, not fighting. At least the engines are in tip-top condition," Lando said. "The *Falcon* hasn't been this pampered since *I* owned her."

"How fast can we get out of here?" Luke asked.

Jacked next to the copilot's chair, Artoo chittered and bleeped. Luke glanced down and saw rows of flickering red lights on the navigation panel. "Uh oh."

"What is he saying?" Lando said. He flicked his gaze from the ships swarming by the front viewport to the little astromech droid. "What's wrong with him?"

"The navicomp's not working," Luke said.

"Well, fix it!"

Luke had already dashed around the bend in the corridor to pry off the access panel to the *Falcon*'s navicomputer. He glanced at the boards, feeling his heart sink into a black hole as deep as the Maw. "They've pulled the coordinate module. It's not here."

Lando groaned. "Now what are we going to do?"

In response to Lando's concussion missiles, the Kessel fighters formed into tighter battle groups, striking at the *Falcon* with a firestorm of blaster bolts. Luke had to shield his eyes from the blinding flashes of near misses and deflected hits.

"I don't know, but we'd better do it as fast as we can."

"They're from the New Republic!" Moruth Doole fumed in his rage, stomping up and down. "They'll go back and report everything!" He straightened his mussed yellow cravat to regain his composure, but it didn't work. He wanted to squash the escapees like a pair of bugs to eat. Spies and traitors! They had led him along, lied to him, taunted him.

"Send out every ship we have!" he screamed into the open channel that broadcast to his forces. He had managed to make it to the command center on the garrison moon. "Surround them, crush them, smash into them. I don't care what it takes!"

"Sending out every ship might not be a good strategy," responded one of the captains. "The pilots don't know the formations, and they'll just get in each other's way."

Doole's mechanical eye lay in pieces scattered about the top of the console, and he could not see well enough to put it back together. With the blurry focus of his one half-blind eye, Doole could not identify the dissenting mercenary.

"I don't care! I don't want to lose these like we lost Han Solo!" He pounded his soft fist on the console, jarring the pieces of his mechanical eye. The primary lens bounced, then slid off the edge to shatter on the floor.

The *Falcon* ran straight toward the Maw, leaving Kessel behind.

"We'll be all right," Luke said. "I can use the Force to guide us through on a safe path."

"If there *is* a safe path," Lando muttered.

Sweat stood out on Luke's forehead. "What other choice do we have? We can't hide anyplace else, we can't outrun all those fighters, and we can't go into hyperspace without a navicomp."

"What a great selection of options," Lando said.

Finally mobilized, the capital ships came after them, firing ion cannon blasts powerful enough to clear a path through an asteroid field. The two big Lancer frigates made a deadly web in front of the *Falcon* with their twenty quad-firing laser cannons; but the Lancers were sluggish, and the *Falcon* increased its lead.

Somehow the other capital ships anticipated their run to the black hole cluster and converged ahead of them as Lando pushed the *Falcon*'s engines. "Come on, come on! Just squeeze a little more speed out."

Ten system patrol craft, originally designed for maximum speed to combat smugglers and pirates, surged past the *Falcon* and lined up in a blockade. But in the three-dimensional vastness of space, Lando managed to slip under their grasp. Laser blasts erupted all around them.

"Our shields are edging the redlines," Lando said.

Three *Carrack*-class light cruisers—midway in size between the Lancer frigates and the larger Dreadnaughts such as the ones in Bel Iblis's lost *Dark Force*—formed a triple-pronged pincer, right, left, and top.

In hot pursuit behind the *Falcon* came the jagged ovoid of a Loronar strike cruiser, the largest ship in the Kessel fleet. As the chase plowed through the net of system patrol craft, the strike cruiser harmlessly took stray fire meant for the *Falcon*.

Lando stared out the viewport windows at the horrifying spectacle of the

Maw and the giant battleships moving to meet them. Artoo bleeped something that even Luke could not translate.

"Only a complete idiot would go into a place like that," Lando said. He squeezed his eyes shut.

"Then let's just hope they're not idiots, too," Luke said.

27

Admiral Daala stood in the bridge tower of the Star Destroyer
Gorgon, looking out at her fleet and feeling the energy build inside her.
The time was at hand! The Empire might have fallen, but with it went all
the people who had squashed her. Now she could show her worth. Daala
could fight her own battle.

She gazed at the misty colors of the Maw and the clump of strung-
together rocks that had spawned the weapons for her assault. In formation
the *Hydra,* the *Basilisk,* and the *Manticore* powered up, waiting to spring out
upon the galaxy with swift and deadly precision. The New Republic would
fall to its knees.

She had no interest in ruling the former Empire herself—Daala never
had any such aspirations. Her main intent right now was just to cause them
pain. She licked her lips, and her hair hung heavy down her back, serpentine
like the demon for whom her flagship had been named. Grand Moff Tarkin
would have been proud.

Commander Kratas, the man who ran the subsystems of the *Gorgon,*
spoke to her from a communication terminal. "Admiral Daala, I have a
priority message from the detention level!"

"Detention level? What is it?"

"The prisoners Han Solo and Kyp Durron have escaped! One guard was
found stunned in Solo's detention chamber, and another is dead in Durron's

cell. Both were stripped of their armor. We are attempting to question the survivor now."

Daala felt a jolt of anger disrupt the eagerness singing through her veins. She drew herself up taller, raising her eyebrows and focusing intently on Kratas. "Track the service numbers of the stolen uniforms. Maybe they've logged in somewhere." Her orders came like staccato laser blasts.

Kratas consulted his terminal, spoke into the comlink. Daala clasped her hands behind her back and paced, barking orders to the bridge personnel. "Put together a search party immediately. We'll comb every deck of the *Gorgon*. They can't have gotten off the ship. There's no place else they could have gone."

"Admiral!" Commander Kratas said. "The surviving guard claims that one of the scientists from the Installation came to see Solo. Qwi Xux. The guard insists that Dr. Xux had an authorization directly from you."

Daala's jaw dropped; then she clamped her lips together in a bloodless, iron line. "Check on the Wookiee! See what's happened to him."

Kratas queried the database. "The keeper says that the new Wookiee prisoner has been requisitioned and taken to a higher-priority assignment." He swallowed. "Qwi Xux was the one who requisitioned him. She used your authorization code again."

Daala's nostrils flared, but then another thought struck her like a crashing asteroid. "Oh no!" she said. "They're after the Sun Crusher!"

Alone in the guarded hangar holding the Sun Crusher, Han clambered into the hatch. "Can't remember the last time I had to use a *ladder* to get inside a ship! Pretty primitive for such a sophisticated weapon."

"It works." Qwi hauled herself up the rungs behind him. "The sophistication is inside. All the rest is just window dressing."

Han sat down in the pilot's chair in the cockpit and looked at the controls. "Everything seems to be labeled the way it should be, though the placement is a little odd. What's this for? Wait a minute, I'll figure it out."

Kyp reached the top of the ladder, paused, then pulled off his stormtrooper helmet. "Those mask filters stink!" he said, then with obvious pleasure tossed the skull-like helmet to the floor of the chamber. It clattered and bounced like a severed head. Kyp's dark hair was curled with sweat and mussed from the confining helmet, but his face shone with a grin.

Chewbacca swung into the compartment, ducking his head and squeezing through the narrow hatch. He looked at the skylights in the chamber's ceiling, then growled at the shape of a Star Destroyer orbiting overhead.

Han dropped his own helmet to the floor of the cockpit. Kyp kicked it under the seat and out of the way. Han touched the Sun Crusher's navicomp, switching it on. "This thing is in better shape than the Imperial shuttle we stole. Are all the coordinates burned into the database, Doc?"

Qwi nodded, sitting down primly and strapping herself into her seat. "The Sun Crusher has been ready to go for years. We've just been waiting for orders from the Empire. Good thing nobody came back, right?"

Han pursed his lips, scanning the controls. "Everything here looks pretty standard," he said. "I won't have much time for practice."

Chewbacca gave an ear-splitting Wookiee bellow of challenge. Below, Han heard the heavy armored door grind open and then clattering footsteps as a squad of stormtroopers charged into the chamber.

Standing at the door, Kyp stuck his head out of the narrow hatch. "Here they come!"

"Seal that hatch, kid," Han shouted. "We're in here for the duration now! Chewie, have you found the weapons controls yet?"

In the copilot's chair, Chewbacca ran his huge hands over the buttons and dials. Finally finding what he wanted, he let out a yowl. Defensive laser cannons mounted at different targeting angles swiveled as he tested the aiming mechanisms.

Small thuds banged against the Sun Crusher's hull as the stormtroopers fired their blaster rifles, causing no damage. Han looked at Qwi. "We don't even have the shields on!"

"This armor will hold against anything they can throw against us," she said with a smug smile. "It was designed to."

Han grinned and cracked his knuckles. "Well, in that case let's take an extra few seconds and do this right!" He worked the controls, activating the repulsorlift engines. The interior of the Sun Crusher wobbled as the entire craft rose into the air, floating on its repulsor cushion. Outside they could hear the faint screeching of an alarm.

"Chewie, point those laser cannons straight up. Let's give ourselves a twenty-one-gun salute—right through the roof!"

The Wookiee roared to himself; then, without waiting for Han to give the order, he fired all of the Sun Crusher's weaponry at once. Kyp scrambled for his seat, strapping himself in. Qwi stared at the roof of the cockpit with wide eyes.

The ceiling of the hangar chamber blasted outward under the barrage of laser energy. Some of the larger chunks of rubble fell downward, clanging against the Sun Crusher's hull, but most of the skylights burst into space with the outrushing of contained air that spewed into the Maw.

Stormtroopers, flailing their arms and legs, were sucked out through the breach, flotsam among the rock and transparisteel debris in low orbit around the clustered rocks. Their armor might protect them against massive decompression for a few minutes, but every one of them was doomed.

Han raised the Sun Crusher up, accelerating through the escape hole they had blown through the top of the chamber. They shot into open space, and Han felt an exhilaration he had not felt since they had first arrived at Kessel.

"Here goes nothing!" he said. "Now for the fun part."

Staring down at the Installation from the *Gorgon*'s bridge, Admiral Daala felt her stomach knot. For years her entire duty had been to protect that small clump of planetoids, to pamper the scientists. Grand Moff Tarkin had said these people held the future security of the Empire, and she had believed him.

Daala had been stepped on, abused, taken advantage of at the Caridan military academy. Tarkin had rescued her from that. He had given her the responsibility and the power she had earned through her own abilities. She owed Tarkin everything.

She would avenge him by destroying the New Republic as she caused their star systems to go supernova one by one. They could hide nowhere. At the same time, she would make her mark on the history of the galaxy, a warlord who had succeeded where an entire Empire had failed. The thought made Daala's pale lips curl upward in a grim smile.

As she watched, Daala saw the puff of an explosion on one of the rocks of Maw Installation. Then the tiny form of the Sun Crusher streaked by, a characteristically angular speck fleeing the confines of the planetoid containing it.

"Red alert!" she shouted. "Mobilize all forces. They have the Sun Crusher, and we can't let them take it away. That is our most valuable weapon!"

"But . . . Admiral," Commander Kratas said, "if the technical reports are correct, nothing can harm the Sun Crusher."

"We must find some way to capture them. Mobilize the other Star Destroyers. We'll try to blockade them, cut off their escape. Release enough small fighters to overwhelm them."

She fixed Kratas with her gaze. Her hair seemed to rise by itself, as if threatening to become a garrote for his throat. "Make certain you understand this, Commander. I don't care how many losses we take, we cannot forfeit the Sun Crusher. That one weapon is worth more to me than all six TIE fighter squadrons onboard this Star Destroyer. Retrieve it at all costs."

Three Star Destroyers closed in behind the stolen Sun Crusher.

"Didn't take them long to figure something was up," Han said.

Clouds of TIE fighters spewed out of the launching bays of the *Manticore* and the *Gorgon*, swarming toward them in formations so dense that Han could not see through them. Flashing, splattering laser bolts struck like pelting raindrops on the viewscreen.

"I always wanted to see if I could fly blindfolded," Han said.

"What are they doing? Trying to smother us or just confuse us?" Qwi said.

The Sun Crusher, undamaged, rocked left and right from the pummeling of blaster strikes. "No, but they can wipe out our external weaponry—in fact, they already have," Han said, checking the readouts. "Every one of our lasers is offline."

"We just have to outrun them then," Kyp said.

Another Star Destroyer, the *Basilisk*, unleashed its squadrons of TIE fighters in wave after wave out of the launching bay.

"Those ships are going to clog space so we can't even move!" Han wrenched the Sun Crusher's controls, trying to dodge but just squeezing his eyes shut most of the time. "Whoever heard of a traffic jam in the middle of a black hole cluster?"

Kyp grabbed his shoulder. "Watch out, Han."

The fourth and last Star Destroyer reared up between them and the outside universe, blocking their passage. The *Hydra* lanced out with its enormous turbolaser cannons, aiming concentrated firepower at the single small ship. The remaining three Star Destroyers pressed in from behind to cut off their escape through the maze of the black hole cluster.

"Now what?" Kyp asked. The great arrowhead shape of the *Hydra* filled space in front of them.

"Qwi, you said this armor could take anything, didn't you?" Han asked.

"Everything I could test it with."

"All right, hold on. Time to accelerate for whatever this fancy toy is worth." He jammed the control levers back. The sudden force shoved the four escapees back into their seats as the Sun Crusher surged forward, straight toward the *Hydra*.

The huge battleship grew larger and larger, filling their entire field of view, and still expanding. Great green turbolaser bolts shot out at them, but the cannons could not refocus their aimpoints fast enough to compensate for the ship streaking directly at them.

"Han, what are you doing?" Kyp cried.

"Trust me," Han said. "Or actually, trust *her*." He nodded toward Qwi. "If she messed up her test measurements, we're all going to be one big organic pancake!"

The *Hydra*'s trapezoidal bridge tower rushed toward them, directly in their path. One suicidal TIE fighter rammed into the Sun Crusher to deflect its course, but merely exploded upon hitting the invincible quantum armor. Han had no trouble compensating for the error in trajectory.

"Look out!" Qwi yelled.

Details of the bridge tower filled their view now as they screamed toward the Imperial battleship. Han could actually see the windows of the bridge, the tiny figures of the command crew, some of them paralyzed in horror, others fleeing madly.

"Han!" Qwi and Kyp screamed in unison. Chewbacca gave a wordless roar.

"Right down their throat!" Han said.

The armored Sun Crusher tore through the *Hydra*'s control bridge like a bullet. Flying debris sprayed in their wake. The ship shot out the other side, shredding the superstructure on its way out.

The impact, the inferno, and a sound like a thousand gongs knocked them into a temporary stupor. Han finally whooped. "We made it!" Behind them the great battleship erupted in flames.

"You're crazy!" Qwi said.

"Don't thank me yet, Doc," Han said.

Burning, out of control, the decapitated *Hydra* wheeled backward, drifting helplessly toward the gravitational trap of one of the black holes. A flurry of escape pods shot out of the crew decks, but the low-power lifeboat engines could not generate sufficient acceleration to take them free of the black holes, and their trajectories began to spiral in.

The lower decks and the immense hyperdrive engines of the doomed Star Destroyer began to explode as it toppled into the unstable trap of the Maw cluster. Clouds of belching flames stretched out and elongated, mingling with the swirling gas as the *Hydra* began its infinite plunge into the singularity.

"We're not home free by a long shot," Han said as he soared into the soup of ionized gas. "Okay, Kyp," he said. "Now it's your turn to take the controls. Get us out of here."

Moments later the other three Star Destroyers rallied behind them in howling pursuit.

28

On the *Gorgon's* bridge, Admiral Daala watched in horror as the *Hydra* crumpled into destruction, its command bridge blown apart from the impact of the Sun Crusher. The battleship's only survivors would be the fighters in the six TIE squadrons; otherwise, all hands would be lost.

Though her expression was carved in ice, hot tears burned unshed in Daala's eyes. Thousands of people crashed to their deaths as the *Hydra* fell like a great slain dragon into the black whirlpool.

Glinting with its maddening invincibility, the Sun Crusher streaked through the wreckage, arrowing for the outer wall of the Maw.

"After them!" Daala snapped. "Full pursuit."

Failure crashed down on her like an anvil. She had been hiding in the Maw for too long, drilling her troops, putting them through practice exercises and dress rehearsals—but that had not been enough. In her first actual battle Daala had lost a quarter of her command—against *four* escaped prisoners!

Grand Moff Tarkin would have struck her sharply across the face and relieved her of her rank. Daala's cheeks stung with the imaginary blow. "They will regret the day they ever unleashed us!" she whispered.

But without the Sun Crusher, her plans to spread havoc among the New Republic would fall apart. She took a deep, sharp breath. No time to panic now. Think fast. Make decisions. Salvage the situation.

The communications dais shimmered, and an image of Tol Sivron appeared. The transmission flickered with staticky disruptions caused by the laser blasts flashing around them. "Admiral Daala! If you intend to deploy your fleet, I insist that you take the scientists of Maw Installation with you."

Not bothering to turn and look at the image of the Twi'lek, Daala continued to watch the *Hydra*'s fiery death. She thought of all the run-ins she'd had with the administrator—Sivron's incompetence, his delays, his excuses, his insistence on reports and tests ad nauseum. "You're on your own, Tol Sivron. It is time we do our duty as Imperial soldiers."

Tol Sivron flicked his head-tails straight out behind him in agitation. "Are you just going to leave us undefended? What about the orders Grand Moff Tarkin gave you? You are supposed to protect us! At least leave one of your Star Destroyers behind."

Daala shook her head, making coppery hair stream around her. "Tarkin is dead, and I'm making all the decisions now. I need every ounce of firepower to deal a fatal blow to the New Republic."

"Admiral Daala, I must insist—"

Daala yanked out the blaster pistol at her hip and pointed it at Sivron's image on the communications dais. If the Twi'lek had been on the bridge in person, she would have killed him; but she would not destroy valuable equipment in a fit of anger. Keeping the blaster pointed directly into Tol Sivron's image, as if to threaten him, she strode forward. "Request *denied,* Director Sivron," Daala said, then disconnected the dais. She turned back to watch her fleet, undisturbed.

"Commander Kratas, we are going to leave the Maw in pursuit of the Sun Crusher. Recall all TIE fighter squadrons, now!"

Kratas gave the order, and she watched as the tiny ships streamed back toward their bays. Daala fidgeted, hating the delay. "Have all three Star Destroyers link into the same course computer. I will call up the specific coordinates from my own personal records, coded to my password."

The last time anyone had left Maw Installation, it had been the construction engineers—and they had been given the wrong course, dooming them to fall into one of the black holes. This time, though, Admiral Daala and all the firepower at her disposal would spring out upon the unwary galaxy, ready to take it back.

The Sun Crusher vibrated from a thousand stresses as it rode the razor's edge of gravity through the maelstrom of the Maw.

Kyp Durron sat at the simplified controls, next to the watchful eyes of Han Solo, but Han didn't dream of interfering with Kyp's intuition, no matter how nightmarish the path ahead seemed.

Kyp half closed his eyes as he looked through a mental vision of the perilous maze to safety. He jerked the ship to starboard, then plunged down, frantically avoiding unseen obstacles. Han kept a firm, reassuring pressure on the kid's shoulder. Hot gas blazed around them like hell's furnace.

Qwi Xux stared at Kyp and his blind piloting, her dark-blue eyes wide and her face transfixed with terror.

"Don't worry," Han said. "The kid knows what he's doing. He'll get us through, if anybody can."

"But how is he doing it?" Qwi's voice sounded flutey, like high-pitched notes played by an amateur performer.

"Not in any way your science can explain. I'm not sure I understand the Force myself, but I don't question it. I used to think it was a hokey religion, but not anymore."

Abruptly the curtains of gas parted in front of them, peeling away to reveal the black infinity of open space. At last they were free of the Maw!

In their mad run away from the forces of Kessel, Luke and Lando tried to push through the clustered capital ships. They winced simultaneously every time a bolt impacted the *Falcon*'s shields.

The mammoth form of the Loronar strike cruiser lay directly across their path, cutting them off from a dubious escape into the Maw. The ten ion cannons mounted in front of the strike cruiser belched destruction at them.

One bolt struck the *Millennium Falcon* dead on, and their systems flickered as sparks flew out of the control panels. Lando grabbed at the overrides and yelled to Luke, "Our shields are failing, and these guys don't want to take prisoners."

"Just get us into the Maw," Luke said. "It's our only chance."

"I never thought I'd be keeping my fingers crossed for *that* to happen!" Lando hunched over the controls. "Artoo, see if you can pump up the front shields. We're going to take quite a pounding from that strike cruiser when we pass by. One good hit and we're fried."

"Wait," Luke said, squinting at the swirling gases ahead of them. "Something's coming *out!*"

The thornlike form of the Sun Crusher streaked away from the cluster, leaving a trail of hot gases. A few moments later three fully armed Imperial-class Star Destroyers charged out of the Maw like banthas on fire.

Han's sigh of relief turned into an exclamation of dismay as he saw the array of Kessel's battle fleet massed in front of them, weapons already blazing. "Where did all those ships come from! They can't still be waiting for us!"

Exhausted from his piloting ordeal, Kyp said, "Han, why is it that every time we escape, we end up in a worse situation than the one we left?"

"Just good timing, kid." He slammed his fist down on the armored controls. "This isn't fair! They should have given us up for dead days ago!"

Chewbacca yowled and jabbed his hairy finger at the viewport, pointing to a ship at the vanguard of the gathered attack forces. The *Millennium Falcon.*

Han's lip curled downward. "I'm going to get that slime merchant who's flying my ship. Don't we have *any* of our laser cannons still operational?"

After rechecking the banks of instruments, Chewbacca grunted a negative.

"Then we'll ram them like we did that Star Destroyer."

"Han," Kyp said, "it looks to me like those other ships are *chasing* the *Falcon*. They're shooting at it."

Han leaned forward to take a closer look. Qwi agreed with Kyp's assessment. "That light freighter doesn't appear to be part of the attacking fleet."

Green turbolaser bolts streaked toward the *Falcon* from the system patrol craft, the big strike cruiser, and the Carrack-class light cruisers. Han's expression changed immediately. "Hey, what's going on here? They better not blow up my ship!"

Then Daala's Star Destroyers emerged behind them, plowing their way out of the clutches of the Maw.

"Look on the rear screens, Han!" Kyp said.

The Star Destroyers *Gorgon, Basilisk,* and *Manticore* burst out like monsters leaping from a closet, giant demons loaded with destructive weaponry from the fallen Empire.

The pell-mell mercenary forces of Kessel, already firing their laser cannons at the *Falcon,* ran headlong into the Imperial fleet. Some peeled sideways, turning to flee back toward the sanctuary of Kessel. Others panicked and opened fire on the Star Destroyers.

Admiral Daala tried to control the actions of her entire fleet from a single station on the bridge. Encountering the strange warships on the other side of the Maw shocked her, but she reacted quickly. "Shields up! This was a trap. The Rebels had their forces here waiting."

How had Han Solo deceived her interrogation droid? Had the Rebels somehow found out about the Installation and sent Solo inside with a cooked-up story to lure Daala's fleet out where they could be destroyed?

She saw the enemy fleet opening fire on her ships, but they were no match for her firepower. After all, Grand Moff Tarkin had given her enough weaponry to slag whole planets.

"Battle stations! Let's mop up this rabble once and for all." She pointed to the conglomeration of fighters swarming across her path. "Open fire!"

Luke and Lando spared a moment to glance at each other as the crossfire erupted around them. "This could be our chance to get out of here!" Lando said.

"Yeah, they might not even notice us leaving," Luke said.

"But where in the universe did those Star Destroyers come from?"

Suddenly a beep sounded from the *Falcon*'s comm-channels, distinctive because it sounded so innocent amid the warning tones of overloading systems and failing shields. Artoo whistled, calling attention to it. Lando looked down.

"We're getting a message over the *Falcon*'s private comm frequency." Lando frowned. "How would anybody know to transmit that? How would anybody even *know* the *Falcon*'s private code?"

Then Han Solo's angry voice burst over the speaker. "Whoever is on the *Falcon* better have a damned good reason for flying my ship!"

"Han! Is that you?" Lando said. A sudden thrill surged through Luke.

"Lando?" Han said after a pause. Over the speakers Chewbacca's roar drowned out Han's own exclamation. "What are you doing here?"

In space around them, blinding lances of light flashed as the weapons of two fleets were brought to bear. Like rival krayt dragons in mating season, the Kessel and Imperial forces slammed into each other in a total free-for-all space brawl.

"Han, listen to me. Luke is here, too," Lando said. "We've got to get away from Kessel, but the *Falcon*'s navicomputer is disabled. We can't make the jump into hyperspace."

An explosion rocked them from the starboard side, but most of the Kessel fighters concentrated their firepower on the much larger threat of Daala's Imperial fleet. Though hopelessly outmatched, the three Carrack cruisers lined up and began to blast the *Basilisk*.

Over the private comm channel Han spoke to someone else behind him, then answered Lando. "We can dump the coordinates to your navicomp, and we'll fly tandem back to Coruscant."

Lando checked the computer, saw the numbers scrolling through, and raised a fist in triumph. "Got it! Artoo, get ready to go."

"You'd better keep my ship safe, Lando," Han said. "On my signal."

"You have my word, Han." Lando's hands flew over the *Falcon*'s familiar controls.

"Ready to enter hyperspace!" Han said.

The Kessel forces flanked and attacked the far larger Star Destroyers, pummeling the Imperial ships with blasts from their ion cannons and turbolaser banks. But the Star Destroyers disgorged their own squadrons of TIE fighters to butcher the unregimented forces from Kessel.

"On your mark, Han!"

"Punch it!"

The last thing they saw was Kessel's massive Loronar strike cruiser exploding under the concerted fire from the *Manticore* and the *Gorgon*. They watched the flaming hulk reel and ram into the Star Destroyer *Basilisk*, causing the bottom of the arrowhead hull to buckle and burn.

Then the universe filled with starlines.

29

The reunion was everything Han had imagined. He had spent a lot of time thinking about it during the long hyperspace flight back to Coruscant.

Leia and the twins met him the moment the Sun Crusher and the *Millennium Falcon* touched down side by side at the high landing platform. Han backed out of the Sun Crusher's hatch and began climbing down the ladder, but Leia ran forward and hugged him before he managed to get all the way down.

"Glad I'm back?" he asked.

"I missed you!" she said, kissing him.

"I know," he said with a roguish smile.

She put her hands on her hips. "What? You didn't miss me?"

Han turned away sheepishly. "Well, first we crashed on Kessel, then we were stuck in the spice mines, then we got captured by a bunch of Imperials in the middle of a black hole cluster. I really didn't have a whole lot of—"

When Leia looked as if she were going to punch him, Han reacted with a grin. "But even through all that I don't remember more than about two seconds when I didn't miss you with all my heart."

Leia kissed him again.

Artoo trundled down the *Falcon*'s ramp, and Threepio bustled to greet him. "Artoo-Detoo! I'm so glad you're back. You wouldn't believe the difficulties I've had while you were gone!"

Artoo bleeped something nobody bothered to translate.

Kyp Durron and Qwi Xux climbed down from the Sun Crusher and stared out at the endless spires and towers of Imperial City, the metropolis of glinting transparisteel and alloy that stretched to the horizon. Above them the tiny lights of shuttles winked across the sky. "Now *that's* a city!" Kyp said with a sigh.

Qwi looked overwhelmed. The Sun Crusher would be transferred to a high-security hangar for study by the scientists of the New Republic. Qwi did not like abandoning it, but she had no choice.

Han strode over to his two children, bending his knees and gathering Jacen and Jaina into his arms. "Hey, kids! Do you remember your daddy? It's been a long time, huh?"

He mussed their hair and stared down at them with the wide-eyed astonishment he always felt when seeing how much they had grown between the visits Winter arranged to the hidden planet of Anoth. Now, though, Jacen and Jaina's two years of isolation and protection were over, and the children were home to stay, leaving only baby Anakin in need of special protection.

Jacen nodded; then a moment later Jaina nodded as well. Han wasn't sure he believed their answer, but he hugged them anyway. "Well, if you don't remember me, I'll try to make it up to you from now on."

A puffed-up official wearing the bright uniform of an offworld administrative office finally cornered Lando in a high-brow diplomatic lounge. The official held an armored briefcase similar to the type credit investigators carried, and he had the same pinch-faced demeanor of a person being given a mission whose importance he drastically overestimated.

"Are you Lando Calrissian?" the official said. "I have been attempting to locate you for several days. You've made my job most difficult." He bustled forward.

Lando saw that he could not slip out the back entrance of the lounge. Beside him at the table Han raised his eyebrows. Both of them had gone to the lounge to relax and settle down after their long debriefings by the Alliance High Command. Unfortunately, the lounge catered to bureaucrats and political functionaries, and served only cloyingly sweet drinks. Han and Lando sipped theirs slowly, trying to keep from grimacing.

Lando had heard rumors about an investigator trying to track him down and had managed to avoid him thus far. He feared some debtor coming after him, or a complaint regarding the tibanna gas mining operations he had abandoned on Bespin or the hot metal mines he had recently lost on Nkllon.

"Yes, you finally caught me," Lando said with a sigh. "What do you want? I can get the best legal representation in the galaxy here in Imperial City."

"That won't be necessary," the investigator said, heaving his armored briefcase onto the table, then fiddling with the cyberlock. "I'll be glad to be rid of this."

He lifted the lid of his case, and glittering light sparkled out. Other people in the lounge turned to gape.

The briefcase brimmed with carefully sorted packets of firefacet gems and shimmering chrysopaz.

"I am from the planet Dargul, and this is the reward owed to you by the Duchess Mistal for the safe return of her beloved consort Dack. You can have them appraised, but I am told these jewels are valued at approximately one million credits. Plus the briefcase, which is worth another forty."

Lando stared, hunched over the briefcase and dazzled by its contents. "A *million*?" he said.

"A million, plus forty for the briefcase."

"But I was only supposed to get half of the reward."

The investigator reached into his pocket. "I neglected to give you this. It is a message wafer for you from Slish Fondine, the owner of the blob stables where you assisted apprehending our consort Dack." He handed Lando a small rectangular object.

Lando turned it over in his hand, frowning, then ran his fingernail along the crease in its center. He cracked the message wafer open, then folded the two halves back to stand it upright on their small table.

An image of the blob-stable owner wafted up. "Greetings, Lando Calrissian. Since you are listening to this message, I will assume you've received your reward. I'm happy to say that your suggestion of not executing the criminal Tymmo has proved advantageous to all concerned. Duchess Mistal was so delighted to receive her consort back that she insisted on paying you the full reward, as well as offering to build a subsidiary blobstacle course for me in the main stadium on Umgul. We are already hiring creative engineers to design even tougher blobstacles for the new course, which, at the Duchess Mistal's request, will be called the 'Dack Track.'

"I am forwarding these firefacet and chrysopaz gems to you and hope you will spend the reward wisely. Why not come to Umgul and do some gambling? I'd be happy to be your host."

As the message dissolved into wisps of light, Lando could do little more than stare open-mouthed at his fortune.

Han laughed, then gestured for the short investigator to sit down. "Join us for a drink. In fact, here—you can have mine! It's too sweet for me anyway."

The investigator shook his head, the hard expression remaining on his face. "No, thank you. I don't think I would enjoy that. I'd rather get back to my work." With that the investigator left the lounge.

Han clapped Lando on the shoulder. "What are you going to do with all that money? Still thinking of investing it in spice mining?"

Lando came back to reality with a streak of defensiveness. "I hate to say this, but when Moruth Doole showed us around, I *was* rather impressed by the potential there. Spice has plenty of good uses, too—perfectly legitimate alternatives in psychological therapy, criminal investigation, communication with alien races, even artistic inspiration and entertainment. You knew that, Han, or you wouldn't have run spice yourself in the old days."

"You've got a point, Lando."

But Lando's imagination kept working on the problem. "I don't see why the spice mines have to be run as some sort of slave-lord operation. A lot of that could be automated. Even if there are more of those energy spiders running around, we could just use supercooled droids down in the deeper tunnels. No big investment. I don't see what the problem is."

Han looked at him skeptically, took a gulp of his sweet drink, then puckered his lips. "Uh-huh."

"Besides," Lando said, "I'm in the market for a new ship. I had to leave the *Lady Luck* stranded on Kessel. I may never get her back. What am I supposed to do for the time being?"

Seeing the eager stares from the others in the lounge, Lando snapped shut the lid of the armored briefcase. "Well, anyway, it's wonderful just to be solvent again!"

"Everybody in!" Wedge Antilles called inside the echoing Imperial City spaceport. "Let's get ready to go."

The last of the New Republic colonization specialists, sociologists, and survival instructors hauled their personal packs up the ramp of the medium transport. The ninety-meter-long ship occupied the better part of an entire bay in the supply sector, but the group needed a transport large enough to haul the Eol Sha survivors and their meager possessions, as well as the supplies necessary to set up a new home on Dantooine.

Wedge kept track of the final details of the operation, skimming a checklist on his datapad. At least this was a better assignment than knocking down ruined buildings—for the time being. He was glad to be flying again, even if it was only a sluggish transport carrier instead of a fighter.

But he knew tougher assignments lay in the near future. Admiral Daala and her three Imperial Star Destroyers had devastated the Kessel system, then vanished into hyperspace. The New Republic had sent its best trackers to find where she had gone to hide. Han insisted she was bound to make destructive guerrilla strikes, popping out of hyperspace and blasting a random planet. A loose cannon like Daala would not follow a predictable overall strategy. The entire New Republic had to be on its guard.

Chewbacca insisted that a New Republic occupation force head out to the Maw Installation to free the other Wookiee slaves. The Alliance High Command also wanted to get their hands on any other plans and prototypes remaining in the secret weapons lab. *So much for relaxing and picking up pieces,* Wedge thought. *Things are going to get a lot more interesting.*

But right now his assignment was to get the people of Eol Sha to safety on their new homeworld.

When everything checked out onboard, Wedge noticed Gantoris standing alone beside supply containers piled next to the wall. The displaced colony leader looked tall and powerful, but didn't seem to know how to react to seeing the relocation ship leave.

"Don't worry," Wedge called, "we'll take your people to their new home. After living with volcanoes and earthquakes all their lives, Dantooine will seem like a paradise to them."

Gantoris nodded, furrowing his smooth forehead. "Give them my greetings."

Wedge waved to him. "You just go and become the best of the new Jedi Knights."

Luke looked deep into the eyes of Kyp Durron, searching for the core of a Jedi. The younger man flinched but continued to meet Luke's gaze.

"Are you nervous, Kyp?" Luke asked.

"A little. Should I be?"

Luke smiled as he remembered boasting to Yoda that he wasn't afraid of his impending Jedi training. "You will be," Yoda had said, "you *will* be!"

Han interrupted them, clapping his hand on Kyp's shoulder. "You should have been there to watch him zipping through the dark spice tunnels. And he navigated us right through the Maw with his eyes closed! This kid has a lot of potential, Luke."

Luke nodded. "I was about to do that trick in the Maw myself. I know how difficult it must have been."

"Does that mean you'll take me for your Jedi academy?" Kyp asked. "I want to know how to use this power I have. While I was sitting in a cell on the Star Destroyer, I vowed never to be helpless again."

Luke withdrew the power pack and sheet-crystal sensor paddles from the old Imperial scanner that had once been used to detect Jedi descendants. "Let's try this scanner first." Untangling the cords, Luke stretched out the sheet-crystal paddles on either side of Kyp. "This won't hurt or anything. It just maps the potential of your senses."

He tripped the scan switch on the control pack, and a narrow line of coppery light traveled down Kyp's body as a smaller image of the copper scan-line reappeared in reverse motion in front of them, digitizing its analysis of Kyp Durron.

Kyp's reproduction hung in the air, bathed with the pale-blue corona Luke had found on the others with genuine Jedi potential. But the aura waxed and waned, knotting itself, turning darker, growing brighter, streaked with red, then becoming tangled.

"What does that mean?" Kyp said.

"He's okay, isn't he?" Han seemed eager to have his protegé accepted.

Luke wondered at the anomalous mapping, disturbed because he didn't know how to interpret it. The shimmer could be a result of faulty scanning equipment, since the instrument had been roughly treated and could no longer be calibrated—or it could be that because of the strain and pressure on Kyp for so many years, he hadn't quite sprung back to his full potential yet.

"I see a lot of power there. A lot," Luke said, and Kyp sighed at the reassurance. "Let me try one other test."

Luke stretched out his hands to touch the curly black hair on Kyp's head. "Let him do what he needs to," Han whispered to the young man. "Trust him."

Luke closed his eyes and sent a tendril of thought to the back of Kyp's mind where the deep primal memories hid, leaving little room for conscious thought. Luke touched inward to the isolated nub in his subconscious. He pushed—

—and suddenly found himself hurled backward, tossed aside like a piece of fluff in a Bespin wind storm. He landed flat on his back on the other side of the room, gasping.

Han and Kyp ran toward him as he struggled to prop himself up on his elbows. Luke shook the daze from his head.

"I'm sorry!" Kyp said. "I don't know what I did! I didn't try to. Honest!"

"What happened?" Han said. "What does that mean for Kyp?"

Luke blinked, then smiled at the others. "Don't worry about me. I triggered that myself." He shook his head. "Kyp, you have *amazing* power!"

Luke stood up and gripped the young man's hand. "You're definitely welcome to train at my academy. I just hope I know how to handle it when you come into full control of your abilities!"

EPILOGUE

Luke Skywalker, Jedi Master, stood atop the Great Temple on the fourth moon of Yavin.

Below his feet lay the empty throne room and grand audience chamber with skylights open to the sun. Garbed in a new Jedi cloak, wearing his lightsaber at his side, Luke felt warmth bathing him. Spicy, lingering scents rose as steam from the lush rain forest below.

The ancient ruins left behind by the vanished Massassi race sprawled out in great geometrical edifices, now overgrown by voracious jungles. Luke stood on top of the ziggurat that had once been a towering lookout station when the Rebel base had been housed on Yavin 4.

In the sky a swollen sphere of pale orange filled most of his view, the looming planet Yavin. The bloated gas giant had been a shield for the Rebel base as the first Death Star orbited into position to fire with its planet-destroying superlaser. The Yavin base had been abandoned by the Rebels years before. But many of the broken stone structures were still serviceable.

With the unleashed might of the Maw fleet, and the expected depredations of Admiral Daala, the New Republic desperately needed a strong force beyond pure military might, a group of guardians to maintain order in the galaxy.

Luke intended to bring together everyone he could, immediately—not just Gantoris and Streen, but also Kyp Durron, Mara Jade, several of the witches of Dathomir, Kam Solusar, and others he had encountered since the Battle of Endor. And the search for new people with Jedi potential would have to be intensified. He needed candidates, as many as possible.

The top levels of some of the flat-roofed Massassi structures had been clear enough for Luke to land his ship. On the broad courtyard once used as a launching pad by the Alliance, Luke's old X-wing fighter lay cooling in the rising mists from the Yavin jungles.

When Mon Mothma and Leia had offered Luke the abandoned Rebel base, he had jumped at the chance.

To begin his actual training, Luke tried to recreate all the exercises Yoda had taught him on Dagobah, as well as the practice sessions Obi-Wan Kenobi had begun. Luke also had the ancient Jedi Holocron, the visual historical database Leia had taken from the resurrected Emperor's stronghold. He had studied the information from the hidden repository of Jedi knowledge on Dathomir. He had many tools, and his students carried inside themselves doorways to great power.

But again Luke worried. If one of his trainees—or more than one!—fell to the dark side, would he himself have the power to bring him back? And who was this "dark man" who haunted Gantoris's dreams with prophesies of destruction?

As Luke looked across the sweeping vista of dense wilderness, he saw wide burned scars where fires had ravaged the rain forests. But the ecology of the moon struck back with a vengeance, healing itself. Dense clusters of sharp-smelling blueleaf shrubs, Massassi trees, and climbing ferns clogged the ground in an impenetrable mesh that stretched as far as he could see, broken only by scattered temple ruins poking through the greensward.

The alien constructions left behind by the Massassi seemed filled with secrets and knowledge of their own. Luke blinked his eyes and felt the power of the place around him, the wonder, the mystery of it all. He could not wait to begin bringing his students here.

It was the perfect place to train a new order of Jedi Knights.

DARK
APPRENTICE

1

The huge orange sphere of the gas planet Yavin heaved itself over the horizon of its fourth moon. Soft, misty light shone across the ever-stirring jungles and the ancient stone temples.

Luke Skywalker used a Jedi refreshing technique to remove weariness from his body. He had slept soundly—but the future of the New Republic and the fate of the galaxy weighed heavily upon him.

Luke stood atop the squared pyramid of the Great Temple that had been abandoned millennia before by the lost Massassi race. During the Alliance's early struggles against the Empire, they had built a secret base in the ruins, from which they had launched their desperate attack against the first Death Star. Now, eleven years after the Rebels' departure, Luke had returned to the fourth moon of Yavin.

Now he was a Jedi. A Jedi Master. He would be the first of a new generation, like those who had protected the Republic for a thousand generations. The old Jedi Knights had been respected and powerful, until Darth Vader and the Emperor had hunted and slaughtered virtually all of them.

Luke had received support from Mon Mothma, the New Republic's Chief of State, to seek others who had a potential to use the Force—trainees who might become part of a new order of Jedi. Luke had managed to bring a dozen students to his "academy" on Yavin 4, but he felt uncertain about the best way to train them.

His own instruction by Obi-Wan and Yoda had been abbreviated, and Luke had since discovered facets of Jedi lore that made him realize just how much he still did not know. Even a great Jedi like Obi-Wan Kenobi had failed with his student and had let Anakin Skywalker become a monster named Darth Vader. Now Luke was expected to instruct others and make no mistakes.

Do or do not, Yoda had said, *there is no try.*

Luke stood on the smooth, cool stones of the rooftop and looked out across the awakening jungle, smelling the myriad sharp and sweet scents as the air warmed in the morning light. The spicy tang of blueleaf shrub and the perfume of lush orchids drifted up to him.

Luke closed his eyes and let his hands hang at his side, his fingers spread. He let his mind open and relax; he drew strength from the Force, touching ripples made by the life-forms crowding the jungles below. With heightened senses he could hear the rustle of millions of leaves, twigs scraping, small animals scurrying through the underbrush.

Letting out a yelp of pain and terror, a rodent thrashed and died as a predator crushed it in its jaws. Flying creatures sang mating songs to each other through the dense treetops. Large grazing mammals fed on leaves, tearing tender shoots from high branches or grubbing for fungi in the forest debris.

A wide warm river, sapphire-blue overlaid with muddy swirls of brown, flowed past the Great Temple, barely visible under the thick trees. The river bifurcated to send a tributary past the old Rebel power-generating station, which Luke and Artoo-Detoo had repaired during their preparation for the Jedi academy. Where the river sloshed around a submerged, half-rotted tree, Luke could sense a large aquatic predator lurking in the shadows, waiting for smaller fishlike creatures to swim by.

The plants grew. The animals flourished. The moon awakened to a new day. Yavin 4 was *alive*—and Luke Skywalker felt energized.

Listening intently, he heard two people approaching from far off in the dense foliage. They moved quietly, without speaking, but he could sense the change in the jungle as two of his Jedi candidates made a path through the undergrowth.

Luke's introspective moment had ended. He smiled and decided to go down and meet them.

As he turned to go back into the echoing stone halls of the temple, Luke looked up at the sky to see the streaking trails of a shuttlecraft descending through the humid atmosphere. He realized with a start that they were due for another delivery of supplies.

Luke had been so focused on training new Jedi that he had lost touch with galactic politics. Upon seeing the shuttle, he felt a deep longing to know about Leia and Han and their children. He hoped the pilot would bring news.

He shrugged down the hood of his brown Jedi cloak. The garment was too warm for the jungle humidity, but Luke had stopped noticing minor physical discomfort. He had walked across fire on Eol Sha and gone to the spice mines of Kessel, and he could not be bothered by a little perspiration.

When the Rebels had first set up their hidden base in the Massassi temple, they had scoured the thick plant life from the chambers. Across the river stood another prominent temple, and according to orbital surveys, more structures lay buried under the implacable vegetation. But the Alliance had been far too wrapped up in its war against the Empire to bother with detailed archaeological inspections. The vanished race of temple builders remained as much a mystery now as when the Rebels had first set foot on Yavin 4.

The temple's flagstoned corridors were uneven but remarkably unscathed after centuries of exposure to the elements. Luke took a turbolift from the pinnacle down to the third level, where other students slept or meditated in the early morning. As he stepped out of the turbolift, Artoo-Detoo puttered out to greet him. The droid's wheels hummed along the bumpy flagstones, and his hemispherical head rotated back and forth, chittering at Luke.

"Yes, Artoo, I saw the shuttle coming down. Would you go down to the clearing to meet it for me? Gantoris and Streen are returning from their sojourn in the jungle. I want to greet them and learn what they've found."

Artoo acknowledged with a bleep and trundled over to a stone ramp. Luke continued through the cool confines of the temple, smelling the mustiness of the enclosed air, the powdery tang of crumbling stones. Along the halls, some of the old Alliance banners still hung outside empty quarters.

Luke's Jedi academy was by no means luxurious; in fact, it was barely even comfortable. But he and his students had concerns that absorbed their energy far more than simple conveniences. Luke had not repaired all of the damage caused by time, but he had refurbished the glowpanels, water systems, and food-prep facilities the Alliance had installed.

When he reached the ground level of the temple, the partially raised hangar-bay doors stood like the dark slit of a mouth. Luke sensed echoes of the past inside the hangar bay, a faint residue of starfighter fuel and coolant, clinging dust and grease in the corners. He stepped outside to the jungle, blinking in the washed-and-faded sunlight as evaporating mists rose from the damp undergrowth.

Luke's timing was perfect. As he walked through the lush foliage, he heard his two Jedi trainees approach.

As an exercise in resourcefulness and as an opportunity for uninterrupted concentration, Luke sent his students in pairs into the wilderness. Alone, with no other abilities but their own, they worked on powers of concentration, sensing and studying other life-forms, touching the Force.

Luke raised his hand in greeting as the two stepped through feather ferns and thick blueleaf shrubs. Tall, dark Gantoris parted heavy branches and came forward to meet Luke. His high forehead had been shaven clean of eyebrows; his skin looked chapped and weathered. Though Gantoris had calmly lived among geysers and lava flows on Eol Sha, he seemed startled to see the Jedi Master; but he covered his reaction instantly.

On his hellish world, Gantoris had used an innate talent with the Force to keep a small group of forgotten colonists alive. Gantoris had had nightmares of a terrible "dark man" who would tempt him with power and then destroy him. At first he had thought Luke was that man—Luke, who appeared in his dark Jedi robe, striding through a geyser field to ask Gantoris to come to his academy. Gantoris had tested Luke by making him walk across lava and climb through geysers.

Behind Gantoris came Streen, the second candidate Luke had found in his Jedi search. Streen had lived as a gas prospector in an abandoned floating city on the planet Bespin. Streen had been able to predict eruptions of valuable gases from deep within the cloud layers. Luke had tempted him with the ability to shut off the clamoring voices Streen heard in his head whenever he went to populated areas.

As the trainees bowed, Luke clasped their hands. "Welcome back. Tell me what you've learned."

"We found another Massassi temple!" Streen said breathlessly, looking back and forth. His wispy pale hair was tangled, matted with flecks of vegetation.

"Yes," Gantoris said. The man's ruddy face and his braided dark hair were smudged with sweat and dirt. "The new temple isn't as large as this one, but it seems more potent somehow. It's made of obsidian, sitting out in the middle of a shallow glassy lake, with a tall statue of a great lord."

"A site of great power!" Streen said.

"I felt the power too," Gantoris added. He straightened, tossing his thick braid behind him. "We should learn all we can about the Massassi race. They seem to have been very powerful, but they vanished entirely. What happened to them? Is there something we need to fear?"

Luke nodded gravely. He, too, had sensed the power in the temples. The first time he had come to Yavin 4, Luke had been little more than a boy thrust headfirst into the Rebellion against the Empire. He had barely realized the extent of the Force; in fact, he had learned of its existence only days before.

But he returned to the jungle moon a Jedi Master, and he could sense many things that had been hidden to him before. He knew the dark power that Gantoris had detected, and although he told his students they must share what they learned, Luke felt that certain knowledge could be deadly.

Darth Vader had discovered the wrong kind of knowledge. Luke could not dismiss the possibility that one of his students would be seduced by the dark side.

Luke clapped his hands on their shoulders. "Come inside. Take a drink. A supply shuttle is landing, so let's go greet our guest."

When they reached the cleared landing pad, Artoo-Detoo waited next to the grid-control kiosk, chittering coordinates to a descending X-23 StarWorker space barge.

Craning his neck, Luke watched the craft descend with a grinding whine of engines and a blast of jets. The StarWorker barge looked like a trapezoidal cargo container with Incom sublight engines strapped on. The intrasystem craft had seen better days: its gray metallic hull showed discolorations from blaster fire and countless pitted scabs from meteor encounters. But the engine sounded loud and strong as the landing gear kicked in.

The space barge flashed its running lights around its belly, then settled down gently. Luke tried to squint through the tiny front port as a group of flying creatures in the treetops burst into flight, screeching and scolding the metal thing that had lumbered into their forest.

Heavy plasteel support struts extended, locking to the ground with a hiss of hydraulic pressure. The bitter-oil smell of exhaust hung in the humid air, mixing with the peppery and sweet scents of jungle flowers and leaves.

The mechanical smell reminded Luke of the bustling metropolis of Imperial City, the governmental center of the New Republic. Though he had been at peace for months now on Yavin 4, Luke felt a tingle of sweat down his back. He could not let his guard slip for one second—he had a mission to do for the New Republic. This was not a vacation.

The hull of the space barge continued to mutter to itself as it settled. With a coughing hiss the rear cargo doors slid apart slowly as if two giants pushed them back one step at a time. Bluish-white light shone down on crates and boxes wrapped in storage nets or bolted to the walls—food, communications equipment, clothing, and amenities.

Moving softly across the packed clearing, Gantoris and Streen came up beside him. Streen's eyes went wide with a sense of wonder, but Gantoris wore a puzzled, sour expression. His skin remained dark, as if in a constant angry blush. "Do we need these things, Master Skywalker?"

Luke glanced at the contents. Judging from the material—the unnecessary material—included in the shipment, Leia herself must have compiled the cargo list. Exotic food synthesizers, comfortable clothes, heaters, humidity-neutralizers, even a few hollow Ithorian wind chimes.

"We'll make do," he said.

A narrow ramp extended with a groan of pistons and rollers from the raised pilot compartment. The silhouette of a man appeared on the ramp, booted feet, wrinkled and padded flightsuit, rounded helmet. He descended, yanking his white helmet off as his gloved hands covered the blue scooped-arc symbol of the New Republic. The pilot shook his head, tossing short dark hair from side to side.

"Wedge!" Luke grinned and shouted. "Doesn't the New Republic have anything better for its generals to do? A delivery driver in space!"

Wedge Antilles stuffed his helmet under the padded orange sleeve of his flightsuit and extended a hand to Luke. Luke embraced Wedge in the greeting of two friends who had not seen each other in far too long.

"You've got to admit I'm qualified for the job," Wedge said. "Besides, I got tired of doing demolition work in the armpit of Imperial City, and before that I got tired of cleaning up wrecked spacecraft in orbit around Coruscant. I figured a delivery driver was better than a garbageman."

Wedge flicked a glance over Luke's shoulder, and another smile dimpled his cheeks. Gantoris came forward from the cargo bay and gave Wedge a quick, almost brutal handshake as he locked eyes with the pilot. "General Antilles, have you any word from my people? I trust they have all been safely shuttled to their new home on Dantooine?"

"Yes, Gantoris, they're all settled in and doing fine. We drop-lifted an entire settlement of self-erecting living modules. We sent them programming units and agricultural droids so they could establish a viable colony right away. Dantooine is a very mild planet—plenty of animals to hunt and native vegetation to eat. Trust me, they'll be much more comfortable than they were on Eol Sha."

Gantoris nodded solemnly. "That I do not doubt." His glittering eyes looked past Wedge to the treetops. Orange light from the rising gas giant made his eyes flicker like the lava pools he had made Luke walk across on Eol Sha.

"Gantoris, Streen—please start unloading the supplies," Luke said. "I don't think you'll have trouble lifting the crates with a little nudge from the Force. Consider it a test. Artoo, please call Kirana Ti and Dorsk 81 from their quarters to help."

Streen and Gantoris moved to the corrugated ramp from the loading bay. Artoo-Detoo hummed across the landing grid and disappeared into the shadowy hangar of the Great Temple in search of the other Jedi candidates.

Luke clapped his friend on the shoulder. "I'm starving for news, Wedge. I hope you brought some gossip with you."

Wedge raised his eyebrows. His narrow chin and soft features made him look more youthful than Luke. They had been through a lot together: Wedge had flown beside Luke on his triumphant run down the Death Star corridor, had assisted in the defense of Echo Base on the ice planet Hoth, and had fought against the second Death Star over Endor.

"Gossip?" Wedge asked, laughing. "That doesn't sound like something that would interest a Jedi Master."

"You got me there, Wedge. How are Leia and Han? How is Mon Mothma? How are things on Coruscant? When is Han going to bring Kyp Durron to my training center? That boy had enormous potential, and I want to start working with him."

Wedge shook his head at the volley of questions. "Kyp will be here, Luke, don't worry. He spent most of his life in the spice mines of Kessel, and he's only been out a month. Han's trying to show the kid how to live a little first."

Luke remembered the dark-haired teen Han had rescued from the black spice mines. When Luke had used a Jedi testing technique to see if Kyp had potential to use the Force, the boy's response had knocked Luke across the room. In his entire Jedi search, Luke had never encountered such power.

"And what about Leia?"

Wedge considered, and Luke appreciated that he didn't just answer with a simple "Of course everything's fine." "She seems to be spending more and more time with her duties as Minister of State. Mon Mothma has been handing off a lot of important responsibilities to Leia while she herself stays in her private chambers and rules from a distance. It's got a lot of people disturbed."

That behavior seemed highly unusual for the strong, compassionate ruler Luke remembered. "And how is Leia handling it?" He longed to know a thousand things at once, wishing he could be in the thick of it all again . . . while another part of him preferred the peace of Yavin 4.

Wedge sat on the edge of the sloping ramp. He propped one leg next to a support strut, then balanced his helmet on his knee. "Leia's doing a wonderful job, but she's trying to do too much, if you ask me. Even with baby Anakin still in hiding, she does have the twins to watch over now. Threepio helps, but Jacen and Jaina are still only two and a half years old. It's more than a full-time job, and Leia is getting exhausted."

"She could come here for a rest," Luke suggested. "Have her bring the twins, since I need to get them started on basic Jedi skills."

"I'm sure Leia would love to come here," Wedge said. They turned and watched as Streen and Gantoris emerged from the barge carrying tall crates. The two Jedi candidates walked smoothly, carrying loads that seemed impossible, and Wedge's eyes widened at the impressive feats of strength. "I had to have labor droids put those boxes onboard. I couldn't budge one myself."

"Then my students must be showing some progress." Luke nodded. "What about you, Wedge? You going to be a delivery driver the rest of your career?"

Wedge smiled; then with a flick of his wrist he tossed the helmet up the ramp and into the open cockpit. It clacked and thumped across the floor. "No. In fact I came here because I have a new assignment, and I won't get a chance to see you again for some time. The New Republic Council feels that Dr. Qwi Xux may be in danger from espionage. Admiral Daala is still out there somewhere with her fleet of Imperial Star Destroyers, and any time now I expect her to start blasting planets at random with hit-and-run strikes. She may try to get Qwi back."

Luke nodded gravely. Qwi Xux had been the top scientist in the Imperial research facility from which Han Solo had escaped—with Qwi's help. "If Admiral Daala doesn't want Dr. Xux back, I'm sure someone else will."

"Yeah," Wedge said, "that's why I've been assigned as her personal bodyguard and escort. In the meantime the Council still hasn't decided what to do with the Sun Crusher weapon that Han captured." Wedge sighed. "That's just scratching the surface of everything going on back on Coruscant."

Luke stared at Gantoris and Streen as they continued to unload the cargo bay, marching across the clearing to deposit their crates in the empty, cool hangar. Artoo-Detoo rattled out of the temple, leading two other students.

"Sounds like you need the new Jedi Knights more than ever," Luke said.

Wedge agreed emphatically. "More than you can know."

2

Fidgeting from the long voyage in the expanded B-wing fighter, Leia Organa Solo rode in silence beside Admiral Ackbar. The two of them sat in the cramped, metallic-smelling cockpit as the ship plunged through hyperspace.

Being Minister of State kept Leia on the move, shuttling from diplomatic event to ambassadorial reception to political emergency. Dutifully, she hopped across the galaxy, putting out fires and helping Mon Mothma hold together a fragile alliance in the vacuum left by the fall of the Empire.

Leia had already reviewed the background holos of the planet Vortex dozens of times, but she could not keep her mind on the upcoming Concert of the Winds. Diplomatic duties took her away far too often, and she used quiet moments to think about her husband Han, her twin children Jacen and Jaina. It had been too long since she had held her youngest baby, Anakin, who remained isolated and protected on the secret planet Anoth.

It seemed that whenever Leia tried to spend a week, a day, even an *hour* alone with her family, something interrupted. She seethed inside each time, unable to show her feelings because she had to wear a calm political mask.

In her younger days Leia had devoted her life to the Rebellion; she had worked behind the scenes as a princess of Alderaan, as Senator Bail Organa's daughter; she had fought against Darth Vader and the Emperor, and more recently against Grand Admiral Thrawn. Now, though, she felt torn between her duties as Minister of State and her duties as Han Solo's wife and as mother to three children. She had allowed the New Republic to come first. This time. Again.

Beside her in the cockpit Admiral Ackbar moved his amphibious hands fluidly as he manipulated several control levers. "Dropping out of hyperspace now," he said in his gravelly voice.

The salmon-colored alien seemed perfectly comfortable in his white uniform. Ackbar swiveled his gigantic glassy eyes from side to side, as if to take in every detail of his craft. Through the hours of their journey, Leia had not seen him fidget once.

He and the other inhabitants of the watery world Calamari had suffered much under the Empire's iron grip. They had learned how to be quiet, yet listen to every detail, how to make their own decisions, and how to act upon them. Working as a loyal member of the Rebellion, Ackbar himself had been instrumental in developing the B-wing class of starfighters that had taken such a huge toll on the Imperial TIE fighters.

As Leia watched him pilot the stretched-out, cumbersome-looking fighter, Ackbar seemed an integral part of the gangly craft that appeared to be all wings and turbolaser turrets mounted around a dual cockpit. Ackbar's crew of fishlike Calamarians, led by his chief starship mechanic, Terpfen, had expanded the former one-man craft into Ackbar's personal diplomatic shuttle, adding a single passenger seat.

Through the curved dome of the cockpit windows, Leia watched as multicolored knots of hyperspace evaporated into a star-strewn panorama. The sublight engines kicked in, and the B-wing streaked toward the planet Vortex.

Leia's dress uniform felt damp and clingy, and she tried to adjust the folds of slick fabric to make herself more comfortable. As Ackbar concentrated on the approach to Vortex, Leia pulled out her pocket holopad, laying the flat silvery plate on her lap.

"Beautiful," she said, peering out the viewport to the planet beneath them. The blue and metallic-gray ball hung alone in space, moonless. Its atmosphere showed complex embroideries of cloudbanks and storm systems, racing spirals of clouds that swirled in horrendous gales.

Leia remembered her astronomical briefings about Vortex. The sharp tilt of the planet's axis produced severe seasonal changes. At the onset of winter, a vast polar cap formed rapidly from gases that froze out of the atmosphere. The sudden drop in pressure caused immense air currents, like a great flood going down a drain; clouds and vapor streamed southward in a battering ram to fill the empty zone where the atmosphere had solidified.

The Vors, hollow-boned humanoids with a rack of lacy wings on their backs, went to ground during storm season, taking shelter in half-buried hummock dwellings. To celebrate the winds, though, the Vors had established a cultural festival renowned throughout the galaxy. . . .

Deciding to review the details one more time before they landed and the diplomatic reception began, Leia touched the icons etched into the synthetic marble frame of her datapad. It would not do for the New Republic's Minister of State to make a political faux pas.

A translucent image shimmered and grew out of the silvery screen in a miniaturized projection of the Cathedral of Winds. Defying the hurricane gales that thrashed through their atmosphere, the Vors had built a tall ethereal structure that had resisted the fierce storm winds for centuries. Delicate and incredibly intricate, the Cathedral of Winds rose like a castle made of eggshell-thin crystal. Thousands of passageways wound through hollow chambers and turrets and spires. Sunlight glittered on the structure, reflecting the rippling fields of windblown grasses that sprawled across the surrounding plains.

At the beginning of storm season, gusts of wind blew through thousands of different-sized openings in the honey combed walls, whipping up a reverberating, mournful music through pipes of various diameters.

The wind music was never the same twice, and the Vors allowed their cathedral to play only once each year. During the concert thousands of Vors flew into or climbed through the spires and windpipes, opening and closing air passages to mold the music into a sculpture, a work of art created by the weather systems of the storm planet and the Vor people.

On the holopad Leia skimmed to the next files. The music of the winds had not been heard for decades, not since Senator Palpatine had announced his New Order and declared himself Emperor. Objecting to the excesses of the Empire, the Vors had sealed the holes in their cathedral and refused to let the music play for anyone.

But this season the Vors had invited representatives from the New Republic to come and listen.

Ackbar opened a comm channel and pushed his fishlike face closer to the voice pickup. Leia watched the bristly feelers around his mouth jiggle as he spoke. "Vortex Cathedral landing pad, this is Admiral Ackbar. We are in orbit and approaching your position."

A Vor voice like two dry twigs rattling together crackled back over the speaker. "New Republic shuttle, we are transmitting landing coordinates that take into account wind shear and storm systems along your descent. Our atmospheric turbulence is quite unpredictable and dangerous. Please follow precisely."

"Understood." Ackbar settled back into his seat, rubbing broad shoulder blades against the ridged back of the chair. He pulled several black restraint strands across his chest. "You'd better strap in, Leia," Ackbar said. "It's going to be a bumpy ride."

Leia switched off her holopad and tucked it beside her seat. She secured herself, feeling confined by the webbing, and took a deep breath of the stale recycled air. The faintest fishy undertone suggested Calamarian anxiety.

Staring ahead, Ackbar took his B-wing into the swirling atmosphere of Vortex, straight toward the storm systems.

Ackbar knew that humans could not read expressions on broad Calamarian faces. He hoped Leia did not realize how uneasy he felt flying through such hellish weather patterns.

Leia did not know that Ackbar had volunteered to take the mission because he trusted no other person to pilot someone as important as the Minister of State, and he trusted no other vehicle more than his personal B-wing fighter.

He turned both of his brown eyes forward to watch the approaching cloud layers. The ship cut through the outer layers of atmosphere, zooming into buffeting turbulence. The sharp wings of the starfighter sliced the air, curling wind in a rippling wake. The wing edges glowed cherry-red from the screaming descent.

Ackbar gripped the controls with his flipper-hands, concentrating on fast reactions, split-second decisions, making sure everything worked just right. In this landing there would be no room for error. He cocked his right eye down to scan the landing coordinates the Vor technician had transmitted.

The craft began to rattle and jitter. His stomach lurched as a sudden updraft knocked them several hundred meters higher and then let them fall in a deep plunge until he managed to wrestle control back. Blurry fists of high-rising clouds pummeled the transparisteel viewports, leaving trails of condensed moisture that fanned out and evaporated.

Ackbar tracked from side to side across the panels with his left eye, verifying the readouts. No red lights. His right eye cocked back to catch a glimpse of Leia sitting rigid and silent, held in place by black restraint cords. Her dark eyes seemed almost as wide as a Mon Calamarian's, but her lips were pressed together in a thin white line. She seemed afraid, but afraid to show it, trusting in his ability. Leia said no word to distract him.

The B-wing headed down in a spiral, skirting an immense cyclonic disturbance. The wind hooked the rattling wings of the fighter, knocking the craft from side to side. Ackbar deployed the secondary aileron struts in an attempt to regain stability and retracted the laser-cannon turrets to minimize wind resistance.

"New Republic shuttle, we show you off course," the brittle-twig voice of the Vor controller came over the speaker, muffled by the roaring wind. "Please advise."

Ackbar turned his left eye to double-check the coordinate display, and saw that the starfighter had indeed veered off course. Calm and focused, he tried to force the craft back onto the appropriate vector. He couldn't believe he had gone so far astray, unless he had misread the coordinates in the first place.

As he yanked the B-wing toward a wall of spiraling clouds, a blast of gale-force winds hammered them into a roll and slammed Ackbar against his pilot seat. The fighter spun end over end, battered by the wild storm.

Leia let out a small scream before clamping her mouth shut. Ackbar hauled with all his strength upon the levers, firing stabilizer jets in a counterclockwise maneuver to counteract the spin.

The B-wing responded, finally slowing its crazed descent. Ackbar looked up to see himself surrounded by a whirlwind of mist. He had no idea which direction was up or down. He accordioned out the craft's set of perpendicular wings and locked them into a more stable cruising position. His craft responded sluggishly, but the cockpit panels told him that the wings were in place.

"New Republic shuttle, please respond." The Vor did not sound at all concerned.

Ackbar finally got the B-wing upright and flying again, but found he had missed his coordinates once more. He angled back into them as easily as he could. His mouth felt desiccated as he checked the altitude panels and saw with alarm how far the ship had dropped.

The metal hull plates smoked and glowed orange from tearing through the atmosphere. Lightning slashed on all sides. Blue balls of discharge electricity flared from the tips of the wings. His readouts scrambled with racing curls of static, then came back on again. The cockpit power systems dimmed, then brightened as reserve power kicked in.

Ackbar risked another glance at Leia and saw her fighting wide-eyed fear and helplessness. He knew she was a woman of action and would do anything to help him out—but there was nothing she could do. If he had to, Ackbar could eject her to safety—but he did not dare risk losing his B-wing yet. He could still pull off a desperate but intact landing.

Suddenly, the clouds peeled away like a wet rag ripped from his eyes. The wind-whipped plains of Vortex spread out below, furred with golden-brown and purple grasses. The grasslands rippled as the wind combed invisible fingers through the blades. Concentric circles of bunkerlike Vor shelters surrounded the center of their civilization.

He heard Leia gasp in a deep wonder that sliced through even her terror. The enormous Cathedral of Winds glinted with light and roiling shadows as clouds marched overhead. The high lacy structure seemed far too delicate to withstand the storms. Winged creatures swarmed up and down the sides of the fluted chambers, opening passages for the wind to blow through and create the famous music. Faintly distant, he could hear the lilting, eerie notes.

"New Republic shuttle, you are on the wrong course. This is an emergency. You must abort your landing."

With a shock Ackbar saw that the displayed coordinates had changed again. The B-wing did not respond as he fought the controls. The Cathedral of Winds grew larger every second.

Cocking an eye to look through the upper rim of the domed viewport, Ackbar saw that one of the perpendicular wings had jammed at a severe angle, yielding maximum wind resistance. The angled wing slapped against the turbulence and jerked the starfighter to the left.

His cockpit panels insisted that both wings had deployed properly, yet his own vision told him otherwise.

Ackbar jabbed the controls again, trying to straighten the wing, to regain control. The bottom half of his body felt cold and tingly as he channeled reserves of energy into his mind and his hands on the control levers.

"Something is very wrong here," he said.

Leia stared out the viewport. "We're heading straight for the cathedral!"

One of the aileron struts buckled and snapped from the plasteel hull, dragging power cables as it tore free. Sparks flew, and more hull plates ripped up.

Ackbar strangled an outcry. Suddenly the control lights flickered and dimmed. He heard the grinding hum as his main cockpit panels went dead. He hit the second auxiliary backup he had personally designed into the B-wing.

"I don't understand it," Ackbar said, his voice guttural in the confines of the cockpit. "This ship was just reconditioned. My own Calamarian mechanics were the only ones who touched it."

"New Republic shuttle," the voice on the radio insisted.

On the crystalline Cathedral of Winds, multicolored Vors scrambled down the sides, fleeing as they saw the craft hurtling toward them. Some of the creatures took flight, while others stared. Thousands of them were packed into the immense glassy structure.

Ackbar hauled the controls to the right, to the left—anything to make the craft swerve—but nothing responded. All the power had died.

He couldn't raise or lower the ship's wings. He was a large deadweight falling straight toward the cathedral. Desperately he hit the full battery reserves, knowing they could do nothing for the mechanical subsystems, but at least he could lock in a full-power crash shield around the B-wing.

And before that, he could break Leia free to safety.

"I'm sorry, Leia," Ackbar said. "Tell them that I am sorry." He punched a button on the control panel that cracked open the right side of the cockpit, splitting the hull and blasting free the tacked-on passenger seat.

As it shot Leia into the clawlike winds, Ackbar heard the wind screech at him through the open cockpit. The crash shield hummed as he hurtled toward the great crystalline structure. The fighter's engine smoldered and smoked.

Ackbar stared straight ahead until the end, never blinking his huge Calamarian eyes.

Leia found herself flying through the air. The blast of the ejection seat had knocked the breath out of her.

She couldn't even shout as the wind caught and spun her chair. The seat's safety repulsorlifts held her like a gentle hand and slowly lowered her toward the whiplike strands of pale-hued grasses below.

She looked up to see Ackbar's B-wing shuttle in the last instant before it crashed. The starfighter smoked and whined as it plunged like a metal filing toward a powerful magnet.

In a frozen moment she heard the loud, mournful fluting of winds whistling through thousands of crystalline chambers. The breeze picked up with a gust, making the music sound like a sudden gasp of terror. The winged Vors scrambled and attempted to flee, but most could not move quickly enough.

Ackbar's B-wing plowed into the lower levels of the Cathedral of Winds like a meteor. The booming impact detonated the crystalline towers into a hail of razor-edged spears that flew in all directions. The sound of tinkling glass, the roar of sharp broken pieces, the shriek of the wind, the screams of the slashed Vors—all combined into the most agonizing sound Leia had ever heard.

The entire glasslike structure seemed to take forever to collapse. Tower after tower fell inward.

The winds kept blowing, drawing somber notes from the hollow columns, changing pitch. The music became a thinner and thinner wail, until only a handful of intact wind tubes were left lying on their sides in the glassy rubble.

As Leia wept with great sobs that seemed to tear her apart, the automatic escape chair gently drifted to the ground and settled in the whispering grasses.

3

The polar regions of Coruscant reminded Han Solo of the ice planet Hoth—with one crucial difference. Han was here *by choice* with his young friend Kyp Durron for a vacation while Leia went off with Admiral Ackbar on yet another diplomatic mission.

Han stood atop the crumpled blue-white ice cliffs, feeling warm in his insulated charcoal-gray parka and red heater gloves. The ever-present auroras in the purplish skies sent rainbow curtains flickering and refracting off the ice. He drew in a deep breath of crackling cold air that seemed to curl his nostril hairs.

He turned to Kyp beside him. "About ready to go, kid?"

For the fifth time the dark-haired eighteen-year-old bent over to adjust the fastenings on his turbo-skis. "Uh, almost," Kyp said.

Han leaned forward to peer down the steep turbo-ski run of rippled ice, feeling a lump form in his throat but unwilling to show it.

Blue and white glaciers shone in dim light from the months-long twilight. Below, ice-boring machines had chewed deep tunnels into the thick ice caps; other excavators had chopped broad terraces on the cliffs as they mined centuries-old snowpack, melting it with fusion furnaces to be delivered via titanic water pipelines to the dense metropolitan areas in the temperate zones.

"You really think I can do this?" Kyp said, straightening and gripping his deflector poles.

Han laughed. "Kid, if you can pilot us single-handed through a black hole cluster, I think you can handle a turbo-ski slope on the most civilized planet in the galaxy."

Kyp looked at Han with a smile in his dark eyes. The boy reminded Han of a young Luke Skywalker. Ever since Han had rescued Kyp from his slavery in the spice mines of Kessel, the young man had clung to him. After years of wrongful Imperial imprisonment, Kyp had missed the best years of his life. Han vowed to make up for that.

"Come on, kid," he said, leaning forward and igniting the motors of his turbo-skis. With thickly gloved hands Han held on to the deflector poles and flicked them on. He felt the cushioning repulsorfield emanating from each point, making the poles bob in the air to keep his balance.

"You're on," Kyp said, and fired up his own skis. "But not the kiddie slope." He turned from the wide ice pathway and pointed instead to a side run that branched off over several treacherous ledges, across the scabby ice of a rotten glacier, and finally over a frozen waterfall to a receiving-and-rescue area. Winking red laser beacons clearly marked the dangerous path.

"No way, Kyp! It's much too—" But Kyp launched himself forward and blasted down the slope.

"Hey!" Han said. He felt sick in the pit of his stomach, sure he would have to pick up Kyp's broken body somewhere along the path. But now he had no choice but to blast after the boy. "Kid, this is really a stupid thing to do."

Crystals of powdery snow sprayed behind Kyp's turbo-skis as he bent forward, touching the ground at occasional intervals with his deflector poles. He kept his balance like an expert, intuitively knowing what to do. After only a second of the thundering descent, Han realized that Kyp might be more likely to survive this ride than he was.

As Han rocketed down the slope, the snow and ice hissed beneath him like a jet of compressed air. Han hit a frozen outcropping that sent him flying, and he somersaulted through the air, flailing with his deflector poles. Stabilizer jets on his belt righted him just in time as he slammed into the snow again. He continued down the slope with the speed of a stampeding bantha.

He squinted behind ice goggles, concentrating intensely on keeping himself upright. The landscape seemed too sharp—every razor-edged drift of snow, the glittering sheared-off face of ice—as if every single detail might be his last.

Kyp let out a loud *whoop* of delight as he slewed left onto the dangerous offshoot turbo-ski path. The whoop echoed three times around the sharp-edged cliffs.

Han began cursing the young man's recklessness, then experienced a sudden inner warmth as he realized he had expected little else from Kyp.

Making the best of it, Han let out an answering whoop of his own and turned to follow.

Red laser beacons flared, warning and guiding the foolish turbo-skiers along the path. The rippled surface whispered beneath the soft cushioning fields of his turbo-skis.

Ahead, the icy roadway seemed foreshortened and continued at a different elevation. Han realized the danger an instant before he reached the precipice. "Cliff!"

Kyp bent low, as if he had simply become another component of his turbo-skis. He tucked his deflector poles close to his sides, then fired up the rear jets of his skis. He rocketed over the edge of the cliff, arcing down in a long smooth curve to the resumption of the trail.

Barely in time, Han activated his own jets and launched himself over empty space. His stomach dropped even faster than gravity could tug him down. Wind ruffled the edges of his parka hood.

In front of him Kyp landed smoothly without so much as a wobble and shot downslope.

Han had time to take only one gulping breath as the plateau of ice rushed up to meet his turbo-skis with a loud *crack*. He gripped his deflector poles, desperate to maintain his balance.

A powdery ribbon of drifted snow curled across their path. Kyp jammed down with his deflector poles, hopping up into the air and cleanly missing the drift—but Han plowed straight through.

Snow flew into his goggles, blinding him. He wobbled and jabbed from side to side with his poles. He managed to swipe a gloved hand across his goggles just in time to swerve left and avoid smashing into a monolithic ice outcropping.

Before he had recovered his balance, Han launched over a yawning chasm in the rotten glacier that fell out beneath him. For a timeless instant he stared down at a drop of about a million kilometers, and then he landed on the far side. Behind him, he heard a *whump* as a block of age-old snow lost its precarious grip on the wall and plunged into the crevasse.

Ahead, Kyp encountered a blocky, rubble-strewn glacier field. More widely spaced now, the laser beacons seemed to give up and let foolhardy turbo-skiers choose their own path. Kyp wobbled as he struck hummocks of ice and snow. He raised the repulsorfield to skim higher over the surface.

As the crusty glacier grew rougher, clogged with grainy blown snow, Han muttered complaints and curses through gritted teeth. He kept his balance somehow, but Kyp had lost ground. Han found himself breathing the boy's wake, pushing closer and faster—and suddenly the race meant something to him again. Afterward, while sitting around in a cantina and swapping stories, he would somehow convince himself that the whole thing had been a great deal of fun.

Feeling a bit of the recklessness he had just cursed Kyp for, Han pulsed the jets, lunging forward in an adrenaline-filled burst of speed that brought him side by side with Kyp.

A snowfield sprawled in front of them, sparkling white and unsullied by other turbo-ski tracks—even though it had not snowed for more than a month in this arid frigid climate—demonstrating exactly how few people had been foolish enough to attempt the dangerous path.

Ahead, the roped-off receiving-and-rescue area lay like a sanctuary: communications gear, warming huts, powered-down medical droids that could be reactivated at a moment's notice, and an old hot-beverage shop that had long since gone out of business. Home free—they had made it!

Kyp glanced sideways at him, his dark eyes crinkled at the corners. He crouched down and blasted his skis at full power. Han hunched over to decrease his air resistance. Pristine snow flew around him, hissing in his ears.

The line of laser beacons switched off like metallic eyes blinking shut. Han had no time to wonder about it before the smooth blanket of snow ahead bulged, then sloughed inward.

A crunching, grinding sound accompanied the straining of massive engines. Gouts of steam erupted from the collapsed snowfield as the glowing red nose of a mechanical thermal borer thrust into the open air. The screw-shaped tip continued to turn as it chewed its way out of the solid ice.

"Look out!" Han yelled, but Kyp had already veered off to the left side, leaning hard on one deflector pole and jabbing at the air with his other. Han punched his stabilizing jets and streaked to the right as the mammoth ice-processing machine chewed the opening of its tunnel wider, clutching the walls with clawed tractor treads.

Han skimmed past the gaping pit, feeling a blast of hot steam across his cheeks. His goggles fogged again, but he found his way to the steep ice waterfall, the final obstacle before the finish line. The edge of the precipice flowed with long tendrils of icicles like dangling cables that had built up over centuries during the brief spring thaws.

Kyp launched himself over the edge of the frozen river, igniting both ski jets. Han did the same, tucking his poles against his ribs, watching the packed snow fly up to strike the bottoms of his skis with a loud slap that echoed along the ice fields in unison with the sound of Kyp's landing.

They both charged forward, then slewed to a stop in front of the cluster of prefab huts. Kyp peeled down the hood of his parka and started laughing. Han held on to his deflector poles, feeling his body tremble with relief and an overdose of excitement. Then he, too, began chuckling.

"That was really stupid, kid," Han managed at last.

"Oh?" Kyp shrugged. "Who was stupid enough to follow me? After the spice mines of Kessel, I wouldn't consider a little turbo-ski slope too dangerous. Hey, maybe we could ask Threepio to tell us the odds of successfully negotiating that slope when we get back."

Han shook his head and gave a lopsided grin. "I'm not interested in odds. We did it. That's what counts."

Kyp stared across the frozen distance. His eyes seemed to follow the arrow-straight lines of nonreflective water conduits ringed with pressure joints and pumping stations.

"I'm glad we've had so much fun, Han," he said, staring into something only he seemed to see. "I've done a lifetime's worth of healing since you rescued me."

Han felt uncomfortable at the thick emotion he heard in Kyp's voice. He tried to lighten the mood. "Well, kid, you had as much to do with our escape as I did."

Kyp didn't seem to hear. "I've been thinking about what Luke Skywalker said when he found my ability to use the Force. I only know a little bit about it, but it seems to be calling me. I could do a huge service to the New Republic. The Empire ruined my life and destroyed my family—I wouldn't mind getting a chance to strike back."

Han swallowed, knowing what the boy was trying to say. "So you think you're ready to go study with Luke and the other Jedi trainees?"

Kyp nodded. "I'd rather stay here and have fun for the rest of my life, but—"

Han said in a soft voice, "You deserve it, you know."

But Kyp shook his head. "I think it's time I start taking myself seriously. If I do have this gift of using the Force, I can't let it go to waste."

Han gripped the young man's shoulder and squeezed hard, feeling Kyp's rangy frame through his bulky gloves. "I'll see that you get a good flight to Yavin 4."

The whirring hum of repulsorlifts broke the quiet moment. Han looked up as a messenger droid approached, streaking like a chromium projectile over the ice fields. The droid arrowed straight for them.

Han muttered, "If that's a representative from the turbo-ski resort, I'm going to file a complaint about that ice-mining machine. We could have been killed."

But as the messenger droid hovered over them, lowering itself to Han's eye level, it snapped open a scanning panel and spoke in a genderless monotone. "General Solo, please confirm identification. Voice match will be sufficient."

Han groaned. "Aww, I'm on vacation. I don't want to bother with any diplomatic mess right now."

"Voice match confirmed. Thank you," the droid said. "Prepare to receive encoded message."

The droid hovered as it projected a holographic image onto the clean snow. Han recognized the auburn-haired figure of Mon Mothma. He straightened in surprise—the Chief of State rarely communicated with him directly.

"Han," Mon Mothma said in a quiet, troubled voice. He noticed immediately that she had called him by his first name instead of his more formal rank. A fist of sudden dread clenched his stomach.

"I'm sending you this message because there has been an accident. Admiral Ackbar's shuttle crashed on the planet Vortex. Leia was with him, but she's safe and unharmed. The admiral ejected her to safety before his ship flew out of control, directly into a large cultural center. Admiral Ackbar managed to power up his crash shields, but the entire structure was destroyed. So far at least 358 Vors are confirmed dead in the wreckage.

"This is a tragic day for us, Han. Come home to Imperial City. I think Leia might need you as soon as she returns." Mon Mothma's image wavered, then dissolved into staticky snowflakes that faded in the air.

The messenger droid said, "Thank you. Here is your receipt." It spat out a tiny blue chit that landed in a puff of snow at Han's feet.

Han stared as the droid turned and streaked back toward the base camp. He squashed the blue chit into the snow with the base of his turbo-ski. He felt sick. The excitement he had just experienced, all the joy with Kyp, had evaporated, leaving only a leaden dread inside him.

"Come on, Kyp. Let's go."

See-Threepio thought that if his fine-motor control had allowed it, his entire golden body would be chattering with cold. His internal thermal units were no match for the frozen polar regions of Coruscant.

He was a protocol droid, fluent in over six million forms of communication. He was able to perform an incredible number of diverse tasks—all of which seemed more appealing at the moment than baby-sitting a pair of wild two-and-a-half-year-olds who saw him as their plaything.

Threepio had taken the twins to the snow-play area at the bottom of the ice slopes, where they could ride tame tauntauns. Little Jacen and his sister Jaina seemed to enjoy the spitting, cumbersome creatures—and the Umgullian rancher who had brought the furry animals to Coruscant seemed delighted to have the business.

Afterward Threepio had stoically endured as the twins insisted on making a "snow droid" of him, packing layers of snow around his shiny body. He still felt ice crystals caked inside his joints. As he enhanced the output from his optical sensors, Threepio thought that his golden alloy had taken on a decidedly bluish tinge from the low temperature.

On a sledding slope the twins spun around, giggling and shrieking as they bounced against padded restraints in a child's snow skimmer. Threepio waited for them at the bottom, then began the long trudge back up the hill so the children could do it all over again. He felt like a low-capacity labor droid with too little computing power to understand the drudgery of its own existence. "Oh, how I wish Master Solo would get back soon," he said.

At the top of the ramp he secured Jacen and Jaina snugly into their seats. In tandem they looked up at him with rosy-cheeked faces. Humans claimed to find the winter chill exhilarating; Threepio wished he had outfitted himself with more efficient low-temperature lubricants.

"Now, you children be careful on the ride down," he said. "I shall meet you at the bottom and bring you back up." He paused. "Again."

He launched the children in the spinning snow skimmer. Jacen and Jaina laughed and squealed as feathers of snow sprayed down the slope. Threepio began to move with a rapid gait down the long ramp.

When he reached the bottom, the twins were already attempting to unstrap themselves. Jaina had managed to disconnect one buckle, though the attendant at the equipment-rental station had assured Threepio that the restraints were utterly childproof.

"Children, leave that alone!" he said. He refastened Jaina's restraint and switched on the hoverfield beneath the snow skimmer. He grasped the handles and began to climb back up the slope to the launching platform.

When he reached the top, both twins shouted, "Again!" in unison, as if their minds were linked. Threepio decided it was time to lecture the children about overindulgence in enjoyment, but before he could formulate a speech with the appropriate levels of sternness and vocabulary, a crowded shuttle skimmer arrived. Han Solo emerged, pulling back the hood of his gray parka and balancing his turbo-skis on his left shoulder. Kyp Durron followed him out of the transport.

Threepio raised a golden arm. "Over here," he said. "Master Solo, over here!"

"Daddy!" Jaina said. Jacen echoed her a fraction of a second later.

"Thank heavens," Threepio said, and started to unfasten the restraints.

"Get ready to go," Han said as he marched forward, his expression unaccountably troubled. Threepio reached forward, about to begin his litany of complaints, but Han dropped the bulky turbo-skis into the droid's arms.

"Master Solo, is something wrong?" Threepio tried to balance the heavy skis.

"Sorry to cut your vacation short, kids, but we have to get back home," Han said, ignoring the droid.

Threepio straightened. "I'm very glad to hear that, sir. I don't mean to complain, but I was *not* designed for temperature extremes."

He felt an impact against the back of his head as a large lump of snow splattered him. "Oh!" he said, raising his arms in alarm, barely managing to keep hold of the skis. "Master Solo, I must protest!" he said.

Jacen and Jaina giggled as they each picked up another snowball to throw at the droid.

Han turned to the twins. "Stop playing with Threepio, you two. We have to get back home."

Down in the repair bays of the revamped Imperial Palace on Coruscant, Lando Calrissian couldn't imagine how Chewbacca managed to cram his enormous furry body inside the *Falcon*'s narrow maintenance crawlway. Standing in the corridor, Lando saw the Wookiee as a tangle of brown fur wedged between the emergency power generator, the acceleration compensator, and the anticoncussion field generator.

Chewbacca let out a yowl as he dropped a hydrospanner. The tool bounced and fell with a series of ricocheting clangs until it landed in a completely inaccessible spot. The Wookiee snarled and then let out a yelp as he banged his shaggy head on a coolant pipe.

"No, no, Chewbacca!" Lando said, brushing back his sleek cape and sticking his arm into the maintenance crawlway. He tried to point toward the circuitry. "That goes here, and *this* goes there!" Chewbacca grumbled back, disagreeing.

"Look, Chewie, I know this ship like the back of my hand, too. I owned her for quite a few years, you know."

Chewbacca made a string of ululating sounds that echoed inside the enclosed chamber.

"All right, have it your way. I can work the access hatches on the outside hull. I'll retrieve your hydrospanner. Who knows what other junk we'll find there?"

Lando turned and made his way to the entry ramp, stomping down into the cacophony of shouted requests and engine noises in the starship mechanic bay. The air smelled oily and stifling, tainted with gaseous coolants and exhaust fumes from small diplomatic shuttles to large freighters. Human and alien engineers worked on their ships. Stubby Ugnaughts clambered inside access hatches and chattered at each other, requesting tools and diagrams for fixing troublesome engines.

Admiral Ackbar's carefully picked crew of Calamarian starship mechanics oversaw special modifications to small vessels in the New Republic fleet. Terpfen, Ackbar's chief mechanic, wandered from ship to ship, status board in hand, verifying requested repairs and scrutinizing the work with his glassy fish eyes.

Lando pried open the access hatch on the *Falcon*'s outer hull. The hydrospanner clattered out and fell into his outstretched hands, along with burned-out cyberfuses, a discarded hyperdrive shunt, and the wrapper from a package of dehydrated food.

"Got it, Chewbacca," he shouted. The Wookiee's answer was muffled inside the cramped access hatch.

Lando looked at the scorch marks along the *Falcon*'s battered hull. The ship seemed to be one massive collection of patches and repairs. He ran a callused hand along the hull, caressing the metal.

"Hey! What are you doing to my ship?"

Lando jerked his hand away from the *Falcon* and looked around guiltily to see Han Solo approaching. Chewbacca bellowed a greeting from the maintenance crawlway.

Han's face reflected a thunderstorm of bad moods as he strode across the debris-strewn floor of the mechanic bay. "I need my ship right now. Is she ready to fly?" Han said.

Lando put his hands at his side. "I was just making some repairs and modifications, old buddy. What's the problem?"

"Who told you you could make any modifications?" Han looked unaccountably angry. "Chewie, we've got to fly right away. Why did you let this clown mess around with my engines?"

"Wait a minute, Han! This used to be my ship, you know," Lando said, not knowing what had provoked such anger in his friend. "Besides, who rescued this ship from Kessel? Who saved your tail from the Imperial fleet?"

See-Threepio hastened stiffly into the mechanic bay. "Ah, greetings, General Calrissian," he said.

Lando ignored the droid. "I lost the *Lady Luck* rescuing your ship. I'd think that deserves a little gratitude, don't you? In fact, since I sacrificed my own ship to save your hide, I thought maybe you'd be grateful enough to give me back the *Falcon*."

"Oh, my!" Threepio said. "That *is* an idea that might warrant some consideration, Master Solo."

"Shut up, Threepio," Han said without glancing in the droid's direction.

"Looks like you've got an attitude problem, Han," Lando said with a grin he knew would annoy his friend. But Han had stepped over the bounds of common courtesy with his snappish accusations, and Lando had no intention of letting him get away with it.

Han looked ready to explode. Lando couldn't figure out what was bothering him. "My problem is you've been sabotaging my ship. I don't ever want you touching her again, do you understand? Get your own ship. Seems to me that with the million-credit reward you got at the blob races on Umgul, you could buy just about any ship you want and stop messing around with mine."

"An excellent idea, sir," Threepio added helpfully. "With that amount of money, General Calrissian, you could indeed buy a fine ship."

"Be quiet, Threepio," Lando said, putting his hands on his hips. "I don't want to buy another ship, old buddy." He stressed the last two words with thick sarcasm. "If I can't have the *Lady Luck*, I want the *Falcon*. Your wife is the Minister of State, Han. You can have the government provide you with any sort of transport you want—why not get yourself a new fighter right from the Calamarian shipyards?"

"I'm certain that could be arranged, sir," Threepio agreed.

"Shut up, Threepio," Han said again, keeping his eyes on Lando. "I don't want any old ship. The *Falcon* is mine."

Lando glowered at Han. "You won her from me in a sabacc game, and to tell you the truth—old buddy—I've always suspected you cheated in that game."

Han became livid, backing away. "You're accusing *me* of cheating? I've been called a scoundrel before, but never a cheat! In fact, it seems to me," he said in a low, threatening voice, "that you won the *Falcon* yourself in a sabacc game before I came along. Didn't you also win the Cloud City Tibanna gas mines from the former Baron Administrator in a sabacc game? What could you possibly have used as collateral for a bet like that? You're a dirty no-good swindler, Lando. Admit it."

"And you're a pirate!" Lando said, stalking forward, his fists bunched at his side. He had made his reputation as an expert gambler.

Chewbacca growled from within the *Falcon*, making loud clangs and thumps as he extricated himself from the cramped passage. He stumbled down the entry ramp and stood gripping the piston supports.

As Han and Lando closed to within striking distance, Threepio wriggled in between them. "Excuse me, sirs, but might I make a suggestion? If indeed you both won the ship in a sabacc game, and if you are contesting the results, could you perhaps simply play another game of sabacc to settle this issue once and for all?" Threepio turned his glowing optical sensors first at Lando, then at Han.

"I just came down here to get my ship," Han said, "but now you've made it into a point of honor."

Lando glared at Han without flinching. "I can beat you any day of the week, Han Solo."

"Not this day," Han said, lowering his voice even further. "But not just sabacc. We'll make it *random* sabacc."

Lando raised his eyebrows, but met Han's gaze stare for stare. "Who's going to keep track of the plays?"

Han jerked his chin to the side. "We'll use Threepio as our modulator. Goldenrod doesn't have enough brains to cheat."

"But, sir, I really don't have the programming to—" Threepio said.

Han and Lando snapped in unison, "Shut up, Threepio!"

"All right, Han," Lando said, "let's do it before you lose your nerve."

"You're going to lose more than nerve before this game is over," Han said.

As Lando set up the cards and the sabacc table, Han Solo ushered the last of the off-duty bureaucrats toward the door of the small lounge. "Out. Come on! We need to use this place for a while."

They grumbled and objected in a variety of languages, but Han assisted them through the entryway with gentle shoves. "File a complaint with the New Republic." Then he closed and sealed the door, turning to Lando. "You ready yet?"

This was far different from the stuffy, smoke-filled parlors where he used to play sabacc, such as the underground game where he had once won a planet for Leia in an attempt to buy her affections.

At the sabacc table Lando spread out a handful of rectangular cards with crystalline screens sandwiched between metal layers. "Ready when you are, buddy." But he looked uneasy. "Han, we don't really have to do this—"

Han sniffed the air, frowning at the cloying smells of deodorizing mists and ambassadorial perfumes. "Yes, I do. Leia's been in an accident on one of her diplomatic missions, and I want to escort her back home, not some hospital ship."

"Leia's hurt?" Lando said, standing up in surprise. "So that's what has been bothering you. Forget it, take the ship. I was just kidding anyway. We'll do this some other time."

"No! We do it now, or you'll never be off my case. Threepio, get in here. What's taking so long?" Han said.

The golden droid scooted in from the back-room computer station, looking flustered, as usual. "I'm here, Master Solo. I was just reviewing the sabacc-rules programming."

Han punched his selections into the console of the bartender droid, smiling as he selected a fruity, prissy drink for Lando—complete with a blue tropical flower as a garnish—and a spiced ale for himself. He sat down, slid the drink across the surface to Lando, and sipped his ale.

Lando took a swallow of the mixture, winced, and forced a smile. "Thanks, Han. Should I deal?" He held the sabacc cards in his hand, leaning over the table's projecting field.

"Not yet." Han held up a hand. "Threepio, double-check to make sure those card surfaces are completely randomized."

"But, sir, surely—"

"Just do it. We want to make sure nobody gets an unfair advantage—don't we, old buddy?"

Lando managed to retain his forced smile as he handed the deck to Threepio, who ran the cards through a scrambler at the side of the table. "They are completely mixed, sir."

Threepio meticulously dealt five of the flat metallic cards each to Lando and to Han. "As you know, this is *random sabacc*, a combination of variant forms of the game," Threepio said, as if reciting the programming he had just uploaded. "There are five different sets of rules, shifted by chance, and changed at random time intervals as determined by the computer's random generator—that's me!"

"We know the rules!" Han growled, but he wasn't so certain. "And we also know the stakes."

Lando's deep, flinty eyes met his across the table. "Winner takes the *Falcon*. Loser takes Coruscant public transit from now on."

"Very well, sirs," Threepio said, "activate your cards. The first player to reach a score of one hundred points will be declared the winner. Our first round will be played according to . . ." He paused briefly as his randomizing function made a selection from the scrambled list of rules. "—Cloud City Casino alternate rules."

Han stared at the images appearing on his cards as his mind raced to remember how Cloud City Casino rules differed from the Bespin Standard form of the game. He stared at a mixed-up assortment of the four suits in sabacc—sabres, coins, flasks, and staves, with various positive and negative scores on each.

"Each player may select one and only one of his cards for a spin-change, and then we tally to see who comes closest to a score of positive or negative twenty-three, or zero."

Han scanned his cards, concentrating, but found no set that would add up to an appropriate tally. Lando wore a broad smile—but Lando *always* carried such an expression when he gambled. Han took a sip of his bitter spiced ale, swallowed hard, and chose a card. "Ready?" He raised his eyes to look at Lando.

Lando pushed the small scrambler button on the bottom left corner of a card. Han did the same, watching the image of the eight of coins flicker and re-form into a twelve of flasks. Together with a nine of flasks in his hand, he added to twenty-one. Not great. But when he saw Lando scowl at his own new card, he hoped it would be good enough.

"Twenty-one," Han said, slapping his cards on the table.

"Eighteen," Lando answered with a scowl. "You get the difference."

"Change of rules! Time has elapsed!" Threepio said. "Three points in favor of Master Solo. Next round is by . . . Empress Teta Preferred system."

Han looked at his new hand of cards, delighted to see a firm straight—but, if he remembered right, under Empress Teta rules the players swapped one card at random, and when Lando reached over to pluck a card from the right side, Han hoped to replace it with a Commander of Sabers—but the hand failed. Lando won the round and came out with a small lead, but before they could tally the scores, Threepio chimed in with another "Change of rules!" This time, scored under the Bespin Standard system, Lando's lead doubled.

Han cursed to himself as he stared at a chaotic mess in the next hand, not knowing what to bid, what to throw away. Before he made his decision, though, the random clock in Threepio's electronic brain forced him to call another rules change. "Corellian Gambit this time, sirs."

Han whooped in delight, for under the new rules the suits fit together with a completely different pattern. "Gotcha!" he cried, laying down his hand.

Lando grumbled, showing a wild card that, while valuable only moments before, now cost him fourteen points under the new scoring system.

Han crept ahead over the next several hands, then lost ground when rules changed back to Cloud City Casino style, which deemed all wild cards forfeit. Han reached forward to snatch one of Lando's cards, just as Lando selected one of his cards to change at random. They both froze. "Threepio, tell us again which rules we're playing under."

"New time interval anyway," the golden droid said. "Change to Bespin Standard. No, wait—new time interval again! Back to Empress Teta Preferred."

Han and Lando looked at their new cards again, minds whirling in confusion. Han took another sip of his spiced ale, and Lando drained his fruity concoction with a grimace. At the bottom the bright-colored flower had begun to sprout writhing roots that crawled on the bottom of his glass.

"Threepio, tell us the scores one more time," Lando said.

"Calculating for the last rules change, sirs, the total is ninety-three points for Master Solo and eighty-seven for General Calrissian."

Han and Lando glared at each other. "Last hand, buddy," Han said.

"Enjoy your remaining few seconds of ownership, Han," Lando said.

"Corellian Gambit rules, last-hand special case," Threepio announced.

Han felt his head pounding, trying to remember what happened in the last hand of the Corellian Gambit. Then he saw Lando locking in the denomination of only one of his cards, making ready to place his hand into the flux field in the center of the sabacc table.

Han studied his high-ranking face cards, Balance and Moderation, either of which would nudge him over the total score of a hundred. He pushed the retainer button on Balance, for eleven points, then thrust the rest of his hand into the flux field.

Han and Lando leaned over, staring in suspense as the images on the cards swirled and changed, flickering from one value to another in a blur until they stabilized, one by one.

Lando stared at low-demonination numeric cards, nothing at all spectacular, while Han got the best deal he had seen throughout the entire game. All face cards, Demise, Endurance, The Star, and The Queen of Air and Darkness, along with the Balance card he had kept. His score handily passed the goal, leaving Lando in the dust.

He cheered at the same instant Threepio declared another "Change of rules!" Han glared at the golden droid, waiting.

"This hand will be scored under the Ecclessis Figg Variation," Threepio said.

Han and Lando looked at each other, mouthing the words. "What is the Figg Variation?"

"In the final round the scores of all odd-numbered face cards are subtracted instead of added to the final score. This means, Master Solo, that while you gain ten points for Endurance and The Queen of Air and Darkness, you forfeit a total of forty-one for Balance, The Star, and Demise."

Threepio paused. "I'm afraid you lose, sir. General Calrissian gains sixteen points for a total score of one hundred three, while you are left with a final score of sixty-two."

Han blinked in shock at his half-empty glass of spiced ale as Lando pounded the tabletop in triumph. "Good game, Han. Now go on off to fetch Leia. Want me to come with you?"

Han kept staring at the table, at his ale, at anything but Lando. He felt hollow inside. Not only had he learned of Leia's tragedy today, but he had also lost the ship he had owned for more than a decade.

"Take her, she's yours," Han mumbled. He finally looked up to meet Lando's eyes.

"Come on, Han. You're distraught. You never should have made the bet in the first place. Just—"

"No, the *Falcon* is yours, Lando. I'm not a cheat, and I made the deal going into the game." Han stood, turning his back on Lando, leaving the rest of his ale untouched. "Threepio, authorize a change of registration for the *Falcon*. And you'd better get in touch with central transportation control. Arrange a diplomatic transport for Leia. I won't be picking her up after all."

Lando shifted uncomfortably. "Uh, I'll take good care of her, Han. Not a scratch."

Without another word Han went to the door of the lounge, unsealed it, and walked out into the echoing halls.

4

With black-gloved hands clasped behind her back, Admiral Daala stood at attention on the bridge of the Imperial Star Destroyer *Gorgon*.

In front of the bridge viewport, brilliant gases illuminated by a knot of blue-giant stars turned the Cauldron Nebula into a spectacular light show. Beside her in parking formation hung the *Basilisk* and the *Manticore*. The ionized gases played havoc with ships' sensors, making the nebula a perfect hiding place for her three fully armed battleships.

Daala heard a tentative bootstep behind her and turned to face Commander Kratas. "Yes, Commander?" As she moved, her olive-gray uniform clung like a second skin, while her mane of coppery hair trailed behind her like the tail of a comet.

Kratas snapped off a perfect salute and remained standing one step below her observation platform. "Admiral," he said, "as of oh-nine-hundred hours we have completed our assessment of the losses suffered during our battle at Kessel."

Daala formed her lips into a tight, emotionless line. Kratas was a short man, recruited into the Imperial Navy from an occupation force on one of the conscripted planets. He had dark hair trimmed to regulation length, wide watery eyes set under beetling brows, and a jutting chin that hung below almost nonexistent lips. The best part of Kratas, though, Daala thought, was that he always followed orders. He had been trained well in the Imperial Military Academy on Carida.

"Give me the breakdown, Commander," Daala said.

Kratas did not blink as he rattled off the numbers from memory. "Together, we lost a total of three TIE squadrons, and of course all hands and resources on board the *Hydra*."

Daala felt a cold stab of anger at the mention of her wrecked battleship. Kratas must have seen something in her expression, because he flinched, though he did not move aside.

The *Hydra*, Daala's fourth Star Destroyer, had been torn apart in one of the Maw cluster's black holes. It had been Daala's first significant loss in combat, one fourth of her destructive capability wiped out by Han Solo and the traitorous scientist Qwi Xux, who had stolen the Sun Crusher superweapon and fled the Empire's closely guarded Maw Installation.

"However," Kratas continued. His voice quavered the smallest bit, then he straightened. "Forty TIE fighters from the *Hydra* did manage to reach safety inside the other Star Destroyers, which makes up somewhat for the other losses."

Daala's Star Destroyers had emerged from the Maw cluster, expecting to engulf and obliterate Han Solo—but her ships had run headlong into Kessel's ragtag fleet like frenzied battledogs. Though her Star Destroyers had defeated nearly two thirds of Kessel's ships, the *Basilisk* had suffered severe damage and had to be linked with the *Gorgon*'s navicomputers for escape to a secret location in the Cauldron Nebula.

"What is the status of repairs to the *Basilisk*?" she said.

Kratas clicked his heels smartly as if pleased to give good news. "Three of the four damaged turbolaser cannons have been refurbished and are now operational. We expect to finish repairs on the fourth battery within the next two days. Armored spacetroopers have completed work on the breached external hull. Decks 7 through 9 are airtight again, and we are currently replenishing the atmosphere. The damaged flight-control circuitry has been rerouted, and the navicomp and targeting consoles are now fully operational."

He drew in a deep breath. "In short, Admiral, I believe our entire fleet is ready for battle again."

Daala leaned closer to the observation window, curling her long fingers around the simulated wood of the railing. She tried unsuccessfully to stop a smile from creeping across her lips. The metallic smell of the air comforted her. She had lived on the *Gorgon* for over a decade now. The air had been reprocessed and replenished until pungent organic odors had been scoured away, leaving only sterile smells, the tang of metal and lubricating oils, the reassuring scent of pressed Imperial Navy uniforms and polished stormtrooper armor.

"If I might ask a question, Admiral," Kratas said, glancing around to see the other personnel at their stations, every head turned studiously away from the conversation, pretending not to listen. Daala raised her eyebrows, waiting for him to continue.

"With the information we gained from interrogating Han Solo, and with transmissions we've received, we know that the Emperor is no longer alive, that Darth Vader and Grand Moff Tarkin are also dead, and that the Empire has fragmented into civil war." Kratas hesitated.

Daala spoke for him. "You are wondering, Commander, who our Commander in Chief is?"

Kratas nodded vigorously. "Grand Admiral Thrawn has been killed, as has Warlord Zsinj. We know of several commanders still fighting over the remnants of the Empire, but they seem more interested in destroying each other than in battling the Rebellion. If I may make a suggestion? The Imperial Military Academy on Carida still appears to be stable and loyal, with a great many weapons at their disposal. Perhaps it would be best to—"

"I don't think so," Daala said sharply, turning from him to smother her scowl. She had been trained and trounced in the harsh military academy on Carida. Because she was female, Daala had been passed over for promotion after promotion; she had been given the worst assignments. She had been brutalized. And that had only increased her drive to succeed.

Finally she had created a false identity for herself through Carida's vast computer networks and used that identity in combat simulation rooms. She had won repeatedly, creating breakthrough tactics that had been adopted by many of the Imperial Army's ground assault forces. After Moff Tarkin had discovered Daala's true identity and realized her talent, he had secretly whisked her away, using his new authority as Grand Moff of the Outer Rim territories. He had promoted her to the rank of admiral—as far as she knew, the only female admiral in the entire Imperial Fleet.

Yet because of the Emperor's own prejudices against women and nonhuman races, Tarkin had kept the truth about his new admiral a secret. Daala and Tarkin had become lovers, and to keep her from coming to the Emperor's attention, he had given her command of four Star Destroyers assigned to guard the supersecret think tank inside the black hole cluster.

But now that she had come out with her battleships, ready to devastate any planet loyal to the Rebellion, Daala could not conceive of handing over that authority to her former persecutors on Carida.

She took a deep breath again and faced Commander Kratas. He stood without moving, still waiting for her response. Around the bridge other crew members looked up from their stations; but when Daala glanced at them, they quickly found other things to do.

"Since the factions seem to have forgotten that our true enemy is the

Rebellion, I think we will set an example for them. We must focus their attention on the appropriate enemy—the Rebels who killed Grand Moff Tarkin, who destroyed the Death Star, who murdered the Emperor. Since Grand Admiral Thrawn was the only person in the Imperial fleet with a rank higher than my own, I must assume that my rank is now at least as high as any of the pretenders."

Kratas's eyes widened, but Daala shook her head. Her long hair swirled like flickering flames. "No, Commander, I have no intention of putting in my bid for what is left of the Empire. That's not a job I would relish. We'll leave that to the petty dictators. I just want to cause damage. Lots of it."

Her lips curled in a snarl, and her voice grew husky. "I think our best chance is to rely on hit-and-run tactics, guerrilla warfare. We have three Star Destroyers. That's enough to wipe out the civilizations on any number of worlds. We must hit fast and run fast. We will continue to pound the Rebels for as long as we can."

She glanced around the bridge to see that all personnel stood staring at her, some with wide eyes and gaping mouths, others grinning. Her crew had been bottled up for so long in the Maw, ready to fight but denied any chance at action because they were forced to guard the group of prima donna weapons scientists.

Daala glanced out at the Cauldron Nebula, saw the bright lights of other star systems piercing the haze of ionized gas. Many targets waited out there.

She turned to the navigator's station. "Lieutenant, I want you to plot a course for the last-known shipping lanes closest to our position."

"Yes, Admiral," the lieutenant said, practically leaping toward his station.

"Inform all personnel on the three ships," Daala said. A bold grin lit her face; she felt as if her blood had become molten copper. Her green eyes seemed to sparkle with laser bolts ready to be fired on unsuspecting prey.

The fight was about to begin.

"Let's go hunting," Daala said, and a spontaneous cheer erupted from the bridge crew.

Deep in space, the pack of Imperial Star Destroyers waited, sensors alert and scanning for the ripples of approaching ships. They hung at a hyperspace node on the far end of the Corellian Trade Spine, where all ships bound for Anoat or Bespin or other planets along the line would drop out of hyperspace to recalibrate their course and set off on a new vector.

Daala paced the *Gorgon*'s bridge, keeping her gaze moving, watching her personnel as they waited. Waited. Her scrutiny kept them on edge, nervous, intent on performing flawlessly. She was proud of her crew. She felt confident that they could wrench a proud victory from the Rebel scum.

One of the lieutenants straightened at his sensor console. "Admiral! Fluctuations indicate a ship arriving in hyperspace. Tracking . . . it's coming through."

Daala snapped commands. "Full alert. Instruct *Basilisk* and *Manticore* to power up their turbolaser batteries."

Commander Kratas whirled from his station to delegate tasks. The intense alarm signal whooped through the decks of the Star Destroyer. Stormtroopers rushed to their posts, armor and boots clattering.

"Gunners," Daala shouted through the intercom, "target to disable only! We must take the ship."

"Here it comes!" said the lieutenant.

Daala spun to stare at the black emptiness of space, at the stars hanging motionless in complex patterns. A ripple appeared, like a scratch on black-painted glass, and a midsized ship broke through into normal space and hung at a preprogrammed halt for navigational recalibration.

Daala smiled, trying to imagine the expression on the captain's face as he suddenly found himself blockaded by three Imperial-class Star Destroyers.

"A Corellian Corvette, Admiral," Kratas said, as if Daala could not identify it herself. She glanced at the distinctive hammerhead shape of the bridge section and the bank of twelve enormous hyperdrive and sublight rocket motors glowing blue-white with exhaust. "They're the most common galactic transports. Might just be merchants."

"What does that matter?" Daala said. "Prepare to fire. Let's test the *Basilisk*'s repaired turbolaser batteries."

"Admiral, the captain of the Corvette is signaling us," the comm officer called.

"Ignore it. *Basilisk*, open fire. Two surgical shots. Take out the rear hyperdrive units."

Daala watched, feeling the electric thrill of command. Two blinding green arrows lanced out. The first bolt spattered and diffused against the Corvette's increased shields, but the second blast punched through the weakened area and crippled the rocket engines. The Corvette rocked in space, then slowly spun like a dead rodent on a wire. Red-yellow glow diffused from a ruptured power core.

The three Star Destroyers loomed over the crippled ship.

"The Corvette's captain is signaling surrender," the comm officer said.

Daala felt a brief twinge of disappointment but brought it under control. She could not allow herself to make stupid mistakes. She had already been overeager in pursuing Han Solo and the stolen Sun Crusher—and that zealousness had caused her to lose the *Hydra*.

Commander Kratas stepped behind her, lowering his voice. "What if this ship is not part of the Rebel Alliance? Many smugglers also use Corellian Corvettes."

"A point well-taken," Daala said. Long ago Tarkin had impressed upon her that a good commander always listened to the opinions and suggestions of her trusted officers. "If the captain has connections with a smuggling network rather than the Rebellion, then perhaps we can put him to work for us. We could hire some spies, saboteurs."

Kratas nodded at the suggestion.

"Engage a tractor beam," Daala said. "Open the lower-bay doors, and we'll draw the Corvette into our hangar."

Daala toggled the narrow-beam comm system by her station, and an image of an Imperial Army general rose from the holo dais. His form flickered blue at the fringes from transmission distortion. Daala bent over the image, like a giant contemplating a toy. "General Odosk, prepare your boarding party. Have you briefed your troops?"

"Yes, Admiral," came the filtered voice. "We know what to do."

Daala whisked his image into thin sparkles of static. It would be fitting to let survivors from the *Hydra* be the boarding party of their first captured ship.

The crippled Corvette, still leaking thermal emissions from its breached power core, rose on invisible strings of the *Gorgon*'s tractor beam. The lower bay of the Star Destroyer slid open like the jaws of an enormous carnivore.

The comm officer spoke again. "Admiral, the captain of the Corvette continues to ask for instructions. She sounds rather distraught."

Daala snapped around. "*She*? The Corvette has a female captain?"

"It's a female voice, Admiral."

Daala tapped her fingers together, pondering the new information. Women seemed to have a much easier time at gaining command in the Rebel Alliance—but the extra burden of brutal struggle had made Daala stronger.

"Keep her in suspense."

"Capture complete, Admiral," Commander Kratas said. "The Corvette offered no resistance. Boarding parties are ready."

"Close the hangar-bay doors," Daala said. "Send a slicer team to drain the prisoner's computer core for information. We need maps, history tapes. We have too much to learn."

"Didn't you just order General Odosk and his special crew to board the ship?" Kratas said.

Daala frowned sharply at him. "They have other orders. You follow yours."

"Yes, Admiral," Kratas said in a small voice.

"Bring the captain of the Corvette to the interrogation chambers. We may need to encourage a bit of truthfulness." Kratas nodded and walked briskly off the bridge.

The door of the grim interrogation room sighed open with a discouraging hiss. When Daala entered, she was disappointed to see the captured captain: a short, mouse-faced Sullustan with thick rubbery jowls hanging around a weak chin. His great glassy eyes, pitch-dark and glittering, reminded her of the black holes in the Maw cluster.

The Sullustan captain jabbered in a panic, his lips wet with foaming drool. Beside him marched an old-model chrome protocol droid that served as his translator. The droid moved arms and legs with humming, ratcheting motivators as if its computer brain was so scrambled it could no longer control all of its systems at once.

The droid spoke in a brusque female voice. "Admiral! I'm so glad we've finally been brought to someone in charge. Can we straighten out this difficulty? We have done nothing wrong."

Beside the droid, the Sullustan captain pushed on the tight skin-cap covering his sloping head. He jabbered away with a monotonous *blub-blub-blub*.

The droid translated, "Captain T'nun Bdu demands an explanation—" The Sullustan babbled in alarm and clutched the platinum arm of the droid. "Correction, the captain respectfully requests that you be so kind as to explain your actions. Please tell us if there is anything he can do to avoid a diplomatic incident, as he has no wish to initiate any conflict."

The Sullustan captain nodded vigorously. A froth of saliva collected on his lips and ran in runnels between his flappy jowls.

"Wipe your chin," Daala said. She looked at the horrendous interrogation chair strapped in the shadows of the room. The walls were covered with unfinished iron plates, held in place by large blocky bolts. Stains marked various places that had not been cleaned after earlier interrogations. The chair itself had angled pipes and tubing, restraints, chains, spikes, most of which served no purpose other than to increase a victim's terror.

"What we would like from the captain right now," Daala said, turning back as if ignoring the chair, "is some information. Perhaps you can provide it to us without our needing to resort to any . . . unpleasantness."

The captain flinched in terror. The platinum female droid shifted from foot to foot and then seemed to reach a decision. The droid looked with apparent adoration at the Sullustan captain and then straightened herself and spoke in a clear, unfluttered voice. "Admiral, I can provide that information. There is no need for you to torture my captain."

The Sullustan *blub-blub-blubb*ed again, but the droid seemed not to hear. "We are on a mission to provide supplies and new living units for a small colony on the planet Dantooine. The colony is not affiliated with the Rebellion as of this moment. The colonists are harmless refugees."

"How many are in this colony?" Daala asked.

"Approximately fifty, taken from the old mining outpost Eol Sha. They are not presently armed."

"I see," Daala said. "Well, Captain, we must liberate your assets. I believe that the cargo hold of a Corellian Corvette routinely carries provisions for up to a year without restocking. I am commandeering those provisions for the service of the Empire. This colony on Dantooine will have to get their supplies some other way."

The Sullustan chittered in dismay, and Daala skewered him with a glare. "Perhaps, Captain, you would like to step outside the airlock and file a complaint?"

The Sullustan shut up instantly.

The door of the interrogation chamber sighed open again, revealing two stormtrooper guards and Commander Kratas. "Take the captain and his droid back to his ship," Daala said, then cocked her head down to stare at the Sullustan. "Our crew is already emptying your cargo holds, but General Odosk has set his men to repairing and bypassing the damaged engine. Enough that you could limp to another system."

The Sullustan bowed, speaking nonstop in his rodentlike language. The female droid stood at attention and spoke in an astonished voice. "Why thank you, Admiral. That is most respectful of you. We appreciate your hospitality."

The stormtroopers took them away, clomping down the sterile halls of the Star Destroyer. The doors sealed shut again, leaving Daala alone with Commander Kratas. He turned to her with wide dark eyes below his beetling brows. "Admiral, have we lowered ourselves to the level of space pirates? Attacking transport ships and stealing supplies?"

Daala removed a datapad from her hip and punched a button to call up her latest readout. She turned it toward him so he could look at the information. "I appreciate your respect for the honor of the Imperial Navy, Commander. However, before I came to see the captives, I received a report regarding the contents of the Corvette's cargo hold. There are indeed supplies for a new colony, but we also found heavy weaponry, communications gear, and prefabricated equipment for starfighter hangars."

She gestured toward the door. "Back to the bridge. I want to see what happens next."

"What do you mean?" Kratas said.

Daala switched off the datapad and looked at him. "You'll see. Be patient for now."

As they left, the door of the interrogation chamber slid shut, sealing behind it the darkness and the smell of fear trapped in the room.

The close-up image of General Odosk flickered, but she could see the self-satisfied grin on his wide, swarthy face. "Mission accomplished, Admiral."

"Excellent, General. I trust you are at a good vantage point?"

Odosk nodded. "I wouldn't miss it. Thank you."

Daala turned back to the viewing window on the bridge. The wounded Corellian Corvette dropped out of the *Gorgon*'s hangar bay and drifted free in space. "Back away," she told the navigator. "Order the *Basilisk* and the *Manticore* to do the same."

"Yes, Admiral."

The three Star Destroyers spread out and moved away from the much smaller ship. The Corvette's damaged rocket engine no longer glowed.

Kratas shook his head. "I still can't believe you're letting him go."

Daala intentionally spoke loud enough for the rest of bridge crew to hear. She rarely felt the need to explain her orders to underlings, but at certain times explaining her reasoning might make them respect her even more.

"Ships vanish all the time, Commander," Daala said. "If we simply destroyed this ship, it could be written off as some accident in transportation. A meteor storm, a breached reactor plate, bad navigation through hyperspace. But if we let this captain send a message first, then the Rebel Alliance will know what we have done. We can accomplish the same task, but increase the terror and chaos. Do you agree?"

Kratas nodded, but he still looked doubtful.

The comm officer spoke up. "The transponder we implanted in his comm system has activated. He's sending a tight-beam transmission to specific coordinates."

Daala smiled. "Good, I didn't think he'd wait until he got clear."

The comm officer pressed an ear jack to the side of his head. "He's reporting the situation, Admiral. Three Star Destroyers . . . fired upon without warning . . . taken prisoner and interrogated."

"I think that's enough," Daala said. She opened the comm channel. "General Odosk, proceed." She shielded her eyes.

The thermal detonators planted against the reactor walls of the twelve rocket pods detonated simultaneously, blasting the inferno open and sending a tidal wave of deadly radiation through the Corellian ship. An instant later the raging heat evaporated the entire hull, turning it into metallic steam. The rocket pods blew up in brilliant sunbursts; then the rest of the ship expanded outward in a blinding glare.

Daala nodded. "I think the survivors of the *Hydra* have had their revenge."

In stunned admiration Kratas smiled. "I believe so, Admiral."

She turned to face the rest of her bridge crew. "We now have accurate maps and information on the political situation of the Rebel Alliance. We have struck our first blow—the first of many."

Daala drew a deep breath, feeling vibrant and alive with euphoria. Grand Moff Tarkin would have been proud of her.

"Our next stop will be the planet Dantooine," she said. "We have a colony to visit."

5

Luke Skywalker, Jedi Master, gathered his twelve students in the grand audience chamber of the Massassi temple.

Diffuse orange light trickled through the narrow skylights. Lush vines climbed the stone walls, spreading out in verdant webs in the corners. Most of the flat stones were a nonreflective smoky gray; other lozenges of dark green and vermilion and ocher stone ornamented the enormous chamber.

Luke remembered standing here as a young man after their brief victory celebration following the destruction of the Death Star. He smiled as he recalled how Princess Leia had presented medals to him and Han Solo and Chewbacca. Now the grand audience chamber stood empty except for Luke and his small group of Jedi candidates.

Luke watched the students file toward him along the broad promenade. Wearing dark-brown Jedi robes, the candidates walked in eerie silence across the slick floor that had long ago been polished smooth by the mysterious Massassi.

Streen and Gantoris moved first, side by side; Gantoris looked full of self-importance. Of all those Luke had gathered at his Jedi training center, Gantoris had so far shown the most progress, the most inner strength—yet the man from Eol Sha did not seem to realize that he stood at a crossroads. Gantoris would soon need to decide exactly how he would proceed in his growth with the Force.

Behind the two of them came Kirana Ti, one of the young and powerful witches of Dathomir, who had left the other Force-wielding, rancor-riding women on her homeworld to learn better control. Kirana Ti and the other witches had been instrumental in helping him recover an ancient wrecked space station, the *Chu'unthor*, in which resided many records of old Jedi training—records that Luke had studied to develop exercises for his Jedi trainees.

Beside Kirana Ti came Dorsk 81, a bald green-and yellow-skinned humanoid from a world where all family units were genetically identical, cloned and raised to carry on the status quo. But Dorsk 81, the eighty-first reincarnation of the same genetic attributes, had somehow been dramatically changed. Though he seemed identical in every way, his mind worked differently, his thoughts moved along different paths, and he could feel the Force working through him. With the hope of becoming a Jedi Knight, Dorsk 81 had left his homeworld of identical people for something new.

Then came Kam Solusar, an older man, son of a Jedi that Vader had slaughtered long ago. Solusar had fled the Empire after the great Jedi purge and had spent decades in isolation beyond the inhabited star systems. Upon returning, Solusar had been captured and tortured by evil Jedi, twisted to the dark side of the Force, but Luke had bested him in the game of Lightsider. Solusar had received advanced training in certain areas, but because of his self-imposed exile, he still knew little about many aspects of the Force.

As the rest of the candidates gathered at the raised platform, Luke shrugged back his hood and tried to mask his pride at seeing the group. If he successfully completed their training, these candidates would form the core of a new order of Jedi Knights, champions of the Force, to help protect the New Republic against dark times.

He heard them stirring, not speaking to each other, each one no doubt wrapped up in thoughts of touching the Force, finding new pathways to inner strength and windows to the universe that only Jedi teachings could open for them. Their collective talent amazed him, but he hoped for even more trainees. Soon Han Solo would send his young friend, Kyp Durron; and Luke had strongly hinted for his former opponent Mara Jade to join them, since they had struck an uneasy truce during the battle against Joruus C'baoth.

At the podium Luke tried to stand tall. He found the core of peace inside him that allowed him to speak with a firm voice. "I have brought you here to study and to learn, but I myself am still learning. Every living thing must continue to learn until it dies. Those who cease to learn, die that much sooner.

"Perhaps it was misleading when I called this an 'academy' for Jedi. Though I will teach you everything I know, I don't want you merely to listen to me lecture.

"Your training will be a landscape of self-discovery. Learn new things and share what you have learned with others. I will call this place a *praxeum*. This word, made up of ancient roots, was first used by the Jedi scholar Karena, distilling the concepts of learning combined with action. Our *praxeum*, then, is a place for the learning of action. A Jedi is aware, but he does not waste time in mindless contemplation. When action is required, a Jedi acts."

Luke repositioned a small translucent cube on the raised dais behind him. He ran his fingers over the cool surface of the ancient knowledge repository Leia had stolen from the resurrected Emperor. The Jedi Holocron.

"We will invoke a past Jedi Master from the Holocron," Luke said. "We have used this device to learn the ways of the old Jedi Knights. Let us see what stories it has for us this morning."

He activated the precious artifact. In the distant past it had been traditional for each Jedi Master to compile his life's knowledge and store it within a great repository such as this, which was then passed to one of his students. Luke had only begun to fathom its depths.

An image formed both inside and outside the cube, a half-tangible projection that was more than just a stored bit of data; it was an interactive representation of the Jedi Master—a stubby alien, part insectile, part crustacean. It seemed to be bent with age or too much gravity. Its head extended into a long funnel, like a beak from which dangled whiskery protuberances. Close-set, glassy eyes stared like glittering pinpoints of knowledge.

The creature leaned on a long wooden staff, its legs spindly and knobby as it swiveled its funnellike face to contemplate the new audience. Tattered rags covered its body, sticking out in odd directions like clothing or external skin. Its voice came out in a reedy melody, like high-pitched music played under fast running water.

"I am Master Vodo-Siosk Baas."

"Master Vodo," Luke said, "I am Master Skywalker, and these are my apprentices. You have seen many things and recorded many thoughts. We'd be honored if you would tell us something we should know."

The image of Master Vodo-Siosk Baas hung his beaklike head on a jointed elbow of neck, as if in contemplation. Luke knew that the Holocron was simply uploading and sifting through reams of data, choosing an appropriate story through a personality algorithm stored with the Jedi Master's image.

"I must tell you of the Great Sith War that occurred—" Here the image paused as the Holocron assessed the current situation. "Four thousand years before your time.

"This war was caused by a student of mine, Exar Kun, who found forbidden teachings of the ancient Sith. He imitated the ways of the long-fallen

Sith and used them to form his own philosophy of the Jedi Code, a distortion of all we know to be true and right. With this knowledge Exar Kun established a vast and powerful brotherhood and claimed the title of the first Dark Lord of the Sith."

Luke stiffened. "Others have claimed that title," he said, "even to this time." *Including Darth Vader.*

Master Vodo-Siosk Baas seemed to lean more heavily on his walking stick. "I had hoped Exar Kun and his kind were defeated once and for all. Exar Kun joined forces with another powerful Jedi and great warlord, Ulic Qel-Droma. Exar Kun worked his invisible threads into the fabric of the Old Republic, bringing downfall through treachery and his distorted abilities with the Force."

Master Vodo looked at the gathered students. Gantoris seemed incredibly eager to hear more, leaning forward and staring with wide, dark eyes. The image of the long-dead Jedi Master turned to face Luke. "You must warn your students to beware of the temptations of conquest. That is all I can tell you for now."

The image flickered and wavered. With a feeling of deep uneasiness Luke silenced the Holocron. The images returned to swirling pearlescence inside its cubical walls.

"I think that's enough for this morning," Luke said. "We all know that other Jedi have followed the wrong path, bringing not only themselves but millions of innocent lives to doom and suffering. But I trust you. A Jedi must trust himself, and a Jedi Master must trust his apprentices.

"Explore yourselves and your surroundings, in teams or alone, whichever makes you comfortable. Go to the jungle. Go to other parts of this temple. Or simply go back to your chambers. The choice is yours."

Luke sat down on the edge of the raised stage and watched the students file out of the grand hall. The translucent cube of the Holocron stood mute beside him, a vessel filled with valuable but dangerous knowledge.

Obi-Wan Kenobi had been Luke's teacher. Luke had listened to every word the old man had said, trusting it; yet Luke had later learned how often Obi-Wan had obscured the facts, had distorted information—or as Obi-Wan explained it, simply offered the truth "from a certain point of view."

Luke watched the robed forms and wondered if his students could handle the knowledge they might discover. What if, like ancient Exar Kun in Master Vodo's story, they were tempted to uncover the forbidden teachings of the Sith, that so subtly yet crucially differed from the Jedi Code?

Luke feared what might happen should one of his students travel down the wrong path. But he also knew that he had to trust them—or they could never become Jedi Knights.

• • •

Deep into the night Gantoris hunched over the cluttered worktable, secretly constructing his own lightsaber.

A blanket of shadows surrounded him, obliterating distractions that might keep him from his task. His dark eyes had adjusted to the tight-beam glowlamp that spilled a harsh pool of light over his debris-strewn work surface, leaving the rest of the room in murk. As Gantoris moved to pick up another precision tool, his shadow flapped like a bird of prey across the ancient stone walls.

The Great Temple sat silent, like an ancient trap to stifle sound. The other students in Master Skywalker's Jedi academy—his *praxeum*, as he called it— had retired to their private chambers to fall into an exhausted sleep or to meditate on Jedi relaxing techniques.

Gantoris's neck ached, and his shoulder muscles burned from holding his cramped position for hours. He breathed in and out, smelling the thickness of old smoke and the scratchy moss that had worked for millennia to pry through cracks in the precisely placed temple blocks.

The moss had withered not long after Gantoris had taken up residence in the chambers. . . .

Outside, the jungle of Yavin 4 simmered with restless life, rustling, chittering, singing, and shrieking, as stronger creatures fed, as weaker creatures died.

Gantoris continued to work. He no longer needed sleep. He could draw the energy he required using different methods, secrets he had been taught that the other students did not suspect. His unbraided black hair stuck out in wiry shocks, and an acrid, gunpowdery smell clung to his cloak, his skin.

He focused on the components scattered across the table: silver electronics, dull metal, glinting glass. He slid his fingertips across the cold bits of wire, picked up a sharp-edged microcontrol box with trembling hands. Widening his eyes in annoyance, Gantoris stared at his hands until the trembling stopped, then set to work again.

He understood how the pieces would all fit together. Once he *knew*, once he had drawn together sufficient Jedi knowledge, everything seemed obvious to him. Obvious.

The elegant energy blade served as the personal weapon of the Jedi, a symbol of authority, skill, and honor. Cruder weapons could cause more random destruction, but no other artifact evoked as much legend and mystery as the lightsaber. Gantoris would settle for nothing else.

Every Jedi built his own lightsaber. It was a rite of passage in the training of a new student. Master Skywalker had not yet begun to teach him, though Gantoris had waited and waited. He knew he was the best of the students— and he chose not to wait any longer.

Master Skywalker did not know everything a true Jedi Master must teach new apprentices. Skywalker had gaps in his knowledge, blank spaces he either did not understand or did not wish to teach. But Master Skywalker was not the only source of Jedi knowledge. . . .

Once he had forsaken sleep, Gantoris had taken to roaming the halls of the Great Temple, sliding barefoot and in silence along the cold floors that seemed to drink heat, no matter how warm the jungle had become during the day.

Sometimes he wandered out into the rain forest at night, surrounded by mists and singing insects. The dew splashed his feet, his robe, making indecipherable patterns across his body like coded messages. Gantoris walked unarmed, silently daring any predator to challenge him, knowing that his Jedi skills would be proof against mere claws and fangs; but nothing molested him, and only once did he hear a large beast charging away from him through the underbrush.

But the dark and mysterious voice that came to him in his nightmares had given him instructions on how to build a lightsaber. Gantoris had been driven with a new purpose. A true Jedi was resourceful. A true Jedi could make do. A true Jedi found what he needed.

Using his ability to manipulate simple objects, he had broken past the seals into the locked Rebel control rooms in the temple's lower levels. Banks of machinery, computers, landing-grid panels, and automated defense systems sat covered with grime from a decade of abandonment. Master Skywalker had repaired little of the equipment. Jedi apprentices had no need for most of it.

Quietly and alone, Gantoris had removed access panels, stripped out microcomponents, focusing lenses, laser diodes, and a cylindrical casing twenty-seven centimeters long. . . .

It had taken him three nights, tearing apart the silent equipment, stirring up dust and spores, sending rodents and arachnids scurrying to safety. But Gantoris had found what he needed.

Now he assembled the pieces.

Under the garish light Gantoris picked up the cylindrical casing. He used a spot laser-welder to cut notches for the control switches.

Each Jedi built his own lightsaber to a range of specifications and personal preferences. Some included safety switches that shut off the glowing blade if the handle was released, while other weapons could be locked on. Gantoris had a few ideas of his own.

He installed a small but efficient power cell. It snapped into place, connecting precisely. Gantoris sighed, concentrated a moment to still his trembling hands again, then picked up another set of delicate wires.

He flinched, whirling to look behind him in the shadows. He thought he had heard someone breathing, the rustle of dark garments. Gantoris stared with his red-rimmed eyes, trying to discern a dim human form in the corner.

"Speak, if you're there!" Gantoris cried. His voice sounded harsh, as if he had swallowed burning coals.

When the shadows did not answer him, he sighed with cool relief. His mouth tasted dry, and soreness worked its way through his throat. But he willed away the feeling. He could drink water in the morning. A Jedi endured.

Building the lightsaber was his personal test. He had to do it alone.

Next, he took out the most precious piece of the weapon. Three corusca jewels, cast out from the high-pressure hell of the gas giant Yavin's core. When he and his addlebrained companion Streen had discovered the new Massassi temple far out in the jungle, Gantoris had found these gems on the steep obsidian walls. Embedded among the hypnotic pictographs etched into the black volcanic glass, the jewels had glinted in the hazy orange daylight.

Though they had remained untouched for thousands of years, these three gems had flaked off as Gantoris stared at them. They fell to his feet in the crushed lava rock surrounding the lost temple. Gantoris had picked up the gems, cupping the warm crystals in his hands as Streen wandered among the obelisks, chattering to himself.

Now Gantoris removed the jewels—one watery pink, another deep red, and the third starkly transparent with an inner electric blue fire along the edges of the facets. He was *meant* to have these jewels; they were destined for his own lightsaber. He knew that now. He understood all of his former nightmares, his former fears.

Most lightsabers had only a single jewel that focused the pure energy from the power cell into a tight beam. By adding more than one gem, Gantoris's blade would have unexpected capabilities to surprise Master Skywalker.

Finally, his fingers raw and aching, Gantoris sat up. Pain embroidered firelines across his neck, shoulders, and back, but he washed it away with a simple Jedi exercise. Outside the Great Temple he could hear the changing symphony of jungle sounds as nocturnal creatures found their dens, and daylight animals began to stir.

Gantoris held the cylindrical handle of his lightsaber and inspected it under the glowlamp's unforgiving light. Craftsmanship was everything in a weapon like this. A barely noticeable variance could cause a disastrous blunder. But Gantoris had done everything right. He had taken no shortcuts, allowed no sloppiness. His weapon was perfect.

He pushed the activator button. With a *snap-hiss*, the awesome blade thrummed and pulsed like a living creature. The chain of three jewels gave the energy blade a pale purplish hue, white at the core, amethyst at the fringes, with rainbow colors rippling up and down the beam.

Accustomed to the dimness, Gantoris squeezed his eyes to block out the glare, then gradually opened them again, staring in amazement at what he had made.

He moved the blade, and the air crackled around him. The hum sounded like thunder, but none of the other students would hear it through the mammoth thickness of the stone walls. In his grip the blade felt like a winged serpent, sending the sharp scent of ozone curling to his nose.

He slashed back and forth. The lightsaber became a part of him, an extension of his arm connected through the Force to strike down any enemy. He sensed no heat from the vibrating blade, only a cold annihilating fire.

He deactivated the blade, awash in euphoria, and carefully hid the completed lightsaber under his sleeping pallet.

"Now Master Skywalker will see I am a true Jedi," he said to the shadows along the walls. But no one answered him.

6

The private investigatory proceedings of the New Republic's ruling Council stood closed against Admiral Ackbar. He waited in the anteroom outside, staring at the tall steelstone door as if it were a wall blocking the end of his life. He stared unblinking at the designs and scrollwork modeled by the Emperor Palpatine after ancient Sith hieroglyphics, and they disturbed him.

Ackbar sat on the cold synthetic-stone bench, feeling only his misery, despair, and failure. He nursed his bandaged left arm and felt pain slice up and down his biceps where tiny needles held the slashed salmon-colored skin together. Ackbar had refused standard treatment by medical droid or healing in a bacta tank programmed for Calamarian physiology. He preferred to let the painful recuperation remind him of the destruction he had caused on Vortex.

He cocked his enormous head, listening to the rise and fall of heated voices through the closed door. He could make out only a mingled murmur of mixed voices, some strident, some insistent. He looked down and self-consciously brushed at his clean white admiral's uniform.

His remaining injuries seemed insignificant compared to the pain inside him. In his mind he kept seeing the crystalline Cathedral of Winds shatter around him in an avalanche of shards, hurling a storm of glassy daggers in all directions. He saw the bodies of winged Vors tumbling around him, slaughtered by the razor-edged crystal sabers. Ackbar had ejected Leia to safety, but he wished he had been brave enough to switch *off* the crash field, because he did not want to live with such disgrace. Ackbar had been piloting the deadly ship, no one else. *He* had crashed into the precious Cathedral of Winds. No one else.

He looked up at the sound of shuffling footsteps and saw another Calamarian approaching tentatively down the rose-hued corridors. The other ducked his head, but swiveled his great fish eyes up to look at his admiral.

"Terpfen," Ackbar said. His voice sounded listless, like words dropped onto the polished floor, but he tried to dredge up enthusiasm. "You've come after all."

"I could never desert you, Admiral. The Calamarian crewmen remain your firm supporters, even after. . . ."

Ackbar nodded, knowing the unshakable loyalty of his chief starship mechanic. As with many of his people, Terpfen had been taken away from his watery homeworld, kidnapped by Imperial enslavers, and forced to work on designing and refining their Star Destroyers with the renowned Calamarian starship-building expertise. But Terpfen had attempted sabotage and had been tortured. Severely. The scars still showed on his battered head.

During the Imperial occupation of the planet Calamari, Ackbar himself had been pressed into service as a reluctant aid to Moff Tarkin. He had served Tarkin for several years until he finally escaped during a Rebel attack.

"Have you completed your investigation?" Ackbar asked. "Have you gone over the records that survived the crash?"

Terpfen turned his head away. He clasped his broad flipper-hands together. His skin flushed with splotches of bright maroon, showing his embarrassment and shame. "I have already filed my report with the New Republic Council." He looked meaningfully at the closed door of the chamber. "I suspect they are discussing it even now."

Ackbar felt as if he had just attempted to swim under an ice floe. "And what did you find?" he said in a firm voice, trying to resurrect the power of command.

"I found no indication of mechanical failure, Admiral. I've gone over the crash tapes again and again, and I have simulated the flight path through the recorded wind patterns on Vortex. I continue to come up with the same answer. Nothing was wrong with your ship." He looked up at the admiral then turned away again. Ackbar could tell that this report was as difficult for Terpfen to say as it was for Ackbar to hear.

"I checked your ship myself before you took off for Vortex. I found no indications of mechanical instabilities. I suppose I could have missed something. . . ."

Ackbar shook his head. "Not you, Terpfen. I know your work too well."

Terpfen continued in a quieter voice. "I can reach only one conclusion from the data, Admiral—" But Terpfen's voice cut off, as if he refused to speak the inevitable.

Ackbar did it for him. "Pilot error," he said. "I caused the crash. It's my fault. I've known it all along."

Terpfen stood; his head hung so low that he showed only the bulging, sacklike dome of his cranium. "I wish there was some way I could prove otherwise, Admiral."

Ackbar extended a flipper-hand and placed it on Terpfen's gray crewman's uniform. "I know you've done your best. Now please do me one more favor. Outfit another B-wing for my personal use and provision it for a long journey. I'll be flying alone."

"Someone might object to having you fly again, Admiral," Terpfen said, "but don't worry. I can find some way around the problem. Where will you be going?"

"Home," Ackbar answered, "after I tend to some unfinished business."

Terpfen saluted smartly. "Your ship will be waiting for you, sir."

Ackbar felt a hard knot in his chest as he returned the salute. He stepped forward to the closed steelstone door and pounded on the ornate surface, demanding to be let in.

The heavy door groaned open on automatic hinges. Ackbar stood at the threshold as the members of the ruling Council turned to look at him.

The flowstone seats were sculpted and polished to a high luster, including the empty chair that still bore his own name. The air was too dry for his nostrils and stank with the underlying dusty smell of a museum. He could detect the pungent nervous odor of human sweat mixed with the peppery steam from their chosen hot drinks and refreshments.

Obese Senator Hrekin Thorm waved a pudgy hand at Ackbar. "Why don't we make *him* lead the reparations team? That seems appropriate to me."

"I wouldn't think the Vors want him anywhere near their planet," Senator Bel-Iblis said.

"The Vors haven't asked us to help them rebuild at all," Leia Organa Solo said, "but that doesn't mean we should ignore it."

"We're lucky the Vors are not as emotional as other races. This is already a terrible tragedy, but it does not seem likely it will turn into a galactic incident," Mon Mothma said.

Gripping the edge of the table, she stood and finally acknowledged Ackbar's presence. Her skin looked pale, her face gaunt, her eyes and cheeks sunken. She had skipped many important meetings lately. Ackbar wondered if the Vortex tragedy had worsened her health.

"Admiral," Mon Mothma said, "these proceedings are closed. We will summon you after we have taken a vote." Her voice seemed stern and cracking, devoid of the compassion that had launched her career in galactic politics.

Minister of State Leia Organa Solo looked at him with her dark eyes. A flood of sympathy crossed her face, but Ackbar turned away with a stab of anger and embarrassment. He knew Leia would argue his case most strongly, and he expected support from General Rieekan and General Dodonna; but he did not know how Senators Garm Bel-Iblis, Hrekin Thorm, or even Mon Mothma herself would vote.

That doesn't matter, Ackbar thought. He would remove their need to decide, remove the possibility of further humiliation. "Perhaps I can make these deliberations easier on all of us," Ackbar said.

"What do you mean, Admiral?" Mon Mothma said, frowning at him. Her face was seamed with deep lines.

Leia half rose as she suddenly understood. "Don't—"

Ackbar made a decisive gesture with his left fin-hand, and Leia reluctantly sat down again.

He touched the left breast on his pristine-white uniform, fumbling with the catch as he removed his admiral's-rank insignia. "I have caused enormous pain and suffering to the people of Vortex. I have brought immense embarrassment to the New Republic, and I have called down terrible shame upon myself. I hereby resign as commander of the New Republic Fleet, effective immediately. I regret the circumstances of my departure, but I am proud of the years I have served the Alliance. I only wish I could have done more."

He placed his insignia on the creamy alabaster shelf in front of the empty Council seat that had once been his own.

In shocked silence the other Council members stared at him like a mute tribunal. Before they could voice their mandatory—and probably insincere—objections, Ackbar turned and strode out of the room, walking as tall as he dared, yet feeling crushed and insignificant.

He went back toward his quarters to pack his most prized possessions before heading to the hangar bay, where he would take the ship Terpfen had promised him. He had one place to visit first, and then he would return to his homeworld of Calamari.

If General Obi-Wan Kenobi could vanish into obscurity on a desert planet like Tatooine, Ackbar could do the same and live out the rest of his life among the lush seatree forests under the seas.

With the pretense of taking out a B-wing fighter to test its response under extreme stress, Terpfen soared away from Coruscant. The other distraught Calamarian crewmen wished him luck before he departed, assuming he intended to continue his desperate work to clear Admiral Ackbar's name.

But just before the jump into hyperspace, Terpfen entered a new series of coordinates into the navicomputer.

The B-wing lurched with a blast of hyperdrive engines. Starlines appeared around him, and the ship snapped into the frenzied, incomprehensible swirl of hyperspace. He reflexively slid the nictating membrane over his glassy eyes.

Terpfen felt shudders pass through his body as he strained to resist the calling. But he knew by now, after all these years, that he could do nothing to fight it. Screaming nightmares never let him forget his ordeal in the hellish conditioning on the Imperial military training planet of Carida.

The scars on his battered head were not just from torture, but from Imperial vivisection, where the doctors had sawed open his skull and scooped out portions of his brain—segments that controlled a Calamarian's loyalty, his volition, and his resistance to special commands. The cruel xenosurgeons had replaced the missing areas of Terpfen's brain with specially grown organic circuits that mimicked the size, shape, and composition of the removed tissue.

The organic circuits were perfectly camouflaged and could resist the most penetrating medical scan, but they made him a helpless cyborg, a perfect spy and saboteur who could not think for himself when the Imperials wanted him to think their thoughts. The circuits left him sufficient mental capacity to play his part, to make his own excuses each time the Imperials summoned him. . . .

After guiding his ship for several standard time units, Terpfen looked at the chronometer. At the precise instant indicated he pulled the levers that switched off the hyperdrive motors and kicked in the sublight engines.

His ship hung near the lacy veil of the Cron Drift, the gaseous remnants of a multiple supernova where four stars had simultaneously erupted some four millennia ago. The wisps of gas crackled with pinks, greens, and searing white. The residual x rays and gamma radiation from the old supernova caused static over his comm system, but it would also mask this meeting from prying eyes.

A dark Caridan ship already hung there waiting for him. With a flat stealth coating on its hull, the Caridan ship looked like a matte-black insect that swallowed starlight, leaving only a jagged silhouette against the starfield. Protrusions of assault blasters and sensor antennas stuck out like spines.

A burst of static came across Terpfen's comm system; then the tight-beam holotransmission of Ambassador Furgan's head focused itself inside the B-wing cockpit.

"Well, my little fish," Furgan said. His huge eyebrows looked like black feathers curling up on his forehead. "What is your report? Explain why our two victims were not killed in the crash you engineered."

Terpfen tried to stop the words from coming, but the organic circuits kicked in, providing all the answer the Imperial ambassador needed. "I sabotaged Ackbar's personal ship, and that should have meant death for both passengers—but even I underestimated Ackbar's skill as a pilot."

Furgan scowled. "So the mission failed."

"On the contrary," Terpfen said, "I believe it is even more successful. The New Republic is far more affected by this chain of events than it would be if a simple crash had killed the Minister of State and the admiral. Their fleet commander has now resigned in disgrace, and the ruling Council is left without an obvious replacement."

Furgan considered for a moment, then nodded as a slow smile spread across his fat, dark lips. He changed the subject. "Have you made any progress in uncovering the location of the third Jedi baby?"

During his torturous conditioning, Terpfen had spent four weeks with his head entirely encased in a solid plasteel helmet that kept him blinded, sent jabs of pain at random and malicious intervals. He could not speak or drink or eat, fed entirely through intravenous nutritional supplements. Now, as he sat trapped inside the cockpit of the B-wing fighter, he felt swallowed up in that black pit again.

Terpfen answered in a steady, uninflected voice. "I have told you before, Ambassador. Anakin Solo is being held on a secret planet, the location of which is known only to a very few, including Admiral Ackbar and the Jedi Master Luke Skywalker. I think it highly unlikely that Ackbar will divulge it in casual conversation."

Furgan looked as if he had just bit into something sour and wanted to spit it out. "Then what good are you?"

Terpfen would have taken no offense even if his organic circuitry had allowed him to. "I have set into motion another plan that may provide the information you seek."

Terpfen had performed the task with parts of his mind he did not own. Flipper-hands moving not of his own volition had completed what the rest of him wanted to scream against.

"Your plan had better work," Furgan said. "And one last question—I've noticed that Mon Mothma has avoided public appearances for several weeks. She has not attended many important meetings, sending proxies instead. Tell me, how is dear Mon Mothma's health?" He began to chuckle.

"Failing," Terpfen said, cursing himself. The laughter in Furgan's face suddenly vanished, and his holographic eyes stared into Terpfen's great watery disks.

"Go back to Coruscant, my little fish, before they notice you've disappeared. We wouldn't want to lose you, when there is so much work left to do."

Furgan's transmission winked out. A moment later the beetlelike ship turned and, with a blue-white flare of its hyperdrive engines, burst into a fold of space and vanished.

Terpfen hung alone in the darkness, looking out at the glowing slash of the Cron Drift, surrounded by the echoing walls of his own betrayal.

7

Bearing only a dim glowlamp, Luke Skywalker led a procession of his Jedi students deep into the lower levels of the Massassi temple. Dressed in hooded robes, none of them voiced objections to Luke's nighttime journey; by now they had grown accustomed to his eccentric training methods.

Luke noted the cold, smooth stone against his bare feet, then dismissed the sensation. *A Jedi must be aware of his environment, but must not let it affect him in ways he does not desire.* Luke repeated the phrase to himself, focusing on the state of perfect control he had learned only gradually through the teachings of Obi-Wan Kenobi, Yoda, and his own exercises of self-discovery.

He initially noted the silence of the temple, then scolded himself as he broadened his perceptions. The Great Temple was not silent: The stone blocks ticked and trembled as they cooled in the deepening night. Air currents danced in faint breaths, slow-motion rivers through the enclosed passageways. Tiny, sharp-footed arachnids clicked across the floors and walls. Dust settled.

Luke led his group down the flagstoned steps until he stood facing a blank stone wall. He waited.

Dark-haired Gantoris was the first to notice a tenuous wisp of pale mist through a flaw in the rock. "I see steam."

"I smell sulfur," Kam Solusar said.

"Good," Luke said. He worked the secret panel that slid aside the stone door to a maze of sunken and half-collapsed passages. The tunnel sloped down, and the students followed as he ducked into the deeper shadows. His glowlamp spilled a flickering pool of light in a faint, washed-out circle. His own shadow looked like a hooded monster, a distortion of Darth Vader's black form against the cramped walls.

The underground passage hooked to the left, and now Luke could smell bright and sharp brimstone fumes; the lumpy rock wept condensed moisture. In a moment he could hear the simmering of water, the whisper of steam, the stone sighing with escaping heat.

Luke emerged into the grotto and paused to draw a deep breath of the acrid air. The stone felt slick beneath the soles of his feet, warm and wet.

The other trainees joined him, looking down at a roughly circular mineral spring. Pearllike chains of bubbles laced the clear water as volcanic gases seeped through the rocks. Steam rose from the pool's surface, twisting in stray air currents. The water reflected the glowlamp with a jewel-blue color from algae clinging to the sides. Ledges of stone and crusted mineral deposits made footholds and shallow seats on the walls of the hot spring.

"This is our destination," Luke said, then switched off the glowlamp.

The underground darkness swallowed them, but only for a moment. Luke heard two trainees draw in deep breaths—Streen and Dorsk 81—but the others managed to restrain their surprise.

Luke stared into the blackness, willing it to peel back. Gradually light did filter back, a distant gleam of reflected starlight from an opening in the ceiling high above.

"This is an exercise to help you concentrate and attune yourself to the Force," Luke said. "The water is a perfect temperature: you will float, you will drift, you will reach out and touch the rest of the universe."

He shed his Jedi robe in the near darkness and slipped without a splash into the spring. He heard the rustle of cloth as the others disrobed and moved toward the edge.

The water's sudden heat stung his skin, and the foam of rising bubbles tingled against him. Ripples traversed the pool as the Jedi candidates slid in one at a time. He sensed them floating, relaxing, allowing themselves to gasp with pleasure and warmth.

Luke drew slow, deep breaths as he lay back, drifting, purging his mind and body. The bite of sulfur in the air scrubbed his throat raw and clean; the heat and bubbles opened his pores.

"There is no emotion; there is peace," he said, echoing words from the Jedi Code that Yoda had taught him. "There is no ignorance; there is knowledge. There is no passion; there is serenity. There is no death; there is the Force."

He heard mingling voices as the twelve others repeated his words. But this was too formal for him, too stiff and stilted—he wanted them to *understand* him, not memorize mantras. "Right now you are floating in warmth, in near darkness. Imagine yourselves totally immersed, surrounded, free. Let your minds wander of their own accord, travel along the ripples in the Force."

He swirled his hands, gently stroking back and forth to generate waves in the pool. The other students stirred. He could sense them around him, concentrating, trying too hard.

"Look up," he said. "First you must find the place where you *are* before you can journey elsewhere."

Overhead, high up in the rocky ceiling, a slash of stars spilled through a crack. The pinpoints winked and shimmered with currents in Yavin 4's atmosphere.

"Feel the Force," he said in a whisper, then repeated the words with greater strength. "*Feel* the Force. You are part of it. You can travel with the Force, down into the core of this moon, and out into the stars. Every living thing strengthens the Force, and everything draws strength from it. Concentrate with me and observe the limitless vistas your skills will show you."

Drifting in the warm water, feeling the fizz of bubbles against his skin, Luke looked up at the confined patch of stars through the broken ceiling, then looked back down to the darkened pool. "Can you see it?" he said.

The bottom of the pool flickered, opening a gateway to the universe. He saw the glory of stars, arms of the galaxy, stars exploding in titanic death throes, nebulae coalescing in a blazing wash of birth.

He heard unbridled gasps as the Jedi candidates saw the same vision. They each seemed to be a self-contained form hovering over the universe, where they could get the ultimate perspective, a true view from a height.

Luke felt the wonder pulsing through him as he identified Coruscant and the Emperor's Core worlds. He saw the embattled systems where tattered Imperial remnants fought each other in civil warfare; he saw the empty systems that had once been controlled by the Ssi Ruuk Imperium, until they had been defeated by the combined Empire and Rebel forces at Bakura. Luke recognized and named planets he had known, Tatooine, Bespin, Hoth, Endor, Dathomir, and many others—including the secret world of Anoth, where he and Admiral Ackbar had hidden Han and Leia's third baby.

But then the names and coordinates of the planets soured in his mind, and Luke scolded himself for thinking like a tactician, like a starship pilot. Names meant nothing, positions meant nothing. Every world and every star was a part of the whole of the galaxy, as were Luke and his trainees at the Jedi *praxeum*. As were the plants and creatures in the jungle above—

His attuned senses picked up a change deep within the subterranean chambers, sleeping volcanic outlets that provided geothermal heat to the mineral spring. Somewhere deep in the crust of Yavin 4, a bubble had burst, spewing hot gases upward, simmering through cracks in the rock, rising, seeking an escape route. Coming toward them.

A dark rift appeared in the image of the galaxy below them. With a sudden wave of alarm, four of the Jedi trainees sloshed in the warm water, attempting to reach the edge. Others clenched themselves in panic.

Luke fought down his own fear and made his voice rich and forceful, as he had once tried to sound when negotiating with Jabba the Hutt. His words came out rapidly, filling the remaining seconds.

"A Jedi feels no heat or cold. A Jedi can extinguish pain. Strengthen yourselves with the Force!" Luke thought of the time he had walked across lava in one of the tests Gantoris had imposed upon him. He willed extra protection into his body, forming an imaginary sheath around his exposed skin, thin as a thought and *strong* as a thought.

He scanned the concerned faces in a flash, saw Kirana Ti close her green eyes and grit her teeth; middle-aged Kam Solusar stared at nothing, yet maintained a confident air; Streen, the Bespin cloud hermit, seemed not to understand, but he instinctively increased his protection.

As the large, shifting bubbles boiled to the surface, Dorsk 81, the yellow-skinned clone from the bureaucratic planet, scrambled toward the edge. Luke saw that he would never make it in time; unless Dorsk 81 set up his personal defenses in the next few seconds, he would be boiled as the hot gas escaped into the air.

Before Luke could move, Gantoris reached Dorsk 81, gripping the alien's naked shoulder with his callused hand. "Ride it with me!" Gantoris said, raising his voice above the hissing noise. Volcanic gas bubbles surged to the surface of the hot spring. Luke saw a wall of protection surround Gantoris and Dorsk 81, incredibly strong—and then the primal, potent gases belched around them, churning the water into a foaming fury.

Luke felt the stab of intense heat, but he willed it away. He could feel the strength grow as the candidates also understood and reinforced each other. The scalding onslaught lasted only a few seconds, and the boiling surface of the pool began to return to stillness.

The window to the universe had vanished.

"Enough for tonight," Luke said, sighing in satisfaction. He heaved himself dripping over the lip of the mineral spring and stood. He could smell sulfurous steam rising from his body as he found the rough folds of his Jedi robe piled on the floor. "Think about what you have learned."

With that the trainees began laughing and congratulating each other. They climbed out, one by one. Gantoris assisted Dorsk 81, who thanked him before donning his robe. "Next time I will be stronger," Dorsk 81 said in the dimness.

"I know you will be."

Luke met the dark-haired man as he pulled the robe over his head. "That was a good thing you did, Gantoris."

"It was only heat," Gantoris said, and his voice became grim. "There are far worse things than heat." He paused, then spoke as if divulging a secret. "Master Skywalker—you are *not* the dark man who haunted my nightmares on Eol Sha. I know that now."

The confession took Luke aback. He could not see Gantoris's expression in the dim light. On Eol Sha, Gantoris had suffered horrifying premonitions, but he had not spoken of his nightmares since arriving on Yavin 4. Luke tried to ask why he had mentioned it now, but the other man turned, gliding past the gathered trainees as they made their way back up the gloomy tunnels.

In the humid morning the trainees gathered in the ship-landing area to continue their exercises. Mists rose to the crown of the Great Temple. Sounds of the stirring jungle buzzed around the students as they practiced preposterous lessons to improve their supernatural balance, to encourage simple feats of levitation.

Luke paced among them as they attempted the things Yoda had taught him in the steamy swamps of Dagobah. He smiled as Kirana Ti and the young minstrel/historian Tionne joined forces. Laughing and concentrating, the two women lifted Artoo-Detoo in the air as the little droid puttered about, clearing the ever-encroaching weeds from the landing grid. Artoo vented electronic beeps and whistles as he floated; his treads spun in the air.

Behind them Gantoris emerged from the shadowy mouth of the temple, striding into the hazy light. Luke turned to watch him approach.

"Glad you could join us, Gantoris!" he said with a combined touch of good humor and scolding as he looked significantly up at how high the orange gas giant had risen to fill much of the sky.

Gantoris's face looked rough and red, as if scorched; tough, smooth skin covered his forehead where his eyebrows should have been. He had braided his thick black hair into a long strand that hung past his shoulders.

"I have been preparing for a new test," Gantoris said, and reached into the folds of his robe. He removed a black cylinder.

Luke blinked his eyes in astonishment at seeing a newly constructed lightsaber.

Artoo crashed to the ground with a terrified squeal as both Kirana Ti and Tionne lost their concentration. The others ceased their lessons and stared in astonishment.

"Fight me, Master Skywalker," Gantoris said. He removed his robe to display the padded captain's uniform he had worn as the leader of his people on Eol Sha.

"Where did you get a lightsaber?" Luke asked cautiously, his mind whirling. None of his students should have been able to master the technology or the discipline yet.

Gantoris fingered the controls on the handle, and with a loud spitting sound the glowing blade extended, a white incandescent core of energy fringed with deep violet. He moved his wrist, flicking the blade back and forth, testing it. A bone-vibrating hum scalded the air. "Isn't it the test of a Jedi to build his own lightsaber?"

Luke proceeded carefully. "The lightsaber may seem the simplest of weapons, but it is difficult to master. An unpracticed wielder is as likely to injure himself as his opponent. You aren't ready for this, Gantoris."

But Gantoris stood like a weathered Massassi colossus, holding the blazing edge of his lightsaber vertically in front of his face. "If you don't ignite your lightsaber and fight me, I will cut you down right here." He paused with a smirk. "That would be a rather embarrassing fate for a Jedi Master, wouldn't it?"

Reluctantly, Luke shrugged out of his robe. He pulled his own lightsaber from the waist of his comfortable gray flightsuit and, feeling the Force thrum through him, ignited the yellow-green blade.

The other trainees watched in amazed silence. Luke wondered how he could have miscalculated so greatly, how Gantoris had gained access to information that only an advanced student should have obtained.

He stepped forward, raising his blade. Gantoris stared unblinking. Luke saw his red-rimmed eyes burn with a depthless intensity, and he felt a twinge of fear.

They crossed blades with a crackle of dissipating power, testing each other. He felt the resistance of the energy blades, the flow of the Force. He and Gantoris struck again, harder this time, and sparks flew.

Abandoning all pretense of testing, Gantoris launched himself at Luke, hacking and slashing with the white-violet saber. Luke blocked each blow, but fought only defensively to keep from provoking his student.

Gantoris made no sound as he struck again and again. The lightsabers intersected with a flash of multicolored lightning. The fury in Gantoris astonished Luke, and he backed toward the jungle's edge, unnerved by the violence.

Gantoris pressed his advantage. Luke blocked away all thoughts of the other trainees watching.

"Am I a Jedi now?" Gantoris asked in a husky voice.

Luke parried, then blocked another blow, locking both blades in a snapping, sizzling spray of discharged energy. He spoke through clenched teeth.

"Training requires diligence and commitment. And control. A Jedi needs to know more than how to build a lightsaber. He must also learn how and when to use it!"

Luke drove forward, suddenly taking the offensive. He struck and struck, careful not to injure Gantoris but confident in showing his mastery. "The lightsaber is the weapon of a Jedi Knight, but a true Jedi rarely uses it to settle a dispute. It is better to outthink and outmaneuver your opponent. But when forced, a Jedi strikes quickly and decisively!" He slashed down, hard.

Clumsily defending himself, Gantoris backed into a tangle of jungle. Dew sprayed from underbrush as they trampled stands of climbing ferns. Startled flying creatures flapped away with squawks. Gantoris swung and slashed wildly at Luke's lightsaber, using brute force but no finesse. He bumped against a wide-boled Massassi tree, and flakes of purplish bark fell to the ground in an uneven patter.

Luke stood over him, intending to call an end to the duel, but Gantoris's eyes blazed brighter. As if springing a trap, he fingered a button on his lightsaber handle—and the violet-edged blade suddenly *extended* like a spear, flashing outward to nearly double its length.

Reacting with lightning reflexes, Luke jerked aside, and the point of Gantoris's energy blade slashed through the sleeve of his gray flightsuit, leaving a smoldering gash.

He stared at Gantoris in disbelief for a precious fraction of a second. Not only had Gantoris built his own lightsaber, but he had constructed a blade with multiple jewels, allowing him to adjust the amplitude of his blade. Such a weapon was at least twice as difficult to make as a traditional lightsaber, and Gantoris had done it by himself!

Without pausing Gantoris pressed his advantage, lunging with his longer blade, knowing that Luke could not come close enough to touch him.

The thin, wavering voice of Streen called out, "Gantoris!" unheeded by Luke or Gantoris. The other students pressed toward the edge of the jungle, but this battle was between Luke and Gantoris alone.

He was dismayed to see the recklessness in Gantoris—it reminded him of his own last battle with Darth Vader as the Emperor gloated, encouraging Luke to feel the anger flow through him. Luke had almost fallen then, almost allowed himself to give in to his anger and begin the journey to the dark side. But he had been strong enough in the end.

Gantoris seemed dangerously close to the edge.

Luke coiled his muscles, gathered his strength, and leaped upward. With a boost of his levitating ability, he soared high enough to reach a thick lower branch of the Massassi tree. He landed gently, keeping his balance as he looked down at the outraged Gantoris.

"How did you learn all this?" Luke called over the hum of lightsabers, trying to break through Gantoris's intensity.

The fiery-tempered man turned his face up, glaring with red-rimmed eyes. "You are not the only teacher of the Jedi way!"

With a low-throated outcry, Gantoris held his lightsaber with both hands and slashed sideways, sizzling through the massive trunk of the tree. Sparks and smoke and the wet cinnamon smell of scalded sap spilled into the air. The ancient tree shifted sideways, then crashed through clinging upper branches as it toppled.

Luke leaped free and landed easily in a rotting tangle of moss and fallen branches. He needed to end this soon. Gantoris seemed possessed by an anger he could not control, and simple Jedi calming techniques could not reach him.

Gantoris shortened his blade to a more usable length, matching Luke's as he came in for the attack. Luke let his student press him back, through climbing ferns and brilliant nebula orchids. He reached out through the Force, sensing the jungle around them, looking for a useful diversion.

And found it.

He faked a stumble against a broken fungus-covered rock and lurched sideways toward a thicket. Gantoris charged after him, slashing vines out of the way in puffs of gray steam. Gantoris would never hear the burbling grunting noises coming from the thicket.

Luke jumped aside as Gantoris hammered down with his lightsaber. The violet-white blade sliced through thorns and interlocked twigs—and a startled, outraged beast charged out of the underbrush with an operatic range of bellows.

The snorting runyip flailed from side to side as it stampeded past them. It was a massive, clumsy creature covered with oily fur and clods of dirt stuck to its flexible nose where it had been rooting among the decaying vegetation.

The outburst distracted Gantoris for only a second. But Luke used the moment to reach out with the Force. Grasping with invisible hands, he yanked the lightsaber handle out of Gantoris's grip and used his skill to push the button that deactivated the blade.

Luke snatched Gantoris's weapon from the air, gripping it with his left hand, and switched off his own lightsaber. Suddenly, without the roaring hiss of dual blades, the jungle seemed disturbingly silent.

Gantoris stared at him, unmoving. Both of them panted with trembling exhaustion. They stood close to each other, within arm's reach. Pearls of sweat appeared on their foreheads.

Reaching his decision, Luke broke the frozen moment. He flipped the handle of Gantoris's lightsaber forward and extended it toward the other man. Gantoris tentatively took his weapon back, glanced at it, then met Luke's gaze again.

"Good exercise, Gantoris," Luke said, "but you must learn to control your anger. It could be your undoing."

8

Through the simmering haze of a security field deep within the steelcrete mazes of Coruscant, Kyp Durron looked at the thorn shape of the Sun Crusher.

He squinted to get a better view, leaning forward until three heavily armed New Republic guards strode to bar his way. Within the hangar he could see another crew of guards standing around the Sun Crusher itself. Just inside the electrostatic security field, a huge blast door hung ready to clang down at a moment's notice.

With his small wiry frame, free grin, and tousled dark hair, Kyp didn't think he could possibly pose any threat, but the three guards pointed their blaster rifles at his chest. "This is a restricted area," the sergeant said. "Leave immediately, or we will shoot."

"Hey, relax," Kyp said, raising his hands. "If I wanted to steal the thing, I would never have flown it here in the first place."

The sergeant looked at him skeptically. It was obvious he didn't have a clue what Kyp was talking about.

"I'm Kyp Durron. I *flew* the Sun Crusher with Han Solo from Maw Installation. I just wanted to have another look."

The sergeant's stony expression did not change. "I don't know General Solo personally," he said, "but I have orders to restrict all access. No exceptions."

Kyp shifted to one side to see between the guards. He disregarded their presence, looking again at the angular superweapon that had been developed by the captive scientist Qwi Xux at Maw Installation.

Dr. Xux had innocently designed a weapon that could trigger a star to explode, wiping out all life in an entire solar system. Qwi had done it as an exercise to test the limits of her scientific abilities; but Han had broken through her brainwashing and made her realize what she had created. Qwi had then helped them steal the superweapon and escape from Admiral Daala and Maw Installation.

Kyp was glad the Sun Crusher was now in the hands of the New Republic, but it concerned him that the Senate couldn't decide what to do with it. The existence of such a powerful weapon seemed to change the attitudes of even good people in the government.

Kyp watched as engineers and mechanics attempted to understand how the Sun Crusher worked. They used laser-welders against the ultradense quantum-plated armor, but nothing could scratch the indestructible craft.

Two mechanics clambered out of the upper hatch, carrying a metal cylinder a meter and a half long and half a meter wide. Three engineers at the bottom of the hangar bay craned their necks to look up at the cylinder and dropped their hydrospanners in horror. Another engineer put down her precision calibrator and backed away very slowly.

"It's one of the supernova torpedoes!" an engineer said.

The two mechanics carrying it suddenly froze. Someone sounded a squawking alarm. The guards inside the security field ran about looking for targets to shoot. The trapped engineers and mechanics screamed for the deadly security field to be dropped so they could evacuate. The three guards outside whirled and leveled their blaster rifles at Kyp, as if he had become a threat after all.

He laughed. "It's only a message cylinder," he said. "Have them open it up—they'll see. It's where the log recorders are kept so vital data can be ejected if the Sun Crusher ever gets destroyed."

But as alarms hammered through the air, and people inside the restricted hangar ran around in panic, the guards showed no interest in Kyp's explanations. "You'd better leave now, young man. Immediately!" the sergeant said.

Shaking his head, part in amusement and part in annoyance, Kyp circled back up the long corridors, wondering how long it would take the supposed experts to figure it out.

Wedge Antilles watched with admiration as the beautiful and ethereal alien scientist, Qwi Xux, stepped forward and prepared to address the New Republic Assembly.

Qwi did not like to talk in front of an audience, and she had been nervous for days after setting up this speech. A solitary person, she had begun to confide in Wedge now that he spent most of his time as her official bodyguard and liaison. Wedge had encouraged her in every way, trying to calm her, insisting that she would do a wonderful job. He supported her belief that she could no longer ignore the Sun Crusher.

Qwi had looked at him gratefully. Her wide indigo eyes were in striking contrast to her pale, pale blue skin and the gemlike cap of pearlescent feathers that draped from her head down to her shoulders.

Now Qwi stared at Mon Mothma and the other ministers. She straightened her back, letting her thin arms hang at her sides. She spoke with a flutey voice that sounded like birdsong.

"Mon Mothma and esteemed representatives of the New Republic government," Qwi said, "when I first came to you seeking sanctuary and bringing the Sun Crusher, you invited me to speak to you whenever I felt the need. Now I must tell you of my grave concerns. I will try to be brief, because you must come to a decision."

Beside Wedge, the enormous form of Chewbacca rumbled a low growl of displeasure; but Wedge was impressed at how quiet and restrained the Wookiee had managed to hold himself. Chewbacca was not known for his ability to sit still.

Threepio spoke in a soft voice. "Calm down, Chewbacca. You'll have a chance to speak soon enough. Are you quite certain you don't want me to edit your words into more appropriate language? I *am* a protocol droid, you know, and I am familiar with the requirements."

Chewie blatted a quiet but definite negative. Wedge shushed them both so he could hear Qwi as she spoke. Her musical voice didn't falter, and Wedge felt a warm pride spreading in his chest.

"The Sun Crusher is the most formidable weapon ever devised," Qwi said. "I know this better than anyone, because I designed it. It is an order of magnitude more dangerous than even the Death Star. It is no longer in the clutches of Imperial powers—but I'm concerned about what the New Republic intends. I have refused to divulge its workings for a reason, but you have kept it locked in your research bays for weeks, tinkering with it, studying it, trying to unlock its secrets. It will do you no good."

She paused to take a long breath, and Wedge worried that she might lose her nerve. But Qwi straightened her slender form and spoke again. "I urge you to destroy the Sun Crusher. A weapon of such power should not be trusted in the hands of any government."

Mon Mothma looked weak and weary as she gazed down at Qwi. Below and to her left, old General Jan Dodonna spoke up. "Dr. Xux, according to reports from our engineers, this weapon cannot be destroyed. The quantum armor makes it impossible for us even to dismantle it."

"Then you must find some other way to dispose of the Sun Crusher," Qwi said.

Sounding flustered, Senator Garm Bel-Iblis, Mon Mothma's old nemesis, rose to his feet. "We cannot allow a weapon of such power to slip *out* of our grasp," he said. "With the Sun Crusher, we have a tactical advantage available to none of our Imperial enemies."

"Enough," Mon Mothma said in a quavering voice. Her cheeks were flushed, which served to highlight the pallor of her skin. "We have debated this many times," she said, "and my opinion stands unchanged. A weapon of such hideous destructive power is a brutal and inhuman device. The Emperor might have been monster enough to consider using it, but under no circumstances will the New Republic be party to such barbarism. We have no need for such a weapon, and its presence only serves to divide us. I shall veto any attempts to study the Sun Crusher further, and I will fight to my last breath any of you who suggest using it against any foe, Imperial or otherwise."

She looked at her military commanders, and Wedge felt intimidated by the anger and sheer conviction in her voice. The vacant seat of Admiral Ackbar, who was normally a voice of sanity and moderation, remained empty and hollow like a deep wound. Wedge silently urged Qwi to speak up again, to tell her idea.

As if on cue, she said in her melodious voice, "Excuse me, but might I make a suggestion? Since the Sun Crusher cannot be destroyed by any normal means, we should use the automatic pilot to send it into the heart of a sun, or at least to the core of a gas-giant planet, where it will be impossible to recover."

General Crix Madine spoke up. "A gas-giant planet would be sufficient. The pressures at the core are far beyond what even our most sophisticated vessels can withstand. The Sun Crusher would be out of reach for all time."

Bel-Iblis looked around, his dark eyes flashing. As if sensing defeat and realizing that a gas planet was marginally more acceptable than the blinding fury of a star, he said, "All right, dump it into a gas giant then, for whatever good it will do."

Mon Mothma raised her hand as if to issue an official directive, but Bel-Iblis interrupted. "On a related topic, I hope you have not forgotten that the Maw Installation itself remains a threat. The Imperial admiral may have taken her Star Destroyers, but the scientists are still there inside the black hole cluster. According to General Solo's report, they have a fully functional Death Star prototype." He sent a challenging look toward Mon Mothma.

Chewbacca lurched to his feet and bellowed. His roar echoed through the chamber, stopping all conversation. Threepio waved his golden metallic arms. "Not yet, Chewbacca, not yet! It's not our turn."

But Mon Mothma looked at the agitated Wookiee and acknowledged him. "You have something to say to us, Chewbacca? Please."

Chewbacca spoke a long rumbling sentence in his Wookiee language. As he spoke, Threepio stood beside him and translated quickly in his prissy synthetic voice.

"Chewbacca wishes to remind this auspicious gathering that not only is Maw Installation the home of numerous highly intelligent Imperial scientists, but it is also a prison for some number of Wookiee captives who have been held for nearly a decade. Chewbacca respectfully wishes to suggest—"

Threepio raised a metal hand in front of the Wookiee's mouth. "Slow down, Chewbacca! I'm doing the best I can." He faced forward again. "Excuse me. Chewbacca respectfully wishes to request that the New Republic Council consider an expedition to Maw Installation, both as a rescue party and as an occupation force for the installation."

Chewbacca roared but Threepio did not seem disturbed. "I know that's not what you said, Chewbacca, but it's what you *meant*—so be quiet and let me finish.

"Ahem, with such an occupation force the New Republic can ensure the security and whereabouts of whatever unpleasant weapons have been developed at Maw Installation. Chewbacca thanks you for your time and consideration, and he wishes you to have a pleasant day."

Chewbacca cuffed him, and Threepio sat down in a stiff-legged tumble of golden arms and legs. "Oh, do be quiet," the droid said. "Every change I made was an improvement."

Mon Mothma looked to the gathered Council members. All of them seemed pleased with the suggestion to send a force to Maw Installation. Qwi Xux backed toward Wedge, nervous and relieved; he squeezed her shoulder in congratulation. She smiled at him, and he smiled back.

"I believe we're all agreed on this matter," Mon Mothma said, and forced a weak smile, "for once. We shall set up a rescue and occupation force to go to Maw Installation. We must move decisively, as soon as possible, but not so quickly that we make mistakes."

As Mon Mothma looked around, she seemed to want nothing more than to leave the chamber and return to her quarters where she could rest. Wedge frowned in concern.

"If there is no other business," Mon Mothma said, "this meeting is adjourned."

9

The Imperial Star Destroyer *Gorgon* entered planetary orbit like a wide-bladed knife ready to strike. Flanking the flagship on either side rode the fully operational cruisers *Basilisk* and *Manticore*.

Commander Kratas relayed a message from the navigation console. "We have achieved orbit around Dantooine."

Daala clasped her gloved hands behind her back and turned to survey the bridge crew. "Sensor sweep," she said, and waited as the lieutenant calibrated his instruments to scan the visible face of the planet.

"A very primitive world, Admiral. No detectable industry. A few nomadic settlements . . ." He paused. "Wait. At the terminator I detect a cluster of people."

Daala studied the swirling olive, blue, and brown face of the planet, observing the edge of daylight creeping across the surface.

"I've found what appear to be the ruins of a larger base that seems mostly abandoned now. The inhabited area is not very well developed—mostly small prefabricated dwellings." The lieutenant scratched his short brown hair and bent closer to his glowing screen.

"I see excavations where new superstructures are being set up," he said, looking up at Daala. "This configuration is consistent with a large transmitting dish. Perhaps even a shield generator."

Daala's brow furrowed as she pondered how her former mentor Grand Moff Tarkin would have handled this situation.

Commander Kratas seemed to sense her hesitation and offered, "It doesn't appear that they could muster much resistance," he said.

Daala pursed her lips. "Even if they did resist, we would still defeat them. That's not the point." She ran a slender finger along her chin, then brushed her coppery hair back behind her shoulders. "To start with, we will target the abandoned base from orbit and level it with our turbolasers. It will be a spectacular display."

Daala's Star Destroyers controlled enough power to turn entire planets to slag, but she didn't want to do that here. "Dantooine is too remote for an effective demonstration," she said, "but we can make use of it nonetheless. Commander Kratas, I want you to lead a strike force. Take two AT-ATs from the *Gorgon* and a pair from each of the other two ships. Six Armored Transports should be enough."

"Me, Admiral? But surely General Odosk or one of the other Imperial Army commanders—"

"Do you have a problem with my orders, Commander?"

"No, Admiral. Not at all."

"I want you to show your versatility. Didn't they put you through those exercises on Carida?"

"Yes, Admiral," Kratas said, "I simply thought it would be more efficient just to blast them from orbit."

Daala fixed him with her emerald stare. "Consider it an exercise, Commander. We've been cooped up guarding Maw Installation for too long, and we won't have another opportunity to catch the New Republic so unprepared."

Now that he was a hopeful colonist, Warton got up in time to watch Dantooine's peaceful pastel sunrise. He stretched and stepped outside his prefab self-erecting home unit, enjoying every moment of dawn. He felt safe and at peace for the first time in his life.

His bones ached, but it was a pleasant soreness from gratifying work. He would never recover completely from his hard life on the tortured world of Eol Sha, but just spending a day without earthquakes or lava flows or scalding geysers made his life happy.

The other colony units, made of brightly colored polymers set with transparisteel windows, looked across the whispering savannas of Dantooine. All the people rescued from Eol Sha agreed that this place seemed like paradise with tall, waving lavender grasses and broad-boled, jagged-branched blba trees.

The southeastern horizon grew bright where Dantooine's amber sun would rise. Overhead in the purplish skies he saw three brilliant stars moving against the other points of light.

A cluster of six meteors streaked through the sky toward the horizon, their bright trails like slashes of claws. Then the supersonic screeching noise of their descent shattered the early-morning stillness. He saw the meteors impact; the savanna glowed with spreading flames not far from the colony.

Other colonists from Eol Sha scrambled out of their huts, roused by the noise from the sky. Not far to the east, the empty ruins of the old Rebel base rose like adobe bulwarks out of the grasses. A small team of New Republic construction engineers bustled about their encampment.

"What is it?" his wife Glena said as she stepped out of the dwelling to stand beside Warton. He shook his head, unable to answer.

Then deadly lightning began to rain down from above.

The singing of mace flies fell into silence. Blinding bolts of green laser fire shot down, striking the abandoned base and ripping up huge clouds of fragmented buildings and shards of synthetic rock.

Turbolaser beams from orbit flashed again, cutting across their earlier path. In seconds they had obliterated the entire abandoned base, leaving only a smoldering rubble-strewn scar.

The colonists ran out of their dwellings. Some screamed; others just stared in stupefied terror. Luke Skywalker had promised he would find a place of safety for the people of Eol Sha—but it seemed the Jedi had been mistaken.

As the ruins of the base continued to crackle and steam, and fires spread across the dry savannas, Warton heard a pulsating, low-pitched sound: the humming of massive engines, the clanking of metal, thunderous footfalls.

He squinted into the brightening morning, still dazzled from the green laser bolts, until he could discern the monstrous silhouettes of gigantic walking machines. Four-legged and camellike, the Imperial walkers—All Terrain Armored Transports—strode from their smoldering landing sites and marched in hulking formation across the savanna.

The cockpit "heads" of the attacking AT-ATs bent lower to aim banks of laser cannons. Precision bolts of green and red fire shot down. The ancient swollen blba trees erupted into flames that spread out in concentric circles across the dry grasses. Greasy smoke curled up, carrying the stench of burning wet vegetation and roasted small animals.

Warton shouted, "Run everyone! Get away from the dwellings. They will target them first."

The refugees from Eol Sha waded across the tall grasses as Imperial walkers plodded forward. The AT-ATs covered more distance with each step than a human could run in half a minute. The walkers took aim at the fleeing colonists, striking each individual with enough firepower to destroy a small fighter ship.

Glena yanked her hand away from Warton and shouted at him, "Wait!" She turned around to run back toward their small dwelling.

"No!" he yelled, unable to imagine anything that would cause her to turn and run into the attack.

Before she could say another word, a blinding lance of turbolaser fire exploded full in her chest, and Warton watched in utter horror as Glena vanished in a blazing, sizzling cloud of red steam.

The six walkers continued to march ahead, firing at blba trees, at colony huts, and at anything that moved. The great machines spread out to encircle the entire settlement.

Over at their encampment the New Republic engineers had managed to set up a single-ion cannon. Warton, still standing stricken and motionless, watched their tiny forms as they scrambled to rig the dish-shaped generator. He knew the people manning the ion cannon were simply construction engineers with no battle training.

"Why?" Warton wanted to know. But so many questions filled his head that he could not be more specific than that: *Why?*

The New Republic engineers powered up the ion cannon and focused a single blast toward the lower section of the closest Imperial walker. The bolt struck and fused the knee joint of the AT-AT's front foreleg, melting the servomotor mechanisms. The walker halted and tried to limp backward in a stiff-legged retreat.

The other five AT-ATs swiveled their heads in unison, targeting the single ion cannon with a river of laser blasts in a great gout of green fire— obliterating communications gear and ion cannon in a single splash of light.

The walkers advanced again, firing indiscriminately. The prefabricated colony huts exploded one by one. Hungry flames raged through the dry grasses on the savanna.

Warton's people screamed as they ran, and stumbled, and died. The roar of destruction rang in his ears, and still he could not move. He stood with his hands at his sides. His entire body trembled.

Even the blasted world of Eol Sha had never been as hellish as Dantooine.

Commander Kratas sat in the AT-AT's unfamiliar cockpit, directing the movement of his six great machines. They fired at anyone who tried to escape, igniting islands of grass and flushing out burning colonists who had attempted to hide there. Kratas intended to leave them no place to hide.

He verified that every one of the huts had been blown to pieces, and all moving colonists had been cut down as they fled. The Rebel engineers and their ion cannon had been taken out with a single strike, and the minor damage inflicted on one walker could be repaired easily in the workshops back on the *Gorgon*.

"I wish he'd move," the gunner said.

Kratas looked down to see a single man standing among the wreckage, motionless and staring.

"It's not much of a challenge to hit a stationary target," the gunner said, lifting the visor of his black helmet. "If he'd run, I could get better practice."

Kratas surveyed the devastation and the black smoke curling up from a thousand different fires. Their job here was done. "Take him out anyway," Kratas said. "We don't have time to play games."

The gunner squeezed his firing buttons, and the lone surviving man vanished in a flare of green fire.

Commander Kratas signaled the flagship, and he nodded to Daala's tiny shimmering form on the transmitter platform. "The mission is a complete success, Admiral. No casualties on our part, very minor damage to one AT-AT."

"You're sure nothing is left alive down there?" Daala said.

"Nothing, Admiral. No structure is left standing. The place is a wasteland."

"Good," Daala said with a slight nod. "You may return to the ships. I believe we've made our point. We've had our practice."

She continued with a smile, "Next time we'll choose a more important world to strike."

10

The sleep of a Jedi was rarely troubled by dreams. Pure rest brought about through concentration and meditation techniques left little room for disturbing thoughts or shadow plays. But this time nightmares did break through to Luke Skywalker.

A voice called him across a misty blank dreamscape. "Luke, Luke my son. You must hear me!"

A shadowy form rose out of the mists even as the surroundings began to sharpen. Luke saw himself in his pale-gray flightsuit, stained with sweat, grime, and pain—as he had looked when he took his father's body from the second Death Star.

The features on the spectral silhouette shimmered with a pale aura. Luke saw the firm face of Anakin Skywalker, restored from the ravages Darth Vader's evil had worked on his body.

"Father!" Luke called. His own voice had an odd, echoing quality, as if it bounced off the mists.

"Luke," the image of Anakin said.

Luke felt tingling amazement surge through him. It was another sending, just like his last contact from Obi-Wan Kenobi. But Obi-Wan had bid him farewell, claiming that he could never contact Luke again. "Father, why are you here?"

Anakin stood taller. His robes rippled in a rising wind that drove back the mists. Suddenly the world surrounding them was no longer featureless. Luke recognized that he and the image of his father stood atop the Great Temple on Yavin 4. The orange gas giant hung overhead, and the timeless jungles below looked unchanged. But the stones of the temple were white and new with bright scars from fresh quarrying. A sketchy framework of scaffolding laced one wall of the ziggurat. Far below, Luke heard mumbling and chanting, incantations from suffering slaves.

He saw people of the vanished Massassi race laboring together, straining to haul enormous stone blocks along roads they had chopped through the jungle. The grayish-green Massassi were humanoid, smooth-skinned, with large lanternlike eyes. Anakin Skywalker stood on the highest point of the temple, as if directing the work gangs below.

"Do not be deceived, Luke. Do not trust everything you think to be the truth." Anakin's words carried an odd, distant lilt, like the faint accent of an ancient race. "Obi-Wan lied to you, more than once."

Luke felt uneasiness well up within him. No matter how much he loved Obi-Wan Kenobi, he knew the old man had not always been completely forthcoming with him. "Yes, I know he hid the truth from me. He told me Darth Vader had killed you, when you had really become Vader."

Anakin turned from the illusory Massassi laborers below. He met Luke's gaze with eyes as bottomless as the universe itself. "Was that the only lie Obi-Wan told you?"

"No. He hid other things from me." Luke looked off into the jungled distance, toward the moon's foreshortened horizon to see another clearing, another tall temple being erected.

"And Obi-Wan rationalized it as being for your own *protection*. Did you ask for such protection, Luke?"

"No." Luke tried to fight back his uneasiness.

"Obi-Wan wanted you to be his student, but he wouldn't allow you the freedom to make your own decisions. Did he trust you so little? Did you always agree with his 'certain point of view'?"

"No," Luke said, feeling the words swallowed up in doubt.

Anakin's voice became tinged with anger. "Obi-Wan fought against the complex Sith teachings I had uncovered. He did not understand them himself, but he forbade me to study them—though he always insisted that I must learn for myself and choose my own path. I rebelled against him for his narrow-mindedness, and I insisted on unlocking secrets for which I was not ready. In the end it consumed me—I fell to the dark side, and I became the Dark Lord of the Sith."

Anakin looked at Luke with an anguished, apologetic expression. "But if Obi-Wan had let me learn the teachings at my own pace, I would have grown stronger. I would have remained uncorrupted. He never understood that."

Anakin's image shook his head. "If you are going to teach other Jedi, Luke, you must understand the consequences of what they may learn. You, too, must study the ancient heritage of the Sith. It is a part of your Jedi training."

Luke swallowed. "I'm afraid to believe you, Father. I have already felt the power of the dark side."

Below, Massassi labor crews hummed and sang in stuporous unison, far beyond exhaustion, as they hauled an enormous block up a mud-covered ramp made of stripped logs.

Atop the dream temple, the wavering image of Anakin Skywalker spoke more forcefully. "Yes, but the ways of the Sith can lead you to a stronger grasp of your own power. You can wipe out the last vestiges of the pitiful Empire that continues to harass your New Republic. You can become more than a mere servant to a frail and corrupt government. You can administer the galaxy yourself as a benevolent ruler.

"You deserve it more than any other person, Luke. You can control everything, if you use the Force as your tool, instead of allowing yourself to become its servant."

Luke stiffened, unable to believe what his father was saying. Then he noticed that with the rising passion in his voice, the image of Anakin Skywalker became less distinct, wavering, until it transformed into only a black outline, an engulfing hooded form that sucked energy from the air.

Slowly, Luke realized the truth. "You are not my father!" he shouted as the illusion began to crumble. "My father was a good man in the end, healed by the light side."

Streaks of brilliant light flashed across the dreamscape sky of ancient Yavin 4. Below, Massassi slaves fled into the jungles in terror as the monumental temples crumbled under a barrage of laser blasts from orbit. Old Republic battleships had arrived, immolating the moon's surface.

"Who are you?" Luke shouted at the figure through the roar of sudden blazing devastation around him. "Who?"

Instead, the hollow shadow laughed and laughed, ignoring the destruction that erupted from the construction sites—or amused by it. The Massassi temples exploded. The thick rain forests burst into flame.

The dark man's silhouette grew larger and larger, swallowing up the sky. Luke backed away from it, but his dream feet reached the edge of the imposing temple, and he stumbled backward, falling away, falling. . . .

Surrounded by the thick stone walls of his quarters, Gantoris did not even attempt to sleep. He sat on his bunk dreading the arrival of the dark man from his nightmares.

He fingered the lightsaber he had constructed, feeling its smooth cylinder, the rough spots where he had welded the pieces together, the buttons that would activate the energy blade. He wondered how he could use it against the ancient spectre who had taught him things that terrified him, things that Master Skywalker would never show his Jedi trainees.

"Do you mean to strike me down with that weapon?" the hollow voice said.

Gantoris whirled to see the oily, infinitely black silhouette ooze out of the massive stones in the wall. His impulse was to ignite the lightsaber and slash the violet-white blade across the dark form. But he restrained himself, knowing it would do no good.

The shadow man laughed, then spoke with his antiquated accent. "Good! I am glad to see you have learned to respect me. Four thousand years ago the entire military fleet of the Old Republic and the combined forces of hundreds of Jedi Masters could not destroy me. You would certainly be unable to do so alone."

The dark man had shown him how to borrow energy from other living things, to shore up his own reserves. His mind was alert, but his nerves were frayed and his body exhausted. "What do you want with me?" Gantoris said. "You don't just want to teach me."

The shadow man agreed. "I want your *anger*, Gantoris. I want you to open the doorways of power. I am barred from the physical plane—but with enough other Sith followers, I could be at peace. I could even live again."

"I won't let you have my anger." Gantoris swallowed, searching for a core of strength within himself. "A Jedi does not give in to anger. There is no passion; there is serenity."

"Don't quote platitudes to me!" the dark man said in a cold, vibrating voice.

"There is no ignorance; there is knowledge," Gantoris continued, repeating the Jedi Code. "There is no passion; there is serenity."

The dark man laughed again. "Serenity? Let me show you what is happening at this moment. Do you recall the people you saved from Eol Sha? How happy you were to learn they had been taken to a place of safety, a paradise world? Observe."

Inside the black cut-out form of the hooded man, an image appeared, displaying the grasslands of the planet Dantooine. The scene looked familiar to Gantoris after seeing the progress tapes delivered by Wedge Antilles.

But now he saw Imperial lasers striking down, leveling colony buildings, giant armored walkers striding across the savanna, blasting anything that moved, igniting the temporary living units. People ran screaming. His people.

Gantoris recognized most of their faces, but before he could name them, they dissolved one by one in brilliant flashes as they tried to flee. The trees blazed in conical bonfires; black clumpy smoke rose in jagged swirls.

"You lie! This is a trick!"

"I have no need of lies when the truth is so devastating. You can do nothing to stop it. Do you enjoy watching your people die? Does that not spark your anger? In your anger lies strength."

Gantoris saw the old man Warton, whom he had known his entire life, standing in the middle of the holocaust. Warton stared around him, hands dangling at his sides, frozen in shock, until a thick green bolt cut him down.

"No!" Gantoris shouted.

"Let loose your anger. Make me stronger."

"No!" he repeated, turning his head away from the images of burned ruins and blackened bodies.

"They are all dead. All of them," the dark man taunted. "No survivors."

Gantoris ignited his lightsaber and lunged at the dark man.

With an insistent bleeping Artoo-Detoo woke Luke from his nightmares. He snapped awake, using a Jedi technique to dispel the weariness and shock of the sudden waking.

"What is it, Artoo?"

The droid whistled, telling him something about a message waiting in the command center. Luke shrugged into his soft robe and hurried across the cold floor in the early light of planetrise. Taking the turbolift down to the second level of the temple, he entered the once-bustling command center.

"Artoo, bring up the lights." He picked his path through the equipment, dust-covered chairs, shut-down computer consoles, document tables cluttered with debris. He powered on the communications station that Wedge had insisted on installing during his last supply run.

The image of Han Solo waited impatiently for him, fidgeting in the holofield. When he saw Luke appear in the transmission locus, Han grinned up at him. "Hey, Luke! Sorry I forgot to account for time differential. Not even dawn there, is it?"

Luke brushed his brown hair into place with his fingers. "Even Jedi need to sleep sometime, Han."

Han laughed. "Well, you'll be getting less sleep when your new student arrives. I just wanted to tell you that Kyp Durron has had enough of his vacation. I think after all that time in the spice mines, he got used to being miserable. The closest thing to the spice mines I could think of was your Jedi academy—that way he can work all day long, but at least he'll be improving himself in the process."

Luke smiled at his old friend. "I'd be honored to have him join us, Han. I've been waiting for him. He has the strongest potential of all the trainees I've seen so far."

"Just wanted to let you know he's coming," Han said. "I'm trying to arrange for the next available transport to Yavin 4."

Luke frowned. "Why don't you just bring him in the *Falcon?*"

Han hung his head, looking extremely troubled. "Because I don't own the *Falcon* anymore."

"What?"

Han seemed filled with embarrassment, eager to end the communication. "Look, I've got to go. I'll tell Leia hello for you and give the kids a hug."

"All right, Han, but—"

Han gave a sheepish grin and quickly terminated the transmission.

Luke continued to stare at the blank space where Han's image had been. First his nightmare of a dark man masquerading as Anakin Skywalker, and now the grim news that Han had lost the *Millennium Falcon*—

Luke heard a disturbance coming down the hall: clumsy footsteps slapping on the stone floor, panicked shouts. He looked up, ready to scold one of his students for such blatant lack of control, when the cloned alien Dorsk 81 rushed into the control center. "Master Skywalker! You must come immediately!"

Luke sensed waves of horror and misery spilling from his candidate. "What is it?" he asked. "Use the calming technique I showed you."

But Dorsk 81 grabbed his arm. "This way!" The yellow-olive alien urged him out of the cluttered control room. Luke sensed widening ripples of alarm traveling like an earthquake through the solid stone of the temple.

They ran along the flagstoned corridors, up the turbolift, and into the section of living quarters where the trainees made their homes.

A sour, smoky stench filled the air, and Luke felt an icy lump in his stomach as he pushed cautiously forward. Hard-bitten Kam Solusar and addled Streen both stood outside the open doorway to Gantoris's quarters, looking pasty and ill.

Luke hesitated for a fraction of a second, then moved through the doorway.

Inside the small stone chamber, he saw what was left of Gantoris. The body lay crisped and blackened on the floor, burned from the inside out. Singed stains on the flagstones showed where he had thrashed about in the conflagration. Gantoris's skin flaked in black, peeling ashes over his powdery bones. Rising wisps of steam curled from the remaining fabric of his Jedi robe.

On the floor the newly constructed lightsaber lay where Gantoris had dropped it, as if he had tried to fight something—and lost.

Luke leaned against the cool stone wall to catch his balance. His vision blurred, but he could not tear his gaze from his dead student sprawled in front of him.

By now the other eleven trainees had gathered. Luke grasped the worn stone bricks at the edge of the door until even the rounded corners bruised his fingers. He applied a Jedi calming technique three times before he felt confident enough to trust his voice. The words tasted like wet ash in his mouth, as Yoda had told him so long ago.

"Beware the dark side," he said.

11

After eight seemingly random hyperspace jumps to shake any possible pursuit, Ackbar took his B-wing fighter along the correct vector to the hidden planet Anoth. Terpfen had "borrowed" the fighter for him, claiming to have purged the records of its existence; Ackbar didn't want to know how his mechanic had gotten through the security systems so easily.

For years isolated Anoth had been a haven for the Jedi children, protected by its perfect obscurity and anonymity. The twins had gone home to Coruscant only a month or two before, but the youngest child—one-year-old baby Anakin—remained under the protection of Leia's devoted servant Winter, far from prying Imperial eyes or dark-side influences that could corrupt the baby's fragile Force-sensitive mind.

As space snapped into sharp focus, Ackbar saw the clustered multiple planet of Anoth. The world was composed of three large fragments orbiting a common center of mass. The two largest pieces hovered nearly in contact, sharing a poisonous stormy atmosphere. The third and more distant fragment orbited in a precarious, almost-safe position where Ackbar, Luke, and Winter had set up a hidden stronghold.

Skittering electrostatic discharges danced from the two touching pieces of Anoth, and the ionized fury bathed the habitable chunk in electrical storms that served to mask the planet from prying eyes. The entire system was unstable, and in a blink of cosmic time it would destroy itself, but for the last century or so it had been possible for humanoid life to establish a foothold there.

Ackbar brought his B-wing in on close approach through the deep-purple skies of Anoth. Sparks discharged from the wing of his fighter, but he felt no threat. This was not like flying through the storms of Vortex.

Inside the cramped B-wing, Ackbar wore only a flightsuit over his big frame, not his admiral's uniform. Later he would leave the "borrowed" fighter in the Calamarian shipyards, where a New Republic pilot could shuttle it back to Coruscant. Ackbar would not be flying a starfighter again, so he had no need of it.

He sent a brief signal to inform Winter of his arrival, but he did not respond to her surprise or her questions. Switching off the fighter's comm unit, he rehearsed how he would tell her all that had happened. Then he concentrated on guiding the B-wing in for a landing.

Below him the surface of Anoth was a craggy forest of rocky spires, sharp ledges, and clawlike peaks that were riddled with caves left behind when volatile inclusions in the rocks had evaporated over the centuries, leaving only glasslike rock.

Inside the labyrinth of smooth tunnels Winter had made a temporary home with the Jedi babies. Now she had only one child left to care for; and in another year, when Anakin reached the age of two, Winter could return to Coruscant and to active service with the New Republic government.

The small white sun never brought much daylight to Anoth, bathing the world in Gothic purple twilight lit by stark flashes of interplanetary lightning discharges. Ackbar and Luke Skywalker had found this planet, choosing it from among the possibilities as the safest place to hide the Jedi children. And now Ackbar had come one last time before returning to his homeworld of Calamari.

He felt sympathy for baby Anakin, who had not known a more welcoming place during his first year. Ackbar had always felt a close attachment to the third child, but he had come to say goodbye before fading from public view forever.

He flew the B-wing in among the spired forests and rock outcroppings. It reminded him of the tall fluted towers of the Cathedral of Winds on Vortex. That thought gave him a stab of pain, and he tried not to think of it further.

He cruised the ship in among the rocks, flying confidently as he arrowed toward the opening to the network of caves. With landing jets and a careful manipulation of repulsorlifts, Ackbar managed to land the starfighter smoothly on the wide grotto floor.

As he powered down the engines and prepared to disembark, a metal crash door swung open. A tall rigid-looking woman stood at the doorway.

Her robes and her white hair clearly identified her as Leia's ageless servant Winter. Even for a human, she looked strikingly distinctive to Ackbar.

He climbed stiffly out of his ship and turned his salmon-colored head away to keep from meeting her eyes. He saw with a backward glance that the one-year-old baby toddled at Winter's feet, making happy noises, curious to see the new visitor. Ackbar felt a shudder go through him as he realized he would probably never see the dark-haired boy again.

Winter spoke in her flat, no-nonsense voice. He had never heard her upset before. "Admiral Ackbar, please tell me what has happened."

He turned to face her, showing his flightsuit, his lack of military insignia. "I am no longer an admiral," he said, "and it is a long story."

Ackbar sat eating a meal of reconstituted rations that Winter had somehow managed to make palatable. As he told her every detail of the tragedy on Vortex and how he had resigned from his service, Winter did not appear judgmental. She simply listened, blinking rarely, nodding even less often.

Baby Anakin crouched on Ackbar's lap, cooing and reaching up in curiosity to pat Ackbar's clammy skin and touch his huge glassy eyes. Anakin giggled as the round eyes swiveled in various directions to avoid being poked by pudgy fingers.

"Will you stay here for an evening's rest—?" Winter said. Her sentence cut off sharply, as if she had been about to call him admiral.

"No," Ackbar said, holding the baby against him with flipper-hands. "I can't. No one must suspect that I have come here, and if I delay too long, they will realize I have not gone directly to Calamari."

Winter hesitated and then spoke in a voice that seemed less able to conceal emotion than it normally did. "Ackbar, you know I have the greatest respect for your abilities. It would honor me if you would stay here with me instead of going into hiding on your homeworld."

Ackbar looked at the human woman and felt a surge of emotion well up inside him. Winter's mere suggestion had been powerful enough to strip away layers of guilt and shame with which he had buried himself.

When he did not answer immediately, she pressed further. "I'm all alone here, and I could use your help. It gets lonely for the baby . . . and for me."

Ackbar finally managed to speak, avoiding Winter's gaze but giving his answer before he could change his mind. "Your offer honors me, Winter, but I am not worthy. At least not at the moment. I must go to Calamari and search for peace there. If I—" The words caught in his throat again, and he realized he was trembling. "If I find my peace, perhaps I shall return to you—and the baby."

"I—we'll be here waiting, if you change your mind," she said, then escorted him back to the hangar grotto.

Ackbar felt her watching him as he climbed back into the B-wing. He lifted the ship on its repulsorlift jets and turned to see her standing at the doorway. He flicked his running lights to signal her.

Winter raised a hand in sad goodbye. Then, with her other hand, she made Anakin's pudgy arm wave to him too.

Ackbar's starfighter soared into space, leaving them behind.

Back on Coruscant, Terpfen lay sick and shivering in his private quarters, trying with all his might to resist. But in the end the organic circuitry inside what was left of his brain took over.

Moving with forced steps, he descended to the dispatching and receiving network in the lower levels of the old Imperial Palace. No one watched him in the echoing, crowded room as diplomatic droids and packages came in and left, streaking off to various embassies and spaceports on Coruscant, bearing important dispatches.

Terpfen coded his secret message, summarizing information he had received from the hidden tracking device he had planted on Ackbar's ship. He sealed the message inside a coffin-sized hyperspace courier tube and shielded the entire apparatus. He glanced around suspiciously before he keyed in Admiral Ackbar's personal diplomatic security code, which would allow it to bypass all checks and tariff points. No one would have thought to revoke Ackbar's access yet.

The routing doors opened up at the far end of the center, and the silvery message canister rose on its launching fields. In a reflex action Terpfen reached out, trying to grasp the slick sides of the canister, scraping with the sharp points of his hands—but the container rocketed out, picking up speed as it soared into the Coruscant sky.

Terpfen had programmed five alternate routes to discourage tracking. The message canister would arrive unhindered and without delay at the Imperial Military Academy on Carida. The coded message would be displayed for the eyes of Ambassador Furgan only—divulging the location of the secret planet where the last Jedi baby was hidden.

12

"You'll do just fine, kid," Han said, trying to maintain his roguish grin.

Standing at the door of Han and Leia's quarters, Kyp Durron nodded. Han noticed a faint trembling around the young man's lips. "I'll do my best, Han. You know that."

Suddenly unable to say another word, Han embraced Kyp, silently cursing the stinging tears that rose to his eyes. "You'll be the greatest Jedi ever. You'll give even Luke a run for his money."

"I doubt that," Kyp said. He broke away and averted his face but not before Han caught the shimmer of tears in his eyes too.

"Wait," Han said, "I've got something for you before you go." He ducked back inside and returned to the door with a soft package. Kyp took it with a tentative smile and unwrapped the top layers of paper.

Han watched the young man's expression. Kyp reached into the package and withdrew a flowing black cape that glittered with subliminal reflective threads, as if it had been woven out of a clear starry night.

"Lando gave it to me—feeling guilty about winning the *Falcon*, I guess— but I can't wear stuff like this. I want you to have it. You deserve something nice, after all those years you spent in the dirty spice mines."

Kyp laughed. "You mean so I can dress up for all those formal occasions at the Jedi academy?" His expression became serious. "Thanks, Han . . . for everything. But I've got to be going. General Antilles is escorting the Sun Crusher to Yavin, and I'll be going with him. He'll drop me off at Luke's academy."

"Good luck," Han said.

Kyp said, "I'm sorry you lost the *Falcon*."

"Don't worry about it," Han said. "She's a hunk of junk anyway."

"You got that right," Kyp said with a smile, but both of them knew he didn't mean it.

"Want me to walk with you down to the hangar?" Han asked, realizing as he said it that he wasn't sure he wanted to.

"Naw," Kyp said, turning away from the door. "I hate long goodbyes. See you around."

"Sure, kid," Han said. He watched Kyp's back for a long time as the young man walked with a feigned bouncy step down the corridors to the turbolift.

Han thought about going back into his room, then decided he'd rather go for a drink instead. Leia was in yet another late-night Council meeting with Mon Mothma, and the kids were already in bed, so Han left Threepio with instructions to remain powered up so he could baby-sit.

Han eventually returned to the lounge where he and Lando had played sabacc for possession of the *Falcon*.

The window looked out across the sweeping geometrical skyline of the rebuilt Imperial City. Towering metal and transparisteel pillars stretched to rarefied heights. Warning beacons and transmitting towers blinked in multicolored patterns as flying craft swooped on the updrafts between the tall buildings.

At another table a hammerheaded Ithorian ambassador sat by himself next to a small musical synthesizer. He hummed along with the atonal noises and plucked small leaves off a fresh ferny-looking snack. A pug-faced Ugnaught chittered and played electronic dice with a well-groomed Ranat. The bartender droid drifted from one table to another, attempting to be of service.

Han soon lost himself in thought, wondering where he had come to, thinking about how much his life had changed since his years as a spice smuggler for Jabba the Hutt and then as a general in the Rebel Alliance.

He continued to do important things with his life, but it just didn't seem as *real* anymore. He had enjoyed spending time with young Kyp Durron. The young man reminded him so much of himself, and now Kyp had gone off to become a Jedi just like Luke.

"You're gonna miss the kid, aren't you?" a deep voice said. Han looked up to see Lando Calrissian standing over him with a big smile.

"What are you doing here?" Han said grumpily.

"I'm buying you a drink, old buddy," Lando said. He shoved forward one of the prissy fruity concoctions, complete with bright tropical flower, that Han had bought Lando on the night of their sabacc game.

Han scowled and accepted it. "Thanks a lot." He took a sip, grimaced, then took a gulp. Lando pulled up a chair.

"I didn't invite you to sit down," Han said.

"Look, Han," Lando said, adding a stern edge to his voice, "when you won the *Falcon* from me in a sabacc game, did I spend years pouting and not talking to you?"

Han shrugged and looked up. "I don't know. I pretty much stayed away all those years." He paused, then added quickly, "And the next time we saw each other, you betrayed us to Darth Vader."

"Hey, that wasn't my fault, and I've more than made up for it since," Lando said. "Listen, I've got a deal for you. Next time you get a chance, why don't the both of us take the *Falcon* and go back to what's left of Kessel? Maybe we can find my old ship there. If we do, I'd gladly take the *Lady Luck* back, and you can have the *Falcon*." He held out his broad hand. "Deal?"

Han grudgingly admitted that it was the best he could hope for. "All right, pal," he said, and shook Lando's hand.

"Solo," a woman's sharp voice said. "They told me I'd find you here."

"Can't a guy get some peace?" he said, and turned to see a trim, attractive woman standing at the lounge entrance. She had shoulder-length reddish brown hair the color of some exotic spice. Her features were finely chiseled: a narrow chin and a mouth that looked as if it had spent too many years frowning and was just now learning the shape of a smile. The shards of ice that were Mara Jade's eyes had warmed somewhat since the last time Han had seen her.

Lando stood up, sweeping his cape behind him and extending his hand. "Well hel-*lo*! Please join us, Miss Jade. May I get you anything? We've met before but I'm not sure you remember me. I'm—"

"Shut up, Calrissian. I need to talk to Solo."

Lando laughed and went to get her a drink anyway.

Dark patches stood out on the shoulders and sleeves of Mara's flight jacket, as if it had once borne the insignia of military service. Mara Jade had been the Emperor's Hand, a special servant to Palpatine himself, and she had seen her life crumble after his death; she had blamed Luke for that and held a vendetta against him until recently.

Now, after the retirement of the great smuggler Talon Karrde, Mara seemed to become more open and ready to participate in broader events. She had managed a tenuous coalition of smugglers to help fight against Grand Admiral Thrawn, and she still maintained a loose alliance, even though some of the worst offenders—such as Moruth Doole on Kessel—refused to have anything to do with the New Republic and the smuggler's alliance.

"What brings you back to Coruscant, Mara?" Han said. Lando returned bearing another one of his fruity drinks for her and a new one for himself. She looked at it, pointedly ignored it, and continued talking to Han.

"I'm bringing a message. You can pass it on to the appropriate people. Your Imperial friend Admiral Daala has been sending out feelers, trying to hire smugglers as spies and saboteurs. A few have taken the offer, but I don't expect many of them to trust Daala after what she did to the forces of Kessel. Even though Moruth Doole wasn't part of our alliance, he was still a smuggler, and smugglers tend to stick together—especially against Imperials."

"Yes," Han said, "we got the message that she had attacked one of the supply ships and destroyed it before it could get to Dantooine."

Mara looked at him, and her gaze became hard again. "Haven't you heard what happened to your colony on Dantooine? Daala's already been there, you know."

"What?" Han said, and Lando echoed his surprise.

"A small group of New Republic engineers is setting up a communications base there," Han said, "but we haven't contacted them in the last week or two."

"Well, there's no need to," Mara said. "Dantooine has been leveled. Every person in your colony *and* all of your New Republic engineers are dead, as of two days ago. Daala attacked with her three Star Destroyers and vanished again to wherever her hiding place is."

"And so you came here just to give us this information?" Han said, trying to recover from his shock.

Mara took a long, slow drink of the cloying concoction that Lando seemed to be enjoying so much. She shrugged. "I have an agreement with the New Republic, and I keep my agreements."

As Han felt anger and shock starting to boil inside him at what Daala had done, Lando changed the subject.

"So where are you off to now, Miss Jade?" he said. Leaning forward on the table, he seemed to be trying to melt her with his big brown eyes. Han rolled his.

"You're welcome to stay here for a while," Lando said. "I'd be happy to show you some of the sights of the city. There's some beautiful views on top of the Grand Towers." Mara looked at him as if considering how much effort it was worth for her to answer his question.

"I'll be leaving immediately," she said. "I'm going to spend some time at Skywalker's Jedi training center. It makes good business sense to learn how to use my Jedi abilities, if only for self-protection."

Han sat up in surprise. "You're going to learn from Luke? I thought you still hated Luke! You've tried to kill him often enough."

Mara's eyes stared back as if ready to blaze through him; then she softened and even smiled. "We've . . . reconciled our differences. You might say we negotiated a truce." She looked down at her drink but did not touch it. "For now, at least," she added, and then smiled even more. She stood up to leave. "Thanks for your time, Solo." She ignored Lando completely and walked out of the lounge.

Lando watched Mara leave, admiring the slick satiny gray fabric of her slacks and tight padded flightshirt. "She sure has gotten beautiful."

"Yeah, I hear that happens to most assassins once they retire," Han answered.

Lando didn't seem to hear him. "How could I have missed her in Jabba the Hutt's throne room? She was there, and I was there, but I didn't notice her at all."

"I was there too," Han said, "and I didn't see her. Of course, I was frozen in a block of carbonite at the time."

"I think she likes me," Lando said. "Maybe I'll volunteer to take the next delivery of supplies to Yavin 4, just so I can see her."

Han shook his head. "Lando, she wanted you to disappear. She didn't even acknowledge your presence."

Lando shrugged. "Sometimes it just takes my charm a little longer to work." He flashed one of his best lady-killer smiles. "But when it does. . . ."

"Oh, brother," Han said. He finished his drink and left Lando sitting there, daydreaming as his own drink sat unnoticed beside him.

13

The next night Leia had just sat down to cherish a relaxing meal with her husband and her children when the summons from Mon Mothma arrived.

As usual, she had been wrapped up in governmental proceedings all day. After the disaster on Vortex, she had been allowed no respite, and the pressure had increased as Mon Mothma withdrew further from her responsibilities, begging off the unimportant receptions and meetings and sending Leia as her proxy.

Living on the peaceful world of Alderaan as the daughter of the powerful Senator Bail Organa, Leia had grown up surrounded by politics. She was used to the constant demands, the communiqués arriving at all hours, the sudden emergencies, the whispered negotiations, and the forced smiles. She had chosen to follow in Senator Organa's footsteps, knowing full well the demands that would be made of her.

But she treasured the scant quiet times she managed to steal with Han and the twins. It seemed ages since she had been able to visit baby Anakin, though Han himself had accompanied Winter twice in the last two months.

Tonight Leia had come home late, flustered and harried, but Han was there waiting with Jacen and Jaina. They had held dinner for her, which Threepio had prepared as a test of his new and dubious gourmet programming at the food synthesizers.

They sat down in the dining area, where illumination strips bathed the room in soft pink and peach colors. Han played the relaxing music of one of her favorite Alderaani composers, and they sat down to eat off fine Imperial china taken from the late Emperor's private stock.

It was not intended to be a romantic dinner with two-and-a-half-year-old twins banging their silverware and demanding constant attention—but Leia didn't mind. Han had done his best to commemorate dinner as a family.

Leia smiled as Threepio delivered their meal, a very passable-looking grazer roulade accompanied by skewers of spiced tubers and sweet marbleberry fritters. "I believe you will be quite impressed, Mistress Leia," the droid said, gently bowing and setting smaller plates in front of Jacen and Jaina.

"Yuck," Jacen said.

Jaina looked at her brother for confirmation, then said, "I don't like this."

Threepio straightened in indignation. "Children, you have not even tasted the food. I insist that you sample your dinners."

Leia and Han looked at each other and smiled. Jacen and Jaina both had bright eyes and well-defined features below thick dark-brown hair—just like their parents. The twins were extremely precocious, speaking in short but complete sentences and amazing their parents with the concepts they had already managed to grasp and communicate.

Jacen and Jaina seemed to share a kind of psychic link, speaking in half sentences to each other or somehow communicating in complete silence. This didn't surprise Leia—as Luke had told her, the Force was strong in their family.

Han claimed that the two kids knew how to use their powers more than they admitted. He had found cabinet doors mysteriously unlocked after he had fastened them securely, and sometimes shiny baubles left on high shelves were suddenly found underfoot as if they had been played with. The food synthesizers, far out of reach, had once been reprogrammed to add a double portion of sweetening to all recipes, even the soup.

Perplexed with the mysterious occurrences, Threepio had dug through diverse and obscure data records, insisting that the best explanation could be found in an ancient superstition of *poltergeists*—but Leia suspected it had more to do with small Jedi children.

She took a bite of her thinly sliced, herb-crusted grazer. It smelled wonderfully nutty as the aroma curled up to her nose. It was tender and perfectly seasoned to counteract the pungent unpleasant aftertaste often found in imported grazer filet. She considered complimenting Threepio, but decided that it would probably make the protocol droid altogether too pleased with himself.

"Look what Jaina's doing!" Jacen said.

Leia stared in astonishment as the little girl balanced her delicate skewer of spiced tubers impossibly on its tip and used the Force to twirl it around like a top.

"Mistress Jaina, please stop playing with your food," Threepio said.

Leia and Han met each other's gaze in amazement. She was glad that Luke had formed his Jedi academy, so these children would learn to understand the powerful and beautiful gift they had been given.

The door chime sounded like a tubular bell through their living quarters. The noise startled Jaina, and her delicately balanced skewer toppled over—which made her begin to cry.

Han sighed, and Leia got up with a scowl. "I didn't think we could sit through an entire meal uninterrupted."

She opened the door, and the ornate plasteel plate hummed aside to reveal a hovering messenger droid that bobbed up and down in the corridor, blinking its lights in a swirl.

"Minister Leia Organa Solo, Chief of State Mon Mothma requests your presence immediately in her private quarters for an important consultation. Please follow me."

Back at the table Han rolled his eyes and glowered at no one in particular as Leia was taken from him again. Jaina continued crying, and now Jacen added his own squalls to the racket. Threepio tried to calm the two children down, completely without effect.

Leia looked imploringly at Han, but he gave a short wave of dismissal. "Go on, Mon Mothma needs you."

She bit her lower lip, sensing the bitterness he tried to cover. "I'll cut it short," she said. "I'll be back as soon as I can."

Han nodded and turned to his eating as if he didn't believe her. Leia felt her stomach knot as she hurried after the hovering droid through the arched, well-lit corridors. She felt a simmering annoyance and stubborn resistance build within her, and she walked with purposeful steps.

She agreed to too many things. She bowed her head and trotted anywhere Mon Mothma asked her to go. Well, Leia had her own life, and she had to spend more time with her family. Her career was important too—crucial, in fact—and she vowed to do both. But she had to reestablish some priorities and ground rules.

As she followed the messenger droid into a turbolift that took her to secluded portions of the old Imperial Palace, Leia was actually glad that Mon Mothma had summoned her. She had a few things to say to the Chief of State, and the two of them would have to work out some sort of compromise.

But when the droid transmitted the special unlocking code that caused Mon Mothma's armored door to grind aside, Leia felt a cold fingernail twist in her chest. Mon Mothma's quarters were too dark, lit only by soft greenish glowing lamps designed to be soothing, restful . . . healing. She breathed the sweet tang of odd medicines, and the clinging aftertaste of sickness caught in her throat.

Leia stepped forward into the chambers and saw that they had been filled with bright nova lilies and nebula orchids that showered heady perfumes into the air, masking the unpleasant medicinal smell.

"Mon Mothma?" she said. Her voice sounded small in the enclosed space.

Motion off to her right made her turn her head to see a bullet-headed Too-Onebee medical droid. Mon Mothma looked gaunt and skeletal as she lay on a broad bed surrounded by diagnostic equipment. Another smaller droid monitored the readouts. Everything hung in silence except for the faint hum of machinery.

Leia also saw—feeling foolish for noticing such a small thing—that Mon Mothma kept an array of makeup jars and synthetic skin-coloring agents on her dressing table in a desperate attempt to make herself look presentable in public.

"Ah, Leia," Mon Mothma said. Her voice sounded pathetically weak, a rustle of dry leaves. "Thank you for coming. I can't keep my secret any longer. I must tell you everything."

Leia swallowed. All her indignant arguments evaporated like mist under a red giant sun. She sat down in the small padded chair next to Mon Mothma and listened.

Han had not had time to put the twins to bed before Leia returned. He had felt angry and distracted during the rest of dinner, listless at having her gone again. He had played with the twins, seeking solace in their company.

Threepio was just finishing the kids' evening ripple bath when Leia came quietly through the doors. Han had been sitting in their main living area, looking at the sentimental "Remembrances of Alderaan" framed images he had given her as a gift. Displayed prominently on a small pedestal sat the ridiculous Corellian fast-food mascot statue Leia had bought for him, thinking it a gaudy but important piece of sculpture from Han's homeworld.

When Leia entered, he sat up quickly, brushing his hair with his fingers. But she turned her back to him and worked the door controls, saying nothing. Leia seemed smaller and drawn into herself. She moved with extreme slowness and caution, as if everything might break at any sudden motion.

Han said, "I didn't expect you back until late. Did Mon Mothma let you off the hook?"

When she turned to him, he saw that her eyes shimmered with bright flecks of light from restrained tears. The skin around her eyes looked puffy, and her mouth was drawn.

"What is it?" Han said. "What does Mon Mothma want you to do this time? If it's too much, I'll go tell her off myself. You should—"

"She's *dying*," Leia said.

Han stopped short, feeling his arguments pop like fragile soap bubbles. His mind whirled. Before he could ask again, Leia began to spill her story.

"She has some sort of mysterious wasting disease. The medic droids can't pinpoint it. They've never seen anything like it, and it's pulling her down fast. It's almost as if something is taking her apart genetically from the inside.

"Remember the four days when she supposedly went to a secret conference on Cloud City? She didn't go anywhere. There was no conference. She spent the time in a bacta tank in a last-ditch effort to be healed—but even though the bacta tank completely purged her system, it could do nothing to help. Her body is falling apart. At the rate the disease is taking over, she could be . . . she could be dead in less than a month."

Han swallowed, thinking of the strong woman who had founded the New Republic, led the political side of the Rebel Alliance. "So that's why she's been delegating so many of her responsibilities," Han said. "Why you've had to take over more and more."

"Yes, she's trying to keep up appearances in public—but you should see her, Han! She looks like she can barely stand. She can't keep up the charade much longer."

"So . . ." Han began, not knowing what else to suggest or what he could say. "What does this mean? What do you have to do?"

Leia bit her lip and seemed to dredge up strength inside herself. She came forward and hugged him. He held her close.

"With Mon Mothma weakening," she said, "and Admiral Ackbar in exile, the moderate side of the Council will be gone. I can't let the New Republic turn into an aggressor government. We have already suffered too much. Now is the time for us to strengthen our ties, to make the New Republic firm through political alliances, with planetary systems joining with us—not to go blasting leftover Imperial strongholds in this sector of the galaxy."

"Let me guess who wants to do that," Han said, thinking of a number of the old generals who had reveled in their days of glory during the major battles of the Rebellion.

"I have to bring Ackbar back," she said, looking up to meet Han's eyes. Her face was pale and as beautiful as he had ever seen it. He remembered her staring at him on Cloud City just before Darth Vader had plunged him into the carbon-freeze chamber. Han had spent months locked in a frozen non-existence with only her words "I love you" ringing in his mind.

He tried not to let his disappointment show. "So you're going off to the planet Calamari?"

She nodded, but kept her face pressed against his chest. "I have to, Han. We can't let Ackbar hide at a time like this. He can't keep blaming himself for an accident. He's needed here."

Threepio interrupted them as he walked into the main room. "Oh," he said, startled. "Greetings, Mistress Leia! Welcome home." Runnels of splashed bathwater trickled down his shiny form and dripped onto the soft floor. He held two fluffy white towels draped over his arms. In the back hall two naked children giggled and ran to their bedroom.

"The twins are ready for their evening tale," Threepio said. "Would you like me to select one, sir?"

Han shook his head. "No, they always cry when you choose." He looked at Leia. "Come on, you can listen too. I'll tell them a bedtime story."

With the twins snuggled in their pajamas under warm blankets, Han sat between their small beds. Leia sat in another chair, looking longingly at her children.

"Which story do you want tonight, kids?" Han said. He held a story platform in front of him that would display words and animated pictures.

"I get to pick," Jaina said.

"I want to pick," Jacen said.

"You picked last night, Jaina. It's your brother's turn."

"I want *The Little Lost Bantha Cub*," Jaina said.

"My pick!" Jacen insisted. "*Little Lost Bantha Cub*."

Han smiled. "Big surprise," he muttered. Leia saw that he had already called up the story on the board before the twins made their decision.

He began to read. "After the sandstorm that drove him from home, the little lost bantha cub wandered alone.

"So he walked, and he walked through the desert heat till noon, when he found a Jawa sandcrawler upon a sandy dune.

" 'I am *lost*,' said the bantha cub, 'Please help me find my herd,' but the little Jawas shook their heads and gave their final word."

The twins leaned forward to watch the accompanying images activated by Han's voice and the scrolling words. Though they had heard the story a dozen times already, they still seemed disappointed when the Jawas refused to help.

"So he walked, and he walked till he met a shiny droid. After walking by himself so long, the cub was overjoyed.

" 'I am *lost*,' said the bantha cub, 'Please help me find my herd.' 'I am not programmed to help you,' said the droid, 'Don't be absurd.'

"The droid kept walking straight ahead, not looking left or right; the bantha cub just watched until the droid was out of sight."

Leia listened as the little bantha cub's adventures continued in an encounter with a moisture farmer, and finally a huge krayt dragon. The twins sat wide-eyed with suspense.

" 'I will eat you,' purred the dragon, then he lunged with snapping jaws! So the bantha cub began to run without the slightest pause."

Jacen and Jaina were delighted when the bantha cub finally found a tribe of Sand People, who reunited him with his parents and his herd. Leia shook her head, marveling at the fascination the children showed.

After Han finished telling the story and switched off the platter in his hands, he and Leia each gave the twins a good-night kiss and tucked them in before quietly walking out to the hall.

"I wish you would let me embellish your tale with sound effects," Threepio said, walking beside them. "It would be so much more realistic and enjoyable for the children."

"No," Han said, "you'll give them nightmares."

"Indeed!" Threepio said in a huff, then moved to the kitchen area.

Leia smiled and held Han's arm, hugging him. She kissed him on the cheek. "You're a good daddy, Han."

He blushed, but didn't disagree with her.

14

Small, but infinitely deadly, the Sun Crusher superweapon entered orbit around the gas giant of Yavin, flying side by side with the armored New Republic transport.

Sitting in the streamlined pilot's seat, young Kyp Durron felt the Sun Crusher's advanced controls respond to his fingertips. He stared through the segmented viewport at the eddying orange planet below, a waiting bottomless pit where the Sun Crusher would be buried forever.

"Ready to send her down, Kyp?" the voice of Wedge Antilles crackled across the comm unit. "Straight-line plunge."

Kyp fingered the controls, feeling a chill of reluctance. The Sun Crusher was such a perfect weapon, well designed, able to withstand any onslaught. Kyp felt a strange attachment to the splinter-shaped craft that had brought him and Han Solo to freedom. But he also knew that Qwi Xux was right in that the temptation to use such power would eventually corrupt anyone. Qwi kept the knowledge in her head, vowing to share it with no one. But the functional superweapon itself had to be taken out of everyone's grasp.

He adjusted the sublight course vectors. "I'm setting the nav systems now," he said. "Prepare to dock."

Kyp programmed a set of coordinates that would fire the Sun Crusher's maneuvering jets and send the small ship down in a sharp ellipse to bury it in the turbulent clouds and the high-pressure core below.

"We're ready for transfer," Wedge said.

"Just a minute," Kyp answered. He locked down the controls and caressed the deceptively simple panel one last time. The New Republic scientists and engineers had not been able to understand the machinery inside. They had not known how to deactivate the resonance torpedoes that would spark supernova explosions. Qwi Xux had refused to help them . . . and now the Sun Crusher would be gone forever.

Qwi's birdlike voice interrupted his thoughts over the comm channel. "Make certain all power systems are shut down," she said, "and seal the containment field."

Kyp flicked a row of switches. "Already done." He heard the muffled thump of hull against hull as Wedge brought the armored transport against the Sun Crusher.

"Magnetic fields in place, Kyp," Wedge said. "Open the hatch and come on over."

"Setting the timer," Kyp said. He activated the autopilot, dimmed the lights in the cockpit, and clambered toward the small hatch. He opened it and met Wedge's waiting arms as the smiling dark-haired man helped Kyp into the transport.

They sealed the Sun Crusher behind them, then disengaged the docking connection. Wedge moved back to the pilot's seat of the armored transport and flopped into the cockpit chair beside the wispy-looking Qwi Xux.

Qwi sat strapped in with crash restraints. Her pale-blue skin looked splotchy, and she was obviously filled with anxiety. Wedge nudged the attitude-control thrusters and swung the armored transport around so they could watch. The elongated crystal shape of the Sun Crusher increased its distance, drifting closer to the gravitational jaws of Yavin.

Kyp hunkered between Wedge and Qwi, watching through the viewport as the Sun Crusher followed its preprogrammed course. Kyp could see the torus-shaped resonance-field generator at the bottom of the ship's long spike.

The Sun Crusher dwindled to a mere speck that approached the chaotic storms of Yavin. He breathed a sigh of relief to know that this weapon would never be used to destroy any star system.

Qwi sat thin-lipped, silent, intense. Wedge reached over to pat her arm, and she jumped.

Kyp continued to concentrate on the Sun Crusher, watching the speck. He was afraid to look away because he might lose the ship against the titanic field of orange-colored clouds.

He saw the shape plunge into the upper atmosphere, plowing down on its unalterable course toward the planetary core. He imagined the Sun Crusher streaking deeper and deeper into the dense atmosphere. Scorching heat generated by atmospheric friction would throw off ripples and sonic booms as the Sun Crusher went down, down to the gas giant's diamond-thick core.

"Well," Wedge said, sounding cheerful, "we never have to worry about that thing again."

Qwi's elfin face seemed to be a catalog of contradictory expressions. She fluttered the lashes of her indigo eyes.

"It's for the best," Kyp agreed, mumbling his words.

Wedge ignited the thrusters of the armored transport and arced them away from close orbit to the fringes of the system of moons. "Well, Qwi and I are due to go inspect the reparation work on Vortex. Still want to go down to the jungle moon, Kyp?" Wedge said.

Kyp nodded, somewhat uneasy but eager to begin a new phase of his life. "Yes," he answered quietly; then drawing a deep breath, he said, "Yes!" to show his enthusiasm. "Master Skywalker is waiting for me."

Wedge turned back to the craft's controls, arrowing for the tiny emerald circle that was the fourth moon of Yavin. He flashed a grin. "Well then, Kyp, may the Force be with you."

Followed by his group of students, Luke Skywalker emerged from the great Massassi temple to watch the arrival of the transport and their new Jedi student.

Luke had told them all of Kyp's coming. They had responded with measured enthusiasm, glad to have another trainee among their number, yet tempered by the clinging memory of Gantoris's dark and fiery death.

A rectangular ship emblazoned with the scooped blue sign of the New Republic approached through the hazy skies. Its tracking lights flickered on, and broad landing struts extended.

Artoo trundled to the side of the landing grid in front of the Great Temple. Luke approached where the ship was about to set down. Blasts of repulsorlift jets fluttered his hood and ruffled his hair. Luke stared at the ship, blinking grit from his eyes until the transport came to rest.

The boarding ramp extended, and Wedge Antilles stepped out, reaching behind him to help the bluish female scientist descend.

Luke raised his left hand in greeting and turned his attention to the young man emerging from the craft. Kyp Durron was a wiry eighteen-year-old full of energy and eagerness, toughened from years of labor in the spice mines of Kessel.

In the mines Kyp had received a small initiation into the Force through another prisoner there, the fallen Jedi woman Vima-Da-Boda. Kyp had instinctively used those skills to help Han and Chewbacca escape from Kessel and from the Maw Installation. When Luke had tested the young man for Jedi potential, the strength of Kyp's response had thrown Luke backward.

Luke had been waiting for a student like this to come to his academy.

Kyp stepped down the landing platform, averting his eyes at first; but then he paused and looked up to stare into Luke's eyes. Luke saw an intelligence, a quick wit, and a quick temper, survival instincts born from years of struggle— but he also saw unshakable determination. That was the most important factor in a Jedi trainee.

"Welcome, Kyp Durron," Luke said.

"I'm ready, Master Skywalker," Kyp answered. "Teach me the Jedi ways."

15

Staring out the observation window of the orbiting station, Leia thought the Calamarian shipyards looked even more impressive than their reputation had led her to expect.

The starship-construction facilities rode high above the mottled blue planet. Supply platforms sprawled in three dimensions, dotted with winking red, yellow, and green lights that indicated landing pads and docking bays. Small girder impellers pushed huge mounds of plasteel extruded from transorbital rubble shipments from the planet's single moon; the girders would be used in the frameworks of the famous Mon Calamari star cruisers. Crablike constructor pods flitted in and around a tremendous spacedock hangar like tiny insects against the mammoth form of a half-built cruiser.

"Excuse me, Minister Organa Solo?"

Leia turned to see a small Calamarian female wearing pale-blue ambassadorial robes. While the males had bulbous and lumpy heads, the females were more streamlined, with olive-colored mottling over the pale salmon of their hides.

"I am Cilghal." When the Calamarian female raised both of her hands, Leia noticed that the webbing between her spatulate fingers seemed more translucent than Ackbar's.

Leia raised her own hand in acknowledgment. "Thank you for meeting me, Ambassador. I appreciate your help."

Cilghal's mottling darkened in a reaction that Leia recognized as humor or amusement. "You humans have called the Mon Calamari the 'soul of the Rebellion.' After such a compliment, how can we turn down any request for help?"

The ambassador stepped forward to gesture out at the bustling spacedock facility. "I see you have been observing our work on the *Startide*. It will be our first addition to the New Republic fleet in many months. We have been devoting most of our resources to recovering from last year's attack by the Emperor's World Devastators."

Leia nodded, looking again at the splotchy organic shape of the Mon Calamari star cruiser, the New Republic's equivalent of the Imperial Star Destroyer. The ovoid battleship had lumpy protrusions for gun emplacements, field generators, viewports, and staterooms placed at seemingly random intervals. Each star cruiser was unique, modeled after the same basic design, yet altered to meet individual criteria that Leia didn't quite understand.

"All the drive units are installed," Cilghal continued, "and the hull is almost complete. We tested the sublight engines just yesterday, hauling the whole spacedock facility once around the planet. It will take another two months to complete the inner bulkheads, staterooms, and crew quarters."

Leia tore her gaze from the activity and nodded at the ambassador. "As always, I'm astonished at the resourcefulness and dedication of the Calamarians. You have given so much after your enslavement by the Empire, after the attacks you've suffered. I feel reluctant to ask for further help—but I desperately need to speak with Admiral Ackbar."

Cilghal straightened her sky-blue robes. "We have respected Ackbar's request for privacy and his need for contemplation after the tragedy on Vortex, but our people remain proud of him and support him entirely. If you wish to bring further charges against—"

"No, no!" Leia said. "I'm one of his greatest supporters. But circumstances have changed since he exiled himself here." Leia swallowed and decided that she would get further if she trusted Cilghal. "I've come to beg him to return."

Cilghal flushed with an olive tinge. She moved quickly, gliding across the floor of the orbital station. "In that case, a shuttle is ready to take you down."

Leia gripped the widely spaced arms of the passenger seat as Cilghal maneuvered the egg-shaped shuttle through sleeting rain and knotted gray storm clouds.

Whitecaps stippled the dull surface of Calamari's deep oceans. Cilghal swung the shuttle lower, seemingly unconcerned with the storm winds. She held her splayed hands over the controls and bent to the viewing panels. The high-resolution viewing instruments had been designed for wide-set Calamarian eyes, and the blunt controls were adapted for the digits of the aquatic people.

Cilghal maneuvered the shuttle like a streamlined fish through water. The vessel curved away from small marshy islands—sparse dots of habitable land where the amphibious Calamarians had first established their civilization. Narrow rivulets of rainwater trickled down the passenger window as Cilghal turned broadside to the wind.

The Calamarian ambassador nudged one of the bulbous control knobs and spoke into an invisible voice pickup. "Foamwander City, this is shuttle SQ/one. Please provide a weather update and an approach vector." Cilghal's voice sounded smooth and soft, as if she hadn't needed to shout in her entire life.

A guttural male voice came over the speaker. "Ambassador Cilghal, we are transmitting your approach vector. We are currently experiencing rising winds that are well within seasonal norms. No difficulties expected, but we are issuing an advisory against topside travel for the afternoon."

"Acknowledged," Cilghal said. "We were planning on making the rest of our journey underwater. Thank you." She signed off, then turned back to Leia. "Don't worry, Minister. I can sense your anxiety, but I assure you, there is nothing to be concerned about."

Leia sat up, trying to quell her nervousness until she put her finger on its cause. "I don't doubt you, Ambassador, it's just that . . . the last time I flew in a storm was on Vortex."

Cilghal nodded somberly. "I understand." Leia sensed Cilghal's sincerity, and the look on her fishlike face was comforting. "We'll be safely landed in a few minutes."

Through the mists and the whipping spray Leia watched them approach a metal island. Lumpy, but smoothed, like an organic coral reef, Foamwander City rose in a hemisphere out of the whitecaps. A forest of reinforced watchtowers and communications antennas rose from the top of the city, but the rest of the drifting metropolis had soft angles and polished outcroppings like a Mon Calamari star cruiser.

The bright lights of thousands of above-surface windows shed jewels of light even through the whipping rain. Below the hemispherical dome Leia knew that the floating cities had underwater towers and descending complexes like the mirror image of a Coruscant skyline. The inverted skyscrapers of dwelling units and water-processing stations beneath the hemisphere made the city look like a mechanical jellyfish.

Starved for raw materials on their marshy islands, the Mon Calamari had not been able to build a civilization until they joined forces with another intelligent species that lived beneath the oceans. The Quarren, a humanoid race with helmet-shaped heads and faces that looked like a fistful of tentacles sprouting beneath close-set eyes, had excavated metallic ores from the ocean crust. Working with the Calamarians, they built dozens of floating cities. Though the Quarren could also breathe air, they chose to remain under the sea while the Calamarians designed starships to explore the bright "islands in space."

Cilghal approached the lumpy hemisphere of Foamwander City, circling to the leeward side, where the bulk of the metropolis protected them from buffeting winds. Whitecaps broke against the dull gray of the city's outer shell, sending arcs of droplets high like a handful of diamonds.

"Open wave doors," Cilghal said into the voice pickup. She aimed the shuttle toward a line of bright lights that guided the ship in. Before Leia could detect the seam, heavy doors split open diagonally like a crooked mouth.

Without slowing, Cilghal shot the vessel into a smooth tunnel, well lit by green illumination strips. Behind them the wave doors closed, sealing the metropolis against the onslaught of the storm.

Leia felt herself swept along as the ambassador moved with a liquid grace, calmly but relentlessly, to the underwater sections of the floating city. Cilghal set a steady, rapid pace that helped Leia hurry but caused no alarm. This was no simple diplomatic mission.

As Leia strode through the curved colorful halls of the upper levels, she was reminded of the corkscrewing chambers inside a gigantic shell. She saw no sharp corners, only rounded edges and smooth, polished decorations made of coral and mother-of-pearl. Even inside the enclosed city, the air had a salty tang, but it was not unpleasant.

"Do you know where Ackbar is?" Leia finally asked.

"Not exactly," the ambassador said. "We allowed him his privacy and did not follow him." Cilghal touched Leia's shoulder with a broad fin-hand. "But do not be concerned. The Calamarians have sources of information that the Empire never suspected. Even during the occupation we were able to keep our collective knowledge intact. We will find Ackbar."

Leia followed Cilghal into a turbolift that plunged down into the deep underwater levels of the floating city. When they emerged, the quality of the corridors had changed. The lighting was dimmer and shimmering, a jewel-blue reflected through faceted glowlamps and thick transparisteel windows that looked out into the ocean depths.

Leia could see divers swimming among the tangle of nets and mooring lines, satellite cages, and small submersible vehicles moving about the inverted towers of the city. The air was thicker and damper. The people in these levels were primarily Quarren, moving about their business, not acknowledging the presence of the visitors.

Though the Quarren and the Calamarians had allied themselves to build this civilization, Leia knew that the two communities did not work together without friction. The Calamarians insisted on their dreams to reach the stars, while the Quarren wished to return to the oceans. Rumors suggested that the Quarren had betrayed their planet to the Empire, but that they had then been treated just as badly under Imperial occupation as the Calamarians.

Cilghal stopped and spoke to a Quarren who stood by a valve-control station. The Quarren looked up at the interruption, flashing dark eyes at Leia, then at Cilghal. The Calamarian ambassador spoke in a high-pitched bubbly language, and the Quarren answered abruptly in kind. He gestured to the left down a steep ramp that corkscrewed to the lower level.

Cilghal nodded her thanks, undisturbed by the Quarren's attitude as she led Leia down the ramp. They emerged into an open equipment bay that had been pressurized to allow easy access to the water.

Five Calamarian males worked on a small submersible hoisted on a tractor beam; they moved together to unload dripping crates from a seatree cargo hold. Quarren, dressed in sleek, flat-black suits that seemed covered with minute scales, dived through access fields into the watery depths. The walls of the equipment bay flickered as traces of dim light wandered up and down the polished surfaces, creating a hypnotic bath of dark green and deep blue.

Cilghal went to a row of small porcelain compartments and opened one. Before she could reach inside, two Quarren workers rushed over, speaking quickly and harshly in their bubbling language. Leia smelled a new, sour scent rising from them.

Cilghal bowed in apology, then moved to a different set of compartments, opening them with more caution. Leia followed, trying to make herself small. She realized she was the only non-native in the entire chamber. The Quarren stared at her, though the Calamarians took no notice.

Cilghal removed a pair of the slithery suits worn by the diving Quarren, handing one to Leia. Leia ran her fingers over the fabric. It seemed alive, clinging and slippery at the same time; the tiny mesh expanded and contracted as if seeking an appropriate shape to best serve the wearer.

Cilghal indicated a narrow closet-sized door. "Our changing compartments are a bit cramped, I'm afraid."

Leia stepped inside, sealing the door behind her as blue-green illumination intensified in the small chamber. She disrobed and slid into the black suit, feeling her skin tingle as the fabric shifted and adjusted, trying to conform. When the crawly sensations stopped, it was the most comfortable garment she had ever worn—warm yet cool, light yet insulating, fuzzy yet slick.

When Leia emerged, Cilghal stood outside the door already wearing her water garment. Without speaking Cilghal fitted a water jetpack over Leia's shoulders, then rigged a crude net for her long hair. Looking at the smooth salmon-and-olive dome of Cilghal's head and the fleshy scalps of the Quarren, Leia said, "I don't suppose you have much need for hair nets around here."

Cilghal made a sound that Leia suspected might be a laugh, and led her over to one of the access fields. Beside a round opening that shimmered with faint static as it held the Calamarian ocean back, Cilghal dipped her broad hands into a bubbling urn. She pulled out a floppy translucent sheet and held it up. Water streamed off its surface, fizzing with tiny bubbles.

"Humans sometimes find this unpleasant," Cilghal said. "I apologize." Without further warning she slapped the gelatinous mass across Leia's mouth and nose. The membrane was cold and wet, clinging to her cheeks, her skin. Leia stiffened in alarm and tried to struggle, but the strange soft gel stuck fast to her face.

"Relax, and you can breathe," Cilghal said. "This symbiote filters oxygen from the sea. It can last for weeks under water."

Starved for air, Leia tried to suck in a deep breath and found that she could indeed inhale clean, ozone-smelling air. Pure oxygen filled her lungs, and as she breathed slowly out, the bubbles percolated back through the symbiote membrane.

Cilghal applied one of the symbiotes to her own angular face and then poked a tiny microphone unit into the soft jelly before adjusting another in her ear hole.

She handed Leia a pair of the small devices. The microphone slid into the gelatinous membrane, but the symbiote held it firmly. When she put the second jack into her ear, Cilghal's voice came through clearly.

"You must take care to articulate your words," Cilghal said, "but this system is quite satisfactory."

Without another word Cilghal took Leia's arm. She could feel the ambassador's grip, every detail of her webbed hands transmitted through the remarkable mesh of the slick suit. Together, they plunged through the containment field and into the deep oceans of Calamari.

As they jetted through the water, Leia felt warm currents on her forehead and around her eyes. The symbiote fed her a steady supply of air, and the fine mesh suit kept her warm and dry and comfortable. Some of her hair broke free of the makeshift netting, and thick strands flipped and flailed around her head as she cruised along.

Behind them, the glittering inverted metropolis of Foamwander City drifted like a huge undersea creature with thousands of tiny figures swimming around it. On the sea floor Leia could see dull orange glows and domed cities, sites of Quarren deep-mining operations in the ocean crust. Above, the light turned milky as it filtered through waves churned by the pelting storm.

Cilghal spoke little, though the radio pickup worked quite well. They left the floating city far behind, and Leia began to feel uneasy at being so far from civilization.

Leia remained close beside Cilghal as their jetpacks bubbled and streamed. Eventually, Cilghal gestured toward a crevasse broken into the ocean crust, surrounded by lumps of coral and waving fronds of red and brown seaweed. "We are going to the Calamarian knowledge bank," Cilghal said through the tiny voice pickup.

They cruised between zigzags of rock overgrown with slow sculptures of coral and hair-fine tendrils of deep plants. The water streamed faster as the rock walls channeled stray currents. Above and around them fleets of bright-colored fish skimmed about, fed upon by larger fish that snapped, swallowed, and returned to feed again.

Leia looked ahead and saw a haphazard bed of shells, polished hulking mollusks a meter across. A faint lustrous glow seemed to come from the shells themselves.

Cilghal unexpectedly switched off her jetpack, and Leia shot past her before managing to stop her own thrusters. Cilghal kicked her broad feet to push herself toward the bottom with long gliding motions.

Leia struggled to keep up as they approached the enormous mollusks. Slowly kicking her feet to maintain her position against the current, Cilghal spread her arms wide as she bent over the largest of the humped shells at the front of the large bed. She hummed, a strange noise that vibrated through the water as much as it moved through the pickup circuit in Leia's ear.

"We have questions," Cilghal said, speaking to the giant shells. "We require access to the knowledge stored here in the great collection of memories. We must know if you have the answers we seek."

The top shell of the largest mollusk groaned open. The crack between its bivalve shells widened until a stream of golden illumination shone out, as if precious sunlight had been captured and held inside the impenetrable shell walls.

Leia couldn't say anything in her astonishment. As the shell cracked open even wider, she saw the soft fleshy mass inside, swirled and curved—not just the meaty lump of a shellfish, but the contours of a brain, an enormous brain that pulsed and shone with yellow light.

A sluggish pulsing sound drummed at Leia's ears through the water, and Cilghal turned to her. "They will answer," she said.

As Leia watched, row upon row of the giant shells opened, shedding rays of warm light into the narrow crevasse and exposing the swirled lumps of other large brains.

"They sit," Cilghal said. "They wait. They listen. They know everything that happens on this planet—and they never forget."

Cilghal began a long, ritualistic communion with the mollusk knowledge bank in a slow hypnotic language. Leia floated in place and watched, mystified and anxious.

Finally Cilghal swam backward, brushing her flipper-hands back and forth as she drifted away. The thick mollusks closed their shells, sealing the golden light away from the shadows of the canyon.

Leia had trouble seeing in the suddenly restored dimness of the depths, but the ambassador's words came crisply through the ear jack. "They have told me where to find him."

Leia could detect no emotion in Cilghal's even voice, but she felt her own thrill of elation.

As they turned to swim upward, Leia stared toward the lip of the crevasse. She froze as she saw a deadly sleek form like an Imperial attack ship above— an enormous living creature with a long bullet-shaped body, spined fins, a mouth filled with fangs. On either side of the mouth streamed whipping tentacles, each tipped with razor-jawed pincers.

Leia began to swim frantically backward. Cilghal grabbed her shoulder and pulled her down. "Krakana," she said.

The monster seemed to notice the bubbles caused by Leia's struggle. A stream of fizz came from the symbiote on Leia's mouth as she panted with terror, but Cilghal held her in a firm grip.

"Will it attack us?" Leia said into the voice pickup.

"If it senses us," Cilghal said. "The krakana will eat anything."

"Then what—" Leia said.

"It won't find us." Cilghal sounded altogether too calm. Fish swam frantically away from the torpedo shape of the predator. Cilghal seemed to be concentrating.

"No, it will get that one," she gestured with one large hand, "the blue-and-yellow-striped kieler. After that it will take that smaller orange one in the middle of the school. By then all the others will have fled, and the krakana will continue on its way. Then we can leave."

"How do you know that?" Leia said, gripping the rough-edged lump of coral on the side of the chasm.

"I know," Cilghal said. "It's a little trick I have."

Leia watched in horrified fascination as the krakana streaked forward, coming unexpectedly from below as it reached out with its mass of tentacles to grab the blue-and-yellow kieler and rip it to ragged shreds before stuffing its fang-filled mouth.

By the time the monster had grabbed the pale-orange fish, the rest of the school had vanished to hidden corners of the crevasse or fled into the broad expanse of the ocean. The krakana slid away as it cruised the depths, constantly in search of a meal.

Leia stared at Cilghal, amazed at her prescient ability, but the Calamarian ambassador squeezed Leia's upper arm before igniting her water jetpack.

"Now we must go find Ackbar," she said.

16

Leia and Cilghal swam closer to the choppy surface after hours of gliding beneath the waves. Around them leathery seatrees veined with iridescent blue and red swirled in the churning current, stirred by the continuing storm.

The seatree fronds formed a tangled forest around them, filled with thousands of strangely shaped blob-fish, crustaceans, and tentacled things; most were small, but others cast large shadows as they drifted among the fronds, feeding on the air-filled fruit bladders that kept the dense weed afloat.

"When Ackbar was younger, he had a small dwelling here in the wild seatree thickets," Cilghal said. "The fish noticed his return, and though they have short memories, they passed the word from creature to creature until it reached the mollusk knowledge bank."

Leia's arms and legs ached as she continued the long swim, though the wonderful clinging mesh suit seemed to revitalize her muscles. "All I want is to talk to him."

Ahead she saw a spherical dwelling made of plasteel covered with algae and draping weed that had grown up from the spray clinging to its hull. Large valves of water-recirculation equipment, desalination devices, and round viewports dotted the open spaces on the curved walls; a bare deck looked clean and bright, as if recently scrubbed. A white utility submersible, ovoid with a mass of articulated working arms, had been lashed to the side of the deck.

Leia treaded water on the surface in the pelting rain and the whipping wind, still breathing through the symbiote. Cilghal tugged her arm, motioning for her to go down. "The entrance will be below," she said.

They stroked down through the water. Thick seatree trunks anchored the dwelling module in place, rocking it from side to side. Traps and nets dangled beneath the water; some held tiny green fish that could easily swim through the open mesh. From inside, shafts of illumination struck down into the depths like watery spears.

On the bottom of the hull they found an opening like a wide mouth. Cilghal went first through the containment field, and Leia followed, brushing her shoulders against the metal lip. When her head plunged through into the dim interior, she stripped off the symbiote, shook herself, and looked into Ackbar's cluttered home.

He stood up in alarm from a bench made of pitted flowstone, speechless as Cilghal and Leia eased themselves out of the water. Leia dripped for a moment, until the wondrous mesh suit absorbed and dissipated the water in its microthin layers.

Leia sighed with relief to see Ackbar, but she sensed his sudden discomfort at her presence—and something more. All her well-rehearsed speeches drained away like so much seawater splashing to the floor. They stood silently staring at each other for a long moment. Finally Leia recovered enough to speak. "Admiral Ackbar, I'm glad we've found you."

"Leia," Ackbar said. He held his hands in front of him, then withdrew them as if completely at a loss. He turned to Cilghal. "Ambassador, I believe we have met twice before?"

"It was an honor both times, Admiral," Cilghal said.

"Please," he said, "just call me Ackbar. I no longer hold that rank."

His dwelling was like a large, solid bubble with extruded knobs for sitting, pedestals for tables, and cubbyholes for storage. Possessions lay strewn about, though the back of the room was neatly organized, cleaned, polished, as if he had methodically begun repairing and organizing the chaos one square meter at a time.

Ackbar gestured toward the warmly lit galley area where delicious-smelling food bubbled over a heater. "Would you join me? I would not insult a potential Jedi by asking how you found me—but I would like to know what has brought you all the way from Coruscant."

Later they sat finishing bowls of simple but delicious fish stew. Leia chewed on the tender meat, swallowed another mouthful, and licked her lips to taste the burning sweet tingle of Calamarian spices.

She had spent the meal trying to work up her courage, but Ackbar finally addressed the question himself. "Leia, you have not yet said why you are here."

Leia drew a deep breath, then sat up straight. "To speak with you, Admira—ah—Ackbar. And to ask you the same question. Why are *you* here?"

Ackbar seemed to deliberately misunderstand her. "This is my home."

Frustrated, Leia was not ready to give up yet. "I know this is your homeworld, but there are many others who need you. The New Republic—"

Ackbar stood and turned away, gathering the empty stew bowls. "My own people also need me. There has been much destruction. Many deaths . . ." Leia wondered if he referred to the Imperial attacks on Calamari, or his own crash at the Cathedral of Winds.

"Mon Mothma is dying," Leia said abruptly before she could change her mind. Cilghal sat up in the most sudden reaction Leia had yet seen from the calm ambassador.

Ackbar heaved his weary eyes to look at her. He set the stew bowls down. "How can you be certain of this?"

"It's a wasting disease that's tearing her apart," Leia answered. "The medical droids and the experts can't find anything wrong with her. She looks bad. You saw her before you left us. Mon Mothma was covering the worst with extensive makeup to hide how ill she really is.

"We need you back, Admiral." Leia used his rank on purpose. She leaned on Ackbar's small table and stared at him, her dark eyes pleading.

"I'm sorry, Leia," Ackbar said, shaking his head. He indicated the newly refurbished workroom and his equipment. "I have important work to do here. My planet was badly damaged during the Imperial attacks, and there have been many tectonic disturbances. I've taken it upon myself to find out if our planet's crust has become unstable. I need to gather more data. My people could be in danger. No more lives will be lost because of me."

Cilghal turned her head from side to side, watching the debate but saying nothing.

"Admiral, you can't just let the New Republic fall apart because of your guilty conscience," Leia said. "Many lives across the galaxy are at stake."

But Ackbar moved about uneasily, as if trying to shut out Leia's words. "There is so much work to do, I cannot delay another moment. I was just preparing to set some new seismic sensors." He shuffled toward a shelf filled with packaged electronic equipment. "Please, leave me in peace."

Leia stood up quickly. "We'll help you set out your sensors, Admiral."

Ackbar hesitated, as if lonely but afraid to have their company. He turned to meet Leia's eyes, then Cilghal's. "Yes, I would be honored to have your assistance. My submersible can carry the three of us." He blinked his large, sad eyes. "I enjoy your company—even though your requests are most difficult."

Strapped into one of the seats in the cramped utility sub, Leia watched as water sloshed around the upper ports. The sea swallowed the craft, and they descended into the isolated seatree forest until the ocean around them looked like panels of dark-green smoked glass. Leia watched in awe as Ackbar picked a course through thick ropy strands and wide pillars.

Underwater, the seaflowers blossomed in shimmering reds and blues to attract darting creatures that flitted in and out of the fronds. As one of the small fish came too close to a brilliant flower, the petals suddenly contracted like a fist, snatching its prey and swallowing it whole.

"I have only begun deploying my seismic network," Ackbar said, as if to divert the conversation. "I've set up the baseline grid beneath my dwelling, but I need to extend into the seatree forest to get higher-resolution soundings."

Cilghal said, "I am pleased with the important work you are doing for our planet, Admiral." Leia was amused at how the ambassador continued— whether consciously or unconsciously—to use his military title.

"It is necessary to do important things with your life," Ackbar said, then said no more, walling himself off with silence. Behind them, stowed seismic equipment rattled beside the empty nets and sea-harvest baskets.

Leia cleared her throat and spoke, keeping her voice gentle. "Ackbar . . . I understand how you must feel. I was there too, remember?"

"You are kind, Leia. But you do *not* understand how I feel. Were you piloting the B-wing that crashed? Are you responsible for hundreds of deaths?" He shook his head sadly. "Do you hear their voices in your dreams each night, calling out to you?"

Ackbar switched on the sub's depth lights, and a bright cone-shaped beam sliced through the water. The funnel of illumination glanced off colorful fish and strips of seaweed.

Leia spoke more from intuition than from knowledge. "You can't hide on Calamari forever."

Ackbar still would not look at her. "I am not hiding. I have my work. Important work."

They drifted toward the silty ocean bottom near one of the gnarled seatree boles. Rounded hummocks of dark rock thrust out from the milky sand. A coating of algae smoothed every surface, making the sea floor appear soft and soothing. Ackbar hunched forward to stare through the murk, searching for a stable place to implant another seismic sensor.

"Important work, perhaps," Leia said, "but not *your* work. Many Calamarians would gladly help with that research, Admiral. Are you equipped to handle such a task by yourself? Remember that old proverb you used to quote when I complained about all those senseless Council meetings? 'Many eyes see what one alone cannot.' Wouldn't it be best to share your concerns with a team of specialists?"

Cilghal interrupted, leaning forward to indicate some curved half-buried sections of metal, like the ribbed shell of some sort of escape pod. "What's that?"

The edges had corroded, and tracings of algae grew in the protected crevices. "Perhaps a wrecked ship," Ackbar said.

Cilghal nodded. "We fought back when the Imperials tried to enslave us. Many of their ships lie beneath our waters."

Ackbar inserted his hands into the waldo control gloves for the automated metallic claws that extended from the front of the small sub. The sharp jerky motions reminded Leia of the vicious krakana monster near the mollusk knowledge bank.

"If that wreckage has been stable here for years," Ackbar said, "this is a good place to deploy another set of sensors."

Watching the external metal arms, Leia saw Ackbar remove a canister from the external storage bin on the submersible. Ackbar lowered the craft until plumes of pale sand drifted up from the disturbance like a slow-motion Tatooine dust storm. The nimble robotic claws positioned the cylinder upright in the soft silt.

Reversing propellers, Ackbar lifted them away. Craning his neck so he could see better through the front viewport, Ackbar pushed the ACTIVATE button. With a vibrating thump that Leia could feel through the sub's hull, the seismic canister detonated its tiny explosive. A long rod plunged deep into the ocean floor while spraying out a web of secondary detectors symmetrically around the core like a shooting star.

"Now we'll send a test signal," Ackbar said. With a whirr he lifted the sub through the densely tangled seatree forest, moving slowly enough so the fronds could be nudged out of the way, slithering over the rounded hull.

Leia fidgeted, swallowing numerous phrases that sounded flat to her. "Admiral, you know better than anyone on this world how important it is to have the right leadership, to have everyone working toward a common goal. You helped lead a band of Rebels from a hundred different planets, turned them into a united fleet that was able to defeat the Empire, and you guided them as they formed a new government."

Ackbar let the sub drift and turned to meet her gaze. She continued rapidly, hoping to cut off any arguments. "At least come with me to Coruscant and *talk* to Mon Mothma. We've been part of the same team for many years, you and I. You won't stand by and watch the New Republic fall apart."

Ackbar sighed and gripped his controls. Seatree branches flapped against the viewing windows. "It seems you know me better than I had thought. I—"

A pinging alarm beeped from the control panel. Ackbar reacted smoothly and swiftly, slowing the sub. He peered into his widely set stereoscopic sensor displays. "This is interesting," he said.

"What is it?" Leia said.

"Another large metallic mass tangled in the weeds right above us."

"Maybe it's part of that crashed ship," Cilghal said.

"If something fell into the seatree forest, it could have been swallowed up for eternity," Ackbar said. He eased the sub ahead.

As Leia saw the outline of a large multilegged thing wrapped with seatrees and overgrown with algae, she thought it was some kind of alien life-form. Then she recognized the squashed elliptical head, the segmented body core trailing jointed mechanical arms, its nonreflective black surface.

She had seen something like this on the ice planet Hoth, when Han Solo and Chewbacca had stumbled upon the Imperial probe droid. "Admiral—" Leia said.

"I see it. Arakyd Viper Series Probot. The Empire dispatched thousands to all corners of the galaxy to hunt down Rebel bases."

"It must have landed years ago on Calamari," Cilghal said. "The wreckage we found below was its landing pod."

Ackbar nodded. "But when the probe droid tried to rise to the surface, it tangled in the seaweed. It must have shut down." He nudged the sub closer, shining his depth light on the outer surface.

But when the beam struck the probot's rounded head, its entire bank of round eyes blinked to life.

"It's been activated!" Leia said. She could hear the high-pitched vibrating hum of powerful generators as the probe droid began to move again. The head swiveled and directed its own glowing beam at the sub.

Ackbar pushed the propellers into reverse; but before the sub could move away, the probot launched out with its spiderlike claws. Mechanical arms latched on to one of the sub's rounded fins. The head of the probe droid rotated slowly, trying to bring its built-in blaster cannons to bear, but the seatree fronds tangled its joints.

Ackbar threw all the sub's power into pulling away and succeeded only in yanking the probe droid along with him, tearing it free of ancient strands of weed.

Ackbar dug his flippers into the wide gloves that controlled his sub's articulated arms. He brought up two of the segmented mechanical tools, wrestling with the probe droid's gripping black claws.

Through the speakers of the comm unit, a sudden static-filled burst of subspace gibberish blasted out from the probe droid in some kind of powerful coded signal. The long chain of data shouted toward space even as the deadly probot wrestled with Ackbar's sub.

The black droid finally succeeded in rotating its head, bending its laser cannons toward the sub.

Ackbar fired the lateral jets, wrenching them and the probe droid sideways as a volley of vicious laser blasts screamed past them, plowing a tunnel of sudden steam through the water. He tugged at the waldos and brought another of his equipment arms to bear, a small cutting laser.

Its tip heated to incandescent red-white as he slashed through the probe droid's gripping metal claw, severing the plasteel and breaking them free. Ackbar pulled the sub away and brought the cutting laser to bear again just as the probe droid turned to fire a second time.

Leia knew it was hopeless. They couldn't get away, and the cutting laser would do nothing against the far-superior weapons of the probot. And unlike Luke, she had not mastered Jedi skills enough to mount even a feeble defense. But Ackbar, still looking cool and in control, fired two blasts from the cutting laser at the head of the probe droid, attempting to blind its optical sensors. The feeble beams struck—

The probot detonated in an unexpected explosion. Bright concentric waves of light hurled the sub back, tumbling it end over end. They were thrown backward; Leia felt the chair's restraints automatically tighten around her. The shock wave rang against the hull, sending a sound like a gong through the enclosed sub. A fury of bubbles and drifting debris surged around them. Large splintered seatree trunks sank to the ocean bottom.

"The probe self-destructed!" Cilghal said. "But we didn't stand a chance against it."

Leia remembered Han's conjecture on Hoth. "The probe droids have programming to destroy themselves rather than risk letting their data fall into enemy hands."

Ackbar finally managed to stabilize the spinning submersible. Four of the mechanical arms extending from the front of the sub had been snapped off, leaving only frayed edges of broken metal and dead circuitry.

Ackbar blew one of the ballast tanks, and the sub rose toward the surface. Leia noticed three hairline cracks in the transparisteel windowport and realized how close they had come to being crushed by the shock wave.

"But the probot already sent its signal," Cilghal said. "We heard it before the self-destruct."

Leia felt a cold fist of fear close around her stomach, but Ackbar tried to dismiss the peril.

"This probe droid has been here for ten years or more, and that would have been a very old code, almost certainly obsolete," he said. "Even if the Imperials could still understand its message, who would be out there listening?"

17

With her three Imperial Star Destroyers safely hidden among the ionized islands of the Cauldron Nebula, Admiral Daala retired to her private quarters to review tactics.

She sat stiffly in a slick lounge chair, refusing to relax into the warm contours. Too much comfort made Daala distinctly uncomfortable.

The holographic image of Grand Moff Tarkin stood with her in the dim room, unchanged after all these years. The gaunt, hard man presented his recorded lectures, his communiqués. Daala had watched them dozens of times before.

In the privacy of her chambers, she allowed herself to miss the one person in the Imperial Military Academy who had seen her talent. Tarkin had raised her rank to admiral—as far as she knew, the highest rank held by any female in the Imperial armed forces.

During her years of exile in Maw Installation, Daala had often replayed Tarkin's messages, but now she studied them intently. Her eyebrows knitted together, and her bright green eyes narrowed as she concentrated on every word he spoke, searching for some indispensable advice for her private war against the Rebellion.

"Liquidating a dozen small threats is easier than rooting out one well-established center of defiance," his image said, in a speech given on Carida explaining the "Tarkin Doctrine." "Rule through the fear of force rather than through force itself. If we use our strength wisely, we shall intimidate thousands of worlds with the example of a select few."

Daala rewound the holotape to listen to his words again, thinking she had been on the verge of capturing a crucial insight. But the door chime interrupted her. She switched off the holoprojector. "Lights up."

Stocky Commander Kratas stood stiffly at her door, his uniform wrinkle free, his hands clasped behind his back. He was trying to mask a smug grin of satisfaction, but the expression displayed itself in a small facial tick and the slight upturn of his vanishingly thin lips.

"Yes, Commander, what is it?" she said.

"We have intercepted a signal," Kratas said. "It appears to be from an Imperial probe droid transmitting covert data gathered on an important Rebel planet called Calamari, the site of one of their prime starship-building facilities. We can't tell how recent the information is."

Daala raised her eyebrows and let her colorless lips form a smile. With both hands she swept her molten-metal hair behind her shoulders, feeling static electricity crackle through her fingertips, as if generated from the excitement building within her. "Are you certain this transmission is genuine? Where was it directed?"

"It was a broad-spectrum signal, Admiral. My assumption is that these probe droids were deployed in a widely scattered pattern. They would not know the location of any particular Star Destroyer when they transmitted a report."

"Could it be a hoax sent by the Rebels? A trap?"

"I don't believe so. It was heavily encoded. We almost couldn't crack it ourselves until we double-checked against one of the new codes Grand Moff Tarkin delivered on his last visit to Maw Installation."

"Excellent, Commander," she said, brushing her palms down the smooth olive-gray of her uniform slacks. "We've been looking for a new target to strike, and if this is an important starship-construction facility, that sounds like a good candidate. As good as anything, I suppose. I want you and the captains of the other two ships to meet me in the war room. Prepare the Star Destroyers for immediate departure. Recharge all turbolaser batteries. Outfit all TIE fighters.

"This time we will follow Grand Moff Tarkin's strategy to the letter." She punctuated the last phrase with an index finger jabbing the air. "Have everyone review their tapes. I want no mistakes. A flawless attack."

She dimmed the lights as she stepped into the corridor. Her two stormtrooper bodyguards fell into ranks behind her. Their boot heels clicked on the floor in perfect echoing unison.

"We are through practicing," Daala said to Kratas. "After our strike the planet Calamari will be nothing more than a rubble heap."

• • •

Leia piloted Ackbar's open-canopied wavespeeder as they rushed over the oceans of Calamari. The sky was still a congealed soup of dark clouds, but the previous day's storm had run out of energy. The wind remained fresh and cool, tossing droplets of salty spray into their faces—but Leia could not stop smiling with relief just to know that Ackbar had agreed to come to Coruscant with her, if only to speak with Mon Mothma.

She and Cilghal would take him back to Foamwander City, where he could turn over his seismic data to other Calamarian scientists. Sitting in the backseat of the wavespeeder, Ackbar seemed deeply troubled and unsure of himself.

The lumpy hemisphere of the Calamarian city looked like a gunmetal-gray island. Other small seaskimmers drifted in and out, gathering up nets and dashing back to access openings.

Ackbar sat up stiffly. "Listen!"

Over the rushing noise of the wind and waves, Leia heard the sharp tones of an all-hands alarm. She grabbed the comm unit, punching buttons for Foamwander City control. "This is wavespeeder seventeen-oh-one/seven. What is the cause of the alarm?"

Before Leia could receive an answer, a curtain of brilliant light sliced through the clouds, slashing the ocean surface near the floating city. Geysers of suddenly vaporized water plumed into the air with a *whoop*.

"Those are turbolasers!" Leia said.

Ackbar gripped the side of his seat. "We're being fired on from orbit."

"Wave doors are closing," said a maddeningly calm Calamarian voice through the speaker system. "All citizens take shelter immediately. Repeat, wave doors are closing."

Most of the other sea vehicles had disappeared inside the various openings around the hull of Foamwander City. Those who could not make it to the doors abandoned their craft and dived overboard to swim down to submerged entryways.

Many wave doors had already clamped shut like diagonal mouths. Leia aimed for one of the remaining openings and punched the wavespeeder's accelerator. The lurch pressed all three of them back against their padded seats.

Overhead, like a flock of razor-winged carrion birds, came an entire squadron of TIE fighters and TIE bombers. They swooped down in a steep descent with a roaring howl of their Twin Ion Engines.

The TIE bombers released glowing energy packets that exploded in the sea, sending out shock waves and foam and spray. TIE fighters roared over

Foamwander City, strafing with their laser cannons. Lances of green light etched smoldering damage into the city shell.

One of the shock waves tossed a wall of water at Leia's wavespeeder. She fought for control but did not slow down, keeping her eyes fixed on the closing wave doors. If they didn't make it through the gap, they would be helpless out on the water, ready targets for the Imperial bombardment.

Ackbar said, "We left a squadron of B-wing fighters to defend the orbiting shipyards. Where are they? I have to learn what's happening up there."

Cilghal maintained a quiet, steady voice. "Perhaps they are otherwise occupied."

"Hang on!" Leia said, and fired emergency thrusters.

The wavespeeder lifted another meter above the surface of the ocean as it flew in a last-ditch effort to get through the closing gap. Leia ducked as the diagonal metal wave doors ground closer and closer. . . .

The bottom layer of plasteel plating scraped off the wavespeeder as Leia struck the sharp edge of the heavy door; then they shot into the protected green-lit tunnel. With the vehicle traveling at such high speed, even that minor impact was enough to send them spinning. Leia wrestled with the controls, trying to slow the vehicle as it caromed off one wall and then the opposite wall, sending out showers of sparks. Finally it ground to a halt. Behind them, with a thunderous echo, the wave doors slammed shut.

Pausing only long enough to confirm that they were all unharmed, Leia picked her way out of the wreckage. Through the thick armor of the floating city she heard the repeated thuds of explosions from TIE bombers and the screams from firing laser cannons.

Ackbar stepped away from the wreckage and turned to Cilghal. "Take me to the control center immediately. I want to be linked with the orbital defense forces." He already looked more alive, more alert. "If I can see what's going on, maybe I can figure out a way to help us all."

"Yes, Admiral," Cilghal said. Leia wondered if she had used his rank intentionally.

Flashing lights and alarm sirens echoed as they hurried through the serpentine corridors. Groups of Quarren rushed past, burbling exclamations through their tentacled faces as they scrambled down access shafts to the underwater levels. Leia had no doubt they were abandoning the city structure, swimming down to where they thought they were safe.

When Cilghal reached a turbolift door, other Calamarians flocked to it, trying to get to the city's protected inner chambers. Cilghal raised her voice, the first time Leia had heard her do so. "Make way for Admiral Ackbar! We must get to Central Command."

"Ackbar," several Calamarians echoed, stepping aside to allow him passage. "Admiral Ackbar!"

Ackbar seemed taller now, without the haunted look he had worn since the crash on Vortex. Leia knew that all Calamarians remembered the nightmare of Imperial attacks—but if anyone could mount a successful defense with what little resources they had, it would be Ackbar.

After the turbolift spilled them out onto the proper level, Ambassador Cilghal led the way. She used her diplomatic access codes to let them into the core of Foamwander City until they finally emerged into the chaotic Central Command.

Seven Calamarian tactical experts sat at command stations, watching the battle overhead. In the center of the room a holographic wireframe diagram of the planet and its moon hovered amid sparkling pinpoints of fighters flying in defensive formation.

Leia stared in awe at the two Imperial Star Destroyers that orbited the planet side by side, firing turbolaser blasts into the oceans. Overhead, TIE squadrons continued to harass Foamwander City. External viewers showed smoldering holes where proton bombs had punctured the city's armored plating. Foamwander's defensive lasers fired upward, burning ship after ship out of the sky—but more attackers kept coming down.

Reeling with shock, the city commander turned from his post and noticed them for the first time. "Admiral Ackbar! Please, sir, help us with our defense. I cede my position."

"Give me a tactical update," Ackbar said, stepping to the holographic projection.

"Cilghal," Leia said, raising her voice over the hubbub, "get me to the comm system. I can use my priority codes to send for New Republic military assistance. On a low frequency the codes can punch through any interference from those Star Destroyers."

"Can their battleships get here in time?" Cilghal asked.

"Depends on how long we can maintain our defenses here," Leia said.

Though Leia could read no specific emotion on Cilghal's face, she sensed some measure of pride. "The Mon Calamari broke the first Imperial occupation using only common tools and scientific implements. This time we have real weapons. We can hold them off as long as necessary." Cilghal motioned to a nearby control panel. "You may use that communication station to send your message."

Leia hurried to the comm station and punched in the override codes to send a tight-beam encoded signal directly to Coruscant. "This is Minister Leia Organa Solo," she said. "The planet Calamari is currently under attack by two Imperial Star Destroyers. We request immediate assistance. Repeat, *immediate* assistance! If you don't get here soon, don't bother to come."

The city commander thrust a webbed hand into the holographic display of the battle. "We positioned the entire squadron of B-wing fighters to defend the shipyards, because we thought that would be the most likely target. But when the Star Destroyers came out of hyperspace, they went into orbit and began an assault on the floating cities. Right now both Star Destroyers are concentrating their firepower on Reef Home City. They've left two squadrons of TIE fighters and TIE bombers to cover Foamwander City. Another three squadrons are currently pummeling Coral Depths."

"Commander," one of the Calamarian tacticians spoke up, touching an implanted microphone at his ear hole. "We've lost all contact with Reef Home. Their last transmissions showed the outer hull breached in at least fifteen separate places, water rushing in. The final image showed a large-scale explosion. Static signature analysis implies that the entire city has been destroyed."

A quiet moan of dismay rippled through Central Command. The city commander said tentatively, "I was about to withdraw defenses from the shipyards to attack the Star Destroyers."

Ackbar looked at the swarms of B-wings still harrying the Imperial fighters. "Good decision, Commander," he said, but stared intently at the map, at the moon, at the two Star Destroyers on the far side of the planet. "Wait a moment," he said. "Something looks very familiar to me."

He paused, nodding slowly as if his great head were too heavy for his shoulders. "Yes, Commander—withdraw the B-wing fighters, all of them. Send them to fight the Star Destroyers. Leave the shipyards entirely undefended."

"Is that wise, Admiral?" Leia asked.

"No," he said, "it is a trap."

On the bridge of the Star Destroyer *Gorgon*, Admiral Daala watched the battle unfold below her, exactly as planned.

In her heart she felt a warm glow of pride for the tactical genius of Grand Moff Tarkin. Beside her ship the *Basilisk* mowed a swath of death across the watery surface. Like a swarm of angry insects, the TIE fighters swept away the pitiful resistance the Calamarians managed to mount.

The Rebel B-wing fighters and some of the midsized capital ships in orbit proved only a minor nuisance. As the *Gorgon* and the *Basilisk* went through their carefully choreographed misleading attack, the Calamarian defense forces had followed along as expected, like marionettes pulled by strings.

She turned to the communications officer at his station. "Contact Captain Brusc on the *Manticore*," she said. "The Calamarian forces have finally left their shipyards undefended. He may begin his attack at once."

• • •

Ackbar gestured with his hands and spoke with an undignified rapidity, as if he knew he didn't have much time. "Before I was liberated by the Rebel Alliance, I was Moff Tarkin's indentured assistant. He took great pleasure in telling me exactly how he was going to enslave other worlds. By observing him I learned the fundamentals of space-warfare tactics, including Tarkin's own favorite strategies."

He pointed a flipper-hand into the images of the two Star Destroyers. "Tarkin is dead, but I recognize this trick. I know what the Imperial commander plans to do. Do we have a sensor network on the far side of the moon?"

"No, Admiral," the city commander said. "We had considered it years ago but—"

"I didn't think so," Ackbar said. "So we're blind there, correct?"

"Correct."

"What are you getting at, Admiral?" Leia said.

"There's a third Star Destroyer hiding behind our moon."

When Ackbar said that, half of the chattering voices in the room fell silent. The others turned toward him in amazement. "What proof do you have?"

Leia tried to use her fledgling powers with the Force to sense the hidden enemy ship, but either it was too distant, or she was not skilled enough . . . or it wasn't there.

"The actions of the Imperial commander tell me all I need," Ackbar said. "Their main target is indeed the shipyards. Moments after these two Star Destroyers came out of hyperspace, a third also emerged, concealed in the shadow of our moon. The vanguard attack is designed to lure us away from the shipyards, tricking us into throwing our entire defenses against a feint. When the third Star Destroyer comes in at full sublight speed, the shipyards will be helpless. With one run the third Star Destroyer can obliterate our starship assembly facilities with virtually no losses of its own."

"But, Admiral," the city commander said, "why did you just withdraw all of our forces from the shipyards?"

Ackbar nodded. "Because you are going to give me remote command of *that* ship." He indicated the huge spacedock hangar where the skeletal hull of the new battle cruiser *Startide* hung in orbit.

"But, sir, none of the *Startide*'s weapons are functional."

"But its engines work, if I am not mistaken?"

"Yes," the city commander said, "we tested the sublight engines only last week. The hyperdrive reactor core has been installed, but we have never taken the ship into hyperspace."

"Not necessary," Ackbar said. "Have all the construction engineers been evacuated?"

"Yes, at first sign of the attack."

"Then give me remote operations."

"Admiral—" the city commander said tentatively, then punched in a command-code sequence. "If it were anyone other than you . . ."

Taking control, Ackbar stepped into the field where virtual images were projected with a parallax designed for wide-set telescopic eyes.

The half-constructed ship powered up its engines and locked into drone mode. With an inaudible roar of massive sublight engines the unarmed battleship crawled away from the orbital shipyards, picking up speed as it ascended from the planet's gravity well. The engines were powerful enough to haul along the entire connected framework of the spacedock.

Ackbar didn't mind. The more mass, the better.

Leia bit her lip as the echoes of attack thundered from above, as the external imagers showed the damage to Foamwander's outer shell, as another wave of TIE fighters swooped down to scorch any exposed surface.

Cilghal seemed to have gone into a kind of a trance. Leia wondered if the shock had numbed her. The ambassador stood before the orbital images of swarming fighters, both the B-wing defenders and TIE attackers. She reached out with her fingers, touching seemingly random blips of light.

"This one, now this one . . . now this one," she said. Barely a moment after she touched each one, the screen flared bright, marking the destruction of the indicated ships.

Leia was amazed, unable to believe that Cilghal could pick them so accurately. But with the fledgling abilities Luke had taught her, Leia could feel a tug in the female ambassador, an instinctive working of the Force. She asked, already suspecting the answer, "How are you doing that?"

"Just like with the school of fish," Cilghal said quietly. "It's only a trick—but I wish I could get in contact with our fighters. This one, this one!" With a long finger she traced one of the B-wing fighters that seemed perfectly safe in the midst of its own squadron, but then a damaged TIE fighter out of control spiraled through the group of ships and impacted the doomed B-wing. Cilghal had done the same thing with the school of fish as the krakana monster fed.

The female ambassador looked astonished and stricken. "There's not enough time," she said. "I can't figure it out soon enough."

Despite the fury of the Imperial attack, Leia felt a thread of wonder pass through her. Even without further testing, she knew that Cilghal had the potential to use her powers as a Jedi. Leia would have to send Cilghal to Luke's training center on Yavin 4—if they somehow survived here.

Ackbar felt as if he were part of the massive derelict ship as he controlled it from the core of Foamwander City. He paid no attention to the loud status reports and alarms in Central Command. His entire body was an extension of the *Startide*, and he stared through sensor eyes.

Its engines added velocity to the great hulk. Calamari's moon grew larger as he approached it, then began to streak by close to the airless cratered surface and out of sensor range to the dark side of the moon. Where the third Star Destroyer lay in wait.

Ackbar powered up the *Startide*'s hyperdrive reactors and shut off the automatic coolant systems. Alarms ran through his body as the ship's warning routines screamed at him. But Ackbar increased the power output, trying to hold it in, restraining the seething energy that waited to explode from the great uncompleted battleship.

As he brought the *Startide* around the curve of the moon, Ackbar saw the arrowhead shape of a third Star Destroyer just powering up its weapons batteries. "There it is."

The third Star Destroyer suddenly detected the Mon Calamari battle cruiser and began unleashing a flurry of turbolaser bolts—but Ackbar didn't care.

One of the blasts detonated a joint in the spacedock framework surrounding the *Startide*, and a network of girders dropped into space. Molten droplets flew from the starboard flank where a direct hit vaporized part of the hull.

Ackbar drove on at full speed on his suicide run, heading directly down the Star Destroyer's throat. The Imperial ship continued to fire.

Ackbar released the last safety mechanisms that held the unshielded hyperdrive reactor in check. The superheated energy furnace would reach its flash point within seconds.

He disconnected himself from the command console and let the laws of physics take their course.

Admiral Daala shouted into the comm system. "Captain Brusc, tell me what's going on!"

The *Manticore* had just begun its triumphant run to destroy the Calamarian shipyards when all havoc broke loose. Alarms interrupted her transmission.

The captain scrambled and shouted orders. "It's another ship, Admiral!" Brusc said, flashing a glance and wanting to bark orders, yet not quite daring to ignore Daala. "It came out of nowhere. They must have known we were here."

"Impossible," Daala said. "They couldn't have known we were there. We left no sensor trace. Ops! Give me the *Manticore*'s tactical sensors."

On the screen Daala saw her third Star Destroyer and the skeletal Calamarian star cruiser. It looked ridiculously cumbersome, dragged back by heavy construction frameworks—yet it moved inexorably. Daala understood the suicide tactic immediately.

"Get out of there!"

The *Manticore* veered to get out of the *Startide*'s path, but the Calamarian cruiser came on too fast. The *Manticore*'s turbolaser batteries did nothing to slow its approach.

Daala held her back rigid, forcing herself not to wince. She gripped the cold rail at her bridge station. Her knuckles whitened. The plasteel floor seemed to drop out from under her. Her dry mouth opened in a wordless shout of No!

The Calamarian battleship struck the underbelly of the *Manticore*. Just before the impact, though, the *Startide* went nova, erupting into blinding waves of energy that tore the *Manticore* apart.

Captain Brusc's transmission cut off abruptly.

Daala turned away, gritting her teeth and refusing to let acid tears of failure well up in her green eyes. She thought of all the weaponry, all the personnel, all the responsibility that had just been destroyed.

She stared into space, blinded by the brilliant double explosion that flowed out behind Calamari's moon, creating an artificial eclipse.

18

Kyp Durron felt exhilarated, yet foolish at the same time. The other Jedi students had stopped their own exercises and dropped back to watch Kyp at work.

Surrounded by the dense foliage of the jungle, with humid air wrapped like sweat around him, Kyp balanced his body. His feet extended straight up into the air, his back rigid; he held himself upright with one hand resting flat on the rough ground. The heel of his palm sank into the soft dirt. Blades of sharp grass stuck between his fingers.

He could balance himself with less difficulty on a more level piece of ground—but that would be too easy. His dark hair hung around his face; droplets of perspiration ran in tiny trickles along his scalp.

With his free hand Kyp supported a moss-covered boulder he had uprooted from the ground. Clumps of dirt pattered to the grass. He held the rock in the air with only a small effort, using the Force to do most of the work.

Artoo-Detoo bleeped in alarm, chittering from high in the branches above. Kyp had levitated him up there as a warm-up exercise, and he would get the little droid down in good time; for now he maintained his concentration.

He blocked out his awareness of the other Jedi trainees. He let his eyes slit halfway closed as he concentrated and raised a fallen, fungus-shrouded tree limb, yanking it from a tangle of blueleaf shrubs and standing it on end beside him.

Kyp blew out a long, slow breath and concentrated on keeping every piece in its place. The rest of the universe focused around him. Highly attuned, he felt a vibration in the Force, a ripple of amazement and pride.

Master Skywalker had come to watch him.

Kyp knew how to feel the Force, how to use it. It came naturally to him. It seemed instinctive, just as navigating the Sun Crusher through the black hole cluster had been. He felt that he had been ready for this all his life, but he could not see it simply because he had never been shown how to use his abilities. But now that Master Skywalker had nudged him, the new skill came flooding into him as if a long-closed valve had been twisted open.

In little more than a week of intensive work, Kyp had surpassed the achievements of the other Jedi students. Kyp shut himself off from socialization among the trainees. He spoke to few of the others, focusing every moment upon honing his Jedi ability, increasing his concentration, developing a rapport with the Force. He hounded Master Skywalker to give him new tasks, to set him greater challenges so he could continue to learn and grow stronger in the Force.

Now, enclosed by the jungle and observed by other trainees, Kyp did not see his exercises as showing off. He didn't care whether Master Skywalker watched him or not. He simply meant to push the boundaries of what he could do. After he completed one set of exercises, he tried another more difficult routine, adding greater challenges. In that way he could continue to improve.

While trapped in the detention levels of the Star Destroyer *Gorgon*, when he had been sentenced to death by Admiral Daala, Kyp had vowed that he would never again allow himself to become so helpless. A Jedi was never helpless, since the Force came from all living things.

Still balancing, dark eyes closed, Kyp felt the other creatures in the jungle, traced their ripples in the great tapestry of the Force. He smelled the plants and flowers and small creatures in the rain forest. He ignored the tiny gnats swarming around his head and body.

He felt the tidal vibrations of the gas giant Yavin and its other moons as he extended his thoughts outward to space. He felt at peace, a part of the cosmos. He pondered what difficulties he could add to his balancing act. But before he could decide, Kyp sensed Artoo-Detoo being lifted from his perch high in the Massassi trees and lowered gently to the ground. The little droid made relieved beeping sounds.

Then Kyp felt the mossy boulder invisibly removed from his hand and set back in its depression. The rotting branch also drifted down, replaced exactly in its former place on the mulch of the jungle floor.

Kyp felt a slash of annoyance at having his exercise forcibly stopped, and he opened his eyes to see Master Skywalker grinning proudly at him.

"Very good, Kyp," Master Skywalker said. "In fact, it's incredible. I'm not sure even Obi-Wan or Yoda would know what to do with you."

Kyp nudged with his levitating skills to flip himself upright so that he landed on his feet. Staring into Master Skywalker's eyes, he felt his heart pounding with exhilaration, filled with far more energy than he knew how to contain.

He spoke breathlessly, blinking as if he had suddenly opened his eyes into the brighter daylight on Yavin 4. "What else can you teach me today, Master?" He felt his skin flush. Droplets of sweat trickled from his dark hair and along his cheeks.

Master Skywalker shook his head. "Nothing more for today, Kyp." The other Jedi candidates stood slumped in exhaustion, resting on broken stumps and overgrown rocks.

Kyp tried not to let his disappointment show. "But there is so much more to learn," he said.

"Yes," Master Skywalker answered with a barely contained smile, "and patience is one of those things to learn. The ability to do a thing is not all there is. You must *know* the thing. You must master every facet of it. You must understand how it fits with everything else you know. You must possess it for it to be truly yours."

Kyp nodded solemnly at the spoken words of wisdom, as Jedi students were expected to do. But he promised himself that he would do everything necessary to make all of these new abilities *his*.

Even in the deepest hours of the night, Kyp did not sleep. He had eaten a bland but filling meal by himself, then retired to his cool quarters to meditate and practice the skills he had already learned.

As he concentrated, with only a small glowlamp in the corner, he sent his mind out to feel between the cracks of all the stone blocks in the Great Temple. He followed the life cycles of the strands of moss. He tracked tiny arachnids skittering through the corridors and vanishing into dark spaces, where his delicate touch could follow them through the blackness into their hidden homes.

Kyp felt as if he had plugged into a network of living things that expanded his mind and made him feel both insignificant and infinite at the same time.

As Kyp thought and dabbled with his fledgling abilities, he felt a great cold *rip* in the Force, like a black gash opening the structure of the universe. He snapped himself back to the present.

Kyp whirled and saw behind him the looming shadow of a tall cloaked figure. Even in the dim room the dark man's silhouette seemed intensely black, a hole that swallowed up all glimmers of light. Kyp said nothing, but as he continued to gaze, he saw the tiny starpoints of distant suns within the outline of his mysterious visitor.

"The Force is strong in you, Kyp Durron," the shadowy figure said.

Kyp looked up, feeling no fear. He had been imprisoned and sentenced to death by the Empire. He had lived in the pitch-dark spice mines of Kessel for over a decade. He had fought against a predatory energy spider. And he had flown through a black-hole cluster. As he looked at the imposing liquid-black outline, though, he felt awe and curiosity.

"Who are you?" Kyp asked.

"I could be your teacher," the dark shape said. "I could show you many things that even your Master Skywalker does not comprehend."

Kyp felt a thrill rush through him. "What things?"

"I could show you techniques that were lost thousands of years ago, secret rites and hidden doorways of power that no weak Jedi Master like Skywalker dares to touch. But *you* are strong, Kyp Durron. Do you dare to learn?"

Kyp felt reckless, but he trusted his instincts. They had served him well in the past. "I'm not afraid to learn," he said, "but you have to tell me your name. I won't learn from a man who is afraid to identify himself."

Kyp felt foolish even as he said it. The shadowy form seemed to ripple as if with silent laughter. His voice boomed out again, full of pride.

"I was the greatest Dark Lord of the Sith. I am Exar Kun."

19

Han Solo dashed into his and Leia's empty sleeping chambers. "Lights!" he shouted so loudly that the voice receptors didn't understand his words. Han forced himself to articulate with brutal clarity through clenched teeth, "Lights," until the illumination came on in the room.

He glanced from side to side, trying to think of everything he would need to bring. After unsealing the coded security chamber atop one of their closets, he snatched a fully charged personal blaster, then grabbed an extra power pack. He pulled out a clean set of clothes, felt a startled pang as he saw Leia's garments hanging untouched in the storage unit.

"Chewie!" he bellowed. "In here."

For some reason the voice-response lights went off again. In disgust he snapped, "Lights on!" for the third time.

See-Threepio strutted into the room with two bawling children in tow. "Sir, must you be so rushed? You're upsetting the children. Will you *please* take a moment to explain what's going on?"

Chewbacca roared from the outer room, and Han could hear him knocking furniture aside as he ran to the bedroom. The Wookiee stood in the doorway, his tan fur ruffled. He opened his wide pink mouth, showing his fangs, and roared again so loudly that it startled the children.

The bedroom lights went off for a second time.

Han saw that Chewbacca carried his deadly bowcaster and a pack of concentrated emergency rations, ready to go. Fumbling in the dimness, Han opened up another small compartment beside the closet and pulled out the trusty automatic medikit he had removed from the *Millennium Falcon.*

"Lights," Threepio said in a calm voice, and the illumination stayed on this time.

"Threepio, where's Lando?" Han said. "Find him for me."

"He's down in the starship bays, sir. He left me a message to tell you that he is not impressed with your standards of maintenance on your former ship."

"Well, he'd better have the *Falcon* running now, that's all I can say," Han said.

Jaina sniffed loudly and between sobs cried out, "Where's Mommy?"

Han stopped as if hit with a stun beam. He knelt, looking into his little girl's face. He brushed aside the tears on her cheeks and placed his hands on her tiny shoulders, giving a squeeze of confidence.

"Daddy's going to rescue her," Han said.

"Rescue her? Oh, dear!" Threepio interrupted. "Why does Mistress Leia need rescuing?" Chewbacca bellowed in answer, but Threepio waved mechanical hands at him. "You're not helping, you know!"

Han turned to the Wookiee. "Not this time, buddy. I need you here to watch over the kids. There's no one else I trust as much." Chewbacca blatted a response, but Han shook his head. "No, I don't have a plan yet. All I know is I need to get to Calamari before the Imperials destroy it. I can't just stay here and let Leia face them alone."

Han stuffed what he needed into a lightweight mesh sack and grabbed the emergency rations from Chewbacca's hairy arms, glancing at the labels to make sure the food was compatible with human digestive systems.

"How long will you be gone, sir?" Threepio asked, trying to stop Jacen from climbing into the open closets.

"As long as it takes to rescue my wife," Han answered.

He sprinted toward the door, taking two steps before he froze. He spun around and returned to his two children. He bent down again and gathered Jacen and Jaina in a big hug. "You two behave for Chewie and Threepio. You have to watch out for each other."

"We *are* good," Jacen answered with a touch of indignation. At that moment the little boy looked heart-wrenchingly like Leia.

"I have recently updated my child-care programming, sir," Threepio said. "We'll have no trouble at all." The golden droid nudged the twins as he tried to usher them back to their own room. "Come, children, I will tell you an entertaining story."

Jacen and Jaina began crying again.

Han took a last longing look at the twins and then ran out of the living quarters, pausing only a moment to straighten the soft chair Chewbacca had knocked over.

The cyberfuse made a popping sound as it clattered on the cockpit floor of the *Millennium Falcon*. Lando Calrissian stared at it in disgust, then turned back to the control panels.

He had finished updating the navicomputer software, but somehow that had caused the cockpit lights to short out. He rummaged around in the small bin of old greasy-smelling replacement fuses and yanked out one that looked appropriate.

The *Falcon* had been cobbled together from so many different parts, he could never keep track of how much spit and monofilament wire kept the ship running. He wondered for the hundredth time why he loved the craft so much.

He popped in the fuse, activated it, and flicked a row of switches that remained glassy dead. "Come *on*," Lando said, smacking the panel hard with the flat of his left palm.

With a humming *whirr* and a blast of cold chemical-smelling air from the recirculating ducts, the controls winked to life. Lando closed his eyes with a sigh. "Good old emergency repair procedure number one," he said.

"Hey, Lando!"

He heard the loud, determined voice from outside in the repair bay. Without looking Lando knew Han Solo had come to shout at him about something.

He felt tired, itchy from sweat and frustrated at how long it was taking to get the *Millennium Falcon* performing up to his exacting standards. He stood up from the open control panels and walked across the short corridor, his boots making impatient clangs on the deck plates. He bent down on the entrance ramp to stick his head out.

"Lando," Han said again, hurrying toward him, his face red with agitation. Sweat clumped his dark hair together, and he marched forward with the unstoppable attitude of an Imperial construction droid.

"Han," Lando said, scowling, "you didn't tell me this junk heap was in such bad shape when we played sabacc."

Han ignored the comment and sprinted up the ramp, carrying a mesh sack of supplies and wearing a blaster at his hip. Lando raised his eyebrows. "Han—"

"Lando, I need the *Falcon*. Now." He pushed past Lando, dropped his sack on the deck plates, and hit the controls for the entrance ramp. Lando had to jump inside as the greased cylinders hauled the slanted metal ramp back into position.

"Han, this is my ship now. You can't just—"

Han went directly to the cockpit and threw himself into the pilot seat. Lando charged up behind Han. "What do you think you're doing?"

Han spun around in the pilot chair and fixed Lando with a stare that skewered him like a pair of stun bolts. "The planet Calamari is being attacked by Admiral Daala at this very moment. Leia's trapped there. Now, are you going to help me go rescue her in the *Falcon*, or do I pick you up by your scruffy neck and throw you off the ship?"

Lando backed off, holding both palms up in a gesture of peace. "Whoa, whoa, Han! Leia's in trouble? Let's go—but I'm flying," he said, motioning for Han to move into the copilot's chair. "It *is* my ship."

Grudgingly, Han unbuckled his restraints and slid over to the right-hand seat normally reserved for Chewbacca. Lando toggled on the comm system. "*Millennium Falcon* requesting clearance for immediate departure."

He raised the modified light freighter off the floor on its repulsorlift jets, hovered, and punched the sublight engines the moment Coruscant Control gave them permission to depart. The *Falcon* shot through the atmosphere and headed out to the stars.

On the planet Vortex, Qwi Xux wandered on the fringes of the reconstruction site of the Cathedral of Winds. Her companion, Wedge Antilles, had joined the other New Republic cleanup crews. The workers wore thick gloves to protect their hands from the razor edges of the crystal shards they hauled to the materials-reprocessing bins, dissolving broken fragments and synthesizing new building material.

Overhead the swirling gray clouds warned of the rapidly approaching storm season. Soon all the winged Vors would take shelter in their low-to-the-ground bunkers and wait out the hurricane-force gales. Already cold gusts hissed across the unbroken plains of pale grasses. Qwi feared that her own ethereal form might take flight, whisked into the air by a sudden powerful gust to join the lacy-winged inhabitants.

The Vors kept away from the New Republic teams, working at the site of the devastated cathedral, reinforcing the foundations and preparing to erect a new network of hollow musical towers. The aliens followed no plan that anyone could see, and had answered only with silence when the engineers asked to study the architectural drawings.

Qwi watched the activity, wishing she could help. The Vors had not demanded aid from the New Republic; in fact, they had barely acknowledged it, simply accepting the new workers and continuing the breakneck pace of their project. The seemingly emotionless Vors had filed no formal protest, made no threats of cutting off relations. It was as if they understood the

New Republic bore them no ill will; but as a race they had been stunned and could not return to normal activities until their Cathedral of Winds sang again.

As she walked among the scattered shards of crystal pipes, Qwi found a small, narrow tube, a broken piece of one of the high-pitched windpipes from the tallest pinnacles of the towers. She bent and picked it up with her long fingers, careful to avoid the sharp edges.

The wind gusted around her, rippling the fabric of her tunic, tossing her pearlescent feathery hair around her head. She stared at the tiny flute. Back at Maw Installation, Qwi had often programmed her own computers using musical notes, whistling and humming to set subroutines in motion. She had not played music in a long time. . . .

Over at the materials-reprocessing station, Wedge and two helpers accidentally dropped a large section of crystal pipe, which crashed to the ground. Wedge shouted, and the others jumped out of the way to escape the fragments.

At the construction site the Vors fluttered up in the air in a panic, alarmed by the sound of breaking crystal.

Qwi put the flute to her mouth, taking a tentative breath. The smooth crystal felt cool against her thin blue lips. She blew into the unbroken end and held a finger over one of the holes, letting a test note whistle through the tube. She tried another, and a third, gaining a feel for the songs the crystal flute could sing.

She planted her feet among the crushed glassy fragments on the ground, steadying herself against the blowing wind, and she played. It took her several tries to work the notes into the shapes she wanted, but she closed her large indigo eyes and let the music flow from her.

The Vors flapped through the air, approaching her, circling overhead. Some landed in the whipping lavender grass nearby, turning their angular faces toward her, blinking horny eyelids over pupilless obsidian eyes. They listened.

Qwi thought of the destruction of the Cathedral of Winds, the loss of a great artifact and work of art, the deaths of so many Vors; the music took on a keening tone. In her mind she also saw her own home planet of Omwat, when Moff Tarkin had placed her in an orbital training habitat as a child so she and other talented Omwati children could watch as he destroyed their families' honeycomb settlements if ever the children failed an examination. . . .

Music skirled out of the flute, rising and falling. She heard the flap of Vor wings over the sound of the notes and the wind. Qwi blinked nervously and looked up at her silent audience, but she kept playing.

From his position with the New Republic workers, Wedge came running over to see if she needed help. The other human engineers noticed the attention she had drawn.

As Wedge approached, breathless and wide-eyed, Qwi stopped playing. She took a deep breath and lowered her crystal flute.

Surrounding her, the Vors did not speak. They stared at her, fluttering their wings to keep their balance. Segmented, leathery armor covered their faces, masking any readable expressions. She couldn't think of anything to say.

A large male Vor, obviously a clan leader of some kind, stepped forward and extended his hand to take the flute from her. Still nervous, Qwi placed the delicate instrument in his leathery palm.

With a sudden, violent gesture, the Vor squeezed his hand shut and crushed the flute. The thin crystal sides of the tube shattered. He opened his hand to let the fragments fall to the ground. Thin lines of blood blossomed on his palm.

"No more music," he said. Her entire audience of Vors spread their wings and leaped into the winds, flying back over to the construction site.

The leader kept his gaze on her. "Not until we are finished here," he said, and flew off to join the others.

Stuck in hyperspace, Han Solo could do nothing but wait. He couldn't hurry the passage of time.

He paced around the common area, looking at the battered holographic game board and thinking of when he had first seen Artoo-Detoo playing with Chewbacca. That had been before he had even met Leia, when Luke Skywalker was a wet-behind-the-ears moisture farmer and Obi-Wan Kenobi was just a crazy old man. If he had known how his life would change after that day in the Mos Eisley cantina, Han wondered if he would have taken the risk to pick up two passengers and their droids bound for Alderaan.

But then he would never have met Leia. Never have married her. Never have fathered three children. Never have helped defeat the Empire. Yes, he thought: despite all the turmoil, Han would make the same choices all over again.

And now Leia was in great peril.

Lando came from the cockpit. "She's on autopilot." He looked at the dejected expression on Han's face and shook his head. "Han, why don't you rest? Let's kill some time." Then, as if the idea had just occurred to him, "How about we play a round of . . . sabacc?" Lando raised his eyebrows and flashed one of his famous grins.

Han wondered if his friend was just trying to cheer him up and decided to see how serious Lando really was. "I'm not interested in sabacc right now."

He sat down and lowered his voice. "I don't suppose you'd put up my ship as a stake?"

Lando scowled. "It's *my* ship, Han."

Han leaned forward across the holographic chess table. "Not for long, buddy—or are you afraid?"

The *Falcon* shot through hyperspace on autopilot, oblivious to the fact that her ownership was being decided.

Tiny pearls of sweat tickled the back of Han's neck as he stared at his cards. Lando, who prided himself on a perfect bluffing expression, showed concern and uneasiness. For the third time in as many minutes, he wiped a hand across his brow.

The scoring computer held them at ninety-four points each. The time now passed in a flash, and Han found himself so intent on the game that he had not thought about Leia's desperate situation for at least fifteen seconds.

"How do I know you don't have some trick programmed into these cards?" Lando said, staring at the aluminized plates but holding the displays out of Han's line of sight.

"You suggested this game, buddy. These were my old cards, but you degaussed them yourself. They're straight, no tricks." He let a smile creep across his lips. "And this time there's no sudden change of rules during the final scoring round."

Han waited a second longer, then impatiently took the initiative. "I'm keeping three cards," he said, and put two others facedown in the center of the randomizer field. He pressed the scan button to change the value and suit on his cards, then slid them back out of the field to look at what he had drawn.

Lando held out two cards and thought better of it, biting his lower lip, and pulled out a third. Han felt a wave of jubilation. Lando's hand was even worse than his own.

Han's heart pounded. He had a flush of Staves, a low flush with no face cards; but if he could beat Lando, this hand would give him enough points to pass the target score. Lando stared at his own cards, smiling a little bit, but Han thought it was forced.

"Go on," Han said, and slipped his cards one at a time onto the platform.

"Do I get extra points for having a completely random hand?" Lando said, then sighed. He put his elbows on the table and frowned.

Han slapped a hand on his flush. "The *Falcon*'s mine again!"

Lando smirked, as if losing the ship were a mixed blessing. "At least you're getting her back in better condition."

Han clapped his friend on the back and with a light step danced back toward the cockpit. Slowly, with a sigh of satisfaction, he lowered himself back into the pilot's seat.

Now, he thought, if he could just get to Leia in time, this would be a perfect day.

20

Kyp Durron trudged through the dense rain forest of Yavin 4, trying to find hidden paths where the jungle would allow him to pass. He knew exactly where to go. The dark spirit of Exar Kun had shown him.

With the stirring of the underbrush, reptilian predator birds burst squawking into flight, disturbed from the bloody carcass of a kill they had dragged into the canopy.

Kyp's assigned companion Dorsk 81 stumbled beside him. The thin, smooth-skinned alien had a much more difficult time with the steamy air and the steep climbs.

A purple-furred woolamander clambered through the overhead network of Massassi trees. Dorsk 81 looked up, startled—but Kyp had sensed the beast minutes before, feeling its primal panic and indecision build until finally it had to flee.

Kyp wiped sweat out of his eyes and shook his head, sending droplets of perspiration flying. He squinted again and moved forward with greater speed, knowing they had almost reached their destination—though Dorsk 81 had no idea yet.

Insects and small biting creatures buzzed and scuttled around them, but none bothered Kyp. He consciously exuded a shadow of uneasiness around him so that lower creatures had no incentive to come nearer. Exar Kun had taught him that trick too.

Dorsk 81 opened his lipless mouth, panting as he tried to keep up with the vigorous pace. His yellow and olive-green skin was unblemished, his nose flattened and smooth, his ears tucked back against his head as if someone had designed his race in a wind tunnel. The alien looked miserable; his wide-set eyes blinked, and his face gleamed with a sheen of moisture. "I was not bred for this," Dorsk 81 said.

Kyp slowed, but not enough to bring relief to his companion. He softened the tone of his instinctive retort. "You were not bred for anything but bureaucracy and a comfortable life. I don't understand how the planet Khomm could have survived unchanged for a thousand years. Or why your people wanted it to."

Dorsk 81 took no offense and followed Kyp. "Our society and our genetics reached their perfection a millennium ago, or at least that's what we decided at the time. To prevent undesirable changes, we froze our culture at that level. We took our perfect race and cloned them rather than risking genetic anomalies.

"I am the eighty-first clone of Dorsk. Eighty generations before me have been identical, doing the same jobs with the same level of skill, maintaining our level of perfection and not slipping back." Dorsk 81 frowned, and with a burst of surprising energy he pushed around Kyp. He flung himself into the effort of making a path through the dense brush with all the strength he possessed. "But I was a failure," he said. "I was different."

Kyp gestured to an identical-looking thicket of raventhorns, spotting the invisible maze of a relatively simple path. "You have the potential to become a Jedi Knight," he said. "How can you consider that a failure?"

Dorsk 81 clawed his way out of the tangle he had become trapped in. Stains from crushed berries and flower petals dotted his uniform. "It is unsettling . . . to be different," he said.

Kyp spoke partly to himself and partly to his companion. "Yes, but sometimes it's exhilarating to know you can rise above the others who are trapped down below."

He ducked into the low tunnel of gloomy foliage and dangling mosses. Tiny gnats flew away from his face. The deep shadows suddenly made him think of the black spice mines of Kessel where he had been forced to work as a slave.

"The Empire ruined my life," Kyp said. "My parents were political resisters. They marked the anniversary of the Ghorman Massacre, and they protested the destruction of Alderaan—but by that time the Emperor had lost all patience with political objections.

"Stormtroopers came in the middle of the night, battered their way into our home on the colony of Deyer. They took my parents, stunned them in front of our eyes, leaving them paralyzed and twitching on the floor. My father couldn't even close his eyes. Tears ran down his cheek, but his arms and his legs kept jittering. He couldn't get up. The stormtroopers dragged him and my mother out.

"My brother Zeth was five years older than me. They took him. He was only fourteen, I think. They put stun-cuffs on his hands. They kicked him, pushed him out, and then they stunned me.

"I found out later that they took Zeth to the Imperial Military Academy on Carida. They put my parents and me in the Correctional Facility on Kessel, where we had to work in the spice mines. I spent most of my days in pitch-darkness because any light straying into the mine shafts spoils spice crystals. My parents died there after only a few years.

"I had to take care of myself even when the prisoners overthrew the Correctional Facility and took over. The crime lord there, Moruth Doole, tossed the captured Imperials down into the spice mines. Doole let some of the prisoners out—but not many and not me. Our masters had changed, but we remained slaves."

Dorsk 81 looked at him with his glittering wide-set eyes. "How did you escape?" he said.

"Han Solo rescued me," Kyp answered; warmth filtered into his voice. "We stole a shuttle and fled into the black hole cluster. There we stumbled upon a secret Imperial research installation, and we were captured again— this time by Admiral Daala and her fleet of Star Destroyers. Han got us out of there after Daala had placed a death sentence on me."

Anger curled through him, making his head buzz, making him feel stronger. He tapped into that strength. "You can understand why the Imperials make me so furious," he said. "It seems that every step of my life the Empire has tried to beat me into submission, tried to take away the rights and pleasures that other life-forms enjoy."

"You can't fight the Empire alone," Dorsk 81 said.

Kyp didn't answer for a long moment. "Perhaps not yet," he said.

Before Dorsk 81 could say anything, Kyp parted a dense clump of blueleaf branches. He felt an electric thrill down his spine as the Force told him they had arrived.

"This," Kyp whispered, "this is our destination."

In front of them the jungle gave way to a circular pond that shone like a flat quicksilver mirror, completely free of ripples. In the center of the lake stood a small island dominated by an obsidian split-pyramid of sharp angles showing the distinctive markings of Massassi architecture: another temple, the same one Gantoris and Streen had located weeks before, but Luke Skywalker had not yet explored it. Exar Kun had told Kyp all about it.

Between the bifurcated spire of the tall pyramid stood a colossus, a polished black statue of a dark man, with long hair swept back behind him, the tattoo of a black sun emblazoned on his forehead, and the padded garments of an ancient lord, the Dark Lord of the Sith.

Kyp swallowed hard at seeing the image of Exar Kun.

"Who do you think he was?" Dorsk 81 asked, squinting to stare across the water.

Kyp answered in a quiet, husky voice. "Someone very powerful."

The great orange sphere of Yavin lurked on the horizon with only a fuzzy curve peeping over the tops of the jungle. The system's small sun would also be setting soon. The twin lights in the sky cast intersecting glitter paths across the still lake.

Kyp gestured toward the temple. "We can spend the night there if you'd like," he said.

Dorsk 81 nodded with more eagerness than Kyp had expected. "I would like to sleep inside shelter again," he said, "rather than up in a tree tangled in vines. But how are we going to get out there? How deep is the lake?"

Kyp went to the edge. The water was as transparent as diamond and so deep that it reflected the bottom like a lens, making it impossible to determine how far down the water went. Just below the surface he saw columns of rock rising from the bottom like submerged stepping stones that stopped just barely beneath the water.

Kyp stepped out onto one. The clear water rippled around the bottom of his shoe, but he did not sink in. He took another step to the second stone.

Dorsk 81 stared at him; Kyp knew that he must appear to be walking directly across the surface of the water. "Are you using the Force?" Dorsk 81 said.

Kyp laughed. "No, I'm using stepping stones."

Without hesitation he splashed to the next stone and then the next, eager to reach the temple—a source of new knowledge and secret techniques. On the island he stepped onto mounds of pitted volcanic rock splotched with orange and green lichen that looked like droplets of alien blood. He could already feel the power.

Kyp turned to watch his companion pick his way across the lake. It looked very much as if Dorsk 81 balanced on the fragile membrane of the pool's surface. The illusion was very effective. Around him silence blanketed the island, as if none of the jungle creatures or insects dared to come near the empty temple.

"It's cold here," Dorsk 81 said, shaking water off his feet and looking around. The smooth-skinned alien hunched his head closer to his shoulders.

"You were complaining before about how hot it was," Kyp said. "You should be grateful."

Dorsk 81 clamped his lipless mouth shut and nodded once, but said nothing else.

Kyp walked around, looking at the polished black glass angles of the pyramid, the jutting point at the top. The architecture had been designed as an angular funnel to concentrate the Force, assembled to enhance the powers of Sith rituals.

He stared up at the frozen statue of Exar Kun. The brooding dark lord looked so real to him, so awe inspiring, that Kyp expected the sculpture to bend down and grasp him.

Kyp knew now that the Great Temple was the focal point for the entire Massassi civilization that Exar Kun had built up from primitive decay. The Great Temple had been the headquarters, the prime focus of Kun's battles in the Sith War. But this small, isolated temple had been more of a private retreat, the place where Exar Kun had concentrated on improving his own abilities, strengthening himself.

A cool wind breathed out of the wedge-shaped opening as if the silent temple were some kind of sleeping monster. "Let's go inside," Kyp said.

He ducked his head and took one step into the enfolding darkness. But when he blinked his eyes, the light gradually grew inside the chamber as if lightning bolts trapped within the black slabs of glass continued to send faint sparks visible only from the corner of his eye. When Kyp faced the polished dark walls, he saw nothing in them, only faint etched markings of hieroglyphics in a long-forgotten language. He could not read any of the words.

Deep green tendrils of moss grew like frozen biological flames that worked their way up the polished stones. Against one wall stood a smooth rounded cistern filled with water.

Kyp stepped over to the cistern and dipped his fingers in, surprised and delighted to find the liquid cold and clean. He splashed his sweaty face, and then he drank, savoring the sweetness of the water as it slid down his throat. He sighed.

Dorsk 81 stood just within the opening, looking out at the jungle beyond the lake. The sphere of Yavin had vanished below the treetops, and the sky began to thicken with purple twilight as the distant sun also set. "I'm very sleepy all of a sudden," he said.

Kyp frowned, but thought he knew what was happening. "You've traveled a long way today," he said. "It's cool and dark in here. Why don't you sleep? The floor looks smooth and comfortable. You can curl up against the wall."

As if hypnotized, Dorsk 81 shambled over to a corner and slithered down against the wall until he lay with his back pressed against the obsidian slab. He fell asleep almost before he had settled into place.

"Now you and I can continue in a more appropriate setting." The deep, loud voice echoed like distant thunder inside the chamber.

Kyp turned to see the hooded silhouette of Exar Kun like a black oil stain shimmering in the air. Kyp stood tall, squashing a thrill of terror every time the ancient Lord of the Sith spoke to him.

Kyp indicated Dorsk 81. "Will he wake up? Will he see you?"

Exar Kun raised his shadowy arms. "Not until we have finished," he said.

"All right." Kyp squatted on the cool floor, tucking his robe around him as he found a comfortable position. He knew that his relaxed attitude might appear to be haughtiness or defiance of Exar Kun, but he didn't care.

The ancient Sith Lord began to speak. "Skywalker has taught you everything he knows. He makes excuses, but he can go no further because he has denied himself other options. He cannot grow as a Jedi by blocking out possibilities, by wearing blinders to what can be and what should be."

Exar Kun loomed over Kyp, hovering closer even though he didn't appear to have taken a step. "You have already learned more than Skywalker will ever know, my student."

Kyp felt enthusiasm and pride burn through him, and he tensed his body, wanting to leap to his feet. But he restrained himself.

"Look at what I can show you today," Exar Kun said, gesturing toward the obsidian walls and the incomprehensible hieroglyphs barely visible, black lines against black volcanic glass. But as Kyp looked at them, the words filled with white fire, standing out against the bottomless, opaque background until they burned into his eyes.

And suddenly Kyp could *understand*. The words snapped into focus and filled his mind, an incredible history from four thousand years ago, telling how Exar Kun had begun to learn forbidden teachings, how he had come to the fourth moon of Yavin to find a lost Sith power object, and how he had enslaved the timid and weak Massassi people, making them build enormous temples for him as focal points for the dark forces he played with.

"The Brotherhood of the Sith could have ruled the galaxy, could have squashed the doddering Republic and turned the other Jedi Knights into mere parlor magicians—but I was betrayed." The shadow of Exar Kun drifted about the floor of the temple, making no sound as he moved. He hovered over the sleeping and helpless form of Dorsk 81.

"When the Jedi combined their might and came here to this moon to fight me, they unleashed such power that I had to drain dry every last one of the Massassi just to trap my spirit within these temples—to survive so that one day I could come back."

Kun's coal-black arms reached down, as if to strangle Dorsk 81. The smooth-skinned clone stirred uneasily in his spellbound sleep, but he made no move to defend himself.

With a thrill of fear and reluctance, Kyp called out, "Exar Kun! *I'm* the one you're trying to teach. Don't waste your time with him."

He was enthralled by the new wonders Kun had shown him, but Kyp was savvy enough to know when he was being manipulated. Exar Kun thought he was playing Kyp like a mesmerized convert. But Kyp was skeptical—Han Solo had taught him that much. He could play his own part, however, to get what he so desperately wanted.

As Exar Kun turned back to face him, leaving Dorsk 81 unharmed, Kyp spread wide his arms in complete acceptance of his new instructor. "Teach me more about the ancient Sith ways."

Kyp swallowed, then made his voice strong, because this was what he really wanted. "Tell me how to use these new powers so I can crush the Empire once and for all."

21

On Coruscant, Chewbacca and Threepio took the twins through the
sculpted duracrete columns at the entrance to the Holographic Zoo of Extinct
Animals.

At home the pestering children had rapidly worn down even Threepio's
patience programming and had driven Chewbacca into a roaring frenzy.
Getting Jacen and Jaina outside seemed like a good idea for all concerned.
The foursome took transit tubes across the upper skyscrapers in old Imperial
City to reach the rooftop levels of the Holographic Zoo.

At the Zoo's gaudy archway Chewbacca let his furry arms dangle behind
him; his huge paws engulfed the tiny hands of the children. Chewbacca took
two sprawling strides forward, then waited for the twins to catch up before
he took two more steps and waited again. Threepio scuttled ahead as if he
were in charge. He had just undergone a deep oil bath so that his gold alloy
plating gleamed in the artificial lights.

They stepped under the grandiose arches. Threepio went to the cashier
kiosk, punching in Han and Leia's credit code. Chewbacca, impatient with
Jacen's and Jaina's short legs, scooped up the twins, one in each arm, and
strode forward.

They endured a dull preshow in an empty waiting room filled with chairs,
cages, and sockets to accommodate the bodies of all alien visitors, until the
far doors automatically clicked open. Chewbacca, still carrying the twins,

marched down a sloped tunnel to the lower levels. Threepio hurried after, trying to lead the way, but he could not get past the bulky Wookiee.

Arcing, glowing lights shot overhead, inept simulations of stars and comets and planets. As they passed motion sensors, booming godlike voices echoed in stereo from microspeakers in the walls.

"Journey down the corridors of time! Travel the lanes of space! You will experience forgotten wonders from a long time ago and far, far away. You will see extinct creatures lost from our galaxy but recreated here—and now!"

The walls around them darkened. Streaks of light shot out, funneling down in a crude animation of starlines for a fake journey into hyperspace. The floor beneath their feet rumbled and vibrated in the simulation. The children were startled, but Chewbacca groaned at the corniness of it. The illusion ended, and the recorded voice spoke in a conspiratorial whisper. "We have arrived . . . at a universe of possibilities!"

They stood before a choice of several doorways.

"This way children, this way," Threepio said, stepping forward. He had already scanned the data brochures about the exhibits, and after correlating them with the twins' interests, decided exactly which dioramas he would show them first. "Let us go see the mammoth krabbex of Calamari."

As they stepped through the portal, holograms flared, surrounding them with a turbulent oceanscape, a jagged reef thrusting out from white foamy waters. Standing in a swirl of green-and-purple seaweed battered by the rushing waves stood a segmented crustacean, a ten-legged krabbex with dual mandibles in its mouth, twin rows of spines down its back, and eighteen glossy black eyes, four of which were on its front grasping claws. The krabbex reared up and let out a bellow like a wampa ice creature set on fire.

The twins watched as three green-skinned mermen thrashed out of the foaming waves, cocking jagged spears made of pale bone. The mermen hauled themselves onto the reef and attacked.

The spears pierced the exoskeleton of the krabbex, and the monster clipped at them with its pincers. It swung to the left and grabbed one of the mermen, slicing into his smooth green flesh and dragging him out of the water, where his fused finned legs thrashed like the tail of a fish.

"Let's go," Jaina said.

"Next one," Jacen said.

"But, children, I haven't told you the biological background of these creatures yet," Threepio said.

"Go now," Jaina insisted.

They walked right through the surrounding illusion to the far wall, where several more openings presented themselves. Chewbacca urged the children through the left-hand door.

"Oh, not that one, Chewbacca," Threepio said. "I'm not certain—"

But they had already entered the second chamber to be surrounded by the illusion of a desert planet. Waves of invisible heat rippled from a scabbed, dried clay surface. A strange creature scuttled atop a rocky outcropping with a bloodcurdling roar. It had a squarish humanoid head and a massive feline body, huge curved claws, and a segmented tail that thrashed back and forth, capped with a wicked-looking scorpion stinger. As it opened its mouth to bellow again, cracked yellow fangs dripped with venom.

"A manticore?" Threepio said in disbelief. "Well, really! I'm astonished they haven't updated their display yet. That creature was proved to be a jumble of mismatched fossils long ago. Manticores never existed."

Directly behind them in the hologram another manticore echoed the bellowing challenge and climbed over the baked rocks. The twins tugged on Chewbacca's furry arms and headed through the nonexistent creatures toward the next set of openings.

"Let me choose this time, children," Threepio said.

Chewbacca groaned. The twins didn't seem to care.

"Go home," Jacen said.

Jaina nodded in agreement. "I want to go home."

"But, children," Threepio said, "I'm sure you'll enjoy this next one. Let me tell you all about the mournful singing fig trees of Pil Diller. . . ."

After three more dioramas and three more of Threepio's boring lectures, the twins decided that they would much rather play hide-and-seek than continue the tedious expedition through the Holographic Zoo.

While they couldn't communicate telepathically with each other word for word, they did know in a clear but general way what the other was thinking. When Jacen broke away from Chewbacca to run through the glacier eyries of the Snow Falcons, he headed to the left. At the same time, Jaina sprinted in the opposite direction, brushing past a startled Threepio. The twins used their fledgling talent with the Force to guide them into one of the other openings that led to an exit corridor.

Chewbacca bellowed; Threepio called after the children, but Jacen and Jaina met up outside the dioramas, pleased with their escape and giggling. They trotted down the white-tiled corridor as fast as they could go, past icons for refreshments, rest-and-recharge rooms, repair facilities.

At an intersection of corridors, an old maintenance droid worked in an open turbolift. Jacen and Jaina had seen turbolifts before. That was how they got back home once they reached the Imperial Palace.

The maintenance droid was gunmetal-gray with two heads and numerous mechanical arms, each studded with a handful of attachments. The droid's two heads faced each other. One head bore a set of bright optical sensors, while the other face was a blank screen that displayed data, statistics, and official Imperial Building Code specs.

Muttering to itself in binary, the droid searched its back compartment for a particular tool, found it missing from its bin, then puttered down the corridor. It left the turbolift wide open with only a small dangling sign saying Out of Service.

The children ran for the turbolift and ducked inside. They had watched their parents and Threepio use the controls many times.

The panel looked different from the one in the Imperial Palace: much less ornate, discolored with age and rough use, with a wall of buttons marking hundreds of different floors in the kilometer-high metropolis. Since the lower levels of the city had been abandoned and buried long ago, a thick metal plate had been welded onto the bottom half of the panel, sealing off the first 150 floors. But the maintenance droid had removed the barrier plate to check the turbolift circuits.

The children barely knew their numbers, though Threepio had been trying to get them to recognize the primary numerals. The lessons frequently frustrated the protocol droid, but the twins were bright. They had picked up more than Threepio had realized.

The rows of buttons looked like shiny colorful circles to Jacen and Jaina. They stared at them, not knowing which to push, but they did recognize some of the numbers.

Jaina spotted it first. "Number one," she said.

Jacen pushed the button. "Number one," he repeated.

The turbolift door closed, and the floor fell away as the elevator shot downward, humming as it accelerated. Jacen and Jaina looked at each other in momentary terror; then they giggled. The turbolift descent went on and on, until finally the platform came to a stop. The door whisked open.

Jacen and Jaina stood blinking. They stepped out into the shadowy bottom levels of the forbidden metropolitan wilderness. Around them they heard large startled creatures clattering through the fallen debris.

"It's dark," Jacen said.

Behind the twins the turbolift door slid shut as the elevator reset itself and returned to the upper floors, leaving Jacen and Jaina alone.

Chewbacca blasted through the exhibits like a landspeeder out of control. He howled and called out for the two lost children. Threepio scurried behind him, trying to keep up.

"I can't see anything through these holograms," Threepio said. Chewbacca sniffed for the twins. He charged through another opening.

All the shouting and chaos finally brought one of the Bothan zoo attendants. The Bothan fluffed up his white fur and flailed his arms as he tried to get Chewbacca to calm down. "Shhhh! You are disturbing our other patrons. This is a quiet place for enjoyment and education."

Chewbacca roared at him. The Bothan, much smaller, stood on his pointed toes, trying to draw himself up in a laughably ineffective attempt at meeting Chewbacca's eyes. "We never should have let Wookiees into the Holographic Zoo."

Chewbacca grabbed the Bothan by the white chest hairs and hefted him off the ground. He let loose a string of growls, grunts, and howls.

Threepio rushed up to them. "Excuse me, if I might be allowed to translate," the droid said, "my friend Chewbacca and I are currently searching for two small children who appear to be lost. Their names are Jacen and Jaina. They are two-and-a-half years old."

Chewbacca roared again.

"Yes, yes, I was just getting to that. This is really something of an emergency. The children just ran off from us, and any assistance you could offer—"

Chewbacca used both hands to shake the Bothan attendant like a rag doll.

"—would be most appreciated," Threepio finished.

But the Bothan had fainted.

Jacen and Jaina hiked through a forest of fallen girders, orange and yellow toadstools, and lumpy fungus growing in ancient garbage. Unseen feet skittered across fallen beams and webwork structures overhead.

The massive foundations of the buildings looked indestructible, overgrown with thick moss. Things moved in the shadows, but nothing came clear, even as the childrens' eyes adjusted to the shadowy light. Drips of warm, bad-tasting water fell around them in a slow arrhythmic rain.

Jacen looked up, and the enormous buildings seemed to rise forever and ever. He could glimpse only a blurred slice of what might have been the sky.

"I want to go home," Jaina said.

The wreckage of abandoned equipment lay in piles, rusted and corroded. The twins scrambled over crashed vehicles, the hulks of discarded battleships and fighting machines, deep debris left from the previous year's civil warfare.

Jacen and Jaina came upon a half-collapsed wall that had once contained a computer screen. The terminal lay tilted on its side with the screen smashed inward, leaving broken teeth of transparisteel. But the twins recognized it as a data unit similar to the ones inside their own quarters.

Jacen stood in front of the broken panel and put his small hands on his hips, trying to look like his father. He addressed the computer screen—and he knew exactly what to say, after having heard the bedtime story many times before. "We are lost," he said. "Please help us find our home."

He waited and waited but received no response. No lights illuminated the panels. He heard no answer from the torn speaker unit, where glistening black beetles had made a nest.

Jacen sighed. Jaina took his hand, and the two turned around as they heard a slithering sound down the cramped alleyway.

A formless gray-green creature paused behind them, a granite slug with two eyes protruding on gelatinous stalks as if assessing the two children. As it moved, it scoured green sludge off the cracked duracrete alleyway, trailing thick translucent slime.

The granite slug slithered toward them, and the twins backed away. From the bottom of the slug's underbelly, a jagged crack opened up, a quivering lipless mouth that sucked in a long hollow whistle of air.

Jaina stepped up to it. It was her turn this time.

"We are lost," she said. "Please help us find our home."

The granite slug reared until it towered over the little girl. She blinked up at it. Jacen stood by her side.

Then the granite slug seemed to deflate again, hooked its body into a broken passage to the right, and landed on the stones with a wet slapping sound.

A rustle of wind suddenly kicked up, and the granite slug churned down the side alley in alarm. Jacen looked up just in time to see the sharp mantalike wings of a hawk-bat that swooped down from high above, metallic talons outstretched.

The granite slug attempted to burrow into the rusted debris, but the hawk-bat landed on top of the wreckage, ripping and tearing at the fallen hunks of metal with its claws. Its triangular beak bobbed up and down like a piston until it had exposed the granite slug and slashed at the slimy creature. The hawk-bat flapped its broad wings again, heading toward the sky with its squirming, dripping prey.

Jacen and Jaina looked up at the creature, then at each other. The two began trudging through the dark underworld of Coruscant again.

Jaina said, "And he walked, and he walked . . . "

"We must sound the alarm *immediately*, Chewbacca!" Threepio said. But the Wookiee seemed reluctant to admit they had lost the two small children.

They left the unconscious Bothan attendant in one of the holographic dioramas, then made their way to the white-tiled corridor leading to the souvenir shops, refreshment stands, and other parts of the museum. Threepio wondered what the poor Bothan would think when he woke up lying inside the web lair of a cannibal arachnid from Duros.

A maintenance droid finished its turbolift repairs and removed the Out of Service sign. Its two heads began humming a duet to themselves at having completed a satisfying menial task.

Chewbacca pointed to the maintenance droid, but Threepio became indignant. "What could a low-level maintenance droid possibly know about this situation? Those models aren't much smarter than loader vehicles." But a large Wookiee hand dragged him along. "Oh, all right, if you insist."

Chewbacca sprinted ahead and stood in the path of the trundling maintenance droid. Automatic sensors instructed the droid to swerve one way, then the other, but Chewbacca forced it to stop. The maintenance droid emitted a high-pitched whine of confusion.

Threepio came up behind it. "Excuse me," he said, and garbled out a long series of crude binary questions. The maintenance droid answered with a *blat* like a stepped-on steam whistle. Threepio repeated his question, but got the same answer.

"I told you he'd be no use," Threepio said. "Maintenance droids aren't programmed to notice anything. They just do their repairs and wait for new instructions."

Chewbacca moaned, shaking his big hairy head.

Threepio said, "Oh, be quiet, you . . . you big walking carpet—I was *not* talking too much! Besides, *you're* the one who has the life debt to Han Solo."

The maintenance droid continued, oblivious to their bickering. Threepio wished that he could simplify his own programming and be so blissfully ignorant in the ways of the galaxy. He felt his circuits overheating as the full impact of what might happen to him slammed down on his poor head.

"Master Solo will probably remove my legs and make me recompile and alphabetize all the fragmented files in the Imperial Information Center!"

In the dim underworld Jacen pointed to a noisy machine in front of them as the cluttered street widened. "Look," he said. "Droid."

The children ran, waving their hands and hoping to get the droid's attention. But they stopped as the machine continued along a polished path worn through the debris.

The droid was vastly older than the maintenance model up at the turbolift. It had bulkier joints, squarish limbs; large bolts held the pieces together. The antique repair droid was little more than a mobile cart of tools with a torso, arms, and an angled hexagonal head. One of its optical sensors had fallen off. Thick cables ran down its spine and along its neck, corroded and caked with dust and dirt. Moss had begun to grow on its sides. It moved with a stuttering motion as if desperately in need of lubricant.

Along the street a line of corroded poles stood a meter taller than the twins. Atop each pole rested an old glowcrystal, engraved with magnifying facets, but each crystal was a dead translucent gray, shedding no light into the dim streets. Some poles had come loose from their ground-level moorings and tilted sideways.

The repair droid worked its way to the end of the street, stopped at an appropriate position, and ratcheted its torso high on accordion joints so its arms could reach the darkened glowcrystal. The droid removed the burned-out crystal, cradling it carefully in segmented pincers. After placing it in the back of the cart, the repair droid removed another thick glowcrystal from an open bin. Following complex programming, the droid positioned the replacement crystal on top of the pole and activated it.

The new glowcrystal remained as dead and lightless as the first, but the repair droid didn't seem to notice. It moved to the next pole, repeating the process.

Jacen stood in front of the droid, addressing it in his best Daddy voice. "We're lost," he said.

Jaina came up beside him. "Please help us find our home."

The repair droid ratcheted up as if in alarm, then lowered itself down to study the children with its single optical sensor. "Lost?" it said in a clanking voice.

"Home," Jaina insisted.

"Not in my programming," the droid said. "Not my main task." It ratcheted up again and moved to a third malfunctioning glowcrystal pole. "Not in my programming."

Jaina and Jacen began to cry. But upon hearing each other, rather than reinforcing their tears, the twins stopped. "Be brave," Jaina said.

"Brave," Jacen agreed.

The two exhausted twins sat down on a time-smoothed chunk of duracrete in the middle of the open street. They watched the repair droid continue removing dead glowcrystals from poles and replacing them with equally useless lights.

The droid moved all the way to the end of the street, unsuccessful in getting any of the streetlights to work again. Then, picking up speed, it whirred down the worn path it had traveled for a hundred years, back to where it had started.

The droid stopped in front of the first dead glowcrystal pole all over again, ratcheted itself up, and replaced the lightless crystal it had changed only a short while earlier with another one. . . .

22

Still reeling from the destruction of the *Manticore,* Admiral Daala slumped against the bridge rail. She found herself at a loss for words as the battle on Calamari continued.

"Wipe them out," she said. "Open fire with all turbolaser batteries from orbit. Target every floating city." She stared with glassy eyes out the *Gorgon*'s wide viewport. "Destroy them all."

She couldn't understand what had gone wrong. She had followed Grand Moff Tarkin's tactics exactly. He had trained her carefully, giving her all the information she should have needed. But since Daala had emerged from Maw Installation, she had met with one disaster after another. The Sun Crusher fallen into Rebel hands, the *Hydra* destroyed, and now the *Manticore*. True, she had been successful in hijacking a small supply vessel, and she had obliterated an insignificant colony on Dantooine—but now on her first major attack against a Rebel world, she had again lost a Star Destroyer through her own overconfidence.

She had failed. Utterly.

Beside the *Gorgon* in a companion flightpath rode the *Basilisk*. Together, they fired volleys of turbolasers into the oceans, incinerating submerged Calamarian structures. In moments they would cross the terminator line between day and night, where they could fire down upon two more of the massive floating cities. They would vaporize the structures, sending all the inhabitants to a watery death.

"Dispatch the last TIE squadron," she said, staring at the fiery battlefield of the ocean world below. "I want to lay this entire planet waste."

"Admiral!" Commander Kratas ran between the sensor and tactical stations and up the two steps to the observation platform. "Rebel battleships have just come out of hyperspace, an entire fleet, more than we can hope to fight."

Daala whirled in disbelief. "They responded to a distress call that quickly?" Then she too saw the glinting figures of large battleships streaking like comets toward them in planetary orbit.

Her breath caught in her throat. The shipyards remained unscathed except for minor sorties. She had not met her primary objective in the attack on Calamari. Still . . . they had destroyed at least one floating city, wrecked another, damaged two more.

"Recall all TIE squadrons," Daala said. "Plot a straight-line vector through hyperspace to the Cauldron Nebula. We'll go back and reassess our tactics, determine our losses." She paused, then raised her voice like a torch of anger. "And we'll prepare our next attack!"

The TIE fighters streamed back into the holds of the Star Destroyers. The Rebel defensive forces swung around in orbit like a pack of carnivores. Daala did not dare risk fighting them, though she wanted nothing more than to rip the throats out of their commanders with her bare hands.

"Ready for hyperspace," she said before the reinforcements could swoop in to attack. Daala watched the starfields elongate into bright white lines that funneled into a vanishing point on the other side of the universe.

Her Star Destroyers entered hyperspace, leaving the New Republic forces hopelessly behind.

Han Solo and Lando Calrissian soared through the skies of Calamari in the *Millennium Falcon,* searching for columns of smoke rising from devastated floating settlements.

They had found Foamwander City, but when they landed on one of the emergency pads, they learned that Admiral Ackbar, Leia, and Ambassador Cilghal had already departed on a rescue mission to the sunken city of Reef Home.

Han, wrapped up in dismay at the devastation caused by Admiral Daala's forces, felt no particular jubilation at being the pilot and owner of the *Falcon.* All exhilaration at winning his ship back had evaporated upon seeing the destruction that had been wreaked on the ocean world.

Lando sat at Chewbacca's station, staring at the navigation charts. "Looks like Reef Home City should be coming up somewhere below. I detect plenty of scattered metallic masses, but nothing that might be a metropolis."

"No, just the remains," Han said in a low voice.

As they skimmed low, he looked out the *Falcon*'s viewports at floating wreckage scattered on the waves. Blackened tracings of blaster scars showed prominently on the fragmented metal. Broken chunks of the floating city, sealed and airtight with flood bulkheads, remained afloat like buoyant coffins; Calamarian and Quarren rescuers swarmed over the self-contained segments, trying to break through to free those inside.

"That used to look like Cloud City," Han said. "Now it looks like leftovers from a garbage masher." He pointed to a smooth chunk of Reef Home's outer shell. "Think we can set down on that section over there?"

Lando gave a nonchalant shrug. "Nobody'd even notice the *Falcon* among all this other junk."

"Hey," Han said.

Lando looked at him. "She's your ship, Han. I just wish I had the *Lady Luck* back."

Han set the *Falcon* down on the rocking plasteel debris, locked down the stabilizers, then broke open the door seals. As he clambered down the exit ramp, he scanned the rescuers to see if he could find Leia. He hadn't held her in his arms in so long.

As usual, when they were forced apart, he thought of all sorts of things he wanted to say to her, the promises and sweet nothings she deserved, though he usually didn't manage to force them through his gruff exterior.

Lando followed him, and they both stared at the wounded who had been dragged onto the floating wreckage of the Calamarian city. Although waves sloshed over the metal edges, for now they had been designated infirmary areas, relatively stable platforms on which the medics could tend the injured.

The smell of blood and salt filled the air, mixed with the chemical stench of laser burns, molten metal quenched in the sea, and smoke from fires that continued to burn.

Tentacle-faced Quarren bobbed up from the waves. Water trickled down their heads as they brought up important components from Reef Home's computer core or personal items rescued from breached living quarters. The Quarren would no doubt claim salvage rights for the entire hulk, and they would sell personal belongings back to the Calamarians.

Han stood with his legs spread wide for greater balance on a drifting fragment. The choppy sea made the platform lurch in slow motion, rocking up and down. He finally noticed a wavespeeder skimming toward the wreckage. Leia piloted it, accompanied by Ackbar and a female Calamarian.

Han waved frantically, and the wavespeeder veered toward him, coming alongside. Leia leaped off the vehicle as Ackbar lashed it to a ragged stump of torn metal. She walked confidently, then ran, keeping her balance as she flung herself into Han's arms. He hugged her against his chest as he kissed her again and again. "I'm so glad you're safe!"

She looked at him. "I know."

"Stop that," Han said. "I'm serious. Daala did this, didn't she?"

"We think so, but we have no proof yet."

He cut her off. "No question in my mind about it. Daala has no political motives—she just wants to destroy things."

The female Calamarian climbed out of the wavespeeder and went to the triage area, glancing at the bleeding Calamarians as far too few medics attempted to tend them. She walked among the injured, making quick pronouncements, as if she could somehow determine their chances for survival.

Two medics worked desperately to resuscitate a Quarren whose arm had been amputated and his chest crushed. She took one glance and said, "He won't survive, and you can do nothing more to make him survive." The two Calamarian healers looked at her and, seeing the absolute conviction on her face, moved to another patient and let the Quarren die.

Like an angel of life and death, she walked among them, staring down, tilting her head and swiveling her round Calamarian eyes from side to side.

Han watched her as she moved. "Who is that?"

"Her name is Cilghal. She's the Calamarian ambassador," Leia said, then lowered her voice. "I think she has Jedi powers. She doesn't know it yet. I'm going to make sure she goes to see Luke." Leia hugged her husband again. "I'm so glad you came."

"I was on my way the moment I heard," Han answered. He cocked an eyebrow as he looked at Lando. "By the way, we played another little game of sabacc en route. This time I won." He offered an arm to his wife. "Would you like a ride home in *my* ship, Leia?"

"The *Falcon*'s yours again?" she said with delight, then slipped her arm through his. Still grinning, she looked at Lando. "Sorry to hear that, Lando."

He shrugged. "It was one way to get him off my back."

Ackbar climbed out of the skimmer and stood on the rocking wreckage. He raised one broad hand to shield his lumpy brow as he looked over the scattered debris of Reef Home City. Han had never been good at telling expressions on the Calamarian admiral's face, but Ackbar seemed devastated.

He went to where Ackbar stood all alone. "Admiral," Han said, "I heard what you did, how you defeated an entire Star Destroyer. Great work."

Leia moved beside him in her white robes. "Admiral, your victory here *must* make up for the simple accident on Vortex. I hope you aren't considering going back into hiding?"

Ackbar shook his massive head. "No, Leia. You've reminded me of one thing with your friendly insistence. I am not the type of person who can hide. I must do what I can, and as much as I can. Hiding is for others. Action is for myself."

Leia placed a hand on the Admiral's thick bicep. "Thank you, Admiral. The New Republic needs you," she said.

But Ackbar shook his head. "No, Leia, I won't be returning to Coruscant. After this attack I can see just how much my own people need me. I must stay here on Calamari to help my people rebuild, to strengthen their civilization, and to tighten their defenses against future Imperial strikes.

"We still have not recovered from the onslaught of the World Devastators, and now a new fleet has laid waste to our floating cities. I can't just leave Calamari now and go back." He turned his circular eyes up into the leaden sky and said, "This planet is my home. These are my people. I must devote my energies to helping them."

Han slipped his arm around Leia's waist and squeezed her. She felt stiff and cold; he knew exactly what she was thinking. "I understand . . . Ackbar," Leia said, finally dropping his military title.

Han could sense her tension, knowing how the loss of Ackbar devastated her. Han gripped her shoulder, feeling iron cords of tension rippling beneath her smooth skin.

With Ackbar's refusal to return to Coruscant, and with Mon Mothma growing weaker day by day, that meant Leia had to face all the problems of the New Republic alone.

23

Daylight shone through the rectangular skylights of the Great Temple. Kyp sat on an uncomfortable stone bench in the grand audience chamber, listening to Master Skywalker. He pretended to pay attention, though it became more and more difficult as his opinion of Skywalker's knowledge dwindled.

The other Jedi trainees sat in rapt attention as Master Skywalker placed the small white Holocron on its pedestal. It told yet another story of the ancient Jedi Knights, extolling their heroic adventures, their battles against the dark side—all ultimately ineffectual, because the Emperor and Darth Vader had been stronger than the Jedi Knights, squashing them.

Skywalker refused to learn from that failure. If he meant to bring the new Jedi Knights to greater power, he would have to recognize new abilities, make his Order of Jedi Knights powerful enough to resist a purge like Vader's.

Exar Kun had shown Kyp the ways of the Sith. But Master Skywalker would never adopt those teachings. Kyp wondered why he bothered to keep listening to Skywalker. He seemed so weak, so indecisive.

The other students were a potential wellspring of strength. They had learned how to tap the Force, but they had gone no further than a novice level, mere magicians, playacting in a role that was too big for any of them. They refused to peek behind the doors of greater power; but Kyp was not afraid. *He* could handle the responsibility.

Another holographic gatekeeper of the Holocron appeared and began telling the story of how young Yoda had become a Jedi. Kyp stifled a yawn, unable to understand why they had to keep watching these trivial histories.

He craned his neck to look at the walls of the enormous stone temple. In his mind he tried to imagine the Great Sith War four thousand years ago. He thought of the damp-skinned Massassi race enslaved by Exar Kun, used by him as tools to build the temples that he had reconstructed from even more ancient and forgotten Sith records. Kun had revitalized the dark teachings, granting himself the title of Dark Lord of the Sith, a tradition passed down all the way to Darth Vader, who had been the last Sith Lord.

Exar Kun's temples had been erected across Yavin 4—the last archaeological resting place of the incredibly ancient Sith race—as focal points for his power. Kun had ruled here on the jungle moon, controlling forces that had nearly defeated the Old Republic. But the warlord Jedi Ulic Qel-Droma had betrayed him; and all the united Jedi had swept down in a final battle on Yavin 4, exterminating the Massassi natives, leveling most of the Sith temples, razing most of the rain forest in a holocaust from the skies. But Exar Kun had managed to encyst his spirit here, waiting four thousand years until other Jedi came to awaken him. . . .

Kyp fidgeted and pretended to pay attention. The temple chamber seemed extremely hot. The Holocron droned on and on.

Luke listened with a beatific smile, and the other students continued to observe the images. Kyp gazed at the walls and wondered why he was there.

As half night fell across the jungles of Yavin 4, Luke Skywalker sat back and allowed himself to relax in one of the meeting halls. Smaller than the grand audience chamber, the hall had arched stone ceilings and polished tables, along with serviceable furniture left behind by the Rebel occupation. Bright glowlamps hung in old torch sconces.

Luke felt bone weariness seeping though his body and hunger gnawing in his stomach. For now the students relaxed, recharging their mental energy.

All day long Luke had supervised them through Force exercises, levitation training, visualizing battles and conflicts, sensing other animals and creatures in the forest, learning Jedi history from the Holocron. He was pleased with how well they were doing; though the death of Gantoris still felt like an open wound, he saw that his other students were making great progress. He felt confident in being able to bring back the Jedi Knights.

One of the trainees, Tionne, sat in the corner preparing to play a stringed musical instrument: two hollow resonating boxes separated by a shaft strung with tonal cords.

"This is the ballad of Nomi Sunrider," she said, "one of the historical Jedi Knights." She smiled. Long silvery hair streamed past her shoulders, hanging down to her chest and splitting like a white-capped river down her back. Her eyes were small and close set, glinting with a mother-of-pearl sheen. Her nose was small, her jaw squarish. Luke thought she looked more exotic than beautiful.

Tionne had a great passion for the old Jedi legends and ballads and histories. Even before Luke found her, she had dedicated her life to resurrecting the old stories, digging them out of the archives and popularizing them. Luke had tested Tionne's Jedi talent, and while her potential was perhaps less than the other students', she made up for it with absolute devotion and enthusiasm.

The others found chairs, benches, or just a smooth spot on the floor to hear Tionne sing. She laid the instrument in her lap, and as the trainees listened, she plucked the strings with both hands, setting up an echoing music that fed and subtracted from her lyrics as she sang.

Luke closed his eyes and heard her tale about young Nomi Sunrider, who, after her husband's murder, attended the Jedi training that had been meant for him. Nomi had become a pivotal character in the devastating Sith War that pitted Jedi against Jedi in the ancient days of the Old Republic.

Luke smiled as he heard the music, the resonating notes, Tionne's soft and watery voice as she sang with passion. From the far side of the room, Luke heard a restless stirring and turned to see Kyp Durron, his face stormy with a scowl. The young man sighed, scowled again, and finally stood up, interrupting Tionne's song.

"I wish you wouldn't perpetuate that ridiculous story," Kyp said. "Nomi Sunrider was a victim. She fought in the Sith Wars without ever understanding what the battles were about. She listened blindly to her Jedi Masters, who were afraid because Exar Kun had discovered a way for the Jedi to increase their power."

Tionne set her musical instrument on the flagstones and gripped her knees through the fabric of her robe. Her face looked stricken, her small eyes glinting with confusion. "What are you talking about?" Her voice was thick with discouragement. "I've spent weeks reconstructing that legend. Everyone here knew what I was doing. If you had other information, Kyp, why didn't you share it with me?"

"Where did you learn all this history, Kyp?" Luke said, standing up. He put his hands on his hips, trying to stare Kyp down. The young man had become more and more volatile as he acquired Jedi knowledge. *Calm, you must be calm,* Yoda had said, but Luke didn't know how to make Kyp calm.

Kyp flashed his glance across the trainees, who looked at him in astonishment. "If the Sith War had turned out differently," he said, "perhaps the

Jedi Knights would have learned how to *defend* themselves when Darth Vader came hunting, and they wouldn't all have been slaughtered. The Jedi would never have fallen, and we wouldn't be *here*, taught by someone who doesn't know any more than we do."

Luke remained adamant. "Kyp, tell me where you learned all this."

Kyp pushed his lips together and narrowed his eyes. He drew several deep breaths, and Luke could sense the turmoil inside him, as if his mind were working rapidly to come up with an answer. "I can use the Holocron too," he said. "As Master Skywalker keeps telling us, we are all obligated to learn everything we can."

Luke didn't quite believe the young man's words, but before he could ask another question, Artoo trundled in, warbling and chittering in alarm. Luke deciphered some of the electronic language. "No idea who it is?" he said.

Artoo whistled a descending hooting negative.

"We have a visitor," Luke announced. "A ship is landing on the grid right now. Shall we go out to greet the pilot?" He turned to place a firm hand on Kyp's shoulder, but the young man shrugged away. "We'll discuss this later, Kyp."

Relieved to have a distraction that would shatter the tension, Luke led the way. The other Jedi students followed him down the stone steps and through the hangar bay to the cleared landing grid.

A small personal fighter—a Z-95 Headhunter, a sleek metallic cruiser often used by smugglers—circled and eased down into the clearing. The other students stood at the edge of the grid, but Luke came forward.

The cockpit doors swung up like the wings of a great insect and the pilot emerged. Luke saw a sleek silvery suit clinging to the curves of a young woman's body. She stepped down, pulled off an opaque helmet and shook her dark reddish-brown hair. Her angular face had once been pinched with determination, but now seemed softened, her eyes wider, her full lips not entirely unaccustomed to a smile.

"Mara Jade," Luke said.

She tucked the helmet under her left arm, squeezing it against her rib cage. "Hello, Luke." She looked at him with just the hint of a friendly expression, then raised her eyebrows. "Or do I have to call you 'Master Skywalker' now?"

Luke shrugged, holding out his arms to welcome her. "That depends on why you're here."

She left the Headhunter open behind her as she strode across the clearing to take his hand in greeting. Then she swiveled in a military-style maneuver to survey the dozen students that had come to Luke's training center.

"You told me I had the ability to use the Force," she said. "I came here to learn more about it. Jedi powers could help me run the smugglers' guild."

She unzipped a flexible pouch at her side and tugged out a packet of microcompacted folds of cloth, more than Luke could believe would fit inside a tiny package. She shook the brownish folds, unwrapping her garment.

She looked at the identical garments on all of Luke's trainees and then back at him. "See," she said. "I even brought a Jedi robe."

Over a generous meal of spiced runyip stew and bowls of chopped edible greens, Luke watched Mara Jade feed herself as if she were famished. Luke savored every bite, sensing the nutrients and energies as they slowly permeated his body.

"The New Republic is counting on your Jedi Knights, Luke, and things are getting much worse out there," she said.

Luke leaned forward, lacing his fingers together and trying to pick up echoes of her emotions. "What's happening?" he said. "We're starved for news."

"Well," Mara Jade said, still chewing a mouthful of greens. She swallowed and took a drink of cold spring water, frowning at it as if she had expected something else.

"Admiral Daala has continued her depredations. She doesn't seem to be allied with any of the Imperial warlords. From what we can tell, she's just trying to cause a lot of damage to anyone who opposed the Empire—and she *is* causing plenty of damage. You know that she has been hitting supply ships, blowing them out of space? She leveled the new colony on Dantooine."

"Dantooine!" Luke said.

Mara looked at him. "Yes, isn't one of your students from that group of people?"

Luke sat rigid. Some of the trainees gasped in shock. His mind whirled, thinking of all the refugees he had helped relocate to a supposedly safe place from the treacherous world of Eol Sha. But now they had been wiped out.

"Not anymore," he said. "Gantoris died. He was . . . unprepared for the powers he tried to use."

Mara Jade raised her thin eyebrows, waited for him to explain further. When Luke said nothing else, she continued. "The worst part was when Daala struck the planet Calamari. Seems she meant to take out the orbiting shipyards, but Admiral Ackbar recognized her tactics. He blew up one of her three Star Destroyers—but Daala still managed to sink two Calamarian floating cities. Countless thousands died."

Kyp Durron stood up at the far end of the long table. "Daala lost another one of her Star Destroyers?"

Mara Jade looked at him as if noticing the young dark-haired man for the first time. "She still has two Star Destroyers, and no inhibitions. Admiral

Daala can still cause incredible destruction, and she has a weapon no one else seems to have: she knows she's got nothing to lose."

"I should have sacrificed myself," Kyp said. "I could have killed her with my bare hands when I was on the *Gorgon*."

He lowered his voice, relating the story Luke already knew. "We stole the Sun Crusher out from under her nose, and we wasted our opportunity. We had a weapon that could have struck a decisive blow against the worlds still loyal to the Empire—but what did we do with it? We threw the Sun Crusher into a gas planet where it won't help us at all."

"Calm," Luke said. He gestured for Kyp to sit back down, but Kyp placed his hands flat on the veined stone table, leaning over to glare at Luke.

"The Imperial threat is not going to go away!" he said. "If we pool our Jedi powers, we can resurrect the Sun Crusher, tear it out from the core of Yavin. We can take it and go hunt the Imperials. What could be a clearer mission for us? Why are we just hiding here on this backwater moon?"

He paused, fuming. When the other students looked at him, Kyp glared back at them. "Are you all stupid?" he shouted. "We don't have the luxury to fine-tune our levitating abilities, or balance rocks, or sense rodents out in the jungle. What good does that do? If we aren't going to use our powers to *help* the New Republic, then why bother?"

Luke looked at Mara Jade, who seemed greatly interested in this discussion. He refocused his attention on Kyp. The young man's meal was practically untouched.

"Because that isn't the Jedi way," Luke said. "You've studied the Code. You know how we must approach a difficult situation. The Jedi do not set out to destroy recklessly."

Kyp turned his back on Luke and stormed toward the door of the dining chamber. At the arched stone entrance to the room, Kyp whirled and said, "If we don't use our power, then we may as well not have it. We're betraying the Force with our cowardice."

He gritted his teeth, and his words came out much more quietly. "I'm not certain what else I can learn here, Master Skywalker." With that, he vanished into the corridor.

Kyp felt his skin tingling with barely contained power, as if his blood had begun to fizz inside of him. He moved down the temple corridors like a projectile, and when he reached the heavy door to his quarters, he used the Force to fling it open and slam it against the far wall with enough strength to flake a long splinter of stone from the blocks.

How could he ever have admired Master Skywalker? What did Han Solo see in him as a friend? The Jedi teacher was blind to reality, ignoring problems, covering his eyes with his Jedi cloak, and refusing to use his own powers for the good of the New Republic! The Empire remained a threat, as Daala's attacks on Calamari and Dantooine demonstrated—if Skywalker refused to use his powers to wipe out the enemy, then perhaps his convictions were not strong enough.

But Kyp's were.

He could stay at the Jedi academy no longer. He yanked at the collar of his robe to tear it off. From his stash of personal belongings Kyp pulled out a satchel that contained the flowing black cape that Han had given him as a good-bye gift. During his training at the *praexum,* he had been content to wear the rough old robe Master Skywalker provided. But now he wanted nothing more to do with it.

Exar Kun had shown him how to unleash great powers. Kyp did not trust the Sith Lord, but he could not deny the truth of what the shadow man taught. Kyp could see the power actually working.

For now he had to get away to ponder and sort through the conflicting thoughts in his mind.

He opened up the satchel to look at the black cape. A pair of small, lightning-fast rodents dashed out from their nest in his garment and vanished like hot liquid through a chink in the stone wall.

Alarmed, Kyp lost control of his anger for an instant and let fly a searing blast of power that followed the two rodents down their narrow tunnels and incinerated them as they ran. Blackened bones tumbled forward with the momentum, then slumped to dust in the stone tunnel.

Paying no more heed to the distraction, Kyp pulled out the flowing cape, holding it in front of him. Its embedded reflective threads sparkled as if with hidden power. Kyp wrapped it around himself and gathered a few of his other possessions.

He had to go far away. He had to think. He had to be strong.

Later that evening, when Artoo sounded all the alarms, Luke awoke instantly. He sprinted down the corridors to the outside landing area. Mara Jade ran beside him, already alert, as if she had a good idea of what might be happening.

Luke's eyes adjusted rapidly to the star-strewn sky, which was fuzzy and pale in the south with skyshine from the gas giant Yavin. Mara and Luke stood outside the half-open hangar doors as they watched her Z-95 Headhunter rise from the landing grid with all its running lights darkened.

"He's stealing my ship!" Mara Jade shouted. The Headhunter's sublight engines kicked in, burning white-hot behind the craft as it shot into the sky.

Luke shook his head in disbelief and realized that he had unconsciously extended one hand, beckoning for Kyp Durron to return.

The small ship became a white streak of light that grew smaller and smaller as it reached orbit, then set out among the stars.

Luke felt a devastating emptiness, knowing that he had lost another of his Jedi students forever.

24

Every flagstone gleamed. Every Imperial column had been scrubbed white. Every colorful banner representing the Empire's most loyal worlds hung absolutely straight, displayed without a wrinkle. Everything was in order at the main citadel of the Imperial Military Academy on Carida.

Ambassador Furgan nodded. Just the way he liked it.

Three hundred crack stormtroopers stood at attention in the echoing hall, motionless in perfect ranks. Their white armor glistened like polished bone. They were identical, intensively trained, precise military machines. These stormtroopers were the best of the best in the academy. Only the top Imperial recruits even began stormtrooper training, and these three hundred had excelled in every way.

Ambassador Furgan moved toward the podium to address them. The smell of oils and waxes on the synthetic wood seemed potent in the otherwise sterilized air. Furgan drew himself up, trying to look larger than his stocky stature allowed. The white helmets turned in unison to track him with their black goggles.

"Imperial troops," he said, "you have been chosen to lead the most important mission since the fall of our beloved Emperor. You have endured hardship and passed many tests during your training. I have chosen you as the elite, the best trainees remaining on Carida."

They did not stir, did not congratulate each other. They remained like ranks of statues—which itself attested to the thoroughness of their training.

Since receiving the long-awaited coordinates of the secret planet Anoth, Furgan had plotted this operation with extreme caution. He had studied the personnel data of thousands of his best troops. He had analyzed the records of their training exercises: mock combat in the harsh ice caps of Carida; prolonged sieges out in the baked and waterless deserts; jungle survival tours through dense and uncharted rain forests filled with primitive predators, carnivorous plants, and poisonous insects.

Furgan had culled the names of those stormtroopers who had shown the most stamina, the most initiative, the greatest success, coupled with the strongest willingness to follow every order.

He was proud of his assault force.

"We have obtained secret information regarding the location of a certain baby. A child with enormous potential for using the Force." He paused, expecting to hear them groan, but the stormtroopers made no sound.

"This child is the son of Leia Organa Solo, the New Republic's Minister of State. If we were to apprehend this child, it would deal an enormous psychological blow to the Rebellion—but beyond that, *this boy is the grandson of Darth Vader.*"

There, finally, he thought he heard a rustle of superstitious fear or awe.

"This child could be extremely valuable to the rebirth of the Empire. A child such as this, raised properly and trained properly, could become a worthy successor to the Emperor Palpatine."

Furgan kept talking, faster now as he felt the excitement within him. He was more than just an ambassador; he planned to go along on this assault himself. He would not expose himself to any part of the attack, of course, but he would be there to snatch the young child named Anakin.

"Your unit leaders will provide you with specific assignments. This expedition is currently being provisioned. We have secured transports to take you to the secret location of this world."

Furgan allowed himself a broad grin with his thick purplish lips. "It is also my pleasure to announce that this assault will mark the first combat use of our new Mountain Terrain Armored Transports on which you have been training these past months. That is all. Hail to the Emperor!"

The thunderous response of filtered stormtrooper voices came back at him, rocking the hall. "Hail to the Emperor!"

Furgan slipped behind the hanging purple curtains into a walkway that led down empty glow-lit corridors toward his secure office. Inside his chambers he closed the blast-proof door and sealed it with a cipher lock. He brushed aside models and plans of the deadly new MT-AT attack vehicles. He felt immensely pleased with himself and eager for the assault to start.

Sitting on Carida during the years of turmoil, Furgan had been upset with all the squabbling Imperial commanders since the Emperor's death. Many of the warlords in the Core Systems were extremely powerful, yet they spent their time wrestling for dominance among the remnants of the Imperial fleet rather than fighting against their real enemy, the Rebellion.

Grand Admiral Thrawn had seemed their greatest hope, but he had been defeated; and a year later even the resurrected Emperor had been defeated. The power vacuum of leadership left the Imperial forces with no leadership, no goal, battling only for their own advancement.

Even this surprise new threat by renegade Admiral Daala disturbed Furgan. At least Daala was putting her Star Destroyers to an appropriate use, attacking Rebel worlds and creating as much havoc as possible. But Daala had no overriding plan, no strategy that would bring her ultimate success. She was simply a juggernaut, striking target after target for the satisfaction of causing pain.

Furgan had discovered to his surprise that Daala herself had been trained on Carida. Digging through old records, he had uncovered many disciplinary actions taken against her, reprimands in her file. Even then she had been a maverick, performing admirably but refusing to learn her place, insisting that she deserved promotions instead of others. Furgan had no record of her advancement to admiral, but Moff Tarkin had transferred her to his personal staff after one of his brief inspection tours. Furgan had no other information about Daala since that time.

It angered him that this admiral continued her attacks on the Rebellion without even attempting to get in touch with Carida. Perhaps Daala considered herself a vigilante, but the Empire needed its soldiers to fight as parts of an immense whole. The Empire did not need vigilantes.

Furgan had tried to contact some of the other battling Imperial commanders to get capital ships for his assault on Anoth. The Emperor and Grand Admiral Thrawn and other depredations had already taken most of the ships available to Carida. On the military training planet, Furgan had access to some of the most sophisticated weaponry and soldiers in the entire galaxy—but because of the perpetual squabbles between the Imperial Army and the spacefaring Imperial Navy, he had no place to go with his troops. This left Furgan in a position of being on the most heavily armed—but useless—planet still loyal to the Empire.

Furgan absently played with one of the articulated models of the MT-AT fighting vehicle. It would be fascinating to see the marvelous new machine in operation. Even with the death of the Emperor, his loyalty to the Empire and the New Order had never been shaken, not even slightly.

Furgan kept doing his best to strike vital blows against the New Republic, one way or another. He was pleased to watch indirect reports that gave him evidence of the inexorable progress of Mon Mothma's "mysterious illness." She would be dead before long.

And as soon as Furgan had the grandson of Darth Vader in his possession, all those still loyal to the Empire would have to listen to him.

25

When Wedge Antilles wasn't looking, Qwi Xux stole a glance at the coordinates displayed on his navigation panel. Sitting in the copilot's seat of the disguised personal space yacht, Qwi used her nimble fingers to tap the coordinates into the navicomputer, requesting a full display.

Wedge looked away from the starfield and caught what she was doing. "Hey!" he said, then grinned sheepishly as he lowered his gaze. "This was supposed to be a surprise."

Qwi laughed, a cascade of short musical tones. "I just wanted to know the name of the planet." She frowned as the display came up. "Ithor? Never heard of it."

Wedge chuckled and reached over to squeeze her slender shoulder. She felt the warmth of his touch linger for several moments after he removed his hand. "Qwi, you've never heard of *most* places in the galaxy. You spent your entire life cooped up in Maw Installation."

"Is Ithor a nice place?" she asked.

He sighed. "It's beautiful. A pristine natural world covered with forests and jungles, rivers and waterfalls. We'll be incognito, and you won't have to worry about anybody knowing who you are."

Qwi looked around at the metal-edged control panels of the space yacht, at the synthetic fabric of the seats that felt so smooth and soft. She smelled the recirculated air. Qwi had lived for years inside a completely enclosed environment; she knew nothing about plants and animals and other life-forms. She hoped it would be fascinating.

"Are you sure we'll be safe?" she asked, swallowing hard. Her greatest nightmare was that some Imperial spy might recapture her and haul her back to the black-hole research lab where they would tear the weapons knowledge out of her head, no matter how much she resisted.

"Yes," Wedge said after a long pause. "Ithor is an isolated paradise. It's a world where many young couples"—he paused, then swallowed as if embarrassed by the word he had just spoken—"uh, *tourists* go for vacations. Many people come and go, and the Ithorians welcome everyone.

"The Empire blockaded this world during the Rebellion, causing some damage as a show of force. But after one of the Ithorians gave the Empire access to the agricultural and cloning information they wanted, Ithor was basically left alone."

Wedge looked out at the starfield where the brilliant sun of the Ithorian system gleamed a whitish blue. He increased the thrust from the sublight engines and vectored them toward a bright green planet veined with blue and swathed with white clouds.

"Just pretend we're on vacation," Wedge said. "We'll be tourists, and I'll show you what you've been missing. I can't think of a better place to start."

"I really look forward to it." Qwi smiled warmly at him.

Wedge blushed, then seemed to concentrate furiously on the relatively simple task of entering a low orbit.

Qwi placed her pale-blue fingers against the side viewport as she stared at the lush vistas below. She had never seen such exotic scenery before, so different from the sterile white-walled rooms in Maw Installation.

Below her, between the treetops of a tropical paradise, broad rivers furled with white rapids as the current flowed over broken rocks. The space yacht soared above broad meadows splattered with brilliant colors, blooming flowers in red and yellow, blue and purple. The sheer vibrancy of the growing things dazzled her eyes.

They passed over a chain of oval lakes that glittered and reflected the sunlight, like the string of jewels on the necklace Wedge had given her as a gift a few days earlier. Overhead the sky was a muted lavender.

"Beautiful," she said.

"Told you so," Wedge agreed, giving her a half smile. "You can trust me."

She looked at him, then blinked her indigo eyes. "Yes, Wedge, I trust you."

He cleared his throat and turned away quickly, pointing out the front viewport. "The Ithorians allow no damage to their environment," he said as if reading a data summary. "In fact, they consider it sacrilege even to set foot on the ground of their mother jungle."

"Then how do they live?" Qwi asked.

"Look," Wedge said.

As they soared above the treetops, Qwi made out a strange shape coming over the horizon, rapidly growing larger as they approached. "Is that a city?" she said.

"More than just a city," Wedge said, "an entire enclosed environment. The Ithorians call it the *Tafanda Bay*."

The enormous disk-shaped construction swelled to fill their front viewport, looking larger and larger—and larger, like a fat coin greater in diameter than the entire Maw Installation. Though the city appeared to be made of plasteel, it also seemed at least partially alive.

A chaos of platforms, flight decks, transmission antennas, and roving machinery studded the hull of the Ithorian floating city—but the exposed surfaces were covered with hanging moss; large trees grew out of special pockets on the side walls, rising to the sky and looking thicker and greener than the metallic towers.

On the top flat surface of the disk, greenhouse domes sparkled like a thousand eyes in the sun. Qwi could see through the transparent domes to dense botanical gardens in carefully manicured rows. Small ships flitted like gnats about the landing ports and shipping bays.

Underneath the *Tafanda Bay*, banks of diffused repulsorlift engines kept the entire city hovering over the treetops, casting an elliptical shadow over the leafy surface. The Ithorian city slowly drifted along a wandering course with no destination in particular, without touching the sacred ground.

Wedge keyed in his request for landing coordinates and was answered by an odd echoing voice that Qwi thought sounded like someone speaking through a long, empty tube. After a moment the comm system crackled again with the voice—or was it another one?—changing the coordinates.

"Excuse us for the oversight, sir. A special representative will meet you at the landing bay. We hope you enjoy your stay here on our homeworld."

Wedge looked suspiciously at the comm unit. "Why would they be giving us special treatment?" he said to Qwi. "Nobody is supposed to know who we really are."

Qwi looked around, and suddenly the cockpit of the space yacht seemed smaller. "Do you think we're in danger? Should we turn around and find some other place to go?"

Wedge looked as if that was indeed what he wanted to do. "No, it's all right," he said bravely. "I can protect you. Don't worry."

They landed on the pad indicated, and Wedge extended the passenger ramp. He climbed down the gangway first and reached up to take Qwi by the hand, leading her gently down. She could easily have disembarked by herself, but she enjoyed the attention he showered on her.

Surrounding the space yacht were wide-boled gray-barked trees with low branches that spread out to form a long, flat platform. Brilliant white and blue flowers spangled the leaves. Staring around her, Qwi took a deep breath of the moist air. Everything smelled fresh and alive, filled with a symphony of scents that startled her imagination.

"Greetings." Qwi turned to see an exceedingly strange-looking alien hulking toward them, flanked by two ten-year-old human boys. The hunchbacked alien wore a white cape trimmed with braid. Its head looked like a long ladle, as if someone had taken a face made of soft clay and stretched it into an S-curve, looping the front up and yanking out two eye stalks. The mouth was hidden far under the sloping canopy of its head. As Qwi watched, the cumbersome-looking creature took steps forward with a gentle, careful grace.

The two human boys beside the creature wore similar white capes, over bright-green jumpsuits. Pale-haired and blue-eyed, both wore beatific expressions, but neither of them spoke.

Wedge must have seen how startled Qwi was by the alien's appearance. "I guess I should have warned you. The Ithorians are commonly called Hammerheads."

Qwi nodded slowly, thinking about other strange creatures she had seen, from the fish-faced Admiral Ackbar to the tentacle-headed Tol Sivron who had run Maw Installation. Perhaps not all intelligent creatures in the galaxy could be as attractive as some humans . . . such as Wedge.

"Actually," the alien said, stepping closer, "we dislike the name Hammerheads. It seems deprecating to us."

"My apologies, sir," Wedge said, bowing slightly.

"I am Momaw Nadon, and I am honored to be of service to you, Wedge Antilles and Qwi Xux."

Wedge took one step back in panic. "How do you know our names?" he said.

Momaw Nadon made a hollow bubbling sound that came from both sides of his mouth in a stereophonic echo. "Mon Mothma asked me to give you special accommodations."

"Why would Mon Mothma tell you we were coming here?" Wedge said. "We're supposed to be keeping a low profile." As Nadon gave a slight bow, his ladle-shaped head see-sawed up and down. "I have sympathized with the Rebel Alliance since my days of exile on Tatooine, more than a decade ago. My people banished me to the desert planet, where I could tend the sands rather than our beautiful forests. The Empire had demanded certain agricultural information, and I gave it to them to save our forests from being obliterated—but still my people exiled me. I returned here after the Emperor's death, and I have continued to make amends ever since."

Nadon gestured to the two human boys. "Take their luggage. We will show them their staterooms."

The youths moved in unison—without the pell-mell franticness of young boys—entering the space yacht and returning with the slick silvery containers of vacation clothes.

Nadon led them away from the landing bay, ducking his head under the low-hanging branches that surrounded the landing pad. The passage seemed like a living green tunnel.

"I was also in the cantina in Mos Eisley when Luke Skywalker and Obi-Wan Kenobi first met Captain Solo. I did not know my brush with history at that time, but I remember it clearly, though I was preoccupied with . . . other concerns at the time."

"I'm amazed you could recall a meeting like that after so many years," Wedge said.

Nadon indicated a disguised turbolift that opened like a great leafy pod in the wall. They all stepped inside and began to descend deeper within the *Tafanda Bay*.

After a long pause Nadon finally said, "Ithorians have long memories."

He led them through winding corridors, past small domes that contained specimens of plant life from different parts of the planet. Near a delicately spraying fountain, Nadon pointed to two doors across the corridor from each other.

"I have assigned you these staterooms," he said. "Please contact me if you desire other amenities. I am here to serve you." The two mysterious boys deposited the luggage in the corridor and stepped back to stand on either side of Nadon.

Qwi finally said, "You haven't introduced us to the children. Are you their caretaker?"

Nadon made a rumbling bubbly sound in his twin throats. "They are . . . seedlings, grown from the flesh of my enemy. They are also a memory of my days on Tatooine." Nadon hung his ladle-shaped head.

The two boys remained impassive, and Nadon ushered them off. Without a backward glance he left Wedge and Qwi standing outside their staterooms, wondering what he meant.

After nightfall on the upper observation deck of the *Tafanda Bay*, Qwi went with Wedge to watch the moons rise. The lavender skies had turned a deep violet, punctuated by brilliant stars in a wash across the heavens.

A small moon in full phase climbed over the eastern horizon, while the fingernail crescent of a much larger moon hung close to the western sky, following the brilliant colors of sunset over the edge of the world. High up, two other moons showed swollen quarter phases.

Qwi took a deep breath of the humid air, smelling a plethora of spicy perfumes from green plants and night-blooming flowers, like a complex mixture of all the perfumes and all the pleasant cooking herbs she had ever smelled.

The breeze grew paradoxically warmer with nightfall, and she felt her feathery hair drifting about. She straightened it with her slender fingers, knowing that Wedge liked to see her pearly strands glisten in the light. She had changed into a soft wrap swirled with pastel colors that accentuated the ethereal beauty of her wispy body.

The Ithorian eco-city cruised slowly over the treetops. The gentle hum of the *Tafanda Bay*'s banks of repulsorlift engines blended with the simmering night sounds of the jungle below. The breeze rustled leaves in the tall hedges and stands of scale trees around the observation deck.

Other Ithorians arrived, standing in silence or thrumming in their strange stereo language. Wedge and Qwi said nothing to each other.

She stepped closer, brushed against him, then finally let herself snuggle up to his side. Nervously, it seemed, Wedge slipped an arm around her waist and she—Qwi Xux, inventor of the Sun Crusher, co-creator of the Death Star—felt honored to be under the protection of General Wedge Antilles.

She knew that Imperial loyalists would be desperate to regain the secret knowledge locked in her brain. But Qwi realized that here, at least, she felt completely safe.

26

Jacen and Jaina continued their trek across Coruscant's dank underbelly. They couldn't tell if the dim half light that filtered down from high above signified nighttime or day. The air smelled thick with rotted garbage, dead things, corroded metal, and stagnant water. They walked along the widest streets, dodging rubble, clambering over fallen and ancient wreckage. They had seen nothing familiar for hours, and neither of them knew what to do next.

"I'm hungry," Jaina said.

"Me too," Jacen said.

The deep underground was smothered in a silence overlaid with white noise. Shadowy creatures, startled by the twins, fled into darker hiding spots. Bumping one pile of debris, Jacen and Jaina sparked an avalanche of frightening clatters. The twins ran from the noise, generating further junkfalls that tinkled and clanged from great heights.

"My feet hurt," Jacen said.

"Mine don't," Jaina answered.

Up ahead they finally saw a welcome sign: a cave dwelling made of shored-up wreckage, walls built from piled chunks of duracrete mortared together with a paste of dried algae, mud, and darker substances. Smoky lights burned deep inside the cave, looking enticing in contrast to the forbidding bleakness of the undercity.

Jacen and Jaina moved forward at the same time. "Food?" Jacen asked. His sister nodded.

Outside of the strange slumped cave they saw cables running through lichen-clogged eye bolts mounted at various points. Along the walls and ceilings, metal bands like long fingerbones dangled in a decoration, linked together by sagging segments of chain.

"In here," Jaina said, taking the lead. Dimness folded over them, leading them toward the enticing lights.

Near her head a scratching, scuttling sound came from the shadows. The girl looked to see an elongated spider-roach nearly the size of her head. Bumping against her, Jacen leaned forward to get a better look at the creature. The spider-roach clambered up the lumpy wall and hesitated, turning three glassy amber eyes at them.

Suddenly, with a ratcheting clatter, a fistful of metal flanges from the ceiling swung loose like a prehensile mechanical hand dangling on chains. Dozens of steel fingers slammed against the wall to trap the spider-roach, clamping it into a makeshift metallic cage. The creature thrashed and flailed, clacking its mandibles. Sparks flew as chitinous forelimbs scrabbled against the impenetrable bars.

In panic Jacen and Jaina hurried down the tunnel toward the flickering orange lights. But the twins stopped, simultaneously sensing a thrill of danger. They looked up just in time to see a much larger cage, all prongs and sharp metal edges, collapse down around them. Mechanical metal claws surrounded them like dozens of fists chained together.

"Trap!" Jaina said.

Shuffling footsteps came toward them—a thud, then a scrape as a large hulking creature emerged from the depths of the lair. The silhouette appeared first, a massive tufted head with enormous arms dragging almost to the ground. One thickly muscled thigh looked the size of a tree trunk, but the other leg was much shorter, twisted and withered.

Jacen and Jaina rattled the sharp metal edges of the cage, but the mechanical claws drew tighter together like scissors. "Help!" Jacen said.

Then their captor came into full view, lit from the side by reflected smoky lights. The creature was covered with a pelt of shaggy hair, showing no distinction between its enormous head and the rest of its torso, as if both pieces had been smashed together into one barrel-shaped mass.

The thing's mouth hung in a long crooked slash, twisted sideways and straightened back only partway. Its left eye was overgrown with a mass of tumors and rotting flesh; the other eye, nearly as large as the twins' fists, shone a sickly yellow, streaked with red lines.

Jacen and Jaina were too afraid to say anything. Their ogrelike captor shambled past, ignoring them for the moment as he rocked back and forth on his stubby withered leg. He picked up the small trap to inspect the frantic spider-roach.

The children could smell the stink from the monster as he next bent toward the bars of their cage, thrusting his giant yellow eye close, but Jacen and Jaina scrambled to the other side of the cage.

The ogre disconnected long chains from the wall, draped them over his shoulder, and dragged the twins' cage clattering down the corridor into his firelit den. The cage rolled and crashed against unseen obstacles, and the twins had to scramble to keep themselves upright.

Inside, gnawed bones from large and small creatures cluttered the monster's lair, some piled in baskets, others cracked and strewn over the broken floor. Smoky red flames came from smoldering pots filled with a rancid-smelling fat.

Chained in a cleared area of the pit sat a tusked ratlike creature covered with bristling fur. Its black rubbery lips stretched back in a perpetual snarl. Gobbets of drool flew from its mouth as it snarled and threw itself to the end of its chain.

A set of broken manacles from a detention area hung on the spike-encrusted walls of the chamber. As the ogre moved about in the brighter light, tatters of an old prison uniform could be seen among his greasy curls of body hair.

The ogre pried open the metal fingers of the small spider-roach trap. He picked up the arachnid with his lumpy bare hands and tossed it to the giant rat-monster. The glossy spider-roach flailed its long legs as it tumbled end over end, and the rat-monster snapped it out of the air. But the bug managed to grab on to the rubbery lips with its sharp legs, and it stung hard.

The rat-creature yelped, gnashing its tusks until it chomped down and split the exoskeleton of the spider-roach with a cracking pop. Then, contented, it slurped the juicy soft meat and licked its black lips. The rat-creature panted and rolled its wet red eyes at the two children.

Hopeful, the twins peered out from the cage. "We are lost," Jaina said, calling to the ogre from between the bars.

"Please help us find our home," Jacen added.

The ogre fixed its yellow eye on them. A foul wet stench came from his mouth, like slime scraped from the bottoms of a thousand sewers. He spoke in a bubbling voice, slurring the words. "No," the ogre said. "Gonna *eat* you!"

Then he tottered off on his shriveled leg toward a smoldering fireplace. The ogre found a pair of long sharp tongs resting in the hot coals. Holding the implements high, the ogre turned back to the twins.

Jacen and Jaina both looked at the top of their cage. The articulated finger joints were held together by small pins clogged with grease and rust, but smooth enough that the cage could open and close.

The twins each knew which pins the other concentrated on—and used their rudimentary ability with the Force, just as they did when they played tricks on Threepio and played the games that their Uncle Luke showed them.

They popped out the cage pins two at a time in rapid succession. Small pieces of metal flew like tiny projectiles in all directions. Suddenly without support, the long metal fingers fell open to the ground with an incredible clang.

"Run!" Jacen cried. Jaina took his hand and they scrambled toward the tunnel.

The ogre let out a furious roar and stumped after them, but he could not keep up on his uneven legs. Instead he grabbed the thick chain holding the rat-monster to the wall and yanked out the long spike that held its collar together.

Set free, the rat-creature lunged. Turning, it tried to snap its teeth at the ogre—but he used a muscle-swollen arm to bash the rat-thing away from him. He gestured toward the fleeing children.

And they ran, and they ran.

The rat-creature came howling and slavering after them. The twins ran out of the firelit opening and dashed down an alley. Behind them they could hear the steam-engine sounds of the creature as it snorted, following their scent. Its claws clattered on the pavement.

Jaina found a small dark gash in the wall, a hole broken into the layered duracrete. "Here," she said.

Jaina dived into the tiny hole headfirst, and her brother clambered after. Only a second later the rat-creature jammed its tusked snout against the jagged opening, but it could not get its head through the hole.

By that time Jacen and Jaina had scrambled on their hands and knees, burrowing deep into the unexplored darkness.

"Oh, we never should have agreed to baby-sit!" Threepio wailed. "I wonder how often baby-sitters actually lose their children." Chewbacca growled at him.

"Why didn't you listen to me, Chewbacca? Mistress Leia will have all your fur shaved off so she can make a new rug. You will be the first bald Wookiee in history."

Chewbacca bellowed a suggestion as they stormed down the corridors, still searching the Holographic Zoo for Extinct Animals.

"You can go to the control room if you like. I think we should sound the alarm here and now. It is perfectly acceptable to summon help. This is an emergency."

Threepio found the fire alarm and activated it with one golden hand; next, he searched among the holographic exhibits until he also found a security alarm. Without hesitation he pressed the button. "There, that should do it."

Chewbacca growled in Threepio's face with enough force that the droid's audio sensors shut down to reset themselves. Then he manhandled Threepio in his furred Wookiee arms, carrying him bodily down the hall at a fast lope.

"All right, have it your way, then," Threepio said. "We'll go to the control center and shut down all the holograms."

Jacen and Jaina felt the slimy surface of the tunnel as they crawled downward. They had no idea where they were going, but they knew they had to find some other way home.

Jacen reached up, felt no close ceiling, and climbed to his feet. The twins could see nothing in the darkness, only a faint glow ahead. They made their way toward it—cautiously this time, afraid they might find another ogre. Jacen smelled sizzling meat, and he heard guttural words, the first human voices they had heard since deciding to go home without Threepio and Chewbacca.

Jacen started toward the light, but Jaina held on to his arm. "Careful," she said. Jacen nodded and put a finger to his lips as a reminder. They inched forward, hearts hammering. They smelled the delicious scents of cooked food, heard the crackle of fire, the chattering voices.

They reached a corner and peered around it to see a large blasted-out room, a low-level reception area used thousands of years ago. Jacen and Jaina could see a bonfire, tattered figures moving between light and shadow, banks of dimly functioning glowcrystals, and a glimpse of blinking computer equipment. Then suddenly, from all sides, silent hands reached out to grab them.

Firm grips, wiry arms. Five sentries struck at once, snatching Jacen and Jaina and whisking them off their feet before they had a chance to struggle.

The sentries laughed even as the children squealed in terror. A cheer went up from the people around the bonfire as the sentries carried the twins out into the bright light.

Alarms pulsed and whooped in the control center of the Holographic Zoo. Red signals flashed; yellow lights blinked on and off in indecipherable patterns.

Threepio was impressed at the commotion he had managed to cause just by activating a few security systems.

The zoo's control droid sat in the center of an octagonal computer bank. It had a spherical head encircled by optical sensors mounted every thirty-six degrees. From its central station the control droid sprouted eight segmented limbs that scrambled over the panels, pecking at the buttons in a blur of motion like fire-linked blaster cannons.

"Permission denied," the control droid said to them.

Chewbacca roared, but the control droid merely spun its spherical head and ignored the Wookiee's outburst.

"I feel required to warn you," Threepio said to the other droid, "that when Wookiees lose their tempers they are known to rip limbs out of their sockets. I believe Chewbacca here is on the verge of losing his temper."

Chewbacca leaned forward on one of the segmented control panels, gripped it with his hairy paws, and roared again into one set of the multiple eyes.

"Permission still denied," the control droid said.

"But you don't understand!" Threepio insisted. "There are two lost children inside your Holographic Zoo. If you would just shut down the image generators, we could search the habitats and find them."

"Unacceptable," the control droid said. "It would cause too great a disturbance among the other guests."

Threepio indignantly propped his metallic arms on his hips. "But the zoo looked empty when we toured it. How many other patrons are currently using the facility?"

"Irrelevant," the control droid said. "Such an action is strictly forbidden except in conditions of extreme emergency."

Threepio waved his golden hands in the air. "But this *is* an emergency!"

Chewbacca had apparently had enough of formal requests. He bunched his fists together and brought them down on the first control bank, smashing the glossy black coverings and shattering circuit connections.

Sparks flew. The control droid's head spun around like a planet knocked out of its orbit. "Excuse me," the control droid said, "please don't touch the controls."

Chewbacca went to the second segment of the octagonal board and smashed it as well. The control droid flailed its eight articulated limbs, trying to bypass circuits in the remaining systems.

"I must admit, Chewbacca, that your enthusiasm makes up for any lack of finesse," Threepio said.

In no time the Wookiee had ruined the entire set of panels. Without a single functioning hologram-generating system, the control droid folded all eight of its articulated arms like a dead insect and seemed to sulk.

Chewbacca yanked Threepio's mechanical arm and hauled him back down to the holographic habitats. Now every chamber was empty, white-tiled walls with strategically mounted hologram generators at the vertices of the room. Various guests had dropped garbage in among the illusions, refreshment wrappers, torn scraps of paper, and half-eaten nonorganic treats that had failed to decompose.

"Jacen! Jaina!" Threepio called.

Alarms continued to squawk as Chewbacca and Threepio passed from one habitat to the next. Threepio called up the data brochure inside his computer brain and guided the search, methodically moving from one room to another. Every cell in the deactivated Holographic Zoo looked identical, and they found the children in none of them.

When they finally hurried to the last chamber, hoping against hope that they would discover the twins crouched in the corner and waiting to be rescued, they were suddenly met by the New Republic militia charging toward them in response to all the alarms.

"Halt!" the captain of the guard said.

Threepio instantly counted eighteen humans, all wearing blaster-proof armor. The militia members drew their weapons and leveled them.

In all his adventures Threepio couldn't recall ever having seen so many blaster barrels pointed directly at him.

"Oh, my!" he said.

The feral humans brought Jacen and Jaina before their king. The flickering warmth of the junk-heap bonfire made a pleasant smell. The strips of unrecognizable meat roasting on long skewers caused both children to lick their lips.

Grimy-faced sentries looked down at the twins and smiled. Their mouths seemed a checkerboard of yellow teeth and black gaps. The king of the underground humans sat on a tall pile of ragged cushions. He laughed. "*These* are the fearsome intruders?"

Jacen and Jaina looked around themselves, gathering details. The refugees in the former reception area had bedrolls, tattered clothing, and stashes of scavenged possessions. Some sat mending rags, others worked on spring-loaded animal traps. Two old men crouched holding small musical instruments cobbled together from old pipes; they blew into the mouthpieces, comparing high whistling notes.

The feral people wore torn and threadbare clothing, some mended, some not, all very old. They had long hair; the men wore bushy beards. Their skin was pale, as if they had not seen sunlight for decades. Some of them might never have seen natural light at all.

The king seemed to have the best materials. He wore shoulder pads and polished white gloves taken from a stormtrooper. His eyebrows were large, his reddish-brown beard wispy. Though his face was the color of raw bread dough, his eyes were bright and alert. His smile also showed gaps from missing teeth, but it contained real humor.

Around and behind the king hung jury-rigged electronic equipment, computer panels, holographic display modules, even one old-model food-processing unit. Ancient generators had been wired into the frayed energy grid of the skyscrapers, skimming power from the main flow through Imperial City. The lost people had obviously been down here a long time.

"Get these children some food," the king yelled, bending down to look at them. "Well, now, my name is Daykim. What're your names?"

"Jaina," Jacen said, indicating his sister.

Jaina pointed to her brother. "Jacen."

A sentry with gray-blond hair tied in a long ponytail brought a smoking skewer of the roasted meat. He yanked off the red-black pieces of meat with his fingers and dropped them onto a squarish metal platter that had originally been some sort of cover plate. The sentry blew on his fingers, licked the juices, and grinned at the children. He set the platter down in front of them, and the twins sat on the floor, crossing their legs.

"Blow on the meat before you put it in your mouths," the king said. "It's hot."

The twins picked up small morsels, dutifully blowing until the meat was cool enough to chew. King Daykim seemed to delight in just watching them.

"So what were you doing down here all alone? It's dangerous, you know. Would you like to stay here with us?" the king said. "We're all growing old. It's been too long since young people joined us down here."

Jacen and Jaina shook their heads. "We are lost," Jaina said around a mouthful of meat. A thick welling of tears appeared on the edge of her eyelids.

Jacen also started to cry. "Please help us find our home," he said, looking toward the high ceiling. Somewhere up in the distance lay their living quarters.

"Up there?" King Daykim said, comically incredulous. "Why would you want to go back up there? The Emperor lives up there. He's a *bad man*." Daykim shook his head and gestured around him. "We have everything we want here. We have food, we have light, we have . . . our things."

Jacen shook his head at Daykim. "I want to go home."

With a sigh Daykim glanced back at his banks of computer terminals and then flashed them a defeated smile.

"Of course you want to go home. Just finish up your supper. You'll need your strength."

• • •

The sergeant of the militia escorted Threepio and Chewbacca back to Han and Leia's quarters in the old Imperial Palace. "Our records indicate that Minister Organa Solo and her husband returned not more than an hour ago," the sergeant said.

Chewbacca moaned dejectedly. Threepio shot a sharp glance at him. "I think *you* should be the one to tell them what happened, Chewbacca. After all, I'm only a droid."

"Rest assured we're doing everything we can," the sergeant said. "We've had our teams combing the Holographic Zoo and the adjoining floors just in case the twins found an emergency staircase. We're checking the logs of the maintenance droid just to be sure that no one used the turbolift that was being serviced." He snapped to attention. "We'll find them, don't you worry."

Threepio used the override code on the doorway to open it. Then he and Chewbacca stepped into the living quarters—to find Han and Leia sitting on the self-conforming chairs, with the twins balanced on their knees.

"Children! Oh, thank goodness, you're home!" Threepio cried. Chewbacca thundered a high-pitched bellow.

Han and Leia both turned to look at them. "Well, there you two are."

Threepio noticed at once that one of the panels from the air-ventilation system had been knocked off, apparently from the inside. A stranger, a large man, dressed in tattered but ornate clothing dashed to shelter behind one of the larger pieces of furniture. He had long reddish-brown hair, a wispy beard, and uncommonly pale skin.

Leia returned her attention to the rag-clad man. "Seriously, Mr. Daykim, I can't tell you how much we appreciate what you've done. I assure you the New Republic will do everything it can to repatriate all your people."

Daykim shook his head. "The Emperor never forgave mistakes, not even accounting mistakes. We saw many of our fellow civil servants either executed or sent off to horrendous penal colonies. As soon as we caught ourselves in a simple but irrevocable filing error, we knew we didn't have long to live—so we grabbed what we could and fled to the underlevels of Imperial City. My people have been living there for years. We're just a bunch of feral bureaucrats who don't know any other life."

"We could find a place for you in the New Republic. We don't punish people for simple mistakes. We could bring you all back," Leia said again. "Look around you, we could give you your own quarters like these. Many of the buildings in the old Imperial City are abandoned."

"We know," Daykim said, "we live there ourselves sometimes. Thank you for your offer." He stood up and cast a suspicious glance toward Threepio and Chewbacca. He patted Jacen and Jaina on the head and flashed his gap-toothed smile. "You're good little children. Your mommy and daddy should be proud of you."

Han cleared his throat and extended his hand in thanks. The tattered man grabbed it and shook vigorously as if pleased to give a firm, businesslike handshake.

"I still don't understand why you want to stay down in those murky lower levels," Han said.

Daykim swung one leg into the ventilation duct and looked around. "It's very simple," he said. "Up here I was just a file clerk—down there I am a *king!*"

With a last smile for all of them, Daykim vanished into the ventilation ducts. They heard him thumping and scrambling as he disappeared down the access tubes.

"Well, everything turned out right after all," Threepio said. "Isn't this wonderful?"

In answer Han and Leia both glared at him.

"We want a story!" the twins said in unison.

27

Kyp Durron brought his stolen ship into orbit around the small forest moon of Endor, where the second Death Star had been destroyed.

Ignoring the sensors on board his stolen Z-95 Headhunter, he let his eyes fall closed. He reached out with his sense ability, seeking across the entire landscape for shadows or ripples in the Force. He had to find the last resting place of the only other Dark Lord of the Sith he knew of.

Darth Vader.

Exar Kun, who had lived long before Vader, was pleased to know that the Lords of the Sith had continued for millennia. But Kyp still felt driven to find answers to the clamoring questions in his mind.

Master Skywalker said that Darth Vader, his own father, had returned to the light side in the end. From this Kyp concluded that the powers of the Sith were not permanently connected with evil. That gave him a thread of hope. He recognized full well that the dark spirit of Exar Kun had lied to him, or at least misled him. The risk was terrible, but the reward would benefit the entire galaxy.

If he succeeded.

Here on Endor, Kyp felt he could hide from the watchful eyes of Exar Kun. He didn't know how far Kun's power extended, but he didn't think the ancient Sith Lord could leave Yavin 4. Not yet at least.

Kyp instinctively worked the controls of Mara Jade's fighter, bringing the Headhunter lower as he scanned the forests. After the Rebel celebration of their victory over the Emperor, Luke Skywalker had built a pyre for his father near the towering trees, not far from the Ewok villages. He had watched the roaring flames consume the remnants of Darth Vader's mechanical attire.

But perhaps something had survived. . . .

As the Headhunter cruised over the tops of the immense Ewok father trees, Kyp searched with his mind, ironically making use of the exercises Master Skywalker had taught him, how to reach out and touch all life-forms.

He caught the stirrings of the furry Ewoks in their tree cities. He sensed large predators on the prowl: one humanoid behemoth, a giant Gorax, crashed through the trees, black hair swinging from side to side as he searched for Ewok dwellings low enough to grab.

As he flew onward, Kyp's mind ranged far and wide across the Endor wilderness. Then he felt a ripple, an echo of something that definitely did not . . . belong.

Everything else seemed to have its place, but this did not conform. A stain that seemed to absorb all other senses, casting waves of leftover darkness that caused the creatures on Endor to avoid the place instinctively.

Kyp changed course and arrowed to the coordinates, circling once until he found an appropriate clearing. The repulsorlifts whined, and his landing jets kicked up fallen forest debris as he landed the Headhunter in the underbrush.

Afraid and yet eager, Kyp swung out of the cockpit and hopped down, landing with a crunch in the twigs and dead leaves. The breeze died, as if the evening forest were holding its breath around him. Silvery planetshine trickled through the dense leaves, lighting the clearing with a wan, milky glow.

Kyp took four steps and stopped before the scorched site of Vader's funeral pyre.

The ground surrounding the old burned area remained dead and brown. Though the thick forests of Endor were tenacious and fast-growing, no plants dared approach the scar—even after seven years.

The bonfire had been large and hot, incinerating Vader's uniform. Only a few heat-warped bits of body armor had survived, along with tatters of a black cape tangled in broken rocks and time-packed ashes. A twisted lacing of steel reinforcement lay like a torn spiderweb covered.

Kyp swallowed and knelt in the dirt. He reached out tentatively, afraid, until he let his fingertips brush the age-crumbled ashes.

He jerked his hand away, then brought it back. The spot was cold, but the coldness seemed to go away as his hands grew numb.

Kyp used the Force to scatter bits of ash, blowing clear the tiny, buckled residue that had survived the fire, an unrecognizable lump of black plasteel that might have been Vader's helmet. Growing more desperate, Kyp increased his power, scouring away debris and leaving only a sad jumble of wires, melted plasteel, and shreds of tough cloth.

Darth Vader, former Dark Lord of the Sith, had been reduced to only pathetic scraps and nightmarish memories.

Kyp reached out to stroke the remnants. Electric tingles went through his hands. He knew he shouldn't be touching these relics, yet he could not turn away now. Kyp had to find answers to his questions, even if he had to answer them himself.

"Darth Vader, where did you go wrong?" he asked, staring down at the fragments of armor. His voice, unused for more than a day, croaked at him.

Vader had been a monster, with the blood of billions on his hands. According to Exar Kun, Anakin Skywalker had been unprepared for the power he had touched, and it had overwhelmed him.

Kyp recognized that he had begun to walk down a similar path—but he was not so naive. Unlike Anakin Skywalker, he understood the dangers. He could guard himself. He would not be tricked by the temptations and the brutalities that had lured Vader deeper and deeper into the dark side.

Feeling cold and alone in the night, Kyp returned to the ship and took out the long cape Han Solo had given him. He wrapped the fabric around his dark jumpsuit to keep warm, then went back to sit on the barren ground by the ashes of Vader's pyre. The peaceful sounds of the forest gradually returned, chirping and whistling around him like a lullaby.

Kyp was in no hurry. He could wait here on Endor. He needed to make sure he wasn't kidding himself. He was no fool. He knew the dangerous edge he was walking, and it frightened him.

As he sat in peace, running his fingers along the slick, fine fabric of his cloak, Kyp thought of how his friend Han Solo had freed him from the spice mines . . . but even that happy thought twisted around to make him realize just how much of his life the Empire had stolen from him.

Kyp rarely recalled the diamond-edged memories of his youth, when he and his older brother Zeth had lived on the colony world of Deyer. He thought of the raft cities anchored in a complex of terraformed lakes stocked with fish.

Zeth had taken him out many times on a pleasure skimmer to sink crustacean nets or just to swim under the ocher-colored skies. His brother Zeth had long dark hair, eyes narrowed against the brightness of the sun, his body wiry and rippling with lean muscles, his skin tanned from long days spent outside.

The colonists had tried to build a perfect society on Deyer, fully democratic with every person serving a term on the council of raft towns. Unanimously, the representatives on Deyer had voted to condemn the destruction of Alderaan, to request that Emperor Palpatine rescind his New Order. They had worked through the appropriate political channels, naively believing that with their votes they could influence the Emperor's decisions.

Instead Palpatine had crushed the "dissidents" on Deyer, overrunning the entire colony, scattering the people to various penal centers, and taking Zeth away forever. . . .

Kyp found his hands clenched tight, and he thought again of the powers that Exar Kun had shown him, the dark secrets that Master Skywalker refused to consider. He frowned and took a deep breath. The cool night air bit into his lungs, and he let it out slowly.

He vowed not to let Exar Kun twist him into another Vader. Kyp felt confident in his determination, in his own strength of character; he could use the power of the dark side for the benefit of the New Republic.

Master Skywalker was wrong. The New Republic stood on the moral high ground and was justified in using any weapon, any force, to eradicate the last stains of the evil Empire.

Kyp stood up and wrapped the black cape around his chest. He could make amends. He alone could show how well those powers could be used.

Exar Kun was long dead, and Darth Vader lay in ashes on Endor. "Now *I* am the Lord of the Sith," Kyp said. With that admission he felt a cold strength creep up his backbone, as if his spine had turned into a column of ice.

He clambered back aboard his small spacecraft. The determination felt like flames in his feet, making him move, making his heart pound, focusing his resolution into a laser-bright beam.

Now he, and he alone, had the opportunity to solve all of the New Republic's problems—by himself.

28

Reflected glows from the Cauldron Nebula made slow dancing patterns on the polished surface of the *Gorgon*'s war-room table. Admiral Daala sat alone at the far end, separated from Commander Kratas, Imperial Army General Odosk, and Captain Mullinore of the *Basilisk*.

Daala stared at her own drawn and distorted reflection in the liquid sheen of the table. She kept her emerald eyes fixedly ahead as she squeezed her fist, feeling the supple black leather of her gloves. Her head pounded with a dull ache, like the imagined echoes of screaming troopers on the exploding *Manticore*. Hot blood roared through her veins as she thought of how she had also lost the Star Destroyer *Hydra*. Half of her force obliterated!

What would Tarkin think of her? In her nightmares she pictured his spectre drawing back his open hand to strike her across the face for her miserable failure. Failure! She had to make up for it.

Commander Kratas drew his bushy eyebrows together in an expression of concern. His Imperial cap rested against his short dark hair. He turned away from Daala's stare, then looked toward the general and the captain of the other Star Destroyer. No one spoke. They waited for Daala, and she tried to summon the courage to speak.

"Gentlemen," she finally said. The words felt like rusty nails catching in her throat; but her voice was strong, startling the three commanders into attention. She eyed each one in turn, then swiveled her chair so she could gaze out at the seething Cauldron gases. A knot of bright blue-giant stars at the heart of the nebula poured out intense energy that illuminated the cloud of gas.

"I have reassessed our mission." Daala swallowed. The words already sounded like defeat to her, but she would not give in to it. "We must somehow differentiate between conflicting priorities. Our original command from Grand Moff Tarkin was to protect the Maw Installation at all costs. That is why we were given four Star Destroyers. Tarkin considered the scientists there a priceless resource for the ultimate victory of the Empire."

She clenched her teeth and hesitated again. Her body betrayed her and started to tremble, but she gripped the edge of the polished table with her glove, gripped it hard until the cramped muscles in her fingers steadied her again.

"But we allowed the Sun Crusher, the most powerful weapon ever designed, to be stolen from our grasp, and we lost one fourth of our fleet in a failed attempt to recapture it. Upon learning of the changed situation with the Rebellion, I decided that it was more important to fight the enemies of the Empire. We left Maw Installation undefended as we harried Rebel worlds. Now, after the disaster at Calamari, I see we have failed in that too."

Commander Kratas rose partway to his feet as if he felt compelled to defend her actions. His skin flushed darker, and Daala noticed a disgraceful hint of stubble on his jaw. If these had been normal disciplinary conditions inside Maw Installation, she would have reprimanded him seriously.

"Admiral," he said, "I agree that we've suffered severe losses, but we have also struck crushing blows against the Rebel traitors. The assault on Dantooine—"

Daala's hand swung up to silence him with the finality of a vibroaxe. Kratas clamped his thin lips shut and slithered back into his chair.

"I am fully aware of the battle statistics, Commander. I see the numbers in my sleep. I have studied the datapads over and over." Her voice rose and became molten with anger. "No matter how much damage we have done to the Rebellion, their losses have been insignificant compared to ours."

Then her voice dropped to such a sudden quiet coldness that she saw General Odosk's watery eyes widen in fear. "And so I intend to use my last resources in one final assault. If successful, it will fulfill both of our missions."

Her gloved fingers worked the controls at the end of the table. From a holoprojector in the center of the black slab rose the computer-generated image she had worked up that afternoon in her private quarters while the image of Grand Moff Tarkin droned on with his prerecorded lectures.

"I mean to stab at the *heart* of the Rebellion," she said. "Coruscant itself."

A high-resolution mapping of the last-known surface topography of the Emperor's planet focused on a world-sized metropolis with frozen polar caps and sparkling chains of city lights on the night side of the planet. She saw spacedocks, curved solar mirrors that warmed the upper and lower latitudes of the planet, communications satellites, large freighters, streams of orbital traffic.

Daala gestured, and two fully rendered images of her Star Destroyers appeared traveling side by side at high speed toward Coruscant.

"I intend to take all ships and all personnel onto the *Gorgon*, leaving only a skeleton crew—of volunteers, of course—on board the *Basilisk*. Our Star Destroyers will come out of hyperspace just beyond the moons of Coruscant. We will drive in at full sublight speed, without hesitation, straight toward our target.

"We will give no warning, and we will fire every turbolaser battery we have, clearing a corridor to head directly for Imperial City. Any ship that stands in our way will become a cloud of ionized metal."

As she spoke, the computer animation demonstrated her tactics. The two Star Destroyers arrowed toward the capital city of the New Republic.

"The Calamarian commander who defeated the *Manticore* gave me an idea with his suicide run, and we shall turn the tables on them." Daala watched the stony face of General Odosk, the appalled look of disbelief on Captain Mullinore, and the stern support of Commander Kratas.

"This will be our deadliest hit-and-run," Daala said. "It will cause enough damage for our names to live forever in the annals of Imperial history. We shall deal a death blow to the Rebel government.

"As we approach in-system, the *Basilisk*'s small volunteer crew will begin a self-destruct countdown. The *Gorgon* will run interference until we reach our target, at which time we will turn aside. At full speed the *Basilisk* will plunge into the atmosphere of Coruscant. It will be unstoppable."

On the simulated image one Star Destroyer split away before touching the skin of air, curving in a tight orbit around Coruscant and then streaking off into space as the first ship plummeted flaming into the atmosphere toward the most heavily populated center on the planet.

"When the *Basilisk* detonates . . . " Daala said. She paused as the planetary image flashed with a brilliant ring of fire that sent ripples igniting through the atmosphere. All the lights on the night side of the planet went dark. Cracks of fire appeared across the land masses.

"The explosion will be sufficient to level the buildings on half a continent. The shock wave traveling through the planetary core could topple cities on the other side of the world. The underground reservoirs will break open. Tidal waves will cause damage along the coasts. For the price of one Star Destroyer, we can lay waste to Coruscant."

Odosk looked grimly admiring at the simulation. "A good plan, Admiral."

"But my ship—" Captain Mullinore said.

"It will be a glorious sacrifice," Commander Kratas said. He steepled his fingers and leaned across the polished table. "I agree."

The simulated death of Coruscant continued, showing spreading fires across the cities, seismic disturbances and destruction that continued long after the *Gorgon* vanished into an incandescent spot of light in hyperspace.

"But what of us?" Kratas said. "What will we do then?"

Daala folded her arms across her chest. "We will accomplish both of our missions, as I said. When the *Basilisk* has destroyed Coruscant, the *Gorgon* and all of our personnel shall return to Maw Installation, where we will defend it to the death with every resource available. The Rebels know it is there—they will be sure to come sniffing around."

Daala's need for vengeance forged her heart into a white-hot brand that threatened to burst its way steaming and pulsing out of her chest. "Grand Moff Tarkin once said that setbacks are merely an opportunity for us to do twice as much damage the second time around."

Captain Mullinore looked even paler than usual; pinpricks of blood vessels speckled his milky-white skin. His blond hair had been cropped severely close to his head, making him seem bald in a certain light.

"Admiral," he said, "let me volunteer to remain onboard the *Basilisk* for this mission. I will be proud to captain my ship until the end."

Daala looked at him and tried to determine if he sought some sort of compassion from her. She decided he wanted none. "I accept, Captain," she said.

Mullinore sat down and gave a tight nod that jerked his chin toward his throat.

Daala rose to her feet. The muscles in her thighs and back felt like tightly bundled wires. Her entire body had been a clenched fist since the debacle on Calamari, and she knew the only way to release the crushing tension would be to strike a devastating blow against the Rebellion.

"Begin the transfer of personnel and equipment," she said. "We must strike Coruscant at once."

Daala glanced once more at the seething nebula that hid her ship, and then she left the war room. She headed to her quarters, where she would review Tarkin's tactical tapes, searching for lost and secret wisdom that would guarantee her victory.

29

The Calamarian female emerged from her teardrop-shaped transport pod and swiveled her head as she took in the thick jungles of Yavin 4, the tall ancient temples. She waited.

Luke hurried out of the hangar bay and tried to maintain a careful pace across the cleared landing area. Artoo accompanied him across the packed ground.

He noted that the Calamarian female had a smaller stature than Admiral Ackbar. She wore yellow-and-turquoise robes that hung loosely about her frame, sleeves that flowed like waterfalls. He sensed a sad determination from her.

The Calamarian female saw Luke and gestured with a flipper-hand to the unseen pilot of the transport pod. Behind her the craft rose skyward with a magnetic hum, leaving her behind. She did not look up to watch the pod streak back into the low-lying clouds, but seemed intent on staying right where she was.

"Master Skywalker," she said with a velvety burr that put him at ease. "I am Ambassador Cilghal from Calamari. I have a message for you." She reached into one of her flowing sleeves and withdrew a gleaming disk traced with patterns of copper and gold.

"Artoo?" Luke said.

The little droid trundled forward, and Cilghal bent down to insert the message disk into Artoo's drive. After a momentary whir Artoo projected a flickering image of Leia in the air in front of him.

Luke stood back surprised, then looked at Cilghal with a deeper interest as Leia started speaking.

"Luke, I hope all is well with you. I think I've found someone for your Jedi training center. Ambassador Cilghal comes with my highest recommendation. She has demonstrated to my satisfaction that she has a true proficiency in using the Force. She seems to have a knack for healing and for short-range prediction. She was a great help during the recent battle on Calamari. Please help her and train her. We need more Jedi Knights."

Her image smiled up at him. "We hope to hear soon that some of your students are ready to help with our struggle against the Empire. These are still desperate times. We can't let our guard slip for a moment."

Her expression softened, and she seemed to look directly into his eyes. "I miss you. The twins keep asking when they'll see their Uncle Luke again. I hope you can visit—or maybe we'll come to Yavin 4." She straightened, taking a formal tone again. "I'm sure you'll find Cilghal to be one of your most promising candidates." She crossed her arms and smiled as the message flickered and vanished.

Cilghal stood in silence, waiting for Luke to respond. His mind spun. "Uh, welcome," he finally said.

He had been disturbed since his confrontation with Kyp Durron; Luke did not know where the young man had gone after stealing Mara Jade's ship. The gruesome death of Gantoris, coupled with Kyp's rebellion, had been more than enough to resurrect the old fear in Luke again. His best students were going sour, getting impatient, trying to push the limits of their abilities.

But he had sensed a greater, deeper menace that vibrated within the very stones of the Great Temple itself . . . evil, and well hidden. Working alone, Luke had attempted to find its source, running his fingers along the stone blocks of the walls, trying to tap the cold shadow—but he had found nothing. He had only his suspicions.

How could Kyp have known the details of the Great Sith War? How could Gantoris have learned how to build his own lightsaber? What had Gantoris seen that last terrible night before he was consumed? What dreaded magic had he attempted? Luke was missing an important piece of the puzzle, and until he found it, he could not strike against the threat.

Ambassador Cilghal shifted and looked at him again. "Master Skywalker, you seem preoccupied. Perhaps Leia was wrong in suggesting that I come here to stay?"

Luke looked at her, feeling the weight of responsibility on his shoulders. "No, no," he said, "that's not it. If Leia thinks you have Jedi potential, then I would be honored to teach you here. In fact," he said jokingly, "an even-tempered Calamarian will be a welcome change." He smiled. "Follow me. We'll find quarters for you inside the temple."

The students at Luke's training center continued their lessons of self-discovery, working eagerly or meditatively, honing their skills.

Newcomer Mara Jade listened intently to Cilghal's firsthand descriptions of the attack on Calamari, pressing the ambassador with detailed questions about the Star Destroyers and the number of TIE squadrons they had carried. Old Streen sat next to Kirana Ti on a rounded bench, listening to silver-haired Tionne practice new ballads. The remaining students sat in other common rooms, or studied in their private chambers, or walked out in the jungles.

Satisfied at their activities, Luke slipped back into the deserted corridors and headed toward his own rooms. Artoo came around the corner and whistled a question at him, but Luke shook his head. "No, Artoo, I don't want to be disturbed for a while."

He stepped inside his stone-walled chamber, the small room where he had stayed as an X-wing pilot in the Alliance. Luke had removed the other bunks, furnished the room to his taste; but the room seemed barren, with only a sleeping pallet and some small Massassi artifacts.

On a ledge of black stone laced with blood-colored impurities sat the translucent cube of the Jedi Holocron.

Luke sealed his door, the first time he had ever locked it since returning to the abandoned temple. He held the Holocron in his palm and activated it, digging deep to seek his information.

"I wish to see Master Vodo-Siosk Baas," he said.

The ghostly image of the nozzle-faced, stunted Jedi Master rose out of the cube, robed and covered with bangles, leaning on a long gnarled stick. "I am the gatekeeper, I am Master Vodo-Siosk Baas," the image said.

Luke squatted in front of the interactive holographic image. "I need information from you, Master Vodo. You were a Jedi during the time of the Great Sith War. You have told us about your student Exar Kun and how he created the Brotherhood of the Sith. You've told us that he fought for dominance over the other Jedi loyal to the Old Republic."

Luke took a deep breath. "I need you to tell me more. How did Exar Kun fall at the end of the war? What happened to him? How did he die— or were you finally able to bring him back to the light side?"

"Exar Kun was my greatest student," Master Vodo said, "yet he was corrupted. He was seduced by the powers available to him through studies of ancient Sith teachings."

Luke nodded gravely. "I am afraid that the same thing might have happened to some of my own students, Master Vodo. Did Exar Kun ever return to the powers of good?"

"That was not to be," the image of Master Vodo said. "Because I was his Master, I alone of the allied Jedi went to confront him, hoping that I could turn him back. I knew it was a foolish mission, but I had no choice. I had to try."

"What happened?" Luke asked.

The image flickered, as if something had sparked inside the Holocron; then Master Vodo reappeared. "Exar Kun destroyed me. He slew his own master."

Luke was suddenly jarred out of the story, remembering that the gate-keeper images in the Holocron were interactive simulacra with personalities imprinted upon them—not the real spirits of long-dead Jedi Masters.

"Then what happened to Kun at the end of the Sith War?" Luke asked.

"All the Jedi banded together and came to the jungle moon in a united front against the Sith stronghold Exar Kun had built. The allied Jedi combined their power into a massive annihilating strike."

Master Vodo's image flickered again, dissolved into static, then reassembled itself. " . . . which obliterated the surviving Massassi natives and . . . " The image broke up, flickered, re-formed, then broke up again—as if something were jamming it.

"But Exar Kun—what happened to Exar Kun?" Luke demanded. He couldn't understand what was going wrong with the Holocron. He shook the Holocron, tapped it a few times, then set it down on the flat, hard table and stepped back to get a better view of the holographic Jedi Master.

Inside the static-filled cube a dark knot appeared, like a storm gathering within its translucent walls. Master Vodo-Siosk Baas reappeared. "—but Kun was able to—"

Suddenly Master Vodo's image shattered into a thousand glittering fragments of colored light, as if a greater force had torn it apart from within.

The darkness inside the Holocron grew deeper and larger, swelling like a slow-motion explosion. Arcs of red fire struck out in all directions from the black fist. With a high-pitched shrieking noise of discharged energy, the faces of the cube split. The Holocron steamed as it collapsed with a shower of sparks, a stream of black curling smoke, and a stench of melted electronics and organic components.

Luke backed away, raising his hands to shield his eyes from the blaze. For a moment it seemed that a solid black hooded form like a walking silhouette rose up from the Holocron, laughing in a deep subsonic voice. Then it drifted away, dissipating into the stone walls.

Luke felt cold fear grip him. The small white cube of the treasured Holocron lay in a melted lump on the table.

Luke would have to find his own answers—and soon.

30

"Luke, I've had enough of this!"

Luke looked up as Mara Jade emerged from the turbolift in the hangar bay of the Great Temple. She had stayed on the jungle moon a few days, long enough to learn *how* to use her own Jedi skills, but the incident with Kyp Durron and the loss of her personal ship had soured the experience for her.

Luke turned from where he stood next to Artoo-Detoo and two Jedi trainees. Kirana Ti bent over to heft a pack of wilderness supplies as she and Streen prepared for a short sojourn out in the jungles. She wore the reptile-skin garments and ornate lacquered battle helm she had brought from her harsh world of Dathomir.

Streen fidgeted and glanced toward the shaft of sunlight that came in under the half-opened hangar door. He wore the many-pocketed jumpsuit he had kept from his gas-prospecting days on Bespin.

Mara walked briskly toward them, cinching her Jedi robe tighter around her waist. Luke looked at her and thought how different she looked from when he had first met her on the hostile smuggler world of Myrkyr.

Mara stopped in front of him, glanced at the two Jedi trainees waiting to depart on their jungle trek, then ignored them completely. "I can't deny what I've learned here, Luke. But Talon Karrde gave me control of the smugglers' alliance, and I've got too much to do. I can't just meditate all day long." Her narrow chiseled face seemed flushed even in the dim light. "I need to send for another transport to get out of here, since your prize student ran off with my ship."

Luke nodded, partly amused at her predicament but stung by the mention of Kyp Durron's betrayal. "We've got a communications setup in the second-tier war room. You can call Karrde and request a new ship."

Mara snorted. "Karrde only lets me contact him at prearranged intervals. He keeps moving around—says it's because he's afraid someone has a bounty on his head. I suspect he just doesn't want to be bothered. He claims that he's retired from the smuggling life and wants to live as a private citizen."

"You can always contact Coruscant," Luke said in a congenial voice. "I'm sure they'll send a shuttle for you. In fact, we're probably due for another supply run anyway."

Mara pursed her generous lips. "It would be nice to have the New Republic chauffeur *me* around for a change."

Luke searched for any hidden sarcasm in her comment but saw only wry humor instead. He shook his head. "I don't know who you'd get to volunteer for a brutal job like that."

When Lando came rushing into Han and Leia's quarters without knocking, Han Solo was intent on studying a list of interactive entertainment options for the twins. On the floor Jacen and Jaina played impatiently with shiny self-aware toys that kept trying to run away from the children's grasping hands.

See-Threepio stood nervously next to him. "I am perfectly qualified to make selections, sir. I'm certain I can find something to amuse the twins."

"I don't trust your choices, Threepio," Han said. "Remember how much they enjoyed the Holographic Zoo for Extinct Animals?"

"That was an anomaly, sir," Threepio said.

Lando rushed into the room, looking around. "Han, old buddy! I need a favor—a big favor."

With a sigh Han turned the selection process over to Threepio. "Okay, pick something—but if the kids don't like it, *I'll* let them amuse themselves by running a maintenance check on you."

"I . . . understand completely, sir," Threepio said, and bent to the task.

"What kind of favor?" he asked Lando warily.

Lando flung his cape over his shoulder and rubbed his hands together. "I, uh, need to borrow the *Falcon*—just for a little while."

"What?" Han said.

Lando answered in a rush. "Mara Jade is stuck on Yavin 4, and she needs a lift. I want to be the gallant gentleman who rescues her. Let me take the *Falcon*. Please?"

Han shook his head. "My ship isn't going anywhere without me. Besides, if you're trying to impress Mara Jade, taking a ship like the *Falcon* isn't the way to do it."

"Come on, Han," Lando said. "I took you to rescue Leia when Calamari was under attack. You owe me one."

Han sighed. "I suppose I could use an excuse to go see Luke and Kyp at the Jedi academy." He turned and smirked at Threepio. "Besides, this time at least *Leia's* here to watch out for the children."

When the *Millennium Falcon* landed in front of the great Massassi temple, Han emerged to see Luke sprinting toward him wearing an expression of boyish delight. Han grinned and stepped down the entry ramp, his boots clomping on the metal plates. Luke came forward to hug him in an enthusiastic embrace that was distinctly undignified for a Jedi Master.

Han said, "Enjoying your little vacation away from the thick of galactic politics, Luke?"

Luke's expression became troubled. "I wouldn't exactly say that."

Lando Calrissian emerged from the *Falcon* after taking an extra few moments to groom his hair, straighten his clothes, and make certain his appearance was as dashing as he could make it. Han had rolled his eyes, convinced that suave gentility was no way to win the affections of Mara Jade.

Though her scalding anger seemed to have cooled somewhat, Mara still showed a rough-edged hardness that made Han wonder why Lando would get so excited about the woman who had once called herself "The Emperor's Hand." With a flash of insight Han realized that Leia herself had come across as a mixture of fiery temper and icy coolness when he had first met her—and look at how that had turned out!

Mara Jade's slender figure emerged from the half-open hangar doors at the base of the blocky stone ziggurat. She carried a satchel slung over her shoulder.

Lando hurried down the ramp and cursorily clapped Luke on the back. "How you doing, Luke?" He practically tripped over himself as he trotted across the landing pad to meet Mara. "We hear you need a lift," he said, offering to take her satchel. "What happened to your own ship?"

"Don't ask," she said, then smiled wryly at him before handing over her heavy bag. "So you finally found something you're qualified to do, Calrissian. Baggage handler."

He carried her satchel over his shoulder and gestured to the *Falcon*. "Right this way to the VIP shuttle, madam."

Han stepped back from Luke and looked around at the steaming jungles and the vine-covered Great Temple. "So, where's Kyp?" he asked.

Luke looked down at his feet, and then, as if gathering courage through some kind of Jedi exercise, he looked up to meet Han's gaze. "I've got bad news for you. Kyp ... disagreed with me about how fast he should learn dangerous new skills and how best to develop his ability with the Force."

"What do you mean?" Han asked. He grabbed one of the piston supports of the entry ramp to keep himself upright. "Was he hurt? Why didn't you call me?"

Luke shook his head. "I don't know what happened to him. He's been practicing certain techniques that I fear may lead him to the dark side. I'm very concerned, Han. He's the most powerful of all the students I've had here. He stole Mara Jade's ship and left Yavin 4. I have no idea where he is now or what he's doing."

Han forced his mouth into a thin line, but Luke continued. "Kyp has a great deal of power, and a great deal of anger and ambition—but little understanding or patience. That's a dangerous combination."

Han felt helpless. He barely noticed as Lando escorted Mara Jade up the ramp into the *Falcon*. "I don't know what to do, Luke," Han said.

Luke nodded grimly. "Neither do I."

The *Millennium Falcon* cruised through hyperspace with a vibrating hum of hyperdrive engines. Lando tried to keep his voice down as he leaned close to Han in the cockpit.

"Just let me tinker with the food-processing units, Han. Please? I've memorized some programming from the finest Cloud City casinos, and I can generate recipes that would make Mara Jade float with pleasure."

"No." Han scanned the chronometer that counted down how much time remained on the journey back to Coruscant. "I like the food processors the way they are."

Exasperated, Lando slumped into the copilot's chair and sighed. "They're all programmed for greasy, heavy Corellian recipes. Someone like Mara needs exotic food, special preparation. Not nerf sausage and dumplings with soggy charbote roots."

"Lando, that's the food I was brought up on—and on *my* ship, I want the food-prep units to make dishes that *I* like. I already wasted the whole journey to Yavin helping you scrub the living compartments in the back, polishing the holochess table, and perfuming the whole ship with disinfectant."

"Han," Lando said, "the ship was filthy, and it stank."

"Well, I *liked* it that way," Han insisted. "It was my dirt, and my stink, on my ship."

"Only because you got lucky in sabacc." Lando stood up, straightened his cape, and smoothed his purplish jumpsuit. "I let you win. You could never do it again."

Han and Lando glared at each other across the hastily cleared game board. Lando kept flicking glances toward Mara Jade as he randomized the rectangles of Han's old sabacc deck.

Mara had ignored Lando for most of the journey to Coruscant. She had rebuffed his attempts to prepare dinner, find musical selections for her, and engage her in conversation. Now as she watched them playing cards to settle a dispute over the ownership of the *Falcon,* she scowled as if they were no more than two little boys scuffling in a child's amusement pen.

Lando took the pack of glittering metallic cards so that the crystalline faces showed and held them toward Mara. "My lady, would you care to cut the cards?"

"No," she said, "I would not."

"I'm getting tired of this, Lando," Han said. "First I won the *Falcon* from you in a sabacc game on Bespin, then you won her back from me in the diplomatic lounge on Coruscant, and I won her back from you en route to Calamari. Enough is enough. This is our *last* hand."

"Fine with me, old buddy," Lando said, and started dealing the cards.

"No rematches," Han said.

"No rematches," Lando agreed.

"Whoever wins this time keeps the *Falcon* from now on."

"You got it," Lando said. "The *Millennium Falcon* belongs to the winner to do with as he pleases. No more borrowing, no more arguing."

Han nodded. "Loser gets a lifetime of Coruscant public transport." He picked up his cards. "Shut up and play."

Han tossed down the cards that had betrayed him and stood up to hide the devastating sense of loss coursing through him. He felt as if his heart had been crumpled like a piece of discarded paper and then stuffed back into his chest. "Go ahead and gloat, Lando."

Cool-faced, Mara Jade had watched the entire game with less indifference than she pretended to show. Now she scowled as if she expected Lando to stand up and cheer in triumph. Han anticipated the same reaction.

Halfway to his feet, Lando stopped and calmed himself, straightening in a dignified fashion. "That's it," he said in a slow, rich voice. "End of game. We'll never play for the *Falcon* again."

"Yeah," Han said in a barely audible voice, "that's what we agreed."

"And the *Falcon* is mine, to do with as I please," Lando said.

"Go ahead and gloat," Han said, again, using sarcasm to mask his own despair. He kicked himself for being lured into another stupid game. He had been an idiot, with nothing to gain, and now he had lost everything. "I should have known better than to play with you."

"Just like vornskyrs hissing at each other in a territorial dispute," Mara said, shaking her head. Her exotic spice-colored hair hung to one side. She did nothing to make herself look attractive, yet somehow it worked to her advantage.

Lando glanced at Mara, then turned partly aside as if ignoring her. With a grand flourish he spread his hands wide and gestured to Han.

"But since you're my friend, Han Solo, and since I know that the *Falcon* means even more to you than she does to me"—Lando paused for effect and stole another glance at Mara Jade before continuing—"I choose to *give* the *Millennium Falcon* back to you. A gift from me to you. A testimony to our years of friendship, and all that we've been through together."

Han collapsed back into his chair, feeling his knees turn weak and watery. His throat shriveled, and he opened and closed his mouth several times, completely at a loss for what to say.

"I'm going to the food-prep units," Lando said gallantly. "*If* Han will let me adjust the programming, I'll see if I can prepare the finest repast your units can manufacture, and we'll all have a nice meal together."

Han felt too stunned to argue, and Lando didn't wait for an answer. He cast a second look back at Mara Jade as he went toward the galley.

Still in shock, Han saw her raise her eyebrows and look after him with a surprised and mystified smile, as if completely reassessing her opinion of Lando Calrissian—which, Han concluded, must have been Lando's plan all along.

31

The Hammerhead Momaw Nadon arranged for Wedge Antilles and Qwi Xux to go sight-seeing across the pristine Ithorian landscape in an open-air skimmer. On the transit landing platform, the dazzling morning sky was a pale whitish purple with high wisps of cloud that masked several dim moons still riding the sky.

Qwi strapped herself into the plush vegetable-fiber seat and looked into the sunshine. "Why didn't you want Momaw Nadon to guide us?" she asked, studying the topographic information and the scenic highlights Nadon had suggested. "He seems very proud of his world."

Wedge concentrated on the control panel, though the vehicle looked rather simple to operate. "Well, because he's very busy, and because . . ." His voice trailed off, and he looked up at her with a faint smile. "I kind of wanted to be alone with you."

Qwi felt a giddy elation rising within her. "Yes, I think that would be nicer."

Wedge lifted their skimmer off the pad, and they soared away from the great disk of the Ithorian eco-city and across the treetops. The *Tafanda Bay* had drifted many kilometers during the course of the night, and Wedge had to recalibrate the skimmer's coordinates. Daylight warmed their faces as the wind breathed cool drafts against their skin.

They headed for a low ridge where the dark-green jungles fell away into a paler forest. "What are you taking me to see?" Qwi asked.

Wedge leaned forward, staring at the horizon. "A large grove of bafforr trees that was half-destroyed by the Imperials during their siege many years ago."

"Is there something special about those trees?" Qwi asked.

"The Ithorians worship them," he said. "They're semi-intelligent, like a hive mind. The greater the forest grows, the more intelligent the trees become."

As they skimmed closer, Qwi could see that an aquamarine crystalline forest glowed faintly in the sunlight, covering part of the hillside. Wedge let the skimmer hover as they bent over the sides to gaze down at the glassy trunks, at the smooth yet sharp webs of bafforr branches. Scattered around the perimeter, large, dark cylinders had toppled to the ground and broken like tubes of burned transparisteel. It reminded her of the debris scattered around the site of the smashed Cathedral of Winds on Vortex. Tiny saplings like inverted icicles protruded from the rocky earth.

"The forest seems to be growing back," Wedge said. The thin saplings glowed a whiter blue than the rest of the forest.

"I see people down there!" Qwi said, pointing off to the side. The smooth grayish forms of four Ithorians dashed for the cover of the thick undergrowth on the side of the ridge. "I thought they weren't supposed to set foot in the jungle."

Wedge stared down at them, baffled. He raised the skimmer higher, but the four renegade Ithorians had already vanished into the tree cover. His brow furrowed as if searching for an answer. He drew in a quick breath.

"I seem to remember something about the Mother Jungle summoning certain Ithorians. It's a rare calling that no one can explain. They leave everything behind and live in the wilderness, forbidden to return to their eco-cities. In a way, they become fugitives. Since the Ithorians consider it such sacrilege to touch the forest, the calling must be pretty strong."

Qwi looked down at the burned glasslike trunks of the bafforr trees destroyed by Imperial turbolaser fire. "I'm glad to know they're tending the forest, though." She wondered how much of the bafforr forest's collective intelligence had returned. "Let's go somewhere else, Wedge, so they can get back to their work."

Wedge took Qwi to a high plateau studded with flat gray and tan rocks, covered with vermilion scrub brush and black vines. A confluence of three rivers came together in a great sinkhole on the edge of the towering cliff, pouring into a spectacular triple waterfall that plunged into the plateau's deep pit. At the bottom of the plateau, water spilled out of a thousand broken caves, flowing into a turgid, foamy marsh filled with swaying reeds and leaping fish.

Wedge circled the open-air skimmer above the enormous sinkhole on the plateau, and Qwi gaped at the fabulous waterfall. Curtains of spray rose from thundering echoes of plunging water. Rainbows sparkled against the lavender sky.

Qwi turned her head this way and that, trying to look at everything at once. Wedge grinned like a daredevil and took them over the center of the three waterfalls, hovering and then lowering them down the core of the sinkhole.

Qwi laughed as the thick, cold mist blanketed them, drenching their clothes. Wedge dropped the skimmer to where all three rivers crashed against the rocks with a sound like exploding planets. Green batlike creatures flitted through the spray, catching insects and tiny fish that tumbled over the falls.

"This is fantastic," Qwi shouted.

"It gets better," Wedge said, "if Momaw Nadon gave us good information."

He steered the skimmer toward a cluster of slick black outcroppings that jutted from the side of the pit. The overhang sheltered them from most of the cold spray and cyclonic winds swirling in the rock-walled chimney. The booming echo of water became a constant background.

Wedge brought the skimmer in among the rocks to a sheltered place where shafts of sunlight pierced the rising swirls of spray. "Nadon said we could land here."

He reached into a compartment under the seat, pulled out two translucent waterproof capes, and removed two packages of self-heating meals Nadon had also provided. Wedge helped Qwi fasten one of the waterproof garments over her narrow shoulders, then fastened his own. He picked up their lunches and indicated the smooth rocks under the overhang.

"Let's have a picnic," he said.

At the end of an exhausting day Qwi stood outside her vine-covered stateroom door on the *Tafanda Bay*. Wedge looked into her indigo eyes and shuffled his feet.

"Thank you," Qwi said. "This has been the most wonderful day of my life."

Wedge opened his mouth and closed it three times, as if searching for something to say. Finally he bent forward, touched her silky mother-of-pearl hair, then kissed her. He let his warm lips linger on hers for a long moment. She pushed closer to him and felt delight surge through her.

"And now you've given me one more interesting thing," she said in her quiet musical voice.

Blushing, Wedge backed away from her and said, "Uh, I'll see you in the morning." He turned and practically fled back to his own stateroom.

With a wistful smile Qwi watched his door close. She opened her stateroom and slipped inside, feeling as if she had repulsorlifts in her feet. She leaned against the door as it closed and shut her eyes as the gentle illumination in her room slowly brightened. She heaved a contented sigh.

And opened her eyes to see a dark man rising from his crouch in the shadowy corners of the room.

The looming silhouette approached her, and she froze in terror at the sight of the swirling black cape that flowed around his body.

Darth Vader!

She tried to shout for help, but her voice locked in her throat as if an invisible hand had stilled her vocal cords. She whirled for the door and hung in midstride, yanked back by unseen spiderwebs.

The dark man was closer now, gliding toward her. What did he want? She couldn't scream. She heard his hollow breathing echo like the snarl of a beast.

A hand reached out for her, and Qwi couldn't move, couldn't duck away as the fingers wrapped around the top of her head. She felt him pressing there. The other hand, cold and supple, grasped her face. She blinked her wide eyes and looked up to see the face of Kyp Durron, eyes blazing, his expression soulless.

He spoke in a freezing voice. "I have found you, Dr. Xux. You hold too much dangerous knowledge," he said. "I must make certain no one can ever again create the weapons you've been responsible for. There must be no more Death Stars. No more Sun Crushers."

His fingers clamped down harder on her forehead, on her face. Her skull seemed ready to shatter. Waves of pain plunged through her brain like the claws of a nightmare monster. She felt the sharp points of metal talons scraping through her mind, digging, prying up, and ripping out memories and scientific knowledge she had accumulated over the course of many years.

Qwi finally managed a scream, but it was a weak, watery cry that faded as she fell down a long, dark tunnel into forgetfulness. She slumped against the vine-covered wall of her quarters.

As her sight turned dim in front of her, the last thing she saw was the black-shrouded form of her attacker as he opened her stateroom door and stalked out into the night.

Next morning Wedge whistled to himself as he dressed, smiling into a reflection plate as he straightened his dark hair. He ordered an exotic breakfast for two. Qwi was an early riser, especially now that she was excited about the sight-seeing they would do on Ithor. Momaw Nadon had promised them the open-air skimmer for another day.

He sauntered across the corridor, signaled at her stateroom door, and waited. No answer.

He signaled again and again until, alarmed, he tried to open the door. Finding the entrance to Qwi's room unlocked, he was even more alarmed. Had someone come to assassinate her in the night? Did the Imperials know her location, after all? He pushed the door open and rushed inside. Darkness and shadows filled her quarters.

"Lights!" he yelled. Sudden illumination bathed the room in pale peach-colored light.

He heard Qwi before he saw her. She sat crouched in a corner, sobbing. She clutched her pearlescent hair with both hands, squeezing her temples as if trying to hold thoughts inside that kept slipping through her fingers.

"Qwi!" he shouted, and ran to her. Bending down, he took her wrist and gently forced her to turn her head. He stared into her wide, blank eyes. "What happened?"

She didn't appear to recognize him, and Wedge's stomach sank with horror. Qwi looked confused and devastated. She frowned as if searching her memory. She shook her head slowly, then closed her big eyes, squeezing them tight as she fought with her own thoughts. Tears ran down her cheeks, oozing in small drops, then larger splashes as she bit her lip in furious concentration. She blinked up at him again, finally finding the name that had eluded her.

"Widj? *Wedge?*" she said at last. "Is your name Wedge?"

He nodded numbly, and with another great weeping cry she threw herself into his arms. He held her, feeling her body tremble with sobs. "What happened?" he repeated. "Qwi, tell me!"

"I don't know." She shook her head, and featherlike hair flowed in a slow wave from one shoulder to the other. "I barely know *you*. I can't remember. My mind feels so empty . . . filled with blank spots."

Wedge held her tight as she said, "I've lost everything. Most of my memory, my life—is gone."

32

Kyp Durron returned to the fourth moon of Yavin in the heartbeat stillness of the jungle night. Filled with a power he had decided to use to its fullest, he felt ready to explode in an exhilarating outpouring of the Force—but he could not let such childish demonstrations seduce him. He had a mission to accomplish, one that would affect the future of the entire galaxy.

Without running lights or landing beacon, he brought the Z-95 Headhunter he had taken from Mara Jade to a gentle rest on the slightly overgrown landing pad in front of the Great Temple. Kyp had no interest in reacquainting himself with the other weak Jedi trainees or even with the misguided and cowardly Master Skywalker. He simply needed access to the ancient Massassi temples Exar Kun had designed as focal points for concentrating the power of the Sith.

Above him the night sky was lush with stars, and the stirrings of the surrounding jungle wove a tapestry of hushed sounds. But the insects made their music more quietly, and few large animals crashed through the underbrush. The entire rain forest seemed stunned by Kyp's return.

Kyp tossed the oddly glittering black cape over his shoulders. Time to be about his business.

Leaving the Headhunter fighter behind him, he approached the monolithic ziggurat of the Great Temple. Rust-colored vermiform vines writhed out of his way, avoiding Kyp's footsteps, as if his entire body exuded a deadly heat.

Chisel-cut stone steps ran up the side of the pyramid. He set one foot in front of the other, climbing slowly, listening to the soft echoes of his breathing. Anticipation built within him.

In his mind Kyp heard cheering ghosts, saw visions like a videoloop from four thousand years ago when Exar Kun had found the last resting place of the ancient Sith. Kun had rediscovered their teachings. He had built great temples, establishing the Brotherhood of the Sith among disillusioned Jedi Knights. Here on Yavin 4, Kun had used the Massassi people as expendable resources, power conduits to redefine the chaos and corruption of the Old Republic. He had challenged the foolish Jedi who followed their incompetent leaders without thinking simply because they had sworn to do so. . . .

Now Kyp would finish the battle, though the enemy was no longer the incompetent, decaying Republic, but the fraudulent New Order and the repressive Empire that had taken the Old Republic's place. While Master Skywalker limited the training of his new Jedi Knights, Kyp Durron had learned more. Much more.

He reached the second tier of the ziggurat and paused to look down at the insectile shape of his Z-95 fighter resting in the center of the landing grid. No one had yet stirred from inside the temple.

A pastel glow crept into the sky at the horizon as the rapid rotation of the jungle moon brought planetrise closer. Kyp continued to climb the long series of steps, staring toward the apex of the Great Temple.

Kyp had already struck his first blow by erasing dangerous knowledge from the Imperial scientist, Qwi Xux. Only Qwi had known how to build another Sun Crusher—but Kyp, using his bare hands and his newfound power, had torn that knowledge from her brain and scattered it into nothingness. No one could ever find it again.

Next, he would apply a poetic justice that delighted his sensibility, that made him thrill with revenge for all that the Empire had done against him and his family and his colony world. Kyp would resurrect the Sun Crusher itself and use it to obliterate the remains of the Empire. He would be accountable to no one but himself. He trusted no one else to make the hard decisions.

Kyp reached the summit of the Great Temple just as the huge orange ball of Yavin heaved itself over the horizon. Misty and pale, the gas giant swirled with tremendous storm systems large enough to swallow smaller worlds.

The temple's diamond-shaped flagstones covered the small observation platform above the grand audience chamber. Vines and stunted Massassi trees poked up from the corners of the old stones.

Kyp looked skyward. The small plants and animals filling the jungles of Yavin 4 were insignificant to him. They mattered nothing in the grand scheme of what he was about to undertake. The importance of his vision far exceeded the petty needs of any single planet.

As the sphere of Yavin rose into the sky, Kyp lifted his arms, and the slick black fabric of his cape fell behind him. His hands were slender and small, the hands of a young man. But inside, power sizzled through his bones.

"Exar Kun, help me," Kyp said, closing his eyes.

He reached out with his mind, following the paths of the Force that led to every object in the universe, drawing power from the cosmic focal point of the Massassi temple. He searched, sending his thoughts like a probe deep into the storm systems of the gas giant.

Behind him Kyp felt the black-ice power of Exar Kun arise, tapping into him and reinforcing his abilities. His own feeble exploratory touch suddenly plunged forward like a blaster bolt. Kyp felt larger, a part of the jungle moon, then a part of the entire planetary system, until he burrowed into the heart of the gas giant itself.

Pale orange clouds whipped past him. He sensed pressure increasing as he plummeted down, down to the incredibly dense layers near the core. He sought the tiny speck of machinery, a small, indestructible ship that had been cast away.

When he reached the bottommost levels of the atmosphere, Kyp finally found the Sun Crusher. It stood out like a beacon, a bull's-eye in the funneling field lines of the Force.

Size matters not, Master Skywalker had repeated. Kyp engulfed the Sun Crusher with his mind, surrounding it, touching it with his limitless, invisible hands. He thought about heaving it back up, dragging the Sun Crusher out of the depths of Yavin. But he discarded that thought.

Instead, with the assistance of Exar Kun, he used his innate skill to power up the controls again, to move control levers, push buttons to alter the course stored in the Sun Crusher's memory, bringing it out of its entombment.

Kyp continued to watch the weapon's progress, focusing on the sphere of the enormous planet as it crested the misty treetops. The Sun Crusher appeared as a silvery dot, seeming no larger than an atom as it emerged from the highest cloud layers and streaked across space toward the emerald-green moon where Kyp waited.

He stared upward and waited, opening his arms to receive the indestructible weapon.

The Sun Crusher approached like a long, sharp thorn of crystalline alloy, cruising upright on its long axis. The toroidal resonance-torpedo launcher hung at the bottom of the long hook. It looked beautiful.

The Sun Crusher descended through the jungle moon's atmosphere, straight down—like a spike to impale the Great Temple. Kyp controlled it, slowed its descent, until the superweapon hovered to a stop, suspended in front of him.

As the sky brightened with planetrise, the alloy hull of the Sun Crusher seemed as pristine as a firefacet gem, scoured of all oxidation and debris by the intense temperatures and pressures at the core of Yavin. The Sun Crusher looked clean, and deadly, and ready for him.

"Thank you, Exar Kun," Kyp whispered.

Luke Skywalker awoke from another series of nightmares. He sat bolt upright on his pallet, instantly aware. He had felt a great disturbance in the Force. Something was not right.

He got up, moving cautiously as he sent out his thoughts to check on his students: Kirana Ti, Dorsk 81, the new Calamarian arrival Cilghal, Streen, Tionne, Kam Solusar, and all the others. Nothing seemed amiss. They slept soundly—almost too soundly, as if a net of sleep had been cast over them.

When he reached out farther, he was stunned to feel a cold, black whirlpool of twisted Force around the peak of the temple. It stunned him.

Luke sprinted to the door of his chambers, hesitated, then stepped back to retrieve his lightsaber. He marched down the corridors, smoothing his fear as he rode the turbolift to the upper levels of the ancient pyramid.

Calm, Yoda had said, *you must remain calm.*

But the sight that greeted him under the dawn sky nearly overwhelmed Luke.

The Sun Crusher hung suspended over the temple, still steaming in the morning air, resurrected from its tomb at the core of the gas giant. Kyp Durron spun around to stare at Luke, his black cape swirling with the rapid motion.

Stunned, Luke reeled backward. "How dare you bring that weapon back!" he said. "It goes against all the Jedi knowledge I have taught you."

Kyp laughed at him. "You haven't taught me very much, Master Skywalker. I've learned a great deal beyond your feeble teachings. You pretend to be a great instructor, but you're afraid to learn for yourself."

He looked back at the Sun Crusher. "I will do what must be done to eradicate the Empire. While I make the galaxy safe for everyone, you can stay here and practice your simple Jedi tricks. But they are no more than children's games."

"Kyp," Luke said, keeping his voice even and taking a step toward him, "you've been lured by the dark side, but you must return. You were deceived and misled. Come back before its grip becomes too strong." He swallowed. "I went over to the dark side once, and I came back. It *can* be done if you're strong enough and brave enough. Are you?"

Kyp laughed in disbelief. "Skywalker, it's embarrassing for me to listen to you talk. You are afraid to risk anything yourself, yet you want to call yourself a Jedi Master. It doesn't work that way. You've stunted the training of your other Jedi candidates because of your own narrow-mindedness. Perhaps I should just defeat you here and now, and then *I* can take over their training."

With trembling hands and a deep-seated dread in his heart, Luke reached to his side and wrapped his hand around the slick handle of his lightsaber. He pulled it free, igniting it with the familiar *snap-hiss*. The brilliant green blade extended, humming and ready for battle.

A Jedi could not attack an unarmed opponent, could not resort to violence before all other avenues had been exhausted—but Luke knew the deadly potential of his most talented student. If Kyp had fallen to the dark side, he could become another Darth Vader. Perhaps even worse. . . .

"Don't make me do this," Luke said, raising his lightsaber, but unsure what to do. He couldn't just cut down his student, who stood unarmed at the top of the temple. But if he didn't . . .

"We have to send the Sun Crusher back," Luke said. "At one time you yourself insisted that it should never be used."

"I spoke out of ignorance," Kyp said, "just as you do."

"Don't make me fight you," Luke said in a low voice.

Kyp made a dismissive gesture with one hand, and a sudden wave of dark ripples splashed across the air like the shock front from a concussion grenade.

Luke stumbled backward. The lightsaber turned cold in his hand. Frost crystals grew in feathery patterns around the handle. At the core of the brilliant green blade a shadow appeared, a black disease rotting away the purity of the beam. The humming blade sputtered, sounding like a sickly cough. The black taint rapidly grew stronger, swallowing up the green beam.

With a fizzle of sparks Luke's lightsaber died.

Trying to control his growing fear, Luke felt a sudden brush of cold behind him. He turned to see a black, hooded *silhouette*—the image that had impersonated Anakin Skywalker in Luke's nightmare . . . the dark man who had lured Gantoris into a devastating loss of control.

Kyp's voice came as if from a great distance. "At last, Master Skywalker, you can meet my mentor—Exar Kun."

Luke dropped his useless lightsaber and crouched. His every muscle suddenly coiled and tensed. He rallied all the powers of the Force around him, seeking any defensive tactic.

With the Sun Crusher looming behind him, Kyp stretched out both hands and blasted Luke with lightning bolts like black cracks in the Force. Dark tendrils rose up from gaps in the temple flagstones, fanged, illusory vipers that struck at him from all sides.

Luke cried out and tried to strike back, but the shadow of Exar Kun joined the attack, adding more deadly force. The ancient Dark Lord of the Sith lashed out with waves of blackness, driving long icicles of frozen poison into Luke's body.

He thrashed, but felt helpless. To lose control to anger and desperation would be as great a failure as if he did nothing at all. Luke called upon the powers that Yoda and Obi-Wan had taught him—but everything he did, every skillful technique, failed utterly.

Against the full might of Kyp Durron and the forbidden weapons of the long-dead spirit of Exar Kun, even a Jedi Master such as Luke Skywalker could not prevail.

The black serpentlike tentacles of evil force struck at him again and again, filling his body with a pain like lava coursing through his veins. As he screamed, his voice was swallowed by a hurricane from the dark side.

Luke cried out one last time and crumpled backward to the blessedly cool flagstones of the Great Massassi Temple, as everything turned a smothering, final black around him. . . .

33

Near the center of the Cauldron Nebula, the two surviving Star Destroyers hung poised and ready to launch their attack on Coruscant.

Admiral Daala stood tall on her bridge platform, filled with an electrifying new self-confidence and determination. She had not slept in the past day.

Her officers sat at their stations, keyed up and anxious. A double complement of stormtroopers marched up and down the *Gorgon*'s halls, fully armed and battle ready. They had had a decade of drills, and now they would use their training to strike the greatest blow they could imagine for their cause.

"Commander Kratas, report," Daala said.

Kratas snapped to attention, barking out his report. "All equipment and weaponry have been transferred from the *Basilisk* to the *Gorgon*. Only a skeleton crew of volunteers—all stormtroopers—remains on the *Basilisk*. Captain Mullinore reports he is ready for his final mission."

Daala turned to the lieutenant at the comm station. "Patch me through to Captain Mullinore."

The image of the *Basilisk*'s captain appeared in front of her. The hologram wavered, but the man himself seemed completely rigid and in control, looking stoic as he met Admiral Daala's emerald eyes. "Yes, Admiral," he said.

"Captain, is your ship ready?" She paused, clasping her hands behind her back. "Are *you* ready?"

"Yes, Admiral. We have reconfigured all weapons systems to increase power to our shields. The stormtrooper crew has rigged the self-destruct mechanism into our primary hyperdrive reactors." He paused as if gathering courage, but his close-cropped blond hair showed not a glimmer of sweat. "The *Basilisk* is ready whenever you give the word, Admiral."

"Thank you, Captain. History will remember your sacrifice—I swear it."

She turned to the rest of her crew and switched on the intraship comm system. Her clipped voice rang throughout the *Gorgon*. "All hands, battle stations! Prepare to begin our run. We will destroy Coruscant and strike a death blow to the heart of the Rebellion."

Kyp Durron piloted the Sun Crusher to the core of the Cauldron Nebula, where Exar Kun had told him Admiral Daala's fleet lay in wait.

The controls of the Sun Crusher felt cool and familiar as he sat forward in the hard, uncomfortable pilot seat, looking through the segmented viewpanels. He had helped fly the superweapon during the escape from Maw Installation with Han Solo.

During that battle they had taken out one of Daala's Star Destroyers. Now he would use the Sun Crusher to obliterate the rest of her fleet.

Igniting an entire nebula seemed like an excessive blow to squash an Imperial insect, but Kyp appreciated the irony of destroying them with their own weapons. And it would signal to the rest of the fragmented Empire what was about to befall them as Kyp continued his purge.

The Sun Crusher's sensor panels became useless in the ionized discharge from the knot of blue-giant stars that illuminated the Cauldron Nebula. The front viewscreens dimmed to filter out the blazing light.

Kyp stretched out with the Force, dropping his inhibitions and letting the power burst from him like compressed gas. After the effort of yanking the Sun Crusher from the core of Yavin, finding a few Star Destroyers seemed a simple exercise.

After only a moment he sensed the arrowhead-shaped silhouettes of two Imperial battleships.

He piloted the Sun Crusher toward the bloated supergiants at the heart of the nebula. The titanic blue stars were huge, and young, and ripe for destruction. On a cosmic timescale they would burn hot, but briefly, ending their lives in supernova explosions that would send shock waves through an entire region of the galaxy.

With the Sun Crusher, though, Kyp could ignite the supernovas *now*, rather than in a hundred thousand years.

He stared across the soothing rainbow sea of gas and thought of the splashed-color sunsets on his colony world of Deyer, the placid terraformed lakes around the peaceful raft towns where he and his brother Zeth had played. But the Empire had broken into Kyp's home and taken him and his family away—without warning.

Years ago the Death Star had approached the quiet and pristine planet of Alderaan and had blown it to pieces with its planet-destroying superlaser—without warning.

Admiral Daala had captured Kyp and Han and Chewbacca after they had passed through the black-hole maze; but because Kyp had possessed no "worthwhile" information for her, she had sentenced him to death.

Daala deserved no warning. None at all.

Kyp increased the radiation shields on the Sun Crusher and approached the mammoth blue-giant stars, seething in their ocean of star material. He powered up the targeting display in front of him.

A recessed section of the control panel slid aside. A screen popped up, displaying a diagram of closely orbiting spheres. Seven enormous stars crowded in the middle of the nebula, circling in complex orbits as they stole gas from each other. Their intense radiation shone through the scattered hydrogen, oxygen, and neon clouds.

Kyp's face was a grim mask as he flicked a row of red activator switches. He knew exactly how the Sun Crusher worked; he had stolen those memories from Qwi Xux.

Warning beacons flashed across the command-system panels, and Kyp confirmed his intentions to the onboard computer. The torus-shaped generator at the long end of the Sun Crusher powered up, crackling with blue plasma.

Kyp remembered the New Republic engineers attempting to determine how the superweapon worked, how they had panicked at the sight of a simple message cylinder. The resonance torpedoes that triggered stellar explosions were dense packets of energy, programmed and modulated to make the core of a star unstable. The torpedoes could initiate a collapse and rebound of the outer layers of star material, unleashing a tremendously violent explosion that would rip a star apart.

Kyp targeted the cluster of blue-giant stars. He did not hesitate. He knew in his heart what he had to do.

He pushed the activation buttons. The Sun Crusher shuddered as the superweapon launched seven high-power resonance torpedoes.

Against the muted swirls of the Cauldron Nebula, he saw sizzling ovoid shapes of electric green, white, and yellow fire. The energy torpedoes streaked out, plunging into the boiling surfaces of the giant stars.

Kyp dimmed the segmented viewport and fixed his gaze on the blue giants. The cluster would explode simultaneously, and the shock waves would ignite vast oceans of nebular material in a galactic wildfire. It would be a perfectly clear signal to the remnants of the Empire.

But it would take hours for the torpedoes to tunnel to the stellar cores and set up the chain reaction. The wave of destruction would boil up from the depths of the stars until a flash of incredible force spewed brilliant light, high-energy radiation, and star matter into the Cauldron. The entire sector would become an inferno.

Kyp felt a cold fist clench inside his stomach. He could not turn back now. Once launched, the resonance torpedoes were irrevocable. These seven stars were doomed to explode in a few hours.

He pulled away at a leisurely pace, killing time. The Sun Crusher was so small that few sensor systems could detect it, especially within the electromagnetic chaos of the Cauldron Nebula. The weapon was designed to flit into a system, drop its torpedo into a star, and vanish without a battle, without loss of ordnance or personnel. A simple first—and final—strike.

Admiral Daala would never detect his presence.

Kyp's gaze wandered back to the chronometer, impatient to watch Daala's ships being wiped out in the murderous waves ripping through the nebula. He had the most powerful weapon ever invented, and he had the powers of the Sith that Exar Kun had shown him.

Where others had failed against the Empire, Kyp Durron would succeed. Completely.

As he drifted away from the blue-giant cluster, he noted that only about an hour remained before the massive explosions would begin. The waiting seemed to go on forever. He sent out his thoughts again, wishing he could taunt Daala.

Then, unexpectedly, her Star Destroyers began to move. The *Basilisk* and the *Gorgon* powered up their sublight engines and started a slow drift, aligning themselves to a hyperspace path, as if they were ready to launch another attack.

Kyp felt a flame of anger sear through him. "No—she can't leave now!"

He could not go back and stop the explosion of the core stars. Daala *had* to stay where she would be trapped!

Kyp slapped at the Sun Crusher's weapon-control systems, powering up the defensive laser cannons mounted at sharp angles on the weapon. Then he shot forward at full thrust.

When he and Han had first escaped from the Maw cluster, Daala had thrown all of her fighters at him in a desperate attempt to recapture the Sun Crusher.

Kyp figured it would take little more than a few potshots to give her the incentive to stay around.

•   •   •

Admiral Daala raised her right hand, looking at the navigator. "Prepare to engage hyperdrive," she said.

"Admiral!" the lieutenant at the sensor station cried. "I've detected an intruder!"

A tiny ship streaked across the bow of the *Gorgon*, blasting at them with puny laser strikes.

"What?" Daala said, turning. "Viewscreen," she called, "Enhance."

A shimmering image of Captain Mullinore from the *Basilisk* appeared at the comm station beside her. "Admiral, we have just detected the Sun Crusher," he said. "Shall we engage?"

"The Sun Crusher!" Daala took a second to accept the information. She could not answer before the small ship flitted in front of the *Gorgon*'s bridge tower again, blasting at the turbolaser batteries. She instantly recognized the thorn-shaped ship, the tiny superweapon bristling with defensive laser turrets. But the Sun Crusher's lasers had too little power to cause damage to a Star Destroyer.

"Launch two TIE squadrons," Daala said, feeling a new excitement. "I want the Sun Crusher recaptured. This changes everything in our strategy against the New Republic."

The stormtroopers, already keyed up from a day's worth of red-alert status, swarmed across the decks. Moments later the bottom bay of the *Gorgon* opened and spewed out a hundred plane-winged TIE fighters soaring through the curling gas of the nebula.

Daala watched the small battle unfold. The Sun Crusher had been designed to be extremely swift and maneuverable. With its indestructible quantum armor, the superweapon seemed to laugh at the attack she sent against it. It was only a matter of time, though.

"But why does he attack us at all?" Daala said, tapping black-gloved fingers on the bridge railing. "Something's wrong here. He provoked us, but he has no way of causing us damage. Why did he call attention to himself," she mused, "and how did he find us here?"

Commander Kratas answered her, though she had been muttering to herself. "I can't speculate on that, Admiral."

"Bring the Star Destroyers about," she said. "Lock a tractor beam on the Sun Crusher next time it passes."

"The Sun Crusher's pilot is maneuvering at speeds much too high for us to be certain of a firm lock," Kratas said.

Daala glared at him. "Does that mean you're unable to try?"

"No, Admiral." Kratas turned and clapped his hands, directing the tactical officers on the bridge. "You heard the Admiral! Set to it immediately."

"Admiral, the Sun Crusher is signaling us," the comm officer said. "Voice-only transmission."

Daala whirled. "Put the pilot on."

With a crackle the thin voice of a mere boy echoed through the *Gorgon*'s command center. "Admiral Daala, I'm Kyp Durron—remember me? I hope so. You put me under a death sentence. That made quite an impression on me. I hope it made some sort of impression on you."

Daala recalled the wiry, dark-haired youth who had been taken prisoner along with the Rebels who had blundered into the Maw Installation. She motioned for the comm officer to open a channel.

"Kyp Durron, if you surrender immediately and deliver the Sun Crusher intact, we will take you to the planet of your choice. You can be free. Don't be foolish."

"Not a chance, Admiral." Kyp laughed at her. "I'm thumbing my nose at your supposed Imperial superiority. I'll take my chances." He cut off the transmission and streaked by again, firing darts of laser energy that bounced harmlessly off the shielded hull of the Star Destroyer.

"Tractor-beam lock—" the tactical officer said, ". . . lost it."

"Admiral!" the sensor chief broke in, his voice filled with urgency. "I'm picking up unusual readings from the star cluster. The blue giants are fluctuating, all seven of them, I've never seen anything like—"

Daala froze. Her mouth dropped open in horror as she suddenly realized the terrible plan this . . . this *boy* had put into effect against her fleet.

"Full about!" she shouted. "One hundred eighty degrees, maximum speed. Get out of the nebula, now!"

"But, Admiral—?" Commander Kratas said.

"He's used the Sun Crusher!" she screamed. "The stars are going to explode! He's just trying to stall us here so we'll be trapped."

Kratas scrambled to the navigation station himself. The *Gorgon* lurched as the sublight engines kicked in, spinning the enormous Star Destroyer about.

"We no longer have our navicomputer lock on Coruscant," the navigation officer said. "When we turned to strike at the Sun Crusher, we lost our alignment."

"Get us out of here now," Daala said. "Any vector! Inform the *Basilisk*."

The sublight engines powered up, blasting as they lumbered away from the center of the nebula, picking up speed. The hyperdrive engines were primed, gathering power. The Star Destroyers began to move away—

Then all the stars exploded.

Kyp Durron watched the Star Destroyers wheel about and flee like wounded banthas.

"You can't get away fast enough." He smiled. "Not fast enough."

The *Gorgon* and the *Basilisk* began to heave themselves through the nebula at top speed, abandoning scores of TIE fighters. The small Imperial fighters veered off in a panic when their mother ships suddenly turned to run.

Kyp ignored the rest of the TIE fighters and punched his engines to twice the Sun Crusher's maximum-rated capacity, shooting straight up and out the plane of the nebular cloud.

When the cluster of blue giants detonated, concentric shock waves of blinding light and searing radiation blasted outward like a cosmic hurricane.

The *Gorgon* had managed to pull two ship lengths ahead of the *Basilisk*.

Hauling on the controls, Kyp continued the Sun Crusher's race upward, confident that the quantum armor would protect him from the worst. The incredible surge of energy from the supernovas darkened his viewports to near opacity.

Curtains of fire overtook the *Basilisk,* washing over the Star Destroyer and igniting it like another tiny nova erupting in the nebula, as the firestorm front swept on.

The viewscreen blackened, but where the *Gorgon* had been Kyp saw another flash—and then the firestorm obliterated all detail.

After his screens opaqued completely, Kyp used the onboard navicomputer to set a new course. This was just the beginning.

Leaving the galactic inferno behind him, and awed by the power of the Sun Crusher, Kyp moved off to seek out those remaining worlds that still swore allegiance to the Empire.

Now, without doubt, he had all the power he needed.

34

With the morning coolness of Yavin 4, Ambassador Cilghal rose in her austere quarters and basked in the shadowy dampness of the stone temple.

She had been at the Jedi *praxeum* for only a few days, but already she felt as if the whole universe had opened for her. Master Skywalker's exercises in attuning her mind to the Force had shown her how to turn her gaze in a new direction, to see things in full view that she had previously only glimpsed out of the corners of her eyes. He had given her a nudge down a long, smooth slope of discovery; the more she learned, the easier it was to learn more.

She splashed tepid water across her face, moistening her rubbery skin, scrubbing the delicate tendrils that hung beneath her slit of a mouth. Though the air of the jungle moon was thick with humidity, she still felt more comfortable when she could keep her exposed skin moist.

Cilghal left her quarters and moved to join the dozen other Jedi candidates in the dining hall, where each would consume a small breakfast of fruits or meats compatible with his or her biochemistry.

Dorsk 81 sat at a table contemplating colored rectangles of processed nutrients. Because he had lived for so long on a self-contained, environmentally controlled world, the cloned Jedi trainee could not digest foods that had not been heavily processed.

The gaunt, hardened Jedi Kam Solusar attempted to talk to wild-haired Streen, who kept flicking his gaze from side to side as if distracted.

The rest of the Jedi trainees sat by themselves or in small groups, talking uneasily. Cilghal did not see Master Skywalker among them. He was usually the first to enter the dining hall, waiting for his students to join him. The other Jedi trainees seemed disconcerted by the change of routine.

Cilghal worked the food-processing unit to prepare a breakfast of diced smoked fish and a pungent-tasting grain mash she enjoyed. Finally she asked the students in general, "Where is Master Skywalker?"

The trainees looked at each other as if they had been wanting to ask the same question.

Streen stood up and looked around in alarm. "It's too quiet," he said. "Too quiet. I wanted it quiet, but this is too much. I can't hear Master Skywalker. I could always sense voices in my head. I *hear* all of yours. It's too quiet." He sat down again as if embarrassed. "Too quiet."

Tionne rushed into the dining hall, clutching her twin-boxed musical instrument. Her silvery hair streamed behind her in a wild mass, and her pearly eyes were wide and panic-stricken. "Come quickly! I've found Master Skywalker."

Without question, without confusion, all the Jedi trainees rose in a coordinated, flowing movement. They moved together and sprinted after Tionne as she ran down the winding moss-grown halls. Cilghal attempted to keep up with the more athletic members, such as Kirana Ti and Tionne.

They ran through the echoing grand audience chamber where vines covered the walls and the long polished seats stood empty in shafts of sunlight.

"This way," Tionne said. "I don't know what's happened to him."

They reached a back staircase of worn stone steps that led to the observation platform at the top of the ziggurat.

Cilghal drew up short as she noticed the robed figure sprawled on the flagstones under the sky. His hands were thrown back as if to defend against something.

"Master Skywalker!" she called. The other trainees rushed forward. Cilghal pushed through the gathered students and knelt beside the fallen man.

Luke's face seemed curdled in an outcry of pain or fear. His eyes were squeezed shut, his lips were curled back in a grimace.

On the stone floor beside him lay his lightsaber, as if it had proved useless against whatever enemy he had fought.

Cilghal propped Luke's head up, touching his pale-brown hair. Rivulets of cold sweat glistened on his face, but she felt no warmth on his skin. She probed, using her newfound abilities in the Force, desperately searching.

"What happened to him?" Dorsk 81 said in great alarm.

"Is he alive?" Streen asked. "I can't hear him."

Cilghal probed with her sensing abilities and shook her orange and muddy-green head. "He's breathing. I can sense very little heartbeat, just the faintest pulse. But I can't find *him* inside. When I touch him with the Force, all I find is a great empty spot. . . . "

She turned to look at the others with her sad round Calamarian eyes. "It's as if he has left us."

"What can we do?" Kirana Ti asked.

Cilghal cradled Luke's motionless head in her lap and blinked her huge Calamarian eyes, unable to speak for a long moment.

"We are all alone now," she finally said.

CHAMPIONS

OF THE

FORCE

1

The Sun Crusher plunged into the Caridan system like an assassin's knife into an unsuspecting heart.

Old beyond his years, Kyp Durron sat hunched over the controls with dark eyes blazing, intent on his new target. With the might of the superweapon—as well as powerful techniques his spectral mentor Exar Kun had taught him—Kyp would extinguish all threats against the New Republic.

Only days before, he had annihilated Admiral Daala and her two Star Destroyers in the Cauldron Nebula. On the fringes of the explosion, he had dropped off one of the Sun Crusher's coffin-sized message pods so that the galaxy would know who was responsible for the victory.

As his next target, Kyp would challenge the Imperial military training center on Carida.

The military planet was a largish world with high gravity to toughen the muscles of potential stormtroopers. Its untamed land masses provided an appropriate range of training environments: arctic wastelands, trackless rain forests, splintered mountain crags, and searing desert hardpan crawling with venomous multilegged reptiles.

Carida seemed the opposite of Kyp's peaceful homeworld of Deyer, where he and his family had lived in raft colonies on the calm terraformed lakes—but that peace had been shattered years ago when Kyp's parents had chosen to protest the destruction of Alderaan. Stormtroopers had crushed the colony, whisking Kyp and his parents to the spice mines of Kessel while conscripting his brother Zeth for the stormtrooper training center.

Now, as he orbited the military planet, Kyp's face bore the tight, hardened look of a person who has been through the raging fire of his own conscience. Shadows rimmed his eyes. He did not expect to find his brother still alive after so many years—but he intended to learn the truth.

And if Zeth was not there, Kyp had enough power to destroy the whole Caridan solar system.

A week ago he had left Luke Skywalker for dead atop the Great Temple on Yavin 4. He had stolen design parameters of the Sun Crusher from the mind of its naive creator, Qwi Xux. And he had blown up five stars to incinerate Admiral Daala and her two Star Destroyers. At the last moment Daala had tried to flee the exploding stars, but to no avail. The shock waves had been intense enough to blank the Sun Crusher's viewscreens even as fire overtook Daala's flagship, the *Gorgon*.

Since that awesome victory Kyp's obsession had gained momentum, and he had set out on a hyperspeed course toward annihilating the Empire. . . .

The Caridan defense network spotted the Sun Crusher as Kyp entered orbit. He decided to transmit his ultimatum before the Imperial forces tried anything stupid. He broadcast on a wide range of frequencies.

"Caridan military academy," he said, trying to deepen his voice. "This is the pilot of the Sun Crusher." His mind searched for the name of the ambassadorial buffoon who had caused a diplomatic incident on Coruscant by tossing his drink in Mon Mothma's face. "I wish to speak to . . . *Ambassador Furgan* to discuss the terms of your surrender."

The planet below made no response. Kyp stared at the comm system, waiting for noise to burst from the speaker.

His alarm consoles flashed as the Caridans attempted to lock on to the Sun Crusher with a tractor beam, but Kyp worked the controls with Jedi-enhanced speed, oscillating his orbit at random so they could never get a positive lock.

"I am not here to play games." Kyp's hand bunched into a fist and slammed down on the comm unit. "Carida, if you do not answer within the next fifteen seconds, I'll fire a torpedo into the heart of your sun. I think you're familiar with the capabilities of this weapon. Do you understand?"

He began counting out loud. "One . . . two . . . three . . . four . . ." He got up to eleven before a brusque voice came through the comm system.

"Intruder, we are transmitting a set of landing coordinates. Follow them precisely or you will be destroyed. Relinquish control of your ship to the stormtroopers immediately upon landing."

"You don't seem to understand what's going on here," Kyp said before he bothered to stop laughing. "Let me talk to Ambassador Furgan *now* or your planetary system is going to be the galaxy's newest bright spot. I've already blown up a nebula to wipe out a pair of Imperial battle cruisers—don't you think I'd destroy one minor star to get rid of a planet full of stormtroopers? Get Furgan, and give me a visual."

The holo panel flickered, and the wide, flat face of Furgan appeared, shoving aside the comm officer. Kyp recognized the ambassador by his heavy eyebrows and fat purplish lips.

"Why have you come here, Rebel?" Furgan said. "You are in no position to make demands."

Kyp rolled his eyes, losing patience already. "Listen to me, Furgan. I want to find out what happened to my brother, Zeth. He was conscripted on the planet Deyer about ten years ago, and he was brought here. Once you have that information, we'll discuss terms."

Furgan stared at him, knitting his heavy spiked brows. "The Empire does not negotiate with terrorists."

"You don't have any choice in the matter."

Furgan fidgeted and finally backed down. "It will take some time to access information that old. Maintain your position in orbit, and we'll check."

"You have one hour," Kyp said, then signed off.

On Carida, in the main citadel of the Imperial military training center, Ambassador Furgan looked down at his comm officer, frowning with lips the color of fresh bruises. "Check that boy's words, Lieutenant Dauren. I want to know the capabilities of that weapon."

A stormtrooper lieutenant marched in with a precise military stride that sent shivers of admiration down Furgan's spine. "Report," he said to the captain.

The helmet speaker amplified the stormtrooper's voice. "Colonel Ardax announces that his assault team is ready to depart for the planet Anoth," he said. "We have eight MT-AT vehicles loaded into the Dreadnaught *Vendetta,* along with a full compliment of troops and weaponry."

Furgan tapped his fingers on the polished console in front of him. "It seems an extravagant effort to kidnap a baby and overcome a single woman who's watching him—but this is a *Jedi* baby, and I will not underestimate the defenses the Rebels may have emplaced. Tell Colonel Ardax to prepare his team for immediate departure. I have a minor irritation that needs to be dealt with here—and then we can go fetch a young, malleable replacement for the Emperor."

The stormtrooper saluted, whirled on one polished boot, and exited through the chamber doors.

"Ambassador," the comm officer said, scanning readouts, "we know from our spy network that the Rebels had a stolen Imperial weapon called the Sun Crusher, which can supposedly trigger the explosion of a star. And there was a mysterious multiple supernova in the Cauldron Nebula less than a week ago—just as the intruder claims."

Furgan felt a thrill of anticipation as his suspicions were confirmed. If he could get his hands on the Sun Crusher *and* the Jedi baby, he would have more power at his disposal than any of the squabbling warlords in the Core Systems! Carida could perhaps become the center of a blossoming new Empire—with Furgan at its helm as regent.

"While the Sun Crusher pilot is distracted and awaiting news of his brother," Furgan said, "we shall mount a full-fledged assault to cripple his craft. We can't let such an opportunity escape us."

Kyp stared at the Sun Crusher's chronometer, growing angrier with each ticking interval. If it weren't for the hope of learning news about Zeth, Kyp would have launched one of his four remaining resonance torpedoes into Carida's sun and backed off to watch the system explode in a white-hot supernova.

With a surge of static, the Caridan comm officer's image appeared before him, contrite and businesslike. "To the pilot of the Sun Crusher—you are Kyp Durron, brother of Zeth, whom we recruited on the colony world Deyer?" The officer spoke with a plodding voice, enunciating each word with unnecessary precision.

"I gave you that information already. What have you learned?"

The comm officer seemed to fade out of focus. "We regret that your brother did not survive initial military training. Our exercises are very strenuous, designed to discourage all but the best candidates."

Kyp's ears filled with a roar like rushing water. He had expected the news, but confirmation sent despair through him. "What . . . what were the circumstances of his death?"

"Checking," the comm officer said. Kyp waited and waited. "During a mountain survival tour he and his team were snowed in by a sudden blizzard. He appears to have frozen to death. There is some indication he made a heroic sacrifice so other members of his team could survive. I have the full details in a file. I can upload it if you like."

"Yes," Kyp said, his mouth dry. "Give me everything." He recalled an image of his brother: two boys throwing small reed boats into the water and watching them drift toward the marshes—then the look on Zeth's face after stormtroopers had crashed into their home and dragged him away.

"This will take a moment," the comm officer said.

Kyp watched the data scroll across his screens. He thought of Exar Kun, the ancient Lord of the Sith who had shown him many things that Master Skywalker refused to teach. The news of Zeth's inevitable death was like severing the remaining threads of Kyp's fragile restraint. Nothing could stop him now.

He would show murderous Carida no mercy. Kyp would remove this Imperial thorn from the New Republic's side and then move on to topple the big Imperial warlords gathering their forces near the galactic core.

He waited for Zeth's files to finish uploading into the Sun Crusher's memory. It would take a long time for him to absorb all those words, to imagine every detail of his brother's life, the life they should have had together. . . .

Emerging from the thin veil of atmosphere at the limb of the planet, a battle group of forty TIE fighters roared toward him. Another cluster of twenty came from the opposite horizon in a pincer formation. The ploy of Zeth's files had merely been a delaying tactic to keep him preoccupied as the Caridans launched an attack!

Kyp didn't know whether to be amused or outraged. A grim smile flickered across his face, then vanished.

The TIE fighters came in, firing what must have been intended as crippling laser blasts. Kyp felt the *thumps* of their impacts against the Sun Crusher, but his special quantum-layered armor could withstand even a turbolaser blast from a Star Destroyer.

One of the TIE pilots contacted Kyp. "We have you surrounded. You cannot escape."

"Sorry," Kyp said. "I'm fresh out of white flags." He used his sensors to track the lead TIE fighter from which the message had come. He targeted with his defensive lasers and let loose a volley that strafed across the ship's flat solar panel. The TIE ship broke apart in a flower of white-and-orange flame.

The other fighters retaliated from all sides. Kyp targeted with his own defensive lasers, selecting five victims. He managed to strike three.

Using the extreme mobility of the Sun Crusher, he accelerated upward just as the surviving TIE fighters sent return fire through the expanding explosions of his first round of victims. Kyp laughed out loud as two of the fighters hit each other in the cross fire.

The wall of anger rose and strengthened in him, increasing his reservoir of power. He had already given more warning than the Caridans deserved. Kyp had stated his ultimatum, and Furgan had sent out attack ships.

"That's the last mistake you'll ever make," he said.

The TIE fighters continued to fire, missing more often than not. Laser bolts *spang*ed off his armor, causing no damage. The pilots did not seem to know how to target and shoot properly. They had probably spent all their time practicing in simulation chambers, without ever fighting an actual space battle. Kyp relied instead on the Force.

He shot back, obliterating another ship, but decided that further fighting was not worth his time. He had a bigger target. Two fast TIE interceptors streaked after him as he pulled out of planetary orbit and set a course for the star at the heart of the system.

The only damage they could possibly do to the Sun Crusher would be to take out its tiny laser turrets. Daala's forces had once succeeded in disabling the Sun Crusher's external weaponry, but New Republic engineers had repaired it.

Another breached TIE fighter spurted flash-frozen atmosphere as it exploded. Kyp darted through the debris, straight toward the sun. The surviving Imperials charged after him, still firing. He paid them no heed.

Over and over in his mind he rolled images of Zeth, imagining his brother frozen and hopeless in a training exercise for an army he had never wanted to join. The only way for Kyp to cauterize that memory was to purge the entire planet with fire, a fire only the Sun Crusher could unleash.

He activated the firing systems for his resonance torpedoes. The high-energy projectile would be pumped out in an oval-shaped plasma discharge from the toroidal generator at the bottom of the Sun Crusher.

Last time Kyp had fired the torpedoes into supergiant stars in a nebula. Carida's sun was an unremarkable yellow sun, but even so, the Sun Crusher could ignite a chain reaction within the core. . . .

As Kyp swooped in toward the blazing ball of yellow fire, flickering prominences reached out of the star's chromosphere. Boiling convection cells lifted hot knots of gas to the surface, where they cooled and sank back into the churning depths. Dark sunspots stood out like blemishes. He sighted on one of the black spots as if it were a bull's-eye.

Kyp primed the resonance torpedo and spared a moment to glance back. His TIE pursuers had split off, unwilling to come so close to the glaring sun.

Fail-safe warning systems flashed in front of Kyp, but he disregarded them. When the control system winked green, he depressed the firing buttons and shot a sizzling green-blue ellipsoid deep into Carida's sun. Its targeting mechanisms would find the core and set up an irrevocable instability.

Kyp leaned back in the comfortable pilot's seat with a sigh of relief and determination. He had passed the point of no return.

He should have felt elated, knowing it was only a matter of time before the military academy was finally extinguished. But that knowledge could not wash away the grief he felt for the loss of his brother.

• • •

Alarms screamed through the citadel of the military training center. Stormtroopers ran along flagstoned halls, taking emergency positions at strategic points as they had been drilled; but they didn't quite know what to do.

Ambassador Furgan's face held a comical expression of shock. His bulging eyes looked as if they might pop out of their sockets. His lips scraped together as he fought for words. "But how could all of our TIE fighters miss?"

"They didn't miss, sir," Comm Officer Dauren said. "The Sun Crusher seems to have impenetrable armor, better than any shielding we've ever encountered.

"Kyp Durron has reached our sun. Although our readings are scrambled from coronal discharges, it appears that he has launched some sort of high-energy projectile." The comm officer swallowed. "I think we know what that means, sir."

"If the danger is real," Furgan said.

"Sir—" Dauren wrestled with rising agitation, "we have to assume it's real. The New Republic was pointedly uneasy about being in possession of such a weapon. The stars in the Cauldron Nebula did explode."

Kyp Durron's voice broke over the intercoms. "Carida, I warned you— but you chose to trick me instead. Now accept what you've brought upon yourselves. According to my calculations, it'll take two hours before the core of your sun reaches a critical configuration." He paused for a beat. "You have that amount of time to evacuate your planet."

Furgan slammed his fist down on the table.

"Sir," Dauren said, "what are we going to do? Should I organize an evacuation?"

Furgan leaned over to flick a switch, toggling to the hangar bay in the lower staging area of the citadel. "Colonel Ardax, muster your forces immediately. Get them aboard the Dreadnaught *Vendetta*. We will launch our Anoth assault team within the hour, and I will accompany them."

"Yes, sir," the reply came.

Furgan turned to his comm officer. "Are you certain that boy's brother is dead? Nothing we can use for leverage?"

Dauren blinked. "I don't know, sir. You told me to delay him, so I made up a story and sent a fake file. Do you want me to check?"

"Of course I want you to check!" Furgan bellowed. "If we can use the brother as a hostage, perhaps we can force that boy to neutralize the effects of this Sun Crusher weapon."

"I'll get on it immediately, sir," Dauren said, and hammered his fingertips on the datapads.

Six of Furgan's training commanders, summoned by the wailing alarms, marched into the control center and saluted briskly. Standing shorter than his commanders, Furgan clasped his hands behind his back, pushing his chest out as he addressed them.

"Take an inventory of all functional ships on Carida. Everything. We need to download the data cores from our computers and take as many personnel as possible. I doubt we'll be able to evacuate them all; therefore, choices will be made on the basis of rank."

"Are we just going to abandon Carida without a fight?" one of the generals said.

Furgan screamed at him, "The sun is going to blow up, General! How do you propose to fight that?"

"Evacuation on the basis of rank?" Dauren said in a small voice, looking up from his panel. "But I'm only a lieutenant, sir."

Furgan scowled down at the man hunched over his control panels. "Then that gives you all the more incentive to find that kid's brother and force him to rescind that torpedo!"

Through half-polarized viewports Kyp watched the surviving TIE fighters pull away and swoop back toward Carida. He smiled with satisfaction. It would be good to watch the Caridans' panicked scramble as they tried to grab everything of value on an entire planet.

Over the next twenty minutes he watched streams of ships launch away from the main training citadel: small fighters, large personnel transports, StarWorker space barges, and one deadly looking Dreadnaught battleship.

Kyp was annoyed at himself for allowing the Imperials to haul so much weaponry away. He was sure it would eventually be used against the New Republic; but at the moment Kyp took his pleasure from eradicating the solar system.

"You can't escape," he whispered. "A few might get away, but you can't all escape." He glanced at his chronometer. Now that instabilities had begun pulsing out of the star, he could get a more accurate determination of how long it would take for the sun to explode. The Caridans had twenty-seven minutes before the first shockwave struck.

The flow of ships had petered out, and only a few scrap-heap vessels struggled out of the gravity well. Carida did not appear to be well supplied with vessels; most of their prime equipment must already have been commandeered by Grand Admiral Thrawn or some other Imperial warlord.

The holopanel flickered, and the image of the comm officer appeared. "Pilot of the Sun Crusher! This is Lieutenant Dauren calling Kyp Durron—this is an emergency, an urgent message!"

Kyp could well imagine that anyone still on Carida might have an urgent message! He took his time answering just to make the comm officer squirm. "Yes, what is it?"

"Kyp Durron, we have located your brother Zeth."

Kyp felt as if someone had thrust a lightsaber through his heart. "What? You said he was dead."

"We checked thoroughly and found him in our files after all. He is stationed here in the citadel, and he has not managed to find transport off Carida! I've summoned him to my comm station. He'll be here in a moment."

"How can that be!" Kyp demanded. "You said he died in training! I have the files you sent me."

"Falsified information," Lieutenant Dauren said bluntly.

Kyp squeezed his eyes shut as hot tears sprang to fill his vision: sudden overwhelming joy at knowing Zeth was still alive, anger at having committed the most fundamental mistake of all—*believing* what the Imperials told him.

He snapped a glance at the chronometer. Twenty-one minutes until the explosion. Kyp wrenched at the Sun Crusher's controls and shot back toward the planet like a laser blast. He doubted he had enough time to rescue his brother, but he had to try.

He stared at the time display ticking away. His vision burned, and he felt a jolt go through him every time a number ticked down.

It took five minutes to get back to Carida. He orbited around the massive planet in a tight arc, crossing over the line from night into day. He set course for the small cluster of fortresses and buildings that made up the Imperial training center.

Lieutenant Dauren appeared again in the small holographic field, dragging a white-armored stormtrooper into view. "Kyp Durron! Please respond."

"I'm here," Kyp said. "I'm coming to get you."

The comm officer turned to the stormtrooper. "Twenty-one twelve, remove your helmet."

Hesitantly, as if he had not done so in a long time, the stormtrooper tugged off his helmet. He stood blinking in the unfiltered light as if he rarely looked at the world through his own eyes. Kyp saw a heartrending image that reminded him of the face he saw when he looked in a reflection plate.

"State your name," Dauren said.

The stormtrooper blinked in confusion. Kyp wondered if he was drugged. "Twenty-one twelve," he said.

"Not your service number, your *name!*"

The young man paused for a long time, as if pawing through rusty, unused memories until he came out with a word that sounded more like a question than an answer.

"Zeth? Zeth Dur . . . Durron."

Kyp didn't need to hear him speak his name, though. He remembered the tanned, wiry boy who swam in the lakes of Deyer, who could catch fish with a small hand net.

"Zeth," he whispered. "I'm coming."

The comm officer waved his hands. "You can't make it in time," he said. "You must stop the Sun Crusher torpedo. Reverse the chain reaction. That's our only hope."

"I can't stop it!" Kyp answered. "Nothing can stop it."

Dauren screamed, "If you don't, we're all going to die!"

"Then you're going to die," Kyp said. "You all deserve it. Except for Zeth. I'm going to come for him."

He plowed like thunder through the high atmosphere of Carida. Heated air pearled off the sides of the superweapon as a shock front pushed a shield in front of him. Sonic booms rippled behind him.

The planet surface approached with gut-wrenching speed. Kyp soared over a cracked, blasted wasteland with craggy red rocks and fractured canyons. Out in the flat desert he saw geometric shapes, tracks of precise roads laid down by the Imperial corps of engineers.

The Sun Crusher shot like a meteor over a cluster of bunkers and metallic huts. Isolated stormtroopers marched about in drills, unaware that their sun was about to explode.

On the chronometer seven minutes remained.

Kyp called up a targeting screen and found the primary citadel. The air tugged at his ship, buffeting him with heavy winds, but Kyp did not care. Flames from the ignited atmosphere flickered off the quantum armor.

"Give me your specific location," Kyp said.

The comm officer had begun sobbing.

"I know you're in the main citadel building!" Kyp cried. "Where exactly?"

"In the upper levels of the southernmost turret," Zeth answered precisely, responding in a military manner, slipping back into stormtrooper training.

Kyp saw the jagged spires of the military academy rising from a cluttered plateau. Kyp's scanners projected an enlarged image of the citadel, pinpointing the turret Zeth had mentioned.

Five minutes remained.

"Zeth, get ready, I'm coming in."

"To rescue us both!" Dauren said.

Kyp felt a twinge inside. He wanted to leave the comm officer who had lied to him, who had made him despair and forced him into the decision to destroy Carida. He wanted to let the lieutenant die in a burst of incinerating solar flame—but that man could help him, for now.

"Get yourselves into an open area. I'm going to be there in less than a minute. You can't get up to the roof in time, so I'm going to blast it off."

Dauren nodded. Zeth finally overcame his own confusion and said, "Kyp? My brother? Kyp, is that you?"

The Sun Crusher streaked over the jagged minarets and pinnacles of the Caridan citadel. A mammoth wall surrounded the entire fortress. Out in the courtyard hundreds of low-ranking refugees scrambled about in tiny fliers aiming up into the skies, though with no hyperdrive capability they could never outrun the fury of the supernova.

Kyp decelerated abruptly until he hovered over the fortress. Suddenly the Sun Crusher lurched from side to side as automatic perimeter lasers targeted him and fired.

"Shut down your defenses!" he screamed at the comm officer. He wasted time targeting and firing at the perimeter lasers. Two of the weapon emplacements blew up in roiling smoke, but the third, a blaster cannon, scored a direct hit against the Sun Crusher.

The superweapon spun end over end, out of control until it smashed into one of the tall turret walls. Kyp managed to get control again and raised the vehicle up. No time to vent his anger. No time to do anything but get to the tower.

Kyp watched the chronometer click down from four minutes to three.

"Take shelter!" he said. "I'm going to blast open the roof."

He targeted with one of his weapons and fired—but he received an ERROR message. The laser turret had been damaged by his collision with the tower. Kyp swore and spun the ship around so he could target with a different laser.

After a short controlled burst, the roof of the tower melted inward. Chunks of synrock and metal reinforcement girders sprayed into the air. Kyp flicked on his tractor beam to yank the debris away before it could collapse into the lower floors.

He brought the Sun Crusher over the smoking crater that had been the rooftop. He pointed his scanners down and saw two people scramble out from under the desks where they had taken shelter.

Two minutes.

Kyp hovered over them. If he lowered his ship, they could reach the ladder to the hatch, where they could climb into the shielded Sun Crusher. He already had an escape route programmed in.

As Kyp dropped toward them, Lieutenant Dauren stood up and battered Zeth on the back of the skull with a broken plasteel shard. Zeth fell to his knees, shaking his head and pulling out his blaster in reflex. The comm officer ran to the Sun Crusher's ladder, but Kyp—furious at seeing what Dauren had done—raised the ship out of the man's reach.

Scrambling, waving his arms, the comm officer jumped up to reach the rungs of the ladder, but he missed and slapped his hands across the hull instead. The quantum armor was still smoking hot from Kyp's fiery plunge through the atmosphere. Dauren screamed as it burned his hands.

Falling back to the ground, Dauren turned just in time to see Zeth point the blaster at him. With precise stormtrooper training Zeth targeted and fired. The comm officer flew backward, his chest a black hole. He collapsed among the debris.

One minute.

Kyp maneuvered the Sun Crusher back into position, lowered the ladder; but Zeth collapsed to his knees; blood streamed down the back of his head, streaking the white stormtrooper armor. Zeth could not move. He had been too badly injured by the comm officer.

Thinking rapidly, Kyp locked on to his brother's limp form with the tractor beam, yanking him up off the floor and drawing him toward the Sun Crusher. This would be it. Kyp left the controls and scrambled to the hatch. He would have to open the hatch, climb down the ladder, and haul his brother up inside. He reached for the locking mechanism that would open the Sun Crusher—

And then Carida's sun exploded.

The shock wave roared through the atmosphere, bringing instant incinerating fire. The entire citadel turned into a storm of flames.

The Sun Crusher tumbled end over end, and Kyp flew against the far wall of the cockpit, his face plastered against one of the external viewscreens. He saw the faint afterimage of Zeth's body disintegrating into a fading silhouette as the stellar energy ripped across Carida.

Kyp hauled himself into the pilot seat. In shock, he used his Jedi instincts to punch the sublight engines. The first wave from the supernova had been the prompt radiation, high-energy particles shot out with the explosion of the star. A minute or so later the heavier radiation would come.

As rippling waves from the second hurricane of energy struck Carida and cracked the planet open, the Sun Crusher accelerated far beyond its red lines along the preprogrammed escape route.

Kyp felt gravity stretching his face into a grimace. His eyelids squeezed closed, and anguished tears flowed backward across his temples with the pull of acceleration.

The Sun Crusher blasted out of the atmosphere and entered hyperspace. As starlines formed around him and the supernova made one last grab with hands of flame, Kyp let out a long anguished cry of despair at what he had done.

His scream vanished with him into hyperspace.

2

Leia Organa Solo emerged from the *Millennium Falcon* on Yavin 4, ducking her head as she walked down the landing ramp. She looked toward the towering edifice of the Great Massassi Temple.

It was a cool morning on the jungle moon, and mist rose from the ground, clinging to the low treetops and brushing against the stone ziggurat like a thin white shroud. *A funeral shroud,* she thought. For Luke.

It had been a week since the trainees at the Jedi academy had found Luke Skywalker's motionless body atop the temple. They had brought him inside, done their best to care for him—but they did not know what to do. The best New Republic medics had found no physical damage. They agreed that Luke still lived, but he lay in complete stasis. He responded to none of their tests or probes.

Leia had little hope of doing anything herself, but she could at least be with her brother.

The twins came clomping down the *Falcon*'s ramp, seeing who could make the loudest banging noises with their small boots. Han stood between Jacen and Jaina, holding their hands. "Be quiet, you two," he said.

"Are we going to see Uncle Luke?" Jaina asked.

"Yes," Han answered, "but he's sick. He won't be able to talk to you."

"Is he dead?" Jacen asked.

"No!" Leia answered sharply. "Come on. Let's get into the temple." The twins scampered ahead down the ramp.

The sharp jungle smells brought warm and fresh memories to Leia as she walked across the clearing. Fallen trees, decaying leaves, and flowers mixed into a potent brew of scents. She had proposed the empty ruins as a site for Luke's academy, but Leia had never managed to visit—and now she had come only to see her brother lying in state.

"I'm not looking forward to this," Han mumbled. "Not at all." Leia reached over to squeeze his hand; he gripped hers, holding tighter and longer than she expected him to.

Robed figures emerged from the temple, drifting out of the early-morning shadows. She quickly counted a dozen. In the lead she recognized the rusty-orange face of a Calamarian female, Cilghal. Leia herself had seen Jedi potential in the fishlike woman and had urged her to join Luke's academy. Cilghal had managed to use her proven ambassadorial skills to hold the twelve students together in the terrible days following the fall of their Jedi Master.

Leia recognized other candidates gliding across the dew-damp ground: Streen, an older man with wild hair tucked haphazardly beneath a Jedi hood; he had been a gas prospector on Bespin, a hermit hiding from the voices he heard in his head. She saw tall Kirana Ti, one of the witches of Dathomir whom Leia and Han had encountered during their whirlwind courtship. Kirana Ti stepped forward, flashing a bright smile at the twins; she had a daughter of her own, only a year or so older than the twins, who remained in the care of others back on her homeworld.

Leia also identified Tionne, with long silvery hair that flowed down the back of her robe. Tionne was a student of Jedi history who wanted desperately to be a Jedi herself.

Then came hard-bitten Kam Solusar, a once-corrupted Jedi whom Luke had dragged back to the light side. And Dorsk 81, a streamlined, slick-skinned alien who had been cloned generation after generation, because his society believed they had already developed the perfect civilization.

Leia didn't recognize the other handful of Jedi candidates, but she knew Luke had been diligent in his Jedi search. The call still rang out across the galaxy, inviting those with the potential to become new Jedi Knights.

Even though their teacher now lay in a coma.

Cilghal raised a flippered hand. "We are glad you could come, Leia."

"Ambassador Cilghal," she said. "My brother—has there been any change?" They walked heavily back toward the oppressive temple. Leia believed she already knew the answer.

"No." Cilghal shook her squarish head. "But perhaps your presence will do something that ours cannot."

Sensing the solemn mood, the twins refrained from giggling and exploring the musty, stone-walled rooms. As the party entered the gloomy ground-level hangar bay, Cilghal led Leia, Han, and the twins to a turbolift.

"Come on, Jacen and Jaina," Han said, grabbing their hands again. "Maybe you can help Uncle Luke get better."

"What can we do?" Jaina asked, her liquid-brown eyes wide and hopeful.

"I don't know yet, honey," he said. "If you come up with any ideas, let me know."

The turbolift doors flowed shut, and the platform rose to the top levels of the temple. The twins clung to each other in sudden uneasiness. They had not recovered from their fear of turbolifts since the last time they had ridden one all the way down to the decaying bottom levels of Imperial City. But the ride was over in a moment, and they stepped out into the grand audience chamber of the Great Temple. Skylights spilled sunlight on a broad, polished-stone promenade that led to a raised stage.

Leia remembered standing on that stage years before, after the Death Star had been destroyed, presenting medals to Han, Chewbacca, Luke, and the other heroes of the battle of Yavin. Now, though, her breath caught in her throat. Han groaned beside her, a deep, grieving tone that she had never heard him make before.

On a bier at the end of the room lay Luke—like a body stretched out for a funeral in an echoing, empty chamber.

Her heart thumped with dread. She wanted to turn around so she wouldn't have to look at him—but Leia's feet compelled her forward. She walked with a rapid step that became a run before she reached the end of the promenade. Han followed, carrying the twins, one in each arm. His eyes were red as he fought to keep tears from flowing. Leia already felt a wetness on her cheeks.

Luke lay in repose, swathed in his Jedi robe. His hair had been combed; his hands were folded across his chest. His skin looked gray and plasticlike.

"Oh, Luke," she whispered.

"Too bad you can't just thaw him out," Han said, "like you rescued me from Jabba's Palace."

Leia reached out to touch Luke. Using her own abilities with the Force, she tried to reach deeper, to brush against his spirit—but she felt only a cold hole, an emptiness as if *Luke himself* had been taken away. Not dead. She had always felt she would somehow know if her brother died.

"Is he sleeping?" Jacen said.

"Yes . . . in a way," she answered, not knowing what else to say.

"When will he wake up?" Jaina asked.

"We don't know," she said. "We don't know how to wake him up."

"Maybe if I give him a kiss." Jaina clambered up to smack the motionless lips of her uncle. For an absurd moment Leia held her breath, thinking that the child's magic just might work. But Luke did not stir.

"He's cold," Jaina mumbled. The little girl's shoulders slumped with disappointment when her uncle failed to wake.

Han squeezed Leia's waist so hard that it hurt, but she didn't want her husband to stop holding her.

"He's been unchanged for days," Cilghal said behind them. "We brought his lightsaber with him. We found it beside his body on the rooftop."

Cilghal hesitated, then moved to stare down at Luke. "Master Skywalker told me I have an innate talent for healing with the Force. He had just begun to show me how to develop my skills—but I've tried all I know. He is not sick. There's nothing physically wrong with him. He seems frozen in a moment of time, as if his soul has left and his body is waiting for him to come back."

"Or," Leia said, "waiting for us to find a way to help him return."

"I don't know how," Cilghal said in a thin, husky voice. "None of us knows—yet. But perhaps working together we can figure it out."

"Do you have any inkling about what really happened?" Leia asked. "Have you found any clues?"

She could sense the sudden spike of Han's turmoil. Cilghal looked away with her big Calamarian eyes, but Han answered with grim certainty. "It was Kyp. Kyp did this."

"What?" Leia said, whirling to stare at him.

Han answered in a tumble of words. "The last time I saw Luke, he told me he was afraid for Kyp." Han swallowed hard. "He said that Kyp had started dabbling in the dark side. The kid stole Mara Jade's ship and took off somewhere. I think Kyp came back here and challenged Luke."

"But why?" Leia asked. "What for?"

Cilghal nodded, as if her head were too heavy for her. "We did find the stolen ship in front of the temple. It is still here, so we don't know how he flew away again . . . unless he fled into the jungles."

"Is that likely?" Leia asked.

Cilghal shook her head. "We Jedi trainees have pooled our talents and searched. We do not detect his presence on Yavin 4. He must have left on another ship somehow."

"But where would he get another ship?" Leia asked, but suddenly she remembered astonished New Republic astronomers reporting the impossible news that an entire group of stars in the Cauldron Nebula had gone supernova at the same time.

She whispered, "Could Kyp have resurrected the Sun Crusher from the core of Yavin?"

Han blinked. "How could he possibly do that?"

Cilghal hung her head gravely. "If Kyp Durron has managed that, then his power is far greater even than we feared. No wonder he was able to defeat Master Skywalker."

Han shuddered, as if afraid to accept what he knew was true. Leia could sense his emotions like a maelstrom within him. "If Kyp is on the loose with the Sun Crusher," he said, "then I'll have to go and stop him."

Leia snapped around to look at him, thinking how Han always leaped headfirst into challenges. "Are you getting delusions of grandeur again? Why does it have to be you?"

"I'm the only one he might listen to," he said. He looked aside, staring down at Luke's cadaverous face. She saw his lips trembling.

"Look, if Kyp doesn't listen to me, then he won't listen to anyone—and he'll be lost forever. If his power is as great as Cilghal thinks, that kid is not an enemy the New Republic can afford to have." He gave one of his lopsided grins. "Besides, I taught him everything he knows about flying that ship. He couldn't possibly do anything to me."

It was a somber dinner with the Jedi trainees.

Han used the *Falcon*'s food synthesizers to create a repast of heavy Corellian food. Leia picked at some spiced, fried strips of a woolamander that Kirana Ti had hunted in the jungle. The twins stuffed themselves with messy fruits and berries. Dorsk 81 devoured a bland and unappealing-looking meal of heavily processed food cubes.

Conversation was minimal, little more than forced pleasantries. They all feared to discuss what really preoccupied them—until Kam Solusar said in a hard-edged voice, "We hoped you would bring us news, Minister Organa Solo. Give us some guidance as to what we should do here. We are Jedi students with no Master. We've learned a little, but not enough to continue training on our own."

Tionne broke in. "I'm not sure we should try to learn things we don't understand. Look what happened to Gantoris! He was consumed by some evil thing he inadvertently found. And what about Kyp Durron? What if we get lured to the dark side without knowing it?"

Old Streen stood up and shook his head. "No, no. *He's* here! Don't you hear the voices?" When everyone turned to look at him, Streen sat down and hunched his shoulders, as if trying to hide under the Jedi robe. He snuffled and cleared his throat before continuing. "I can hear him. He's whispering to me now. He talks to me always. I can't get away from him."

Leia felt a rush of hope. "Luke? You can hear Luke talking to you?"

"No!" Streen whirled at her. "The Dark Man. A dark man, a shadow. He talked to Gantoris. He talked to Kyp Durron. You shine the light, but the shadow always stays, whispering, talking." Streen placed his hands against his ears and pressed his temples.

"This is too dangerous," Kirana Ti said, knitting her eyebrows. "On Dathomir I've seen what happens when a large group falls to the dark side. The evil witches on my planet made things terrible for centuries—and the galaxy was saved only because they had no spaceflight. If the witches had managed to spread their dark workings from star system to star system . . ."

"Yes, we should all stop our Jedi exercises," Dorsk 81 said, blinking his large yellow eyes. "This was a bad idea. We shouldn't have even tried."

Leia slapped both her hands hard on the table. "Stop this talk!" she said. "Luke would be ashamed to hear his students saying such things. With attitudes like that, you'll never become Jedi Knights."

She fumed. "Yes, there is a risk. There will always be risks. You've seen what happens to someone who isn't careful—but that simply means you must *be careful.* Don't be seduced by the dark side. Learn from the sacrifice that Gantoris made. Learn from how Kyp Durron was tempted. Learn from the sacrifices your Master made in an attempt to protect you all."

She stood and looked at each one of them. Some flinched. Some met her gaze.

"You are the new generation of Jedi Knights," she continued. "That is a great burden, but you must bear it, because the New Republic needs you. The old Jedi protected the Republic for a thousand generations. How can you give up after the first challenge?

"*You* have to be the champions of the Force, with or without your Jedi Master. Learn as Luke learned: step by step. You must work together, discover the things you don't know, fight what has to be fought. But the one thing you can't do is give up!"

"She is right," Cilghal said in her maddeningly calm voice. "If we surrender, the New Republic will have one less weapon against evil in the galaxy. Even if some of us fail, the rest of us must succeed."

"Do or do not," Kirana Ti said, and Tionne finished the phrase that Master Skywalker had drilled into them. "There is no try."

Her heart pounding, her stomach watery, Leia slowly sat down. The twins stared at their mother in amazement, and Han gripped her hand in admiration. She breathed deeply, began to let herself relax—

When suddenly a strangling outcry of death shattered her soul. It sounded like an avalanche within the Force, an outcry of thousands upon thousands of lives wiped out in an instant. Around the table the other Jedi candidates, all those sensitive to the Force, clutched at their chests or their ears.

Streen let out a long wail. "It's too many, too many!"

Leia's blood burned through her veins. Painful claws skittered down her spine, plucking her nerves and sending jolts through her body. Both of the Jedi twins were crying.

Baffled, Han grabbed Leia's shoulders and shook her. "What is it, Leia? What happened?" He apparently had felt nothing. "What?"

She gasped. "It was . . . a great disturbance . . . in the Force. Something terrible just happened."

With a cold wash of dread Leia thought of young Kyp Durron, turned to the dark side and now armed with the Sun Crusher.

"Something terrible," she said again, but she could not answer Han's other questions.

3

The Force moved through all things, weaving the universe into an
invisible tapestry that tied the smallest living creature to the largest star
cluster. Synergy made the total far greater than the sum of its parts.

And when one of those threads was torn, ripples spread through the
entire web. Actions and reactions . . . great shock waves that affected all who
could hear.

The destruction of Carida screamed through the Force, building power
as it reflected off other sensitive minds. It rose to a tumult that struck—

And woke.

Sensory perceptions rushed back to Luke Skywalker like a storm, freeing
him from the smothering nothingness that had trapped and frozen him. His
final shout still echoed in his ears, but now he felt strangely numb.

The last thing he remembered was the serpent-shaped tendrils of black
Force wrapping around him. Rising from the summons of Exar Kun and
Luke's misguided student Kyp Durron, the serpents of Sith power had sunk
their fangs into him. Luke had been unable to resist their combined might.
He had tried to use his lightsaber, but even that had failed.

Luke had fallen into a bottomless pit deeper than any of the black holes in
the Maw cluster. He did not know how long he had been powerless. He remembered only an emptiness, a coldness . . . until *something* had jarred him loose.

Now, as the sudden clamor of sensory impressions filled him, it took him some time to sort out and make sense of what he could see: the walls of the grand audience chamber, the lozenge-shaped stones, the translucent tiles set out in hypnotic patterns, the long promenade and the empty benches spread like frozen waves on the floor, where once the entire Rebel Alliance had celebrated their victory over the first Death Star.

Luke's head buzzed, and he felt giddy. He wondered why he should feel so insubstantial, until he looked down—and saw his own body still lying prone and motionless below him, eyes closed, face expressionless.

Astonishment and disbelief blurred Luke's vision, but he forced himself to focus again on his own features. He saw the faded scars from when the wampa ice creature had attacked him on Hoth. His body was still draped with the brown Jedi robe, his hands crossed lightly on his chest. The lightsaber lay at his hip, a cylinder of silent plasteel, crystals, and electronic components.

"What's going on?" Luke said out loud. "Hello?"

He heard the words thrum through his head like vibrating transmissions, but they made no sound at all in the air.

Finally Luke looked at *himself*—the part of himself that was aware—and saw an insubstantial image, like a ghost reflection of his body, as if he had reconstructed a hologram using his impression of what he looked like. His spectral arms and legs appeared to be garbed in a flowing Jedi robe, but the colors were washed-out and weak. Everything was sketched with a lambent blue glow that sparkled as he moved.

With a rush of awe and astonishment Luke suddenly *knew* what had happened. Several times he had encountered wavering spirits of Obi-Wan Kenobi and Yoda, and his own father, Anakin Skywalker.

Was he dead, then? It sounded ludicrous because he didn't *feel* dead— but he had no point of comparison. He recalled how Obi-Wan's and Yoda's and Anakin's bodies had all vanished upon their deaths: Obi-Wan and Yoda leaving only crumpled robes, Anakin Skywalker leaving only the empty body armor of Darth Vader.

Why, then, had his own body remained intact, stretched out on the raised platform? Could it be because he was not yet entirely a Jedi Master, completely given over to the Force—or could it be that he was not truly dead?

Luke heard a whirring as the turbolift rose to the top chamber. The sound seemed eerie and unnatural, as if he were using senses other than his ears to hear.

The turbolift doors slid open. Artoo-Detoo extended his front wheeled foot and rolled out, moving slowly, almost respectfully, along the polished stone promenade. The droid proceeded toward the raised platform.

Luke's shimmering image stood in front of his body where it lay in state, and he watched with joy as the little astromech droid came to him.

"Artoo, am I glad to see you!" he said. He expected the droid to bleep with wild excitement. But Artoo gave no indication that he heard or detected Luke.

"Artoo?"

Artoo-Detoo trundled up the ramp to Luke's shrouded body. The droid hooted, a low, mournful sound that expressed deep grief—if droids could feel such emotions. It tore Luke apart to see his mechanical friend looking at the body; his optical receptor winked from red to blue and back again.

Luke realized that the droid was taking readings, checking on his body's condition. He wondered if Artoo would detect anything different, now that Luke's spirit had been set free; but the droid gave no sign.

Luke attempted to move over to Artoo, to touch the polished barrel-shaped body. It took him a moment to figure out how to move his ghostly "legs." His image skimmed across the floor with a dizzying fluidity. But when he stroked Artoo, his hand passed directly through.

He felt no contact with the plasteel of the droid's body, no sensation of the floor against his ethereal feet. Luke tried walking completely through the droid, hoping somehow to scramble Artoo's sensors, but Artoo continued to take readings, unperturbed.

The droid gave another sad hoot as if in farewell, then spun around and whirred slowly back toward the turbolift.

Luke called out. "Wait, Artoo!" But he held little hope the droid would hear.

A quick idea came to him: rather than using his illusory hands, he reached out with the Force. He thought of how he and Gantoris had used little nudges from the Force to rattle metal antennas in the airborne ruins of Tibannopolis on Bespin.

Luke reached out invisibly to tap Artoo's shell, hoping to make a loud *spang* that would at least let the droid know something was amiss. He pushed and thumped with all his intangible might, and succeeded only in what he thought was a barely audible bump against the droid's metal casing.

Artoo paused, but while Luke gathered strength to make another Force assault, the droid dismissed the unexplained sound and entered the turbolift. Inside the turbolift, Artoo turned his optical sensor once more toward the body of his master, made a low, sliding whistle, and then the doors whisked closed. Luke heard the humming of the platform as it dropped back down to the lower levels of the Great Temple.

Luke stood in the echoing grand audience chamber all alone—awake again, but insubstantial and apparently powerless. He would have to find some other way to solve his predicament.

He looked out through the temple skylights into the blackness of the jungle moon's deep night, and he wondered what he could do to save himself.

4

With a Wookiee bellow of impatience, Chewbacca urged the last members of the Special Forces team onto the remaining troop transport. The other transports had been shuttling up and down from Coruscant orbit all day, carrying weapons, equipment, and personnel to the strike force already assembled in space.

The heavily armed battle group consisted of one escort frigate and four Corellian corvettes—enough firepower to occupy the secret Imperial think tank, Maw Installation, and to overcome any resistance from the weapons scientists stranded there.

The last three stragglers hustled up the ramp, clad in light armor and securing tight packs onto their shoulders. Chewbacca watched the soldiers strap into their seats before he punched the ALL CLEAR button to raise the boarding ramp.

"Your impatience is not helping, Chewbacca," See-Threepio said. "The tension level is already substantial, and you're simply making things worse. I have a bad feeling about this mission already."

Chewbacca growled at him, disregarding his comment. Impatient, he picked up the droid and dropped him with a metallic clatter into the only remaining spare seat—which was, unfortunately, next to Chewbacca's own.

"Indeed!" Threepio said as he dutifully hooked himself in. "I'm doing my best. This isn't my area of expertise, you know."

Chewbacca settled into a seat that had never been designed to accommodate a creature of his massive proportions. He bent his hairy knees nearly to chest level. He wished he could be with Han in the *Millennium Falcon*, but Han and Leia had gone to see Luke Skywalker, and Chewbacca felt his stronger duty was to go rescue the Wookiee prisoners left inside Maw Installation.

The rest of the assault team shifted in their seats, looking around, double-checking their mental lists of equipment and procedures. Page's Commandos, a crack assault troop, would be handling most of the front-line mission, with plenty of New Republic firepower to back them up. The Special Operations Commander, General Crix Madine, had given the Special Forces thorough briefings on strategy for the planned occupation. The soldiers were fully trained and competent.

Chewbacca just wished the pilot would hurry up and take off. He blew out a long sigh through his rubbery lips, thinking uneasily of Han. He had waited a long time for an opportunity to rescue the tortured Wookiee slaves, though.

When he, Han, and young Kyp Durron had been captured by Admiral Daala at Maw Installation, Chewbacca had been forced to work with captive Wookiees aboard the Star Destroyers and down in the Installation itself. The Wookiees had been imprisoned for more than ten years, working at hard labor, and the resistance had gone out of them. The thought of their ruined lives made Chewbacca's blood boil.

Not long ago, with Threepio's dubious abilities as translator, Chewbacca had addressed the New Republic Council. He urged them to occupy the Installation and rescue the Wookiee prisoners, as well as to keep the new weapon designs from falling into Imperial hands. Seeing Mon Mothma's support, the Council had agreed.

With a mechanical whir and a thump of metal against metal, the landing struts of the transport drew up inside the hull. With a lurch the transport rose on its repulsorlifts, then headed off the landing platform, rising into the sky as the metropolis of Imperial City glittered below.

Threepio began talking to himself. Chewbacca marveled at how sophisticated the droid's electronic brain must be to consistently find so many things to complain about.

"I simply don't understand why Mistress Leia ordered me to go with you. I am always happy to serve in any capacity, naturally, but I could have assisted greatly in watching the children while she visited Master Luke on Yavin 4. I've been doing a good job of taking care of the twins, haven't I?"

Chewbacca grunted. Threepio continued. "True, we misplaced them at the Holographic Zoo for Extinct Animals, but that was only one time, and it all turned out right in the end." He swiveled his golden head.

As the acceleration increased, Chewbacca closed his eyes and growled at him to be quiet. Threepio ignored him. "It would have been nice to see Artoo-Detoo again at Master Luke's Jedi academy. I haven't spoken to my counterpart in a long time."

Threepio did not slow down as he changed subjects. "I really don't know what use I'm expected to be on this military mission. I've never been very skilled at combat. I don't like combat. I don't like excitement in any form, though I seem to have encountered enough of it."

Inertia pushed Chewbacca back against his uncomfortably small seat as the transport accelerated toward the congregation of battleships in orbit around Coruscant.

Threepio continued, and continued. "Of course I understand that I am technically supposed to help sift through the data in the Maw Installation computers, and I suppose I could be of some use translating the languages of alien scientists—but certainly there must be some other droid better qualified for that type of work? Isn't General Antilles taking along an entire team of slicer droids to get encrypted information? Page's Commandos are experts in this sort of thing. Why do I have to go along and do all the hard work? It seems unfair to me."

Chewbacca barked a sharp command. Threepio turned to him with his yellow optical sensors glowing in indignation. "I will *not* be quiet, Chewbacca. Why should I listen to you after you put my head on backward in Cloud City?

"If you yourself had spoken up during the preparations for putting this team together, you could have convinced them to let me stay with Mistress Leia. But you thought I might be an asset to this mission, and now you're just going to have to listen to me."

With a sigh of annoyance Chewbacca reached over and hit the power switch on the back of Threepio's neck. The droid fell silent, his words slurring to a stop as he slumped forward.

On the troop transport Page's Commandos—noted for their intense training, cold efficiency, and utter professionalism—took a moment to applaud Chewbacca's action.

On the command bridge of the escort frigate *Yavaris,* General Wedge Antilles looked across space. Sunlight reflected off the metal hulls of his fleet. He had asked for command of this mission because he wanted to return to where Qwi Xux had spent so much of her life—to where the secrets of her lost memory might lie hidden.

The *Yavaris* was a powerful ship, despite its fragile appearance caused by the thin spine that separated its two primary components. At the frigate's aft end a boxy construction contained sublight and hyperdrive engines and the power reactors that drove not only the engines but also twelve turbolaser batteries and twelve laser cannons. On the other end of the connecting rod, separated from the engines, was the much larger command section, hanging down in an angular structure that contained the command bridge, crew quarters, scanners, and cargo bays that carried two full X-wing fighter squadrons for the assault.

The escort frigate held a crew of about nine hundred seasoned soldiers, while the rest of his fleet—four Corellian corvettes—carried one hundred on each vessel.

Wedge brushed his dark hair away from his forehead and set his square jaw. The last of the troop transports had docked on the frigate, bringing the remainder of the handpicked raiders.

Han Solo had reported that Maw Installation was no longer protected by Admiral Daala's Star Destroyers, which had been lured out of the black hole cluster to wreak havoc across the galaxy. The precious weapons information and scientists inside the Installation were undefended. Probably. Wedge was prepared for surprises, especially from a congregation of Imperial weapons designers.

On the command bridge of the *Yavaris*, Wedge toggled on the intercom. "Prepare to depart," he said. The four corvettes folded around the escort frigate in a diamond formation. Ahead, Wedge saw throbbing blue-white light as banks of heavy engines pulsed to life.

The corvettes' huge engines were twice as large as the living compartments and the hammerhead-shaped control section. Princess Leia had been riding a corvette when Vader's Star Destroyer had captured her, demanding that she return the stolen Death Star plans, so long ago.

He watched the light-embroidered nightside of Coruscant veer away from the fleet as they angled up out of orbit, past metallic docking stations and heavy parabolic mirrors that directed magnified sunlight to warm the higher frozen latitudes.

He wished Qwi had stayed with him to watch the departure, but she was down in their quarters reviewing information tapes, studying . . . studying. Since her memory would not come back of its own accord, Qwi intended to fill the gaps with the missing information as quickly as possible.

She also had a deep revulsion toward watching a planet from orbit. It had taken Wedge much quiet encouraging before she finally told him that the sight reminded her of her youth, when she had been held hostage aboard an orbital training sphere under the harsh tutelage of Moff Tarkin. Qwi had been forced to watch as Victory-class Star Destroyers obliterated the honeycomb settlements of her people whenever students failed their examinations.

Thinking of the terrible things the Empire had done to the delicate and lovely Qwi made Wedge clench his teeth. He turned to the bridge crew. "Ready for hyperspace?"

"Course set, sir," the navigation officer answered.

Wedge vowed to do what he could to fill Qwi's life with joy . . . once they had conquered Maw Installation.

"Move out," he said.

Inside windowless quarters in the protected lower decks of the *Yavaris,* Qwi Xux stared into the tutorial screen and blinked her indigo eyes. She skimmed file after file, absorbing the information as enthusiastically as a Tatooine desert sponge grabbed droplets of moisture.

A small portrait holo of Wedge sat inside a cube atop her worktable. She glanced at it frequently, reminding herself what he looked like, who he was, how much he meant to her. None of her memories were certain after Kyp Durron's assault on her mind.

She had initially forgotten Wedge himself, forgotten the times they had spent together. He had desperately told her everything, showed her pictures, taken her out to the same places that the two of them had visited on the planet Ithor. He had reminded her of the reconstruction site of the Cathedral of Winds they had visited on Vortex.

Some of these things caused elusive images to flicker in the back of her mind, enough that she knew they had been there once . . . but she could not grasp them anymore.

Other things Wedge told her exploded back into her thoughts with full clarity, enough to bring stinging tears. Whenever that happened, Wedge was there to hold her in his arms and comfort her.

"No matter how long it takes," he had said, "I'll help you to remember. And if we can't find all of your past again . . . then I'll help you make new memories to fill those spaces." He brushed her hand, and she nodded.

Qwi reviewed the tapes of her speech before the New Republic Council, where she had insisted that they dispose of the Sun Crusher and stop trying to analyze it. The Council members had grudgingly agreed to mothball the project by plunging it into the core of a gas-giant planet. But now it appeared that this had not been sufficient to keep the superweapon away from an anger and determination as powerful as Kyp Durron's.

As she reviewed the holotaped speech she had given, she heard the words in her own voice, but did not remember speaking them. She placed the memories in her mind, but they were external views of herself as seen and recorded by others. She heaved a deep breath and scrolled to the next data file. A cumbersome method, but it would have to do.

Much of her basic scientific knowledge remained intact, but certain things were completely gone: insights she had gained, new weapons designs and new ideas she had developed. It seemed that when Kyp had rummaged around in her brain, yanking out anything that had to do with the Sun Crusher, he had erased whatever he found questionable.

Now Qwi had to rebuild what she could. It didn't bother her that knowledge of the Sun Crusher had been obliterated. She had previously vowed to tell no one how the weapon worked—and now telling would be impossible, even if she wanted to. Some inventions were better erased. . . .

The Maw assault fleet had been under way for almost a full day, heading toward the Kessel system. Qwi had been studying much of the time, sparing only a moment to talk to Wedge when he came to visit after completing his duties on the command bridge. When he brought her food, they ate together, making small talk, spending their time looking into each other's eyes.

As she sat at the data terminal, Wedge would come and stroke her narrow shoulders, massaging until her tense muscles turned buttery and warm. "You're working too hard, Qwi," he had said more than once.

"I have to," she answered him.

She recalled her youth, when she had studied desperately, cramming knowledge of physics and engineering and weaponry into her pliable young brain for Moff Tarkin. She alone had survived the rigorous training. Kyp's heavy-handed scouring of her mind had left her with those painful childhood memories—memories she would just as soon forget.

There were some things she could not recapture from data tapes or tutorial programs. She had to go back inside Maw Installation, into the laboratories where she had spent so many years. Only then could she determine which memories would come back and how much of her past she would have to sacrifice forever.

The intercom rang out, and Wedge's voice flooded into their quarters. "Qwi, would you come up to the bridge, please? There's something I'd like you to see."

She acknowledged, smiling at the sound of his voice. She took a turbolift up to the frigate's command towers and stepped out onto the bustling bridge. Wedge turned to greet her—but her indigo eyes were drawn to the broad viewport at the front of the *Yavaris*.

She had seen the Maw cluster before, but her mouth still dropped open in awe. The incredible maelstrom of ionized gases and superheated debris screamed past the edges of the bottomless black holes in a great whirlpool of color.

"We came out of hyperspace near the Kessel system," Wedge said, "and we're lining up our vector to go in. I thought you might want to watch."

She swallowed a lump in her throat and stepped forward to take his hand. The black holes formed a maze of gravity wells and dead-end hyperspace paths; only a few dangerously "safe" courses made passage possible through the tangled labyrinth.

"We downloaded the course from the Sun Crusher," Wedge said. "I hope nothing's changed, or we'll all have a big surprise when we try to make it through."

Qwi nodded. "It should be safe," she said. "I double-checked the route."

Wedge looked at her warmly, as if her verification gave him more confidence than all the computer simulations.

The black hole cluster was an impossible astronomical oddity; for thousands of years astrophysicists had attempted to determine its origin—whether some freak galactic combination had led to the birth of the black holes, or whether some impossibly ancient and powerful alien race had assembled the cluster for its own purposes.

The Maw sent out deadly radiation and was even now drawing the Kessel system to its eventual doom. For the present, though, the Empire had found a stable island within the cluster and had built its secret laboratory there.

"Let's go then," Qwi said, looking out at the brilliant gases flaring in incredible slow motion. She had much to learn—and a score to settle. "I'm ready."

The ships of the Maw assault fleet spread apart, arrowing one by one into the heart of the black hole cluster.

5

One wing of the rebuilt Imperial Palace had been converted into a crèche for the water-loving Calamarian people, humid quarters for those brought by Admiral Ackbar and trained as his specialized starship mechanics.

The crèche had been built of smooth plasteel and hard metal fashioned to look like a reef within the towering palace. Some of the round portholes looked out upon the glittering skyline of Imperial City, while others gazed in on an enclosed water tank that circulated around the rooms like a trapped river.

A loud venting of mist from the humidity generators startled Terpfen out of nervous contemplation. He looked around his quarters wildly, swiveling his circular eyes, but he saw nothing in the shadows, only a jewel-blue light shining through the water windows. He watched as a gray-green glurpfish oozed its way along the channel, filtering microorganisms from the brine. No sound intruded other than the steam generators and bubbling aerators in the wall tanks.

Terpfen had heard nothing in his mind, felt no compulsion from his Imperial masters on Carida for more than a day, and he didn't know whether to be frightened . . . or hopeful. Furgan usually taunted and jabbed him regularly, just to remind him of his constant presence. Now Terpfen felt alone.

Rumors flew around the Imperial Palace. Distress signals had been detected from Carida, and then all contact had broken off. New Republic scouts had been dispatched to inspect the area. If Carida had somehow been destroyed, then perhaps the Imperial hold on his brain had been severed. Terpfen could finally be free!

He had been taken prisoner during the vicious Imperial occupation of the water world Calamari. Like many of his people, Terpfen had been dragged to a labor camp and forced to work at the starship-construction facilities.

But Terpfen had been damned to undergo a special kind of training. Taken off to the Imperial military planet of Carida, he had suffered weeks of torture and conditioning as xenosurgeons removed portions of his brain and replaced them with vat-grown organic circuits that allowed Furgan to use Terpfen as a perfectly disguised puppet.

The poorly stitched scars on his swollen head had served as badges of his ordeal once he was released. Many Calamarians had also been severely tortured during the occupation, and no one suspected Terpfen of treachery.

For years he had tried to resist his Imperial masters; but half of his brain was not his own, and the Imperial controllers could manipulate him at will.

He had sabotaged Admiral Ackbar's expanded B-wing fighter so that it crashed on Vortex, destroying the precious Cathedral of Winds and disgracing Ackbar. Terpfen had planted a tracer on another B-wing, which had allowed him to obtain the location of the secret planet Anoth, where baby Anakin Solo lived in isolation, protected from prying eyes and minds. Terpfen had passed that crucial information to a greedy Ambassador Furgan—even now the Caridans must be mounting an attack to kidnap the third Jedi child.

Terpfen stood before the aquarium window in his dim quarters, watching the glurpfish sluggishly go about its business. An aquatic predator swooped toward it, flailing spear-tipped fins and jagged jaws. The predator would fall upon the glurpfish . . . just as the Imperial forces would fall upon the helpless child and his lone protector, Winter, who had once been Leia's close companion and confidant.

"No!" Terpfen smashed his flipper hands against the thick glass. The vibrations startled the fanged predator, and it shot away in search of other prey. The protoplasmic glurpfish, unaware of what had just happened, continued on its way, sifting the water for microscopic food.

Perhaps his Caridan masters had only been distracted temporarily by other things . . . but if Terpfen hoped to accomplish anything, he had to make his move now. He swore that it didn't matter what damage it did to his own brain.

Ackbar himself remained in self-imposed exile on Calamari, working with his people to repair the floating cities that had been devastated in

Admiral Daala's recent attack. Ackbar claimed to have no further interest in New Republic politics.

Since an assault was to be launched against young Anakin, Terpfen would go directly to Leia Organa Solo. She could mobilize New Republic forces and thwart the Imperials. But she and Han Solo had just departed for the jungle moon of Yavin. . . .

Terpfen would have to go there, commandeer a ship, and meet her face-to-face. He would confess everything and put himself at her mercy. She might execute him on the spot, as would be her right. But even that would be a just punishment for the damage he had already done.

His mind made up—at least for as long as it remained *his* mind—Terpfen took a last look around his quarters. Turning from the aquarium windows that reminded him of the homeworld he had left behind, he took a last glance at the faceted skyline with its kilometer-high skyscrapers, winking landing lights, gleaming shuttles rising toward the aurora that blanketed the night.

Terpfen doubted he would ever see Coruscant again.

He didn't have time for a ruse.

Using his own security access codes, Terpfen entered the starfighter servicing bay and walked briskly, confidently. His body odor was laced with tension, but if he moved fast enough, no one would notice until it was too late.

The large launch doors had been sealed for the night. Two Calamarian starship mechanics stood around one of the B-wing fighters. A group of chattering Ugnaughts worked under the hyperdrive motors of a pair of X-wing fighters that had been jacked together to exchange navicomputer information.

Terpfen walked toward the B-wing. One of the Calamarians saluted him as he approached. The other lowered herself out of the pilot compartment, slinging down a webbed sack of tools. From his own terminal Terpfen had already checked the status of this fighter, knew it was ready to launch. He didn't have to ask the question, but it distracted them.

"Repairs completed as planned?"

"Yes, sir," the male Calamarian said. "What are you doing up so late?"

"Just attending to some personal business," he said, and reached into a pocket of his flightsuit. He whipped out a blaster pistol set to STUN. He fired in a sweeping arc, catching both Calamarians with blue ripples. The male slumped to the ground without a sound. The female dangled on the rung, unconscious as she thumped against the side of the B-wing; finally her elbow went slack, and she dropped to the hard floor in a tumble.

Over by the X-wings the Ugnaughts stopped chattering and stood up in amazement; then they began squealing. Three ran to the comm alarm next to the controls of the launch doors.

Terpfen took aim and squeezed the firing button again, cutting the Ugnaughts down. The others raised their stubby hands in surrender; but Terpfen could not risk taking captives, so he stunned them as well.

Moving purposefully, he hurried across the slick-plated floor to the controls of the launch door. From the enameled badge on his left breast, he withdrew a disguised slicer chip the Imperials had provided months ago, in case he should need to make a quick escape. Now, though, Terpfen used the Imperial technology for the benefit of the New Republic.

Terpfen jammed the small wafer into the input slot and punched three buttons in succession. The electronics hummed, scanning the information in the chip. The slicer chip convinced the controls that Terpfen had the appropriate override codes, that he had authorization from both Admiral Ackbar and Mon Mothma.

With a groan and a thud, the heavy launch doors split apart. The night winds whistled outside the hangar bay, gusting into the chamber and bringing the chill air.

Terpfen strode to the repaired B-wing, slid his broad hands under the arms of the fallen male Calamarian, and dragged him across the slick floor. He dumped the mechanic beside the slumped bodies of the stunned Ugnaughts.

When Terpfen moved the female mechanic, she moaned softly. Her arm hung at an awkward angle, broken in the fall. Terpfen hesitated a moment in guilty misery, but the accidental injury couldn't be helped. A few hours in a bacta tank would patch her up just fine.

By then Terpfen would be on his way to Yavin 4.

He clambered into the pilot seat of the B-wing and powered up the controls. All the lights winked green. He sealed the hatch. With the speed of the B-wing's engines, he could make it to the Yavin system in record time. He had to.

Terpfen raised the awkward-looking craft on its repulsorlifts and maneuvered toward the open launch doors.

Screeching alarms penetrated the enclosed cockpit, vibrating from the servicing bay. Terpfen twisted his head to see what had gone wrong—and spotted another Ugnaught, one who had apparently been hiding inside the cockpit of an X-wing. The lone Ugnaught had squirmed out in a panic and scurried over to the alarm panel.

Terpfen cursed under his breath and knew that he had to hurry. He had hoped not to fight his way out.

He punched the maneuvering jets and shot out of the wide mouth of the launching bay. His stolen B-wing streaked away from the immense towers of Coruscant and headed out on a high-energy straight-line path to orbit.

He couldn't waste time fooling the New Republic security monitors. Terpfen would appear to be an Imperial saboteur stealing a starfighter. If they captured him, they would interrogate him until it was too late to help young Anakin Solo. Terpfen had done many terrible things against his will, but now that he was free from Imperial control, any failure would be his own fault. He could blame no one else.

It surprised and dismayed him how rapidly the Coruscant security forces scrambled to intercept him. Four X-wings soared by at low altitude and vectored in on his single fighter.

Terpfen's comm buzzed. One of the pursuing pilots said, "B-wing, you have made an unauthorized departure from the palace. Return immediately, or you will be fired upon."

Terpfen merely increased power to the shields surrounding his ship. The B-wing was one of Ackbar's prize contributions to the Rebellion, and it was far superior to the old-model X-wings. Terpfen could outrun them, and his shields could probably survive several direct hits—but he didn't know if he could withstand the combined firepower of four X-wings.

"B-wing fighter, this is your last chance," the X-wing pilot said, and fired a low-energy bolt that spattered against Terpfen's shields. The warning shot nudged the B-wing, but caused no damage.

Terpfen punched the throttle, kicking in the afterburners that launched him toward the aurora and a low planetary orbit that his onboard navigational systems marked with heavy red danger lines.

A year before, the battle to regain Coruscant and overthrow the warring Imperial factions had been won only at the cost of incredible destruction. Many ruined battleships remained in low orbit, collected there in a great garbage pile. Crews had been dismantling them for months, repairing those that could be salvaged, sending others down to burn up as they made their spectacular descent through the atmosphere. Such work, though, had low priority during the crisis phase of the formation of the New Republic. A large junkyard of debris still orbited in well-marked lanes.

Terpfen, however, had previously scanned the placement of the twisted hulks and made his own personal orbital chart. He had found a dangerous path through the maze, so narrow he would have to fly with no margin for error—but it seemed his best chance. He was certain the alarm had sounded across Coruscant's full security systems, and before long squadrons of fighters would come screaming in to converge on him.

Terpfen didn't want to fight. He didn't want to cause more death and damage. He wanted to escape as quickly and as painlessly as possible.

As he left the blanket of atmosphere behind him, the X-wings followed in his wake, firing in earnest now. Terpfen refused to shoot back, although if he crippled one or more of the starfighters, he would have an easier time escaping. But he did not want the death of an innocent pilot on his conscience. He had too many deaths to deal with already.

In the blackness of space he flitted past glimmering shards of metal, reactor pods, and hull plates from blasted freighters. He skimmed up and over a tangled cluster of girders and a largely intact planar solar array from a destroyed TIE fighter.

Up ahead the breached hull of a capital ship—a Loronar Strike Cruiser— hung as little more than a framework of structural beams and split plating after its hyperdrive engines had blown up during a direct hit.

Terpfen streaked toward the hulk, knowing that the blast cavity in its middle was wide enough for a B-wing to pass directly through. He had already studied the path, and he hoped the risk would cause his pursuers to pull back and give him just enough time to launch into hyperspace.

Without slowing Terpfen shot through a gaping opening in the Strike Cruiser's hull. Two X-wings peeled off, another managed to follow directly in his wake. The fourth shifted a micron too far and clipped its wings against a ragged strut. The X-wing spun and slammed into the wreckage; its fuel cylinders detonated.

Terpfen felt claws of dismay sink into his heart. He had never meant for anyone to die.

The last X-wing hung hotly behind him, firing repeatedly in outrage at the death of his partner.

Terpfen checked his shields and saw that they had begun to fail under the pummeling. He did not blame the other pilot for his anger, but neither could he surrender now. He studied his control panels. The navicomputer had plotted the best course to the Yavin system.

Before his shields could buckle, Terpfen took a short course directly out of the orbital debris field. The X-wing came at him again with all weapons blazing. Upon reaching open space Terpfen punched the hyperdrive engines.

In an instant the B-wing shot forward, impossibly out of the reach of the other fighter. With white starlines that looked like spears to impale him, Terpfen vanished into hyperspace with a silent bang.

6

Standing in front of the _Millennium Falcon_, Han Solo held Leia in a long embrace. The oppressive humidity of the jungle moon clung to them like wet rags against their skin. Han hugged Leia again, smelling her scent. The corners of his lips drifted upward in a wistful smile. He could feel her trembling against him—or perhaps it was his own hands.

"I really do have to go, Leia," he said. "I've got to find Kyp. Maybe I can stop him from blowing up more star systems and killing more people."

"I know," she said. "I just wish we could arrange to have our adventures _together_ a little more often!"

Han tried unsuccessfully to give her his famous no-care grin. "I'll work on it," he said; then he kissed her long and hard. "Next time we'll manage."

He bent down to gather the twins in his arms. Jacen and Jaina clearly wanted to go back inside and play in the temples.

The children had found a small group of furry woolamanders nesting in an unused wing of the Great Temple, and Jacen claimed in his broken sentences that he knew how to talk to the creatures. Han wondered just what the hairy and noisy arboreal animals were saying back to the boy.

He backed toward the boarding ramp. "You know I need you to stay here in safety with the kids," he said to Leia. "And with Luke."

She nodded. They had been through this all before. "I can take care of myself. Now, get going. If you can do anything to stop Kyp, you shouldn't be wasting time here."

He kissed her again, waved goodbye to the twins, and vanished into the ship.

In a rotating cocktail lounge high up in Imperial City, Lando Calrissian yanked the fruit stick out of his drink before it could take root at the bottom of the glass. He sipped the fizzy concoction and smiled across the table at Mara Jade.

"Sure I can't get you another drink?" he asked. She looked absolutely beautiful with her exotic hair, high cheekbones, generous lips, and eyes the color of expensive gemstones. She hadn't touched her first drink yet, but he made certain he still shone with confidence.

"No thanks, Calrissian. We've got business to discuss."

The windows of the observation lounge showed the glittering former Imperial Palace and crystallike spires and skyscrapers that extended to the fringes of the atmosphere. Hover barges drifted above the buildings, flashing announcements in numerous languages, ferrying tourists out to watch the sunset and the brightening aurora. A pair of mismatched moons hung in the sky, shining down on the bustling city.

Musical notes drifted into the air from a complex multilayered bank of keyboards in the middle of which sat a purplish-black, tentacled creature. With a flurry of cilia, the creature played a staggering number of keys at a time. Instead of eyes on its lumpy head, it was studded with tympanic membranes of varying sizes so it could hear music over an incredible range. Its tentacles flailed, striking upper keys, drawing out lower resonances, playing tunes both too high and too low for the human ear.

Lando took another sip and leaned back in his chair with a sigh and a soft smile. He had draped his slick burgundy cape over the back of his chair. Mara Jade wore only a tight-fitting jumpsuit; her curves looked like hazardous paths through a complicated planetary system.

Lando looked across at her. "So you think the Smugglers' Alliance would be interested in an arrangement for distribution of glitterstim spice from Kessel?"

Mara nodded. "I think I can guarantee that. Moruth Doole let the spice mines fall into a shambles. Black-market smuggling from the Imperial Correction Facility has made the entire planet a pain in the soft parts for any self-respecting runner trying to earn a living. It took powerful crime lords like Jabba with enough strong-arm just to make it worthwhile."

"I'll make it worthwhile," Lando said, folding his hands together on the tabletop. "I received a million-credit reward from the Duchess of Dargul, and I can invest it to bring the systems up to a more sophisticated level."

"What exactly are your plans?" Mara asked, leaning closer to him.

Lando responded by leaning over the table himself, bringing his large brown eyes close to hers. His pulse raced. She frowned and sat up straight again, still waiting for him to answer.

Rebuffed, Lando looked for words. "Uh, I don't have any great fondness for the prison where Doole centered his operations, but I think I can use that as a starting point. Dismantle most of the old correction facility, but use the buildings for a new base.

"And I don't plan to use slave labor, either. I figure we can get worker droids. On Nkllon I got familiar with some sophisticated mining systems, and if I use supercooled devices, the infrared signatures won't attract those energy spiders that caused so much trouble before."

"Droids can't handle everything," Mara said. "You're going to need some people down there. Who will you get to run a miserable operation like that?"

"Miserable to humans maybe," Lando said, locking his hands behind his back and sitting straight, "but not to some other species. In particular, I've got in mind an old friend of mine, Nien Nunb, who was my copilot on the *Falcon* during the Battle of Endor. He's a Sullustan, a little creature who grew up living in tunnels and warrens on a tough volcanic world. He'd consider the spice mines a luxury resort!" Lando shrugged at Mara's skeptical look. "Hey, I've worked with him before and I trust him."

"Sounds like you've got most of the answers, Calrissian," Mara said. "But so far it's all just talk. When are you planning to go to Kessel and get to work?"

"Well, I lost my ship there. I've got to get back to Kessel to pick up the *Lady Luck* and start my operations." He raised his eyebrows. "Say, you wouldn't be willing to give me a lift to the system, would you?"

"No." Mara Jade stood up. "I would not."

"All right, then. Will you meet me on Kessel in one standard week? By then I should have a good feel for how things are going to go. We can lay down the foundation for a long and lasting relationship." He smiled at her again.

"*Business* relationship," she said, but not quite as sharply as she might have.

"You sure you won't have dinner with me?" he asked.

"I've already eaten a ration bar," she said, and turned to leave. "One standard week. I'll see you on Kessel." She turned and left.

Lando blew her a kiss, but she didn't see him . . . which was probably a good thing.

At the keyboards the tentacled musician played a mournful tune of unreciprocated emotional resonances.

● ● ● ●

In the stuffy Council chambers Han Solo swallowed a lump in his throat before he addressed the gathered senators and generals and Mon Mothma herself.

"I don't often talk to this"—he tried to think of the appropriate flowery language Leia would use in front of politicians—"this, um, august assemblage, but I need some information fast."

Mon Mothma sat up weakly. Nearby a medical droid tended the silent monitoring and life-support systems attached to the Chief of State's body. Her skin looked grayish, as if it had already died and was waiting to fall off her bones. As she declined, she had given up all pretense of hiding her failing health.

According to Leia, Mon Mothma had only a few weeks to live with her strange, debilitating disease. Seeing the woman now, though, Han wouldn't have laid odds she would survive even that long.

"What exactly," Mon Mothma began—then paused to heave a deep breath—"do you need to know, General Solo?"

Han swallowed again. He couldn't hide the truth, though he hated to admit it. "Kyp Durron was my friend, but he went wrong somehow. He attacked Luke Skywalker. He took the Sun Crusher and blew up the Cauldron Nebula to destroy Admiral Daala's fleet. Leia and all the Jedi trainees on Yavin just experienced what they called 'a great disturbance in the Force,' and she's convinced that Kyp might have done something else."

General Rieekan spoke in his gruff voice, looking at Han with weary eyes. Rieekan had been the commander of Echo Base on Hoth, and he had seen many hard times. "Our scouts have just come back, General Solo. Your friend *did* use the Sun Crusher again. He destroyed the Caridan star system, site of the Imperial military academy."

Han felt his throat go dry, though the news was no great surprise, considering how much Kyp hated the Empire.

"This slaughter must stop. It goes beyond even the Emperor's atrocities," the aging tactician, General Jan Dodonna, said. "The New Republic does not employ such barbarous tactics."

"Well, *he* does!" interrupted Garm Bel-Iblis. "And he has obliterated two crucial Imperial targets. While we may not agree with Durron's methods, his success rate is nothing short of astonishing."

Mon Mothma interrupted, somehow finding the energy to speak a harsh sentence. "I will not allow this young man to be portrayed . . . as a war hero." She paused for a deep breath and raised her clenched hand to signal that she had not yet finished. "His personal crusade must stop. General Solo, can you halt Kyp Durron?"

"I've got to find him first! Give me the reconnaissance information your scouts gathered from the Cauldron Nebula and Carida. Maybe I can track him down. If I could just talk to him face-to-face, I'm sure I could make the kid see reason."

"General Solo, you will have access to everything you desire," Mon Mothma said, spreading her palms on the synthetic stone surface in front of her, as if to support herself. "Do you require . . . a military escort?"

"No," he said, "that might scare him off. I'll take the *Falcon* and go myself. If I'm lucky, maybe I can bring the Sun Crusher back, too." Han gazed slowly around the Council chamber. "And this time let's make sure we destroy it completely."

Packing the *Falcon*, Han had almost finished his last-minute emergency preparations when he heard a voice behind him. "Han, old buddy! Need some help?"

He glanced over his shoulder to see Lando Calrissian striding toward him across the hangar bay, ducking under the flat aerofoil of an X-wing starfighter.

"Just leaving, Lando," he said. "Don't know how long I'll be gone."

"I heard," Lando said. "Hey, why not let me come along? You'll need a copilot, with Chewbacca gone on the Maw mission."

Han hesitated. "I'm doing this by myself. I can't ask anyone else to go with me."

"Han, you're crazy to fly the *Falcon* alone. You don't know what sort of hostile situations you're going to get into. Who'll be at the controls if you need to go up into the gun well?" Lando flashed his most winning smile. "You've got to admit, I'm the obvious choice."

Han sighed. "Chewbacca would be my first choice—I miss that fuzzball, you know? At least he doesn't try to gamble the *Falcon* away from me."

"Awww, we don't do that anymore, Han," Lando said. "We promised, remember?"

"How could I forget?" Han groaned. Lando had beaten him in their last round of sabacc, claiming ownership of the *Falcon*—and then he had given the ship back to Han, just to impress Mara Jade. "But what's your take on this, you old pirate?" Han said, raising his eyebrows. "Why do you want to come along so bad?"

Lando shuffled his feet on the polished floor of the landing bay. At the other end of the chamber a sublight engine started up, blatted, then coughed as a team of mechanics scrambled over the fuselage of a dismantled A-wing.

"To be honest . . . I need to get to Kessel within a week."

"But I'm not going anywhere near Kessel," Han said.

"You don't know *where* you're going yet. You're looking for Kyp."

"Point taken. What's at Kessel?" Han asked. "I didn't think you'd want to go back there soon, after what happened last time. I sure don't."

"Mara Jade's going to meet me there in a week. We're partners in a new spice-mining operation." He beamed, tossing his burgundy cape over his shoulder.

Han tried to cover his skeptical smile. "And does Mara herself know about this partnership, or are you just talking big?"

Lando looked hurt. "Of course she knows . . . sort of. Besides, if you get me to Kessel, maybe I can find the *Lady Luck* again, and I can stop hitching rides with people. This is getting old."

"That's for sure," Han said. "All right, if we go near Kessel, I'll take you there—but my priority is tracking Kyp."

"Of course, Han. That's understood," Lando said, then mumbled under his breath, "just as long as I get to Kessel within a week."

7

As a disembodied spirit, Luke Skywalker could only watch as his Jedi trainees and his sister Leia filed into the grand audience chamber. Artoo-Detoo trundled ahead, like an escort, silently coasting to a stop before the platform on which he lay.

The other Jedi trainees stood in a row in front of the motionless form. They stared respectfully at his motionless body as if they were attendees at a funeral. Luke could sense emotion pouring from them: grief, confusion, dismay, and deep anxiety.

"Leia," he called in his echoing otherworldly voice. "Leia!" he screamed as loud as he could, trying to break through the other-dimensional walls that restrained him.

Leia flinched, but didn't seem to hear. She reached forward to grip the arm of his cold body. He heard her whisper, "I don't know if you can hear me, Luke, but I know you're not dead. I can sense you're still here. We'll find a way to help you. We'll keep trying."

She squeezed his limp hand and turned away quickly. She blinked to cast away the tears welling up within her eyes.

"Leia . . . ," he sighed. He watched as the other Jedi candidates followed her back to the turbolift. Once again he found himself all alone with his paralyzed body, staring at the echoing walls of the Massassi temple.

"All right," he said, looking for another solution. If Artoo couldn't hear him, and if Leia or the other Jedi trainees could not identify his presence, then perhaps Luke could communicate with someone on his own plane of existence—another glistening Jedi spirit he had spoken to many times before.

"Ben!" Luke called. "Obi-Wan Kenobi, can you hear me?"

His voice hummed through the ether. With all the emotional firepower he could dredge from the bottom of his soul, Luke shouted into the silence. "Ben!"

Growing more concerned at hearing no answer, he called for others. "Yoda! Father—Anakin Skywalker!"

He waited, but there was no response.

. . . Until he sensed a *coldness* ripple through the air like an icicle slowly melting. Words trembled from the walls. "They can't hear you, Skywalker—but I can."

Luke spun around and saw a crack form in the stone walls. It grew darker as a tarlike silhouette oozed out and congealed into the shape of a cowled man whose features were distinct now that Luke could see him in the spirit plane. The stranger had long black hair, shadowed skin, and the tattoo of a black sun emblazoned on his forehead. His eyes were like chips of obsidian and just as sharp. His mouth bore a cruel scowl, the expression of one who has been betrayed and has had much time to think bitter thoughts.

"Exar Kun," Luke said, and the dark spirit understood him perfectly well.

"Do you enjoy having your spirit trapped away from your body, Skywalker?" Kun said in a mocking voice. "I have had four thousand years to get accustomed to it. The first century or two are the worst."

Luke glared at him. "You corrupted my students, Exar Kun. You caused the death of Gantoris. You turned Kyp Durron against me."

Kun laughed. "Perhaps it was your own failings as a teacher. Or their own delusions."

"What makes you think I'll stay like this for thousands of years?" Luke said.

"You will have no choice," Kun answered, "once I have destroyed your physical body. Trapping my own spirit inside these temples was the only way I could survive when the final holocaust came. The allied Jedi Knights devastated the surface of Yavin 4. They killed off the few Massassi people I had kept alive, and they destroyed my own body in the inferno.

"My spirit was forced to wait and wait and *wait* until finally you brought your Jedi students here, students who could hear my voice once they learned how to listen."

An echo of fear rang through Luke's mind, but he forced himself to sound calm and brave. "You can't harm my body, Kun. You can't touch anything physical. I've tried it myself."

"Ah, but I know other ways to fight," Kun's spirit said. "And I have had endless millennia to practice. Rest assured, Skywalker, I will destroy you."

As if finished with his taunting, Kun sank like smoke through the cracks in the polished flagstones, descending to the heart of the Great Temple. In his wake he left Luke alone but more determined than ever to break free from his ethereal prison.

He would find a way. A Jedi could always find a way.

When the twins suddenly started crying on their cots beside her, Leia woke up with a feeling of dread.

"It's Uncle Luke!" Jaina said.

"He's gonna be hurt," Jacen said.

Leia bolted upright and felt a series of whistling, tingling vibrations through her body, unlike anything she had ever encountered before. She sensed more than heard the howling wind, a gathering storm trapped inside the temple—centered in the grand audience chamber where Luke lay.

She threw on a white robe, cinched it around her waist, and dashed into the hall. Several other Jedi trainees emerged from their quarters, also sensing an indefinable dread.

The twins jumped out of their beds, and Leia called back to them, "You two stay here." She doubted they would. "Artoo, watch over them!" she shouted to the droid, who was buzzing in confusion down the corridors, lights flashing.

"Come to the grand audience chamber," Leia cried to the Jedi trainees. "Hurry!"

Artoo spun around in the hall and returned to the children's quarters; the droid's confused bleeps and warbles followed Leia down the hall. She rode the turbolift to the top. When it stopped and opened its doors, storm winds howled around the vast, open chamber. Leia stumbled out into a cyclone.

Cold rivers of air gushed through the horizontal skylights high in the walls. Ice crystals sparkled as the temperature plummeted. Wind drawn in from every direction struck the center of the room and spun around, corkscrewing, picking up speed in an irresistible force.

Streen!

The old Bespin hermit stood on the outskirts of the storm with his brown Jedi robe flapping around him. His wild gray hair writhed around his head as if charged with static. His lips mumbled something incomprehensible, and his eyes remained closed as if he were having a nightmare.

Leia knew that even powerful Jedi could not manipulate large-scale phenomena like the weather; but they could move objects, and she realized that was what Streen did now. Not changing the weather, but simply moving the air, drawing it in from all directions, creating a self-contained but destructive tornado that struck toward Luke's body.

"No!" she shouted into the starving wind. "Streen!"

The cyclone struck Luke, buffeted his body, and lifted it into the air. Leia ran toward her paralyzed brother, feet barely touching the ground as the powerful winds knocked her sideways. The storm wrenched her off balance, and she found herself thrown through the air, flying like an insect toward the stone walls. She spun around and reached out, calming herself enough to use her own abilities with the Force, to nudge her body away. Instead of being crushed against the stone blocks, she slid softly to the floor.

Luke's body continued rising, tugged upward by the hurricane. His Jedi robe wound around him as the winds spun him like a corpse launched out of a star-freighter air lock into the grave of space.

Streen didn't seem aware of what he was doing.

Leia staggered to her feet again and jumped. This time she rode the circling air currents, flying around the fringe of the cyclone toward her helpless brother. She reached out to grab the tail of his robe, felt her fingers clutch rough fabric, and then burn as the robe was snatched away from her. She fell back to the floor.

Luke had been drawn up into the tornado's mouth, rising toward the skylights.

"Luke!" she cried. "Please help me." She had no idea if he could hear her, or if he could do anything. Gathering strength in her leg muscles, she leaped into the air again. It might be possible to use her Jedi skills of levitation for a brief moment; Luke had done it several times, although she herself had never mastered the skill. Now, though, it mattered more than it ever had before.

As Leia sprang upward, the wind caught her. She rose high enough to grab Luke's body. She wrapped her arms around his waist, twisted her legs around his ankles, holding him, hoping her weight would drag him down.

But as they started to drop, the winds picked up in intensity, howling and roaring. Leia's skin went numb from the blinding wintry cold. They shot toward the roof of the grand audience chamber, toward the widest skylight, where jagged icicles hung like javelins.

Leia suddenly knew what Streen intended to do to them, whether consciously or unconsciously. They would be sucked out of the Great Temple, tossed high into the sky, and then allowed to crash thousands of feet to the spear-pointed branches of the jungle canopy.

The turbolift door opened. Kirana Ti charged out, followed by Tionne and Kam Solusar.

"Stop Streen!" Leia shouted.

Kirana Ti reacted instantly. She wore thin but supple red armor from the scaled hides of reptiles from Dathomir. She had been a warrior on her own world, fighting with untrained and unhoned skill in the Force, but she had also fought in physical combat as well.

Kirana Ti launched herself forward on long, muscular legs, ducking her head as she charged into the cyclonic wind that surrounded Streen. The old hermit stood entranced, spinning slowly around with his arms dangling at his sides and his fingertips spread apart, as if trying to catch something.

Kirana Ti staggered as she hit the wind, but she wrenched her head aside, spread her legs, and dug the toes of her bare feet against the stone floor for traction. She shoved forward into the wind and finally shattered through into the dead zone of the storm. She tackled Streen to the flagstoned floor and locked his arms behind his back.

Streen cried out, then blinked his eyes open. He looked wildly around in confusion. Instantly the wind stopped blowing. The air fell still.

High up at the ceiling of the grand audience chamber Leia and Luke plunged toward the unforgiving flagstones below. Luke fell like a doll, and Leia tried to remember how to use her levitation skills, but her mind went blank with panic.

Tionne and Kam Solusar raced forward, stretching out their arms, using what they had been taught. Less than a meter above the crushing stones, Leia found herself slowed, pausing in the air beside Luke's body. They drifted gently to the floor. Leia cradled Luke against her, but her brother did not respond.

Streen sat up, and Kam Solusar ran over to help Kirana Ti hold him. The old hermit began to weep. Kam Solusar gnashed his teeth and looked as if he wanted to kill the old hermit then and there, but Kirana Ti stopped him.

"Don't hurt him," she said. "He doesn't know what he was doing."

"A nightmare," Streen said, "the Dark Man talking to me. Whispering to me. He never lets go. I was fighting him in my dream." Streen looked around for sympathy or encouragement.

"I was going to kill him and save us all, but you woke me." At last Streen realized where he was. He looked around the grand audience chamber until his gaze fell upon Leia holding Luke.

"He tricked you, Streen," Kirana Ti said in a hard voice. "You weren't fighting the Dark Man. He was manipulating you. You were his tool. If we hadn't stopped you, you would have destroyed Master Skywalker."

Streen began sobbing.

On the raised platform Tionne helped Leia lift Luke back onto the stone table. "He doesn't seem injured," Leia said.

"By sheer luck," Tionne said. She wondered aloud, "Did the ancient Jedi Knights have to deal with challenges like this?"

"If they did," Leia said, "I hope you manage to find the old stories. We need to learn what those Jedi did to defeat their enemies."

Streen stood, shaking himself free of the gripping hands of Kirana Ti and Kam Solusar. The old man's face was filled with outrage. "We must destroy the Dark Man," Streen said, "before he kills all of us."

Leia felt a grip of unbearable cold in her heart, knowing that Streen was right.

8

Being Chief Administrator of Maw Installation was a great enough burden under normal circumstances, but Tol Sivron had never counted on doing it without Imperial assistance. Standing inside the empty conference room, Sivron stroked his sensitive Twi'lek head-tails and stared out the viewport into the empty space around the secret facility.

He had never liked Admiral Daala and her overbearing manner. In the years they had been stranded in the Maw, Sivron had never felt as though she understood his mission to create new weapons of mass destruction for Grand Moff Tarkin—to whom they both owed enormous favors.

Daala's four Star Destroyers had been assigned to protect Sivron and the precious weapons scientists, but Daala had refused to accept her subordinate position in the scheme of things. She had let a few Rebel prisoners steal the Sun Crusher and kidnap one of Sivron's best weapons designers, Qwi Xux. Then Daala had abandoned her post to chase after the spies, leaving him alone and unprotected!

Sivron paced the conference room, puffed with pride and saddled with disappointment. He shook his head, and his two wormlike head appendages slid across his tunic with a tingle of sensory perceptions. He gripped one of the head-tails and wrapped it heavily around his shoulders.

The handful of stormtroopers Daala had left behind served little purpose. Tol Sivron had compiled a full tally of the soldiers: 123. He'd filled out official reports, gathered their service records, compiled information that might someday be useful. It wasn't clear to him exactly *how* this information would be useful, but Sivron had based his career on compiling reports and gathering information. Someone, somewhere, would find it worthwhile.

The stormtroopers obeyed his orders—that was what stormtroopers *did*, after all—but he was no military commander. He didn't know how to deploy the soldiers if Maw Installation was ever attacked by Rebel invaders.

During the last month he had kept the Maw scientists working harder to come up with better prototypes and functional defenses, writing contingency plans and emergency procedures, outlining scenarios and prescribed responses to every situation. *Being prepared is our best weapon,* he thought. Tol Sivron would never stop being prepared.

He had requested frequent progress reports from his researchers, insisting that he be kept completely up-to-date. The storage room adjacent to his office was piled high with hardcopy documents and demonstration models of various concepts. He didn't have time to review them all, of course, but it comforted him just to know they were there.

He heard footsteps approach and saw his four primary division leaders escorted to the morning briefing by their designated stormtrooper bodyguards.

Tol Sivron did not turn to greet them, staring with a thrill of pride at the huge spherical skeleton of the Death Star prototype rising over the cluster of rocks like a framework moon. The Death Star was the Installation's greatest success. Grand Moff Tarkin had taken one look at the prototype and given him a medal on the spot, along with Bevel Lemelisk, its main designer, and Qwi Xux, his primary assistant.

The four division leaders took their seats around the briefing table, each bringing a hot beverage, each munching on a reconstituted morning pastry. Each carried a hard-copy printout of the morning's agenda.

Sivron decided he would keep the meeting brief and to the point—no longer than two, possibly three, hours. They didn't have much to discuss anyway. As the Death Star orbited out of sight overhead, he turned to face his four top managers.

Doxin was a man wider than he was tall, completely bald except for very dark, very narrow eyebrows that looked like thin wires burned into his forehead. His lips were thick enough that he could have balanced a stylus on them when he smiled. Doxin was in charge of high-energy concepts and implementations.

Next to him sat Golanda. Tall and hawkish with an angular face, pointed chin, and aquiline nose that gave her face the general shape of a Star Destroyer, she was about as beautiful as a gundark. Golanda led the artillery innovations and tactical-deployments section. In ten years she had not stopped complaining about how foolish it was to do artillery research in the middle of a black hole cluster where the fluctuating gravity ruined her calculations and made every test a pointless exercise.

The third division leader, Yemm, was a demonic-looking Devaronian who excelled in saying the right thing at the right time. He supervised documentation and legal counsel.

Last of all, seated at the far corner of the table, was Wermyn, a tall, one-armed brute. His skin had a purplish-green cast that left his origin in question. Wermyn was in charge of plant operations and keeping Maw Installation up and running.

"Good morning, everyone," Tol Sivron said, seating himself at the head of the table and tapping his needle claws on the tabletop. "I see you've all brought your agendas with you. Excellent." He scowled at the four stormtroopers standing outside the door. "Captain, please step outside and close the door. This is a private, high-level meeting."

The stormtrooper made no answer as he ushered his companions outside and sealed the door with a hiss of compressed gases.

"There," Tol Sivron said, shuffling papers in front of him. "I'd like you each to report on recent activities in your division. After we've discussed the possible implications of anything new, we can then brainstorm strategies. I take it our revised Emergency Plans have been distributed to all members of this facility?" Sivron looked at Yemm, the paperwork person.

The Devaronian smiled pleasantly and nodded. The horns on his head bobbed up and down. "Yes, Director. Everyone has received a copy of the full three-hundred-sixty-five-page hard-copy document with instructions to read it diligently."

"Good," Sivron said, checking off the first item on his agenda. "We'll leave time at the end of the meeting for new business, but I'd like to move right along. I still have a lot of reports to review. Wermyn, would you like to begin?"

The one-armed plant operations division leader rumbled through a detailed report on their supplies, their power consumption rates, the expected duration of fuel cells in the power reactor. Wermyn's only concern was that they were running low on spare parts, and he doubted they would ever receive another shipment from the outside.

Tol Sivron duly noted that fact in his log pad.

Next, Doxin slurped his hot beverage and gave a report of a new weapon his scientists had been testing. "It's a metal-crystal phase shifter," Doxin said. "MCPS for short."

"Hmmmm," Tol Sivron said, tapping his chin with a long claw. "We'll have to think of a catchier name before we present it to the Imperials."

"It's just a working acronym," Doxin said, embarrassed. "We've constructed a functioning model, though our results have been inconsistent. The tests have given us reason to hope for a successful larger-scale implementation."

"And what exactly does it do?" Tol Sivron asked.

Doxin scowled at him. "Director, I've filed several reports over the past seven weeks. Haven't you read them?"

Sivron flinched his head-tails instinctively. "I'm a busy man, and I can't recall everything I read," he said. "Especially about a project with such an uninspired name. Refresh my memory, please."

Doxin grew animated as he spoke. "The MCPS field alters the crystalline structure of metals—e.g., those in starship hulls. The MCPS can penetrate conventional shielding and turn hull plates into powder. The actual physics is more complicated, of course; this is just an executive summary."

"Yes, yes," Tol Sivron said. "That sounds very good. What were these problems you encountered?"

"Well, the MCPS worked effectively over only about one percent of the surface area on our test plate."

"So it might not be terribly useful?" Tol Sivron said.

Doxin rubbed his fingers across the polished table surface, making a squeaking sound. "Not exactly true, Director. The one percent effectiveness was distributed over a wide area, leaving pinhole failures over the entire surface. Such a loss of integrity would be enough to destroy any ship."

Sivron grinned. "Ah, very good! Continue your studies and continue filing those excellent reports."

Golanda, the hatchet-faced woman in charge of artillery deployment and tactical innovations, talked about cluster-resonance shells based in part upon preliminary theoretical work for the Sun Crusher.

Yemm interrupted Golanda's summary by standing up and crying out. Sivron frowned at him. "It's not time for new business, Yemm."

"But, Director!" Yemm said, gesturing madly toward the viewport. The other division leaders stood in an uproar.

Tol Sivron finally whirled to see silhouettes against the gaseous backdrop of the Maw. His Twi'lek head-tails uncurled and stood out straight behind him.

A fleet of Rebel warships appeared inside the Maw. The invasion force he had dreaded for so long had finally arrived.

With two Corellian corvettes at point and two at his flanks, General Wedge Antilles brought the escort frigate *Yavaris* toward the mismatched cluster of rocks that formed Maw Installation.

Qwi Xux stood pale blue and beautiful at the observation station beside him, looking tense yet eager to ransack her old quarters for clues to her lost memories.

"Maw Installation," Wedge said into the comm channel. "This is General Antilles, Commander of the New Republic occupation fleet. Please respond to discuss terms of your surrender."

He felt arrogant as he said it, but he knew they had no way of fighting off his fleet. Hidden in the midst of the black holes, without Admiral Daala's Star Destroyers to defend it, the Installation depended on inaccessibility rather than firepower for protection.

As his ships approached the cluster of rocks, Wedge received no response. But when the open metal framework of the Death Star prototype orbited up from behind the planetoids, he felt a stab of terror.

"Shields up!" he said instinctively.

But the Death Star did not fire, gracefully orbiting back out of view again.

As Wedge brought his fleet in closer, a tracery of laser fire shot toward them from small buildings and habitation modules on the misshapen asteroids. Only a few of the beams managed to strike, reflecting harmlessly off the ships' shields.

"All right," Wedge said. "Two corvettes. Surgical strikes only. We want to remove those defenses, but don't damage the Installation itself." He shot a glance at Qwi. "That place holds too much important data to risk losing it."

Wedge watched the enormous banks of engines behind the foremost two corvettes as they rained destructive blasts upon the asteroids. Bright-red spears lanced down to pulverize the rocks.

"This is too easy," Wedge said.

A desperate signal came from one of the corvette captains. His image flickered as he beamed a transmission on the emergency channel. "Something's happening to our hull! Shields aren't effective. Some new kind of weapon. Hull walls are weakening. Can't pinpoint where—"

The transmission cut off as the corvette became a ball of fire and shrapnel.

"Back off!" Wedge shouted into the open channel, but the second corvette plunged forward, choosing instead to use his full complement of dual turbolaser cannons as well as a pair of proton torpedoes that had been specially installed for the occupation mission. "Captain Ortola! Back off!"

The captain of the second corvette blasted the nearest planetoid. Proton torpedoes sizzled with uncontained energy. Turbolaser blasts ignited volatile gases and flammables, reducing the small planetoid to incandescent dust.

"That won't be a problem anymore, sir," Captain Ortola said. "You may deploy the strike forces at your leisure."

• • •

Howling warnings shrieked through the Maw Installation's intercom so monotonously that Tol Sivron found it difficult to plan his speech.

"Your attention, please," he said into the intercom. "Remember to follow your emergency procedures."

Outside, stormtroopers hustled up and down the white-tiled corridors. The stormtrooper captain was yelling and directing his troops to set up defensive positions at vital intersections. No one bothered to refer to the carefully written and tested contingency scenarios Tol Sivron and his managers had spent so much time developing.

Gritting his pointed teeth in annoyance, Sivron raised his voice into the intercom. "If you need another copy of your emergency procedures, or if you have difficulty finding one, contact your respective division leader immediately. We will see to it that you receive one."

Hanging above Maw Installation, the Rebel ships looked like nightmarish constructions, brushing aside the Installation's defensive lasers as if they were mere insect bites.

Doxin sat by an interlaboratory communication station and cheered as he saw one of the Rebel corvettes crumble, disintegrating into a cloud of pulverized metal plate and escaping fuel and coolant gases.

"It worked!" Doxin said. "The MCPS worked!" He tapped the receiving jack in his ear, listened, and frowned with his enormous lips. When Doxin wrinkled the brow on his bald head, the ridges rippled all the way up to his crown like rugged-terrain treads.

"Unfortunately, we won't get a second shot, Director. The MCPS seems to have malfunctioned," Doxin said. "But I do believe the original success against an actual target has proved the system worthy of additional development."

"Indeed," Tol Sivron agreed, looking admiringly at the expanding cloud of debris from the corvette. "We must have a follow-up meeting."

"The system is presently off-line," Doxin said.

The second Rebel corvette came in with all weapons blazing, and the asteroid housing the offices and labs of the high-energy concepts incinerated under the barrage.

"It appears to be unquestionably out of commission," Sivron said.

Doxin was deeply disappointed. "Now we'll never conduct a post-shot analysis," he said with a sigh. "It's going to be hard to compile a full report without actual data."

A loud *whump* reverberated through the facility. Tol Sivron peered out into the hall as his division leaders crowded to get a view. White-and-gray smoke curled down the corridors, clogging the ventilation systems.

The screens on the computer monitors inside the conference room went blank. As Sivron stood up to demand an explanation, the lights in all the offices winked out, replaced by a pale-green glow of emergency systems.

The stormtrooper captain rushed up with a clatter of boots on the tiled floor.

"Captain, what's going on?" Tol Sivron said. "Report."

"We have just successfully destroyed the main computer core, sir," he said.

"You did *what*?" Sivron asked.

The captain continued in his staccato voice. "We need your personal codes to access the backup files, Director. We will irradiate them to erase the classified information."

"Is that in the emergency procedures?" Tol Sivron looked from right to left for an answer from his division leaders. He picked up the hardcopy of the Emergency Procedures manual. "Captain, which page did you find that on?"

"Sir, we cannot allow our vital data to fall into Rebel hands. The computer backups must be destroyed before the invaders take possession of this facility."

"I'm not sure we addressed that contingency when we wrote the manual," Golanda said with a shrug, flipping pages as well.

"Perhaps we'll have to put that in an addendum?" Yemm suggested.

Standing, Wermyn shuffled through the papers with his one meaty hand. "Director, I see here in Section 5.4, 'In the Event of Rebel Invasion,' Paragraph (C). If such an invasion appears likely to succeed in gaining possession of the Installation, I am to lead my team in a mission to the power-reactor asteroid and destroy the cooling towers so that the system will go supercritical and wipe out both this base and the invaders as well."

"Good, good!" Tol Sivron said, finding the right page and verifying the words for himself. "Get to it."

Wermyn stood up. His swarthy greenish-purple skin flushed darker. "All these procedures have been approved, Director, but I don't quite follow our next step. How is my team going to get to safety? In fact, how are any of us going to get to safety once I've set up the chain reaction?"

A stormtrooper's voice cut through the alarm chatter on the intercom. "Rebel troops have entered the base! Rebel troops have entered the—" The words ended in a squawk of dead static.

"Sound the evacuation order," Sivron said, beleaguered. He stared out the sweeping viewing window with his close-set, beady eyes. Rebel battleships pummeled the Installation. Then a glinting metal framework rose into view, an armillary sphere the size of a small moon.

"Just go and take care of the reactors, Wermyn," Tol Sivron said. "We'll fall back and evacuate to the Death Star prototype. We can swing by and pick you up, then make our escape. We'll abandon the Rebels to their deaths and take our precious knowledge back to the Empire."

Three transports bearing New Republic strike teams landed on the Installation's central asteroid, blasting through the closed bay doors with their forward laser cannons. As the transports opened egress doors like mechanical wings, the teams flooded out of the passenger compartments and fanned into defensive phalanxes. Crouched low, heads ducked behind blaster-resistant armor, they held high-energy rifles in front of them.

Chewbacca let out a Wookiee bellow as he thumped down the ramp, holding his bowcaster in front of him. He squeezed a hairy paw around the stock and pointed the crossbow-shaped weapon. His fur bristled. He smelled smoke, oil, and coolant fumes. Chewbacca scooped the air with his hairy paw, gesturing for the elite team of Page's Commandos to follow.

Blaster shots rang out as four stormtroopers fired from ambush. A member of one of the other strike teams went down, then forty blaster bolts converged on the Imperial soldiers.

Chewbacca remembered being a prisoner in the Maw Installation, when he had been forced to perform maintenance on Admiral Daala's ships. He had been tempted to sabotage one of their gamma-class assault shuttles, but knew that it would only get him killed while causing no irreparable harm to the Imperial forces.

Now, though, Chewbacca kept thinking of the other Wookiee slaves. He remembered their bowed heads and patchy fur, their gaunt frames. The fire in their eyes had gone out after years of hard and hopeless labor.

With a barely contained snarl he also remembered the sadistic lump of a man who served as the Wookiee "Keeper," watching over the slave detail no matter where they were assigned. His blazing eyes, broken-glass voice, and deadly force whip had kept the Wookiees in line through intimidation.

Alarms shrieked through the intercoms, pumping Chewbacca's adrenaline and anger. He growled for the teams to hurry. He thought about See-Threepio still onboard the flagship *Yavaris* and was glad the protocol droid would not be in all the cross fire now. Chewbacca didn't want to have to put Threepio back together all over again.

He approached a vast rock-walled workroom, where he remembered performing endless hours of heavy labor. The doors stood sealed by heavy blast shields with rivets the size of Chewbacca's knuckles.

He hammered on the metal door with his flat palm. Behind him Page's Commandos rummaged in their packs. Two members rushed forward with thermal detonators in each hand. They placed the detonators at critical junctures on the blast door and flicked the timer switches. Amber lights winked on and off, counting down.

"Back away!" one yelled.

Chewbacca loped after the team as they ran around the corner just in time to hear a muffled explosion. An instant later a much louder sound reverberated as the heavy blast door clanged to the floor.

"Move out," the strike-team leader said.

Chewbacca charged forward through the smoke as he pushed into the sealed bay. He heard thin hissing sounds, like lightning strikes mixed with outraged bellows of pain. The captive Wookiees were in such a frenzied state that they had forgotten their own language.

As the smoke cleared, Chewbacca was disappointed to find the battle already over—but he was elated that the Wookiees had finally taken a stand upon hearing the alarms and sensing that the tide of their misery had turned.

Nine Wookiees had converged on the Keeper, who now stood backed against a half-disassembled *Lambda*-class Imperial shuttle. The Keeper was barrel-shaped with oily skin enhanced by a sheen of terrified sweat. His lips pulled back in a snarl of defiance, and he kept lashing out with serpent strikes of his force whip. The Wookiees growled, trying to come close enough to rip him apart with their claws.

Chewbacca let out his own roar of challenge. Some of the Wookiees glanced up at the rescue force, but other hairy giants were so transfixed by their chance to get the Keeper that they paid no heed.

"Drop your weapon," the commando-team leader said to the Keeper. All of the blaster rifles were directed toward him. It amused Chewbacca to see the cruel man glance at the New Republic force with an expression of relief.

The Wookiees continued to snarl. They looked worse now than they had appeared only months earlier. No doubt without the protection of Admiral Daala's fleet, the Keeper had forced the slaves to work even harder to arrange other defenses for Maw Installation.

"Drop your weapon, I said!" the strike-team commander insisted.

The Keeper flicked his force whip once more, driving the Wookiee mob back. Chewbacca saw the three largest males in front, their fur streaked and patchy, burned from lashes of the whip and shiny with waxlike welts from old scars. The oldest gray-furred Wookiee, whom Chewbacca remembered as Nawruun, crouched by the edge of the shuttle, hiding under the sharp panels of the ship's upfolded wings. The old Wookiee's bones seemed twisted and crushed from years of labor, but the anger in his eyes was brighter than a star.

The Keeper raised his force whip, stared at the Wookiees, then at Page's Commandos. The human team leader fired a warning shot, which *spang*ed off the chamber walls. The Keeper raised his other hand in surrender, then let the handle of his force whip fall to the ground. It clinked on the smooth deck plates.

"All right, now, back away," the team leader said.

Chewbacca offered his own words in the Wookiee language. The astonished prisoners stood tense for a moment. The Keeper looked ready to collapse in terror, when suddenly old Nawruun dived to the floor, lunging with a hairy paw to snatch the handle of the whip. He fumbled the activation switches.

The Keeper shrieked and backed against the wall, looking for someplace to hide. Chewbacca yowled for the Wookiees to stop, but they didn't hear him as they all surged forward, claws extended, ready to shred the Keeper into bloody pieces.

Nawruun sprang upon the man's barrellike form. Though he was misshapen and old, the hunched Wookiee gripped the force whip like a club and tackled the Keeper to the floor. The burly man screamed and flailed.

The other Wookiees fell upon him. Nawruun jammed the handle of the force whip into the Keeper's face and switched on the weapon at full power.

The lance of lashing energy drilled into the Keeper's head, skirling fireworks inside his brainpan. Sparks came out of his eye sockets, until the Keeper's skull shattered, showering the hysterical Wookiee prisoners with gore.

Silence thundered down upon the chamber.

Chewbacca walked carefully forward as the surviving Wookiees withered. Without any stamina or fury, they backed away from the corpse of their tormentor. Old Nawruun stood again and stared blankly down at the force whip in his hand. He let it drop.

It struck the floor with a hollow sound, and Nawruun crumpled beside it. His body shuddered, and he made hollow sounds as he wept.

Tol Sivron tried to find a comfortable place to sit back and relax in the pilot compartment of the Death Star, but the prototype had not been designed for niceties.

Racks of equipment stood surrounded by bare wires and clumsy welds. Girders and reinforced framework blocked his view of most of the embattled Installation, but he could see that the Rebel forces had overrun the facility.

At the outer perimeter of the clustered planetoids, the tangled cooling towers and radiation vanes of the power reactor suddenly glowed bright and began to collapse.

Wermyn's gruff voice came over the radio. "Director Sivron, our explosives have destroyed the coolant systems. The power reactor will soon go supercritical. I don't think the attackers can stop it. Maw Installation is doomed."

"Very well, Wermyn," Sivron said, dismayed at the loss of capital equipment—but what could he do, after all? His Imperial guardians had deserted him. He and his division leaders had done quite a creditable job of putting up a fight. Without any military help they couldn't be expected to succeed against a well-armed strike force, could they? Besides, they were following established procedure. No one could fault them for that.

Sivron looked at the stormtrooper captain and at the other three division leaders. The rest of the Maw scientists and stormtrooper contingents had taken refuge inside the prototype's supply and control rooms.

"I have not had a chance to read the complete technical readouts of this battle-station prototype." Tol Sivron looked around. "Does anyone know how to fly this vessel?"

Golanda looked at Doxin, who in turn looked at Yemm.

The stormtrooper captain said, "I have had some experience flying attack vehicles, sir. Perhaps I can interpret the controls."

"Good, Captain," Tol Sivron said. "Ummm . . ." He stood up from his command chair. "Do you need to sit here?"

"No need, sir. I can handle it from the pilot station." The captain went over to a bolted-together row of controls.

"They must have detected Wermyn's explosions," Doxin said, watching the Rebel attack ships clustered around the reactor planetoid. Two more shuttles descended as teams were deployed down to the power station. The combined Rebel firepower would block all rescue attempts.

"Now, how are we supposed to get Wermyn?" Sivron said.

Yemm began to flip through the Emergency Procedures manual again. "I don't think we addressed that contingency either."

Tol Sivron's head-tails thrashed in extreme annoyance. "That's not very good, is it?" He scowled, trying to figure out how he could adapt on the spot. Twi'leks were good at adapting. Sivron had managed to adapt when he left his home planet of Ryloth; he had adapted when Moff Tarkin had assigned him as director of the think tank. Now he would adapt his plans again to make the best of a situation that was growing worse by the minute.

"All right, so there's no time to rescue Wermyn. Change of plans. Our duty is to the Empire. We must take this Death Star prototype and make a rapid retreat."

Wermyn himself had seen the Rebel strike teams coming down to retake the reactor planetoid, and he contacted Tol Sivron again with a more frantic tenor in his voice. "Director, what can I do to assist you? How are you planning to rescue us?"

Tol Sivron opened the channel and said in his gravest, most sincere voice, "Wermyn, I just want you to know how much I admire and respect you for your years of service. I regret that your retirement cannot be as long and as happy as I had hoped it would be. Once again, accept my appreciation. Thank you."

He signed off, then turned to the stormtrooper captain. "We need to get out of here now."

When the heaviest fighting began to die away, Qwi Xux shuttled down to the Installation with Wedge Antilles. Qwi saw the planetoids growing larger as they approached. She had spent most of her life down there, but she remembered little of it.

Other than the destruction of the first corvette, the New Republic fleet had suffered minimal losses. The Maw scientists had put up even less resistance than Wedge had feared. Qwi looked forward now to going through her old labs, eager to find her own files in hopes of answering some of her questions . . . but afraid to learn the answers.

Wedge reached over to hold her hand. "It'll be fine. You'll be a great help. Wait and see."

She looked longingly at him with her large eyes. "I'll do my best." But something caught her attention, and she pointed quickly. "Look, Wedge! We've got to stop it."

The Death Star prototype rose away from Maw Installation under its own power, glistening in the reflected light of the gas cloud.

"According to my own records, Maw Installation had a fully functional prototype," Qwi said. "If they take that Death Star into New Republic space—"

Before she could complete her sentence, the gigantic sphere of the Death Star shot away toward the edge of the black hole cluster and vanished into the masking clouds of superhot gas.

9

Terpfen stood in the looming shadow of the Great Temple as Yavin's early daylight increased, warming the jungles until mists rose in the air.

Paralyzed with fear in front of the towering, ancient ziggurat, Terpfen swiveled his circular eyes to look back to the landing area where his stolen B-wing fighter rested, humming and ticking as it cooled among the cropped weeds. He saw discolored smears on its hull from where the pursuing X-wing fighters on Coruscant had scored direct hits.

Looking up, he spotted several of the Jedi candidates, tiny figures atop the temple. As the jungle moon orbited around the gas giant, the configuration of the system set up an unusual phenomenon that had filled the Rebels with wonder when they first established the small moon as a secret base.

Bright sunlight streaming through the upper layers of the Yavin primary refracted in many different colors, then struck the moon's atmosphere, filtered through the rising mists to let loose a shower of rainbows that lasted only minutes with each dawn. The Jedi trainees, gathered to watch the rainbow storm high above, had seen his ship land. They were coming.

In a slick fighter jumpsuit that bore no insignia, Terpfen felt his heart pounding, his mind whirling. Confessing his traitorous acts frightened him the most—but Terpfen had to face it. He tried to rehearse his words, but decided that it would not help. There was no good way to share the terrible news.

He felt dizzy, ready to faint, and grasped the cool, moss-covered blocks of the temple with one flippered hand. He feared that Carida had somehow found him again, that Furgan was sinking his clutches into the organic components that had been substituted for parts of Terpfen's brain.

No! It was *his* mind now! He had not felt the tug from his Imperial controllers for over a day now. He'd forgotten what it was like to think his own thoughts, and he had tested the new freedom with growing wonder. He fantasized about overthrowing the Empire, about throttling bug-eyed Ambassador Furgan.

And during these thoughts no shadowy presence squashed his mind. He felt so . . . free!

He realized the faintness was just his numbing fright. The feeling passed, and Terpfen stood straight again as he heard footsteps approach.

The first to emerge into the bright daylight was Minister of State Leia Organa Solo herself. She must have run to the turbolift, expecting that the B-wing fighter carried some emergency message from Coruscant. Her hair looked mussed and windblown, and shadows haunted her eyes. Her face wore a concerned frown, as if something else already troubled her.

Terpfen felt the cold despair increase within him. She would be even more agonized after he told her that the Imperials knew the location of her son Anakin.

Leia stopped and looked gravely at him, sizing him up. Her brows drew together in thought, and then she said his name. "I know you. Terpfen, right? Why have you come here?"

Terpfen knew that his battered bulbous head and the lumpy mappings of scars made him recognizable even to humans. Behind Leia came several Jedi students Terpfen did not recognize, until he saw Ambassador Cilghal. The female Calamarian's large round eyes seemed to bore into his soul.

"Minister Organa Solo . . . ," Terpfen said in a quavering voice. Then he collapsed to his knees, partly in abject misery and partly because his legs refused to support him any longer. "Your son Anakin is in grave danger!"

He hung his scarred head. Before she could fire off laser-sharp questions, Terpfen confessed everything.

Leia stared down at Terpfen's scarred head and felt as if she were being strangled. Luke and Ackbar's intricate security and secrecy about Anoth had been breached! The Empire knew where to find her baby son.

Leia understood little about the defenses on the sheltered, hellish world. Now her servant and friend Winter was the only protection baby Anakin had.

"Please, Minister Organa Solo—we must go to Anoth at once," Terpfen said. "We must send them a message, evacuate your child before an Imperial strike squad can reach him. While I was under Furgan's influence, I transmitted Anoth's coordinates to Carida, but I did not keep a copy of them. I destroyed that information. You must take us there yourself. I will do whatever I can to help, but we must move quickly."

Leia made ready to leap into action, ready to do anything necessary to save her son. But a paralyzing realization brought her up short. "I can't contact Anoth. Even *I* don't know where the planet is!"

Terpfen stared at her, but she couldn't read expressions on his angular, aquatic face. She continued. "It was kept secret from me, too. The only ones who knew were Winter—and she's *on* Anoth—and Ackbar, who is now hiding on Calamari, and Luke, who's in a coma. I don't know how to get there!"

She steadied herself, trying to recall how fast-thinking she had been in her younger days. On the first Death Star she had taken charge during Han and Luke's ill-planned rescue. She had known what to do then. She had acted quickly and without hesitation.

But now she had three children to care for, and her new priorities seemed to scramble her single-mindedness. Han had already departed to search for Kyp Durron and the Sun Crusher. She'd been left here with the twins, supposedly to keep them safe. She couldn't just leave now.

Ambassador Cilghal seemed to sense her thoughts. "You must go, Leia. Go save your son. Your twin children will be safe here. The Jedi students will protect them."

As if suddenly freed of something she hadn't known was binding her, Leia felt plans plunge into her conscious mind. Relaxing, she became cool and decisive. "All right, Terpfen, you're coming with me. We'll go to Calamari as fast as we can. We'll find Ackbar, and he can take us to Winter and Anakin." She looked at the traitor with a complex mixture of anger and hope, pity and sorrow.

He turned away. "No. What if the Imperials activate me again? What if I am forced to commit some new sabotage?"

"I'll keep my eyes peeled," she said in a hard voice. "But I want you to come see Ackbar." She thought of the Calamarian admiral's misery, how he had gone to hide in the wilderness of his planet so others would not have to look at his shame. "You're going to explain to him that he wasn't at fault in the Vortex crash."

Terpfen worked his way back to his feet. He wobbled on his feet, but finally stood firm. "Minister Organa Solo," he said. His voice sounded as if he had swallowed something unpleasant. "I—I am sorry."

She shot a look at him, but she felt adrenaline pumping through her, a need to be on the move, to do anything possible. Hesitation could mean the loss of everything.

"Apologize when this is all over," she said. "Right now I need your help."

10

The *Millennium Falcon* emerged from hyperspace near the coordinates of the destroyed Caridan star system.

Han Solo polarized the segmented viewport to look out at the rubble that had recently been a group of planets and a burning sun; now he saw only a slash of still-glowing gases, a sea of radiation from the supernova. The sheer destruction was on a scale greater even than when he had emerged from hyperspace to find Alderaan reduced to broken debris—back before he had even met Leia, before he had thrown his lot in with the Rebellion, and before he had believed in the Force.

Carida's exploded star had spewed stellar material in a thick band around the ecliptic, vast curtains of roiling gases that glowed and crackled with intense energy across the spectrum. A shock wave plowed through space, where it would dissipate over thousands of years.

Under his high-resolution scanners Han spotted a few twisted cinders, burned-out lumps of worlds that had been the outer planets in the system. Now they shone like embers in a dying fire.

Lando Calrissian sat beside him, his mouth open in amazement. "Boy, that kid sure knows how to cause damage."

Han nodded. His throat felt dry and raw. It felt strange not to have Chewbacca in the copilot's seat. He hoped his Wookiee friend was having an easier time on his mission than Han was.

The *Falcon*'s sensor banks barely coped with the overloading energies that pulsed through the wreckage of the Caridan system. X rays and gamma rays hammered against his shields. But Han saw no sign of Kyp.

"Han, what do you think you'll find with all this static? If you're real sharp and real lucky, you might detect an ion trace from the Sun Crusher's sublight engines, but in the middle of a supernova you'll never pick up the track. Odds are—"

Han cut him off with a raised hand. "Never quote me the odds. You know better than that."

Lando grinned. "Yeah, I know, I know. So what are we going to do? What was the point of coming to this system?"

Han pressed his lips together, searching for an answer. It had felt right to come to Carida to pick up Kyp's trail. "I want to see what he saw," he said, "think like he might have been thinking. What was going through his mind?"

"You know him better than I do, buddy. If he ignited the Cauldron Nebula to wipe out Admiral Daala, and now he blew up the Imperial military training center, where would he go next? Think for yourself. What would be your next target?"

Han stared out at the inferno of what had been Carida's sun. "If my goal was to strike out at the Empire, causing as much damage as possible . . . I would head for . . ." He turned sharply and looked at Lando.

Lando's deep-brown eyes flew open. "That's too dangerous. He wouldn't go there!"

Han said, "I don't think dangerous has anything to do with it."

"Let me guess. Next, you'll say that we're going to follow him to the Core Systems."

"You got it, old buddy." Han set the coordinates in the navicomputer, and he heard Lando mumble to himself.

"Now I'll never get to Kessel on time."

The glowing gases of Carida's exploded star funneled around them as space elongated. The *Falcon* shot into hyperspace, heading far behind enemy lines and deep into the heart of the remaining forces of the Empire.

Near the bright heart of the galaxy, where stars lay close together in uncharted configurations, the resurrected Emperor had gathered his defenses to make a last stand. But since Palpatine's destruction, the Imperial warlords had fought each other for control. With no military genius like Grand Admiral Thrawn to unify the remnants, the Imperial war machine had withdrawn into the protected Core Systems. The warlords had left the victorious New Republic to lick its wounds while they vied for supremacy in their own corner of the galaxy.

But when one military leader managed to come out on top, the forces would strike against the New Republic. Unless Kyp Durron destroyed them first.

Han and Lando found an exploded red-dwarf star on the fringes of the Core. The small, dim sun had been unremarkable, and according to the *Falcon*'s planetary atlas, had no habitable worlds. However, scouts had determined that the red-dwarf system sheltered a starship-construction yard, weapons depot, and storage for archives shielded in thick vaults deep within several lifeless, rocky planets.

Han looked out the viewport and saw that the small star had exploded in a less-spectacular fashion than Carida's sun, a fizzle without enough mass to generate a significant chain reaction. But the shock fronts had still pulverized and incinerated the closely orbiting planets.

"He's done it again," Han said. "You can't miss a trail like the one Kyp is leaving."

Lando squinted at the scanners. "I'm tracking eleven Victory-class Star Destroyers heading out of the system."

"That's just great," Han said. He had enough to worry about with Kyp and the Sun Crusher; he didn't want to tangle with an Imperial fleet at the same time. "Have they picked us up yet?"

"Don't think so. There's still a lot of radiation and interference from that explosion. Looks to me like they just packed up and ran."

Han felt hope blossom in him. "You think this happened recently? Kyp just triggered the star explosion?"

"Could be."

"All right. Then you'd better scan for—"

"Already got him, Han. The Sun Crusher is sitting high above the ecliptic like he's just . . . watching."

"Plot a course," Han said, sitting up straight. "We're going after him. Full speed."

He punched the thrusters, and the *Falcon*'s bank of sublight engines blazed white. The acceleration shoved Han and Lando back into their seats as the ship made a graceful loop, heading above the orbital plane and approaching the blip on their sensors. As the *Falcon* closed the gap, though, the Sun Crusher began to flit away.

"He's spotted us. After him!" Han said. "If he jumps to lightspeed, we've lost him."

The *Falcon* shot forward. Han sighted on a bright speck moving across their path against the starfield.

"Want me to power up the lasers, Han?" Lando asked. "We're not going to shoot him, are we? What if he doesn't stop?"

"Wouldn't do any good to shoot him—not with that quantum armor of his." Han opened a comm channel. "Kyp, it's me, Han Solo. Kid, we've got to talk to you."

In answer the Sun Crusher winked as it changed course and increased speed.

"Punch it," Han said. "Let's go."

"We're already pushing the red lines," Lando said.

"She'll hold together," Han answered, then bent to the comm system again. "Hey, Kyp, listen to me."

The Sun Crusher arced around and began to grow larger in the viewport.

"Ah . . . Han?" Lando said. "He's coming right at us."

Han felt exhilarated, glad that Kyp was turning around to talk with them.

"I think he's going to ram us," Lando said.

Han blinked in disbelief. He bent over the transmitter. "Kyp, don't do this. Kyp! It's me, Han."

The Sun Crusher hurtled past them, swerving at the last moment to fire a burst of lasers from the defensive weapons mounted on its hull. Han heard the blasts thump against the *Falcon,* but they caused no damage.

"Must have been a warning," Lando said.

"Yeah, some warning," Han answered. "Kyp, why don't—"

The young man's brittle voice finally came at them. "Han, leave me alone. Go away. I've got work to do."

"Ummm, Kyp—that's what I'd like to talk with you about," Han said, suddenly at a loss for words.

The Sun Crusher hurtled toward them as if for another strafing run. As the small craft rushed past, Han worked the controls and yanked out with the *Millennium Falcon*'s tractor beam, latching on to the small superweapon. "Hey, I caught him!" Han said in surprise.

The momentum of the Sun Crusher was enough to jerk the *Falcon* around, but the tractor beams held. Han pumped up the power, increasing his invisible grip. Finally both ships came to a relative dead standstill high above the orbital plane of the exploded red-dwarf star.

"All right, Han," Kyp said. "If this is the way you want it . . . I can't let you stop me." The comm system fell silent.

"I don't like the sound of that," Lando said.

Kyp's voice returned. "One of these resonance torpedoes is enough to make a whole star blow up. I'm sure it'll make short work of a piece of junk like the *Falcon.*"

Han looked out at the crystalline shape of the Sun Crusher. The toroidal projector glowed a crackling blue and green, powering up to launch one of its projectiles at point-blank range.

"I've got a bad feeling about this," Han said.

11

The midmorning light shone through open skylights into the temple's grand audience chamber. Golden sunbeams dappled the polished flagstones, reflecting onto the rough-hewn walls.

From the raised platform behind his motionless body, the spirit of Luke Skywalker watched as Cilghal led the young twins on another visit. Cilghal held the twins' hands, gliding forward with fluid steps. This morning she wore her bluish ambassadorial garment instead of her drab Jedi robe. Behind the Calamarian ambassador came a guilt-ridden Streen beside muscular and supple Kirana Ti.

Artoo-Detoo hovered close to Luke's body, like a sentry rolling back and forth. The astromech droid had taken it upon himself to guard the Jedi Master after the devastating storm. Luke found the little droid's loyalty deeply touching, though not surprising.

Han and Leia's twin children stared wide-eyed at Luke, and his spirit watched them back longingly. Unable to communicate, he felt trapped. What would Obi-Wan have done in such a situation? He believed the Force would give him an answer, if he knew where to look.

"You see, children? Your Uncle Luke is safe. We rescued him last night. Your mother helped. We all helped. We're still trying to find some way to wake him up."

"I am awake!" Luke shouted into the empty spirit plane. "I've got to find a way to communicate that to you."

The twins stared at the motionless body. "He is awake," Jacen said. "He's right there." The little boy tilted his dark eyes up to gaze directly at Luke's spirit.

With a jolt Luke stared back at Jacen. "You can see me, Jacen? Can you understand me?"

Both Jaina and Jacen nodded their heads.

Cilghal wrapped her hands around their shoulders and steered them away. "Of course he is, children."

Thrilled and suddenly hopeful, Luke started to drift after them, but Streen came to the platform and threw himself to his knees, looking so stricken that waves of confusion rippled from him like a physical blow to Luke.

"Master Skywalker, I am deeply sorry!" Streen said. "I listened to the wrong voices in my head. The Dark Man tricked me. He will never do that again." Streen looked up, his eyes unfocused, flicking from side to side. He seemed to stare at Luke as well.

"Can you see me too, Streen? Can you hear me?" Luke thought fast, wondering if his abilities had changed.

"The Dark Man came to me," Streen said. "But I sense you're here too, Master Skywalker. I will never doubt you."

Kirana Ti squeezed Streen's shoulder. Luke's mind raced. Exar Kun could communicate with the others, if only in subtle ways—and now Luke knew that was possible for him too. He could already speak to the twins. Elation swept over him.

He began to make plans as the other Jedi candidates filed out of the echoing room. Now he was confident he could save himself, perhaps with the help of his Jedi students, his new generation of Jedi Knights.

From the stone walls behind him an otherworldly voice said, "How touching. Your clumsy students still imagine they can save you—but I know more than they do. My training wasn't limited by cowardice, as yours was."

Exar Kun stood black and wavering. "Gantoris was mine, and he is destroyed. Kyp Durron remains under my tutelage. Streen is already mine. The others will also begin to hear my voice." He raised his spectral arms. "It is all falling into place.

"I shall resurrect the Brotherhood of the Sith, and with your Jedi trainees I shall form the core of an invincible Force-wielding army."

Luke rounded on him, still not knowing how to fight this intangible enemy. Exar Kun laughed, as if an idea had just occurred to him. "I came to you first in a dream disguised as your fallen father, Skywalker . . . perhaps I should appear to them in your own form. They will certainly follow the teachings of the Sith if the words come from your mouth."

"No!" Luke said. With his astral body he leaped to tackle the shimmering silhouette of the Sith lord. But though his sparkling body passed smoothly through the shadow, Exar Kun did seem to discorporate momentarily.

Luke felt a spear of ice plunge through his core as he touched Kun, but he stood firm while the Dark Lord reeled against the stone wall, seeping back into the cracks to escape.

"I've already been tempered by the dark side," Luke said. "I came out stronger. You are weak because you know *only* the evil teachings. Your understanding is no greater than that of my apprentices."

Before he vanished, Exar Kun called back, "We shall see who is stronger."

The sun had set behind the giant ball of Yavin. With the onset of the moon's half night, the sky was lit only by an orangish glow reflected from the gas giant, giving the jungle a ruddy appearance.

Colonies of jabbering woolamanders settled down in the high branches for the night. In the underbrush, predators and prey moved through dances of survival. Sapphire-blue piranha beetles buzzed low over the sluggish rivers in search of victims. Other insects hummed their mating songs.

Far deeper in the jungle, though, night creatures rose out of shadowy caves and flapped their jagged wings. Hissing and mindless, they followed a burning compulsion that drove them toward the Great Temple. . . .

The creatures' wings made sounds like wet cloth striking stone as they flapped against downdrafts in the rapidly cooling air. Purplish veins pulsed as their black hearts beat swiftly, giving them energy for the long flight.

Two heads spread out on long, sinuous necks from each muscular torso. A wicked tail dangled behind each creature, ending in a hooked stinger that glistened with crystals of poison. Iridescent scales glittered in the coppery dusk light, as if illuminated by stoked embers. Yellow reptilian eyes widened their pupil slits, seeking their target.

Alchemical monsters created long ago during the dominion of Exar Kun on Yavin 4, these creatures had lived for generations in the black and dripping grottoes of distant mountains. Now three of them had awakened, called to destroy the body of Luke Skywalker.

The flying creatures struck the open skylights at the apex of the ziggurat. With metallic claws they scrabbled on the weathered stones that framed narrow windows. Each creature's double heads bobbed up and down, hissing and snapping in anticipation.

Folding their batlike wings against them, they squirmed through the skylights into the open chamber. Moving together, the creatures descended toward Luke's helpless body, long talons extended. . . .

●   ●   ●

Luke's image shimmered but cast no light in the dim chambers where the twins lay sleeping. The door was open. Cilghal sat up studying in her own room across the corridor, but she could not yet hear Luke's voice. The boy Jacen could—and Luke had no time.

"Jacen," he said with his muffled inside-the-head voice. The boy stirred. Beside him Jaina sighed and rolled over in her sleep. "Jacen!" Luke said again. "Jaina, I need your help. Only you can help me."

The boy woke up, blinking his dark eyes. He scanned the room, yawned, then fixed his eyes upon Luke's image. "Uncle Luke?" he said. "Help? Okay."

"Wake your sister and follow me. Tell her to raise the alarm and bring all the other Jedi. But you have to help me now! Maybe you can hold them off long enough."

Jacen didn't ask questions. By the time he shook his sister, she had already started to awaken. She too saw Luke, and the boy needed only a few words to explain the situation.

Jacen trotted down the hall on his little legs. Luke drifted in front of him, urging Jacen faster, faster, toward the turbolift.

Jaina ran into Cilghal's quarters and screamed, "Help, help!" at the top of her lungs. "Uncle Luke needs help." The Jedi trainees surged out of their quarters.

Suddenly alarms rang out. Luke realized that Artoo, still standing sentry duty in the grand audience chamber, must have triggered them. He didn't know, though, what the astromech droid could do against the monstrous winged creatures summoned by Exar Kun.

Jacen hesitated inside the turbolift while Luke showed which button to push. "Hurry, Jacen!" Luke said. The turbolift shot upward and spilled them into the vast, dim chamber.

Down at the end of the promenade, Artoo hummed back and forth, whistling and warbling shrilly. His arc-welding arm extended, flashing blue sparks, but the reptilian creatures flapped into the air, circling around the sluggish droid as if they considered Artoo to be no threat.

Two of the creatures flapped up from the raised platform upon hearing the turbolift doors open. They honked and hissed, spitting at the very small boy who emerged alone to challenge them.

Artoo squealed, as if thankful for any sort of help. The alarms continued to hammer through the temple.

The third creature perched at the edge of the long stone table on which Luke's body lay. Its two heads bobbed forward to let out a dual squeal of annoyance. One of the heads snapped down to tear a mouthful of cloth from

Luke's robe. The other head curled back scaled lips and flashed a jagged row of fangs.

"They're angry," Jacen said as if he had some kind of empathy with the creatures. "They're . . . wrong."

"Chase them away from my body, Jacen," Luke said, eyeing the poisonous stingers on their tails, the vicious teeth, the sharp claws. . . . "Go help Artoo. The others will be here in just a few seconds."

Without fear Jacen shrieked like a wild warrior as he ran toward the monsters on his stubby legs. He flailed his arms, yelling.

Two of the creatures squawked and swooped into the air, then flapped their leathery wings to dive at him. Artoo whistled a warning.

Jacen ducked at the last moment. The creatures dragged their hooked metallic claws on the flagstone floor, sending up showers of sparks. The boy didn't slow. He ran toward the last of the reptilian creatures, who stared hungrily down at Luke's soft, closed eyelids.

Jacen reached the raised platform. The third creature rose into the air, thrashing with its scorpion tail and snapping with both heads full of clacking fangs.

Unable to fight for himself, Luke paralleled the boy as Jacen struggled up onto the raised platform. Grim and determined, the boy stood guard by his uncle's motionless form. Artoo came up beside Jacen, his welding arm still crackling.

Then Luke saw what to do—if it was possible, if he could manage to use his skills in such a way. Next to his robed body lay a black cylinder studded with power buttons.

"Jacen," Luke said, "take my lightsaber."

The three flying creatures circled the chamber, croaking at each other as if receiving instructions from the Exar Kun.

Without hesitation the boy picked up the lightsaber handle. It was as long as his small forearm.

"Don't know how," Jacen said to Luke.

"I'll show you," Luke said. "Let me guide you . . . let me *fight* with you."

Talons extended, the three flying creatures plunged toward the boy, squealing with bloodlust in their eyes.

Jacen held the smooth handle in front of him and pushed the activation button. With a loud *snap-hiss* the lightsaber's deadly shaft blazed in the dimness. The little boy planted his feet apart, raised the glowing blade, and prepared to defend the Jedi Master, Luke Skywalker.

Cilghal scooped Jaina up in her arms and ran down the halls as Dorsk 81 and Tionne joined her at the turbolift. They rose to the highest level, ready to battle for their Master, as they had done against the unleashed storm. But even Cilghal's greatest fears did not prepare her for the astonishing sight that greeted her as she entered the grand audience chamber.

Little Jacen held a lightsaber in his hand with all the grace and confidence of a master swordsman. The trio of flying creatures came at him, jabbing with their dripping stingers, snapping with long teeth, reaching with hooked claws. But Jacen pirouetted with the energy blade, wielding the lightsaber as if it were an extension of his arm. The blade crackled and hummed through the air.

Artoo-Detoo, agitated, buzzed back and forth, doing his best to keep the creatures from coming too close to Master Skywalker's body. Jacen continued to fight.

One of the lizard creatures darted in with gnashing fangs, but Jacen deftly cleaved off a head with one smooth stroke. He left only a smoking neck stump as the other head of the two-headed monster writhed and flailed and spat. The creature crashed to the floor and flopped its leathery wings against the flagstones.

The remaining two monsters struck with their scorpion stingers. The little boy swung the lightsaber, neatly slicing off one pointed stinger, then rolled out of the way as gouts of black poison spurted from the amputated end. The evil liquid burned on the ancient Massassi stones like acid, boiling with greasy gray-and-purple smoke.

Maddened with pain, the injured thing flapped in the air until it grappled against its companion, rending with claws and snapping with two heads full of tearing teeth. It struck with the useless stump of its stinger, but the stronger creature stabbed with its own stinger—leaving a burning hole in the torso of its attacker, a hole that continued to burn and sizzle as the poison ate deeper and deeper.

The stronger flying lizard latched its jaws on to the scaly throat of the other. When its victim had ceased its struggles, the survivor released its claws, flapping higher as the dead carcass fell with a thud onto the floor. Artoo came forward to zap the limp creature, making certain it was dead.

Cilghal, Tionne, and Dorsk 81 froze on the threshold of the turbolift, watching the impossible tableau. "We've got to help him!" Dorsk 81 said.

"How?" Tionne asked. "We have no weapons."

Cilghal assessed the furious battle. "Perhaps Jacen doesn't need our help."

Jaina snatched her hand free from Cilghal's grip and scrambled down the promenade even as the others hesitated for a fraction of a second. Cilghal ran after her.

The last of the reptiles shrieked through double throats, infuriated by the attack of its companion. It dived down in an unstoppable plunge. Jacen stepped back to meet it, holding the lightsaber poised at his shoulder, waiting for the right moment.

Coolly, as the creature came in with dripping fangs and outstretched claws, Jacen swung in a clean arc with grace and skill, perfectly in command of his reflexes. The glowing blade struck and severed both throats in one sizzling flash. The carcass of the creature, reflexively convulsing its wings, crashed into Jacen and drove him to the floor.

Artoo rolled forward to help, bleeping.

"He is all right," Jaina called, finally reaching the raised platform. "Jacen!"

"Jaina!" Cilghal shouted, catching up with her.

The tip of the lightsaber appeared, smoking and blazing through the carcass as Jacen cut his way free of the stiff wings. Cilghal assisted him.

In surprise Jaina looked up to see the first fallen creature lurch back up, clinging to life with its remaining head, still desperate to kill Luke. With one stump of its severed neck still oozing dark blood, it clutched the edge of the stone table and hauled itself up, snapping its scorpion tail in convulsive twitches and preparing to sting. Its wings flapped, helping it balance on the table where it could rip apart Luke's body.

In one last moment of defiance, pushed on by the evil spirit controlling it, the wounded creature struck toward Luke's unprotected throat.

But Jaina arrived first. The little girl jumped up and grabbed its wings, yanking backward with all her weight. Writhing and snapping, the creature tried to bite down on the hands holding its leathery wings.

A mere second behind Jaina, Cilghal wrapped her powerful Calamarian hands around the creature's long serpentine throat even as Jaina continued to yank backward at its wings. Cilghal let out a high grunt as she wrung its neck, crushing a succession of vertebrae as if they were dry twigs.

The thing slumped down across the table, finally dead.

Jaina panted and slid into a squat. Jacen climbed to his feet and looked around as if confused. He blinked his eyes sleepily, then, with a deft movement of one small finger, deactivated the lightsaber. The humming sound of the blade vanished into the sudden silence of the chamber.

The turbolift opened, and the remaining Jedi trainees rushed out, drawing up short as they saw the carnage.

Tionne reached the raised platform. Her silvery hair flowed behind her like a comet's tail. She bent over Luke's body and, with an expression of disgust, gripped the still-oozing reptilian carcass of the last slain creature and flung it away from the Jedi Master.

Cilghal rushed to Jacen just as he calmly replaced the lightsaber beside Luke's motionless form. She grabbed him, hugged him, and then stared in awe at the little boy. Only moments ago this not-quite-three-year-old child had fought like a legendary lightsaber duelist.

Dorsk 81 and the other Jedi trainees came forward. "He fought as well as a Master!" Dorsk 81 said. "It reminded me of the duel between Gantoris and Master Skywalker."

"Uncle Luke was with me," Jacen said. "He showed me. He's here."

Cilghal blinked her large round eyes.

"What do you mean?" Tionne asked.

"Can you see him now?" Dorsk 81 said.

"Yes, he's right there," Jaina pointed to thin air. "He says he's proud of us." She giggled. Jacen giggled too, but he looked exhausted, covered with dark ichor. He slumped down on Cilghal's lap.

The Jedi trainees looked at each other, then gazed at the open air above Luke's prone body. Artoo whistled in confusion.

"What else does he say?" Cilghal said.

Jacen and Jaina both sat still for a moment, as if listening. "Exar Kun. He's making the trouble," Jacen said.

Jaina finished, "Stop Exar Kun. Then Uncle Luke can come back."

12

Leia sat next to Terpfen in uneasy silence during the entire journey
from Yavin 4 to the ocean world of Calamari. Terpfen said virtually nothing,
crouched over the controls as if unable to bear the weight on his shoulders.

The small ship descended through the cloud-swirled atmosphere of the
sapphire world toward one of the wrecked floating cities where Ackbar had
been overseeing heroic salvage operations. As the ship streaked toward the
sunlit water, Leia saw golden trails reflected off the choppy waves.

She felt an eerie sense of déjà vu, thinking of when she and Cilghal
had come to this planet in search of Ackbar in his exile. She felt this time
she was coming full circle, riding with the unwilling Calamarian traitor to
redeem Ackbar . . . but more important, to enlist the admiral's assistance in
a rescue operation to save her son.

"Reef Home salvage team, this is—" Terpfen hesitated. "This is Minister
of State Leia Organa Solo's ship. We must speak with Ackbar. Do you have
a place for us to land?"

After only a moment Ackbar's own voice responded. "Leia coming to
see me? She's certainly welcome here." Then Ackbar added, "Terpfen, is
that you?"

"Yes, Admiral."

"I thought I recognized your voice. I would delight in seeing both
of you."

"I'm not so sure, sir," Terpfen said.

"What do you mean? Is something wrong?" Ackbar replied.

The Calamarian hung his scarred head, wrestling with his answer. Leia leaned over to the microphone. "It's best if we explain face-to-face, Ackbar," she said in a soft but firm voice. It still felt awkward not to address him by his rank.

Terpfen nodded a painful thanks to Leia. He brought the ship down in a steep dive toward the ocean surface, then pulled up with room to spare and cruised over the wavetops until they approached a cluster of floating vessels and a turmoil in the slate-gray water.

Organic-looking barges with articulated crane apparatus extended down into the water. Bloated, inflated ships like enormous bellows blazed exhaust fire as their engines drove fans to pump air into the submerged hulk of Reef Home, one of the majestic Calamarian floating cities that had been sunk in Admiral Daala's recent attack.

Leia had been on Calamari trying to convince Ackbar to reclaim his rank when Daala's Star Destroyers had struck. Squads of TIE bombers had managed to sink Reef Home and damage several other cities. But Ackbar had come out of his seclusion and rallied the Calamarian forces to victory.

Now Leia watched the white froth as the hulk of the city heaved itself to the surface. Bubbles simmered around the lumpy dome of Reef Home. Figures clambered over the exposed metal, attaching grappler cables from the towering cranes on the surrounding barge ships. The bellows pumps continued to gush air into Reef Home's sealed compartments, forcing out the water that had flooded deck after deck.

In the water, groups of dark figures—tentacle-faced Quarren—worked at the edge of the derelict city, prying open wave doors, patching breaches in the hull, and scavenging the ocean floor to find lost possessions.

As Terpfen brought the ship to land on the wet expanse of the main crane barge, the domed city shouldered its way higher above the choppy ocean.

Leia emerged from the small ship and stopped to catch her balance on the gently swaying deck. Cool salt spray struck her, making her gasp at the cutting wind and the iodine tang of drifting seaweed. One of the figures in the water used a jetpack to scoot away from the salvaged city, climbing a long ladder up the side of the crane barge.

Leia recognized Ackbar as he scrambled with enthusiasm onto the barge deck and stood dripping before them. He peeled off a thin translucent membrane from his face and took a deep breath of fresh air.

"Leia, I greet you," he said, raising a flipper hand. "We're making great progress in resurrecting Reef Home City. Our crews should have it refitted and ready for habitation within a few months.

"And Terpfen!" he said with heartbreaking joy as he strode to embrace his former chief starship mechanic. Terpfen stood stiffly, unable to speak a word.

Leia's immediate need was too great for pleasantries. "Ackbar," she said, "the Imperials have learned the location of Anoth. Winter and baby Anakin are in grave danger at this very moment. You must take us to them right away. You're the only one who knows the location."

Ackbar stood in shock, and Terpfen broke away from his embrace. "I have betrayed us, Admiral," he said. "I have betrayed us all."

Working hard to appear useful and important, Ambassador Furgan stood on the control deck of the Dreadnaught *Vendetta*. As they came out of hyperspace and approached the planet Anoth, he stepped forward. "Shields up," he said.

"Already done, sir," Colonel Ardax answered from the command station. Ardax wore a crisp olive-gray Imperial-navy uniform with his cap firmly planted on his short-trimmed hair. He drew in a deep breath to broaden his shoulders.

Throughout the journey to Anoth the colonel had annoyed Furgan by making decisions for himself without asking for input. Ardax was altogether too independent for Furgan's tastes. True, Furgan was merely the administrative head of the Caridan military academy—*former* military academy, now that the Rebel terrorist Kyp Durron had destroyed it—but he was still the most important person on this entire ship; his opinion should be valued.

He still thought of the roaring explosion of Carida's star, the echoed screams of those low-ranking individuals and all the valuable equipment he had left behind. Furgan's glorious dreams of resurrecting the Empire had dwindled to a point—but it was a laser-bright point. If he could just get his hands on the Jedi baby, there would be hope for the galaxy once more.

The *Vendetta* passed through a broken belt of asteroids scattered along Anoth's orbit. The planet itself had shattered into three components: two large chunks in contact, scraping and creating static discharges so that titanic lightning bolts blasted between them; farther out circled a smaller, misshapen rock that held a breathable atmosphere in its lowlands. In a century or two the three chunks would pulverize each other to space dust, but at the moment Anoth was a hidden and protected haven.

Until now.

"Looks like a rather . . . rugged place to raise an infant," Colonel Ardax said.

"It'll toughen him up," Furgan said, "an appropriate beginning to the rigorous training he will undergo if he is to be our new Emperor."

"Ambassador Furgan," Ardax asked, raising his eyebrows, "do you have any indication of exactly where we should look for this alleged stronghold?"

Furgan thrust out his purplish lower lip. The spy Terpfen had provided the planet's coordinates, nothing more. "You can't expect me to do your entire job for you, Colonel," he snapped. "Use the Dreadnaught's scanners."

"Yes, sir." The colonel gestured toward the technicians at the analysis and sensor panels.

"We'll find it, sir," a wide-eyed corporal said, staring at a screen that showed a simplified computer diagram of the Anoth system's three components. "There's not much down there, so it shouldn't be hard to pick them out."

Furgan stumped to the turbolift at the rear of the control deck. "Colonel, I'm going down to inspect the MT-AT vehicles. I trust you can handle everything here without me?"

"Yes, sir," Ardax said, a bit too emphatically.

As the turbolift swallowed him, Furgan thought he heard a muttered comment from the Dreadnaught captain, but the words were cut off by the closing metal doors. . . .

Down in the *Vendetta*'s hangar bay and staging area Furgan stepped into a flurry of stormtrooper activity. White-armored troopers jogged in tight formation across the metal-plated floor, carrying weapons, stashing siege gear and power packs inside the cargo holds of the MT-ATs.

On Carida, Furgan had followed the design and development of the new Mountain Terrain Assault Transports, and he relished the opportunity to see them used in actual combat. He would follow in the rear of the assault, letting fully trained troopers face the initial hazards, though there was little to worry about—a woman and a child hiding on a rock? How much resistance could they offer?

Furgan ran his stubby fingers across the polished knee joint of one of the MT-AT walkers. Designed for ground assaults on remote mountain citadels, the MT-ATs' articulated joints and sophisticated claw footpads could scale even vertical surfaces of rock. On each joint were mounted supercharged lasers that could penetrate a half-meter-thick blast door. Two small blaster cannons hung on either side of the low-slung pilot's compartment to shoot down harrying fighter ships out of the sky.

Furgan stared at the beautiful construction, smooth lines, and glossy armor, marveling at the MT-AT's incredible capabilities. "Splendid machine," he said.

The stormtroopers paid no attention to him as they finished their preparations.

Colonel Ardax's voice came over the intercom. "Your attention, please! After some difficulty with electrical discharges and ionization interference in this system, we have pinpointed the secret base. Prepare to deploy the strike force immediately. Let's make this a clean and quick kill. That is all." Ardax signed off.

"You heard the colonel," Furgan said as the stormtrooper teams began to clamber aboard their MT-AT vehicles. They would be dropped from orbit on a thunderous plunge through the atmosphere, encased in a thermal-resistant cocoon that would detach upon striking the surface.

One trooper scrambled alone into his cockpit, hauling extra weapons, interrogation devices, and intelligence-gathering equipment.

"You!" Furgan said. "Stow all that in the cargo compartment. I am riding with you."

The stormtrooper looked at him in silence for a moment, his polished eye visor staring blankly.

"Do you have a problem with that order, sergeant?" Furgan asked.

"No, sir," the voice crackled through the helmet speaker. The stormtrooper methodically removed the equipment and stowed it in the undercompartment.

Furgan heaved himself into the second seat and strapped in. He pulled two sets of the crash webbing around his body to make sure he landed without injury. He didn't want to limp in triumph into the defeated Rebel stronghold. He waited impatiently as the rest of the stormtroopers completed preparations, slipped aboard their assault transports, and locked themselves down.

When the launching bay dropped out from beneath his feet like a trapdoor, Furgan grabbed the arms of his chair and cried out. The transports plunged like heavy projectiles into the waiting atmosphere. Even in its thick cocoon the MT-AT jounced and rocked as if it were being struck by cannon blasts. He tried unsuccessfully to stop his yell of panic.

Beside him the stormtrooper pilot said nothing.

Inside the stronghold on Anoth, Leia's personal servant Winter glanced at the chronometer and at the giggling dark-haired baby. It was time to put young Anakin to bed.

Though the triple planet Anoth had its own unusual cycle of days, nights, and twilights, Winter insisted on keeping their chronometers set to Coruscant standard time. Outside, the thin skies rarely brightened to more than a dark purple with flashes of searing yellow as electrical discharges blasted across space.

The planetoid was a stormy world, its surface covered with stone pinnacles like mammoth cathedrals reaching up to the limits of Anoth's low gravity. Riddled with caves from thousands of geological inclusions that had weathered and volatilized away during centuries of planetary stresses, the rock spires provided a sheltered hiding place.

Winter picked up the baby in her arms and bounced him against her hip as she went deeper into the facility. Anakin's shielded bedroom was brightly lit and decorated with soothing pastel colors. Tinkling music filled the air, a cheerful melody mixed with quiet wind and rushing water.

A boxy rectangular GNK power droid waddled from station to station in the room, charging the batteries of Anakin's self-aware toys. "Thank you," Winter said out of habit, though the droid had only minimal interactive programming. The power droid burbled a response and shuffled out in a slow walk on accordioned legs.

"Good evening, Master Anakin," said the caregiver droid in Anakin's chambers. An enhanced protocol model, the TDL droid was programmed to perform a majority of the functions required to care for a young child. TDL models had been marketed across the galaxy as nanny droids for busy politicians, space military personnel, and even smugglers who had children but too little time to spend with them.

The TDL droid had a silvery surface with all corners and sharp edges smoothed for comfort. Because nannies and mothers were expected to need more than the usual set of hands, TDL nanny droids had four fully functional arms, all of which were covered with warm synthetic flesh—as was the torso—to provide a more nurturing experience for a baby held in robot arms.

Anakin cooed with pleasure to see the droid, said a word resembling its name. Winter patted the baby on the back, saying good night.

"Do you have a preference from the large selection of lullabies and bedtime music I have available, Mistress Winter?" the droid said.

"Make a random selection," Winter answered. "I want to get back to the operations room. Something . . . doesn't feel right tonight."

"Very well, Mistress Winter," the nanny droid said, cradling Anakin in her arms. "Wave good night." She plucked up Anakin's pudgy hand and puppeted a wave.

Winter made it to the door of the operations room just before the intruder alarms went off. She rushed into the control center, scanning the big screens that showed outside images of the stark landscape.

Sonic booms thundered through the thin air, as large objects streamed down in a tight cluster. Winter saw the last of a group of projectiles impact at the base of the nearest spire of rock.

Winter activated the automated defense systems. She closed the massive shield doors that covered the entrance to the hangar grotto. Through the rock she could feel the heavy vibration as the metal doors slammed together.

She saw movement below, just out of range of the cameras. Then a long metal leg bent up on a huge articulated joint; a foot spiked with claws smashed into the rockface, creating traction with explosive bolts. Then the huge machine levered itself out of view around an outcropping.

Winter enhanced the audio pickup, listening to the groaning sounds of straining machinery, pulleys and grinding engines, the clank of treads.

Working rapidly, she switched to another set of image enhancers mounted on a distant pinnacle. The picture that appeared made her gasp in amazement and fear—an extreme reaction, considering her usual unemotional and inflectionless manner.

The smoldering hulks of protective reentry pods lay strewn about the landscape. The metal shells had cracked open like black vermin eggs and unleashed mechanical monstrosities—eight-legged, arachnidlike machines.

Each of the heavily jointed legs moved along different axes as the clawed feet helped the ellipsoid body scuttle over rugged terrain, finding footholds in the rock and scaling the sheer peak in which Winter and Anakin hid.

Eight Imperial Spider Walkers swarmed up the stone pinnacle, firing bright-green blasts against the thick walls of the stronghold, searching for a way in.

13

The Jedi trainees gathered in the dusty, abandoned war room of the Great Temple. They had chosen it as the most fitting place to plan their battle against Exar Kun.

On the third level of the ancient ziggurat the war room had once been used by the Rebel Alliance as a control center for their secret base. Here the tactical genius General Jan Dodonna had planned the strike against the first Death Star.

Cilghal and the others had cleared away much of the debris that had collected in the decade since the Rebels had left the base behind. Multicolored lights flickered on the control panels of the few functional sensor networks; grime-caked viewing plates and cracked transparisteel screens made the signals refract and glitter. Atop a tactical map the tiny hash-mark footprints of a skittering reptile were overlaid with the larger clawed prints of some predator that had chased after it.

Sealed behind the protection of thick stone walls, the war room allowed no outside illumination. Newly restored glowpanels in the corners made the place shine brightly, but also enhanced the shadows.

Cilghal looked at the group of Jedi trainees. A dozen of the best . . . but now they were gripped with fear and indecision, unprepared for the trial forced upon them.

Some—such as Kirana Ti, Kam Solusar, and, surprisingly, Streen—reacted with outrage to the long-dead Lord of the Sith. Others, particularly

Dorsk 81, were filled with an unreasoning fear, afraid to challenge the dark power that had been sufficient to warp other students and defeat Master Skywalker. Cilghal herself did not look forward to the fight, but she vowed to do everything she could against their unwanted enemy.

"What if Exar Kun can hear our plans?" Dorsk 81 said, his large eyes shining in the harsh lights. "Even here he might be spying on us!" His voice rose, and his yellow-olive skin mottled with panic.

"The Dark Man can be everywhere," Streen said, leaning across the cluttered table. His frizzy gray hair still looked windblown. He fidgeted as he glanced around the room, as if afraid someone were watching.

"There's no other place we can go," Cilghal said. "If Exar Kun can find us here, he can find us wherever we go. We must operate on the assumption that we can still fight him." She gazed at the candidates. She had taken great pains to develop her oratory skills as ambassador for Calamari. She had used her voice and her wits to great success in the past, and now she took advantage of her gift. "We have enough real problems to confront—there's no need to manufacture worse ones from our imagination."

The others murmured in agreement.

"Tionne," Cilghal said, "much of our plan depends on your knowledge of ancient Jedi lore. Tell us what you know about Exar Kun."

Tionne sat up in a battered and uncomfortable chair beside one of the dilapidated tactical stations. Across her lap lay the double-boxed musical instrument on which she played old ballads to anyone who would listen.

Tionne had only a small amount of Jedi potential. Master Skywalker had made that clear to her, but she would not be swayed from her resolve to become one of the new Jedi Knights. She had become enamored of Jedi legends, traveling from system to system, digging through ancient writings and folktales, compiling tales of the Jedi from thousands of years before the Dark Times.

The Jedi Holocron had been a treasure trove, and Tionne had spent much of her time studying it, replaying forgotten legends, clarifying details. But the Holocron was destroyed when Master Skywalker had asked the simulated gatekeeper, the ancient Jedi Master Vodo-Siosk Baas, to tell of his student Exar Kun, who had rebuilt the Brotherhood of the Sith. . . .

Tionne flicked molten-silver hair over her shoulders and looked at the other trainees with her eerie mother-of-pearl eyes. Her lips were thin and pale, bloodless with tension.

"It's very difficult to find verifiable legends from the Great Sith War. That was four thousand years ago, and it was incredibly devastating—but apparently the old Jedi Knights were ashamed of how they had failed to protect the galaxy. Many of the records were distorted or destroyed, but I think I've pieced together enough." She swallowed, then continued.

"Kun seems to have built his primary stronghold on this jungle moon. He enslaved the Massassi race to build all these temples as focal points for his power."

She looked around, sizing up the Jedi trainees. "In fact, this gathering reminds me of the Great Council on the planet Deneba, when most of the old Jedi Knights met to discuss the dark tide rising through the galaxy. Master Vodo-Siosk Baas—who had trained Exar Kun—became a martyr when he tried to turn his student back to the light side. When Master Vodo did not succeed, the other Jedi banded together in a massive strike force such as had never before been gathered.

"Though Kun had enormous power, it seems that the key"—Tionne tapped the side of her instrument with a glistening fingernail—"the *key* was that the other Jedi combined their might. They fought together as a unit where all the pieces fit together, as components in a much larger machine powered by the Force.

"I've found only sketchy information, but it seems that in the final battle the unified Jedi wiped out most of the jungles on Yavin 4, laying waste to everything in their efforts to destroy Exar Kun. Kun drained dry the life force of all his Massassi slaves in one last gambit. The ancient Jedi succeeded in destroying much of what he had built and obliterated Kun's body, but he somehow managed to preserve his spirit within the temples. For all these years."

"Then we must finish the job," Kirana Ti said, standing up. She wore her reptilian body armor all the time now, unencumbered by a Jedi robe because she did not know when she might need to fight at a moment's notice.

"I agree," Kam Solusar said. His gaunt face held the expression of a man who had long ago forgotten how to smile.

"But how?" Streen said. "Thousands of Jedi could not obliterate the Dark Man. We are only twelve."

"Yes," Kirana Ti said, "but this time Exar Kun doesn't have a race of enslaved people to draw upon. He has no resources but himself. Besides, Kun has already been defeated once—and he knows it."

"And," Cilghal interjected, gesturing around the table, "all of us have trained together from the beginning. Master Skywalker made us to be a team. Leia called us champions of the Force—and that is what we must be."

Standing at the pinnacle of the Great Temple, Luke Skywalker's shimmering form could not feel the cool twilight breeze as the lumbering orange hulk of the gas giant cast fading light across the jungles. Luke watched a flock of batlike creatures take to the air and swarm across the treetops in search of night insects.

He remembered his nightmare when Exar Kun, disguised as Anakin Skywalker, had urged Luke to dabble in the dark side. Against the backdrop of history Luke had seen the labors of the broken Massassi erecting mammoth temples, working until crushed by sheer labor. Luke had cast off that nightmare, but he had not interpreted its warning soon enough.

Now he turned to see the hooded form of Kun standing black against the jungle landscape, but the sight no longer had the power to make him afraid. "You're growing bolder, Exar Kun, to keep showing yourself to me—especially when your attempts to destroy my body continue to fail."

In the aftermath of the reptilian creatures' attack, Luke had watched Cilghal tend his body's minor wounds, cleaning them and binding them with the meticulous care and empathy he had sensed from her first days at the Jedi academy. Cilghal was a born Jedi healer.

She had spoken aloud to Luke's spirit, though she couldn't see him. "We will do whatever we can, Master Skywalker. Please keep faith in us."

Luke had indeed maintained his faith. He felt it throbbing within him as he confronted Exar Kun atop the temple, where the Sith Lord and Kyp Durron had defeated Luke once before.

"I have been toying with you." Kun waved his silhouette hand. "Nothing will affect my plans. Some of your students are already mine. The others will soon follow."

"I don't think so," Luke said with fresh certainty. "I have instructed them well. You might show them easy ways to glory, but your tricks carry a high price. I have taught them diligence, confidence in their own worth and abilities. What you offer, Exar Kun, is mere parlor magic. I have given them the true strength and meaning of the Force."

"Do you think I don't know of the laughable plans they make against me?" Kun said. The spirit of the Dark Lord seemed to be growing more full of bluster and threats. Perhaps his confidence was shaken.

"It doesn't matter," Luke answered. "They will defeat you anyway. Your imagined power is your weakness, Exar Kun."

"And your faith in your friends is yours!" Kun snapped back.

Luke laughed, feeling his strength and determination increase. "I've heard talk like that before. It was proved wrong then, and it will be proved wrong now."

The black outline of Exar Kun rippled in an unseen breeze. As the shadow vanished, Kun's last words were, "We shall see!"

14

Standoff.

Han Solo felt cold sweat spring from his forehead as he looked out from the cockpit of the *Millennium Falcon*. In front of him the Sun Crusher powered up its supernova torpedo launcher.

Han pounded his fist on the console. "Hold it, kid!" he shouted. "Just hold it. I thought you were my friend."

"If you were my friend," Kyp's voice croaked through the speaker, "you wouldn't try to stop me. You know what the Empire did to my life, to my family. The Empire lied to me one last time—and now even my brother is dead."

At the copilot's station Lando scrambled at the controls. His big eyes flicked back and forth, and he turned to Han, waving frantically for him to shut off the voice pickup.

"Han," he whispered, "remember when you and Kyp took the Sun Crusher away from Maw Installation? And Luke and I were there waiting to intercept you?"

Han nodded, not sure what Lando was getting at. "Sure."

"Back then we linked the ships together because the *Falcon*'s navi-computer wouldn't work." He raised his eyebrows and spoke very slowly. "Listen . . . we've still got the Sun Crusher's control codes in here."

Suddenly Han understood. "Can you do anything with that? You're not even familiar with the Sun Crusher's systems."

"Don't have much choice, do we, buddy?"

"All right," Han said in a needlessly low voice, because the voice pickup was switched off. "I'll keep him talking—you work to deactivate the Sun Crusher." Lando, with a skeptical but determined frown, continued his programming.

Han toggled on the comm system again. "Kyp, don't you remember when we went turbo-skiing at the poles of Coruscant? You led me down one of the dangerous paths, but I went after you because I thought you were going to fall on your face. Don't you remember that?"

Kyp didn't answer, but Han knew he had struck home.

"Kid, who got you out of the spice mines of Kessel?" he said. "Who broke you out of the detention cell on the *Gorgon*? Who was with you during the escape from the Maw? Who promised to do everything he could to make your life worth living again after your years of misery?"

Kyp answered in a halting voice. "It didn't work."

"But why not, kid? What went wrong? What happened on Yavin 4? I know you and Luke didn't get along—"

"It had nothing to do with Luke Skywalker," Kyp snapped so defensively that Han knew it wasn't true. "There in the temples I learned things Master Skywalker would never teach. I learned how to be strong. I learned how to fight the Empire, to turn my own anger into a weapon."

"Look, kid," Han said, "I don't claim to understand anything about the Force. In fact I once said it was a hokey religion full of mumbo jumbo. But I do know that what you're saying sounds dangerously close to the dark side."

After a deep pause Kyp said haltingly, "Han . . . I—"

"Got it!" Lando whispered.

Han nodded, and Lando punched in the control sequence.

A rapid succession of lights twinkled on the control panel as the override command was transmitted across the narrow bridge of space. In the black gulf lit only by a backwash of dull light from the exploded red-dwarf star, the Sun Crusher suddenly went dark: the lights in its cockpit, the aiming beacons on its laser cannons, and the blaze of plasma at the end of its toroidal torpedo generator.

"Yes!" Lando shouted. Han gave a whoop of triumph, and the two of them reached out to slap their hands together.

"Let me talk to him," Han said. "Does he still have power to his comm system?"

"Channel open," Lando said. "But I don't think he's very happy—"

"You tricked me!" Kyp's voice screamed through the speaker panel. "You claimed to be my friend—and now you've betrayed me. It's just like Exar Kun said. Friends betray you. A Jedi has no time for friendship. You should all die."

Astonishingly, the power in the Sun Crusher surged back to life again, despite Lando's overrides. The lights came on in a blaze.

"It's not my fault!" Lando squawked, scrambling to reroute the command. "I didn't know he could bypass it so fast!"

"Kyp can do things with the Force that you and I can't understand," Han said.

The energy torpedo launcher fired up with a flare of intense plasma, brighter than before, ready to launch at the *Falcon*.

And this time Kyp did not hesitate.

15

Streen dozed cross-legged on the cold flagstone floor before Master Skywalker. He folded his arms over his knees, comfortable in the many-pocketed jumpsuit he had brought with him from his lonely days as a gas prospector on Bespin. He could no longer smell the bitter sulfurous taint of rich plumes of deep-layer gases.

Now Streen had a greater mission—to guard Master Skywalker.

Low-slanted light from outside elongated the shadows in the grand audience chamber. Twelve candles, one placed by each of the Jedi trainees, flickered around Luke's body, shedding a faint but protective glow into the motionless air. The small bright points glittered as the darkness gathered all around.

Streen muttered to himself. No, he would not listen to the Dark Man's words. No, he would not serve Exar Kun's purposes. No, he would not do anything to harm Master Skywalker. No!

In his lap, cool and hard against his callused hands, he held the handle of Luke's lightsaber.

This time he could fight it. This time the Dark Man would not win. Some of the other Jedi trainees had expressed grave misgivings about letting Streen near Master Skywalker, especially armed with a lightsaber. But Streen had begged for his chance at restitution, and Kirana Ti had spoken on his behalf.

The others would watch over him. Master Skywalker would be in danger, but they had to take the risk.

Streen let the fuzzy caress of sleep work its way into his mind. His grizzled head nodded to his chest. Whispering voices sounded like breezes in his mind, forming gentle words, soothing phrases . . . cold promises.

The words demanded that he wake up, but Streen resisted them, not knowing if they were evil suggestions or the insistences of his companions. When Streen felt he had waited long enough, he allowed himself to snap awake.

The voices fell silent as he blinked his eyes. Another voice, external this time, replaced the silence. "Wake up, my student. The winds are blowing."

Streen focused on the black form of Exar Kun in the center of the throne room. In the flickering candlelight and dim rays from the dying day, Streen could see chiseled features on the onyx silhouette, more detailed than he had ever seen before on the shadow of the Dark Man.

Exar Kun turned a well-defined face toward him, completely ebony as if molded from lava stone: high cheekbones, haughty eyes, a thin, angry mouth. Long black hair like carbon wires swept across his shoulder, gathered in a thick ponytail. Padded armor covered his body, and the pulsing tattoo of a black sun burned from his forehead.

Streen climbed slowly to his feet. He felt calm and strong, angry at how the Dark Man had set a sharp hook in his own weakness and had dragged him along. "I won't do your bidding, Dark Man," he said.

Exar Kun laughed. "And how do you propose to resist? You are already mine."

"If you believe that," Streen said, and took a deep breath, strengthening his voice, "then you have made your first mistake." He brought up the handle of Luke's lightsaber, igniting it with a loud *snap-hiss*.

Exar Kun's shadow flinched backward, much to Streen's surprise and satisfaction.

"Good," Kun said with false bravado, "now take the weapon and cleave Skywalker in two. Let us be done with this."

Streen took one step toward Exar Kun, holding the green lightsaber before him. "This blade is meant for you, Dark Man."

"If you think that weapon will have any effect on me," Kun said, "perhaps you should ask your friend Gantoris—or have you forgotten what happened to *him* when he defied me?"

A vision flashed through Streen's mind: Gantoris's crisped corpse incinerated from the inside out, his body turned to ash from the incredible fires of the dark side. Kun must have intended for that memory to drive Streen to despair; Gantoris had been his friend; he and Gantoris were the first two trainees Master Skywalker had found on his Jedi search.

But rather than causing panic or dismay, the memory increased Streen's determination. He strode forward, staring down the shadowy man. "You are not wanted here, Exar Kun," he said. To his continued surprise the shadow of the ancient Sith Lord drifted back from him, down the promenade.

"I can find other tools, Streen, if you prove difficult. I will show you no mercy when I have gained control once more. My Sith brothers will use the power stored within this network of temples. If you defy me, I can find new ways of inflicting pain far beyond the capabilities of your imagination—and you will endure all of them!"

Kun's shadow drifted farther away . . . and a tall figure emerged from the left stone stairwell into the grand audience chamber: Kirana Ti clad in her polished reptilian armor, her muscles rippling in the pale candlelight, her curves making her look supple yet deadly.

"Are you running away, Exar Kun?" Kirana Ti said. "Frightened off so easily?"

Streen held his position, still gripping the lightsaber.

"Another foolhardy student," Kun said, whirling to face her. "I would have come to you in time. The witches of Dathomir would be fine additions to a new Sith Brotherhood."

"You'll never get a chance to ask them, Exar Kun. You are trapped here. You won't leave this chamber." She pressed forward to intimidate him by her very closeness.

Kun's shadow distorted, but he held his ground. "You cannot threaten me." Kun loomed over her.

Streen felt a stab of cold fear at the movement, but Kirana Ti ducked swiftly, fluidly, into a fighting stance. She reached to her waist and snatched one of the tools hanging there.

A loud crackle seared the air, and she stood holding another ignited lightsaber. A long amethyst-and-white blade extended from the handle, humming like an angry insect. She thrashed the lightsaber from side to side.

"Where did you get that weapon?" Kun demanded.

"It belonged to Gantoris," she said. "He once tried to fight you and failed." She slashed with the lightsaber, and Kun flinched back toward Streen. "But I will succeed."

Kirana Ti stalked toward the platform where Luke's body lay, where Streen stood on guard with the other lightsaber. Kun was trapped between them.

Another Jedi trainee emerged from the right-side stairwell—grim and wiry Kam Solusar. "And if she fails," he said, "*I* will pick up the lightsaber and fight you." He marched forward, closing the distance to join her.

Then Tionne came from the opposite stairwell, throwing her challenge at Exar Kun as she walked up to the platform. "And I will fight you as well."

Cilghal stepped in with Jacen and Jaina, each holding one of her hands. "And we will fight you. We will all fight you, Exar Kun."

The remaining Jedi trainees flooded into the chamber, converging in a group that surrounded the Dark Lord of the Sith.

Kun raised his opaque arms in a sudden brisk gesture. With a flicker of wind the twelve candles around Master Skywalker's body snuffed out, plunging the room into deep shadow.

"We're not afraid of the darkness," Tionne said in a firm voice. "We can make our own light."

As his eyes adjusted, Streen saw that all twelve of the Jedi candidates were limned with the faintest sheen of an iridescent blue glow that grew brighter as the new Jedi converged around Exar Kun.

"Even joined together, you are too weak to fight me!" the shadowy man said.

Streen felt his throat constrict, his windpipe close. He choked, unable to breathe. The black silhouette turned, staring at those who resisted him. The Jedi trainees grasped their throats, straining to breathe, their faces darkening with the effort.

Kun's shadow expanded, growing darker and more powerful. He towered over Streen. "Streen, take your lightsaber and finish these weaklings. Then I will allow you to live."

Streen heard the blood sing in his ears as his body strained for oxygen. The rushing sound reminded him of blowing wind, gale-force storms. Wind. Air. He grasped the wind with his Jedi powers, moving the air itself and making it flow into his lungs, past Kun's invisible stranglehold.

Cool, sweet oxygen filled him, and Streen exhaled and inhaled again. Reaching out with his power, he did the same for all the other Jedi students, nudging air into their lungs—helping them breathe, helping them grow stronger.

"We are more powerful than you," Dorsk 81 said, gasping, in a tone that mixed challenge with amazement.

"How you must hate me," Exar Kun said. Desperation tinged the edges of his voice. "I can feel your anger."

Cilghal used the silken ambassadorial voice she had worked so hard to develop. "There is no anger," she said. "We don't hate you, Exar Kun. You are an object lesson for us. You have taught us much about what it is to be a true Jedi. By observing you we see that the dark side has little strength of its own. You have no power that we do not have. You merely used our own weaknesses against us."

"We have seen enough of you," Kam Solusar said grimly from the edge of the circle, "and it's time for you to be vanquished."

The Jedi trainees stepped closer together, cinching the circle around the trapped shadowy form. Streen held his lightsaber high, while across the circle Kirana Ti raised hers to a striking position. The nebulous glow around the new Jedi Knights grew brighter, a luminous fog that joined them in an unbroken ring, a solid band of light forged by the power of the Force within them.

"I know your flaws," Kun said stridently. "You all have weaknesses. You—" The shadow lunged toward the streamlined form of Dorsk 81. The cloned Jedi candidate flinched, but the other trainees gave him strength.

"You: Dorsk 81, a failure!" He sneered. "Eighty generations of your genetic structure were perfect, identical—but you were an anomaly. You were an outcast. A flaw."

But the olive-skinned alien would not back down. "Our differences make us strong," he said. "I've learned that."

"And you"—Exar Kun whirled to Tionne—"you have no Jedi powers. You are laughable. You can only sing songs about great deeds, while others go out and actually do them."

Tionne smiled at him. Her mother-of-pearl eyes glittered in the dim light. "Someday the songs will tell of our great victory over Exar Kun—and I will sing them."

The glow continued to brighten as the synergy between the trainees grew more powerful, weaving threads to reinforce their weak spots, to emphasize their strengths.

Streen wasn't sure exactly when another image joined the Jedi candidates. He saw a new form without a physical body—short and hunched, with withered hands held in front of it. A misshapen funnel face, whiskered with tentacles, stared with small eyes hooded by a shelf of brow. Streen recognized the ancient Jedi Master Vodo-Siosk Baas, who had spoken to them from the Holocron.

Kun's image also saw the ancient Jedi Master, and his expression froze in a sculpted grimace of astonishment.

"Together Jedi can overcome their weaknesses," Master Vodo said in a bubbly, congested voice. "Exar Kun, my student—you are defeated at last."

"No!" the shadow screamed in a night-rending voice as the silhouette fought to discover a part of the circle he could breach.

"Yes," came another voice, a strong voice. Opposite Master Vodo glimmered the faint, washed-out form of a young man in Jedi robes. Master Skywalker.

"The way to extinguish a shadow," Cilghal said in her calm and confident voice, "is to increase the light."

Kirana Ti stepped forward with the lightsaber that had been built by Gantoris. Streen met her with Luke Skywalker's lightsaber. The two stared into each other's eyes, nodded, and then struck with the brilliant luminous blades.

Their beams crossed in the middle of Exar Kun's shadowy body—pure light intersecting pure light with an explosion of lightning. The flash of dazzling white seemed as bright as an exploding sun.

Darkness flooded out of the shade of Exar Kun. The blackness shattered, and fragments flew around the circle, seeking a weak heart in which to hide.

Streen and Kirana Ti kept their lightsabers crossed, the energy sizzling and searing.

With the Force, Streen touched the winds again. The air inside the grand audience chamber swirled with increasing coriolis force to form a whirlwind. The cyclone grew tighter in an invisible knot around the shredded shadow, trapping it and carrying it up toward the rooftop and out, flinging it into the vast emptiness.

Exar Kun vanished with only a brief, curtailed scream.

The Jedi Knights stood joined together for a final moment, relishing the shared Force. Then, in exhaustion and relief and triumph, they separated from each other. The unearthly glow dissipated around them.

The image of the alien Master Vodo-Siosk Baas stared toward the ceiling, as if to catch a last glimpse of his conquered student, and then he too disappeared.

With a wheezing cough as he expelled long-trapped air from his lungs and drew in a fresh breath, Master Skywalker groaned and sat up on the stone platform.

"You've—done it!" Luke said, gaining strength with each lungful of cool, clean air. The new Jedi Knights surged toward him. "You have broken the bonds."

With squeals of delight Jacen and Jaina ran to their Uncle Luke. He pulled them into his arms. They giggled and hugged him back.

Luke Skywalker smiled out at his students, his face glowing with pride for the group of Jedi Knights he had trained.

"Together," he said, "you make a formidable team indeed! Perhaps we need no longer fear the darkness."

16

In the Sun Crusher's pilot seat Kyp Durron crouched over the controls.
He stared at the *Millennium Falcon* as if it were a demon ready to spring
at him. His fingernails scratched down the metallic surface of the navigation
panels like claws trying to dig into flesh.

His mind had been swimming with the bittersweet memories of happy
times with Han, how the two of them had careened over the ice fields
in a frantic turbo-ski run, how they had made friends in the blackness of
the spice mines, how Han had pretended not to be all choked up when
Kyp left for the Jedi academy. Part of him was appalled at the idea of
threatening Han Solo's life, that he would want to destroy the *Millennium
Falcon*.

It had seemed an easy threat, the obvious thing to do. But it came from
a dark shadow in the back of his mind. The whispering voice chewed at his
thoughts, haunted him constantly. It was the voice he had heard during his
training on Yavin 4 in the deepest night and in the echoing obsidian pyramid
far out in the jungles, and on top of the great ziggurat from which Kyp had
summoned the Sun Crusher out of the core of Yavin.

Troubled by that voice, Kyp had stolen a ship and fled to the forest moon
of Endor to meditate beside the ashes of Darth Vader's funeral pyre. He had
thought to go far enough away to escape Kun's influence, but he no longer
thought that was possible.

Kyp had traveled to the Core Systems, but still he felt the chains binding him to the Dark Lord, the malevolent obligations required by the Sith teachings. If he tried to resist and think for himself, the angry tauntings returned with full force, the snapped words, the coercions, the veiled threats.

But Han Solo's words tugged at him too—weapons of a different sort that made his heart grow warm, melting the ice of anger. Right now Exar Kun's voice seemed distracted and distant, as if preoccupied with another challenge.

As Kyp listened to Han's words, he realized that his friend, knowing little about Jedi teachings, had put his finger on the truth. He *was* following the dark side. Kyp's weak justifications crumbled around him in a storm of excuses built on a fragile foundation of revenge.

"Han . . . I—"

But just as he had been about to speak warmly to Han, to open up and ask his friend to come talk with him—suddenly his controls went dead. An override signal from the *Falcon*'s computer had shut down the Sun Crusher's weapons systems, its navigation controls, its life support.

The black net of anger fell over him, smothering his kind intentions. In outrage Kyp found the power to send a burst of controlling thought through the integrated circuits in the Sun Crusher's computer. He flushed the alien programming, wiping pathways clean and rebuilding them in an instant. He remapped the functions with a sudden mental pinpoint that made the Sun Crusher whole again. The systems hummed as they returned to life, charging up.

Exar Kun had also been betrayed by his supposed partner, the warlord Ulic Qel-Droma. Now Han had betrayed Kyp. Master Skywalker had also betrayed him by failing to teach the appropriate lessons . . . appropriate defenses against Exar Kun. In his head the voice of the Sith Lord shouted for him to kill Han Solo, to destroy the enemy. To let his anger flow through and be strong.

It overwhelmed Kyp. He squeezed his dark eyes shut, unable to watch as his hands gripped the control levers for launching the torpedo. He primed the system. The screens blinked with warning signals, which he disregarded.

He needed to destroy something. He needed to kill those who had betrayed him. His fists gripped the firing handles. His thumbs rested on the launch buttons, squeezing, ready—

Squeezing—

And then the haunting voice of Exar Kun rose to a wail in his mind, an utterly forlorn scream as if he were being torn out of this universe and exiled to another place entirely, where he could torment Kyp Durron no more.

Kyp snapped backward in his control seat as if an invisible tow cable had been severed. His arms and head dangled like a puppet with suddenly snipped strings. The cool wind of freedom whistled through his mind and body. He blinked his eyes and shuddered with revulsion at what he had been about to do.

The *Millennium Falcon* still gripped the Sun Crusher in its tractor beam. As Kyp saw the battered old ship, Han Solo's prize possession, he felt a tidal wave of despair.

Kyp reached out to the energy torpedo controls and vehemently canceled the firing sequence. The plasma generator flickered and faded as the energy died away.

Without the presence of Exar Kun inside him, Kyp felt isolated, suddenly in free fall—but independent.

He opened the communication channel but couldn't form words for a few moments. His throat was dry. It felt as if he hadn't had anything to eat or drink in four thousand years.

"Han," he croaked, and said louder, "Han, this is Kyp! I . . ." He paused, not knowing what next to say—what else he *could* say.

He hung his head and finally finished, "I surrender."

17

The Twi'lek Tol Sivron still felt jangled from his horrendous passage through the Maw, escaping from the Rebel invasion force and riding the gravity between black holes.

His long head-tails tingled with a rush of impressions, delighted to see that the information he had long ago stolen from Daala's secret files—the list of tortuous safe routes through the black hole cluster—had been accurate. If the course map had been the least bit imprecise, he and his retreating crew would not be alive now.

The Death Star prototype lurched under full power as it emerged safely from the cluster, but just as it sped away from the sinuous, brilliant gases, the propulsion systems fizzled and went off-line.

Sparks showered from panels as the stormtrooper captain shut down the engine power and rerouted systems. Yemm attempted to use a manual fire-extinguishing apparatus to squelch flames licking out of a nearby console, but he succeeded only in short-circuiting the intercom systems.

Golanda and Doxin flipped furiously through repair manuals and design specifications.

"Director," the stormtrooper captain said, "we have successfully broken free from the Maw, though the strain has caused a good deal of damage."

Doxin looked up, scowling. "I remind you that this was a nonhardened prototype, never meant to be actually deployed."

"Yes, sir," the stormtrooper said in an inflectionless voice. "As I was about to say, I believe the damage can be repaired in only a few days. It is a simple matter of bypassing circuits and reinitializing computer systems. I believe after this shakedown the prototype will be in much better shape for combat."

Tol Sivron rubbed his hands together and smiled. "Good, good." He leaned back in the pilot's chair. "That will give us time to select a suitable target for our first attack."

Golanda called up a navigational chart, displayed across the viewscreen. "Director, the Kessel system is very close, as you know. Perhaps we should—"

"Let's get the propulsion units up and running again before we plan too far ahead," Doxin interrupted. "Our ultimate strategy may depend on our capabilities."

Yemm tore the cover off the communications panel and squinted down into the morass of blackened wires, sniffing the burned insulation.

Golanda kept studying her station, calling up readings from the prototype's exterior sensors. "Director, I've found something puzzling. Looking at the gas turbulence that surrounds the black hole cluster, it appears that another very large ship has recently entered the Maw, only moments ago. It seems to have followed one of the other paths Admiral Daala designated as a safe route through to the Installation." She looked at him, and Tol Sivron flinched away from her unpleasant face. "We just missed them."

Sivron didn't know what she was talking about, nor why it should concern him. All of these frantic problems were like stinging insects buzzing around his head, and he swatted at them.

"We can't do anything about that now," he said. "It's probably another Rebel ship coming to mop up the invasion of our facility." He sighed. "We'll get back at them, as soon as we get the Death Star up and running again."

He leaned back in his pilot's chair and closed his beady eyes, longing for just a moment's peace. He wished he had never left his home planet of Ryloth, where the Twi'lek people lived deep within mountain catacombs in the habitable band of twilight that separated the baking heat of day from the frigid cold of endless night.

Tol Sivron thought of more peaceful days, breathing the stale air through gaps in his pointed teeth. The heat storms on Ryloth brought sufficient warmth into the twilight zone to make the planet habitable, though desolate.

The Twi'leks built their society around the governorship of a five-member "head-clan" who led the community in all matters until such time as one of them died. At this point the Twi'leks cast out the remaining members of the head-clan to the blasted wasteland—and presumably to their deaths—while they selected a fresh group of rulers.

Tol Sivron had been a member of the head-clan, pampered and spoiled by the benefits of power. The entire clan was young and vigorous, and Sivron had expected to reap the benefits of his position for many years—spacious quarters, Twi'lek dancing women renowned throughout the galaxy, delicacies of raw meat that he could tear with his pointed teeth and savor the spicy liquid flavors. . . .

But the good life had lasted barely a standard year. One of his idiot companions had lost his balance on a scaffolding while inspecting a deep-grotto construction project and had fallen to impale himself upon a ten-thousand-year-old stalagmite.

According to their custom, the Twi'lek people had exiled Tol Sivron and the other three members of the head-clan into the blasted deserts of the dayside to face the heat storms and the scouring wind.

They had resigned themselves to death, but Tol Sivron had convinced the other three that if they worked together, they could survive, perhaps eke out an existence in an uninhabited cave farther down the spine of mountains.

The others had agreed, clinging to any hope; and then, as they slept that night, Tol Sivron had killed them all, taking their meager possessions to increase his own chances of survival. Covering himself with thick layers of garments stripped from the dead bodies of his companions, he had trudged across the fiery landscape, not knowing what he was searching for. . . .

Tol Sivron had thought the glittering ships were mere mirages until he stumbled into the encampment. It was a rugged training base and refueling station for the Imperial navy, frequented by smugglers but supported by the Empire.

Tol Sivron had met a man named Tarkin there, an ambitious young commander who already had several ships and who intended to make the small outpost on Ryloth a strategically important refueling station in the Outer Rim.

Over the years, Tol Sivron had worked for Tarkin, proving himself to be an unparalleled manager, a skillful arranger of the complex business that Tarkin—then *Moff* Tarkin, then *Grand* Moff Tarkin—had under way.

Sivron's career had culminated in his directorship of Maw Installation—which he had now fled in the face of a Rebel invasion. If Tarkin was still alive, the embarrassing retreat would no doubt figure negatively in Tol Sivron's next performance appraisal.

He had to do something to make up for it, posthaste.

"Director," Yemm said, interrupting his thoughts. "I think the comm system is functioning again. It will be ready to use as soon as I log the modifications into its maintenance record."

Sivron sat up. "At least something works around here."

Yemm entered numbers into one of the computer stations and nodded his horned head at Tol Sivron. "Ready, Director."

"Turn it on," he said. "Let me speak to the crew." His last words echoed through the speakers, startling him. He cleared his throat and leaned closer to the voice pickup on the pilot's chair.

"Attention, everyone! Hurry with those repairs," he snapped into the intercom. His voice sounded like the commands of a deity as he spoke through all levels. "I want to destroy something as soon as possible." He switched off.

The stormtrooper captain turned to him. "We will do our best, sir. I should have final repair estimates within a few hours."

"Good, good." He stared across the open emptiness of space, looking at all the possible starpoint targets.

Tol Sivron had in his possession one of the most devastating weapons in the galaxy. But it remained untested. For now.

18

The second timed detonation occurred just as Wedge Antilles and his assault squad charged into the Maw Installation's power-reactor complex. Shaped charges planted by a sabotage crew exploded at the base of the reactor's cooling towers, shutting down the enormous generator that powered the facilities, the laboratories, the mainframe computers, and life-support systems.

Wearing mottled brown-and-gray body armor, Wedge had led his assault team across the connector-tube catwalks to the power asteroid. But just as the squad entered, gouts of gray smoke spurted through the tunnels, carrying dust and debris along with a hot wind.

Wedge shook his head to clear his ringing ears. He climbed to his knees and then to his feet again. "I need an assessment of the damages," he shouted. "Quick!"

Three of the leading soldiers raced down the hall only to encounter a group of Maw Installation personnel fleeing the wreckage. The saboteurs were led by a one-armed brute of a man with purplish-green skin and a sour expression.

Wedge's team snapped up their weapons, training the barrels of their blaster rifles on the saboteurs, who halted with a clatter like machine components locking into place. The one-armed man skidded to a stop and looked around wildly. The rest of his crew glared at the New Republic soldiers.

"Drop your weapons!" Wedge said.

The large brute raised his single hand, palm outward, to show that he carried no weapons. Wedge was surprised to see that the others were also unarmed.

"It's too late to stop anything," the one-armed man said. "I am Wermyn, Division Leader for Plant Operations. Accept my surrender. My team and I would appreciate it if you'd get us off this rock before the whole thing explodes."

Wedge pointed to four of his soldiers. "Use binders, see that the prisoners are secured. We've got to get that power reactor functioning again, or we'll have to evacuate."

The Maw saboteurs did not resist as the squad took them into custody, though Wedge's men looked confused about how to apply binders to Wermyn's single arm.

Wedge and the technicians proceeded cautiously into the reactor housing. The heat struck him like a sandwhirl during the hot season on Tatooine. The air smelled thick with acrid lubricants, molten metal, and charred high-energy explosive.

Red warning lights flooded the chamber, reflecting from whistling jets of steam like droplets of flying blood. Laboring pumps and engines thudded with a pounding beat that made Wedge's skull ache. A large reactor component had been slagged, left with ragged, dripping edges.

He squinted as the techs ran forward, yanking handheld detectors from their belts to study radiation leaks. One trotted up to Wedge. "Both the primary and the backup cooling pumps have been destroyed. Our friend Wermyn was right. He has initiated a meltdown, and there's nothing we can do to stop it. We can't fix this equipment."

"Can we shut down the reactor?" Wedge said.

"It's been locked on, and the controls are destroyed," the tech answered. "I suppose there's a chance we could reroute and rig up temporary systems in an hour or two, but if we shut the reactor down, we also terminate power and life support to the Installation."

Wedge looked around the wreckage as his stomach sank. With his boot he kicked a broken piece of plasteel shielding. It clattered hollowly across the floor until the throbbing engines swallowed the sound.

"I didn't lead this strike force just to let all the scientists and the Death Star get away while the whole Installation is destroyed under my feet." He drew a deep breath and tapped his fingers together in an attempt to concentrate, as Qwi often did, though he wasn't sure it worked.

Then he yanked the comm link from his hip and gripped it, toggling on the frequency for the flagship *Yavaris*. "Captain," he said, "get me some engineering experts right away. We need to rig up emergency cooling pumps for the main power reactor.

"I know we don't have much equipment, but our hyperdrive cooling systems shouldn't be too dissimilar to what this reactor uses. Take one of the corvettes off line and remove the engine pumps. We've got to get something working down here to hold us until we can remove everything of value."

The two technicians looked up at Wedge and smiled. "That just might work, sir."

Wedge ushered them back to where the prisoners were held, vowing not to let the Imperials win so easily.

Qwi Xux felt like a stranger in her own house. She walked timidly into the room she had identified as her former laboratory, expecting something to jump out at her, memories to come flooding back.

The illumination came on, shedding a cold white glow on the design apparatus, her computer terminals, her furniture. This place had been her home, the center of her life for more than a decade. But it looked like a foreign land to her now. She stared in amazement and sighed.

See-Threepio whirred as he followed her into the room. "I still don't know why I'm here, Dr. Xux. I can assist you in assimilating the leftover data, but I'm a protocol droid, not a slicer. Perhaps you should have brought my counterpart Artoo-Detoo? He's much better at this sort of thing than I am. He is a fine model, but a bit too headstrong for a droid, if you catch my meaning."

Qwi ignored him as she stepped farther into the room, walking on tiptoes. Her skin felt cold and clammy. The air smelled stale, empty. She trembled as she ran her fingers along the cool synthetic stone of the thick support pillars. She caught a flash of distant memory—a ragged Han Solo tied to this pillar, barely able to hold his head upright after the "deep interrogation" Admiral Daala had performed on him. . . .

Qwi went over to the lab table, picked up her spectral-analysis sensors, materials-properties analyzers, stress and strain simulators, and a holographic 3-D design projector that glittered darkly under the bright lights.

"My, this appears to be a completely adequate workspace, Dr. Xux," Threepio said. "Spacious and clean. I'm sure you accomplished a great deal here. Believe me, I've seen far more cluttered research areas in facilities on Coruscant."

"Threepio, why don't you take an inventory of the equipment you see," Qwi told him, just to keep the droid quiet so she could think. "Pay particular attention to any demonstration models you find. Those could be significant."

Qwi discovered a small musical keypad lying half-hidden in a pile of printouts and handwritten notes. Beside the keypad stood the milky eye of a powerless computer terminal.

She switched the terminal on, but the screen demanded her password before it would allow her access to her own files. So much for that.

Qwi picked up the musical keypad and cradled it. The instrument felt familiar and yet alien. She touched a few of the keys and listened to the soft, high notes that issued from it. She remembered standing in the shattered debris of the Cathedral of Winds, picking up a fragment of one of the windpipes and blowing a slow, mournful melody through it. The winged Vors had snatched the flute from her, insisting that there be no more music until the cathedral itself was rebuilt. . . .

But this keypad held her own music. Qwi vaguely recalled using it, but she couldn't quite picture for what. A flickering image came to mind, like a slick, wet fruit that slipped from her fingers every time she tried to grasp it—*setting the keypad down, suspecting she might never come back.* . . . She winced, drew a breath, and tapped her fingers together, trying to think.

Han Solo! Yes, she had left everything untouched as she attempted to rescue Han and escape with the Sun Crusher.

She let her long blue fingers dance across the musical keys. Her mind remembered no particular sequence, but her body knew. Her hands moved by habit, tapping out a quick loop of melody. She smiled—it seemed so familiar to her.

When she finished the sequence of notes, her computer screen winked, PASSWORD ACCEPTED. She blinked her indigo eyes, astonished at what she had done.

ERROR, the computer printed. MAIN DATABASE UNAVAIL-ABLE . . . SEARCHING FOR BACKUPS. FILES DAMAGED.

Qwi suspected Tol Sivron might have destroyed the computer core before fleeing in the Death Star prototype. But she must have left *something* stored within the temporary memory of her own terminal.

RECOVERED FILES FOLLOW, the screen said.

Qwi looked through a window into her own journals, her personal notes. Her heart pounded as she scanned words she herself had typed—but it was *not* herself. It was another Qwi Xux, a Qwi from the past who had been brainwashed by Imperials, a Qwi who had been twisted as a child and forced to perform to the utter limits of her mental abilities.

Taking shallow breaths, she read her daily accounts with growing uneasi-ness: the experiments she had performed, simulations she had run on the computer, meetings she had attended, endless progress reports she had filed for Director Sivron. Though she remembered none of it, it appalled her to realize that she had done nothing but work. Her only joy had come from completed experiments—her only moments of excitement, when tests proved her designs to be reliable.

"Was this all my life was?" Qwi asked. She scrolled down, scanning day after identical day. "How . . . empty!" she muttered.

"Excuse me?" Threepio said. "Did you ask for assistance?"

"Oh, Threepio." She shook her head and found tears stinging her eyes.

She heard footsteps in the outer corridor and turned as Wedge entered the lab. His face was smudged with grime, his uniform rumpled. He looked sweaty and exhausted, but she rushed to him and hugged him. He squeezed her shoulders, then ran his fingers through her feathery pearlescent hair.

"Is it bad?" he said. "Sorry I couldn't be here when you first entered the lab. I had an emergency."

Qwi shook her head. "No, I had to face this myself anyway."

"Find anything useful?" He stepped away from her, becoming the general again. "We need to know how many scientists were at the Installation. Most got away on the Death Star, but any information you have . . ."

Qwi stiffened and looked back at her computer terminal. "I'm not sure I can help you." Her voice carried a desolate, lost quality. "I've been looking over my daily life. It doesn't look like I *knew* any of the other scientists. I . . . I had no friends here." She looked at him, widening her depthless eyes.

"More than ten years of my life, and I knew no one. I worked. I thought I was dedicated. Defeating universal challenges meant a great deal to me— but I didn't even know what it was for. All I cared about was finding the next solution. How could I have been so naive?"

Wedge gave her an encouraging hug. He felt so warm and comforting against her. "That's all over, Qwi. It'll never happen to you again. You've been let out of a cage, and I'm here to help show you the rest of the universe— if you'll come along with me."

"Yes, Wedge." She looked up at him with a faint smile. "Of course I'll come with you."

Wedge's comm link beeped at him from his waist, and he pulled it out with a sigh. "Yes, what is it?" he said.

"General Antilles, we've brought down some temporary equipment to the reactor facility. We modified the critical components taken from one of the corvettes, as you suggested. We've managed to emplace them, and the systems are marginally functional. The core temperature levels of the reactor have begun dropping, and we expect them to go below the red lines within the next several hours."

"Good. Do we have a time limit here, then?" Wedge said.

"Well . . . ," the technician's voice answered, "the reactors are still shaky, but they're stable for now."

"Good work," Wedge said. "Pass along my commendations to your people."

"Yes, sir."

Wedge switched off and smiled at Qwi. "See, everything's working out after all," he said. She nodded, raising her face to look through the long, narrow window at the top of the wall. Pools of hot gas drifted around the Maw's black holes.

They seemed safe here, walled off from the conflicts of the galaxy. Qwi had fought her greatest personal battles, and now she could allow herself to relax just a little.

But before she could turn away, she saw a shadow appear in the multicolored nebula—a huge triangular shape, like a spear point plunging through the gases and emerging into the safe gravitational island.

Qwi stiffened, biting back an outcry of panic.

Wedge let go of her and whirled, looking up.

"Oh, dear!" Threepio said.

Battered and blackened, an Imperial Star Destroyer came through the Maw with its weapons already powering up. Its once-white hull was blistered and streaked with burn marks; its shielding plates damaged by an inferno of destruction.

Admiral Daala's flagship, the *Gorgon*, had returned to Maw Installation.

19

The Imperial Spider Walkers ascended the steep, pitted stone pinnacle. Their long metal legs bent at odd angles as their claws hauled them toward the heavy blast doors protecting Winter and baby Anakin.

Winter stood in the operations room, her jaw clenched, her eyes narrowed, as she viewed the progress of the assault transports. They had reached her first line of defenses.

When establishing the Anoth hiding place, Admiral Ackbar and Luke Skywalker had been unwilling to rely entirely on secrecy. They had tried to plan for every possible attack scenario. Winter had hoped she would never need to test those contingency plans, but now she had to fight for the child's life—and her own.

Winter looked down at her status panels: the Foreign Intruder Defense Organism was primed and ready for automatic strike. She anticipated that FIDO could take out at least two of the Spider Walkers. She watched, gripping the edge of the consoles to steady herself.

Scuttling up the rock wall with insectile legs, the Spider Walkers reached a line of caves, small openings to a labyrinth of dead ends and grottoes within the stone.

Winter tensed as the first two MT-ATs passed, unsuspecting, over the black openings. The uppermost assault walker paused and fired a preemptive strike against the blast doors above with two forward lasers. A muffled thump and clang reverberated through the sealed installation.

As the second Spider Walker also prepared to fire, masses of whip-like tentacles lashed out of the hidden caves, long ropes each ending in a razor-sharp pincer claw. The tentacles took the Spider Walkers completely by surprise.

Two of FIDO's writhing arms locked around the first walker and ripped it from the cliff face. Before the machine could use its pneumatic claws to grasp the rock again, FIDO tossed the Spider Walker over the edge.

The MT-AT tumbled in a long clatter of wildly gesticulating legs. On its way down the Walker clipped another of the assault transports; the two plummeted together and exploded in a fiery crash on the jagged ground below.

The second Spider Walker fired with its laser cannon into the dark caves. One of FIDO's tentacles, black and smoking, withdrew like a flicked whip, vanishing deep into the tunnels; but other tentacles emerged from different openings to wrap around the Walker in a stranglehold. In desperation the turbolaser fired again, dislodging chunks of rock. FIDO squeezed, bending the articulated legs until their hinges groaned and thick rivets popped out.

Sensor-tipped tentacles comprehended what the cockpit of the MT-AT was for. FIDO's heavy plasteel claws smashed through the armored canopy, tearing open the roof and plucking out two stormtroopers to toss them over the precipice like gnawed bones discarded after a feast. Unmanned, the walker skidded down the cliff face as the remaining five assault transports scuttled out of the way.

Winter clenched her fist and slowed her shallow breathing. She tried to calm herself. The defending semiorganic droid had succeeded in removing three of the attacking machines, but the remaining five would almost certainly destroy FIDO.

Ackbar had proposed modeling a guardian droid after the dreaded sea monster from Calamari, the krakana. Calamarian scientists had designed a resilient, partially sentient machine that mimicked many of the krakana's most fearsome traits. Its tentacles were threaded with durasteel cables, its pincers plated with razor-edged alloys. FIDO's existence centered on protecting the base. The droid tentacles writhed out from the cavern, searching for more prey.

Three of the remaining assault walkers hauled themselves up on either side of the catacomb openings to fire repeatedly into the caves. Unexpectedly, from an apparently empty side hole, another trio of tentacles grabbed one of the Spider Walkers, dragging it toward the central cluster of cave openings.

Winter marveled at the tactic. Not only was FIDO destroying another one of the vehicles, it was also using the MT-AT as a shield. But the other Walkers did not stop shooting. Stormtroopers considered each other expendable for the sake of a mission.

The occupants of the captured Spider Walker continued to fire. FIDO dragged the MT-AT closer, crushing it against the rock like a thick-skinned jewel fruit. At close range the stormtrooper pilot powered up his low-slung, high-power blaster cannons and fired a combined blast into the caves. The enormous explosion ripped out a vast chunk of the catacombed understructure. Flames and dust, broken rocks and volatile gases, sprayed in a plume that rose into the violet skies of Anoth. The backwash vaporized FIDO's body core and, simultaneously, detonated the captured Spider Walker.

Inside the operations room FIDO's diagnostic panel went blank. Winter rubbed her fingertips along the smooth surface of the screen. The first line of defense had taken out half the assault transports. "Good job, FIDO," she whispered. "Thank you."

The multilegged assault transports began pounding against the blast doors. The thumps of turbolaser impacts and the screeching resistance of heavy metal filled the air.

Winter knew what she had to do. She toggled on the other automatic defense systems before fleeing the operations room. With silent footsteps she hurried down to the grotto, where Admiral Ackbar had recently come to visit her in his personal B-wing. Winter wished the Calamarian admiral could be at her side right now. She knew she could always count on him, but right now she had to act for herself and young Anakin.

She ruthlessly clamped down on her personal fears and forced herself to do what had to be done. No time for panic. She ran along the tunnels, leaving the metal hatches open for escape once the stormtroopers saw her. When she emerged into the landing grotto, the repeated thudding explosions from outside nearly deafened her.

The blast doors buckled inward, dented and glowing cherry-red as continued laser fire melted away the outer armor, chewing into the super-dense metal core. The doors bent as she watched; a split appeared in the middle.

Articulated claws pushed through the opening. Laser strikes continued around the attachment bolts until the left-side door twisted. The other door hung askew in its track.

Whistling wind shrieked into the landing grotto as Winter stood ready to face the assault.

With a whir of straining engines, the Spider Walkers clambered into the chamber, bristling with weapons and manned by crack stormtroopers.

The Dreadnaught *Vendetta* maintained its position in orbit. Colonel Ardax touched his fingertips to the voice pickup in his ear, listening to the report from the assault team on the planetoid below.

"We have succeeded in breaching the blast doors, Colonel," the stormtrooper commander said into the radio. "Losses have been heavy. Rebel defenses are stronger than anticipated. We are proceeding with caution, but we expect to have the Jedi child in hand shortly."

"Keep me updated," Ardax said. "Report to me when the mission is completed, and we will arrange for pickup." He paused. "Was Ambassador Furgan one of the casualties?"

"No, sir," the stormtrooper said. "He was in the rearmost assault transport and faced no direct danger."

Colonel Ardax signed off. "A pity."

Ardax was looking out at the three locked planetoids when sudden alarms rang through the *Vendetta*'s control deck. "What's that?"

A lieutenant looked up from his sensor station, his face ashen. "Sir, a Rebel battleship has just come out of hyperspace! It outguns us by a substantial margin."

"Prepare to take evasive action," Colonel Ardax said. "It appears that we've been betrayed." He drew a cold breath through gritted teeth. Furgan must have somehow given away their plans to Rebel spies.

The wide communications screen sizzled with gray static that resolved into the image of a fish-headed Calamarian. "This is Ackbar, in command of the star cruiser *Galactic Voyager*. Surrender and prepare to be boarded. Any New Republic hostages you have taken must be returned unharmed."

"Reply, Colonel?" the communications officer said.

"Our silence is enough of an answer," Ardax said. "Right now our primary objective is to survive. The surface team is forfeit. Set course to fly between the two close components of Anoth. The electrical discharges will mask us from their sensors, and from that point we can escape into hyperspace. Shields at maximum."

"Yes, sir," the tactical officer said. The navigator set a course.

"Full speed ahead when ready," Colonel Ardax said. He paced on the control deck.

With a lurch the *Vendetta* accelerated toward the broken planet. The Rebel battleship fired at them. The Dreadnaught rattled and shook as heavy explosions struck its shields.

"They outgun us, sir, but they are aiming to disable, not to destroy."

Colonel Ardax raised his eyebrows. "Ah, of course—they think we've got the child already! Let's not convince them otherwise."

The *Vendetta* sped into the grinding jaws of the broken world.

Leia squeezed until her nails bit into the smooth fabric of Ackbar's command chair on the *Galactic Voyager*. The battered old Dreadnaught wheeled in its orbit and set a new course. "They're calling your bluff, Admiral," she said.

"They are not responding," Ackbar agreed.

"They won't respond," Terpfen said, sullen at an auxiliary station. "They will run. If they already have the baby, there is nothing to keep them here. They won't risk a fight against a superior battleship."

Leia swallowed, knowing Terpfen was right. She wished Han could be beside her right now.

"Then we must not let them get away," Ackbar said. He had stuck close to Terpfen's side throughout the journey. During the mustering of the rescue force, Ackbar had snatched the most loyal members of his salvage crew on Reef Home City; he had gathered others from the starship construction yards in orbit. In all that time he had not once mentioned Terpfen's treachery.

Ackbar and Terpfen were having some kind of silent conflict, a wrestling of wills. Ackbar claimed he understood how the other had been manipulated. He himself had been a prisoner of the Empire, but instead of being programmed as a spy and saboteur, he had served as an unwilling liaison to Moff Tarkin. Though those times had been oppressive, Ackbar had managed to turn his close association with the cruel strategist into an advantage during Admiral Daala's attack on Calamari. Now, he claimed, it was time for Terpfen to use his misery against the Imperials as well.

As Leia watched from the bridge of the *Galactic Voyager*, the blunt-ended Dreadnaught ignited its sublight engines. She closed her eyes, gripped the back of Ackbar's chair, and sent out a tendril of thought with her mind to seek the presence of baby Anakin, hoping to find him or comfort him.

She sensed her baby across the vast distance of space, but could not pinpoint his location, feeling only his presence in the Force. She could make no direct contact, could not see him. Anakin could still be on Anoth, or he could be a prisoner aboard the Dreadnaught.

"Crippling strikes only. Fire all forward weapons," Ackbar said in a maddeningly calm voice. "Cause only enough damage to prevent them from entering hyperspace."

High-powered energy beams splashed against the *Vendetta*'s heavy shields. Residual radiation glowed from the hits, showing minor damage to the Imperial ship's hull. But the Dreadnaught continued to accelerate.

"He's going between two of the planetoids," Leia said.

Terpfen leaned forward with interest, swiveling his round eyes as he concentrated. "He's trying to use the static discharges as camouflage," he said. "With so much ionization scramble we'll lose him on our sensors. Then he can escape on any heading before we find him again."

Leia breathed deeply to subdue her anxiety. They were so close—why else would the Dreadnaught run, unless they already had Anakin on board? Again she tried to sense where the baby was.

The two atmosphere-swathed fragments of Anoth's primary body loomed ahead of the Dreadnaught, with only a tight channel between the lumps. Fingernails of lightning skittered from one atmosphere to the other as the orbiting shards built up an incredible electrostatic charge.

"Increase speed," Ackbar said. "Stop them before we lose them in the static."

The Dreadnaught captain still refused to respond.

"Fire again," Ackbar said. "Increase power."

Turbolasers struck the starboard side of the *Vendetta*, shoving it visibly to one side with the momentum of the blasts. Its shields buckled; parts of the Dreadnaught's sublight engines were crippled. But the captain continued his flight. The blue-white exhaust glow increased as the engines powered up, readying for a jump into hyperspace.

"No!" Leia cried. "Don't let them take Anakin away!" Before she could finish her sentence, the Dreadnaught passed into the narrow passage between the split planet.

A blinding blue tracery of static blanketed the outer shields of the *Vendetta*, like a half-formed cocoon. The glow of an ionization cone spread out in front of it as it plowed through the thickening atmosphere into spectacular storms.

Leia squeezed her eyes shut, concentrating, concentrating. If she could establish a link between Anakin's mind and hers, she had some minuscule chance of tracking him once the Dreadnaught vanished into hyperspace.

She sensed the people onboard the Imperial battleship—but she felt no glimmer of her own son, nor of her longtime companion Winter. Leia reached out wider with her searching thoughts as the *Vendetta* plowed through the thin bottleneck of atmosphere.

The giant armored ship was like a metal probe between a pair of fully charged batteries. The Dreadnaught became a short circuit across the two supercharged atmospheres.

A colossal lightning bolt blasted through the atmosphere and linked across the warship like a chain of fire. A river of raw power slammed into the *Vendetta* from both sides, obliterating it in a hurricane of searing electricity, leaving only a burned afterimage on the screen.

Ackbar gasped audibly and hung his head. Terpfen slumped in his chair, but Leia observed the destruction with only part of her mind. She cast across space—until at last she found the bright point that was her youngest son, Anakin.

Terpfen stood up as if already bound in thick chains. "Minister Organa Solo, I submit myself to—"

Leia shook her head. "No punishment, Terpfen. Anakin is still alive. He's on the planet. But right now he's in terrible danger. We have to hurry."

20

Winter crouched by the metal hatch outside the landing grotto. She held a blaster pistol in one hand, knowing her white hair and light robes would make her easily visible even in the dimness.

Four huge mechanical assault transports picked their way over the wreckage of the left blast door and halted with hissing engines in the middle of the grotto. Transparisteel canopies flipped up with a high-pitched whir to disgorge stormtroopers.

Flicking her eyes from side to side, Winter took a quick inventory. Each of the four Spider Walkers carried two troopers—eight targets. She steadied her blaster and aimed at the nearest white-armored soldier.

Winter fired off three shots in quick succession. She couldn't tell how many actually hit the trooper, but he flew backward with his armor blasted to pieces. Other soldiers boiled out of the transports, firing in her direction.

Winter hunched down, but could not get another shot in. The last Spider Walker opened up to reveal one stormtrooper and a squat man with huge eyebrows and thick lips.

The other troopers had pinpointed Winter's position next to the door and hammered repeated blasts at her. She backed toward the open hatch.

Winter had two choices: she could either run back and stay with Anakin to defend him with her life—or she could lure the seven remaining invaders away from the baby and do her best to dispose of them.

Winter squeezed the firing button of her blaster without aiming. Bright streaks ricocheted around the grotto. The squat man ducked under the low-slung cockpit of a Spider Walker. "Go get her!" he yelled.

One of the stormtroopers, still in the cockpit of an MT-AT, brought laser cannons to bear and shot at the wall beside her head, leaving a smoking crater.

The squat man screamed from his hiding place under the MT-AT, "Don't kill her. Use stun until you have the child. You"—he gestured to the trooper who had emerged from the Spider Walker with him—"come with me, we'll . . . provide reconnaissance. The rest of you—capture that woman!"

Exactly as Winter had hoped. She fled down the corridor, knowing that most of the assault team would follow her. She sped along the sloping tunnels, ducking low through jagged archways, slamming heavy air-lock doors behind her as she passed into a deeper level of the installation.

The stormtroopers followed, making short work of the thick hatches by using focused thermal detonators that blasted the metal doors out of their seams.

Winter led them through the labyrinth of passages, farther and farther away from baby Anakin. The stormtroopers would be completely disoriented by now.

The troopers fired whenever they got a clear shot, but Winter managed to avoid being blasted to pieces. She heaved a sigh of relief—the only emotional release she allowed herself—when she finally succeeded in leading the troopers into the subterranean generator room and computer core.

The chamber itself was a dim morass of tangled equipment, cooling ducts, metal pipes, and throbbing life-support systems. The computer core glowed with oblong green lights that flickered in a waterfall pattern. The computers themselves, incorporated into the pumping stations and generator housing, formed a surrealistic cluster of twisted metal and plastic and a confusion of transparisteel diagnostic screens, input/output terminals—more equipment than anyone could possibly fathom a purpose for.

Winter knew the equipment was just stage dressing to hide the real purpose of the chamber.

The troopers hesitated at the threshold, as if suspecting a trap within the shadows. Winter pointed her blaster and fired seven rapid shots at them. The stormtroopers dived for cover and then, when Winter did not fire again, charged into the dim room after her.

Winter did not try to hide. She ran to the glowing pillar of the computer core and then into shadows on the other side of the chamber, surrounded by conduits and tubes and flashing lights that served no purpose. The stormtroopers moved toward her, still shooting.

Winter fired several more times, just to provoke them, and to make sure they remained within the chamber. One of her shots ricocheted off a gleaming surface and flew into the side of a stormtrooper, melting the white armor from his right arm.

Winter appeared to be cornered at the far side of the room as the troopers advanced toward her—five of them, one hanging back with an injured arm.

The Imperial soldiers got halfway across the space before the walls began to writhe and move.

Jointed pipelines and conduits, bulky control decks, and spherical readout panels shifted, clicking together into specific components. Winter heard pieces locking into place, metal against metal, connections linking up.

The machine-filled walls suddenly became a squad of burly assassin droids assembled out of disguised components. The droids activated their weapons, forming a shooting gallery whose only purpose was to destroy stormtroopers.

Winter had no need to issue commands. The assassin droids knew exactly what they were supposed to do. They had been programmed to ignore her and the Jedi children, but they knew their targets well.

From all sides the assassin droids opened fire on the five pursuers. The cross fire of deadly beams cut down the white-armored Imperials in less than two seconds, leaving only piles of smoldering wreckage, fused and melted armor, and useless weapons in dead hands. None of the stormtroopers had an opportunity to fire a single shot.

One of the troopers groaned once, hissed in pain, then fell into the silence of death. The shadows cast a blanket over the carnage.

Heaving a sigh of relief, Winter stepped over the bodies, which were still sizzling from the massacre. She looked down at the expressionless black visors of the Imperial enemy. "Never underestimate your opponent," she said.

Ambassador Furgan crouched low as the stormtrooper sprinted ahead of him down the lumpy rock corridors.

Furgan had no combat training and no experience, but he did his best to imitate his companion's fluid movements. He held his blaster rifle in hand, glancing down repeatedly to make sure the weapon was powered up.

The tunnels were dim and shadowy, lit by white glowtubes mounted along the ceilings. The stormtrooper pressed his armor back against the wall and held his weapon around a corner to see if he drew any fire; then he jogged down to the next intersection of tunnels.

They passed door after door, unsealing each room, ready to snatch the helpless child and run back to their MT-ATs. Furgan and the trooper found storage compartments filled with crates of supplies and equipment, the dining room, empty sleeping quarters—but no child.

Far beneath them Furgan heard the patter and distant echo of blaster fire. He glared back toward the sounds. "I told them not to shoot her down. Why didn't they listen to me?" He turned to the stormtrooper. "Now we'll have to find the child all by ourselves."

"Yes, sir," the stormtrooper said, without expression.

The next metal door was locked and sealed. No one responded when the stormtrooper hammered with his white gauntlet. He withdrew a pack of tools from his utility belt, removed a high-powered cutting laser, and slashed open the door's control panel. Moving with nimble fingers despite the thick gloves, he rewired the sparking controls.

The door ground open, exposing the pastel colors of a room filled with toys, a plush bed . . . and a four-armed nanny droid backed into a protective position in the corner to shelter a small child.

"Ah, here we are at last," Furgan said. He stepped inside looking around for booby traps. The trooper flanked him, maintaining his defensive position, blaster rifle in hand. Furgan saw no other defenses, just the TDL droid.

"Please leave," the nanny droid said in a sweet, grandmotherly voice. "You are disturbing the baby."

Furgan let loose with a full-throated laugh. "The only defense they managed was *one nanny droid*?" He chuckled again. "We sent an entire assault team to take a baby away from a nanny droid?"

The TDL droid stood in front of the baby, who sat very still on the floor. The droid used her lower set of arms to unfold a blaster-proof metal apron from the base of her torso to shield the baby from stray laser fire.

"You may not have this child," the droid said. "I must warn you that my programming is to protect him at all costs."

"How touching. Well, I'm going to take that child—at all costs," Furgan said, nodding with a triumphant smile to the stormtrooper. "Go get the baby."

The stormtrooper took one step forward. The droid held out all four hands in an imperative gesture to stop. "I'm sorry, but I cannot allow that," the nanny droid said calmly. "Close your eyes, baby Anakin."

"What are you waiting for?" Furgan snapped at the trooper. "It's only a nanny droid."

With a whir and a click all four of the droid's hands detached and dropped to the floor, exposing the blaster barrels hidden in each of her wrists. "I am an *enhanced* nanny droid," she said with prim emphasis, "and you will not harm this child." She let loose with all four barrels, firing gouts of deadly energy.

The four beams struck the approaching stormtrooper before he could swing up his blaster rifle. He was hurled back against the wall, shards of white armor flying away from smoking black wounds.

Furgan yelled in astonishment and terror. He swung up his blaster rifle and depressed the firing button long before he took time to aim. A flurry of incandescent bolts sprayed across the room, reflecting from the pastel walls, bouncing off the corners.

Furgan ducked, but continued to fire. The nanny droid centered all four blaster arms on him—but Furgan raked his stream of blaster bolts across her rounded head and soft, flesh-encased torso, succeeding more through luck than skill. Sparks flew and molten metal showered in all directions.

Beneath the blaster-proof apron, the baby began to wail.

Bruise-colored lips curved upward in a smile, Furgan stepped over the debris of the nanny droid and the dead stormtrooper to retrieve the child. He reached down to grab one of little Anakin's arms and yanked him into the air by the cloth of his pajamas. Furgan wasn't quite sure how to hold a baby, especially one that continued to squirm as this one did.

"Come with me, little one," he said. "You are about to begin a whole new life of galactic importance."

21

Han Solo longed to get closer to Kyp Durron in the Council chambers on Coruscant, wanting to comfort his young friend—but the armed New Republic guards surrounding Kyp made it impossible for anyone to approach.

Kyp moved slowly, as if walking barefoot across shattered glass. His eyes were dull. His face was seamed with new lines, as if the dark spirit of Exar Kun had shed his four thousand years of existence onto Kyp's shoulders.

The Sun Crusher had once again been impounded by New Republic security, and Mon Mothma had declared the entire area off limits. There would be no further research into the workings of the superweapon. Kyp's chaotic vengeance had demonstrated how horrible the Sun Crusher truly was.

Inside the Council chambers the air smelled thick and oppressive from too much tension and too little ventilation. The stone added a musty old smell to the room. The place made Han uneasy and claustrophobic.

The Council members wore their formal uniforms like armor, frowning like ancient sentinels, passing judgment. Some looked as if they hadn't had any rest. Han felt deeply troubled to be facing them without Leia. She had departed from Yavin 4 with Terpfen, supposedly to go see Ackbar, but he had not been able to learn what had happened to her. Leia certainly knew how to take care of herself, though, and he did not dare leave Kyp alone with the predators here.

Mon Mothma, flanked by her ever-present medical droids, seemed only partially aware of what was going on. None of the other Council members had suggested removing her from office while she was still willing to attend meetings, though Mon Mothma contributed little. Han was stunned by how much the Chief of State had worsened in just the last few days.

One of the functionaries beside the sculpted door arch tapped on a long chime, sending a pure tone into the air to call the attendees to order.

Han didn't know much about the protocol of government, but he didn't plan to stand by and do nothing while Kyp was trounced by bureaucratic bigwigs. Before one of the members could speak, Han stepped forward. "Hey! Could you let me put in a word for my friend, Kyp Durron?"

Aging General Jan Dodonna hauled himself to his feet. Ancient and weathered, like a piece of gnarled driftwood, the bearded general still seemed filled with energy. His eyes flashed at Han. "The prisoner may speak for himself, General Solo. He has certainly shown no reluctance to *act* for himself. Let him answer our questions now."

Chastised, Han stepped back and looked at the floor, tracing patterns made by cracks in the inset flagstones. Since Dodonna had the lectern, he leaned forward to look down at Kyp. The young man lifted his tousled head and blinked sheepishly at the old tactician.

"Kyp Durron," Dodonna said, "you stole the Sun Crusher. You attacked and temporarily incapacitated the Jedi Master Luke Skywalker. You blew up the Cauldron Nebula and obliterated two other inhabited star systems. I will not debate the tactical significance of your actions—but we cannot tolerate juggernauts who make up their own orders and cause wholesale destruction on a whim!"

The other Council members agreed. General Rieekan's deep, thick voice reverberated through the chamber. "This Council had already decided that the Sun Crusher would never be used. We disposed of it in a safe and protected place, but you *knowingly* thwarted our wishes."

The other members fell quiet after Rieekan's words. They seemed eager to add their own condemnations, but realized there would be little point in it.

After a moment of silence Kyp spoke. His voice sounded impossibly thin and small, reminding Han and everyone else there just how young this boy was. "I have no excuse for my actions. I'll accept the consequences."

"Even if your actions demand the death penalty?" the obese Senator Hrekin Thorm asked. "Such destruction as you have caused can warrant nothing less than execution."

"Wait a minute!" Han said. The Council members glared at him, but he ignored their silent rebukes. "I know, I know—but listen to me for a minute. Kyp wasn't himself. He was possessed by the evil spirit of a Sith Lord who has since been defeated. And he did do some good. He destroyed Daala's fleet. How many lives did he save by doing that? We are at war, after all." Mon Mothma's words wheezed from her cracked lips. Her voice came out in a ragged whisper. The rest of the chamber fell into a deep hush as she began to talk. "Kyp Durron," she said, "you have the blood of millions, perhaps billions, on your hands. We are a governing body here, not a judicial council. We have no right to decide your fate. You—" She gasped as if using most of her energy just to fill her lungs. "You must be judged by the Jedi Master. We are not qualified to judge your crimes."

She raised one of her hands to gesture toward Han. "Take him to Yavin. Let Master Skywalker decide his fate."

22

Leia, Ackbar, and Terpfen joined the rescue party from the *Galactic Voyager*, swooping through the violet skies of Anoth. Ackbar took the lead in his own B-wing. His weapons systems were powered up and ready to attack any ground assault team the Dreadnaught had deployed.

The starfighters soared over the fanged landscape toward the stone turret that Ackbar and Luke had chosen for the base. Leia saw signs of damage that made her blood run cold, smoke and debris from an attack. "We're too late," she whispered.

Part of the spire had been blasted away, and soot splattered the eroded surface. Below, she saw the still-smoldering remains of several horrific mechanical spiders.

Ackbar's voice came over the ship-to-ship intercom. "Winter must be putting up a good fight. Our emplaced defensive systems are functioning as planned."

Leia swallowed to clear her dry throat. "Let's just hope that's good enough, Admiral."

The fighters targeted in on where the blast doors had been melted aside. One of the heavy metal shields still hung in place in its tracks. The rescue ships maneuvered around the four Walkers that cluttered the floor of the landing bay. Ackbar, Leia, and Terpfen sprang out of their cockpits as other Calamarian fighters joined them.

"Terpfen, go with Minister Leia and half the fighters directly to the nursery. See if the baby is still there. I will take the other troops down into the lower levels to find Winter. I think I know what her strategy would have been."

Leia, not bothering to argue, yanked out her own blaster pistol. With a hardened expression she took the lead, running to see that her child was safe.

The team swarmed down the maze of convoluted tunnels toward the nursery. Leia glanced around her as she jogged but saw no signs of blaster fire on the walls. Weapons rattled against body armor as the Calamarians ran to keep pace with her.

As they rounded the last corner toward Anakin's room, Leia swerved to keep from tripping over the slow-moving power droid who plodded along on its rounds, unconcerned with the turmoil. Leia paid the walking battery no further heed when she saw the door to the nursery yawning open.

"Oh, no," she said, lurching to a cautious stop just as Ambassador Furgan backed out, clutching a squalling Anakin to his broad chest.

Both Leia and Furgan froze for a moment, staring at each other. Furgan's eyebrows jerked up in a muscular twitch like birds about to leap into flight.

The Calamarian rescuers leveled their weapons at Furgan. He held the baby in front of him like a shield.

"Give Anakin back to me," Leia said, her voice dripping with greater threat than an entire fleet of Star Destroyers could convey.

"I'm afraid not," Furgan said, and wrapped a broad hand around Anakin's fragile neck. His wild eyes flicked from side to side. "Point your guns away from me, or I'll snap his neck! I've gone through all this to get the Jedi baby, and I'm not going to give him up. He's my hostage, and the only way he stays alive is for you to let me go."

He edged along the tunnel. His back scraped against the rough, lumpy wall. Furgan locked his eyes on the weapons pointed at him, but he held the baby out, squeezing the boy's throat. "Even if you stun me, I can still crush his windpipe. Drop your weapons!"

"Back off," Leia ordered, taking a step backward.

The Calamarian defenders stepped to the side, clearing a path for Furgan—all except for Terpfen. He stood holding his hands in front of him like sharp claws.

Furgan saw the swollen, sagging Calamarian head, the tracery of blunt scars—and suddenly recognized him. "So, my little fish, you betrayed me after all. I didn't think you had the strength of will."

"I found the strength," Terpfen said. He stepped toward Furgan. Anakin continued to squirm in the ambassador's arms.

"Stop!" Furgan said. "You have enough on your conscience, little fish. You wouldn't want to add the death of this baby to it."

Terpfen made a low gurgling noise that was some kind of Calamarian snarl. Furgan kept his wild gaze fixed on all those cornering him as he slid backward toward the Spider Walkers and his only escape.

In his grasp baby Anakin's deep-brown eyes flashed, as if he were deep in thought.

Suddenly Furgan cried out as he stumbled against the squarish, waddling power droid that had silently crept up behind him. The power droid gave out a small jolt of electricity, shocking Furgan.

The ambassador tripped and fell, still holding the child. The power droid shuffled out of the way with a squeal of something like terror.

As the Calamarian defenders snatched up their weapons again, Terpfen lunged forward to grab the baby out of Furgan's hands.

The other Calamarians fired at Furgan, but the squat man rolled across the floor, got to his knees, and launched himself around the corner, moving far faster than Leia would ever have thought possible.

"After him!" Terpfen cried. He passed baby Anakin to Leia and dashed off in pursuit of Furgan.

As hot tears flowed from her eyes, Leia hugged her youngest son, trying to find words that would console him—but nothing came to mind, so she just made cooing noises. She sank to the floor, rocking him back and forth.

Ackbar's broad feet slapped on the stone floor as he ran deeper into the catacombs. His lungs burned in the dry air, but still he insisted on more speed. He pulled ahead of the others. So far Winter had followed exactly the guidelines he had established for defense of the base.

He knew from the wreckage outside that the Foreign Intruder Defense Organism had done its job, eliminating half the Spider Walkers before they could breach the blast doors—but it had not been enough. Winter would have proceeded down to trigger the camouflaged assassin droids.

The other team members clattered behind him. He could smell dust and engine oil in the dry air, and also a sharp, damp smell like copper and smoke—blood.

The robed form of Winter sprang around the corner, holding a blaster in front of her, ready to fire. But she froze. For just an instant a smile of delight crossed her face. "Ackbar! I knew you would come."

Ackbar strode toward her, resting his hand on her arm. "I arrived as fast as I could. You are safe?"

"For the moment," she said. "The defenses have eliminated all but two of the intruders, according to my inventory."

"Are you certain?" he said.

"I never forget anything," Winter said, and Ackbar knew it was true.

"Leia and the rest of my team should be getting Anakin now," he said, then continued softly, "We split up so that I could determine if you required assistance."

She nodded. The expression on her face softened. "I will not feel comfortable until I see the baby safe."

"Let's go," Ackbar said, still out of breath. Together they began the long run uphill.

Terpfen raced feverishly up sloping corridors. His feet were raw, bleeding from running on the textured floor, but still he ran. He didn't care if this race killed him. He had to get to Furgan before the ambassador escaped.

Furgan had jerked his controls and made Terpfen reveal damning secrets of the New Republic, forced him to sabotage Ackbar's B-wing so that it had crashed into the Cathedral of Winds, made him betray the location of the Jedi baby.

Terpfen would pay his personal debt in any way he could—but Furgan would also have to pay the price.

With determination coursing through his veins, Terpfen passed the other Calamarian pursuers. Through the dimness he could hear Furgan scurrying forward like a krabbex.

"Follow!" Terpfen wheezed as he shot past the others. Terpfen leaped over fallen hunks of metal shrapnel, blasted doors that the invading stormtroopers had blown away. He emerged into the landing grotto to find Furgan already scrambling into one of the unoccupied MT-ATs.

"You can't escape, Furgan!" Terpfen shouted. He paused to catch his breath against the melted but now cooled hatch.

Furgan slung one leg over the edge of the Spider Walker and settled himself into its cockpit. His face wrinkled as if someone had scrunched it up from the inside.

"We already destroyed your Dreadnaught in orbit," Terpfen said. Finding energy deep within him, he staggered toward the walker. He heard the other troops catching up.

Furgan looked amazed at the news, but then his face smoothed again with disbelief. "I know better than to trust you, little fish. Your whole life is a lie."

Furgan closed the transparisteel canopy. The engines hummed to life. One of the outer blast doors had been completely torn away; the other hung half-open. Wind sighed through the opening. In the clotted purple sky the two larger components of Anoth rode overhead like stone clouds exchanging lightning across the silence of space.

Terpfen snarled and ran to another Spider Walker. He was a chief starship mechanic. He had helped the Imperials work on their combat vehicles and their Star Destroyers. He could run any equipment—probably better than Furgan himself.

In his panic Furgan had trouble making all eight of the walker's legs move in sequence to make progress across the grotto floor, but he finally plowed ahead, swiveling the laser cannons on the joints of the articulated legs to blast one of the B-wing fighters that stood in the way.

Terpfen powered up his Spider Walker and slammed down the canopy. The machine had crude controls and sluggish response, nothing at all like the streamlined controls used on Mon Calamari Star Cruisers.

Furgan's vehicle approached the large opening at the cliff's edge, and Terpfen knew from the design of the MT-AT that it could climb straight down the rockface. He didn't quite know how Furgan would escape once he got to the bottom; he doubted the ambassador had thought that far ahead.

Terpfen found the fire controls and shot his lasers three times, taking out one joint of the other walker's legs. The lower portion of the metal limb sheared off and fell to the grotto floor with a clang.

Off balance, Furgan's walker scuttled in a drunkard's circle until he managed to compensate for the lost limb. Once again he made for the exit.

Terpfen saw the powerful blaster cannons slung beneath his cockpit— if he fired both of them in the enclosed grotto, it would obliterate Furgan's assault transport . . . but the explosion would also destroy him and his own Walker, and probably most of the B-wings as well.

Then Terpfen saw other rescuers streaming into the grotto. Admiral Ackbar himself came from a different entrance and stood with his own team next to a white-clad woman whom he recognized as Leia's companion Winter.

He could never fire the blaster cannons now. But he vowed not to let Furgan escape. Working the controls, Terpfen lunged the eight-legged vehicle forward in pursuit just as Furgan's machine tottered on the edge.

Ackbar arrived in time to see the beginning of the battle between the two Spider Walkers. Terpfen's lasers blasted out, striking the ambassador's MT-AT. Furgan didn't seem to have a plan, intending only to get away. Terpfen's walker scuttled forward. Its clawed footpads struck sparks from the landing-bay floor.

Terpfen blasted again and again with his lasers. Furgan fired back, but his shot missed, scoring sharp flakes of rock from the grotto wall.

Terpfen's MT-AT charged ahead, raising its two front clawed legs, and grabbed the metal limbs of Furgan's transport, raising it partway off the floor.

Furgan's vehicle reached out with its own legs to grasp the edge of the cave opening, trying to haul itself forward and away.

Terpfen fired directly at the transparisteel canopy of the cockpit, but the laser shots could not pass through the shielded surface. His Spider Walker grappled with Furgan's vehicle, four mechanical legs planted firmly on the stone floor, four legs *pushing* with all his engine's capacity.

A large chunk of rock shattered at the claw grip. With a horrible sound of rending, tearing metal, Furgan's walker finally broke free of the grotto opening.

Terpfen's MT-AT pushed forward and forward. Inside the cockpit of the ambassador's vehicle, Furgan frantically grabbed the controls but did not seem to know which to use.

Terpfen continued his relentless blasting with the lasers. He shoved Furgan's walker completely through where the blast door had been blown away and held out the thrashing MT-AT over open space.

Terpfen released his grip.

Ambassador Furgan's multilegged vehicle flailed as it dropped through the air on a long plunge toward the jagged landscape far below. Before the assault vehicle could actually strike the ground, Terpfen fired both of his powerful blaster cannons. The beams blew up Furgan's MT-AT with a blinding flash just above the spiked rocks.

And then, inexplicably, Terpfen's walker continued its own forward motion, moving mechanical legs to drive him over the edge in a suicidal plunge.

Ackbar instantly knew what Terpfen intended. Not wasting time with a shout that would not be heard, he lunged for the blast-door controls.

Just as the thrashing metal legs vanished over the lip of the cliff, Ackbar punched the buttons, hoping that the skewed half of the door still functioned just enough. The heavy metal plate crashed down on top of the last footpad of Terpfen's Spider Walker, pinning it to the cliff and preventing it from falling.

"Help him!" Ackbar cried.

The other Calamarians scrambled forward, accompanied by the admiral himself. Secured with a tow cable from one of the B-wings, they lowered themselves over the cliff to open the canopy of Terpfen's walker. Inside they found him shuddering and nearly unconscious with shock. The team rigged a sling and hauled him to the safety of the grotto.

Ackbar bent over him, looking stern. He called Terpfen's name until the scarred Calamarian finally stirred. "You should have let me die," he said. "My death should have been my punishment."

"No, Terpfen," Ackbar said, "we cannot choose our own punishment.

There is still much you can contribute to the New Republic, still a great many things to do before you will be allowed to give up."

Ackbar straightened, realizing that those words could just as well apply to himself, after he had run away to hide on the planet Calamari.

"Your punishment, Terpfen," he said, "will be to live."

23

The *Falcon* cruised over the lush treetops of Yavin 4, and Han Solo set the ship down in front of the Great Temple. He bounced down the landing ramp.

Leia and the twins practically tackled him as they rushed to greet him. "Daddy, Daddy!" Jacen and Jaina cried in peculiarly overlapping voices. Leia, back from Anoth, cradling the one-year-old against her chest, squeezed Han and gave him a long kiss as Anakin played with her hair. The twins jumped up and down against Han's legs, demanding the attention that was their due.

"Hello there, little guy!" Han grinned down at Anakin; then he looked deep into Leia's eyes. "Are you all right? You've got a lot of details to tell me. That message you sent wasn't very explicit."

"Yeah," she said. "You'll get the whole story, when we have some quiet time, just the two of us. I'm glad all of our children are home to stay, though. We'll protect them ourselves from now on."

"Sounds like a great idea to me," Han said, then chuckled and shook his head. "Say, weren't you telling *me* that I shouldn't go off and have adventures by myself?"

Han stepped away from the *Falcon* as he saw Luke Skywalker striding toward him across the flattened landing grid. Artoo-Detoo puttered along next to him as if reluctant ever to leave his master's side again.

"Luke!" Han cried. He ran to give Luke an enthusiastic hug. "Great to see you up and around again. About time you quit napping."

Luke clapped him on the back and smiled with dark-ringed eyes that shone with an inner brightness stronger than ever before. As he conquered each seemingly insurmountable obstacle, Luke's Jedi powers grew greater and greater—but, like Obi-Wan Kenobi and Yoda, a Jedi Master learned to use his powers even less, relying on wits instead of showmanship.

In the dense jungle surrounding the Massassi temple a squawking racket boiled up as a gang of woolamanders startled a pair of feathered flying creatures; the woolamanders hurled rotten fruit as the flying creatures flapped into the air, shrieking down at their tormentors.

Han glanced toward the disturbance, but Luke's gaze remained fixed on the *Falcon,* as if held by a powerful magnet. Han turned to look—and stopped.

Kyp Durron, still wrapped in the slick black cape that Han himself had given him, descended the boarding ramp. His eyes locked on Luke's, and the two Jedi stared at each other as if psychically linked.

Han stepped away from Luke, and the Jedi teacher silently walked across the weed-strewn landing grid. Kyp reached the end of the ramp, planted his feet on the soil of Yavin 4 again, and stood looking penitent.

Han could tell from Kyp's rigid posture and his set jaw that the young man was terrified at having to face his Jedi Master. Han felt cold, not wanting to be trapped between two people he counted among his dearest friends.

Leia took the children off to one side, watching the encounter warily. Concern furrowed her brow as she flicked her gaze from her brother to Kyp and back again.

Luke walked toward his student slowly, as if gliding over the ground. "I knew you would come back, Kyp."

Han watched him, and it seemed that Luke had no anger in his bearing, no fury or need for vengeance.

"Exar Kun is destroyed?" Kyp asked hoarsely, but he knew the answer already.

"Exar Kun will have no influence on your future training, Kyp. The question is, what will *you* do with your abilities?"

Kyp blinked his eyes in shock. "You—you would let me continue my training?"

Luke's expression softened further. "I had to witness the death of my first teacher. I also had to confront Darth Vader, my own father. I have done other difficult tasks.

"I did not plan these things, but each time I passed through the fire of an ordeal such as those, I emerged a more powerful Jedi. You, Kyp, have been thrown into the flames. I must determine whether you have been consumed— or tempered into a great Jedi. Can you forsake the dark side?"

"I . . ." Kyp stumbled over his words. "I will try."

"No!" Luke shouted with the first glimmering of anger that Han had heard in his voice. "There is no *try*. You must *believe* you will do it, or you will fail."

The jungle fell silent. Kyp hung his head, and his nostrils flared as he took a deep breath. The young man's dark eyes glittered as he looked back up into Luke's face.

"I want to be a Jedi," he said.

24

Lando Calrissian felt as if the million-credit reward was burning a hole in his account. He needed to invest it soon.

It was a new feeling for him to have such a large sum of money and nothing practical to do with it. He had won control of Bespin's Tibanna gas mines in a sabacc game, and he had served for years as Baron Administrator of Cloud City. He had run metal-mining operations on the superhot planet Nkllon, and now with his huge reward from the blob races on Umgul, Lando saw no reason why he could not make a successful operation out of the spice mines of Kessel.

"I really appreciate your taking me, Han," Lando said. He reached over to slap his friend's shoulder in the cockpit of the *Millennium Falcon*. He knew that Han was not terribly pleased to leave Leia and his children again so soon, even if only for a day to drop him off at Kessel. He suspected, too, that Han was also worried about Chewbacca and the Maw occupation force, who had sent no word since advancing into the black hole cluster. Since the Maw lay near Kessel, Han probably hoped to learn some news.

"It'll be worth it, if only to keep you from begging for rides all the time," Han said, looking in the opposite direction. He glanced out the front viewport. "I still think you're crazy to want to go to Kessel—even crazier to want to stay there."

Ahead, the small planet orbited near its faint sun. The misshapen lump of Kessel had too little gravity to hold its own atmosphere, and so the gases streamed into space like a tenuous mane flowing out from its barren rocky outline. A large moon, on which the alien prison lord Moruth Doole had stationed his garrison of pirates, climbed over the limb of Kessel, emerging from the wispy corona of escaping air.

"Last time I came here with Chewie," Han said, shaking his head, "we got shot down. I promised myself I'd never come back—and now it's only been a couple of months, and here I am again."

"That's just because you're a good friend, Han. I really appreciate it. Mara Jade wouldn't want me to be late."

Han smirked. "If she remembers to show up, you mean."

Lando laced his fingers behind his neck, staring at the rising moon as the *Falcon* arrowed in to a close orbit. "She'll be there," Lando said. "I'll bet she's been counting down the days."

"Wish I had Chewie back as a copilot," Han muttered, rolling his eyes. "At least he didn't say such hokey things."

At the mention of Chewbacca, both men subconsciously looked toward the glowing tapestry of ragged gases surrounding the Maw cluster. Somewhere inside, Chewbacca and the rest of the strike force should be mopping up their efforts to retake the Maw Installation. The black holes made communication impossible, so they had no way of knowing what had happened during the occupation.

"I hope he's all right, Han," Lando said quietly.

Han leaned forward to finger the controls on the comm unit. He hesitated, and his face sagged for an instant; he flicked on the transmitter, then cleared his throat, businesslike again. "This is Han Solo on the *Millennium Falcon*, approaching Kessel."

Lando watched Han's left hand drift to the hyperspace controls. A new course had already been programmed into the navicomputer. Han was ready to dash away at a moment's notice if anything suspicious happened.

"We're looking for Mara Jade, a representative of the Smugglers' Alliance," Han continued. "We, uh, request permission to land on the garrison moon. Please acknowledge before we come any closer." Han's face was lined with concern.

"Don't be so nervous, Han," Lando said. "Things have changed on Kessel. You'll see."

Han's voice took on a defensive tone. "I just don't want to take any chances after what's already happened."

Before Lando could respond, Mara Jade's crisp, businesslike voice came over the speaker. Lando felt his heart warm at hearing her subtle tones. He imagined her soft lips moving, forming the words.

"You're half a day late, Solo," she said.

"Well, Lando here wanted to make himself look presentable," Han said, grinning, "and you know how much time that could take."

Mara gave a short, sharp laugh, and Lando glared at Han. "Come on in, then," she said. "I've brought a defensive fleet from the Smugglers' Alliance. The garrison moon is secure. We'll discuss our business there. I have an escort coming for you—something I think Calrissian will appreciate."

Lando smiled broadly. "She's planned some kind of surprise for me! Probably a token of her affection."

"Oh, brother." Han rolled his eyes again.

Han checked the coordinates on his navigation console and vectored in toward the large station on Kessel's moon.

Disguised as potential investors in the spice-mining operations, Lando Calrissian and Luke Skywalker had been shuttled up to this moon by froglike Moruth Doole. Doole had done his best to show off the spice-mining operations in hopes that Lando would sink his blob-won credits into the facility.

With a shudder Lando remembered how all the ships in the hangar bay had launched after them when he and Luke had stolen Han's repaired *Falcon*. The Kessel pirate fleet had run headlong into Admiral Daala's Star Destroyers, as they charged out of the Maw cluster after Han Solo. The two fleets had crashed into each other, inflicting horrendous damage, but Han, Luke, and Lando had fled into hyperspace before seeing the outcome of the battle. . . .

Now a single small ship appeared over the misty horizon of Kessel. "This is Jade. I'm your escort. Follow me."

The space yacht approached, then spun about to dart toward the moon. Han increased the *Falcon*'s speed.

Lando sat up sharply, his eyes blinking in astonishment. "Hey, that's my ship!" he cried. "That's the *Lady Luck*. That's—"

"Well," Han said, "at least that saves us the trouble of looking for it."

Lando grabbed the comm unit. "Mara, you found my ship! I can't thank you enough." He lowered his voice. "If there's anything I can do to repay you, anything in your wildest dreams . . ."

"Keep talking like that, Calrissian, and I might just send this ship on autopilot into the sun."

Lando leaned back in the seat with a sigh and a smile. He flashed a glance at Han. "She's such a kidder."

The space yacht *Lady Luck* looked sleek and angular with propulsion pods slung below. Her hull gleamed, none the worse for wear, somehow unscathed from the devastating battles on Kessel.

Lando fidgeted, anxious to see Mara again, anxious to sit back in the plush cushions of his own pilot chair, to luxuriate in the smell and feel of his own ship.

They entered the cave mouth of the moon garrison, flying past the thick blast doors into the garish light of a large landing bay. The atmosphere-containment fields closed behind them and repressurized the habitable area. The *Falcon* coasted in on its repulsorlifts and landed in a broad polished area beside the *Lady Luck*.

Mara Jade swung out, clad in a tight metallic jumpsuit with a helmet tucked under her right elbow. As she tossed her head to loosen her dark, reddish-brown hair, she narrowed her eyes. Lando stared with a warm-cold shudder at the energy and intelligence that radiated from this woman. He marveled at her generous curves, her tough exterior.

"Hey, Mara," Han said, "where did you find Lando's ship? We thought we were going to have to spend days combing the surface for it."

"Right where Lando claims he landed it. Seems nobody had time to strip her down and remove the identification markings."

Lando glanced around the garrison bay, but all the ships looked unfamiliar, custom designs—not the barely moving scrap heaps that had made up Doole's fleet. These were emblazoned with markings unique to each vessel, though each carried a crosshatched design on the wing.

Mara noticed his inspection. "That's our new insignia for the Smugglers' Alliance," she said. "Not too obvious, but enough for us."

"What happened to all of Doole's ships?" Lando sniffed the enclosed dry air, smelling the powdered rock and spilled hyperdrive fuel that made the air sour and unpleasant.

"Ninety percent of Doole's ships were obliterated in their tangle with Daala's Star Destroyers. Most of the surviving pilots took their ships and fled into hyperspace. No one knows where they are now—and frankly, I don't really care.

"When a few New Republic relief ships came in, they evacuated most of the inhabitants, the prisoners in the Imperial Correction Facility, a few holdouts in the city of Kessendra. Nobody *wants* to make a life on Kessel if they have another option."

"So what you're saying," Lando said, letting his hopes rise, "is that Kessel is deserted, ready for the taking?"

"Yes," Mara said. "I've talked over your proposal with some members of our Alliance, and it sounds good to us. Not only have you proved your ability in your other ventures, but you've also got strong connections with the New Republic, which will allow efficient distribution channels for glitterstim. You've even got enough money to invest in the new infrastructure." She shrugged. "Sounds like a good deal all around."

Lando beamed. "I knew you'd realize that being partners with me is a very good deal."

Mara turned abruptly and continued with her discussion, ignoring his insinuation. "But we need to move right away. We've heard talk of other, less-scrupulous crime lords arranging to take over the mines. The spice tunnels are empty, ripe for the plucking. Frankly, we'd rather deal with *you*, Calrissian, than someone who's going to bring in his own teams and cut the Smugglers' Alliance out of the entire operation. That's why we brought our forces here to hold it, just in case some Hutt crime lord gets any ideas."

"Makes sense to me," Han said.

Lando rubbed his hands together, looking at the other ships in the bay. Various smugglers moved around, humans and aliens, burly-looking men and women, people he wouldn't want to meet alone in the dim lower levels of Coruscant. "Should we go down and have a look at the real estate?"

"Fine." Mara snapped to attention. "Let's go ahead and take your ship, Calrissian. You pilot her."

Lando reveled in the feel of his controls again, running his hands along the soft, polished seats. This was his own space yacht, specially built to his personal design. Now he was riding in the cockpit with a beautiful, intelligent woman, heading down to a planet where he intended to make a fortune. He didn't think the day could possibly get better.

He was right.

When they soared low over the parched and blasted surface of Kessel, they cruised past one of the major atmosphere factories, which had once spewed manufactured air to replenish the constant loss from the low gravity.

But the tall stack stood half-collapsed. Black blaster scorches mottled its pale exterior. The baked, dry ground—already lifeless except for a few tufts of extremely hardy vegetation—had been torn up by TIE bombers and space-based turbolaser strikes.

"Over half of the atmosphere factories are out of commission," Mara explained. "Admiral Daala did a lot of damage. Seems she thought this was a Rebel base, so she struck at anything that showed up on her targeting screens."

Lando had a sinking feeling deep in his chest. "This is going to take more work than I had anticipated," he said. But he consoled himself by calculating the unclaimed wealth within the tunnels below and thinking of how he could get teams of droids, Sullustans, and other races to work for shares in the profits. It might take a little longer to earn back his investment, but the demand for pure glitterstim was so high that he could raise his prices—at least until he turned a profit.

"I'm heading toward the prison," Lando said. "That fortress should have withstood the attack from space. I think I'll use that as my base of operations. It'll take some conversion, but we should be able to adapt it into the control center for our new manufacturing complex."

The speed of the *Lady Luck* rapidly ate the kilometers across the empty landscape until a towering trapezoid stood like a great monument on the barren surface.

The old Imperial prison was made of synthetic rock, flat, unappealing tan veined with other colors. An outcropping of crystal windows jutted from the slanted smooth front. Tubed elevator shafts rode along the angled corners. The place was streaked with burn marks, but appeared undamaged.

Lando heaved a sigh of relief. "At least the building looks intact," he said. "Something's going right for a change. This'll be a great place to start." He smiled at Mara. "You and I should christen our new headquarters!"

Mara Jade frowned and kept looking out the front viewport. "Ah . . . there is one problem, Calrissian."

Lando and Han turned to look at her. The prison loomed higher as the *Lady Luck* continued to approach.

Mara continued. "Well, you see, Moruth Doole has holed himself up inside the prison building. He's scared to death, doesn't know what to do. All of his cohorts have fled or been killed, and now he's using the sophisticated prison-defense systems to keep everyone else out."

The fortress looked impenetrable, a huge hulking mass of stone armor. Lando had no desire whatsoever to see Moruth Doole again, and neither, he knew, did Han.

"I wish you had mentioned that detail a little sooner," Lando said with a grimace as he brought the *Lady Luck* in for a landing.

25

Inside the rigid cleanness of the medical chambers in the old Imperial Palace, Terpfen stood silent and patient. He waited and watched the massaging bubbles in the bacta tank working on Mon Mothma's ailing body.

The medical chambers glowed with sterile whiteness. The tiles on the floor and walls had been acid scoured; utensils and surgical equipment gleamed silver and chrome. Wall monitors blinked with a steady, throbbing rhythm, proclaiming the declining state of Mon Mothma's health.

Outside the chamber doors two New Republic guards stood watch, making certain no one could intrude.

Sound-absorption panels in the ceiling deadened the mechanical whispers in the large chamber. Two bullet-headed medical droids hovered on either side of the tank, tending Mon Mothma and paying no attention to Terpfen.

Beside him Ackbar stood tall and strong. "She'll be finished soon," he said. Terpfen nodded, not eager to speak to Mon Mothma—but resigned to the necessity of it.

In these chambers the Emperor had himself undergone rigorous treatments as dark-side workings rotted his physical body. Perhaps the same facilities could remove the scourge within Mon Mothma's body. Terpfen had little hope of that, though, now that he knew what had caused it. . . .

Mon Mothma blinked her greenish-blue eyes through the murk of the tank solution. Terpfen couldn't tell if she could focus on them standing outside, or if she merely sensed their presence. She moved her head, and the thick air hose drifted with her. Bubbles pummeled her body, forcing invigorating solutions through her pores.

Mon Mothma released her grip on the stabilizers within the tank and floated up. The droids assisted her in getting out. She stood sagging, dripping as her lightweight robes dribbled solution into drainage grates on the floor. Even the thin wet robes seemed as heavy as a leaden shroud to her. Her auburn hair clung like a skullcap. Her eyes were sunken, her face chiseled with deep canyons of pain and weakness.

She filled her lungs and exhaled, resting the flat of her hand against the medical droid's green shoulders. She raised her head with obvious effort and acknowledged her visitors.

"The treatments give me strength for only about an hour. Their effectiveness decreases every day," she said. "Soon it will be useless, I'm afraid, and I will no longer be able to perform my functions as Chief of State. The only question is whether I resign before the Council removes me. . . ." She turned to Terpfen. "Don't worry, I know why you are here."

Terpfen blinked his glassy eyes. "I don't believe—"

She raised a hand to cut off his objections. "Ackbar has spoken to me at great length. He has considered your case thoroughly, and I agree with his conclusions. You were not acting of your own free will, but were merely a victim. You have redeemed yourself. The New Republic can't afford to throw away defenders who are willing to continue the fight. I have already issued a full pardon for you."

She wavered, on the verge of slumping backward. The two medical droids moved to help her to a chair. "I wanted to make sure that got done before . . ."

Ackbar made a grumbling noise as he cleared his throat. "I am also here to tell you, Mon Mothma, that I have decided to stay. I will request that my rank be reinstated, now that it is clear the crash on Vortex was not solely due to my error, as I had originally thought. The people of Calamari are resilient, and they are strong—but if the New Republic is not also strong, my work at home will be fruitless, because we will face a galaxy full of shadows and fear."

Mon Mothma smiled at Ackbar, a sincere expression of relief. "Ackbar, knowing that you will be here makes me feel stronger than any of these treatments ever did." Then she showed a deeper misery and let her chin sink into her hands, a moment of weakness she would never have displayed in front of the Council. "Why did this disease have to strike me now? I'm mortal just like everyone else . . . but why *now*?"

Terpfen walked across the slippery floor, feeling the cold, polished surface on the soles of his broad feet. He bowed his scar-traced head. At the doorway the two New Republic guards stiffened at seeing the known traitor so close to their Chief of State, but Mon Mothma showed no alarm. Terpfen looked down at her.

"That is what I have come to discuss with you, Mon Mothma. I must tell you what has happened to you."

Mon Mothma blinked, waiting for him to continue.

Terpfen searched for the right words. His mind seemed so empty now that the implanted biological circuits had been neutralized. He had hated the insistent compulsions from Carida, but now he was left alone with his own thoughts—no one else inside his skull to taunt him, or to guide him.

"You are suffering from no disease, Mon Mothma. You have been poisoned."

She jerked in sudden shock but did not interrupt him.

"It is a slow, debilitating poison targeted specifically to your genetic structure."

"But how was I exposed to this poison?" She looked hard at him, not accusing, but insisting on answers. "Did you do it, Terpfen? Was this another of your programmed actions?"

"No!" He reeled backward. "I have done many things—but this is not one of them. You were poisoned by Ambassador Furgan himself, as dozens of people watched. During the diplomatic reception at the Skydome Botanical Gardens. Furgan carried his own refreshment because he claimed you might try to poison *him*. He had two flasks, one on each side of his hip. In one flask he carried his true beverage, in the other he carried a poison specifically developed for you. He pretended to propose a toast and then tossed a glassful of the poison into your face. It seeped into your pores and has been multiplying and attacking your cells ever since."

Both Ackbar and Mon Mothma stared at him in astonishment.

"Of course!" she said. "But it's been months. Why did they choose such a slow-acting . . ."

Terpfen closed his eyes, and the words came to him as if he were reciting a script. "They wanted a long, debilitating decline for you because of the damage it would do to the New Republic's morale. If you were simply killed, you could become a martyr. Your death might have galvanized support from otherwise neutral systems. But with a slow, progressive weakening, it could be seen as the decay of the Rebellion."

"I see," Mon Mothma said.

"Very shrewd," Ackbar said. "But what are we to do with this information? What else do you know of the poison, Terpfen? How can we treat it?"

Terpfen heard the silence in his head like a scream. "This is not a true poison. It is a self-replicating swarm of nano-destroyers: microscopic, artificially created viruses dismantling Mon Mothma's cells one nucleus at a time. They will not stop until her life ceases."

"Then what do we do?" Ackbar persisted.

Finally the helplessness and all the pain within Terpfen built until it spilled out of him like a star finally reaching its flash point.

"We can do nothing!" he shouted. "Even knowing about this poison does not help us, because there is no cure!"

26

The battered Star Destroyer *Gorgon* barely survived its passage through
the gravitational whirlpool into the Maw cluster.

Admiral Daala strapped herself to a command chair on the bridge as the
Star Destroyer was buffeted by tidal forces that would rip the ship apart if
their trajectory deviated from its charted path. Daala had ordered her crew to
stand down and take refuge in protective areas, to buckle themselves into their
stations and prepare for a rough ride. Of the very few known paths inside the
Maw cluster, she had chosen the shortest, the "back door," but still her ship
was in no shape to withstand the enormous stresses for long.

Many of the *Gorgon*'s stabilizers had blown in their narrow escape from
the multiple supernova explosion in the Cauldron Nebula. Shields had failed
at the end—but they had held long enough. The *Gorgon*'s once-ivory metallic
hull was now streaked and scarred. Outer layers of armor had boiled away,
but Daala had taken a gamble.

She had been lucky fleeing from the exploding suns, while only seconds
behind her the *Basilisk* had vaporized in flame, disintegrated by the outrushing
supernova shock wave. But Daala had ordered the *Gorgon* to plunge blindly
into hyperspace mere moments before the explosive front had reached her
rear thrusters. The desperate leap knocked them headlong on a reckless
course through the hazards of the universe. The *Gorgon* would have been
obliterated if they had stumbled onto an interdimensional path that passed

through the core of a star or planet. But through some miracle of fate that had not happened.

The *Gorgon* had emerged in an uninhabited void in the Outer Rim. Their shields had failed, life-support systems partly burned out, and the hull had been breached in several areas that let the atmosphere squeal into the vacuum of space until those compartments were sealed off.

Collectively gasping from their narrow escape, Daala's crew had set about effecting repairs. It took her navigators a day just to determine their galactic position because they had gone so far afield. Armored spacetroopers in totally contained environment suits walked over the external skeleton of the *Gorgon,* removing ruined components, patching weak spots in the hull, rigging replacements from their meager inventory of spare parts.

The Star Destroyer had drifted in the uninhabited space between stars. One of the engines was permanently damaged, and three of the aft turbolaser batteries were dead. But Daala had let none of her crew rest until the *Gorgon* was functional again. They had a mission to complete. She did not allow herself the luxury of rest, either, tirelessly marching down corridors, inspecting repairs, making personnel assignments, prioritizing maintenance tasks.

Daala had done well for more than ten years, drilling her stormtroopers and her space navy personnel. They were used to grueling labor, and they performed admirably now that they were faced with a true crisis.

Grand Moff Tarkin had given her command of four Star Destroyers to protect Maw Installation. But her first ship, the *Hydra,* had been lost even before she could bring her fleet out of the Maw cluster. The *Manticore* had been destroyed behind the moon of Calamari, unable to run when some Calamarian tactical genius had second-guessed Daala's strategy. Her third ship, the *Basilisk,* already injured in the battle against smuggler forces at Kessel, had not been able to flee the supernova explosions fast enough.

Daala had been helpless to stop the attrition of her forces. She had planned a fabulous and devastating attack on the Rebel capital world of Coruscant, but before she could strike, Kyp Durron had used the Sun Crusher against her.

During the long days of repairs Daala had come to terms with her failure. She had misplaced her priorities. Her only reason for existence should have been to protect Maw Installation, not to wage a private war against the Rebellion. Once the Rebels knew of the Installation, they would no doubt attempt to steal its secrets. Her priority now was to fulfill the mission that Tarkin had given her.

The *Gorgon* was wounded, unable to proceed at full thrust; but still Daala approached the Maw with all possible speed. She would return to the Installation and protect what remained of it, to the best of her ability. There would be no such thing as surrender. She had a job to do, a duty she had sworn to her superior officer Tarkin.

Now Admiral Daala clung to her command chair and kept her eyes open against the blazing swirls from the inferno of trapped gases. The *Gorgon* plunged through the barrier of black holes and followed a convoluted path. Daala felt her insides tugged as she passed gravity wells so deep they could crush an entire planet to the size of an atom.

The windowports dimmed, but still Daala did not close her emerald eyes. Presumably only she knew the detailed route, but young Kyp Durron had found his way, and she assumed that other Jedi Knights could perform the same feat.

Daala heard a system squeal with automatic alarms as some critical component failed. Sparks shot out of one of the sensor stations, and a lieutenant strained against the pull of acceleration to bypass the systems.

In his seat Commander Kratas spoke through clenched teeth. "Almost there," he said, his voice barely audible above the racket.

A series of automatic warning signals echoed through the bridge—and suddenly the colors washed away from the front viewport like a blindfold being ripped from her eyes. The Star Destroyer had stumbled into the shielded calm at the center of the cluster.

She recognized the isolated clump of interconnected planetoids gathered in a loose configuration. Glittering lights showed that the facility still functioned. In a rapid assessment she saw that the framework of the Death Star prototype was gone—and in its place she saw a Rebel frigate and three Corellian corvettes.

"Admiral!" Kratas said.

"I see, Commander," she answered in a clipped voice.

She unbuckled her restraints and stood up, automatically smoothing down the olive-gray uniform that clung to her trim body. Sweat prickled like tiny insect stings on her skin as she stepped onto the command platform and walked closer to the viewport as if responding to a summons.

Her gloved hands gripped the bridge railing as if to strangle something. Black leather squeaked against enameled metal. The Rebels had come, just as she had feared—and Daala had arrived too late to stop the invasion!

Her lips grew white as she pressed them together. She believed the *Gorgon* had survived for a purpose. And now, as she returned to Maw Installation, it seemed as if the spirit of Grand Moff Tarkin were looking over her shoulder, guiding her. She knew what she was destined to do. She could not fail a second time.

"Commander, power up all functional weapons systems," Daala said. "Shields up. Approach the Installation."

She looked back at large-browed, weak-chinned Commander Kratas, who snapped to attention.

"It appears we have some work to do," Daala said.

27

Kyp Durron ducked under a thorny vine as a flock of scarlet insect-birds thrummed into the air. Acrid stinging thistles brushed against his arm, his face. Overhead, the interlocked branches rustled as arboreal creatures fled from the noise. Sweat dripped from Kyp's dark hair, and the oppressive air felt like a moist blanket, smothering him.

He did his best to keep up with Master Skywalker, who flowed through the jungle thickets, finding secret paths that allowed him to pass unhindered. Kyp had once used dark tricks to dodge spiny debris and find the easiest routes through the underbrush; now, though, even the thought of such techniques made him shudder with revulsion.

Once, when he had gone on a jungle sojourn with Dorsk 81, Kyp had brashly used a Sith technique to generate an unappetizing aura around himself, driving away gnats and bloodsucking pests. Now, though, Kyp tolerated the misery as Master Skywalker led him far from the Great Temple.

They had left the other Jedi trainees to continue their independent studies. Master Skywalker was proud of them. He said that the trainees were reaching the limits of the techniques he himself could teach them. The new Jedi Knights would grow in their own directions, discover their own greatest strengths.

But since the time he had come within a razor's edge of blasting Han Solo with the Sun Crusher, Kyp had been reluctant to use his power, afraid of what it might drive him to do. . . .

Master Skywalker took Kyp alone out into the jungles, leaving the great pyramid behind as Artoo-Detoo wobbled and jittered, bleeping with displeasure at being left behind.

Kyp wasn't sure what the Jedi teacher wanted from him. Master Skywalker said little as they trudged for hour after hour through the dripping rain forest and the oppressive humidity, the insect-laden air, the claw-thorns of brambles.

Kyp was intimidated to be alone with the man he had defeated through Exar Kun's evil powers. Master Skywalker had insisted that Kyp arm himself—that he wear the lightsaber built by Gantoris. Did Luke intend to challenge Kyp to a duel—a duel to the death this time?

If so, then Kyp vowed not to fight. He had allowed his anger to cause too much destruction already. It was only by a miracle that Master Skywalker had survived the onslaught of Sith treachery.

Kyp had recognized the dark side when Exar Kun whispered in his ear, but he had been too overconfident, thinking he could resist where even Anakin Skywalker failed. But the dark side had swallowed him whole—and now Kyp questioned all of his abilities and wished he could just be free of his Jedi talent so he need not fear what he might do with it.

At the edge of a clearing, with tall grasses stroking against each other, Master Skywalker came to a halt. Kyp stopped beside him to see two ferocious-looking predators, iridescent in scales of pale purple and mottled green for camouflage in the thick vegetation. They looked like hunting cats crossbred with large reptiles: their shoulders were square, their forearms as powerful as heavy pistons. They had three eyes across their boxy faces, yellow and slitted, unblinking as they stared at the intruders.

Master Skywalker gazed back at them in silence. The breeze stopped. The predators growled, opening their mouths to expose scimitar fangs, and let out a purring howl before they melted back into the jungle.

"Let's continue," Master Skywalker said, and walked across the clearing.

"But where are we going?" Kyp asked.

"You'll see soon enough."

Unable to bear his feelings of isolation and loneliness, Kyp tried to keep the Jedi teacher talking. "Master Skywalker, what if I fail to distinguish between the dark side and the light side? I'm afraid that any power I use now might also lead me down the path of destruction."

A feathery-winged moth flitted in front of them, seeking nectar from the bright flowers that blossomed among the creeping vines. Kyp watched the moth's flight until suddenly, from four different directions, sapphire-winged piranha beetles zoomed in to strike, ripping the moth's wings to shreds. The moth fluttered and struggled, but the piranha beetles devoured it before it could even fall to the ground. The beetles buzzed so close to Kyp's face that he could see their saw-toothed mandibles ready to tear flesh to shreds; but the beetles ratcheted away to seek other prey.

"The dark side is easier, faster, more seductive," Luke said. "But you can identify it by your own emotions. If you use it for enlightenment to help others, it may be from the light side. But if you use it for your own advancement, out of anger or revenge, then the power is tainted. Don't use it. You will know when you are calm, passive."

Kyp listened and knew that he had done everything wrong. Exar Kun had given him false information. The Jedi Master turned to him; his face looked haggard with the weight on his shoulders. "Do you understand?" Master Skywalker asked.

"Yes," Kyp answered.

"Good." Master Skywalker parted the branches on the other side of the clearing to expose a sight that made Kyp stop cold in his tracks. They had come from a different direction, but Kyp could never forget the site itself. Fragments of burning ice trickled down his spine.

"I feel cold," he said. "I don't want to go back there."

They stepped out to where the vegetation dropped off at the edge of a glassy-smooth lake, a circular reflecting pond where the water looked clear and colorless and reflected the cloudless skies above like a pool of quicksilver.

In the center of the pond sat an island of volcanic rock on which perched a sharply angled split pyramid made of obsidian. Two halves of the steep pyramid had been spread apart to bracket the polished black statue, a towering colossus of a man with flowing hair, bulky uniform, and a long black cape. Kyp knew the image all too well.

Exar Kun in life.

Inside that temple Kyp had received his initiation into the Sith teachings, while Dorsk 81 had lain in an unnatural coma against the wall. The spirit of Exar Kun had meant to destroy the cloned Jedi student on a whim, as a gesture of power, but Kyp had stopped him, insisting instead that the Sith Lord teach him everything. He had seen things that still left yammering nightmares in the depths of his mind.

"The dark side is strong in that place," Kyp said. "I can't go in there."

Master Skywalker said, "In your fear lies caution, and in that caution lies wisdom and strength." He squatted on a comfortable rock at the edge of the crystalline lake. He shaded his eyes against the light reflecting from the surface of the pool.

"I will wait here," Master Skywalker said, "but you must go inside."

Kyp swallowed, terror and revulsion rising within him. This black temple symbolized everything that had rotted his core, everything that had led him astray, all the mistakes he had made. The dark lies and goading of Exar Kun had caused Kyp to kill his own brother, to threaten the life of his friend Han Solo, to strike down his Jedi teacher.

Another shiver passed through him. Perhaps this was his punishment.

"What will I find in there?" Kyp asked.

"Ask no more questions," Master Skywalker said. "I can give you no answers. You must choose whether to carry your weapon with you." He nodded toward the lightsaber handle clipped to Kyp's waist. "You will have only what you bring with you."

Kyp touched the ridged handle of the lightsaber, afraid to turn it on. Did Master Skywalker want him to leave it behind or take it? Kyp hesitated. Better to have the weapon and not use it, he decided, than to need it and be without.

Trembling, Kyp went to the water's edge. He looked down and observed the tall columns of stone that stopped just beneath the surface of the water, providing submerged stepping stones.

Tentatively, he set one foot on the first stone. The water rippled around his foot. He drew a deep breath, raised his head high, and fought back the echoing voices in his head. He had to face this, whatever it was. He did not look back at Master Skywalker.

He crossed the water and climbed onto the lichen-encrusted lava rocks of the island, walking the narrow path that led to the triangular entrance of the temple.

Beneath the towering statue of Exar Kun, the black opening glittered with implanted Corusca gems. Incised runes and hieroglyphics broke the polished brightness of the obsidian. Kyp stared at the writings, finding that he could summon some of their meaning back to him; but he shook his head to clear the words from his thoughts.

The temple seemed to breathe a cool air current that seeped in and out of the enclosed space. Kyp did not know what he would find inside. His body stiffened with anticipation. He looked around, refusing to call out. Kyp took one step into the doorway and looked up at the dour chiseled face of the long-dead Sith Lord. Then he entered the temple chamber.

The walls glittered with an inner light that had been trapped within the volcanic glass. Tracings of frost spiraled in a frozen dance up and down the walls. In the far corner a cistern dripped, filled with chilled water.

He waited.

Suddenly Kyp's stomach wrenched. His skin crawled. He blinked as his vision blurred. The air around him grew grainy as if the light itself had splintered inside the temple.

He tried to turn, but found himself moving sluggishly as if the air resisted him, solidifying around him. Everything flickered.

Kyp staggered deeper into the temple, trying to move quickly, but his body would not respond with its customary speed.

A shadow rose from the black wall, an ominous form, human-shaped. It gained power, growing as Kyp fed it with his fear. The figure rose higher, oozing out of the cracks, out of a blackness from beyond time, a featureless silhouette that nevertheless seemed familiar to Kyp.

"You're dead," Kyp said, attempting to sound angry and defiant, but his voice was uncertain.

"Yes," the oddly familiar voice spoke from within the shadows. "But still I live within you. Only you, Kyp, can make my memory strong."

"No, I'll destroy you," Kyp said. In his hand he felt the black power crackling, the ebony lightning he had used to strike Master Skywalker: the power of fanged serpents, the dark teachings of the Sith. How ironic it would be to use Exar Kun's own power against him! The energy grew stronger, begging to be unleashed, demanding that he give himself over to it so he could eradicate the black shadow for all time.

But Kyp forced himself to stop. He felt his heart pounding, his blood singing in his ears, his anger taking control—and he knew that was wrong. He took deep breaths. He calmed himself. This was not the way.

The black Sith power faded from his fingertips. The shadow waited; but still Kyp forced his power back, smothered his anger. Anger was exactly what Exar Kun would want. Kyp could not give in to it now.

Instead he reached for the lightsaber at his hip, pulled it free, and flicked on the power button. The violet-white blade shone in an arc of cleansing electricity, purest light.

The shadow hovered, as if waiting to do battle with him, waiting for Kyp to make the first move. It lifted its nebulous arms, blacker than anything Kyp had seen before. Kyp raised Gantoris's lightsaber to strike, proud of what he was about to do. He would use a Jedi weapon instead—a weapon of light to strike the darkness.

He made ready to swing. The shadow hung poised, as if stunned—and Kyp halted again.

He could not strike out, not even with a lightsaber. If he attacked Exar Kun, he would still succumb to the temptation and ease of violence, regardless of the weapon he chose.

The lightsaber handle felt cold in his grip, but Kyp switched the power off and clipped the handle to his belt. He stood alone, face-to-face with the shadow that now seemed his own size, merely the black outline of a human wearing a shroud.

"I will not fight you," Kyp said.

"I am glad," said the voice, which became clearer now, more maddeningly familiar. Not Exar Kun at all. It never had been.

The shadowy arms reached up to pull back the cowl, exposing a luminous face that clearly belonged to Kyp's brother, Zeth.

"I am dead," the image of Zeth said, "but only you can keep my memory strong. Thank you for freeing me, brother."

The image of Zeth embraced Kyp with a brief, tingling rustle of warmth that melted the ice in Kyp's spine. Then the spirit vanished, and Kyp found himself alone again in a musty, empty temple that no longer held any power over him.

Kyp stepped into the warm sunlight again, free of the shadows. On the opposite shore he saw Master Skywalker stand up and look at him. Luke's face wore a broad grin, and he opened his arms in a celebratory gesture.

"Come back and join us, Kyp," Master Skywalker called. His voice echoed across the flat surface of the still water. "Welcome home, Jedi Knight."

28

The immense barricade doors of the Imperial Correction Facility did not budge, nor did they open when Han knocked. Naturally.

He stood with Lando and Mara Jade outside on the scoured landscape of Kessel, dressed in an insulated jumpsuit taken from the *Lady Luck*'s stores. Mara leaned closer to Han, her shout muffled through the breath mask covering her mouth.

"We could bring down a full-scale assault team from the moon," she said. "We have enough firepower."

"No!" Lando shouted. His dark eyes shone with excitement and anxiety. "There must be a way to get in without damaging my facility!"

The cold, dry wind stung Han's eyes, and he turned his head to protect them from the breeze. He remembered gasping for air when Skynxnex, Moruth Doole's henchman, had dragged him and Chewbacca into the spice mines without giving them breathing apparatus. Right now Han wanted nothing more than to kick the toadlike Doole out of the prison so that his frog eyes could blink and his fat lips pump together as he tried to fill his lungs.

Doole, an administrator of the Correction Facility, had dealt in black-market glitterstim, making deals with Han and other smugglers to deliver the precious cargo to gangsters such as Jabba the Hutt. But Doole had a habit of delivering his partners into Imperial hands whenever it proved convenient.

Doole had ratted on Han long ago, forcing him to dump his cargo—which had made Jabba very angry. . . .

Han did not want to be back on Kessel. He wanted to be back home with his wife and children. He wanted to have his companion Chewbacca back. He wanted to take a nice, relaxing vacation. For once.

"I've got a better idea," Mara said, interrupting Han's thoughts. She craned her neck to look up at the murky sky. "Up on the garrison moon I brought along Ghent, our slicer. You might remember him. He used to be one of Talon Karrde's top aides. He can crack into anything."

Han remembered the brash young slicer: an enthusiastic kid who knew electronics and computer systems intimately, but didn't know when to keep his mouth shut. Han shrugged. They didn't need social skills now; they needed someone who could crack through the defenses.

"Okay, bring him down along with the *Falcon*," Han said. "I've got a few gadgets inside my ship that might help us out, too. The sooner we can get in, the sooner I can get going."

Lando agreed. "Yes, any way to enter without doing too much damage . . ."

Mara pursed her lips. "I'm also going to bring in a team of fighters. I've got four Mistryl guards and a handful of other smugglers who are getting fidgety with our new alliance. Some of them have been complaining that it's been too long since they had a good, satisfying fistfight."

An hour later, cold and uncomfortable even in the insulated suit, Han sat on the *Lady Luck*'s thruster pod. He saw the faltering plumes from two distant atmosphere-factory stacks, but the rest of the world stood lifeless. He knew from experience, though, that deep within the spice mines lurked hideous energy spiders, waiting to strike any creature they found.

Han heard a sonic boom reverberate through the thin atmosphere, a high-pitched sound mixed with the thunder of sublight engines. He scanned the sky until he saw the pronged disk of the *Millennium Falcon*.

The ship landed in a powdery white clearing beside the *Lady Luck*. The ramp slid out, and five smugglers emerged: two tall, well-muscled women—Mistryl guards—a hairy, tusk-faced Whiphid, and a reptilian Trandoshan; each wore a uniform with the crosshatched insignia of the new Smugglers' Alliance. The smugglers bristled with weapons; their bulging belts contained enough recharge packs for an entire assault.

Last down the ramp, still fumbling to adjust a breath mask over his face, came Ghent the slicer, with tousled hair and rapidly blinking, alert eyes. He nodded cursorily at Mara, then fixed his entire attention on the barricade gates. Slung over his shoulder was a satchel crammed with tools, diagnostic apparatus, splitters, rerouting circuits, and security-cracking equipment. "Should be a piece of cake," Ghent said.

Mara Jade and Lando sat next to Han and watched Ghent fall to work with total concentration, not the least distracted by the miserable environment of Kessel.

Han said, "I certainly never dreamed I'd be trying so hard to break *into* the Kessel prison."

Cowering behind a locked door in the lower levels of the Imperial Correction Facility, Moruth Doole longed for the good old days. Compared to the constant paranoia he had endured for the past several months, even life under the Imperial yoke had been paradise.

After he had taken over the prison years ago, Doole had moved into the warden's office, where he could spend much time staring out at the landscape, observing the desolate purity of the alkali wastelands. He had fed upon tender flying insects. Whenever the whim struck him, he had mated with one of his captive female Rybets in his personal harem.

Now, though, since Daala's attack, he had moved into one of the high-security prison cells for protection. He had tried to make preparations, establish defenses, because he knew someone was going to come after him, sooner or later.

The cell walls were thick and blast proof. The lights shone down, burning shapes into his blurry vision. He tapped the mechanical eye that helped him to focus. The device had broken during the space battle around Kessel. Doole had tinkered with the mechanical components, putting its gears and lenses back together; it no longer worked quite properly, though, and his vision winked out from time to time.

Doole paced the cold stone floor of his cell. Everything had fallen apart. The planet Kessel had been abandoned, leaving only smoking rubble on the surface and destroyed hulks of ships strewn across the system all the way to the black hole cluster. Doole couldn't even get a ship of his own to escape. He didn't *want* to stay here—but what choice did he have?

Even the blind larvae—the large-eyed creatures whom Doole had locked inside pitch-black rooms to process the mind-enhancing spice, glitterstim— were growing restless. He had cared for them, given them food (a meager amount, to keep their growth down, but enough for survival), but now they had begun to struggle.

Doole snorted, making a squeaking sound with his bloated lips. The larvae were his own ungrateful children, immature Rybets who had not yet undergone their final metamorphosis. Blind and wormlike, almost as large as Doole himself, the larvae were perfect workers to wrap the spice fibers in opaque sheaths, since even brief exposure to light would spoil the product.

His children could work in the blackness, and be happy. And what sort of gratitude did they show him?

A few larvae had gotten loose, fleeing blindly through the winding prison passages, hiding in shadowy cells, waiting in darkened wings to ambush Doole if he came looking for them. But he was not going to look. He had more important things to do.

To make things worse, one of the largest male larvae had freed all of Doole's specially picked females! The females had fled into the labyrinth of the prison, so that during this time of greatest terror, Doole couldn't even relieve his tension with an occasional visit to the harem.

He had no choice but to remain locked inside his office cell, pace the floor, and be alternately bored out of his mind and scared out of his wits. When he did make his way to the storerooms, he emerged heavily armed, waddled quickly down the corridors, and came back with as much food as he could carry.

He had an escape tunnel, of course. He had blasted a channel into the spice mines directly under the prison. Doole could lose himself for a long time in that network, but he still couldn't get off-planet. And lately the tunnels had become a far more dangerous place.

After Daala's attack most of the spice miners had fled. Without guards and construction and loud machinery, the spiders had surged upward to lay down their glitterstim webs along the walls. Looking with specially adapted kinetic energy detectors, Doole had spotted swarms of the monsters in the deepest shafts, migrating closer to the surface.

In despair Doole sat on his bunk and smelled the dank air of the dungeon. At another time he might have found it comforting and cool, but now he just rested his sucker-tipped fingers against damp jowls and stared at the monitors.

He was astonished to see a ship land outside. And even though all humans generally looked alike to him, Doole was certain he recognized one of the three intruders pummeling his armored door: Han Solo, the man he hated most in the entire universe, the man who had caused all this misery!

At the ominous prison gates Han watched as Ghent the slicer worked diligently on the problem. He jacked in all manner of equipment, components stolen out of other systems, barely functional combinations that somehow found loopholes around defense systems.

Ghent raised a triumphant fist into the grainy sunlight. The reinforced latticework of the defensive portcullis rode up on invisible tracks. With a hollow clunking sound the shipping and receiving gates split apart, squealing and creaking as they lumbered into the thick walls. A gust of higher-pressure air bled out of the prison.

The four large smugglers shouldered their weapons and plodded forward, crouched over and ready to fight. The two Mistryl guards took the lead, sliding along the walls. The burly Whiphid and scaly Trandoshan strode brashly down the middle of the hall.

No attack came from the dark passageway. "Let's go find Moruth Doole," Han said.

None of his options looked good, but Doole had to make choices. He had watched Han Solo and his group of commandos force their way in—and Kessel was supposed to be the toughest prison in the galaxy. Hah!

Doole didn't know how to use the built-in defense systems, the external laser cannons, the disintegrator fields. He was helpless without his right-hand man, Skynxnex, but the scarecrowish fool had gotten himself killed chasing Solo through the spice tunnels, devoured by one of those energy spiders.

As a desperate measure Doole had come to the conclusion that he must trust his own children, the blind larvae he kept in blackness since the moment they writhed out of the gelatinous egg mass in the harem wing's breeding pools.

Doole rushed down the corridors, gathering weapons from the prison's armory. He carried two satchels of blaster pistols over his shoulder as he opened the protective vaults. Suddenly exposed to the light, the larvae reared back like caterpillars, blind eyes bulging as they attempted to sense the identity of the intruder.

"It's only me, only me," Doole said. Bright light stabbed at them, illuminating their pale skin. Damp vestigial hands reached up, small fingers and arms short and weak, not completely formed. Wormlike tendrils quivered below their mouths as the larvae made soft burbling noises.

Doole herded the oldest and strongest of the larvae along ramps to the lower levels. He would station them as guardians inside his cell. Being blind, they probably couldn't hit anything with the blasters, but he hoped they would at least fire with enthusiasm once he gave them the orders. Given enough cross fire, Doole could hide behind a blast-proof screen and hope the firefight would kill Solo's team.

As Doole ushered them toward his cell, he smelled the musky wetness of their fear and uncertainty. The immature Rybets did not like change, preferring a rigid daily routine until eventually they molted and became adults, gaining intelligence and self-awareness.

Distracted by trying to think of what other defenses he might bring to bear, he was startled by a high-pitched scream echoing from three of the nearby chambers. Several of the freed female Rybets sprang out, wailing and throwing sharp objects at them.

Doole ducked as broken shards of transparisteel, sharpened knives, and heavy paperweights flew at him. Doole tried to grab a blaster from one of the two satchels on his back, but a drinking mug struck him on the soft side of his head. He dropped one of the satchels and ran wildly down the corridor, waving his sucker-tipped hands.

Most of the larvae followed him, but a few split off to stay with their mothers. Doole ran, wanting only to get back to the safety of his cell. Finally slamming the thick door behind him, he emptied his remaining satchel and placed fully charged blasters in the hands of six potential defenders.

"Just point it toward whatever noise you hear," he said. "When they break in, it's up to you to shoot. This is the firing button."

The smooth-skinned creatures shivered and ran their sensitive mouth tendrils over the barrels of the weapons.

"You point it, and it makes a blast." Doole repositioned the pistols in their vestigial hands, pointing them toward the door.

Without warning the vision in his mechanical eye flickered again, and Doole couldn't see a thing. He moaned in terror. The escape tunnel was sounding better and better.

With a growing dread in the pit of his stomach, Han Solo hurried down the prison corridors. The entire place was full of cold shadows, echoing with emptiness.

Over the comm link Mara Jade said, "We've found him, Solo. He's barricaded in one of the dungeons. We tapped into the surveillance cameras. He's got some creatures standing with him, and they appear to be armed."

"On my way," Han said.

When he reached the lower corridors, Han saw heavy barricades thrown in place across a sealed door. Mara watched the operation as the two female Mistryl guards placed concussion detonators around the door seal.

Lando paced nervously. "Don't do any more damage than you have to," he said. "I've got enough repairs to make here on Kessel as it is."

The two women ignored him as they sprinted out of the way. They ducked their heads and covered their ears as a rapid *thud thud thud* echoed from the concussion detonators.

They heard a volley of sudden blaster fire from inside the sealed chamber, a high-pitched shriek of energetic beams striking and ricocheting off the walls.

"No, no! Not yet!" came a howling voice that Han recognized as Moruth Doole's.

With a final *thump* the last concussion detonator blew the bottom off the door. The hairy Whiphid rushed forward to elbow the heavy plates aside.

"Look out," Mara called.

The Whiphid ducked and rolled as the soft larvae flailed, pointing their blasters and firing in every direction. Their huge glassy eyes spun around without seeing anything.

"Get them!" Doole yelled. The larvae whirled at the sound of his voice and fired their blasters toward Doole himself. But he had already ducked behind a thick piece of wall plating. "Not at me!"

Hissing, the reptilian Trandoshan shot inside, cutting down two of the blind larvae. He lumbered into the chamber, but before the other smugglers could rush in, another explosion came from the ceiling. Han, Mara, and the Mistryl guards used the distraction to muscle their way forward, ducking down and firing again. Han took out another of the larvae just as the ceiling collapsed in flaming chunks.

Wailing for revenge, swarms of female Rybets dropped through the ceiling into Doole's private cell. Each bore a blaster of her own and fired repeatedly at the metal shield Doole hid behind until its center glowed a cherry-red.

The blind larvae targeted on the new noise—but then as if suddenly they understood, as if they could communicate with their own mothers, the larvae turned and directed their fire toward Doole as well.

"Stop, stop!" Doole cried.

Han crept in beside Lando, not wanting to draw fire in the midst of this civil war. Doole yelped and dropped the superheated protective shield. His mechanical eye popped off and broke into a thousand bouncing and rattling components on the floor. His long squishy fingers punched a hidden control button, and a trapdoor opened beneath him. With a mindless squeal Doole leaped through an access hatch into an escape tunnel, down into the cold black mines.

"Hurry, before he gets away!" Lando said. "I don't want him running around in my spice mines."

The surviving larvae flowed forward as if they wanted to plunge into the tunnels after Moruth Doole, either to follow him or to chase him. But the amphibious females grasped the larvae and held them back with gentle cooing sounds. Their wide eyes looked on the invading smugglers with apprehension.

Han rushed toward the trapdoor and dropped to his knees, pushing his face into the darkness. He heard Doole's splatting footsteps diminishing as he ran on webbed feet deeper into the catacombs.

The larvae shot several blaster bolts into the passages after him. Long spears of heat bounced along the tunnel walls, knocking boulders loose. The light sparked a scintillating glare of activated glitterstim.

Then Han heard a new sound that turned his blood cold. A faint but chilling noise, hundreds of sharp legs like ice picks scrambling down the tunnel. Han could still hear Doole's footsteps getting fainter and fainter as he fled. Han heard the *tik tik tik* of multilegged creatures, attracted by the heat of a living body . . . and Doole's gasping, ragged breath as the Rybet searched blindly for a way out.

Han heard many more sets of pointed legs scrabbling, like a stampede from converging tunnels as the energy spiders found nourishment after the long silence in the spice mines. Han's skin crawled.

At the tail end of a high-pitched and gut-wrenching scream, Doole's footsteps suddenly stopped. The scream cut off abruptly, as did the sound of running ice-pick feet. The instant silence seemed even more horrible than the scream, and Han quickly pulled up the trapdoor and secured it before the energy spiders could seek other prey.

He sat back, heart pounding. The smugglers looked grimly satisfied at the battle they had won. The Whiphid leaned against a wall with arms crossed. "A good hunt," he growled.

The Trandoshan glanced from side to side, as if seeking something to eat.

The female Rybets hauled away the blasted larvae, tending the injured, mourning over the dead.

Han sighed as Lando sank down next to him. "Well, Lando," he said, "now you can start remodeling."

Han, Lando, and Mara rode back up to the garrison moon in the *Falcon*. Mara and Lando spoke more easily to each other, now that Lando wasn't pushing so hard to get the slightest word or smile from her. Mara had even stopped avoiding Lando's gaze or raising her chin whenever he spoke. She spent most of her time reassuring him that the *Lady Luck* would be just fine behind the security fields of the reoccupied prison. Lando didn't seem to believe her entirely, but he did not want to disagree with Mara Jade.

"We've got a lot of paperwork to do," Mara said. "I have all the standard contracts and agreements up at the moonbase. We can take care of the formalities between us, but there are still a lot of forms to digitize and sign, a lot of records to cross-reference."

"Whatever you say," Lando said. "I want this to be a long and happy partnership. You and I need to figure out how we can best implement production on Kessel. It's in the best interests of both of us to get the glitterstim flowing soon, especially since I'm going to have to sink so much of an investment into the mining work again."

Han listened to them talk but devoted most of his thoughts to his family. "I just want to go home. No more side trips."

The *Falcon* sped away from the wispy corona of escaping air toward the large moon. Once leaving the turbulent atmosphere of Kessel, they coasted smoothly in the vacuum of space as if on glass.

Suddenly an alert flashed on their communications panel from the moonbase. "Warning! We've detected a large vessel approaching Kessel— and I mean *large*."

Han reacted instantly. "Lando, check the scanners."

Lando stared at the copilot station and sat up quickly, his eyes as big as viewports. "Not just large," he said.

Han could see the globe-shaped object through the viewport. Spherical, but skeletal, crossbraced and arched with giant girders. The size of a miniature moon.

"It's the Death Star."

The repairs took longer than expected, much to Tol Sivron's frustration, but the prototype was finally ready to approach, and attack, the nearest planetary system.

Sivron shifted in his seat, pleased to observe the stormtrooper captain giving all the right orders. Delegating responsibility was the first lesson of management. He liked sitting in the pilot's chair while others did the work.

Squat, bald Doxin leaned forward from one of the other chairs. "The target is coming into view, Director Sivron."

"Good," Sivron said, looking at the streaked atmosphere fuzzing around the planet and its close-orbiting moon.

"There seems to be significant ship activity in the area," Yemm, the Devaronian, said. "I'm tracking and documenting it for posterity. We'll want a careful record in case we need to file a report on the performance of this prototype."

"It's a Rebel base," Tol Sivron said. "No doubt about it. Look at those ships. Look at its position. This must be where our prisoner Han Solo came from."

"How can you be sure?" said Golanda.

Sivron shrugged. "We need to test this Death Star, right? We've got a handy target right here—so it might as well be a Rebel base."

The stormtrooper captain sat at the tactical station. "We're picking up numerous alarms from the moonbase. It appears to be some sort of military installation."

A flurry of ships departed from a large opening in the moon, spewing a random collection of well-armed and fast cruisers around Kessel.

"They can't get away from us," Tol Sivron said. "Target the planet. You may fire when ready." He smiled, and his pointed teeth formed a serrated edge against his lips. "I've got a good feeling about this."

Doxin grinned in breathless delight. "I never thought I'd get a chance to see this weapon in action."

"It's never been calibrated, you know," Golanda said with a sour expression.

"It's a planet-destroying superlaser," Doxin shot back. "We can turn that whole world into rubble. How well does it need to be calibrated?"

"Targeting now," the stormtrooper captain said.

In shielded firing chambers below, lit only by flickering blazes of colored light from complex control panels, other stormtroopers functioned as Death Star gunners, after having been told to scour the instruction manuals.

"What's taking so long?" Tol Sivron fidgeted against the uncomfortable fabric of the command seat.

Suddenly the white-noise background hum of the operating systems dropped an octave. The lights dimmed on the panels as the prototype consumed an incredible amount of energy.

Out the front viewport, past main support struts that arched like giant steel rainbows over their heads, smaller superlaser beams fired out of the Death Star's focusing eye, phasing together at the intersection point. The green beam gained in power and lanced out in an immense blast, greater in diameter than a starship.

Its target erupted in a blaze of smoke, fire, and incandescent rubble.

Tol Sivron applauded.

Yemm took careful notes.

Doxin let out a cry of triumph and amazement.

"You missed," Golanda said.

Tol Sivron blinked his small dark eyes. "What?"

"You hit the moon, not the planet."

He saw she was right. The moon that had served as a garrison for the fighter ships had exploded into fragmented rubble that was raining down in spectacular meteor showers on the planet Kessel.

The fighter ships that had evacuated from the moonbase swarmed about in a flurry, like fire-mantids disturbed from their nests during mating season.

Tol Sivron coiled and uncoiled his naked head-tails, feeling tingles along his nerve endings. He leaned back in the chair and waved a clawed hand in dismissal.

"That can be corrected. The target was irrelevant. At least now we know the prototype is fully functional." He nodded approvingly. "Just as all the progress reports said."

Sivron took a deep breath, feeling the thrill build within him. "Now we can put this weapon to use."

29

Leia was amazed that Mon Mothma still clung to life. Anxiously, she stood over the deathbed of the Chief of State, looking at the kaleidoscope of medical apparatus and life-support systems that refused to let Mon Mothma die.

The auburn-haired woman had once been such a fiery rival of Leia's father on the Senate floor; now she could no longer stand on her feet. Her skin was gray and translucent, thin as crumpled parchment on a framework of bones. Her eyelids struggled open as if they were heavy blast doors. Her eyes took a long time to focus on her visitor.

Leia swallowed, feeling hot lead in her stomach. She reached out with trembling fingers to touch Mon Mothma's arm, afraid that the slightest pressure could cause bruises.

"Leia . . . ," Mon Mothma whispered, "you came."

"I came because you asked me to," Leia said.

Han had dropped her and the children off on Coruscant, grumbling about having to go away again with Lando, but promising to return in only a few days. She would believe that when it happened. In the meantime Leia was shocked to see the accelerating decline of Mon Mothma's condition.

"Your children . . . are safe now?"

"Yes. Winter is staying here to protect them. I won't let them be taken from me again."

Leia would be even busier than before; she would see less of Han, less of her children. Momentarily she envied the peaceful life of a lower functionary who could leave work at the end of the day and go home, letting unfinished tasks wait for tomorrow. But she had been born a Jedi and raised by Senator Bail Organa. Her life had been focused toward a greater destiny, and she could not shirk either her public or her private burden.

Leia took a deep breath, tasting the nauseating chemicals that clung to the air, the disinfectants, the medicines, the ozone smell of atmospheric sterilizers.

She felt so helpless. Her excitement at defeating the Imperial strike force and rescuing her son seemed trivial in the face of Mon Mothma's battle against the slow-acting poison. Leia took little consolation in knowing that Ambassador Furgan was no longer alive to gloat.

"I . . . ," Mon Mothma spoke ponderously, "have tendered my resignation to the Council. I will no longer serve as Chief of State."

Leia realized that empty encouragements would be useless. She reacted in a way that Mon Mothma had taught her to respond, thinking of the New Republic first.

"What about the government?" she said. "Won't the Council bicker with each other and accomplish nothing because they can't reach a consensus? Who will they look to for leadership?"

She looked down at Mon Mothma, and the haggard woman blinked at her with shining, hopeful eyes. "*You* will be our leader, Leia," Mon Mothma said.

Leia blinked in shock and opened her mouth. Mon Mothma found the strength to nod slightly. "Yes, Leia. While you were away, the Council met to discuss our future. My resignation is no surprise to anyone, and we voted unanimously that you should be my replacement."

"But—" Leia said. Her heart pounded; her mind whirled. She had not expected this, at least not now. Perhaps after another decade or two of dedicated service, then . . .

"You, Leia, will be the Chief of State for the New Republic. If I had any strength left to give, I would give it all to you. You'll need it to hold this newborn Republic of ours together."

Mon Mothma closed her eyes and squeezed Leia's hand with a surprisingly firm grip. "Even when I'm gone, I will be watching over you."

Speechless, Leia knelt at Mon Mothma's bedside for a long time, far into Coruscant's night.

30

Inside Maw Installation one of the members of Wedge's Special Forces
Team had deciphered enough of the primary controls to sound the facilitywide alarm. Through the intercom system an unfamiliar voice barked, "Red
alert, an Imperial Star Destroyer has entered the vicinity. Red alert! Prepare
for attack."

Wedge stood next to Qwi inside her empty old laboratory as they gaped
at the scarred and blackened hulk of the *Gorgon*. The mammoth ship maneuvered into position over the cluster of lashed-together rocks.

"Oh, my!" Threepio said. "I thought we were supposed to be safe in
here."

Wedge grabbed Qwi's pale hand. "Come on, we have to get to the
operations room."

They ran through the corridors. Qwi did her best to lead him, though
frequently she couldn't remember which direction to go. Threepio, his servomotors whirring, tottered after them as fast as he could go. "Wait for me!
Oh, why does this always happen?"

Inside the operations room Wedge was relieved to see that a dozen of
his troops had gotten there ahead of him and were already scrambling to
operate the controls. A few of the computer banks had malfunctioned, but the
rest had been jump-started. Sensor arrays spilled data across their screens.

Wedge put his hands on Qwi's shoulders, pressing his face close to hers and looking into her big eyes. "Qwi, try to remember! Does Maw Installation have any of its own defenses?"

She looked up through the latticed skylight, seeing the looming arrowhead shape of the Star Destroyer. Qwi pointed up. "*Those* were our defenses. Maw Installation depended entirely upon Admiral Daala's fleet."

She hurried over to one of the deadened computer consoles and used her musical keypad to whistle her password into the system, hoping to bypass the damaged circuits with her own files and select some of the higher-order functioning routines. "We do have shields," Qwi said, "if only we could increase them."

Five harried technicians came over to help her, using their own expertise to access the generators and reinforce the protective force field around the primary planetoids.

"That'll hold for now against an assault," a tech said, "but this makes me very uncomfortable, General Antilles. The power reactor is already unstable, and we're placing a tremendous drain on it. We could be sealing our own fate."

Wedge's gaze flicked to Qwi and then back to the soldiers. "Well, it's certain death if we don't do something to protect ourselves now. We've taken what we need. I think it's time to leave Maw Installation. Have the ships prepare for departure."

"If Daala will let us," Qwi said. "I doubt she'll allow us to walk off now that we've uncovered its secrets."

Wedge's eyes suddenly blinked in realization. "We took one of the corvette engines off-line for spare parts for the power reactor! One of my ships is crippled and can't move." He ran to the communications station and switched on a narrow-beam to the disabled corvette.

"Captain Ortola, launch all starfighter squadrons from your bay—now. Take all personnel and shuttle over to the *Yavaris* or one of the other two corvettes. Without maneuverability, your ship is a prime target."

"Yes, sir," Captain Ortola's voice acknowledged.

The broad trapezoidal viewscreen at the far end of the operations room surged with static, and then an image of fiery-haired Admiral Daala filled the screen. She leaned forward into the viewing area. Her eyes seemed to throw pointed javelins right into Wedge's heart.

"Rebel scum, you'll not leave Maw Installation alive. The information contained in this facility is now forfeit, tainted by your sabotage. I'm not interested in your surrender or your flight. Only your destruction."

Daala ended the transmission herself before Wedge could formulate a reply. He shook his head at the flickering static that faded into a dull gray. He turned back to Qwi and felt his heart pounding. "Qwi, are you sure there's nothing else here we can use? Any other weapon?"

"Wait," Qwi said. "Chewbacca took a team down into the maintenance bay to rescue the Wookiee slaves. There were always several assault shuttles or fighter ships being worked on. Maybe those?"

One of the New Republic commandos snapped his head up. "Assault shuttles? Probably gamma class. They're nothing spectacular, but they are heavily armored and well outfitted with weapons, worth ten of our starfighters. It could be a welcome addition in the battle. Daala's got only one Star Destroyer against us, but she still outguns the combined force of the corvettes and the *Yavaris*."

The squad leader looked down at a scrolling list of equipment on a data screen. "Just as I feared, sir. These are old models. They require a piloting droid to fly complicated maneuvers, especially in this gravitational environment. We could probably do it with only one droid and cross-link to the separate navigational systems."

At that moment, with heavy footfalls and buzzing servomotors, Threepio hurried into the operations room, emitting a loud sigh of relief. "Ah, there you are! I've finally found you."

Wedge, Qwi, and everyone else turned to look at the golden droid.

Threepio moved forward, his arms waving in dismay as he negotiated a steep ramp into the rock-lined maintenance bay. "I don't know why everyone keeps treating me as if I were some sort of . . . property," he said.

Chewbacca grunted a sharp retort, and Threepio snapped at him. "That's quite beside the point. In actual fact, I—"

Chewbacca lifted up the golden droid and set him bodily on the entrance ramp of a gamma-class assault shuttle. The recently freed Wookiee slaves, along with a group of New Republic commandos, scrambled into the five armored shuttles that remained in the bay. Each ship had been maintained in perfect working order by Wookiee crews.

From above sudden hollow thumps echoed through the asteroid as the *Gorgon* pummeled them with turbolaser blasts. Chewbacca and the other Wookiees howled at the ceiling, their bestial noises echoing louder than the thunder of attack. Faint dust trickled down, split from the sealed rock walls.

"I still think I'm going to regret this," Threepio said. "I wasn't designed for this kind of work. I can communicate with other tactical computers and coordinate your flight paths, but putting me in charge of strategy—"

Chewbacca ignored him and climbed into the vehicle. Seeing that his arguments were useless, the golden droid shuffled up the ramp into the confines of the assault shuttle. "But, then again, I am always happy to help, where needed."

The other Wookiees, including stunted old Nawruun, took their places in the gunnery seats, ready to blast TIE fighters.

Chewbacca slumped into the assault shuttle's too-small pilot seat and made Threepio sit beside him in the copilot's chair. "Oh, very well," Threepio said, and inspected the computer, deciding how best to communicate with it.

More explosions from the *Gorgon*'s attack pounded through the thick walls, but those noises were soon drowned out by the growling purr of the shuttles' repulsorlift engines.

Chewbacca raised the heavily armed ship off the floor and guided it down the launching corridor. Atmosphere-containment fields sealed behind them just before the heavy launch doors opened into space like a huge vertical mouth.

Threepio linked up to the guidance computers and the directional programming of all five assault shuttles. Behind them identical vehicles flew in a tight formation, picking up speed. "This is rather exhilarating," Threepio said.

Chewbacca punched at the controls until the shuttle rocketed like a projectile through the launch doors and away from the Installation's protective shield.

Above, swarms of starfighters streamed from the Corellian corvettes. The frigate *Yavaris* began to fire on the Star Destroyer as Daala continued to rain turbolaser bolts upon the Installation. From the lower bay doors of the *Gorgon,* squads of TIE fighters streaked out like spooked mynocks from a cave.

Chewbacca powered up his weapons systems, and Threepio linked into their preprogrammed attack patterns. The five assault shuttles from Maw Installation plunged into the heart of the burgeoning space battle.

"Oh, my!" Threepio said.

31

When Leia answered the summons at the door to her quarters in the rebuilt Imperial Palace, she saw it was the deepest hour of the bustling night. For a moment she had a thrilled thought, that Han might have come back from Kessel already. But when she rubbed sleep from her eyes and opened the door, she found her brother Luke standing there. She paused a moment, utterly astonished, and then rushed forward to embrace him.

"Luke! When did you come to Coruscant?" Out of the corner of her eye she caught sight of another young man standing off to the side in the dim corridor. She recognized the tousled dark hair of Kyp Durron; his eyes were deep-set and averted, no longer the brash teenager that Han had rescued from the spice mines of Kessel.

"Oh, Kyp," she said in a flat, unemotional voice. Seeing the young man unnerved her. He had been Han's dear friend, a companion through enjoyable adventures—but Kyp had also gone over to the dark side, paralyzed Luke, killed millions of people, turned on Han. . . .

Kyp's face and eyes looked old now, exhausted from the traumas he had endured—and caused. Leia had seen eyes like those only once before: on her brother after he had faced the knowledge that Darth Vader was his own father. But Kyp had been through a hell as deep as Luke's had been.

A small courier droid shot down the hall, blinking red lights to warn others to clear the way as it propelled itself along on urgent business, even this late at night.

With a flush of embarrassment Leia remembered her manners. "Please, come in."

From the back room Winter emerged, gliding forward on silent bare feet, wearing only a loose sleeping garment. Winter appeared ready for action lest some other danger throw itself upon the children. She bowed her head formally when she saw Luke. "Greetings, Master Skywalker," she said.

Luke smiled and nodded to her. "Hello, Winter."

Winter backed into her chambers. "I'll just check on the children," she said. She vanished, giving them no chance to say anything else.

Leia looked from Kyp to Luke again, feeling deep weariness behind her eyes, behind her head. She had been relying on too many stimulant drinks, spending too much time negotiating with other Council members, sleeping too little.

Luke closed the door behind him as he and Kyp entered the common room. Leia remembered when her brother had trained her in this room, trying to unlock her Jedi potential. Now, though, she sensed that Luke had a much more ominous agenda.

"Is Han here?" Kyp blurted, looking around the quarters.

Leia noticed that he still wore the black cape Han had given him as a gift; but now Kyp seemed to carry it as a symbol over a light jumpsuit, a reminder to himself of what he could become.

"He's gone off to Kessel with Lando," Leia said, a tired smile tugging at the corners of her mouth. "Lando wants to try running the spice mines."

Kyp frowned uncertainly. Luke sat down on one of the self-conforming cushions and leaned forward, weaving his fingers together. He directed his intense gaze at Leia. "Leia, we need your help," he said.

"Yeah, I figured that out," Leia answered with a touch of irony. "I'll do everything I can, of course. What do you need?"

"Kyp and I have . . . made our peace. He has the potential to be the greatest of the Jedi I am training, but there's one thing he must do before I can consider him completely absolved."

Leia swallowed, already afraid of what he might say. "And what is this 'one thing'?"

Luke did not flinch. "The Sun Crusher must be destroyed. Everyone in the New Republic knows that. But Kyp must do it himself."

Leia simply blinked, unable to say anything. "But . . . how can he destroy it?" she finally said. "As far as we know, it's indestructible. We already dropped it into a gas planet's core, but Kyp"—she turned her exaggerated gaze on the young man—"managed to retrieve it. I don't suppose even dropping it into a sun would have made much difference."

Kyp shook his head. "No, I could have recovered it just as easily."

Leia looked helplessly at Luke, spreading her hands. "So what else—?"

"Kyp and I will fly the Sun Crusher back to the Maw. He will set the autopilot and drop it down one of the black holes. Quantum armor or no quantum armor, it will be obliterated. There's no more definite way of erasing something from this universe."

Kyp piped up. "I know the Sun Crusher must be taken away from both the Empire and the New Republic. I . . . Dr. Xux no longer has any memory of how to reconstruct it. The galaxy will never need to fear such a threat again." His posture stiffened, his chin rose, his eyes grew alive again. The guilt and pain were replaced with a look of pride and determination.

Luke placed a hand on the young man's forearm, and Kyp fell silent, content to let Luke continue.

"Leia, I know you've been appointed the new Chief of State. You can make this happen." He leaned forward, speaking to her with the idealistic, boyish energy she remembered from years before. "You know I'm right."

Leia shook her head, already afraid of the enormous diplomatic battle she would have to face at the mere mention of Luke's preposterous request.

"There'll be a lot of heated discussion. Most of the Council members are going to refuse to let Kyp get within sight of the Sun Crusher again. What's to stop him from rampaging around the galaxy and blowing up more star systems? Can they take that risk? Can *we*?"

"They have to take that risk," Luke said. "It must be done. And I'll be there with him."

Leia bit her lip. Her brother could be so forceful. She knew him well enough that she wasn't simply awed by what the Jedi could do . . . but she was confident that Luke could follow through on his claim.

"Do you know what you're asking?" she said in a soft, pleading voice.

"Leia, just as I had to face our father, this is a test Kyp must complete. Tell the Council that if he passes this test successfully, Kyp Durron could become the most powerful Jedi Knight of this generation."

Leia sighed and stood up. "All right. I'll try—"

Kyp interrupted her and said, "There is no try: do or do not." Then he allowed himself a wry smile, gesturing toward Luke. "At least that's what he always says."

Han Solo gritted his teeth as he yanked on the *Falcon's* **controls. The** modified light freighter flew up and around in a tight backward loop. The blinding flash of the Death Star's superlaser faded to a glowing streak as the rubble of Kessel's moon mushroomed in a rapidly expanding cloud.

"That was gonna be my garrison!" Lando cried. His voice cracked. "First Moruth Doole, now a Death Star—this deal is getting worse all the time."

Mara Jade, her face hard as chiseled stone, quickly leaned between Han and Lando in the two cockpit seats and shouted into the comm unit. "This is Mara Jade. All ships report. How many did we lose? Did the evacuation order go out on time?"

One of the cool-voiced Mistryl guards responded. "Yes, Commander Jade," the warrior woman said. "We scrambled at first sign of the intruder. All but two ships made it away from the base. One more was struck and destroyed by the flying debris."

Mara nodded grimly. "Then we still have enough of a fighting force," she said.

"Fighting force!" Han said. "Against that thing? To do what? It's a Death Star, not a cargo freighter." He looked through the overhead viewport and saw the skeletal prototype over Kessel. The superweapon seemed to be brooding over the destruction it had just caused.

"But, Han," Lando pleaded, "we've got to do something before it blows up the planet, too. Think of all the *spice* down there."

Mara grabbed the comm again. "Attack formation gamma," she said. "We're going to head out and pound that Death Star." She turned to Han and lowered her voice. "If it's just a prototype, my guess is they won't have the defenses the real Death Star had, no squadrons of TIE fighters, no turbolaser fortifications across the surface. That's what did the most damage to your Rebel fleets, wasn't it?"

"Not entirely," Lando said. "The second Death Star used its superlaser against a few of our capital ships."

Mara pursed her lips as she thought. "Then we'll just have to keep them busy. I don't think that superlaser can be very effective at targeting small moving objects."

"I don't like the odds on that," Lando said.

"Never quote me the odds," Han said, hunching over the panel and guiding the ship into position.

"Who, me?" Lando said, raising his eyebrows. "I'm a sucker for lost causes."

The *Millennium Falcon* soared into the vanguard of the smugglers' attack formation. Han was impressed to see the assortment of large and small ships fall into a perfect pattern, as if they were trained and regimented. The motley bunch must have a great deal of respect for Mara Jade, he realized; as a rule, smugglers were notoriously independent and took orders from no one.

One of the other ships, an insectile Z-95 Headhunter—the type of ship Mara herself often flew—streaked in beside the *Falcon*. Its pilot spoke over the open channel. "This is Kithra. I'll take the right-hand prong, Shana will take the left. You fly center, *Falcon*, and we'll hit the Death Star in all three places at once."

Han recognized the no-nonsense voice of another Mistryl guard. How many had she brought along with her?

"Agreed, Kithra," Mara said. She turned to look at Han. "Well, Solo, ready to lead the attack?"

"I never intended to take the *Falcon* against a Death Star," he groaned, even as he prepared for battle. "I was just giving Lando a lift to Kessel."

"Think of it as an added bonus," Mara said.

"Come *on*, Han," Lando urged, "before that Death Star fires again."

"Good thing Leia's not here," he muttered. "She'd probably succeed in talking me out of this."

As the ships converged on the skeletal behemoth, the superlaser struck once more, scorching the fabric of space with emerald fire—but the beam passed through the scattered ships descending upon it, causing no damage.

"Shields up," Han said, "for whatever good it'll do against *that*."

On either side of the *Falcon* two segments of the smuggler fleet peeled off like the skin from a rustle snake: one prong led by Kithra in her Headhunter, the other headed by Shana in an angular blockade runner, a clunkier forerunner of the *Falcon*'s light-freighter design.

The smuggler ships drove in, energy cannons blazing, drawing a deadly tracery of fire across the superstructures and girders of the enormous sphere.

Han launched three proton torpedoes into the labyrinth of cross beams and supports as they charged toward the enormous construction. A few reinforced girders glowed molten as projectiles and energy beams hit.

"It's going to take us a year to chop away at this thing," Han said, firing from the *Falcon*'s forward weaponry.

"I never claimed this was going to be easy," Mara said.

Tol Sivron's head-tails twitched. He squinted his black beady eyes at the oncoming small ships. They appeared so trivial, their weapons systems so minor. "I can't believe they're attacking *us*," he said. "What do they think they're going to accomplish?"

At the tactical station the stormtrooper captain spoke through his white helmet. "If I might point out, Director, this battle station is for proof-of-concept only. It was never designed to defend itself against multiple small threats. In fact, the Death Star was meant to house over seven thousand TIE fighters, not to mention thousands of surface turbolasers and ion cannons and an escort of several Imperial-class Star Destroyers. We have none of these.

"Individually, those Rebel ships may be only a minor threat, but together they can harry us for an extended period and, if we are unlucky, cause significant structural damage."

"You mean we don't have any fighters of our own?" Tol Sivron said with stern disapproval. "That was poor planning. Who wrote that section of the procedure? I want to know right now."

"Director," the stormtrooper said with a tinge of exasperation in his filtered voice, "that doesn't matter at the moment."

"It matters to me!" Tol Sivron said. He turned toward demon-faced Yemm, who was already scouring the records.

"It appears that Dr. Qwi Xux was responsible for that section, Director," Yemm said. "She devoted much of her time to the operation and performance of the superlaser, giving short shrift to tactical considerations."

Sivron sighed. "I see we've found a flaw in our approval system. Such weak spots should never have been allowed to pass through the progress reports and review meetings."

"Director," Doxin said, "let us not allow this to overshadow the marvelous performance of the Death Star superlaser itself."

"Agreed, agreed," Sivron said. "We should have a meeting immediately to discuss the implications of—"

The stormtrooper captain stood up from his station. "Director, we *must* establish certain priorities right now! We are under attack."

An outside explosion made the Death Star framework around the control chamber vibrate.

"That's three direct hits with proton torpedoes," the stormtrooper said. "So far."

As Sivron watched, four Z-95 Headhunters swooped out of the superstructure, their rear engines blazing.

"Well, then fire again with our laser," Tol Sivron said. "Maybe we can hit one of them this time."

"The power core is only half-charged," Doxin pointed out.

Sivron whirled and parted his lips to show pointed teeth. "Isn't that good enough to knock out a few little ships?"

Doxin blinked his piggish eyes as if he hadn't considered the possibility. "Why, yes, sir—yes, it is. Ready to fire."

"At your convenience, Division Leader," Sivron said.

Eagerly, Doxin spoke into the intercom, commanding the gunners to fire. After a few seconds the incredible beam of light seared out; side lasers converged at a focal point and coalesced into a laser battering ram that plowed through the fringe of the oncoming cluster of fighters, vaporizing one old blockade runner in the vanguard of the left prong. Another ship was damaged by the backwash of the blast, but the attacking forces spread out and disappeared into the superstructure like parasites, firing again.

"Did you see that?" Doxin said with obvious pleasure. "We hit one!"

"Hooray," Golanda said sourly from her seat. Her voice carried absolutely no enthusiasm. "Only about forty more to go, and you can't even fire the superlaser again for fifteen minutes."

"Director, if I may make a suggestion," the stormtrooper captain said. "We have successfully tested the prototype laser, but to stay here any longer would serve no purpose. To endure unnecessary damage to this fine weapon is folly. We should protect the Death Star so we may present it intact to the Imperial authorities."

"And what do you suggest doing, Captain?" Tol Sivron said. He dug his long claws into the armrests.

"We should withdraw to the Maw cluster. I doubt these small ships will follow. We are not highly maneuverable, but we can build up considerable speed. Note that we don't need to go all the way back to the Installation, just to the opposite side of the cluster where we can hide." The captain paused, then said slowly, "Once there, you will have time to hold a lengthy meeting, to decide what to do. You can . . . discuss the whole situation by committee if you like."

Tol Sivron brightened. "Good idea, Captain. See to it. Let's head out of here as fast as we can."

The stormtrooper captain fed in a new course for the prototype. The huge open-framework sphere wheeled about on its axis and accelerated away from Kessel, cumbersome but picking up speed as it left the flurry of other ships behind.

After the blaze from the Death Star's third blast faded, Han Solo rubbed sparkles out of his eyes, seeing distorted colors. "That was too close," he said. "The fringe of the beam fried our forward shields."

Shana's old blockade runner had been destroyed, and some ships now flew off in retreat. "We have to regroup," Kithra's voice came over the comm system.

"I think we should just get out of here," Han said.

"Look!" Lando interrupted as the arching framework of the Death Star spun about and began to accelerate away from Kessel. "We've got it on the run."

"For now," Mara said, "but it may just be retreating long enough to recharge its power core so it can strike again."

"Kessel won't be safe while that thing is out there," Lando said. "Han, we've got to go in. Let's take the *Falcon* all the way to the power core."

"Are you crazy, Lando?" Han asked, his voice rising. "This is my ship, remember."

"I'm not contesting that," Lando said, holding his hands up, "but I've flown her into a Death Star before. Remember?"

"I've got a bad feeling about this," Han mumbled, and he shot a sidelong glance at Mara Jade. "But you're right. We can't just run away. If the prototype falls into the hands of the Imperial navy, it could cause a lot more misery than I want to be responsible for. Let's go in."

He punched his accelerators. Mara sent orders to her fleet. "All ships back off. We're going in. Alone."

The *Falcon* cruised through the nightmarish maze of overhanging girders, coolant and ventilation systems, power conduits and substations that formed the inner structure of the Death Star prototype. Catwalks laced the open spaces like so many spiderwebs.

The *Falcon* shot inward, tunneling deeper and deeper into the construction as the framework grew denser, more complex. Han spun the ship left and right to squeeze through narrow passages.

Just ahead, in the middle of a huge open corridor, a mammoth-sized construction crane toppled from its moorings, dislodged by the smuggler attack and the sudden lurching movement of the prototype. The crane fell, tumbling in silence through the vacuum of space, directly into the path of the *Falcon*.

"Look out!" Lando cried.

Han punched the firing buttons and sent out a converging blast from his laser cannons, disintegrating the falling machine into an expanding plume of incandescent gas and metal steam. Lando leaned back and closed his eyes with a shuddering sigh.

As the *Falcon* careened through, the passengers were bumped and jostled. Large debris struck the deflector shields. Sparks flew out of the control panels, and smoke poured from the engine panels beneath the floor plates.

"We've got damage!" Lando yelled.

Han fought for control. "She'll hold together," he said, as if praying.

Suddenly the Death Star jerked and slammed forward as its heavy-duty sublight engines fired up. Han tried to match the speed, spiraling closer to the power core. The *Falcon* lurched, barely responding to Han's attempts to maneuver.

They passed gargantuan girders ringing the outer core, tumbling into a vast enclosed space, a spherical chamber that contained the two gleaming conical sections of the power core. Green-and-blue fire crackled between the contacts as reactors pumped up the energy level, recharging the weapon to fire again.

"Talk about recurring nightmares," Lando said. "I never wanted to see anything like this again in my life."

"I guess we're just lucky," Han said, scanning his damage reports. "We need repairs bad," he said through gritted teeth. "Lousy time for the engines to act up."

The Death Star rotated again, changing course and accelerating once more with equatorial propulsion units. Han narrowly avoided an arc-shaped girder that swung across to slam at them; he maneuvered the *Falcon* around it in a tight loop and limped toward the superstructure that held the reactor core in place.

"I need to check on those engines," Han said, "but I can't do anything while the Death Star is moving and rocking like this. We're going to have to settle in for the ride."

"Settle in?" Mara asked in astonishment.

"Don't get all bent out of shape. I did this once before to elude Imperial pursuit," he said, flashing a lopsided grin. "A nice little trick built into the *Falcon*. Added it myself." Han brought the ship up parallel to one of the thick girders. "It's my landing claw. I used it to hang on to the back of a Star Destroyer, then drifted off with the garbage as the fleet entered hyperspace."

The *Falcon* attached itself with a *clang*. Directly below them the towering cylinder of the power core blazed into the emptiness, shining its deadly light.

"We're secure here for now," Han said. "But if they plan to go back inside the black hole cluster, we could be in for one wild ride."

33

Riding together in the close confines of the Sun Crusher, Luke felt young Kyp Durron draw mentally closer to him as they journeyed toward the black hole cluster.

Kyp was gradually overcoming his fear and preoccupation with Jedi powers and the potential for abusing them. After his epiphany inside the temple of Exar Kun, Kyp had emerged stronger, able to accept the challenge. If he could face this final test, Luke would know that Kyp had passed through the fire of his testing—tempered by forces as dire and powerful as those Luke himself had endured. . . .

Luke smiled as he recalled how Leia had argued for Kyp in the Council meeting, fighting for the chance that Luke offered. During her very first session as leader of the New Republic, Leia had presented her brother's demand; in the uproar that followed she had reasoned, cajoled, or shamed every one of them into giving Luke a chance.

She had emerged from the hours-long meeting in the middle of a bright Coruscant day. Kyp and Luke, waiting for her in one of the high mezzanine cafés within the enormous Imperial Palace, had sipped warm drinks and sampled delicacies from a hundred planets that had sworn allegiance to the New Republic. Leia had brushed aside her two bodyguards and hurried forward to meet them as other bureaucrats and minor functionaries stood up from their tables in recognition of their new Chief of State. Leia ignored the attention.

Her face was haggard and exhausted, but she could not hide her satisfied smile and the twinkle in her large eyes. "The Sun Crusher is yours to dispose of," she had said. "You'd better take it before someone on the Council decides my victory was too easy and moves to reopen the discussion."

Then Leia had turned a stern face toward Kyp. "I'm gambling my entire future administration on you, Kyp."

"I won't let you down," Kyp had promised, holding his head high. Luke did not need Jedi powers to sense the determination in the young man.

They had flown away from Coruscant into hyperspace on a direct course for the Maw cluster near Kessel.

The two of them ate rations and shared a warm silence. When they finished, Kyp fell into a deep rejuvenation trance, a form of deathlike hibernation that Luke taught all his students; the young Jedi awoke after only an hour, looking greatly refreshed.

En route Kyp had shared fond memories of his home planet, Deyer. He spoke in a halting, wistful voice about his brother Zeth. As Luke listened with quiet understanding, Kyp let loose his sorrow and wept cleansing tears, finally allowing himself the freedom granted by the vision of his brother's spirit in the obsidian temple.

"Yoda made me take a test of my own," Luke told him. "I had to go into a cave in the swamps of Dagobah, where I confronted a vision of Darth Vader. I attacked and defeated him, only to find that I was fighting myself. I failed my test, but you succeeded."

Luke looked into Kyp's dark eyes. "I don't promise it will be easy, Kyp, but the rewards of your efforts will be great, and the entire galaxy will benefit from them."

Kyp looked away as if embarrassed and studied the piloting controls of the Sun Crusher. "Ready to come out of hyperspace," he said. "You strapped in?"

Luke nodded with a slight smile. Around them hyperspace looked bruised and distorted from their proximity to all the black holes.

Kyp stared at the chronometer and concentrated as the numbers spun by. "Three, two, one." He released the levers, and suddenly the blur sprang away from their viewport, and real space snapped into crystal focus around them.

Luke saw the distant gaseous knot of the Maw, but he instantly felt a wrenching inside as if something was terribly wrong.

"What happened to Kessel?" Kyp said.

Luke found the much closer, distorted shape of Kessel masked by an expanding debris cloud.

"The garrison moon," Kyp said. "It's gone."

"We've been detected," Luke said. "Ships coming in." He sensed the anger and dismay from the pilots in the attack ships now gathering speed and converging on the Sun Crusher.

The speaker buzzed with a forceful female voice. "This is Kithra of the Mistryl guard, representing the Smugglers' Alliance. Identify yourself and state your business in the Kessel system."

"This is Luke Skywalker," he said, restraining a confident smile. "We're here on business for the New Republic. Our mission is to destroy the Sun Crusher, and we had hoped to hitch a ride back to Coruscant with one of your ships. Mara Jade cleared us by subspace transmission only yesterday."

"Commander Jade is not here now," Kithra said. "But she did notify me you would be coming. As you can see, though, we have recently been under attack."

"Tell me your situation," Luke said. "Where's Mara? Is she okay? What about Han Solo?"

Kyp let his eyes fall half-closed, reaching out with the Force, searching. He jerked his head to the left, toward the swirling mass of the Maw. "Han's there—he's over there."

Kithra's voice came over the speaker again. "A Death Star prototype attacked us," she explained as the smuggler ships swarmed around them in a protective contingent. "We suspect it was fleeing the New Republic occupation force that recently entered the cluster."

"Wedge and Chewie are inside the Maw, too," Luke said to Kyp.

"What happened to Han?" Kyp said into the comm with rising urgency.

"Our ships struck at the prototype and caused some minor external damage, but Han Solo flew the *Millennium Falcon* into the superstructure. Commander Jade ordered us to fall back. The *Falcon* was carried along as the Death Star retreated toward the Maw. They were going to attempt to sabotage its power core, but we've heard no word from them since."

"How long has it been?"

"Only a couple of hours," Kithra answered. "We've been considering our options."

Luke looked to Kyp, and their eyes met in shared concern. "We don't have any options," Luke said.

Kyp nodded. "We've got to help Han."

"Yes," Luke said, swallowing hard. "Into the Maw."

For two Jedi, finding a safe path through the labyrinth of gravity wells proved simple enough. Working together, Luke and Kyp reinforced each other's perceptions, flying the Sun Crusher in tandem, like linked navicomputers.

The Sun Crusher rattled and vibrated with the strain. Luke experienced a stretching of his mind as he let his senses extend outward, as if dragged downward into the bottomless black holes.

Kyp flew with his eyes closed, his jaws clenched, his lips drawn back in a grimace. "Almost through the wall," he said through his teeth.

After passing through an eternity of superhot colors, they fell into the quiet bubble within the center of the cluster.

Clearing his vision, Luke searched for the Death Star prototype, expecting to see it firing at Wedge's assault fleet. But instead he saw quite a different space battle in progress: New Republic forces blasting, starfighters launched in frantic dogfights—arrayed not against the Death Star, but against the deadly spear-point shape of a battered and blaster-scarred Star Destroyer.

"It's Admiral Daala!" Kyp said, his voice thick with hatred.

34

The wire-frame prototype hid, powered down, on the far side of the
Maw cluster as Tol Sivron, Golanda, Doxin, Yemm, and the stormtrooper
captain held a meeting to discuss the implications of their changed situation.

It had taken some time to find an empty storeroom that could be converted into an appropriate conference chamber, and they had to forgo their
hot beverages and morning pastries. But these were emergency times, Sivron
admitted, and they had to make sacrifices in the name of the Empire.

"Thank you, Captain, for pointing out that loophole in our procedures,"
he said, flashing a pointy-toothed smile.

The stormtrooper had shown them in an appendix to the emergency
procedures, under the subheading "Dissemination of Information," a clause
pertaining to the total secrecy of Maw Installation inventions—"Rebel access
to Maw Installation research and development data must be denied at all
costs." This clause, he argued, could be interpreted as mandating the destruction of the facility, now that it had been overrun.

"*At all costs*," the captain repeated, "clearly means we should forfeit the
Installation itself rather than let the Rebels have access to our work."

"Well," Doxin said, "it would give us another opportunity to fire the
superlaser for the good of the Empire." He raised his wire-thin eyebrows so
that his scalp furrowed like treadmarks across a sand dune.

Yemm, the Devaronian, continued to flip through paragraph after paragraph of the procedures on his datapad, studying the terminology. "I see nothing to contradict the captain's assessment, Director Sivron," he said.

"All right, the resolution has passed," Sivron said. "We shall direct the prototype back into the Maw, using our previous flight path. Captain, take care of the details."

"Yes, sir," the stormtrooper captain said.

"So that's all settled, then," Tol Sivron said, clacking his long claws on the tabletop. "If we have no new business, the meeting is adjourned."

Everyone stood to leave, brushing their uniforms and stepping away from the table.

Tol Sivron looked at the small chronometer; barely two hours had passed. He blinked his beady eyes in surprise. This had been one of his shortest meetings ever.

35

Threepio's dizzying preoccupation with battle configurations and tactics and ships swarming around the five gamma assault shuttles absorbed all his concentration. He forgot entirely about his dread.

The *Gorgon* cruised ominously overhead, firing down on the Installation or shooting across at the New Republic ships.

Chewbacca growled, squinting his fur-rimmed eyes to study the Star Destroyer's firing pattern. He chuffed and grunted an idea to Threepio and, without waiting for a response, opened the tight-beam ship-to-ship communications systems.

Chewbacca spoke rapidly in the Wookiee language, which Threepio decided was a tactically wise thing to do. Although he himself was a protocol droid and understood more than six million forms of communication, he doubted that anyone on the *Gorgon* would know what Chewbacca was saying.

Even as acknowledgment came from the Wookiee pilots in the other assault shuttles, Threepio broke away from his full concentration to speak to the Wookiee. "I simply don't see how we can possibly take out all of the starboard turbolaser banks on the Star Destroyer. It's suicide. Why don't we wait for more fighters from the New Republic ships? I think that would be by far the safest strategy."

Chewbacca snarled, and Threepio decided it was unwise to press the point any further.

A combat wing of TIE fighters soared past them, firing bursts from their laser cannons. One of the assault shuttles passed into the crossfire, and as Threepio reconstructed the images an instant later, he determined that it received eight direct hits within two seconds. Its shields failed. Hull plates buckled, and the shuttle exploded as the TIE fighters roared past to face the X-wings and Y-wings pouring from the New Republic battleships.

Chewbacca let out a grief-stricken roar at seeing some of his newly rescued friends die. The cry was echoed across the comm system by the other Wookiees.

With the explosion Threepio experienced a sudden disorientation; he had been partially linked to the destroyed ship. It felt as if a part of him had been disconnected.

"Oh, dear!" he said, then shifted his concentration to managing the other shuttles. "Chewbacca, you have my complete support. We simply cannot allow them to do this sort of thing."

Chewbacca roared agreement and gave Threepio a comradely slap on the back that practically sent the droid through the control panels.

A tiny streak of light shot past them, and Threepio was able to freeze the image in his optical sensors: it was the angular crystalline shape of a tiny two-man ship. He recognized it instantly.

"Oh, my, isn't that the Sun Crusher?" Threepio asked.

Preoccupied, Chewbacca roared a challenge as the four remaining assault shuttles cruised low over the *Gorgon*'s starboard side. They soared above the complex topography of the hull, a blur of indecipherable outcroppings, piping, fuel shafts, portholes, and life-support equipment. Daala's heavy turbolasers shot alternately at the Maw Installation and at the New Republic starfighters.

Seven TIE fighters broke away from the main attack and circled back to head off Chewbacca's squadron. But the Wookiees unleashed a smoking volley from the assault shuttle's heavy blaster cannons. Stunted old Nawruun and several other Wookiees sat in the gunner seats and fired relentlessly.

A web of blaster bolts spewed from the shuttles, clipping four of the attacking TIE fighters. Two others veered wildly away from the sudden firepower and careened into the side of the *Gorgon*. The lone survivor of the attack group peeled off and fled to get reinforcements.

Chewbacca grunted in satisfaction.

The assault shuttles hammered the Star Destroyer's turbolaser batteries as they streaked back and forth, launching their store of concussion missiles. With the smoldering eruptions of hull plates and exploding weapons systems, the *Gorgon* was defenseless on one side.

"Oh, well done, Chewbacca!" Threepio cried. "You did it."

Chewbacca purred in satisfaction. Loud, triumphant roars came from the back of the assault shuttle and the gunner bay. But as TIE reinforcements arrowed toward them, Threepio decided it was time to cease the frivolity.

"Excuse me, sir," he said, "but hadn't we better retreat now?"

Like a master pilot Kyp Durron brought the Sun Crusher into a berth on one of the planetoids. He maneuvered the thorn-shaped ship through the blast doors and into the bay.

Luke let the young man pilot as he himself worked the communications systems, transmitting to the escort frigate and then to the Installation operations center.

"Wedge, are you there? Are you all right? Tell me what's going on. This is Luke."

A response came over the comm, accompanied by a cacophony of alarms and shouted orders, status reports, and the background rumble of direct hits from the Star Destroyer.

"Luke, you're alive! What are you doing here?"

He realized that Wedge had been inside the Maw cluster since before the defeat of Exar Kun. "We brought the Sun Crusher here to destroy it. But it looks like you're having problems of your own."

"I'd need a few hours to tell you everything that's happened since this operation started," Wedge said. His voice was harried. "Are you safe?"

"We're fine for now, Wedge. We're landing in one of your maintenance bays."

"Good. I can sure use whatever help you can offer."

After Kyp secured the Sun Crusher, he popped open the hatch, and the two of them clambered down the metal ladder. They set off at a brisk jog through the curving corridors that tunneled through the dead rock. The rhythmic pounding of Daala's repeated blasts echoed through the tunnels.

The two of them spilled into the operations center, trying to make sense of the frenzy of preparations Wedge had underway.

Wedge Antilles ran forward to embrace his friend. Both men clapped each other on the back. "I'm so glad you're back with us," Wedge said in a voice filled with unasked questions. Then he flashed a distrustful glance at Kyp Durron, who stood contritely on the threshold. "What's *he* doing here?"

Beside him Qwi Xux also saw him and gasped, taking a step backward.

"I'm sorry," Kyp said quietly.

Luke looked sternly at Wedge. "Kyp is here to help us, Wedge. He has returned from the dark side, and I've made my peace with him. If you still hold a grudge, then take it up with him once this is all over."

Wedge looked to Qwi, and her gentle narrow face tightened before she nodded briefly.

"Kyp came here to destroy the Sun Crusher as a form of penance, but now—" Luke gripped his apprentice's shoulder. "Now we are two Jedi offering our services in this fight."

Wedge called to one of the other commandos. "Give me a status update now," he said.

The tactical crew rattled off a list of starfighters deployed, shots fired, a tally of enemy and ally losses. "Chewbacca's team appears to have knocked out the *Gorgon*'s starboard turbolaser batteries."

Wedge looked relieved. "If only we can keep damaging Daala faster than she can damage us." He shook his head.

"Where's Han?" Luke asked. Kyp perked up, eagerly awaiting the answer.

Wedge frowned. "What do you mean?" Luke explained about the prototype and how Han, Lando, and Mara Jade had last been seen inside its superstructure.

Wedge shook his head. "The Sun Crusher and the *Gorgon* are already here—now you're telling me the Death Star is coming back?" He blinked in disbelief before starting to snap out orders to the tactical team. "You heard what Luke said! Looks like we've got another surprise coming our way."

It didn't seem possible, but everyone managed to bustle a little faster. Luke stared through the broad sky-lights of the operations center. He sensed it before he saw it.

Through the flaring lights of battle overhead and the muffled din of repeated explosions, the armillary sphere of the Death Star prototype emerged through the pastel glow of the Maw and entered the fray.

36

The *Millennium Falcon's* landing claw clung to the Death Star's superstructure as the skeletal sphere lurched into motion again and careened through the black hole cluster.

Han, Mara, and Lando sat strapped into their swiveling seats, gritting their teeth from gravity's onslaught. The *Falcon* held on, but the prototype bucked from the enormous tidal pulls.

Once the rough passage was over, Han scanned the diagnostics. "Got to do something about these hyperdrives," he said. "If we fly fast enough, we could just blow the reactor core and run. But the way the *Falcon's* limping along, we'd never get away in time."

Han turned his seat to look at Lando and Mara. He wiped dark hair away from his eyes. "And even if we did get away in time, we'd never make it back through the Maw cluster without top-notch maneuverability."

"Not to mention we don't know the *way* out," Mara said. "My Jedi instincts aren't strong enough for a job like that."

"Uh, now, that's another good point . . . ," Han admitted.

"But Han," Lando said, "we've got to do something. If the Death Star's come back to Maw Installation, it's bound to be up to no good."

"Yeah," Han said, nodding grimly. "Chewie is in here with the rest of the occupation force. I won't just leave him if he's in trouble."

Mara pulled herself to her feet. "So it's obvious," she said. "We've got to deactivate that superlaser." She shrugged. "As long as we're here."

"But the hyperdrive engines—" Han began.

"You've got environment suits, don't you?" she said. "A light freighter like the *Falcon* ought to have at least a couple for emergency repairs."

"Yesss," Han said, drawing out the word, still unable to guess what Mara had in mind. "I've got two suits: one for me and one for Chewie."

"Good," Mara said, cracking her knuckles. "Calrissian and I will go out and plant timed detonators on the reactor core. You work on the hyperdrive engines. The timers will let us get out of the superstructure before they blow."

Lando's mouth dropped open. "You want *me*—?"

Her eyes challenged him. "Got any better ideas?"

He shrugged and grinned. "Why, no. I'd be honored to escort you, Mara."

Lando sneezed as he tugged on the huge padded suit. "This whole thing smells like Wookiee hair," he said. "Did Chewbacca exercise in this thing and put it away wet?"

The sleeves were enormous, and his feet swam in the Wookiee-sized boots. He tugged the bulky fabric around his waist, fold upon fold, and then used the adjustment straps to cinch it tighter around him. He felt as if he were walking inside a giant inflated mattress.

"We've got a job to do, Calrissian," Mara said. "Quit complaining or I'll do it myself."

"No," Lando said. "I want to help you. Really."

"Here." Mara held out a case of the timed detonators. "Carry these."

Lando looked down at them and swallowed. "Thanks."

Han gave a hollow grunt of pain as he bumped his head on something down in the repair crawl space. Lando heard his friend mutter something about wishing for a decent droid to do the dirty work.

"A couple of the components are fried," Han called up to them. His voice sounded tinny through the compartment. "But I've got spares—or at least close enough that I can get the ship running again. We've got three fused circuits. One we can get by without; two I can bypass."

"We'll give you half an hour," Mara said, pulling the helmet on and sealing it over her neck.

Han repositioned himself in the coffin-sized maintenance bay to stick his head above the deck plates. Grease and leaked coolant stained his cheeks. "I'll be ready."

"You better be, if we trigger those timers," Lando said, and secured his own helmet. It seemed as large as a shuttlecraft on his head.

"Come on, Calrissian," Mara said. "We've got some wrecking to do."

●   ●   ●

From his comfortable chair Tol Sivron squinted out at the panorama of the Maw's center, assessing the situation but making no decisions—like a good manager.

"It's the Star Destroyer *Gorgon*, sir," the stormtrooper captain said. "Shall I hail it?"

Sivron scowled. "About time Admiral Daala came back to do her duty," he said. It still rankled him that she had abandoned her primary mission of protecting the Maw scientists. Now that the Rebels had already taken over the Installation, it was too late for her to make amends.

"Why did she come back with only one Star Destroyer?" Sivron said. "She had four. No, wait—one was destroyed, wasn't it? Well, three, anyway. Does she simply want to flaunt her weaponry?" He sniffed. "Well, this time we've got our own Death Star, and we're not afraid to use it."

"Excuse me, Director," the captain said, "but the *Gorgon* appears to be severely damaged. The Rebel forces are attacking her. I believe it's our duty to come to her aid."

Tol Sivron looked at the captain incredulously. "You want us to rescue Admiral Daala after she deserted us? You have an odd sense of obligation, Captain."

"But," the stormtrooper said, "aren't we all fighting the same battle?"

Sivron frowned. "In a sense, perhaps. But we must have different priorities—as Daala herself evidenced by leaving us behind."

He saw the Rebel ships opening fire on the lone Star Destroyer, saw the attack increasing as starfighters met TIE fighters in a flurry of pinpoint laser strikes. The colorful battle had a hypnotic effect—and he thought of the blazing heat storms on the Twi'lek homeworld of Ryloth.

He felt a lump of comet ice form in his stomachs. His career had been long and successful, but he was about to end it by destroying the facility he had so successfully administered for years and years.

In the pilot chair of the Death Star prototype, Sivron said in a cold voice, "All right, let us show Admiral Daala we scientists can hold our own."

Suddenly an alarm ratcheted through the chamber. Sivron sighed. "Now what?"

Yemm and Doxin both flipped through their manuals, searching for an explanation.

"We've detected intruders," the stormtrooper captain answered. "On the power core itself. It seems we picked up one of those smuggler ships near Kessel."

"Well, what do they think they're doing?" Sivron asked.

"According to our sensor cameras, two people have emerged from their ship and—as far as we can tell—are attempting some sort of sabotage."

Sivron sat up in alarm. "Well, stop them!" He snatched the manual out of Doxin's hands and flipped through the pages. "Use emergency procedure number—" He continued to skim over the pages, squinting down at the bulleted lists, flipped a few more pages before tossing the book aside in disgust. "Well, just use the correct procedure, Captain. Do something!"

"We have only a few men and not much time," the captain said. "I'll order two spacetroopers to suit up and take care of the intruders personally."

"Yes, yes," Sivron said, waving his clawed hand, "don't bother me with details. Just get the job done."

Lando tilted the face shield of his enormous helmet back and forth, the better to see with, but the Wookiee-sized suit folded around him in strange and uncomfortable ways. He had to work twice as hard just to figure out where he was going.

His magnetic boots clomped on the metal plating of the gigantic cylindrical power core. Tapered at one end like a spindle with a diamond-hard point, the core pressed against another contact point that rose from the south pole of the Death Star. Between the two points starfire crackled as the charge built up.

The skeleton of girders and access tubes, walled-off compartments, temporary quarters, and storerooms, formed a giant cage around them. Linked catwalks spanned open spaces like a tangled net. Though the prototype was the size of a small moon, it held very little gravity. Lando had to work hard to keep his balance, letting his magnetic boots determine the direction "down."

"We have to go closer to the energy pods," Mara said, her voice buzzing through the tiny earphone.

Lando looked for a way to respond and finally figured out how to activate his own helmet microphone. "Whatever you say. The sooner I get rid of these detonators, the happier I'll be." He sighed partly to himself but also for Mara's benefit. "You'd think destroying one Death Star in a man's lifetime would be enough."

"I prefer men who never settle for *enough*," Mara answered.

Lando blinked, not sure how to take her comment. He allowed himself a broad grin.

Holding out his gloved hand to steady Mara, Lando worked his way down the immense cylindrical core. He tilted his visor to shield himself from the glare pouring from the discharge at the contact points. Above them the pronged disk of the *Falcon* clung to a thick girder.

"Should be good enough here," Mara said, reaching out. "Give me the first detonator."

Lando rummaged in the shielded container and withdrew one of the thick disks. Mara cradled it in her padded glove and bent down to fasten it to the metal hull.

"We'll work our way around and place them on the perimeter," she said, pushing her thumb down on the synchronization button. The detonator lit up with seven lights blinking slowly, like a heartbeat, waiting for final activation.

"When they're all emplaced," Mara's voice said, "we'll give ourselves twenty standard minutes. That should be ample time to get back to the *Falcon* and get away."

Without waiting for him to agree, Mara worked her way around the curving reactor core and turned to take a second detonator from him, planting it squarely against the plating.

Lando felt the faint vibrations of the core throbbing against his magnetic boots. The stored power seemed to be restless, building, waiting to be unleashed.

It seemed to take forever to traverse the circumference of the vast power core, planting the seven detonators. When they returned to their starting point, Mara leaned closer so Lando could see her face through the curved faceplate.

"Ready, Calrissian?"

"Sure thing," Lando answered.

She punched the activator button on the first device. All around the perimeter the detonators winked blue as they began their countdown.

"Back to the *Falcon*. Hurry," Mara said. Lando clomped after her.

A movement caught his eye from the side of the bucket-sized helmet, and he turned his head just in time to see the blocky armored suit of an Imperial spacetrooper. The enemy looked like a man-shaped AT-AT walker with reinforced joints on elbows and knees, heavy boots—and vibroblades like claws in his gloves. One slash and the spacetrooper could rip open Lando's suit, killing him with explosive decompression.

The spacetrooper emerged from an access hatch in the framework above. He let the low gravity cushion his fall as his bulk dropped onto the power core. His heavy boots clanged on the metal as he landed next to Lando and Mara.

"Where did *he* come from?" Lando said, ducking as the spacetrooper lunged with the vibroblades in his gloves. Lando bent backward like a mucus tree in a gale. His magnetic boots held his feet in place, but he threw himself in the opposite direction. Vibroblades slashed past his chest.

Mara reacted more swiftly, swinging the empty padded container that had held the detonators, putting all her momentum behind it. The sharp-edged metal banged against the spacetrooper's thick helmet.

The trooper reached up, stabbing through the plated case with vibroblade claws. Mara used his temporary disorientation to grab Lando and add his mass to her own as she shoved the spacetrooper. With her foot Mara pried free one of the spacetrooper's boots as he fought to regain his balance. She slammed against him, breaking the magnetic grip of his other boot. In an instant the trooper snapped free.

Suddenly unattached to the core, he dropped with the momentum imparted by the force of Mara's attack. The spacetrooper scrabbled to find purchase against the smooth cylindrical hull as he slid down toward the fiery contact points. The vibroblades in his glove made long, silvery score marks on the metal, but did no good.

Sucked inexorably down, the trooper plunged into the flaming discharge between the contact points and vaporized in a bolt of green-and-blue static.

The detonators continued their countdown.

Lando signaled. "We're on our way, Han, old buddy. Make sure you're ready to go."

When he felt a vibration through his boots, Lando looked up to see another spacetrooper drop down from the catwalks. This one carried a blaster rifle, but Lando guessed that the trooper dared not use it in the vicinity of the power core.

The second trooper brought his blaster rifle to bear, motioning for them to surrender, but no voice came over their helmet radios. Lando wondered if the trooper had tuned to a different frequency, or if he merely expected the blaster rifle to be a universal language.

"Can he hear us?" Lando said.

"Who knows? Distract him. Our time is running out." Lando waved his gloved hands and pointed down the expanse of metal to the blinking detonators. He flapped his palms frantically and threw his arms wide to mime an explosion.

As the spacetrooper glanced in the other direction, Mara launched herself forward and grabbed the barrel of his blaster rifle, using it like a lever. In free fall her own momentum knocked him free, sending the trooper tumbling back up toward the catwalks.

"Let's go! Don't worry about him," Mara said, returning to Lando's side. "Get to the *Falcon* before those detonators blow."

Mara and Lando toiled back to the ship still clinging to the support girders. Behind them the second spacetrooper managed to reach out and grab one of the tangled coolant pipes, stopping his reckless tumble. He descended toward the power core again, ignoring Lando and Mara as he hurried to the detonators.

Lando felt Chewbacca's enormous baggy suit folding around him, making it difficult to walk. He looked back and saw the spacetrooper working with the detonators, but he knew Mara had cyberlocked them together. With only a few minutes left, the spacetrooper would be able to do nothing.

Less than a minute before the timed detonation, Lando and Mara sealed themselves inside the *Falcon* just as Han disengaged the landing claw.

"Glad you could join me!" Han said, immediately punching the accelerators.

The *Falcon* raced back out along the Death Star's equator. Its sublight engines flared white-hot behind it.

The surviving spacetrooper managed to reach the ring of detonators. He worked meticulously but rapidly, disconnecting each one, using the built-in laser welder in his suit to remove the explosives. He tossed each one, still blinking, into the open space.

He succeeded in disarming six of the seven detonators. He was standing right above the last one, prying it up, when it exploded beneath him.

Outside, in the midst of the space battle, Admiral Daala gritted her teeth. Her face wore a perpetual look of disdain as she stared at the dizzying firefight.

The attack was not going well. Her forces were being gradually worn away. She hadn't had many TIE fighters to start with; most of them had been left behind in the Cauldron Nebula when she had wheeled the *Gorgon* about to escape the exploding stars. She had only her reserves, and most of those squadrons had been wiped out by Rebel starfighters.

When the Death Star prototype reappeared among the gases overhead, Daala felt a thrill of awe. She rejoiced at the enormous destructive potential suddenly available to her. The tide of the battle had turned—now they could wipe out the Rebel infestation.

But when she determined that the prototype was piloted by the incompetent fool Tol Sivron, her hopes dwindled. "Why doesn't he fire?" she said. "One blast and he could take out all three corvettes and the frigate. *Why* doesn't he fire?"

Commander Kratas stood by her side. "I can't say, Admiral."

She glared to make it clear she hadn't expected an answer. "Tol Sivron has never had any initiative in his entire life," she said. "I should have known

I couldn't expect him to do his duty now. Redouble our efforts against the Installation. Let us show Tol Sivron how it must be done."

She narrowed her brilliant eyes to look around the bridge. "Enough practice," she said. "It's time to destroy Maw Installation once and for all. Open fire!"

37

In the Maw Installation operations room, one of the technicians pounded her fist on a control deck. "Shields are failing, General Antilles!" she announced.

Another engineer ran in from the outside corridor, florid-faced and puffing. Sweat plastered his hair to his forehead, and his blue eyes were glassy with panic. "All this pounding has knocked out the temporary cooling systems we installed on the reactor asteroid! It was never meant to withstand such punishment. The reactor's going to explode—no chance of patching it this time."

Wedge gritted his teeth and looked to Qwi. He squeezed her hand. "Looks like we're about to save Daala the trouble," he said. "Time to evacuate."

Beside him Luke whirled around. "Hey! Where's Kyp?"

But the young man was gone.

"I don't know," Wedge answered, "but we don't have time to look for him now."

Kyp Durron's heart hammered, but he used a Jedi calming routine, forcing himself to relax. He required his bodily systems to operate efficiently, providing strength where he needed it, allowing neither fear nor exhaustion to hinder him.

The tumult of alarms and the external attack rattled the Installation. New Republic soldiers ran across corridors, grabbing equipment and rushing back to their transports.

No one stopped to look at Kyp; if anyone had bothered to question him, he would have used a simple Jedi trick to distract them, blur their memories, making them believe they had never seen him.

Kyp was pleased that Master Skywalker had not noticed his departure. With the sudden appearance of the Death Star prototype and the continued pounding from the *Gorgon*, Kyp had known what he must do.

He also knew Master Skywalker would try to stop him, and Kyp had no time for that.

He had used his own powers—light-side powers, he fervently hoped—to distract everyone while he slipped out into the corridor. He had blanked his thoughts, his keyed-up emotions; unless Master Skywalker made a directed effort to pinpoint him, Kyp would go unnoticed in the chaos.

As he ran, the tempo of the battle outside increased, and he knew that the Installation would not last much longer. If the Death Star prototype managed even one shot, they would be annihilated in an instant. That was the primary threat at the moment.

As he sprinted down the rocky tunnels to the maintenance bay where he had landed the Sun Crusher, he recalled when he and Han had fled through the spice mines of Kessel. The memory of Han brought a deep pang.

The Death Star had reappeared in the center of the Maw, but Kyp had seen no sign of the *Millennium Falcon*. Did that mean Han was dead, destroyed in his sabotage attempt?

Kyp had been cursed with impulsiveness, making his decisions and acting on them without thinking of the consequences. Right now, though, that was a strength. He had to fight against the New Republic's mortal enemies, and he could not ponder and debate the ultimate results of his actions.

Kyp knew he had a great deal to atone for. He had listened to the dark teachings of Exar Kun. He had struck down his teacher and Jedi Master. He had wiped clean the memories of Qwi Xux. He had stolen the Sun Crusher and obliterated entire star systems . . . he had caused the death of his brother Zeth.

Now he would do all he could to rescue his friends—not only to salve his conscience, but because they deserved to live and continue the fight for freedom in the galaxy.

Kyp stared at the oily metallic texture of the Sun Crusher's faceted sides. The quantum armor reflected light in strange directions, distorting it, making the superweapon appear to have been polished with slow light.

With trembling hands he gripped the rungs of the ladder and ascended. Han Solo and Chewbacca had climbed these same rungs to get into the

Sun Crusher during their escape from the Installation. Kyp's brother had attempted to pull himself aboard before Carida's star exploded—but Zeth had not succeeded.

Kyp swung shut the hatch as if he were sealing himself off from the rest of the galaxy for all time. He didn't know if he would ever see the outside again, if he would ever return to Coruscant, or if he would ever speak to Han Solo or Master Skywalker again.

He slumped into the pilot's seat and stilled those thoughts with a Jedi technique. Only a few hours earlier he and Luke had been riding in the Sun Crusher, peaceful companions talking about their lives and their hopes. Now Kyp could not think beyond working the simple controls of the Sun Crusher.

He raised the spike-shaped craft on its repulsorlifts and guided himself through the long launching tunnel into open space where the battle raged.

He approached the giant framework sphere of the Death Star. Kyp had seen the effectiveness of the Sun Crusher's ultrastrong armor when Han Solo had flown at full speed through the bridge tower of the *Hydra*—but even the quantum armor could not possibly withstand a blast from the Death Star's superlaser.

Kyp had two remaining resonance torpedoes that could trigger a supernova. He doubted he could get a critical mass in the prototype's skeletal structure, but a direct hit would still cause a substantial chain reaction.

He accelerated forward, a mere pinprick on the vast canvas of garish-colored gases around the Maw's black holes.

Then, without warning, a bright flower of orange and white erupted from the power core at the center of the Death Star, a small explosion. An instant later, flying in the opposite direction, the *Millennium Falcon* blasted out of the superstructure, gaining speed.

With a warm melting sensation of relief and triumph, he knew that Han Solo had survived! Now Kyp could strike the crippled Death Star with no second thoughts. And then he would go after Daala.

He powered up his targeting and weapons systems. With Jedi senses Kyp could feel the power surging beneath him in the toroidal torpedo generator— energy sufficient to crack open stars.

For one last time, he had to use it.

The explosion in the power core sent the entire Death Star reeling off its axis. The lone spacetrooper attempting to disarm the detonators was hurled backward, already torn to shreds of plasteel armor and incinerated bone.

The detonator had ripped open a gash in the cylindrical core, splitting the armored plating wide and spraying a jet of radioactive fire.

Tol Sivron's head-tails stretched out straight with outrage. "I ordered those two spacetroopers to stop the sabotage!" He whirled to the Devaronian Division Leader. "Yemm, record their service numbers and make a special disciplinary notation in their files!"

He tapped his claws on the chair arm and finally remembered to say, "Oh, and give me a damage assessment."

Doxin ran to the status console and pulled up a visual. "From what I know of the blueprints, Director, there appears to be a relatively insignificant breach in the power core. We can repair it before radiation levels get too high. It's a good thing no more than one of those detonators blew, though. Otherwise we wouldn't be able to contain it."

The stormtrooper captain was on his feet, chattering orders into his radio helmet. "I've already sent a full squadron of troopers down to suit up, sir. I have instructed them that their personal safety is forfeit."

"Good, good," Tol Sivron said absently. "How soon will I be able to shoot again?"

The stormtrooper studied his panels. The white plasteel helmet masked any hint of expression. "The spacetroopers are suited up and on their way. They are descending the catwalks now." He pointed his featureless black goggles at Sivron. "If the repair work goes as planned, you could fire within twenty minutes."

"Well, tell them to hurry," Sivron said. "If Daala destroys Maw Installation before I do, I'll be very annoyed."

"Yes, Director," the captain said.

Tol Sivron watched with simmering frustration as the *Millennium Falcon* disappeared toward the other fighting ships inside the Maw. He noticed the New Republic battleships that had overrun his facility; he noticed the large conglomeration of planetoids where he had spent so many years of his career. And then he looked at Admiral Daala's Star Destroyer. Daala, whom he loathed, who had deserted him and her duty at the time of greatest need.

Tol Sivron muttered to himself as he fidgeted in the command chair. "So many targets," he said, "and so little time."

38

The battle-scarred Star Destroyer cruised so low over the Maw Installation's weakening defensive shields that Luke's instinct was to duck. The complex clutter of the *Gorgon*'s hull flowed like an unending river past the skylights, showing just how immense the battleship was.

"Shields just failed completely," one of the technicians said. "We won't survive another pass, and the reactor asteroid is going critical!"

Wedge punched the facilitywide intercom and shouted orders. His voice echoed through the labyrinth of tunnels in the clustered asteroids of the Installation. "Last call for evacuation. Everyone to the transport ships. Now! We've only got a few minutes to get out of here."

The alarms somehow grew even louder. Luke turned to follow the troops running toward the doors. Wedge grabbed the thin blue arm of Qwi Xux, but she resisted, staring in horror at the computer screens. "Look!" she said. "What is she doing? She can't!"

Wedge stopped to glance at the streams of data flying across the screens at high speed. He blinked and saw rapid-fire images of blueprints, weapons designs, test data.

"Admiral Daala must have known Director Sivron's password," Qwi cried. "She's dumping the data backups we couldn't crack. She's downloading all the weapons information!"

Wedge grabbed Qwi by the waist and yanked her away from the terminal, rushing her toward the door. "We can't do anything about that now. We've got to get out of here."

They ran down the corridors with the assault troops in the lead. Qwi's feathery hair streamed behind her, glinting in the harsh white light from the glowpanels.

Wedge felt overwhelmed, his tension rising, as if his internal chronometer were ticking down the seconds until the explosion of the fragile reactor asteroid, until Admiral Daala's next attack, until the whole Installation bloomed into a white-hot cloud of rubble.

Wedge had never wanted to be a general anyway. He was a good wing man, a fighter pilot. He had flown beside Luke down the trench of the first Death Star, and next to Lando Calrissian to destroy the second one.

By far the best assignment had been to escort the lovely Qwi Xux. Even frightened and dismayed, Qwi looked exotic and beautiful. He wanted to hold her and comfort her—but he could do that on the transport back to the *Yavaris*. If they didn't get out of here immediately, they would all die.

As the refugees scrambled across the takeoff area, one of the transports declared itself fully loaded. Wedge grabbed his comm link. "Go, go! Don't wait for us!"

They charged up the ramp of another waiting shuttle. The remaining troops scattered to their seats. Wedge took a second to make sure Qwi had a safe place to strap herself in. Luke bolted for the cockpit and threw himself into the copilot's chair, powering up the sublight engines.

Wedge took one last glance back at the personnel compartment to verify that everyone was at least close to being seated. "Secure the door!" he cried.

One of the lieutenants slammed a palm against the hatch controls. With an impatient hiss the ramp drew in like a retracting serpent's tongue. The doors clamped shut.

Wedge wasted no time securing himself into his seat before raising the transport off the landing pad. With a scream of acceleration the troop ship launched itself away from the dying Maw Installation.

The bootsteps of Commander Kratas sounded like hammers on sheet metal as he ran up to the bridge observation platform. Admiral Daala turned, anxiously awaiting a favorable report.

Kratas tried to regain his composure but did not succeed in wiping the idiotic grin from his lips. "Transfer successful, Admiral. Complete core dump of all the Maw's backup computer files." He lowered his voice. "You were correct. Director Sivron never bothered to change his password. He was still using the same one you obtained ten years ago."

Daala snorted. "Sivron has been incompetent in everything else. Why should he change now?"

Most of her TIE fighters had been wiped out. None of her starboard turbolasers were functional. Engines operated at only 40 percent efficiency, and many systems were severely overheating.

She had never anticipated the battle would take this long. She had meant to obliterate the Rebel forces and then finish mop-up operations at her leisure. She didn't understand why Sivron and his Death Star didn't do anything. But finally something had gone right; she had retrieved the precious data from the Maw Installation computers.

Daala watched as troop transports fled the cluster of rocks below, but she deemed them insignificant targets.

"Installation shields are completely down," the tactical lieutenant said.

"Good," she snapped. "Wheel about. We'll make a final attack run."

"Excuse me, Admiral," Kratas interrupted. "We're getting anomalous readings from the reactor asteroid. It appears to have suffered severe damage and is highly unstable."

Daala brightened. "Ah, excellent. We'll target that. Perhaps the reactor can do most of the destructive work for us."

She looked out the bridge tower and saw the ocean of screaming gases around the infinitely black pinpoints. The *Gorgon* turned about and headed toward Maw Installation.

"Full ahead," Daala said, standing rigid at her station, gloved hands clasped behind her back. Her coppery hair flowed behind her like spraying lava. "Fire repeatedly, until the Installation is destroyed—or until our turbolaser banks are drained dry."

The lumbering ship picked up momentum as the *Gorgon* accelerated forward on its final run.

Wedge flicked on the open communications unit to contact the New Republic fleet. He didn't care about encryption at the moment—if the Imperial forces could decode his transmissions, they wouldn't have time to take action anyway.

"All fighters, regroup and return to the *Yavaris*. Prepare to retreat. We are leaving the Maw. We have everything we came for."

The huge frigate hung like a jagged weapon waiting to receive the fighter squadrons. X-wings and Y-wings looped around, disengaging from space dogfights and heading back to their primary ships. Wedge accelerated toward the *Yavaris*. The squarish opening of the frigate's lower bays glowed with an atmosphere-containment field, like a welcoming open door.

Without warning four square-winged TIE fighters shot up from Wedge's blind spot, mercilessly battering the front of the transport shuttle with laser bolts.

Before Wedge could react, an assault shuttle bearing Imperial markings flew in from the left, firing multiple beams from its forward heavy blaster cannons. The attack took the TIE pilots by surprise. They scrambled and scattered. Two careened into each other to get out of the way. Two others succumbed to the focused blasts, exploding into molten debris.

Wedge heard a loud Wookiee roar of triumph over the open comm channel, echoed by growls and shouts from the assault shuttle's passenger compartment. The clipped metallic voice of See-Threepio interrupted, "Chewbacca, please do stop showing off! We need to get back to the *Yavaris*."

Luke toggled the communications panel. "Thanks, guys."

"Master Luke!" Threepio cried. "What are you doing here? We need to get away!"

"It's a long story, Threepio. We're doing our best to do just that."

On the opposite side of the Maw, the *Gorgon* spun about and accelerated toward the unprotected Installation like a wild bantha, its rear engines blazing with star fire. A flurry of green turbolaser bolts blurred out from the Star Destroyer's fore section, angling down to strike the Installation's clustered asteroids. With the facility's shields down, ionized rock dust sprayed into space.

Daala fired and fired again, picking up speed in what appeared to be a suicide run. Her strafing beams pummeled the Installation, striking asteroid after asteroid. Metal bridges vaporized, transparisteel shattered and blew outward.

The *Gorgon* came on, unstoppable until—just as she soared over at closest approach—the attack breached the containment housing the unstable power reactor.

Sitting in the cockpit of the personnel transport, Wedge and Luke both flinched as the entire Maw Installation suddenly became a blaze of light, like a miniature exploding star. The center of the Maw was filled with an incandescent purifying fire.

The glare flooded outward, automatically causing the viewscreens to darken. Wedge flew blind, trusting the navigation computer's controls and aiming toward the waiting New Republic flagships.

When his vision finally cleared, he looked back to the stable point that had held the Empire's most sophisticated weapons-research laboratory. He saw only a far-flung swarm of broken rocks and smoldering gases in an expanding backwash of energy. Eventually, the debris would drift far enough to be siphoned down to infinity through one of the black holes.

As the glare faded and the fiery gases cleared, he saw no sign whatsoever of Admiral Daala or her last Star Destroyer.

39

Working like automatons, the team of doomed spacetroopers attached themselves to the breached wall of the Death Star's power core. Intense radiation spewed out, darkening their faceplates so they could barely see, slowly frying their life-support systems.

Moving sluggishly as they weakened under the invisible onslaught, they wrestled thick sheets of plating in the low gravity. They used rapid laser welders to slap patches over the breach, reinforcing it to withstand an energy buildup.

One of the spacetroopers, his control pack sparking with blue lightning as the suit's circuits all broke down, thrashed about in eerie silence; his arm movements gradually slowed until he drifted free. One of the others took his place, ignoring the lost companion. Every one of them had already received a lethal dose of radiation. They knew it, but their training had been thorough: they lived to serve the Empire.

One of the troopers completed a last weld at the hottest point of the breach. His skin blistered. His nerves were deadened. His eyes and lungs hemorrhaged blood. But he forced himself to finish his task.

The cold vacuum of space solidified the welds instantly. With a gurgling voice filled with fluid, the spacetrooper gasped into his helmet radio, "Mission accomplished."

Then the remaining troopers, with failing life-support systems and bodies already savaged by the fatal radiation, released their hold on the power core in unison. They drifted free, dropping toward the brilliant energy discharge like shooting stars.

At the total destruction of Maw Installation and the loss of Admiral Daala's *Gorgon*, Tol Sivron's initial reaction was one of annoyance and disappointment.

"The Installation was supposed to be *my* target," he said. He glared at his other Division Leaders. "How could Daala do such a thing? I have the Death Star; she doesn't."

As the shock waves and light echoes from the huge explosion drifted and faded, Sivron could see the Rebel fleet gathering itself to flee the cluster.

Sivron sighed. "Perhaps we should hold another meeting to discuss options."

"Sir!" The stormtrooper captain got to his feet. "Our power reactor is now temporarily repaired. I lost nine good spacetroopers to bring the weapon back online. I think we should use it. The Rebel fleet is in retreat. We'll lose them if we don't act soon. I know this is nonstandard procedure, Director, but we have no time for a meeting."

Sivron looked from side to side, suddenly insecure. He didn't like to be pushed into snap decisions. Too many things could go wrong if one did not consider the full consequences. But the captain had a good point.

"All right, then, temporary emergency actions. Ad hoc committee decision—shall we use the superlaser to strike out at the Rebel forces? Doxin, your vote."

"I agree," the squat Division Leader said.

Tol Sivron turned to the hatchet-faced woman. "Golanda?"

"Let's cause some damage."

"Yemm?"

The Devaronian nodded, his horns bobbing up and down. "It will look much better in the report if we have a unanimous vote."

Sivron considered. "Since Wermyn is no longer with us, I will act as his proxy and cast my vote along with his. Therefore, the vote is unanimous. We will strike the Rebel forces." He nodded to Yemm. "Please note that in the minutes."

"Director," the stormtrooper captain interrupted, "the Rebel fleet is pulling out. One of the corvettes has already gone into the Maw."

"Captain, you are so impatient!" Sivron snapped. "Can't you see we've already made the resolution? Now it's time to implement it. Go ahead and establish your first target."

He blinked his tiny eyes and spotted one of the Corellian corvettes hanging dead in space. "What about that one?" Sivron said. "It appears to be either crippled or boobytrapped. I don't like it—and besides, it's a stationary target. We can use it to calibrate our aiming mechanisms . . . since you missed a whole planet last time."

"As you wish, Director." The stormtrooper relayed the instructions to the team of gunners in the firing bay.

"I suggest we fire at only half strength, Director," Doxin said, scanning the technical readouts. His bald scalp furrowed again. "Even at reduced power the Death Star superlaser will be more than adequate to destroy a simple battleship. In that way we can manage multiple firings without depleting our reservoir so quickly. We won't have to wait so long between shots."

"Good suggestion, Division Leader," Sivron said with a smile of anticipation. "I'd very much like to shoot more than once."

Down in the firing bay the gunners hunched over sprawling control banks, fingers moving deftly over the arrays of brightly lit squares to call up the targeting cross and lock in on the doomed corvette.

"Hurry up and fire," Tol Sivron's voice echoed through the speakers. "We want to get a second shot at those ships before they all leave."

Together the gunners focused the secondary laser beams and yanked back on the levers to release the pent-up energy within the power core.

Along the focusing tubes a wide beam of incinerating power shot out. It funneled through the focusing eye and blazed into a deadly spear, striking precisely on target.

The crippled Corellian corvette was so insignificant that it absorbed little of the destructive power. The beam went through the vaporized wreckage and continued into the curtains of the Maw.

"Outstanding!" Sivron said. "See what happens when you follow the correct procedures? Now target the frigate. The big ship. I want to see that one explode."

"We have enough energy reserves for several more blasts," the stormtrooper captain said.

Then a tiny, angular blip of light streaked across their targeting viewport— as seemingly insignificant as a gnat—yet it kept coming. Its hull glistened brightly in reflected light. The small ship fired its ridiculously ineffective defensive lasers at the Death Star.

"What's that?" Sivron said. "Give me a close-up."

Golanda magnified the image on the screen and scowled. Her face looked unpleasant enough to shatter planets. "I believe it's one of our own concepts, Director Sivron. You may recognize it yourself."

As he looked at the shard-shaped vessel, his head-tails twitched. Of course he remembered it—not only from the working model he had seen once, but from all the progress reports and computer simulations its creator, Qwi Xux, had delivered during her years of development.

"The Sun Crusher," he said. "But that's ours!"

The torus-shaped resonance field generator glowed with plasma fire at the bottom of its long spike.

"Open a channel," Tol Sivron said. "I want to talk to whoever is there. Hello, hello? You have appropriated property that belongs to Maw Installation. I demand that you return it to the proper Imperial authorities immediately." He crossed his arms over his chest and waited for a reply.

The pilot of the Sun Crusher answered by launching one of the supernova torpedoes into the Death Star.

Kyp felt a rush of satisfaction as he pressed the firing button, ignoring the Twi'lek administrator's pompous posturing. He watched the high-energy projectile shoot from the bottom of the Sun Crusher and burrow deep within the complicated framework of metal girders inside the prototype.

The resonance torpedo vaporized girders as it tunneled deeper and deeper, until it finally struck heavier primary struts that foamed as they disintegrated.

The torpedo dumped its energy in a shower that triggered a small chain reaction within the solid superstructure, splitting atomic nuclei and causing an arc of spreading dissolution. Girders vaporized in a widening hole that ate its way farther and farther through the heavy framework.

But Kyp's elation faded as the chain reaction slowed, and then stopped. The skeletal Death Star had insufficient mass to continue its own disintegration.

He had ruined a good portion of the support framework in one sector of the prototype, but not enough.

Kyp powered up the weapons panel again and prepared to fire. He could annihilate the Death Star piece by piece if necessary. But looking down at his panel, he noted with dismay that only one of his supernova torpedoes remained.

Grim-faced, Kyp zoomed in closer to the prototype. He would have to make this last shot count.

Wheeling the *Millennium Falcon* in a backward arc, Han Solo tried to check how much damage the detonators had done to the Death Star's power core.

He was disappointed. He had expected to see the skeletal prototype bloom into a fantastic flower of fire, but instead the detonators seemed to have fizzled, leaving only a dimming blaze at the center.

The ship drifted in space for a few moments as Mara and Lando shucked their environment suits. Lando rubbed sweat from his forehead and wiped his hands as if disgusted with the griminess of the suit.

"Now what are we going to do?" Han asked when they had finally joined him back in the cockpit.

Lando looked at the Death Star shrinking in the black distance behind them. "Maybe we'd better go see if Wedge—"

Suddenly the Maw Installation and the *Gorgon* were swallowed in a brilliant flare as everything detonated at once.

"Too late," Mara said.

"Now why couldn't the Death Star have exploded like that?" Lando said miserably.

"Maybe we at least caused some permanent harm," Han said hopefully. But moments later they all groaned as a green beam lanced out from the Death Star to destroy one of the corvettes in the retreating New Republic fleet.

"So much for permanent harm," Mara Jade said.

"That Death Star's causing some harm, big time!" Lando said.

"Wait," Han said as he glanced back at the Death Star, squinting. "Move in closer."

"Closer?" Lando said. "You out of your mind?"

"That's Kyp," Han said as the Sun Crusher streaked across the face of the Death Star and launched one of its static-filled torpedoes into the superstructure.

"If he's taking on the Death Star, we've got to go help," Han said.

The Sun Crusher fled toward the gravitational walls of the Maw cluster, and Tol Sivron ordered the Death Star to track the small but deadly ship.

"Get a lock on it," he said. "We'll blast it out of space the same way we did with that Rebel ship."

"Sir," the stormtrooper captain said, "to lock on to a target so tiny and moving so quickly—"

"Then get close enough so you can't miss," Sivron snapped. "One of his torpedoes ate up eleven percent of our superstructure! We can't afford more losses like that. How are we going to explain it when we get back to the Empire?"

"Perhaps that would be a good reason to stay away from the Sun Crusher, sir," the stormtrooper pointed out.

"Nonsense! How would that look on the report?" Sivron said, leaning forward. "You have your orders, Captain."

The equatorial propulsion units powered up and nudged the massive skeletal craft to greater speed as it pursued the flitting superweapon.

"Fire whenever you have a target," Sivron said.

The Death Star picked up speed, and the tiny Sun Crusher slowed down, as if taunting them.

The gases grew hot in the outer shell of the Maw as they approached one of the bottomless singularities. The Sun Crusher danced back and forth, shooting its tiny lasers, destroying minor struts here and there, causing insignificant damage. The Death Star had to fight against the gravity of the nearby black hole.

"What's the matter?" Tol Sivron said to the gunners over the intercom. "Are you waiting to read the serial numbers on his engine parts?"

The Death Star shot again. Its green beam tore through the outer wisps of the cluster, firing point-blank at the Sun Crusher—but the laser curved to the left, tugged by the mighty force of the black hole. The green beam spiraled like a ball bearing falling into a drain.

"You missed! How could you miss?" Tol Sivron ranted. "Captain, give me those flight controls. I'm going to pilot the Death Star myself. I'm tired of your incompetence."

All of the Division Leaders suddenly looked at Tol Sivron, aghast. The stormtrooper captain turned slowly in his chair. "Are you sure that's wise, Director? You don't have the experience—"

Sivron crossed his arms over his chest. "I have read the procedure and I've watched what you're doing. I know everything I need to know. Give me the controls right now. That's a managerial directive!"

Sivron grinned with anticipation as he began to issue commands directing the Death Star. "Now we'll finish this properly," he said.

Just like a pet floozam on a leash, thought Kyp as he flew toward the black hole. The Death Star followed his every move.

He reversed course and arrowed back toward the prototype, increasing speed and calling up his weapons controls. The maze of metal girders and cross braces spun below him—and he launched his last resonance torpedo. The blazing cloud of plasma chewed through the outer layers of the prototype as it plowed ever-widening circles of destruction.

The last shot would make them panic. It wouldn't cripple the Death Star entirely, but merely crippling the prototype would never be enough. He had to go for the full victory.

As the chain reaction initiated by his last torpedo petered out, Kyp sped over the metallic horizon of the Death Star and raced for the Maw's nearest black hole.

Kyp used his onboard tactical systems to estimate the exact position of the event horizon, the point from which no ship, however powerful, could ever escape. He came closer and closer—and the Death Star howled after him.

Han shouted into the comm systems, "Kyp, Kyp Durron! Answer me. Don't go so close. Watch out!"

But he received no reply.

Death Star and Sun Crusher were locked in mortal combat, paying no heed to outside distractions. The Death Star prototype orbited close to the black hole. The Sun Crusher danced from side to side, hammering with tiny laser blasts.

"I think I know what he's doing," Han said with deep uneasiness. "The prototype has greater mass and a much larger volume. If Kyp can lure it near the point of no return . . ."

"Without getting sucked down himself," Lando said.

"That's the catch, isn't it?" Han answered.

The Death Star fired again, and the superlaser beam curved around, bent even more severely in the deep gravity well; but this time the gunner had compensated. The blurred fringes of the beam actually struck the Sun Crusher and knocked it spinning out of control.

Any other ship would have been vaporized instantly, but the quantum armor plating protected the superweapon—just barely.

Kyp's propulsion systems were obviously damaged. The Sun Crusher struggled along on a tangential course, attempting to pull away from the event horizon. But it was too close, and gravity was too strong. It spiraled in a tight orbit, sinking deeper and deeper.

The Death Star pilot couldn't resist making the final kill, and the prototype loomed closer. The Sun Crusher and the giant skeletal sphere orbited the black hole like the ends of a baton, speeding up.

Only then did the Death Star pilot seem to realize his peril, and all equatorial thrusters kicked on at once, attempting to pull the prototype away. But the giant vessel had already crossed the edge of the black hole.

The Sun Crusher could not achieve sufficient velocity to escape its tightening orbit either. It spiraled in the wake of the Death Star, with no hope of getting away.

Han felt as if his chest were being torn apart by the tidal forces. "Kyp!" he cried.

A final streak of light shot away from the Sun Crusher, and then it was too late for the tiny superweapon.

The Death Star prototype plunged into the thickening cascades of superhot gases that shrieked down into nothingness. The spherical prototype elongated like a great egg under the uneven gravitational stresses. The curved girders ripped apart, then were crushed into a cone that stretched into the black hole's funnel.

With a wink of brilliance the tiny Sun Crusher followed its nemesis down into the black hole.

Lando and Mara remained utterly silent. Han hung his head and squeezed his eyes shut. "Goodbye, Kyp."

"It's a message cylinder," Mara said, identifying the small streak shot out by the Sun Crusher. "We'd better get it quick, because it's falling toward the black hole, too."

"Message cylinder?" Han sat up, trying to find his enthusiasm. "Okay, let's snag it before it's too late."

The *Falcon* raced toward the event horizon. Lando and Mara worked together, wrestling to navigate the ship in the buckling jaws of gravity. They detected the metallic container, and Lando swooped in, latching on to it with the tractor beam moments before the small message pod could fall over the brink of the gravitational pit.

"Got it," Lando said.

"All right, pull it inside, and let's get out of here," Han said in a bleak voice. "At least I can hear the last words Kyp had to say."

40

Han and Lando both pulled on stiff gloves before they wrestled the Sun Crusher's message canister into the *Falcon*'s common area. Deep cold had penetrated the canister, and as they brought it into the enclosed atmosphere, tendrils of frost grew like lacy ferns across its surface.

The thin metal hull gleamed bright, splotched in places by electrostatic discharges from when the cylinder had been launched at high speed from the Sun Crusher.

"That's one heavy message," Lando said as they lugged the canister to a flat spot on the floor and set it down with a metallic *thump* on the deck plates.

Little more than a meter long and less than half a meter wide, the message pod was used by the captain of a doomed ship to launch his last log entries and to dump his computer cores and navigation records for later investigations.

Han remembered Kyp telling him that when the Coruscant scientists had stumbled upon the message canisters inside the Sun Crusher, they had panicked, thinking they had uncovered the dangerous supernova torpedoes—even though the cylinder was standard Imperial issue, and any smuggler or starfighter pilot should have recognized it immediately.

On his rampages in the Cauldron Nebula and the Carida system, Kyp had left message cylinders to explain what he had done and why, so that no one would construe his actions as simple astronomical accidents.

Han felt stunned and lethargic with sadness. His friend had been right, but only to a point. Kyp Durron's agenda to destroy the Empire had used tactics as vicious as those of the Emperor's.

Luke Skywalker had claimed the young man would redeem himself fully, but now Kyp's potential as a great Jedi had been extinguished.

Han could not question Kyp's sacrifice, though. Kyp had eliminated both the Death Star prototype and the Sun Crusher. He had bought the galaxy's freedom from terror at the cost of his life . . . one life for potentially billions. That made sense, didn't it?

Didn't it?

Mara Jade knelt beside the message cylinder, running her slender hands over its hull. She popped open the access plate. "Well, it's not encrypted," she said. "Either Kyp didn't have time, or he knew we'd be the ones to pick it up. He left the homing beacon off."

"Just open it," Han said roughly. He'd had enough of this grim waiting. What had Kyp thought to say in his last moments?

Mara punched in the standard sequence. The lights blinked red, then amber, then flashed green. With a hiss of escaping air, a formerly invisible seam appeared down the center of the pod. The long black line widened as the two halves split, opening up.

Inside, looking waxen and emotionless as a statue, lay Kyp Durron. His eyes were closed, his face drawn into an expression of intense—yet surprisingly peaceful—concentration.

"Kyp," Han shouted. His voice cracked with astonished joy, yet he tried to hold back his hope. "Kyp!"

Somehow Kyp had crammed himself inside the small volume of the message cylinder, a vessel barely large enough to hold a child. But Kyp had managed to crush his legs, fold his arms until the bones snapped, pressed down on his rib cage until ribs cracked, compacting himself.

Han leaned closer to the ashen face. "Is he alive? He's in some kind of Jedi trance." In his final desperation Kyp had somehow found the strength to use his Jedi pain-blocking techniques, his determination, and all the knowledge Luke had taught him . . . to do this to himself, as his only chance for survival.

"He's slowed his functions almost to the point of suspended animation," Mara said. "He's in so deep that he might as well be dead."

The message canister was airtight but had no life-support systems, no air other than the small amount that had fit around his own broken body.

"That's impossible," Lando said.

"Let's get him out," Han said. "Careful."

Han gently, meticulously pried the young man free of the tiny cylinder. As Lando and Mara helped him carry Kyp to one of the narrow bunks, the young man's body sagged and flopped from grievously smashed bones, as if someone had crumpled him into a ball and then tossed him aside.

"Oh, Kyp," Han said. As he set Kyp on the bunk and straightened his arms, Han could feel the shattered wrists like jelly under his skin. "We have to get him to a medical center," he said. "I've got first aid here, but not nearly enough for something like this."

Kyp's black eyes fluttered open, glazed and unfocused with incredible pain; but he drove it back. "Han," he said in a voice as faint as beating wings. "You came to get me."

"Of course, kid," Han said, bending down. "What did you expect?"

"The Death Star?" Kyp asked.

"Sucked down into the black hole . . . along with the Sun Crusher. They're both gone."

Kyp's entire body shuddered with relief. "Good."

He looked as if he were about to collapse back into unconsciousness, but then his eyes blinked again, brightening with a new confidence. "I'll be all right, you know."

"I know you will be," Han answered.

Only then did Kyp succumb to the pain and allow himself to sink back into his Jedi trance.

"Good to have you back, kid," Han whispered, then looked up to Mara and Lando. "Let's get him back to Coruscant."

A Wookiee bellow split from the intercom system, and Han stood up straight, rushing back to the cockpit to see a battered Imperial gamma assault shuttle hanging in space in front of the *Falcon*, its engines white-hot and ready to go.

"Chewie!" Han shouted into the voice pickups, and the Wookiee responded with a roar.

"What Chewbacca is saying," Threepio's voice translated unnecessarily, "is that if you would like to follow us out of the Maw, we have the appropriate course programmed into our navicomputer. I believe we are all anxious to go home."

Han looked at Lando and Mara and smiled. "You're sure right about that, Threepio."

41

Inside the dining hall of the Great Temple, Cilghal stood silent and firm,
studiously showing no reaction to Ackbar's insistence.

Clad once again in his white admiral's uniform, Ackbar leaned closer
to Cilghal. He placed his splayed hands firmly on the shoulders of her
watery-blue robe. She could feel the heavy musculature in his hands as he
pressed down. She flinched, afraid of what he would demand of her.

"You cannot surrender so easily, Ambassador," Ackbar said. "I will not
accept that this task is impossible until you prove to me it is impossible."

Cilghal felt small under the probing gaze of his large eyes. No human
would recognize it, but she could see the effects of long-fought stress on
his face, in the mottling of his dark-orange color. Ackbar's skin looked dry,
and his lobes had sunk deeply into the sides of his head. The small tendrils
around his mouth looked frayed and cracked.

Since the terrible crash on the planet Vortex and his resulting disgrace,
Ackbar had lived with an enormous weight on his conscience. But now he
had come back to himself, returning to serve his people and the New Republic
with greater determination—and coming to speak with her on Yavin 4.

"There have been no Jedi healers since the great purges," Cilghal said.
"Master Skywalker believes I possess some aptitude in this area, but I have
had no appropriate training. I would be swimming in murky waters, uncertain
of my course. I don't dare—"

"Nevertheless," Ackbar interrupted sharply. He released her shoulders and stepped back so that his clean white uniform dazzled her eyes in the dimness of the Massassi temple's dining hall.

Dorsk 81 stepped into the chamber, looking surreptitiously at Ackbar. His eyes widened as he recognized the commander of the New Republic Fleet. The cloned alien muttered his apologies and backed out, flustered.

But Ackbar's gaze did not waver from Cilghal. She raised her head to meet his stare but waited for him to speak.

"Please," Ackbar said. "I beg you. Mon Mothma will die within days if you do nothing."

"I made oaths to myself, both when I became an ambassador and when I arrived here to train as a Jedi," Cilghal said, bowing her head with a sigh, "that I would do everything in my power to serve and to strengthen the New Republic."

She looked down at her spatulate hands. "If Master Skywalker has faith in me, who am I to question his judgment?" she said. "Take me to your ship, Admiral. Let us go to Coruscant."

In the former Imperial Palace, Cilghal reviewed the situation with growing dread.

Mon Mothma no longer remained conscious. The infestation of nano-destroyers filled her body, tearing her cells apart one by one. Without the life-support systems that kept her lungs filling, her heart beating, her blood filtered—the human woman would have died days earlier.

Some Council members had begun advising that she be allowed to die, that forcibly keeping Mon Mothma alive in such a state was a lingering torture. But upon hearing that one of Master Skywalker's new Jedi would come from Yavin 4 to attempt healing her, Chief of State Leia Organa Solo had insisted that they wait for this last chance, this slim hope.

Arriving in Imperial City, Cilghal was flanked by Ackbar and Leia as they ushered her down corridors to the medical chambers where Mon Mothma lay surrounded by the growing stench of death.

Leia's dark gaze flicked from Mon Mothma to Cilghal. Her human eyes glittered with gathering tears, and Cilghal could sense her hope like a palpable substance.

The smells of medicines, sterilization chemicals, and throbbing machines made her amphibious skin feel irritated and rubbery. She wanted to swim in the soothing waters of Calamari, to wash the disturbing thoughts and poisons from her body—but Mon Mothma needed that purging even more than Cilghal did.

She stepped to Mon Mothma's bedside, leaving Leia and Ackbar behind her. "You must realize that I know nothing specific about the healing powers of the Jedi," she said, as if offering an excuse. "I know even less about this living poison that is destroying her."

She drew a deep breath of the tainted air. "Leave me alone with her. Mon Mothma and I will fight this together." She swallowed. "If we can."

Murmuring warm wishes and reassurances, Ackbar and Leia faded into the background. Cilghal paid little attention to them as they departed.

Her shimmering blue ambassadorial robes flowed around her like ethereal waves. She knelt to stare at Mon Mothma's motionless form. Reaching out with the Force, but at a loss for what exactly she was supposed to do, she tried to assess the scope of damage inside Mon Mothma's body.

As she began to see deeper, the extent of the poison's ravages astounded her. She could not comprehend how Mon Mothma had managed to stay alive for so long. Uncertainty fluttered in Cilghal's mind like gathering shadows.

How could she possibly combat such a disease? She did not understand how working with the Force could heal living things, how it could strengthen the life of someone as devastated as Mon Mothma. The best available medical droids had not been able to remove the malicious poison. No medicines had been able to cure her.

Cilghal knew only what Master Skywalker had taught her—how to sense with the Force, how to feel living things, how to move objects. She touched Mon Mothma with glowing currents of the Force, searching for some kind of answer, or at least an idea.

Could she use her Jedi skills but in a different manner that might strengthen Mon Mothma? Help her body to heal? Find some method to remove the poison?

Cilghal hesitated as a possibility struck like a meteor. The magnitude of the effort stunned her, and she wanted to dismiss the thought automatically— but she forced herself to study the idea.

Master Skywalker had explained Yoda's teachings, his insistence that "size matters not." Yoda had claimed that lifting Luke's entire X-wing fighter was no different from lifting a pebble.

But could Cilghal turn it the other way around? Could she use her precise control of the Force to move something *so small?*

She blinked her round Calamarian eyes. Millions of the tiny nano-destroyers saturated Mon Mothma's body.

Size matters not.

But if Cilghal could remove the destructive poison molecules, if she could somehow keep Mon Mothma from toppling over the abyss into death—then her body could restore itself, in time.

Cilghal refused to let her thoughts overwhelm her with visions of the sheer number of poison molecules. She would have to move them one by one, tugging each nano-destroyer through cell walls and out of the dying leader's body.

Cilghal placed her broad fins on Mon Mothma's bare skin. She picked up the leader's left hand and raised it over the side of the bed frame, letting the woman's fingertips rest in a small crystal dish that had once been used to dispense medications. Even this gentle touch was enough to cause red bruises to bloom on the woman's fragile skin.

Cilghal opened her mental doors, freeing her thoughts, allowing currents of the Force to flow into Mon Mothma's form. She let the nictitating membranes slide over her Calamarian eyes as she began to see with an inner vision, traveling through the cellular pathways of Mon Mothma's body.

She found herself in a strange universe of rushing blood cells, electrically firing neurons, contracting muscle fibers, laboring organs that could no longer perform their functions. Cilghal couldn't exactly comprehend what she saw, but somehow she understood instinctively which parts were healthy, which molecules were sustaining Mon Mothma, and which were the black scourge.

With the Force, Cilghal could touch with fingers infinitely small, infinitely precise, to grasp one of the nano-destroyers and send it careening out of the dying body.

Cilghal found other microscopic destroyers and nudged them, pushed them, herding the poison away from healthy cells, preventing further damage.

The task was incomprehensibly large. The poison had spread and replicated, scattering itself through the billions and billions of cells in Mon Mothma's body. Cilghal would have to search and remove every one of them.

After succeeding with the first one, Cilghal sought out another.

And another.

And another.

And another.

"Has there been any change?" Leia whispered at the doorway. She had just returned from a meeting where General Wedge Antilles, Doctor Qwi Xux, and Han Solo had given a detailed debriefing on the entire Maw assault.

Leia had listened with fascination, making eyes at her husband Han— whom she had seen too little of in the past several days. But always in the back of her mind was a pressing concern for Mon Mothma.

"No change," Ackbar said in a tired voice. "I wish we understood what Cilghal is attempting to do."

The female Calamarian had not moved in nine hours, kneeling beside Mon Mothma's bedside, flippered hands resting on the dying woman's skin, deep in a trance. The medical droids had not expected Mon Mothma to live for this long, so the mere fact that she still had not succumbed to death meant something.

From outside the door Leia peeked in to see that nothing had changed. The leader's hand lay in a crystal dish as droplets of an oily grayish liquid emerged from the tip of her index finger. The process was too slow to watch, but over the course of half an hour a small droplet would gather at the tip of her finger, dangling, until gradually gravity pulled it off into the dish.

Terpfen walked slowly down the tiled corridors dressed in a dark-green close-fitting uniform that bore no insignia. Even after his full pardon Terpfen had refused to accept his rank again. He had sequestered himself in his rooms for much of the time since returning from Anoth.

The scarred Calamarian stopped several meters away from them, reluctant to go closer to the room that held Mon Mothma. Leia knew that Terpfen still blamed himself for the dying woman's condition, and he refused to let the guilt be assuaged. Though she understood his misery, she was getting impatient with his withdrawal and hoped he climbed back to his feet soon.

Terpfen bowed ponderously, displaying the network of scars on his disfigured head. "Admiral, I have reached a decision." He drew a deep breath. "I wish to return to Calamari and continue your work—if our people will have me. I wish to assist in rebuilding Reef Home. I fear . . ." He looked up to stare at the intricate mosaics on the walls of the Imperial Palace. "I fear that I will never be comfortable on Coruscant again."

"Believe me, Terpfen," Ackbar answered, "I know exactly how you feel. I would not try to talk you out of your decision. It is a fair compromise between your need for healing and your desire to make amends."

Terpfen straightened, as if some measure of self-esteem had been returned to him. "I would like to depart as soon as possible," he said.

"I will arrange a ship," Ackbar replied.

Terpfen bowed again. "If I have your leave, Chief of State?"

"Yes, Terpfen," Leia answered. She turned once again to watch the motionless tableau inside the medical chamber.

At a forgotten hour in the depths of Coruscant's night, Cilghal emerged from the medical chambers. She staggered, cradling in her right hand a shallow crystal bowl half-filled with the deadly poison from the drink that Ambassador Furgan had thrown in Mon Mothma's face.

The two New Republic guards stationed at the door snapped to attention and rushed to help Cilghal. She was so exhausted she could hardly place one foot in front of another. She leaned against the stone doorway, drawing strength from the solidity of the rock.

Her arm trembled as she extended the crystal dish to one of the guards. Cilghal barely had enough strength remaining to lift the small poison-filled container, but she did not dare drop it. She felt a deep, bone-melting relief when the guard took it from her.

"Be careful," she said in a husky, utterly exhausted voice. "Take this . . . and incinerate it."

The second guard scrambled to the intercom system and signaled for all Council members to come immediately.

"Do you have news of Mon Mothma?" the first guard asked her.

"She has been cleansed and she will heal." The lids dropped over Cilghal's glassy eyes. "But for now she must rest." Her flowing robes whispered against the tiled walls as she slid down to collapse on the floor.

"As must I," she said, falling immediately into a Jedi recovery trance.

42

The Star Destroyer *Gorgon* limped through open space like a wounded dragon, leaking radiation from a thousand damage points.

Only one of the *Gorgon*'s primary sublight engines still functioned. Admiral Daala's engineers assured her it would be many days before they could attempt to enter hyperspace.

Life-support systems were down for the lower twelve decks. But Admiral Daala's soldiers were accustomed to harsh and difficult conditions. Cramped living quarters might encourage them to make repairs faster. Heating systems were low, giving the air a frigid edge, making spoken words emerge from her lips accompanied by a plume of steam.

Her precious flagship had been grievously wounded, Daala knew; but she realized she did not need to make the *Gorgon* into a top-flight fighting machine again. Not anymore. This time she merely needed to complete sufficient repairs to crawl back to Imperial-controlled territory, where she could start from scratch.

Daala's best advantage was that the Rebel forces must have assumed her ship had been destroyed in the explosion. Their sensors would have been blinded in the eruption of the reactor asteroid.

Watching Maw Installation vaporize, Daala had ordered full shields and full speed, throwing caution aside as she drove the *Gorgon* straight to the walls of the Maw, seeking her own way out. Now, crawling away from the energetic outbursts of the black hole cluster, the battered Imperial battle cruiser would not be noticed on any Rebel scopes.

Half the consoles on her bridge remained dim, unable to function after sustaining so many overloads. Technicians tore open access plates, bundled in heavy uniforms to keep warm, rubbing their numb hands together as they tinkered with electronics. But they did not complain, at least not while Daala was watching.

A significant percentage of her stormtroopers had been killed in sudden hull breaches or explosions belowdecks. The sick bays were filled with injured personnel. Many of the computer systems were off-line. But they had survived.

Commander Kratas stepped up to Daala and saluted. His face looked devastated, smudged with grease and smoke from his attempts at hands-on repair work.

"The news is not good, Admiral," he said.

"I want to know our true status," Daala said, forcing her concern back inside, where it could increase the pressure in her heart, crystallizing a diamond of her own resolve. "Tell me, no matter how bad it is."

Kratas nodded, swallowing. "We have only seven functional TIE fighters remaining in the hangar bays. All others were lost."

"Seven!" she cried. "Out of—" She gritted her teeth and shook her head so that her hair whirled like an inferno around her face. She drew a short, controlled breath and nodded. "Yes. Continue."

"We don't have sufficient spare parts to repair the damaged external weapons systems," he said. "Our starboard turbolaser batteries have been wrecked, but we may be able to get two guns functional again."

Daala tried to be optimistic. "That might be enough to defend ourselves if we are attacked. But we must hope not to encounter such a situation. We will not initiate any aggressive action at this point. Is that understood?"

Kratas looked relieved. "Understood, Admiral. We can repair most of the hull breaches and repressurize some of the decks, although . . ." He hesitated, and his thick eyebrows knitted together like a giant furworm. "But I don't really see the point in that, Admiral," he finished. "We don't need those quarters, and it would only tax our resources at this point. Our repair crews are working around the clock, and I suggest we devote our efforts to completing only the systems critical to life support and those necessary for us to be on our way."

Daala nodded slowly. "Again I agree, Commander. It is a difficult decision, but we must be realistic. We have lost this battle—but the war continues. We will make no excuses for ourselves but continue to give our best effort for the good of the Empire."

She drew another controlled breath of the frosty air, staring through the bridge viewport at the lush starfield that waited ahead, crossed by a wide swath like a milky river. Looking through the disk of the galaxy toward the dense core, she saw the stars appear to stream like a wide river. The *Gorgon* headed toward the luminous bulge of the galactic center.

"Commander"—she lowered her voice—"what is your opinion of the overall morale on the ship?"

Kratas took a step closer so he could answer in a soft voice. "We have good people, Admiral, as you know. Well trained and well drilled. But they have repeatedly suffered grievous defeats...."

"Have they lost faith in me?" Daala asked. Her face was chiseled in stone. She made herself strong and tried not to show that Kratas's answer could devastate her. She averted her emerald eyes, afraid that he might see something in them.

"Absolutely not, Admiral!" Kratas answered with a tinge of surprise. "They have the utmost confidence in you."

She nodded to cover her long sigh of relief, then raised her voice, turning to the communications lieutenant. "Give me an open-ship channel," she said. "I want to address all of our troops."

Daala gathered her thoughts until the lieutenant nodded to her. She spoke in a loud, firm voice that reverberated through the damaged ship.

"Attention, all crew members of the *Gorgon*. I wish to commend you for your efforts against overwhelming odds, against a foe that continues to gain the upper hand through treachery and uncanny luck. We must now prepare for the next phase in this battle, however. We are making our way to the Core Systems, to the last strongholds that still swear loyalty to the Empire.

"It was not originally my intention to join with one of the Imperial warlords struggling for dominance, but it now appears that we must fight the larger fight. We need to convince them of their real enemy and show those still faithful to the Emperor that we must be united to be strong."

She paused before raising her voice. "Yes, the *Gorgon* has been damaged. Yes, we have suffered severe losses. We have been wounded—but we will never be defeated!

"Trials such as these only strengthen us. Continue your efforts to make the *Gorgon* powerful again. Thank you for your service." She signaled for the communications lieutenant to stop the transmission. She looked out again at the moving stream of stars.

The *Gorgon*'s computer banks held all the information Daala had pulled from Maw Installation's classified computer banks. The weapons designs and new concepts alone would help the Empire win the next phase of the war.

As she stood on the cold bridge with gloved hands clasped behind her back, she watched the universe unfold in front of her.

The Star Destroyer *Gorgon* sailed on toward the Core Systems. Through persistence she could become victorious. One day.

43

The *Lady Luck* cruised low over the jagged surface of Kessel. Bleached sunlight washed across the alkali flats. The sky scintillated with intermittent streaks of light, flaming trails of meteorites—chunks of Kessel's destroyed moon burning down through the thin atmosphere.

"You know, this is all kind of beautiful," Lando said, "in its own way."

Beside him in the space yacht's overly padded passenger seat, Mara Jade frowned skeptically. She looked at him as if she thought he was crazy—not a new thought. "If you say so," she said.

"Of course, it'll take a lot of work," Lando admitted, lifting one hand off the controls so he could rest it on the arm of her chair. She flinched at his move . . . but not too much.

"First order of business will be to get the atmosphere factories up to full capacity again. I'll have to bring in specially modified droids. I've already talked to Nien Nunb, my Sullustan friend, who says he'd love to make his home down in those tunnels. I think he'll make a great crew boss."

Lando raised his eyebrows and flashed her his most dazzling smile. "Defense will be difficult without the moonbase, but I'm sure with the help of the Smugglers' Alliance we can put together a great system. You and I will make quite a team, Mara. I'm really going to enjoy working closely with you."

Mara sighed, but it was more of a resigned, tolerant noise than actual annoyance. "You just don't give up, do you, Calrissian?"

He shook his head, still grinning. "Nope. Giving up is not my style. Not ever."

Mara slumped back in her passenger chair and stared out the *Lady Luck*'s front viewport. "I was afraid of that."

Overhead in the white skies of Kessel, shooting stars continued to rain down.

Two medical droids supported a recovering Mon Mothma. She stood dripping as she emerged from the bacta tank. She wavered a little and held on to the smooth shoulder plates of the droids. Finally she stood on her own again, took a deep breath, and lifted her head to smile.

Leia stood watching, impressed at the rapid improvement. "I never thought I'd see you stand again, Mon Mothma."

"Neither did I," the former Chief of State admitted with a rueful shrug. "But my body is healing itself with a vengeance. The bacta tanks are working overtime, effective again now that Cilghal removed the nano-destroyers. I'm anxious to move about, to see all the things that happened while I was sick. I have a lot to catch up on. But the medical droids say I have to stay here and rest."

Leia laughed. "You have plenty of time, don't worry. Do you—" She hesitated, not wanting to push Mon Mothma, but anxious to know. "Do you have any idea when you'll be ready to take back your duties as Chief of State?"

Assisted again by the droids, Mon Mothma toiled over to one of the padded seats near the bacta tank. She slowly sank into the cushions. Still-damp garments clung to her wasted body. She did not answer for a long time. When Mon Mothma looked up, her expression made Leia's heart skip a beat.

"Leia, I am no longer Chief of State. You are," she said. "I served well for many years, but this wasting illness has made me weak—not only physically, but also in the eyes of the New Republic. The New Republic must not waver in these trying times. Our leadership must be strong and dynamic. We need someone like you, Leia, daughter of the legendary Senator Bail Organa.

"My decision is firm. I won't attempt to regain my title. It's time for me to rest and recover with a great deal of thought on how best to serve the New Republic. Until such time as that changes, our future is in your hands."

Leia swallowed and forced a comically stoic expression on her face. "I was afraid you were going to say that," she said. "But if I can handle a few Imperial renegades, I suppose I can keep the Council members in line. After all, they're on *our* side."

"You may find that the Imperials surrender a bit more readily than Council members, Leia."

Leia groaned. "You're probably right."

The winds sang on the planet Vortex. Leia stared up at the newly rebuilt Cathedral of Winds, which rose like a gesture of defiance against the terrible storms. Beside her Han kept blinking as the breezes stung his eyes, but he seemed awed by the tall structure.

The new Cathedral was different from what had been destroyed by Ackbar's crash, more streamlined. The winged Vors had shown no interest in recreating their previous design, following a plan that seemed to flow from their collective alien minds.

Crystal cylinders glittered in the sunlight, large and small tubes like a towering pipe organ. Notches and windows had been cut into the curved surfaces. The leathery-winged Vors flew about, opening and closing the orifices to shape patterns of music as the winds whistled through. Everything else hunched low to the ground, but the Cathedral of Winds soared, like the spirit of the New Republic.

The impending storm rippled the thick carpet of purple, vermilion, and tan grasses that covered the plains. Low hummocks, underground Vor dwellings for the vicious storm season, lay in concentric rings around the pinnacles of the new cathedral.

Leia and Han stood surrounded by a New Republic formal escort on a patch of grass packed down with polished squares of synthetic marble, laid out to form a low viewing stage. The Vors wheeled about in the air, flapping their wings and circling over the audience.

The winged aliens had allowed no off-worlders to hear the concert of winds since the Emperor Palpatine had established his New Order; but with the success of the Rebellion, the Vors had finally permitted spectators again, not only representatives from the New Republic but also dignitaries from a host of populated worlds. Leia's first attempt to come here with Ackbar had ended in disaster, but she was certain that this time everything would turn out well.

Han stood beside her, dressed in the diplomatic finery that he obviously found uncomfortable, but she thought it made him look dashing. That seemed no consolation to her husband as he chafed under the rough and stiff formal dress.

He must have sensed Leia looking at him, because he glanced down to give her a roguish smile. He snuggled closer, slipping an arm around her waist and pulling her tightly against him. The wind whipped around them.

"Feels good to relax," he said. "And it's good to be with you, Your Highness."

"I'm Chief of State now, General Solo," she said with a twinkle in her eyes. "Maybe I should *order* you to stay home more often."

He laughed. "Think it would make any difference? You know how good I am at following rules."

Leia smiled as the wind stirred her hair. "I suppose the two of us will just have to work out a compromise," she said. "Why does it seem as if the whole galaxy conspires to keep us away from each other all the time? We *used* to have adventures together!"

"Maybe it's payback for all the lucky breaks I've had," he said.

"I hope your luck comes back soon, then." She snuggled against him.

"Never quote me the odds." Han ran his fingers up and down her back, making her skin tingle. "I feel lucky enough right now."

The wind picked up and the hollow music lifted higher.

Chewbacca's matted fur blew in all directions, making him look as if he had toweled off after a steam bath and forgotten to comb his body hair. He bellowed over the winds and the music of the cathedral.

Threepio's tinny voice rang out. "Anakin. Jacen and Jaina! Children, where are you? Oh, please do come back here. We're growing very worried."

Chewbacca and Threepio waded through the thick grasses in search of the twins and their little brother. Anakin had crawled off to hide during the cathedral's opening ceremony. Distracted by the ethereal harmonies, none of the spectators had noticed the baby disappearing into the grasses, including Chewbacca and Threepio.

Upon seeing their little brother missing, Jacen and Jaina had both dashed out into the expansive fields, claiming they would help find baby Anakin— and of course now all three children were lost. Chewbacca and Threepio tried not to cause too much of a distraction as they searched.

"Jacen and Jaina!" Threepio said. "Oh, dear, what are we to do, Chewbacca? This is most embarrassing."

They stumbled through thick rustling grass that rose to Chewbacca's chest. Threepio spread his golden arms to clear a path for himself. "This is scratching up my plating," he said. "I was never meant for duty like this."

Chewbacca cocked his head to listen, ignoring Threepio's complaints. He heard children giggling somewhere among the whispering grass blades. The Wookiee plunged through the thickets, swiping with his hairy paws to knock the blades out of his way. He found no one—only a trampled path from where he had heard the sounds. He would find them sooner or later.

From behind him, swallowed up in the dense grass, he heard another thin voice. "Oh, Chewbacca! Where have you gone? Now *I'm* lost!"

Standing on the polished mosaic platform of synthetic marble squares, Admiral Ackbar held himself rigidly at attention beside white-robed Winter as the cathedral played its music. They sat among other off-world dignitaries and lavishly clad representatives from various planets.

He had been reluctant to come for the christening ceremony, since he had accidentally destroyed the old Cathedral of Winds. He had feared the Vors might hold a grudge against him—but the Vors were a flat, emotionless race who seemed unaffected by individual events. They simply pushed on, recovering and striving to complete their plans. They had not censured the New Republic, had demanded no retribution; they had simply fallen to work reconstructing the Cathedral of Winds.

The wind whistled cold around his exposed skin. The music sounded beautiful.

Nearby, a lovely woman decked in jewels and bright primary colors clung to a haggard, weary-looking young man, who slumped in his chair. Ackbar glanced at them, then bent close to Winter, lowering his voice. "Could you tell me who those people are? I do not recognize them."

Winter studied the pair, and her face took on a distant look as if she were sifting through various files in her mind. "I believe that is the Duchess Mistal from Dargul and her consort."

"I wonder why he appears to be so miserable," Ackbar said.

"Perhaps he is not a music lover," Winter suggested, then settled into an awkward silence. Finally she spoke again. "I am glad you decided to return to the service of the New Republic, Ackbar. You have much to give to the future of our government."

Ackbar nodded solemnly, looking at the human woman who had served so many years as Leia's close personal aid.

"I am pleased that you yourself have been freed from exile on Anoth," he said. "I was concerned for you. Your personal talents and perceptiveness are greatly needed, and I have always valued your input."

Ackbar could see that Winter masked her expression carefully, allowing just a glimmer of a smile to show that she was holding back as much as he was.

"Good, then," Winter said. "We shall be seeing a great deal more of each other in times to come."

Ackbar nodded to her. "I would enjoy that."

* * *

Qwi Xux listened longingly to the music of the winds. The notes rose higher, dipped lower, wove around themselves to form a complex, never-to-be-repeated melody, since the Vors forbade any recording of their storm concerts, and no two were ever alike.

The flying creatures flitted up and down the shafts of crystal, opening hatchways, covering small holes with their hands or bodies as they shaped the symphony, building it as the storm grew closer.

The music seemed to tell Qwi's own life story. It struck her emotional chords, blowing through the hollows and crevices of her heart so that she heard the feelings she had experienced through her life: her childhood loss, her agonized training, her brainwashed imprisonment for years in Maw Installation . . . and her sudden thrill of freedom as she met members of the New Republic who helped her escape . . . then Wedge Antilles, who had opened up more new worlds for her, bright dawns she had never before imagined.

Now, after her time of healing, after she had returned to Maw Installation and walked along the old corridors, set foot in her former laboratory—Qwi no longer chose to mourn those lost memories.

When the misguided Kyp Durron had erased her thoughts, it had been a violent act. But, in hindsight, she thought he might have inadvertently done her a great favor. She did not wish to remember her devastating weapons work. She felt as if she had been reborn, given a new chance to start a life with Wedge, unencumbered by dark thoughts of the deadly inventions she had helped to create.

The music continued: hollow and mournful, then joyous and uplifting, in an eerie counterpoint like nothing she had ever experienced before.

"Would you like to go back to Ithor with me?" Wedge bent close and whispered in her ear. "We can do our vacation right this time."

Qwi smiled back at him. The idea of returning to the lush jungle world sounded wonderful to her: the self-contained cities drifting over the treetops, and the peaceful alien people. The experience would do much to ease the pain from the memories she had lost there.

"You mean we'd no longer have to hide from Imperial spies? From Admiral Daala?"

"We wouldn't have to worry about any of that," Wedge said. "We could concentrate entirely on enjoying ourselves."

The Vors opened up all of the hatchways and windows in the Cathedral of Winds. As the storm center hurled its greatest gales at the structure, the music built to a spiraling crescendo, a triumphant finale that seemed to echo throughout the galaxy.

44

Sunrise on the fourth moon of Yavin.

Artoo-Detoo trundled ahead up the flagstoned ramp, chittering and bleeping as the new Jedi Knights followed him. In silence they gathered atop the Great Temple to look across the mist-covered treetops. The orange gas giant glowed from behind as the system's sun came closer to the limb, suffusing the upper atmosphere with light.

As the jungle moon continued in its headlong orbit, Luke Skywalker took his position in front of the procession to greet the coming dawn. Beside him walked young Kyp Durron, still limping slightly from his newly healed injuries, but moving with an enormous inner strength. His entire attitude had changed in such a short time.

But while Kyp had been through the greatest ordeal of the new Jedi, Luke's other students had also proved themselves to be greater than he had foreseen, greater than he had hoped.

Together they had overthrown Exar Kun, the Dark Lord of the Sith. Cilghal had saved Mon Mothma's life with new techniques in Jedi healing. Streen had recovered his confidence and had shown remarkable adeptness at feeling and touching the weather.

Tionne continued her quest to resurrect Jedi history, a job made more difficult now that the Jedi Holocron had been destroyed—but Luke knew there were other Holocrons to be found, though they might have been lost over the millennia. Many of the ancient Jedi Masters had recorded their lives and their wisdom in such devices.

Others, such as Dorsk 81, Kam Solusar, and Kirana Ti had not exhibited their particular aptitudes yet, though their powers were broad and strong. Some of the new Jedi would stay on Yavin 4 and continue to train and grow; others would take their skills out to the galaxy, as knights to defend the New Republic.

Artoo warbled an announcement, his prediction of when the first sunlight would strike the apex of the temple. The little droid seemed immensely pleased to be at Luke's side.

Luke gathered his Jedi Knights around him, sensed their growing power intertwined. They were a *team,* not just wild cards with powers and abilities they did not understand.

The others stood on the chipped flagstones of the observation platform, looking out toward the hidden sun. Luke tried to find words to express his glowing pride and his high expectations.

"You are the first of the new Jedi Knights," he said, raising his hands as if in a benediction. "You are the core of what will become a great order to protect the New Republic. You are champions of the Force."

Though his students did not speak or respond, he felt the upsurge of their emotions, their swelling pride.

There would be other students, new trainees who would come to his Jedi academy. Luke had to face the fact that he might lose a few to the dark side— but the more defenders of the Force he could train, the stronger would be the legions of the light side.

With a collective gasp the gathered Jedi on the rooftop watched as the sun burst from the fringe of Yavin. Brilliant white rays gleaming like firefacet gems sprayed across the jungle moon, reflecting and refracting from the swirling atmosphere.

Artoo whistled; Luke and the other Jedi simply watched in awed silence.

The rainbow storm cast its glow over all of them as the dawn continued to brighten.